THE LEAVENING

THE LEAVENING

by

ed owen

Copyright © 2000 by Ed Owen
All rights reserved.
No part of this book may be reproduced, stored in a retrieval system, or transmitted by any means, electronic, mechanical, photocopying, recording, or otherwise, without written permission from the author.

ISBN: 1-58721-897-6

1stBooks – rev. 6/28/00

About the Book

There was an era in the history of our nation that was dominated by a work ethic, sacrifice and a sincere effort to pull together. It was the era in which Jim Williams started life's journey, an era of strong family ties, an era that melted away as adversity eased and moved from our national boundaries and families became increasingly separated geographically.

From a moral and loving working class family, Jim's humility, his innocence and unpretentious ruggedness is a challenge to the fair sex. As a teen he experiences the tragedy of great personal loss during WWII, leaving him vulnerable.

Plunging into hedonism with disastrous consequences, Jim feels disgraced and leaves school to join the Marine Corps, yet still, can not escape the allure of the female. In the ancient culture of China, a beautiful prostitute, then back in the States, an innocent lass and at the same time, a psychologist desiring only his virile body, come next. Reflection brings change to Jim, while his sister and his good friend, a black former schoolmate, find love.

Before long Jim is thrown into a new conflict. From Pusan to Inchon and the epoch fight to the sea from Chosin, the Korean War brings forth the fighting spirit and tenacity of the U. S. Marines, but not without great loss to Jim.

Assigned duty in Britain with the Royal Marines, Moira, a wonderful, compassionate and loving Scottish lass captures Jim's heart. With a family started, the Williams volunteer for duty in Malaya during the Communist insurgency. Moira's friendship with a beautiful Chinese girl, tragedy and Ceit, Moira's foster sister, add a new and surprising dimension that builds to a shocking conclusion.

Alice,

So many great memories.

Thank you so much for that day we shared and thank you for reading an earlier manuscript.

For what ever life has in store for me, his memory will remain a part of it.

He was a great guy.

Ed

The Leavening is dedicated to three old buddies.

George, one of the real Marines.

He took part in some of the actions described herein, from Inchon to Hungnam under the legendary Chesty. It is always a pleasure to share with him, reminisce, or attend any function where the Corps is honored. He is a brave and unassuming guy and certainly a diamond in the rough. He is the perfect example of, 'Once a Marine, always a Marine.' He is a true friend and a great guy!

Paul, a Corpsman, as gung-ho as any Marine.

In his later years when he could not see or use his arms and legs, he insisted on being helped to his feet when the Marines' Hymn was played, even if only a recording. Sadly, he did not make it to the end of this book, having spent the last sixteen years of his life in a V A Hospital. His faith and friendship, his never ending sense of humor, was an inspiration to me!

Bill, the one who prodded me and convinced me I could write The Leavening when I laid it out to him.

About fifty years ago in a town where Marines were not always thought of as admirable, he and his family opened their home to two Marines a long way from their homes. We were treated like kings. Though he served in the Air Force, he was a staunch friend to us jarheads and would stand with us in any eventuality. His recent death deprived me of a true and generous friend!

Semper Fidelis, Buddies!

Prologue

Yeast leavens the dough.

Along with genes, our character is shaped by events and people, not unlike the yeast at work in the dough. Abraham Lincoln once said, "I claim not to have controlled events, but confess plainly that events have controlled me."

In our lives, we sometimes see just that, the influence of events and people. Occasionally they have an unfavorable effect and we react badly. The opposite is also true. At either point, those events and people have become a leavening in our lives.

In the words of the Apostle Paul, "A little yeast leavens the whole loaf." That is good when the yeast or leaven is good, but when it is bad, we must again listen to Paul, "Cleanse out the old leaven that you may be fresh dough."

This is such a story.

PART I

* ONE *

On the day before Thanksgiving, the wind was blowing fierce and cold against the bedroom windows in irreverence for the season. The thermometer hovered around freezing, putting the wind chill in the teens. Southern New England could be like that, especially along its shoreline.

Fresh from the shower, he lay on the bed, a towel about his loins. The bedroom was snug and cheerily warm. He was almost smug in his happiness. Their parents and children and grandchildren would join them in a few hours to celebrate a very unusual silver anniversary. It was always a favored event for him when the family was together.

His mind wandered dreamily back in time. As incidents jogged his memory that day, in the year of the Lord, nineteen-hundred and eighty, he felt a lack of reality that what he now remembered had ever happened, ... but it had.

~ ~ ~ ~ ~

Jim Williams was not quite ten years when he stood on the sidelines of the playing field at Collins Park, his attention riveted to his brother Don, seventeen months older and a grade ahead in school. It was 1938 and the two had journeyed many times to the park to observe sandlot football games. The boys who played the unorganized rough and tumble game were a year or two older than Don.

In the early days, Jim was a spectator. At eleven, Don was taller and more quickly allowed to play. He was a ferocious tackler and that got him recognition from the bigger boys. Jim watched his brother play after play make more tackles than anyone on the field. Usually Don was the last to rise from the pile of bodies, his face flushed with excitement, his eyes full of a sparkle that left no doubt of his intense love of the game. It was not long before Don was allowed to carry the ball. When he could not run around someone he plowed into them with a fury, his legs pumping till he was flat on the ground.

The first time an eager and excited Jim was permitted to participate was late in a day when players had departed and bodies were needed to keep the game going. His pleading, coupled with Don's enthusiastic support got him onto the field and into the game. He was trampled instantly. In quick succession his ankle was stepped on, then his hand, followed by a knee to the head and an elbow to the nose, which miraculously did not bleed.

The opposing team was close to scoring. The next play found Jim between the goal line and the biggest kid on the field. The huge lad bore speedily and menacingly upon him. One scared kid desperately wanted to be someplace else, .. anyplace else. In that terrifying instant before their bodies violent encounter, Jim's feet seemed rooted to the earth. His legs immobile, he plunged in panic to the ground hoping to escape instant death.

Too late!

The big kid's knees smashed into his ribs and belly. The impact lifted and spun him 180 degrees to land on his back, stunned, gasping for air, his body filled with pain, his mind disjointed. He lay where he landed, unable to move.

A grinning Don was the first to him. Then he was looking up into the smiling faces of his teammates. They helped him to his feet yelling words he could not make out, all the while slapping him on the back.

The big lad was on his hands and knees. He too could not move. He had been flipped, plunging head first into the turf clouding his consciousness. He too had to be helped erect. Darkness was fast approaching and it was decided to call it a day. The youngsters left the park and went their separate ways.

Jim was thankful for his brother's arm about his shoulder as he and Don journeyed homeward. Groggy and none too steady on his feet it was not only Jim's body that Don's arm supported. Regularly the smiling older brother praised his younger siblings deed to the accompaniment of broad smiles and numerous squeezes across the shoulders. But Don's praise was stirring an unease that tormented Jim with an expanding guilt the closer they got to home.

The two brothers arrived just in time for supper. Mom's scolding was averted when Don walked immediately to her. He kissed her on the cheek and gave her a hug.

"Hi, Mom."

Jim followed his brother's example. Her scowl turned to a soft smile.

"Wash up, boys, supper's almost ready."

Standing side by side at the sink in the very large kitchen, Don continued to grin at his younger brother. After they dried their hands, Don punched Jim lightly on the arm and gave him a wink as their father and two younger children entered the kitchen. Greetings were exchanged. When all were seated, Dad gave thanks.

When their plates were full, Don was first to speak.

"Boy! You shoulda seen Jim today!" All eyes focused on Don's grinning face. "You know Eric Olson, Dad?" Bill Williams nodded to his son and Don excitedly continued, "Well he's gotta be the biggest eighth grader in Shoreford. Well he's got the ball and runnin like heck and Jim hits him and he goes up in the air and comes down on his head. Wow! What a crash!"

"Jimmy!" Sarah Williams blurted, her voice reaching a near scream, "Were you playing football with those big boys? And you, Donald, you too? Oh my! You two will get yourselves maimed for life. Will, can't you do something about this?"

Her face was a huge frown mixed with a fear for her children, always so apparent when they did the things she felt put them in harms way.

Before Dad could answer, Don with a soft smile turned to his mother. It was a warm smile. It was not a smile to con, it was not a fake smile. In a tone somewhat humble and entreating he said, "It's only a fun game, Mom. We won't get hurt. You know that, don'tcha?"

Sarah continued to frown, her words brisk, "No! I don't know that, Donald! You're always so sensible about everything except that stupid football and how could you let your little brother get involved?"

"I'm sorry, Mom, I'm really sorry, we'll try to steer clear of the big guys."

Football was the only thing Don was not completely truthful about with his mother.

Dad cleverly changed the subject, his pride in his sons remaining unknown to his wife. Sometime in the near future, he thought, he would talk to her and try, probably with little success, to help her understand how boys were.

The youngest at the table, Bobbie, the hero worshipping first grader, was caught up in the excitement and beamed his approval at his brothers.

Two years older than Bobbie, Shirley was devoted to her mother and that is where her sympathies lay, but those feelings were in conflict for she adored Don, three years her senior. Jim was another story. He teased her too much and she managed a swift smirk in his direction which wrinkled her nose.

Jim did not respond to his sister's taunt in the usual manner. His nervous attention was on his mother. He grinned weakly at her, grimacing within himself to keep the hurt of his aching body from her awareness.

Sarah Williams grudgingly gave up the frown and allowed a weak and unenthusiastic smile to flit across her face before she picked at the food on her plate.

There was less than the normal conversation at the supper table that night.

*

Later in bed after Bobbie had fallen asleep, Jim whispered to Don in the bed to his other side, "Are you still awake?"

Don rolled to his side, propped his head on his hand and answered, "Yeah."

"I hurt so much I can't sleep."

"Try not to think about it. Think about all the fun you had. Wasn't it worth it?"

Jim was silent a spell. The pain caused him to wonder if it was worth it, but that was not his only thought. His conscience was eating at his innards.

"Don," he said very softly, "I didn't really tackle Eric Olson. When I saw him comin at me, .. I was so scared I tried to drop down in the ground."

As he had done so many times in his young life, Jim confessed to Don, the only person to whom he ever bared his soul or confided his innermost feelings.

Don slid from his bed and came over and sat on the edge of Jim's bed.

"Jim, everybody gets scared, but things gotta get done and ya know, when it's done, bein scared was worse than it shoulda been. Remember when Bobbie was small and Mom and Dad were tryin to get him to walk and how scared he looked? Then he took a step and fell down. Remember? Then he tried again and again. Remember? And he wasn't scared anymore. Now the little guy'd walk a tightrope if it was there."

"But Eric Olson is really big, Don!"

"I know, Jim. I guess the way we have to feel when somebody like him is comin at us is, if we don't stop him, nobody else will. Then he'll score a touchdown."

At eleven, Don was endowed with a mature wisdom and quiet courage that made him the special person he was. To Jim, that was the greatest brother in the world.

"How about tomorrow," Don whispered, "you and me go out in the field in back and we'll practice tacklin and stuff. OK, Jim? You'll see, .. it's not so bad."

There was enough light coming in the window that Jim could make out the broad smile on Don's face. Looking into his brother's lively eyes, Jim smiled shyly and shook his head. Don patted him on the shoulder. He gave Jim a quick wink and added, "We'll have fun, .. you'll see."

*

The next day, just as he said, Don took Jim to the small lot behind their home. It started very seriously, one running at the other and being thrown to the earth. As Don coached Jim, he enthusiastically cheered him on. It lasted for more than an hour. During the rough and tumble play and the bruises that went unnoticed, Jim was caught up in his brother's enthusiasm and cheerfulness.

"That was really great, Jim. Ya know, you did terrific. See how it is when you put your heart to it .. and by golly, Jim, that's what you really did. I'm really proud of ya."

Hesitating, Don looked about, his eyes settling on the western sun.

"Holy Moses, we better get home before Mom skins us alive. Crimany, ya know what she thinks about football."

Both boys grinned. Don put an arm about Jim's shoulder, with the other hand, rumpled his hair, then squeezed him across the shoulders.

They managed to get into the house unseen and clean up before presenting themselves to their mother.

* * *

"Sarah, that was one fine meal!" Ed MacPherson, Sarah's older brother and a widower exclaimed that Sunday in December of 1941. "It sure is a pleasure when you feed us."

"Oh! Ed," was Sarah's self-conscious response.

"You know, Ed, we sure miss you and Kit," Bill Williams said. "We all wish you lived closer." He looked around the table at his family's affirmative nods. "We sure don't see you two enough."

"Actually, Will, both Kit and I would like nothing better than living in Shoreford. She really enjoys being with her cousins." He glanced at his grinning daughter, "But you know how it is when you have to work."

"Yeh, I guess we don't have much choice when it comes to that," Bill replied.

"Will, why don't you and Ed take the children and go into the living room while I clean up here."

"I'll help, Aunt Sarah," said Kit, the same age as Don. Her mother had died when she was nine and she became the lady of the house for her father to whom she was completely devoted.

"That's not necessary, Dear. After all, you're company."

"But I want to help, Aunt Sarah, I really do."

"And I'll help too, Mom." Shirley said, smiling at Kit whom she looked up to and adored.

"All right," Sarah smiled approvingly, winking at her husband, "Well, Will, I guess that means you'll have to leave the women behind."

"OK, guys, you heard your mother. Come on, Ed, the news will be on pretty soon and we can find out what's going on in this crazy world."

Sarah and the girls commenced the clean up, the males adjourned to the living room.

"What number should I turn to, Dad?" Bobbie asked standing in front of the large, floor radio.

"Nine-sixty, Bob, the city station will be fine."

The music of Artie Shaw drifted in over the air waves. Before everyone was comfortably seated, the music was suddenly interrupted by, "Flash! Washington! The White House announces Japanese attack on Pearl Harbor........"

Stunned, speechless, the five were at once joined by the females. Not a muscle moved as they listened intently to the staggering news. Bobbie, the youngest, soon filled with curiosity, yearning for all kinds of answers, but sensing the mood, remained steadfastly silent.

When the news finally ended, the benumbed occupants of the Williams living room, had little to say.

*

As darkness approached Shoreford that eventful day, Ed and Kit MacPherson departed for the hour long drive to their home. Later when Shirley and Bobbie were asleep and Bill and Sarah sat silently in their living room, Don and Jim, too excited to sleep, conversed softly across the space between their beds.

"How long do you think the war will last, Don?"

"I don't know, Jim, it's hard to say. Things don't seem too good right now," the fourteen year old high school freshman answered. "It's kinda hard to imagine, but you know how long it's been going on already."

"Yeah. ... Crimany, Don, if it lasts three years, you might have to go .. and then me."

"Well, Brothe, maybe it won't. .... But I'll tell you one thing. If I have to go, I want to go like Uncle Art."

"Yeah, Don. Me too."

* * *

By his junior year at Shoreford High in 1943, Don Williams had become the best end in the schools history. With great natural ability, he put his skills and tenacity on the line every second, from the beginning of a practice session on Monday, till the end of a game on Saturday. His pass catching was without peer and he was a superb blocker. It was his tackling and defensive play, however, that earned him even greater praise. He made all state that year, the only junior on the squad.

As a sophomore the same year, Jim made the team. He gave completely of himself every practice. He was shorter than Don and did not possess all of his brother's natural ability, but he had come to love the game and worked very hard. He progressed rapidly from those early days at Collins Park. Don was an immense help, not only with his coaching, but in igniting Jim's desire to reach beyond himself. The episodic collision with Eric Olson, the reality which only Don knew, was added stimulus to Jim's dedication. Coach Mullen liked what he saw in Jim and had no reservations about using him. The coach tried him at various positions and Jim steadily got more playing time as the season advanced.

After mid season, late in the fourth quarter of the Crampton game, Dinky O'Brien the starting center got hurt. Jim was the one player who could lead the runners accurately with his snaps. Andy Morris, Shoreford's solid fullback raved about the way Jim got the ball to him in a punting situation. In addition, the center in those days often played behind the line on defense (as the present day linebacker) and that was Jim's forte. He was as willing as his brother to give up his body to plow into a runner, or knock down the interference. That willingness was most evident on the first play after his entry into the game.

The score was 19 to 14 in favor of Shoreford. It was Crampton's third down and they needed just over a yard for a first down at Shoreford's twenty-nine. Jim took his position on the defensive left behind Tony Capoletti at guard, George 'Ole' Olson at tackle and his brother Don at the end. All juniors, these three were already considered one of the finest front trios in the state. The right side of Shoreford's line was almost as good.

When the teams lined up, the ball went to Crampton's speedy right half back. He took one quick step straight ahead, then immediately slanted to his left to slice between his center and left guard. Jim was instantly in motion, his legs churning, his arms pumping with every ounce of energy and will he possessed. With three powerful strides he launched his body over Tony and fellow guard Tim Ryan, smashing into the runner. They crashed to the earth almost a yard behind the line of scrimmage.

Jim saw stars briefly. Grabbed under the armpits he was pulled upright by Ole.

A big grin on his face, Don handed Jim his helmet, jarred loose on impact. His teammates were thumping his back, but all he could see was the smiling face of his brother, his free hand with a thumb up and shouting, "Way to go, Jim! Way to go!"

With time running out, Crampton tried again. This time the entire Shoreford line stopped them at the line of scrimmage, Jim the last to struggle to his feet when they unpiled. Their spirit broken, Crampton could only go through the motions as Shoreford took over on downs and ran out the clock.

Coach Mullen gathered the team together on the locker room benches after their showers.

"I'm proud to be your coach today, guys. You played a great game. I'm sorry I have to send you home with bad news. Dinky O'Brien will be lost for the final two games of the season. He broke his arm today. We wish him a speedy recovery and of course we will miss him on the team." He paused and looked around the room, "As for the team, .. Jim Williams will take Dinky's place and join the starting eleven."

The players, at first sympathetic for Dinky, were soon smiling. Those nearest Jim were quick to give him a hearty slap on the back. Quarterback Andy MacDonald walked over and shook his hand, "You'll do OK, Jim."

Milton Buchanan, the teams fastest man, not only a teammate, but a member of Jim's homeroom was sitting nearby. Grinning broadly he gave Jim an enthusiastic thumbs up.

Jim was squeamish. His face reddened and he looked downward. Then slowly, deliberately, he lifted his eyes and glanced around the room contacting most of his teammates eyes. He said softly and shyly, "Thank you."

Mercifully Coach rescued him, "OK guys, have a great weekend. See you at practice on Monday."

A strong arm went about Jim's shoulder and he heard his brother's voice, "Let's go home, my brother."

He looked into Don's sparkling eyes. All was very well in the world of James Arthur Williams.

*

During the practices in the following week, Tony Capoletti and Tim Ryan, Shoreford's two fine guards who flanked Jim in the offensive line took him under their respective and protective wings. Both juniors, each had nearly eighteen pounds on Jim. Only Olson and Jaskowski the two tackles were bigger. Tony and Tim were good steady ballplayers in an unglamorous roll. Much of their lives had been shared. Their families were friends and neighbors living in the same block. In grade school they shared time as alter boys at St. Augustine. Their immediate joint venture on entering Shoreford High was to join the glee club. Both had great voices and had done solos.

Jim was vulnerable during the snap of the ball and they showed him how they would block with him to keep the offensive center of the line strong. Before the week was out, the three became a close knit group and a hard charging blocking force on offense. Extremely close friends, Tony and Tim accepted Jim into their midst with enthusiasm. On nights when Don worked, Jim often accompanied them to Burndys where the soda jerks were soon heard to call out, "One vanilla, one chocolate and one strawberry shake," when the three entered.

Practice with Milton 'Buck' Buchanan was also essential for Jim. Buck was so fast off the count on a motion play, he had to be well led with the snap. Buck joined the team as a freshman and was soon a starter. He carried the moniker of Buck from his earliest days, because boys as they are wont to do reduce long surnames to the shortest, easiest form of address. As Buck's ability to run and dodge and dart became evident, the nickname became associated with the male deer's skills and his teammates often respectfully referred to him as, 'The Buck'. It caught on throughout the school and when ever his performance was discussed, that nickname was frequently used.

Jim liked Buck from their first encounter. A lad with a ready smile, his white teeth contrasted pictorially with his milk chocolate skin. As they worked more closely, Jim found that Buck was someone pretty special. The wiry kid with the blinding speed and remarkable instantaneous shifts had more than a few of the qualities that made Don what he was.

It was a week of hard practice, but Jim was riding high. He was not only playing with his brother, his brother became an untiring supporter. That drove him even more. The nights Don did not report for work at Myer's Market after practice, the two boys jogged home together. When they reached their destination, their faces alight, their bodies heated, their clothing a trifle damp, it was not only Jim's face that glowed, inwardly he was doing the same. He did like to play the game, but his greater joy was playing it with his brother and it was during these days that

Jim Williams became more deeply and consciously aware of what Don Williams meant to him.

*

Their opponents were older, but the Shoreford Bulldogs won the game on Saturday. Shoreford had but one senior on the team since O'Brien was sidelined. Their opponents did not play to their potential and the intensity they carried onto the field that day was no match for that of the Bulldogs. Jim valiantly displayed the skills that not only endeared him to his coach and teammates, but were soon conspicuous to the loyal spectators.

All that remained was to beat Newville. Both teams had identical records. The winner on Thanksgiving day would wear the league crown.

*

It was a short week. The pep rally was Wednesday after school and the teams were on the field Thursday morning before most of the players had time to be nervous.

Jim lined up between Don on his left and Ole on his right. Andy Morris kicked off for Shoreford. The ball sailed end over end down the field. The Williams boys sprinted side by side slanting to the right to that point where the ball would be caught. Ole, a few yards behind at the instant they smashed into the unfortunate receiver, had to leap over the three jumbled bodies. Two of the players were soon happily on their feet grinning broadly at each other. The third took longer. That would be the first of many similar hits he would take over the course of that Thanksgiving morning.

An older team, Newville struggled to stay in the contest. Shoreford was scrappy, well coached and determined. It was the scrappiness that forced a safety on Newville early in the game. Those two points helped. Shoreford was unable to convert any of its extra points.

With only minutes to go Shoreford led 20 to 14 with possession on their own forty-five. It was second down, two yards to go for a first down.

Scoring one touchdown on a thirty-three yard romp while rushing for over one hundred and twenty yards, Buck was having a pretty good day. He was called on for an end run. He took the snap from Jim, breaking for the outside. Attempting to secure the ball in his outside arm it squirted free. He dove recklessly for the bouncing ball, pulling it under him, but the play lost over five yards.

Now it was Don's turn. Having scored twice on passes, he was picked to catch another out in the flats, ten yards from scrimmage and more than enough for a first down. He was the one person who would somehow get free.

The team broke from the huddle full of confidence. With vigor Jim sent the ball spiraling to Andy MacDonald. Don charged straight ahead, made a superb cut and was in the clear on the sideline. The pass was thrown swiftly and flat and was still rising when Don leaped high in the air and made a sensational catch. He landed well forward of the first down marker, ... but out of bounds.

Shoreford had to punt. The ball went off the side of Andy Morris' foot and traveled but twenty yards. The receiver was hit immediately, but Newville took over on their own forty. There was time for maybe two plays. Clamor from the Newville fans was instantaneous.

The right side of Newville's offense was on the side of the field occupied by their fans. In a practiced and unobserved move, the Newville right end did not enter the huddle, but stayed at the sideline, kneeling just inbounds. With the snap he was on his feet flying straight down the sideline. In the air, the ball sailed, then settled into his outstretched hands.

Jim spotted the move when the lad was beyond scrimmage. Instinct alone sent him racing frantically to the point they would meet. At the final instant he lunged at the runner. With picturesque skill, the speedster halted, sucking in his midsection.

Jim's grip slipped fleetingly and feebly away as he plunged by crashing to the turf, skidding among Newville's screaming fans.

The runner was gone. There was no one close. He crossed the goal line amid a cacophony of wild yells and terrible groans. The game was tied at 20 all.

Jim lay sprawled where he landed amidst the unrestrained jubilation of the Newville spectators. He pulled his hands beneath his body to save them from the jumping feet. Dejectedly, he struggled to his feet and joined his angry teammates in the end zone.

Tim Ryan was trying to shout above the screaming crowd, "They really played us for suckers on that one! It was a real sucker play!"

"Let's get the bastards!" screamed Eddie Jaskowski.

"Get em? Geeze! There's only enough time for the extra point try!" Ole yelled.

"That's just it, guys!" Don was shouting above the noise. Jim could not ever remember seeing his brother's eyes so intense. The team crowded around their charismatic leader. "That's just it! Time is gone! There's just no way, guys, just no way we can let em make that extra point! No way!!!"

As one they nodded solemnly, many yelling with grim determination, "Yeh!" and those who had not, echoed those who had, but louder and more forceful, "Yeah!!"

Newville came out of the huddle clapping and cheering. They had a pretty good place kicker. Every spectator in the bleachers and around the field was on their feet, some yelling wildly, others grim, but shouting encouragement.

With fierce resolve the Shoreford Bulldogs got into their sets, teeth clenched, eyes glaring as one, glued to that place the ball would be spotted. The entire crowd went silent, those on the Newville side in reverent anticipation, those on the Shoreford side in terrible anxiety.

The Newville center sent the ball spiraling like a bullet into the holders hands. The holder placed the ball down. The kicker rushed his foot forward in a powerful arc. Leather met leather. The ball exploded skyward. In that crucial instant the entire right side of the Newville line was crushed by the left side of the inflamed Bulldog defense. Just a hair's breadth behind thundered Shoreford's right side. Too many hands and arms assaulted the ill-fated pigskin. It plummeted harmlessly, impotently to the earth amidst wild animation and dejected silence.

Time had run out.

A few, mostly those players who suffered the agony of misfortune in the final minute, felt cheated with the tie and a share of the league title. But they were cheered by their coach and fellow teammates and before they went home to Thanksgiving dinner, all were in an improved frame of mind, ... all except Jim. He successfully hid his mood from his friends and later, from most of his family.

*

Now in sixth grade, Bobbie went to bed Thanksgiving night before his older brothers. He tried to stay awake. He was excited about the game and he never tired of talking about such things. The Bulldogs outplayed their older opponents for nearly the entire game. He did not feel negative about the tie. He was perfectly placed behind the end zone, dragging his father hurriedly there after the touchdown. He was able to observe his brothers storm through the Newville line leading the charge that blocked the kick. That was enough for him.

The light was on when Don and Jim walked into the room. Bobbie looked as peaceful as could be, a smile on his face, his breathing barely noticeable.

Don smiled and spoke softly, "Look at that, not a care in the world," but knew it would take something like a bomb to wake his youngest brother.

"Yeah," Jim grinned, "he never seems to have the slightest trouble falling asleep."

Don looked at Jim a few seconds, "How're ya doin now, Jim?"

Jim hesitated and glanced curiously at his brother, "I'm doin OK. Why?"

"You don't have to talk about it, but I can see you're eating yourself up." Don sat on the edge of his bed, "Sit down, Jim, .. please."

Jim sat and frowned slightly as he gazed into his brother's eyes.

"Brothe, for whatever reason, I always seem to know when something's troubling you. This time it's that last tackle, ... isn't it?"

Jim's expression turned shy, "Yeah, ... I guess it is," he stopped and looked down. When he raised his head, his eyes locked into his brother's eyes, "Yeh, Don, .. you're right. It sure is."

Don smiled affectionately, but the smile was soon replaced by a concerned expression, "Jim, you can't let something like that keep you down. It's OK to examine something that happened and try to improve, but you gotta get up and go on. That was a game we played today and we played a pretty good one, .. especially you ... and we put on a good show, .. especially you .. and we tied a team that was supposed to beat us. That's not too bad. But it's still just a game. We went out there today, .. especially you .. and we did our very best and we played our hearts out, .. especially you. No one can ask more than that of any team, .. or any person.

"Sure, we think we should have won. If everything happened just the way we thought it would, .. we might have, but it didn't, .. yet still, .. we didn't lose. We really showed the world we weren't going to lose. Now that's not too bad, Brothe. What do you think?" Don was smiling broadly.

Jim's eyes never left his brother's during those words. Slowly he gave into Don's smile and was soon smiling shyly himself, "Ya know, Don, I know you're right. .... I'm really sorry I'm such a sap."

"You're not a sap, Jim, ... but sometimes you're overly hard on yourself ... and when you are ... well, .. I feel bad for you. You're really a pretty good guy ya know ... and I'm glad you're my brother." Don reached across and softly punched Jim in the upper arm, "Now let's get some sleep, .. OK?"

When the light was turned off, there was silence for a few minutes and Jim turned his head on his pillow and spoke softly, "Don?"

"Yeah," his brother quietly replied.

"You must know it's in my heart, .. but is it wrong, ... would you be upset ... if I said out loud .... that .. that I loved you?"

Don rose to an elbow. Jim could not see his smile in the darkness, but it was there in abundance. "Brothe, I'd say it's very right and I'm not only not upset, I'm filled with all kinds of good feelings. I don't know why us guys don't say that to each other. Dad has never said it to us, but we know he really does love us. You can tell. It shows in so many ways, like when he takes us in the woods hunting, the way he looks after us and makes sure everything is done right so we won't get hurt. Maybe someday he'll say it like you just did, Jim. He really is a great dad. Anyway, thanks for telling me, Jim, cause I sure do love you."

All the Williams brothers slept well and peacefully that Thanksgiving night and before 1943 came to a close, Donald Edward Williams was elected captain of the Shoreford football team for the coming season.

* * *

"Whadaya say, Jim?" Don smiled as he spoke, "New Years Eve is almost here and we can celebrate it together with a couple of nice girls. We can go for a burger in the city and see the late night movie that ends at midnight and be home by one."

"But, Don, I don't even know Janet Griswald."

"Sure you do. Crimany, Jim, she's in one of your classes."

"I know that, but what I mean is, I don't know her enough to go out on a date."

"Jim, going out with her will get you acquainted faster than anything else will."

"But how'm I gonna ask her? Supposen she says no."

"You don't have to ask her and she won't say no. She wants to go out with you. Alice told me so. So you see, if you agree, that's all you have to do. Come on, Jim, say yes and we'll double date the Griswald sisters."

Don put his arm about his brother's shoulders. He smiled pleasantly. He knew there were more than a few girls at Shoreford High who would love to date his bashful brother. He knew too that Jim knew nothing of this charm. His innocence was a part of what made him so appealing.

Jim smiled timidly, "OK."

* * *

Closing the door of his locker, Jim caught sight of Don coming down the hall. They always went home together on the nights Don did not have to work. Usually they jogged, enjoying the mild exertion and peaceful companionship and if they felt the need for conversation, it was mostly light hearted. If there was a serious matter to be discussed, that was done mostly at night in their room after Bobbie was asleep.

"Ready, Jim?"

"Sure am," Jim answered, searching his brother's face for the reason behind Don's seriousness, so unusual at this time of day.

They walked silently down the hall and out into the warm air of the late afternoon. Clear of the school grounds Jim asked, "Don't you feel like running tonight?"

"Would you mind if we walked. I'd like to tell you about somethin that's been rollin around in my mind."

"Sure, Don."

They exchanged glances. Jim was puzzled by his brother's demeanor. Don was uncomfortable and this was new to Jim, though he had been aware that something seemed to be on Don's mind of late. They walked at a leisurely pace and covered half a block before Don spoke.

"I've been thinkin about joinin up."

Jim cast a quick glance at his brother, though he was in no way surprised by Don's statement.

"Trouble is, it'll kill Mom when I tell her. There's no way she'll ever understand how I feel and how right I know my decision is." They walked a bit in silence before Don continued, "You know, Jim, they're having to draft more and more guys these days. They need enlistments. I really feel I hafta go. Heck, I'll be seventeen in a few more weeks."

It was what Jim expected of his brother. He smiled to himself. "I guess I know what you'll be joinin," he replied with a grin.

"Yeah, I guess you do."

Normally Don would have smiled and ruffled Jim's hair, but today he was more serious.

"You know," Don continued, "Uncle Art never would talk about his war, except once in awhile he'd tell you and me about the guys he was with and that's the kind of guys I'd like to serve with. I've read so many books about it, Belleau Wood, Soissons, Blanc Mont and how the Germans called them Devil Dogs and the French general who named Belleau Wood after the battle, Bois de la Brigade de Marine. Every time I hear those stories I get a lump in my throat. And now we hear about Guadalcanal and Tarawa."

Jim turned and gave his brother a soft poke to the upper arm. They went the rest of the way in silence. They would talk more tonight and as the time drew near. Both agreed that telling their mother ahead of time would give her that much longer to suffer. When they walked into the house and greeted their mother, Don was slightly ill at ease, something Jim had never seen him be with their mother. Fortunately she did not notice. Both boys breathed easier when they were up in their room changing into after school clothing.

* * *

The day after Allied forces landed at Normandy in France, June the 7th, Don turned seventeen. He did not attend school on his birthday. When Jim and Shirley arrived home, Mom was sitting at the kitchen table, her eyes red and moist with tears. She sobbed a muffled greeting, but refused any further conversation. She did not move from the chair until Dad walked in the side door. She got up and fell into his arms. Veiled conversation passed between them and they went upstairs to their bedroom, their words inaudible in the downstairs.

Supper was late ... and quiet. Don pecked at his food with an unusual expression which caused Bobbie to continually cast glances his way. Shirley did the same, but less openly. Mom toyed with her food.

When Dad realized no one was interested in eating, he put his fork on his plate and leaned back in his chair. Somewhat somber, he spoke, "Today, ... Don joined the Marines."

"That's great, Don!" Bobbie said, instantly animated, "Gee! I'm gonna have a Marine for a brother!"

Shirley kept looking at Mom, not knowing how to react. She said nothing.

Despite his knowledge of Don's plans, Jim acted enthusiastic to hide that knowledge from his parents.

Dad was a little sad, nevertheless, had a father's pride in his oldest son and looked into Don's eyes, "You'll make a fine Marine, Don."

"Will!" Mom replied agitated, "we haven't even signed the papers yet." Turning to her oldest she added unhappily, "Donald, I just don't understand? You could at least finish school. You only have one more year and you're only seventeen. You're class president, on the National Honor Society, captain of your football team and you'll surely be All State again." Her expression showed her deep concern and there was pleading in her voice, "Donald, that's a really rare achievement. You've got everything to stay in school for."

"Mom, I can be part of all that when the war is over. I just feel I have to do this. There's guys all over who've given up all kinds of stuff to serve and I would really feel bad if I couldn't go."

"Oh Donald!" she was close to tears, "You're only seventeen!"

"So are thousands of other kids, Mom! Please, .. I have to do this!"

"Sarah," Dad spoke her name softly, "let's go in the living room with Don. The kids can finish the dishes. Jim, you and Bobbie give your sister a hand."

Jim was stunned by the command. Don was embarking on a great adventure. They shared the secret for weeks and now he was being denied his place at Don's side. Besides, he thought angrily, the dishes only needed Shirley and Bobbie, who after all, did not understand all of this anyway. Likewise, Shirley and Bobbie felt left out and the dish washing was accompanied by some muffled grumbling at first, but ended silent and sullen. Only after, when the clean up was complete, did the hurt disappear when the three youngsters joined their parents and older brother and talked past normal bed time.

*

As the reality of Don's act began to be more fully understood, Jim experienced confused thoughts and conflicting emotions. Don was not just his brother, but his best friend, .. his buddy.

Don had many friends, but he never allowed those friendships to be more important than the one he and Jim shared. Their relationship was a tremendous influence in Jim's young life. Don the scholar prodded him about his studies and Jim fulfilled his potential as a student. Don the athlete pushed him to an excellence he would not otherwise have known. And Jim was too bashful to ask a girl out, but found the courage to make up a foursome with his brother and his date. It took Don's gentle persuasion.

Jim knew of no other brothers with anything like the relationship he and Don shared. Who would take Don's place? No one could take his place. Jim did not want anyone to take his place.

Don was going someplace special and heroic and Jim would not be going with him. They would no longer have the same bond, sharing their daily lives and adventures. Jim was going to be alone for the first time. He felt the pangs of loneliness even before Don left and for the first time he could remember, he was envious of his brother.

* * *

The final week of school went slowly at first, but as Jim started putting his thoughts into proper perspective and it took some doing, normality returned and times passage quickened. One of his first tasks was to speak to Mr. Myers at the market about taking over Don's job. Mr. Myers thought highly of Don and was happy to hire his younger brother as his replacement.

Three days after Don departed for Parris Island, the first letter arrived. This buoyed the entire family, especially Mom and caused Jim to neglect showing his final report card of the year to his parents, his best ever. He passed with high honors. Don's hand had been on his shoulder.

* * *

Arriving home and finding a letter from his brother, especially when it was a personal one for him, became Jim's greatest joy. There were letters to the entire family, but also individual ones to Mom and Dad and each of the siblings. Don told Jim and his father more about the grueling physical and mental aspects of boot camp, though even about that he was low key. Mom was not informed about those parts of her son's training and she never pressured anyone to fill in the details. She did not want to know.

Jim was glad for his job at the market and for football practice which started late in the summer. Likewise, his growing friendship with Buck and Tony and Tim helped. Those activities kept his mind and body reasonably occupied.

School opened the first week in September and football practice went into high gear. Jim threw himself into the practice sessions with a vengeance. In addition to giving so much to football, he did the same to his schoolwork, his work at the market and at home. He was, he believed, filling in some for his missing brother. With all the activities and the step up in his more serious approach to life, teasing his sister diminished, if but a modicum. Shirley was grudgingly and slowly, seeing Jim in a different light

The weeks prior to Don's short leave between Parris Island and reassignment, Dad used the car sparingly to save on rationed gasoline. Mom scrimped on meat and butter. The entire family worked at saving up one thing or another that was rationed. That way, when Don got home, in addition to the normal extras allowed for service personnel, there would be a surplus.

*

The Williams family piled into the '38 Chevy at 8:10PM to drive to the city to meet the shoreline train from New York due at 9:00. They wanted to be early. Mom, usually talkative was silent most of the trip, but in the darkness she was wearing a broad and sweet smile. Dad often allowed Mom the floor, but tonight, he and Shirley and Bobbie kept the conversation lively. Jim spent most of the trip observing his family and quietly sharing their joy. The family's exuberance at their early arrival at the station was quickly blunted when they learned the train was twenty minutes late. They stood on the platform the entire time. They were impatient in the warm night air.

Shirley was the first to hear the whistle as their composure was beginning to slip. The fifty or so people present began to react. A few picked up suitcases to board, but many, like the Williams, responded with smiles and chatter in expectation of pleasant reunions. Six cars passed before the seventh came to a stop in front of the them. Dozens of servicemen began to disembark, mostly in olive drab, with a lesser amount in navy blue.

"There's a Marine!" Bobbie excitedly yelled.

They turned and looked rearward. Walking straight and very lean, the man in the forest green uniform approached. He was a sergeant with a hash mark and two rows of ribbons. His face was gaunt, his eyes somewhat sunken, his skin yellow in the dull artificial light. Malaria and Atabrine had done that. The family was taken aback by his appearance. Sarah winced. It was an awkward moment and so engrossed were they, that all jerked clumsily around at the familiar, pleasant, "Hey!"

He was coming toward them at a rapid pace, Private Donald Edward Williams, USMC. He bounced his seabag from his shoulder to the platform, picked up his mother bodily and swung her twice 360 degrees and replaced her gently on her feet. As quickly, he grabbed his father's hand for a few vigorous shakes and as quickly, a hard embrace. Shirley next, feet lifted from the ground, embraced in a great bear hug. Then Bobbie, his face beaming, shoved his hand into his brother's and squeezed with all his might. Thereupon the two oldest siblings shook hands. Don concluded by placing his free hand on Jim's upper arm and clasping it firmly. It was a supremely happy moment, the family all together in a tight circle jabbering aimlessly.

Jim broke from the group first. He grabbed the seabag and grunted at its unexpected weight as he wrestled it to a shoulder. Dad stepped out in front with Bobbie who kept looking back at his big brother striding with his arms about his mother and sister. Jim brought up the rear, making a valiant effort to cover up his conflict with the seabag and maintain the pace as they hurried to the parking lot. In the car and heading home, Don was bombarded with questions. He answered them with the patience the family took for granted. They stayed up late that night, talking and sharing thoughts and time together.

*

"Jimmy," his mother's voice was soft, accompanied by a gentle shake of his shoulder, "it's time to get up."

"Aah, Mom, .. not yet, .. it's too early," he mumbled groggily.

His mother smiled down at him, sympathetic for his lack of sleep, "It's 6:30, Jimmy, same as always. Get yourself up, breakfast is ready," then left the room.

He looked over at his brother Bobbie, still asleep. Lucky stiff, he could sleep for awhile. Turning to the other side of the room he saw that Don was already up and gone, his bed freshly made.

It was a large bedroom and had been their parents till Bobbie was able to move from crib to standard bed. At that time Bill and Sarah Williams turned the room over to their three sons that they would have ample space to grow in. They took the room Jim and Don shared which was somewhat smaller. Shirley had a small room on the first floor.

As tired as Jim was, he forced his feet to the floor and headed for the bathroom as quickly as he could force his unresponsive body to move. He had lost the race to that sacred room too many times to his sister. He knew from unhappy experience how long he would have to wait for her. He completed his ablutions as Shirley yelled through the door a second time. He opened the door and tweaked her nose, gingerly sidestepping an inaccurate punch that accompanied her high pitched, "Jimmy!"

Taking the steps two at a time, he was in the large kitchen seconds later.

"Jimmy!" Sarah softly scolded, "I wish you wouldn't come down the stairs like that. You could really hurt yourself if you tripped. And besides, Bobbie's still asleep. And will you ever stop pestering your sister?"

"Aw, Mom!" he said as he walked to his mother and gave her a quick, half conciliatory, half zany hug, lifting her off the floor in the process. When he released her, she gave him a sharp slap on the behind. He instantly put a hand over the point of impact, groaned and limped to his chair. His father and Don smiled good naturedly at the antics they had come to expect. It was just like it used to be.

He took his usual seat opposite Don, both boys at their father's elbows. Don had a cup of coffee, a habit acquired in boot camp. He was answering questions from his father. Jim was content to listen.

Jim's parents sometimes treated him less maturely than Don and today he was more aware of that treatment. Don did seem older ... and more serious and Jim accepted that reality. He was the younger brother and worse, no longer connected to Don in their daily existence. He wondered how long it would be till they would again share their lives and if their relationship might be different.

Shirley came in and sat next to Don. She glanced diagonally across the table at Jim and stuck out her tongue. Jim responded by focusing his eyes on the end of his nose and grabbing his throat as if being choked. He pushed his tongue out the side of his mouth and let it hang there. Shirley scrunched up her face and muttered, "Yuuk!" and the game was over. Mom, who just sat down at the end opposite Dad, sighed, glanced upward at the heavens and conversation resumed.

Bill Williams worked at an arms factory in the city and was normally gone before his offspring came to the breakfast table, but today, he would report an hour late, because of Don's homecoming. As Bill was leaving, Bobbie joined the family. He appeared to need additional sleep. He had many questions for Don, but for now he listened to his older brothers converse. He was impatient to get into the conversation, but he knew he would soon have Don to himself.

Sitting opposite Bobbie, Shirley glared scornfully, "Bobbie! Get your elbows off the table!"

Not knowing how he would hold his head up, he reluctantly obeyed. He was relieved when Shirley rose to leave. She was often more harsh about his table manners than his mother. But mostly he was happy to see her leave for Jim too was going. His mother would allow him access to Don.

Robert Owen Williams had difficulty containing his exuberance. This was the first time he had his brother to himself. Last night when the family remained up so late, he had listened and done little talking, a rare practice for him. It was different now and he made the most of it, but alas, the time passed quickly and his mother was hurrying him off to get ready for school.

"I guess you better get going, Bob," Don said, adding affectionately, "we'll finish our talk tonight. OK?"

Bobbie beamed, "If you say so, Don." He grudgingly abandoned his brother, but returned soon, dressed and ready for school. He reached out with his right hand. Don got up and stuck his hand out. When they completed their handshake Bobbie confidently asked, "We'll talk again tonight, right, Don?"

"You bet we will, Bob!" Don gently squeezed his brother's shoulder before Bobbie walked out the door filled with the hero worship that only a seventh grade boy could know.

Sarah was smiling at her eldest when he turned and sat again. They had a second cup of coffee and as the two talked, she experienced a tranquillity she had not known since that eventful day Don turned seventeen. Long after the cups were empty, Don helped her with the dishes, though she protested mightily. When the task was complete and the kitchen in its usual, spotless state, Don put an arm about his mother's shoulders. Turning to face him, she slid her arms about him. They hugged for a very long time. She did not want to let go.

*

Every one of the five nights of Don's leave the two older brothers sat on their beds, or lay in them, talking, well into the coming day. Passionately intent on being part of that brotherly comradery, Bobbie never managed to stay awake as long as his older brothers and they had considerable time to themselves. It was at those moments that Jim realized how much he respected and admired Don. It was not Don's achievements, which were many. It was the gentle patience and understanding he possessed and which rarely deserted him. Some of this was from their mother. He was also endowed with a quiet tenacity which he carried into every undertaking. This came from their father. He had a wisdom well beyond his years and like his Grandfather MacPherson, he had a faith which he rarely talked about, but which motivated so many of the things he did. Jim understood more fully why his parents accepted Don's maturity more readily than his own.

*

The six days passed quickly. There was a party for Don on Saturday night put on by the football team. It was a raucous, happy affair and since Don was not going steady he was fair game for a bevy of the girls present. Surprising for Jim was his own popularity with the opposite sex. He brushed it off and chalked it up to being Don's brother. His good spirits came from being in the company of his brother, his teammates and a crowd of cheerful party goers, ... but mostly, ... it was his brother.

*

The conversation on the station platform was subdued, unlike that night last week when Don arrived. Dad would report an hour late for work. He could do little to keep Mom's spirits up. Shirley, head slightly bowed, cast sympathetic glances at her mother, holding Don's hands while tears formed in her eyes and rolled in ever larger droplets down her cheeks.

Don in his most serious and reassuring manner spoke to her, "Mom, we get the best training in the world and my buddies are the greatest and we really look out for each other."

Sarah could not, .. would not be convinced. Jim stood quietly behind his sister and found he was impatient with his mother. Bobbie was the exception in the group. He grasped at every word his big brother uttered, all the while beaming at his hero, his twelve year old adulation unmindful of the reality of his brother's undertaking.

The 7:00AM Boston to New York was coming to a stop, metal wheels squealing noisily, making conversation difficult. The handshaking and embracing continued most of the five minute stop till the, "All aboard!"

Don slung his seabag to his shoulder, secured the package of goodies under the other arm and climbed aboard. The family walked along the platform following him to a seat near the rear of a packed coach. Then the train was in motion. Sarah waved in a subdued manner and Shirley, mindful of her mother's emotions, mimicked her. Bill, an arm about his wife trying to boost her morale was having trouble with his own. There were strong feelings of pride for his son, but that did not overcome the anxiety that was pricking at his soul. Bobbie beamed and waved enthusiastically. Jim waved cheerfully and gave his brother a keen thumbs up which Don returned, but already, loneliness was creeping into his feelings. There was a smile of confidence on Don's face which only disappeared when he was gone from sight. The family did not move from the platform until the train had vanished.

* * *

It was unusual not to hear from Don right away. When the first letter arrived the family knew why. He reported to Brooklyn Navy Yard and left immediately with a small detachment of Marines under a platoon sergeant. Future letters brought them up to date. The Marines filled every seat in a tourist sleeping car. What contact they had with civilians aboard was most enjoyable. They were treated royally. They landed at Treasure Island five days later and three days after that they were aboard ship with hundreds of other Marines. Seven letters arrived Thursday, their third day at sea.

The following Saturday was the first football game of the season. With Don's letters cheering him on, Jim was driven. From his defensive position behind the line he was learning to read offensive players. He picked out foot, hand, body and eye movements and made up for any lack of speed by knowing where the play was going and being there. His blocking assignments on offense were usually to help the guard on the side the play was run, but his intensity was such that on a pass play or end run that was successful, he often made a second block downfield. The predictions were true and Shoreford won easily. Jim was honored in the weekly town newspaper, a rare occurrence for an interior lineman.

Riding their laurels the following week, the team let down a bit and victory came harder in a closer game. Jim was an exception and the townsfolk began heaping praise on a second Williams kid.

Early in the next week a batch of letters from Don arrived. He was somewhere in the Hawaiian Islands and because of censorship could not be specific. The detachment he sailed with had split up and been fed into various units of the newly created Fifth Marine Division recently landed from the west coast. Though the division was new, about forty percent of its Marines were combat veterans, many from the disbanded Paramarines and some from the disbanded Raiders. While the letters did not contain many specifics they were as usual, cheerful, bright and uplifting to the family, especially Sarah.

Don's letters now arrived on a regular basis. He became Jim's greatest supporter, .. except for young Bobbie. That was for Jim his foremost incentive and his play was sometimes characterized as that of a demon.

*

Victory followed victory for Shoreford High that autumn of 1944 and a tradition was born following the first win, a tradition that intensified as the victories amassed. Tony and Tim sang the Shoreford Bulldog victory song in the showers after each win. Their teammates listened approvingly and happily till they finished, then joined in and started again with great enthusiasm, but allowing Tony's baritone and Tim's tenor the final stanza. It provided a sweet poignancy to the event. As the season progressed it took on an almost spiritual quality. Coach Mullen or anyone not on the team who was present found it impossible to leave till the singing was concluded.

Shoreford was 7 and 0 after the Saturday game before Thanksgiving. Opposing teams had crossed their goal line only three times till now. They were a great team. Nine of the starters had played together for three years. If they had a shortcoming other than lack of depth, it was difficult to find. They had been overconfident on two occasions, but Coach Mullen was able to work them out of it and in the end they were dominant. Don would have made the team unbeatable under any adversity. Of that, Jim was certain. Now all they had to overcome was Newville on Thanksgiving day and that should not be difficult. Having tied Shoreford last year to share the league title, this year, Newville was 4 and 3 and struggling. It should be a foregone conclusion, nevertheless, Jim thought of Don and wished he were here. The Thanksgiving game was always special.

Before the close of school on Wednesday the pep rally was held. The auditorium was packed and the stage was jammed with the team, coaches and cheerleaders, who were at their most animated, boisterous best. There were normally enough seats for the entire student body and staff in the auditorium, but today there was barely standing room. Some selective townsfolk had sneaked in, adding to the clamor and festive atmosphere.

After a few cheers, Mr. Melillo, the principal, gave a short speech and introduced Coach Mullen to the noisy, cheering throng. Another brief speech and Coach introduced quarterback Andy MacDonald who replaced Don as captain. There was more cheering and Mac raised both arms, the index and middle fingers of each hand in the Churchillian V. The noise increased and the jumping cheerleaders lured the excited crowd to greater fervor. The team was glowing.

Mac did a great job. He thanked the coaches and conveyed to the crowd his own pleasure and privilege at playing with such a great team. He took much time to give special attention to the linemen who performed such stellar and unsung duties in front of him. He pointed all of them out and identified them by name. Jim felt the flush mask his face when Mac announced his name. Before the last cheer was completed Coach began herding the team down the back stairs of the stage and up into the locker room. When they were all assembled he spoke in a matter of fact, business like way.

"OK guys, you all know the rules. Go straight home, eat a good supper and be in bed by ten ... and be here by nine tomorrow morning!"

The coach knew that most of his team would not go straight home or be in bed by ten. This was to be their year. They were excited. So was he.

It was a noisy throng that thundered down the stairs and out into the ebbing daylight and cool, fresh air. Small groups conversed briefly before departing. Many headed in the same direction in twos and threes. It was not the direction of their respective homes.

Outside the school Jim conversed with Buck. They were laughing when Tim and Tony joined them.

"OK, Guys, see ya tomorrow at nine sharp," Buck grinned and waved.

"Aren't you comin with us, Buck?" asked Tim.

"Nah. I promised my mom I'd be right home after the rally," then jokingly ran a finger across his throat. "Besides, I don't wanta be caught with you lawbreakers."

All four boys laughed and Buck waved again, "See ya."

"Take care, Buck," Tim waved.

"See ya in the mornin, Buddy," Tony said.

"See ya, Buck," Jim said as the three watched Buck move quickly out to the sidewalk.

"We're a lucky bunch to have a runner like him," said Tim.

"You bet we are," echoed Tony.

"Yeah," Jim responded as the three headed for their destination.

The friendship between Jim and Tony and Tim had matured greatly over the past year. Being smaller and younger, Jim was pleased to count them as friends on the gridiron. They watched over him as they would a younger brother. As he matured they accepted him as a peer. When he blossomed into a defensive standout, they, along with Buck, were the ones to shout his praise the loudest. With Don gone, those friendships helped Jim more than anything else.

The soda fountain at Burndys Drugstore was packed when the three friends walked in. Well over half the team members were present, one or two constantly on watch near the entrance. The alcove at the end of the counter contained six booths and probably sixty or more high schoolers. The counter with eight stools hosted another forty students. They were jammed together belly to back, elbow to elbow. It was nearly impossible to move.

Recognition of Jim, Tony and Tim produced faster service than many of the non team members received. One of the soda jerks yelled, "One vanilla, one chocolate and one strawberry milkshake comin up."

Amidst all the jostling and shouts of encouragement it required considerable skill to get the large, heavy glass containers to the lips, but the three friends did manage to down the shakes without incident.

Reluctantly they detached themselves from the noisy crowd and exited into the cool, clear, afternoon air. The sky was already darkening in the east. They said their goodbyes, shook hands, slapped backs and parted, Tony and Tim going north up Hillside Ave. Jim headed east across town.

It was the first time Jim was alone that day. Still feeling euphoric, he started to jog, his thoughts turning to his brother about 5000 miles away. He knew that as good as this team was, it would be almost invincible if Don were here and most likely no team would have crossed the Shoreford goal line. Ted Jones was OK, but he was not of Don's caliber. The image of his brother dominated his minds eye. He saw him pulling in pass after pass, meeting the ball in perfect rhythm with that graceful stride that was so much a part of his beauty on the gridiron. Then the beauty became terror and Don was tearing into ball carriers with savage ferocity and smashing them to the ground. On the left side of Shoreford's unyielding defense last year, when Jim stood behind his brother on the outside and Ole and Tony on the inside, there was none better in the state. There was little that passed through them or around them and they happily pummeled those who tried.

Suddenly the silence was shattered with a frightening roar as three P-47s flying at what seemed tree top height exploded the tranquillity. Jim's eyes burst wide open. His head swung instinctively trying to follow the thundering trail, but the aircraft were gone in an instant.

"Phew!! That was something!" he said out loud, smiling to himself for being so startled. He was almost home.

Mom and Shirley were setting the table when Jim walked in the door, his mother all smiles. A letter had arrived from Don. With the greetings concluded, Mom excitedly blurted, "Your brother's been promoted ... to Private First Class .. and he's in charge of ... what was it, Shirley?"

"A fire team, Mom, whatever that is. How come Marines have to fight fires, Jimmy?"

Jim chuckled, "A fire team is a BARman and three riflemen, one who's the leader."

"Why do you spell B-A-R? What the heck is a B-A-Rman? Does he serve beer? And how come Don's only in charge of three men?"

More patient with his sister these days and proud that she was asking him and pleased that his mother had stopped what she was doing and likewise, was awaiting his response, his chuckle was replaced with a soft smile. "Shirl, the BAR is a Browning automatic rifle, that's what the B-A-R stands for. It's a heavy duty rifle that can fire fully automatic, .. like a machine gun. Each fire team is built around the BAR. The Marine Corps has three fire teams in each squad, so that means three BARs, which gives their squads some real firepower. Besides the BARman, each team has a Marine who carries extra ammunition for the BAR and also carries an M-1. That's the rifle they make where Dad works, the one he calls the Garand. The other two guys also carry M-1s and one of them is the fire team leader who's supposed to be a corporal, .. so Don must be a pretty good Marine to be a fire team leader already."

Mom was smiling more than before. Shirley cocked her head to one side, uttered an approving, "Hmmph!" and she and Mom finished setting the table as Dad and Bobbie walked in the side door with the turkey. Greetings exchanged, Mom ordered all to wash up. When they were seated, Dad gave thanks, the food was passed around and the conversation immediately focused on Don.

Toward the end of the meal conversation slackened and Shirley shot a quick glance at Jim who was concentrating on cleaning up the last of the food on his plate. She turned and winked at her father.

"Boy! You shoulda seen Jimmy up on the stage today. His head," she spread her hands wide apart, "was this big, he ..," a pea hit her right between the eyes.

"Jimmy!" yelled his mother.

"Enough, Jim!" said Dad.

"Dad! She's askin for it."

"Enough." Dad repeated, though not harshly. "Tell us about it, Shirley." A thinly veiled smile betrayed somewhat his attempt at seriousness.

Jim knew he was having a good season, but like Don, he had never been egotistical about it, never talked much about it except in reply to Bobbie's incessant questions. Actually he tended to be shy, even humble when his deeds came to light in conversation. His sister's comments stung him.

"Ha!" Shirley chirped sticking out her tongue, "You don't like being teased, do you? Honest, Mom, I was just kidding him. I really shouldn't say this in front of him, but my girlfriends sitting with me at the rally were going ga ga and asking me all kinds of stuff about him." She looked across the table at her brother and smiled somewhat tenderly, "Actually, Mom, he wasn't big headed at all. I really think he was embarrassed."

By now Jim was embarrassed. His face red, he mumbled, looking down at his plate, "Aw, I wasn't embarrassed."

Sarah and Bill enjoyed their daughter's remarks and took delight in their son's discomfort, only because it was prompted by his modesty, a modesty they prized. They smiled at each other across the length of the table.

Bobbie loved it. He looked up to Jim's exploits on the gridiron with the same enthusiasm and intensity he followed

Don's career in the Marine Corps. Within seconds he had the conversation centered on tomorrow's game. He gave Jim no respite. Leaning on every word, at any pause, he bombarded Jim with additional questions. He was in an emotional state when he pushed himself from the table and blurted, "Kill em tomorrow, Jimmy!"

"Bobbie," Sarah said softly, shook her head, looked skyward and sighed and started clearing the table.

*

Jim lay awake well into the night, his mind immersed in tomorrow's game. He could not remember the school or the town being so excited about a football game. The school had never owned a championship exclusively its own. Last year during 'the' game, Shoreford thought they had it wrapped up, but did not. This year Newville had many shortcomings and even without Don, Shoreford was much the better team.

Suddenly, unsure, he heard the words of his thoughts, "We can't possibly lose, ... can we?"

As suddenly, his voice burst in the still darkness, "We can't lose! ... We can't!" He turned, fixing his gaze on his younger brother. Bobbie was not disturbed by the outburst and slept peacefully.

Moving his head to the other side he stared at Don's empty bed. "Crimany!" he thought, "I sure miss Don. It would be so good to hear his voice right now." The excitement, the recurring doubts would not go away. He knew his only escape was in sleep. But sleep was a long time coming.

*

George Olson, left tackle and biggest player on the squad was the last to enter the locker room, right at nine o'clock. A mood of confidence filled the room. Andy MacDonald minus his shoulder pads and jersey was going from player to player slapping backs and shouting encouragement. As if that was needed. But he was leaving nothing to chance. Mac had done a good job since taking over as captain. Being quarterback, coupled with his spiritedness, the gregarious boy was a natural leader. When Mac reached Ole's locker, Eddie Jaskowski was standing, looking down at Ole, his expression troubled.

"I don't know, Ski," Ole gloomily said, "I woke up with this bad gut ache and I had the runs. Damn, Ski, I just don't know what it is."

Ski turned to Mac and blurted, "Ole's feelin lousy! We gotta tell Coach."

"No!" Ole shot back furiously, "I'll be OK!"

Mac lost some of his edge instantly. Jim, whose locker was next to Ole's was the only other player to hear the conversation. After a short, heated discussion, Ole convinced Mac and Ski to remain silent. Jim knew that the concern was not just for Ole, but the team. There was no one of Ole's size or talent to replace him. Shoreford had a very good, even excellent first string line, but lacked quality substitutes. Ole was a rock and Tony Capoletti a near equal in performance. With two such teammates in front of him on defense, Jim was able to range more freely and be involved over much of the field.

Jim did not socialize out of school with Ole as he did with Buck, Tony and Tim, but on the gridiron they were great buddies. Because Ole was such a good natured scooch, Jim was less than serious with him. He enjoyed kidding with the cheerful giant. Their banter before the games was a pleasurable occasion for Jim. It started last year when Jim made the starting lineup. Eric Olson, Ole's older brother, had been a star fullback at Shoreford and had told Ole about the little Williams kid who had dumped him on his head at Collins Park knocking him unconscious. Ole never tired of telling the story to their teammates. Today, there was no banter between Jim and Ole.

When all were dressed, the team gathered around Coach. He spoke briefly about individual assignments, plays on which to concentrate and he tried to pry away the overconfidence exhibited by the bulk of his players.

"Remember," he said, "last year we were outplaying them and suddenly we were fighting for our lives. We had to pull off a near miracle to come away with a tie. Every Thanksgiving, Newville plays us tough. It's up to us to be tougher." His voice rose, full of enthusiasm, "Let's see it happen! Go out there and do it!"

The sound of the hard rubber cleats on the stairs and the shouting of the players was thunderous as the Shoreford Bulldogs rushed down and out into the bright sunlit day and onto the field amidst a cheering ovation and some boos from the opposite side of the field.

Newville won the toss and chose to receive. Shoreford did not have a great place-kicker and Newville got good field position on their own forty after a short runback. Three downs and Newville had to punt. From their own twenty-five, Shoreford marched methodically down the field, alternating power plays with their sure handed fullback Andy Morris and sweeps and slants from their left halfback Buck Buchanan.

Jim loved snapping the ball to Buck. No one could ever know when he was going to break loose and be gone. Before the first quarter was over, the Bulldogs scored twice and led, 12 to 0.

About three minutes into the second quarter, Shoreford on offense, ... it happened. On a run between Ole and Tony for a short gain, Tony was next to last getting to his feet.

"Cripes! Ole's puking his guts out!" Tony yelled.

On the field and off all eyes were riveted to the large boy on his hands and knees, scrunched over, retching uncontrollably. The school doctor and Coach were at Ole's side in an instant. It was nearly five minutes before they got him to his feet and supported him to the sidelines, a glaze clouding his eyes

When play resumed, a first down was ground out, all plays run to the right behind Tim and Ski. A short pass and a few more runs and Shoreford was inside Newville's twenty. Mac dropped back to pass. He looked right, then left and saw Teddy Jones had his man beat and let go one of his vintage, sharp passes to meet Teddy in the end zone. Teddy made a quick cut, hit a soft spot in the turf sliding clumsily to the ground, his feet entangled. The Newville defender racing to the spot took the ball at waist height and was on his own thirty-five before being pulled down.

Newville had a fair sized fullback, not fast, but hard nosed, who plowed into the left side of the Shoreford line right at Ole's replacement, picking up two yards.

As the players unpiled, Tony remained down groaning quietly, holding his leg. Again Doc Thompson and Coach sprinted on to the field. A few minutes later, they called for a stretcher. Tony was carried off with a broken ankle.

Play after play the Newville fullback drove into the left side of the Bulldog line with a vengeance. It took about four minutes, almost the end of the first half, but Newville scored and converted the extra point. The half ended, 12 to 7.

At the bottom of almost every play in Newville's touchdown drive, Jim was tired and muscle sore when he left the field with his dejected, disbelieving teammates.

In the locker room Coach was more calm than ever. He was struggling to pick up his team with cool, clear logic, pointing to their mistakes almost kindly and building on their strengths. He knew he had to convince them they could win.

When Shoreford returned to the playing field, not everyone's confidence was restored.

The Bulldogs took the kickoff. Starting from their own thirty they struggled and moved the ball to Newville's twenty. They fumbled. Newville took over and picked up two first downs running almost exclusively at Shoreford's left side. The defense stiffened. As before, Jim was at the bottom of almost every play. Newville punted.

The third quarter and most of the fourth was played between the two thirty yard lines. It was head to head, blow for blow, body weary football.

Jim Williams took on a new role, a role he never attempted before, never dreamed of doing. When the Bulldogs went on defense he led and inspired the second string guard and tackle. His constant encouragement and stellar performance was the driving force in the play of the two substitutes. They exceeded expectations. Standing behind them he slapped shoulders and butts and yelled up close, "If he comes this way, we're gonna nail the bum, nail him real good!" or, "Let's show this guy what it feels like to hit a stone wall!" The two subs answered the call.

With less than two minutes on the clock Newville received a punt on their own fifteen and ran it back to mid field. A quick pass took them to Shoreford's twenty-two. Already stirring, the Newville side of the field came to life with a passion.

Then, there they were, last nights doubts came suddenly to life in Jim's head. But almost as soon the image of Don was there and Jim remembered his brother last year, the look in his eyes, the determination, the indomitable spirit.

On the next play the snap went to the quarterback. Jim saw him glance quickly to his right, something he had seen him do before on a pass play. A halfback rolled out of the backfield making a perfect cut. The ball was in the air heading right for his eager grasp.

Racing in front of the receiver Jim snatched the bullet pass from his hands. He was hit before he could go five yards, but the ball was now Shoreford's and the Shoreford side of the field was pandemonium.

The Bulldogs broke from the huddle. Jim settled over the ball. The snap. With ferocity, Andy Morris slammed between Tim and Ski. There was a roar from the crowd.

For the first time that year Andy fumbled. Newville recovered. The clamor that moments before came from the Shoreford fans now reverberated from the opposite side of the field.

Newville had used its time-outs. The defense expected the air to be filled with flying pigskins. The Shoreford lads expected nothing but a pass.

The ball went to the quarterback. He took a step to the rear and to his right as if to pass, faked beautifully and handed off to his right halfback who dashed frantically to his left racing to the nine yard line before he plunged out of bounds stopping the clock.

Amidst the wild cheering of the Newville fans and the frightened pleading from the opposite side, Shoreford's faithful were suddenly mindful of last year. But this year, if Newville scored a touchdown, they did not need the extra point.

Newville came out of the huddle and lined up the same way. The wild clamor of the crowd blotted out conversation. The last play made over twelve yards. Was it possible they would try it again? They did! As the Bulldogs stormed unhesitatingly, unthinkingly to the right, Newville's other halfback crossed behind his counterpart and took the ball under his left arm. Like a galloping stallion he dashed madly for the safety of the end zone.

Not charging with the defense, expecting something unusual, something Newville seemed to work at, Jim's eyes spot checked every movement.

The swift runner came churning out of the backfield sweeping to the open right. Only one defender close enough burst to the left, an instantaneous thought flashing through his mind, "Not this time, you bugger!"

Jim hurtled into the sprinting zealot with unbelievable power. His left shoulder slammed into the runners solar plexus, his head sliced between body and arm. The ball was torn from the halfback's grasp to land under Jim as the two crashed to the earth.

And so quickly, the bedlam was again on the Shoreford side.

Andy Morris carried one more time straight up the middle. Hercules himself could not have pried the ball loose. The game was over.

The field swarmed with Shoreford High students and townspeople. The wooden goal posts came down easily in the frenzy. Bodies were crushed together all over the field. It was delirium in its purist form. Suddenly Jim was plucked from the ground, crushed in a gargantuan hug and kissed on the cheek by a tearful, naked to the waist Ole who had lost the heavy coat he was bundled in when the crowd erupted.

Despite the soreness and stiffness of the players, Thanksgiving dinner in Shoreford tasted quite good that day.

Townsfolk forgot the war for an instant and shared in the joy of a bounteous feast that Thanksgiving of 1944.

From the Williams home, quietly and quickly, four letters were mailed to P.F.C. Donald Edward Williams, U.S.M.C., along with clippings from the local paper.

*

The student body of Shoreford High School was still euphoric Monday morning. The halls were filled with groups of happy, chatting students. Everyone had relatives or friends in the armed forces and Thursday's game had been a gratifying interlude in the crisis of war.

The praise from his classmates when Jim entered the building made him uncomfortable and the warmth he felt was evident by the flush on his cheeks. He spotted Tony on crutches standing with Tim and a bevy of chattering females. Tony probably would not have to carry his books for awhile.

Stopping to talk to his friends, Jim inquired as to Tony's injury.

Tony gave Jim a quick wink and looking at the floor said, "Ohh, I'll be OK, but it looks like I'll need a lot of help."

Rolling his eyes, Tim smiled at Jim as Ole joined the crowd. Ole was amused at the attention Tony was receiving and some good natured kidding followed till the first bell sounded and the group split up. Jim and Ole walked together to Jim's homeroom. At the door Jim gave Ole a soft poke in the ribs and Ole placed a large hand on his smaller teammates shoulder and squeezed firmly before parting.

Milton Buchanan, star halfback, was in his seat and waved to Jim as he walked through the door. A little out of character, Jim popped Buck a snappy salute. Buck ran for almost sixty yards in the first quarter of the Thanksgiving game and finished the day with over a hundred-forty yards. Every game that year he exceeded one-hundred and twenty yards.

Of the four junior homerooms, this was the only one with starters and two of the games heroes to boot. The occupants of the room were proud. Even the aloof to athletes Mrs. Siptroth was caught up in the spirit.

The final bell rang and the public address system sounded immediately. This morning it was Mr. Melillo. He completed the regular announcements, paused and continued, "We saw Thanksgiving morning a fine group of Shoreford's young men go out and play a splendid game of football. They were visited with some very bad luck, but they did not give up ... and .. they prevailed. In the fifteen years of this high school, we have shared the league title twice. This year, it belongs to us alone and that is as it should be. To the players, Coach Mullen and staff, we say, 'Well done!' You have given us something we won't quickly forget. Happy memories are good always, but especially now, when our nation is involved in a titanic struggle for world freedom. Shoreford High has contributed almost two hundred of its graduates to this just cause, seven of whom will never return to our beautiful town. Coach Mullen informed me last week that following our final game, Edward Jaskowski, Andrew MacDonald and George Olson will be leaving to join the Army. When Anthony Capoletti's ankle heals, he and Timothy Ryan will be leaving for the Navy. We will cling to our Thanksgiving memory tenaciously! Thank you."

*

Almost two weeks later, Jim received a personal letter from his brother, a one page V-mail letter the government designed for both service personnel and their families at home. Thousands of letters could be photocopied to microfilm saving enormous shipping space and on arrival at a destination, recopied to letter size and delivered

    Hi Jim,

    That was some Thanksgiving game you and the Bulldogs played. I always knew you were an outstanding football player and now so does everybody else.

I don't know if you remember the sermon that Reverend Clark gave about pride being 'deadly', I think that's the word he used. But I know it's pride I feel about being a Marine and it sure doesn't seem wrong. It seems like the right way to feel.

But that's not my only pride. I couldn't wait to show the clippings to all my buddies. Many said you should be a Marine. I told them that if you were old enough that is exactly what you would be.

How could that be wrong, the pride I feel for you? It's so great, I think if I'm not careful, I'll pop the buttons right off my shirt.

You played a terrific game, Jim. I really look forward to the day we can play together again. Keep up the great work.

Love Ya, Brothe!

Don

With all the accolades that came before, spoken or in print, none would be held in Jim's heart so fervently or be so memorable as that letter from his brother.

"It sure will be a great day when Don and I can play together again," he happily thought

* * *

Mac, Ole and Ski left school the first week in December. Tony healed quickly and now he and Tim were gone, so Jim missed his brother more than ever. In addition to the loneliness and melancholy that visited him, there was guilt. He had a great football season, but it should have been Don's, he thought. The local weekly suggested that another Williams was a potential all-stater next year, but for Don, it would have been a second selection to that squad. There could have been no greater honor for Jim than to have shared the past season with his brother.

Escaping in his schoolwork and his work at the market, which was his main outside activity, Jim also became an expert on the war, following every news dispatch diligently, especially those from the Pacific.

The family at last knew that Don was in the 28th Marines and was training on Hawaii, the largest island of the group. His letters continued to be upbeat and cheerful. He kept the rumors from his parents, but by various nefarious means, he passed on to Jim what he could. Don had a feeling that something big was afoot.

*

It had always been the happiest time of the year for Jim, but the coming of Christmas in 1944 was very different. Don's absence diminished the event immensely. The Williams household that Christmas lacked the cheerful and cordial air of years past. An atmosphere of thoughtful spirituality was now common.

Mom mostly, but sometimes Dad, were more subdued in demeanor. Often Mom seemed aloof and certainly preoccupied. At other times a kind of tenseness became evident, especially when letters from her eldest did not arrive at regular intervals.

Shirley on occasion mirrored her mother's emotions, but some of that was empathy.

In his last preteen year, Bobbie went the other way. He was more talkative and energetic and was not always easy to take. Every war movie that came to the local movie house, the Centre Theatre, he begged to see. His side of the bedroom was filled with photos of planes, ships, tanks and the Marine Corps. A picture of Don taken during his short leave hung in the center of it all. The face smiled back, full of confidence and cordiality, the garrison cap at the precise angle required by regulation. Millions of similar pictures hung in homes throughout the nation.

*

On the eve of the celebration of the birth of the Prince of Peace, during this time of world conflagration, the family attended the early church service. The hymns and the sermon were full of hope and the congregation, while apprehensive, was warm and friendly and drawn together.

Jim was a bit ashamed of himself. Initially he did not want to attend, though he did not express those sentiments to his parents. After the service the handshakes and smiles relieved him of that burden. His acceptance by the congregation gladdened the sixteen year old boy-man. One of the strongly athletically inclined parishioners remembered his performance on Thanksgiving day and made mention of it. As usual he was uncomfortable with the praise, but afterwards, he found it left him with a pleasant feeling.

It took about twenty minutes to get from the church to Gramma Williams in Newville for a tradition older than Jim. Dad's two older brothers, Arthur and Owen who also lived in Newville, were present with their families when the Williams of Shoreford arrived.

Shirley and Bobbie hurried through the greetings and their grandmother teased them, trying to start a conversation. They stood fidgeting until she grinned, "Would you like to sample the fresh cookies in the kitchen?"

There was a hearty, "Yes!" in unison.

"Go!" their grandmother laughingly commanded and patted Bobbie on the rump as he rushed past.

Their five cousins were already at work devouring the griddle baked, raisin filled, golden brown, delightful Welsh cookies, made the way only Gramma could. Jim seated himself amongst the adults. He did not have long to wait before his uncles started to chide him .. with abundant good-humor. Shoreford they claimed, had been exceedingly lucky to come away with a victory over Newville. Despite the kidding, it was very evident that Art and Owen had enormous pride in their nephew.

Bobbie returned during this time and nearly choked on a mouthful of cookie. Before the remnants had cleared his throat he proceeded to dispute his uncles, two men he loved dearly, in defense of his brother and Shoreford. His face got redder with each word and his father reached out and placed a hand on his shoulder. It took some effort, but Bobbie was finally convinced about the true meaning of his uncles' kidding. His sheepish acquiescence to his father's words was amusing to all.

The cookies, snacks, tea and milk were consumed. Gifts were exchanged that came from a fund to which all the families contributed. The debris was cleared by the men while the women washed the eating utensils and the cousins put them away. With that accomplished, Uncle Art sat at the piano to play carols, so much a part of the Williams' Christmas.

The piano was purchased in 1919 when Art came home from France, a Marine with multiple wounds and a long period of recuperation. He had much time to practice and learned quickly, in demand for singalongs wherever he went. He even played in a band briefly. His two younger brothers had been unable to enlist, because of their age. In this war too, only one, Don, was serving. The other boys in the three families were too young.

Jim did not have the deep, rich Welsh voice of the adult males and some of the cousins. Nevertheless, he truly enjoyed being part of the family chorus. Carols were sung for more than an hour. It seemed that this Christmas Eve everyone was reluctant to break up. The families drew strength and comfort in the bonding of the group.

* * *

After the holidays and the beginning of the new year, 1945, the youngsters returned to school and Jim again immersed himself in his schoolwork. The only diversion he allowed himself was attendance at Shoreford's home basketball games. This was as much to watch his friend Buck perform, as it was to school loyalty. Their friendship had matured during the football season, but Jim was drawn to the cheerful kid for an additional reason. Working at the market he overheard some conversations belittling Buck's ancestry. Mr. Myers, who Jim liked, participated in those conversations. Jim, usually bashful and not quick to offer an opinion, was incredulous and it drove him to champion Buck's cause whenever he heard such conversation, something that did not always endear him to some, but usually put an end to the talk. The two became close and staunch friends.

A very good football player, Buck was in a class by himself on the basketball court. He had fumbled a few times during the football season, but with the round ball, it was like he had glue on his fingertips. His ability to dribble around opponents and shoot from the most contorted position was uncanny. He consistently made three, four or more steals every game. Just under six feet in height, he had blinding speed and adroitness without peer. His complete lack of self grandiosity and his selflessness made him an inspiration to his teammates.

During the war years the games were held after school due to lighting restrictions. There were no street lights and windows were covered. One could attend a local game and be home before supper. Lacking the desire to play basketball and doubting his ability, Jim was content to be a spectator and offer his vocal support to the team which was enjoying a good season. Much of the credit belonged to Buck.

As the teams left the floor after the final buzzer Jim caught Buck's eye, gave him a big wave and smile, put his books under his arm and headed into the cool January darkness. A soft snow with large flakes was falling and he jogged the mile and a half through the unlit streets to his home. He was sitting in the living room doing homework when Shirley walked in the front door.

"Hi Jimmy! Great game, huh?"

"Yeh, it sure was," he answered, smiling.

Shirley was dressed in her J.V. cheerleading outfit. She stayed with the squad as was customary, to watch the varsity game. Jim was becoming more friendly with his sister. His teasing had almost disappeared. She hung her coat in the closet, went into the kitchen greeting and conversing with her parents for a few minutes before returning to the living room to sit opposite Jim.

"Jimmy," he glanced up curiously, "do you like any girl?"

He was surprised at the question and hesitated, cupping his chin in a hand, "Why the heck do you want to know that?"

"Just tell me. Is there any girl you like."

Again a pause. He grinned self-consciously, "I like em all," sheepishly adding, "they're fun to look at."

"I know," Shirley chuckled, "I've seen you trying to sneak a peek at them without their knowledge." She paused a moment, became serious and looked deeply into his eyes, "But is there any girl you really like?"

"I guess not."

He was uncomfortable with his sister's prodding.

"Well, you know Connie Snyder?"

"Course I know her. She's a cheerleader isn't she? And I've seen her swimming at Collins Park. She's good. Course I know her. Why?"

"Just wondering. She asks me a lot of questions about you. Thinks you're sorta special," giggling, she continued, "though I really don't know why." He did not respond, but looked quizzically at his sister when she asked, "Why don't you ask her out?"

"How the heck am I gonna do that?"

"Just walk up to her and ask her."

"I can't do that! Crimany! I've hardly ever talked to her."

"Why are you so afraid of girls, Jimmy?"

"I'm not!"

"You are too!"

"I'm not!"

"You are too! You'd never have had a date if Don hadn't got you started. Come on, Jimmy, take a chance!"

The conversation ended. Their mother called them to supper.

*

The next few weeks went uneasily for Jim. The first few times he saw Connie in the hall between classes he tried to avert eye contact, but was unsuccessful. She smiled easily when their eyes did meet and when they were close, she would offer a cheery, "Hi Jimmy!"

At future basketball games Jim sat closer to the front, on the side Connie occupied during the cheers. He looked only at her when the cheerleaders were on the court. When they were returning to their seats after leading a cheer she always looked straight at him. When their eyes did finally meet, he received a smile that sent his heart into orbit. As he became more daring he returned her look and smile and was soon waving to her, bashfully and unobtrusively at first, but deliberately. She was starting to fill his whole being with her presence. The innocent, unworldly schoolboy was falling in love, the way innocent, unworldly schoolboys have done since the first one room school came into existence.

Constance Snyder was the only sophomore on the varsity cheerleading squad. She was an energetic and athletic girl. An excellent swimmer, she had won many of the girls swimming events in the progressive age groups she competed in, events that took place on Shoreford Beach Days held annually over Labor Day Weekend at Collins Park. She was an average student, only because she spent more time at socializing and doing the things she enjoyed than at her studies. She was somewhat spoiled. Her father was president of the largest bank in the city. The Snyders lived in a large house near the shore in Shoreford's most exclusive area, Silver Beach.

*

By mid February Jim knew he had worked himself into the frame of mind necessary to ask her out. Monday morning he was at school early, becoming fidgety after the first bell sounded. His jitters got worse when he spotted Connie coming in the main entrance moments before the final bell, her usual practice. He became more tense as he moved toward her. He could feel the flush on his face when they quickly exchanged greetings. Blurting out words quite different from those he had rehearsed brought a smile to Connie's face. The relief in his guts was instantaneous. She nodded once and they ran in different directions to their home rooms.

Jim burst through the door as it was being closed by Mrs. Siptroth, slid into his seat, dropped two of his books and picked them up, oblivious to the muffled giggles of his classmates. Unaccustomed to such behavior from Jim, Mrs. Siptroth was still standing open mouthed, her hand on the door knob when the first words sounded from the room's speaker.

"I did it! I did it! I did it!" Jim repeated over and over to himself.

The bell sounded. He had not heard any of the morning announcements. He was unaware of the movement around him as his classmates departed for their first period classes. He felt a hand on his shoulder and looking up saw Buck's bright smile.

"What's up, Buddy?"

"Oh! ... Hi!" Jim responded and jumped to his feet grabbing his books. Walking to the door, Jim got a perplexed stare from Mrs. Siptroth. In the hall he looked at Buck, hesitated shyly, then blurted, "I got a date!"

"You got a date! Connie Snyder, ... right?" Buck answered grinning broadly.

"How the heck did you know that?"

"Crimany, Jim, I've been watching you act funny for a month now and the school gossip has been onto you two for some time. When I was at your house Saturday, waiting for you to go to Burndys, Shirley and I talked about it."

"Geeze!" exclaimed Jim looking down and shaking his head.

Buck gave him a friendly slap on the back when they split up at the stairway heading for different first period classes.

After school Jim went straight to work. At five o'clock he bid Mr. Myers goodnight and started for home. The sky was still light in the west. He broke into a jog as he often did going home. His head was in the clouds and he was full of high spirits.

Turning into the driveway Jim noticed the evening newspaper on the front lawn. He picked it up and entered the side door quietly. Unfolding the paper he began to read. The news on the front page was very positive. The Western Allies and the Soviets had entered Germany from both the west and the east. The days of the Third Reich were numbered. He picked out the details quickly. But what really sent his blood coursing was the headlines. 'U. S. Marines Land on Iwo Jima'. He knew in his heart that Don was there.

Leaving the kitchen Jim went into the living room. The entire family was present, all reading their short V-mail letters. Greetings were cheerful and Mom with a sweet smile handed him a letter from Don.

"We all got letters today," she said happily. Always in a better frame of mind when mail from Don arrived, soon after, she would return to the anxiety she nurtured so deep-rooted in her subconscious.

Conversation was spirited, but short. Mom and Shirley soon left the room to prepare supper and Bobbie returned his attention to his mail. After a chat with his father, Jim went upstairs to read his letter.

Hi, Jim,

Things have been picking up for quite a spell. Our training has been intense. The time has at last arrived. We are now aboard ship and have been told we can send messages home about going into combat. We have at last been told where, but obviously I can't say.

You are the one I'm telling what is permitted. I don't want Dad to know, because I don't want to burden him trying to keep it from Mom. You are the one I know I can trust to keep it under wraps, to bear the burden, for that is something we have done for each other all our lives.

We are really ready for the adventure ahead. I'm a little scared when I think about it, but am so proud to be with these guys. Marines cuss and swear a lot and sometimes drink too much, but they sure are the greatest bunch of guys in the world.

You take care of yourself, Brothe. See you soon. I love you.

>   Your brother and buddy,
>   Don.

When he finished the letter, Jim was more sure than ever that Don was at Iwo Jima. Despite the calm that was always with Don, Jim could sense the excitement his brother was feeling. His own pulse quickened at the realization. His brother was finally there, finally pitting his life against a determined and ferocious enemy. He felt a strong sense of pride for his brother, ... but it also scared him and for an intense moment, he considered mortal life.

When the anxiety passed, Jim was warmed by a different feeling. He sensed the rising pride in himself. Don had put trust in him, trust that required strength, Don said. Sitting on his bed, the letter in his hand, Jim gazed out the window, a gentle smile curling his lips. And Don had said he loved him.

*

Long before his mother called him, Jim awakened. His first excited thoughts were of Connie and Saturday night. They would take a trolley into the city and see a movie. Before making the trip home they would go to a nearby White Tower and have a shake and maybe a hamburg. On arrival back in Shoreford, they had a good twenty minute walk to the Snyder home. It did not matter that he would have a further thirty minute walk to his own bed after eleven o'clock, or twenty three hundred as Don would say.

Crimany! ... Don! Jim jerked up in bed. Bobbie was sound asleep. He got up and tiptoed to the radio the brothers shared. He carried it back to his bed extending the power cord to the fullest. With his ear close to the speaker he searched for the news. Details about Iwo Jima were few, but he did learn it was a small island less than eight square miles in size and less than 700 miles from Tokyo. It did not seem like much of a task to take such a place. As he listened to the news, a sense of shame came over him. Here was he, deliriously happy, while his brother was involved in a great and bloody conflict. But the shame slacked off a bit. He knew that Don was a most capable person and would perform the task at hand with flying colors. That was just the way Don was.

*

Jim and Connie met more frequently in the halls as the week went by. The one night he did not have to report to the market, he walked her home. At the same time that he was falling for her, he was gaining a confidence like none he had ever known. There were girls in his past he had feelings for, but his lack of confidence hindered his ability to do anything about it. The girl he dated with his brother did not excite him greatly and he had no further thoughts of her in a romantic sense. Now, however, he had definite romantic thoughts and they were solidified by the knowledge that Connie showed serious feeling for him. His confidence rose proportionately with that knowledge.

*

Mr. Myers teased Jim when he asked to leave an hour early on Saturday and continued to do so at odd moments during the days ahead.

Glad to finish his cleaning chores early, Jim headed for home which he reached in record time. The shower felt good and he scrubbed his body with an unusual vigor. He stayed under the hotter than normal spray a very long time trying to quell his eagerness. He dressed and went downstairs for a quick snack, thankful he was not joining his family for supper. He could do without Bobbie's constant, prodding questions and Shirley's sweet, yet very smug smiles.

His mother helped him put together a sandwich and glass of milk which he wolfed down. He ran back upstairs to clean his teeth, bounded back downstairs and grabbed his coat from the closet. Standing in the living room amongst his smiling family, his mother walked over to him, straightened his tie and put her arms about him hugging him firmly. He responded cheerfully, unaware of the smiling onlookers.

The knock on the front door sounded as his father was reaching for the knob to open the door for him. When the door swung open, he saw his father blanche, take some change from his pocket and push it through the opening before closing the door.

Holding a yellow envelope, his father opened it with unsteady hands. His mother ripped the telegram from her husband's grasp and Jim, looking over her shoulder read, "We regret to inform you ....."

Sarah Williams turned white. The paper message slipped from her fingers and floated lazily to the floor. She could not control her unsteadiness. She staggered backward and collapsed into a chair. Her head dropped like a lead weight into her hands. Sobbing shook her entire body.

Bill Williams could do nothing, but stand by the door, stunned, his own grief and misery too much for his soul to bear.

Shirley frantically picked up the telegram, read it and ran screaming from the room slamming her bedroom door.

Bobbie sat open mouthed staring into space.

P.F.C. Donald Edward Williams, U.S.M.C., indomitable, indestructible, ... Jim Williams' noble brother ... was dead!

* TWO *

The melancholy dream scene was abruptly interrupted when his wife entered and walked to the bed. "You took your shower early," she said smiling down at him.

"Yeah. I didn't have much else to do. I've been lying here .. just sorta thinking about the things that brought us here."

"I know," she continued to smile, but her face softened. She bent and kissed him on the forehead. Still leaning over him, she sighed almost inaudibly and reached for a tissue on the night stand. From the corners of his eyes to his ears she gently wiped the sides of his face. Only then was he aware of the tears that had silently and sorrowfully escaped through his tightly compressed eyelids.

He grasped her hand, brought it to his lips and kissed it, "God, I love you!"

Again she bent and kissed him, this time full on the lips. Her hair, that still beautiful hair, caressed his face. She slid her lips across his cheek and gently bit his ear lobe and whispered, "Me too!"

Almost certain of what he was thinking, she did not wish to intrude. She straightened and left the room. As her image faded his thoughts slowly returned to the past.

~ ~ ~ ~ ~

Weeks passed and a Navy Cross arrived. On February 22nd, Don had been with a group of Marines from his decimated platoon at the base of a mountain called Suribachi. The deeds stated in the award were so typical of Donald Williams.

The flag raising atop that mountain on Iwo Jima was photographed for all posterity. That photo proclaimed America's victory and the indomitable spirit of United States Marines. Jim knew that while his brother had not witnessed the event, he had been a part of what made it happen. But that thought could do nothing to deaden the pain of his and his family's dreadful loss.

*

It was mid March before a day went by that Sarah did not cry in front of someone. Bill, zombie like after the telegram, suffered silently. He came home from work one day during a snow storm, walked into the back yard and stood, hands at sides, staring at the ground for nearly ten minutes. Shirley was resilient. Had she been alone she would have returned to normality sooner, but her parents mourning affected her deeply. At first dumbfounded and languid, Bob went quickly through his period of grief. He was not aware of the depth of his parents suffering and he focused on his brother and his deeds. His imagination created a demigod he could look up to, one whose footsteps he would gladly follow, one whose example he would seek to emulate.

In those early days of 1945, Bill and Sarah Williams were completely engrossed in their own suffering and did not see the deep agony that Jim was experiencing. Jim did not understand the profound affect his brother's death was having on him. He retreated within himself. His intense grief blocked his ability to understand the meaning of his emotions, the most prevalent becoming self pity. Having always been somewhat shy, his schoolmates, with the exception of Buck, did not recognize his reticence for what it was.

Buck reached out to Jim, calling him frequently on the phone and occasionally asking for his company to share a milkshake. Jim was unaware of this good friend's valiant effort to ease his burden. As time passed Jim did take Buck up on some of his 'requests.'

Connie had a sixteenth birthday party in March. Jim begged off. Their first date had yet to occur. As an excuse not to socialize Jim continually used his job and his schoolwork, which now he was struggling to keep up.

In April Bill Williams decided to take a few courses at the electronics school in the city. He always enjoyed fixing things, most of all, electric appliances, radios and such. By the time the war was over he felt he could leave the factory and start his own radio and electrical repair shop. With television on the horizon he wanted to be ready for that event.

April was mild and warm and Sarah began to return to her old self a little more each day. Reverend Clark, their minister, had steadfastly visited twice a week for more than a month and still showed up weekly at the Williams home. His spiritual guidance was a help to her. As her wounds healed the one noticeable scar that remained was a sadness in her eyes.

By May Jim was sensing a deterioration in his body which was crying out for activity. He did not have to work on Monday and decided to walk to Collins Park after school. He went directly to the beach which was vacant. He sat in the sand looking across the water. As was often the case when he was alone his thoughts turned to his dead brother. He removed his shoes and socks, left them with his books and began to walk. The sand was mildly warm to his feet and he liked the feeling as it squished between his toes and moved beneath his feet, forcing his leg muscles to greater effort. He started slowly and gradually increased his speed. He walked to the west end, all the while forcing himself to greater exertion, turned and traversed about the length of a football field to the starting point. It felt good. After a short break he walked to the waters edge, turned west and took off on the hard packed, wet, cold sand at a trot. He completed one circuit, increased his speed for another circuit, sprinting the final fifty yards.

When the race was over he was gasping for breath. Hands on hips he walked in a small circle, head bobbing up and down, mouth hanging open as he labored to suck in the fresh sea air, the fire in his lungs slowly dying out. When his breathing returned to normal he ceased walking and sat, arms folded around bent knees. Gazing across the water he was exhilarated in his exhaustion and glad to be able to forget, if but briefly. He knew he must do this again .. and again.

*

The following day, May 8th, the entire student body was called into an assembly in the auditorium. Mr. Melillo was on the stage. He announced the surrender of Nazi Germany and the European Axis. There was jubilation mixed with relief. After a brief message of thankfulness he prodded everyone not to let down. The job of bringing Japan to its knees remained a formidable task. Many students left school at the conclusion of the assembly at the risk of disciplinary action. There was a need to celebrate, a need that was absent in Jim.

* * *

Connie Snyder was determined to coax Jim Williams back to life and into hers. As if by accident she commenced to bump into him in the halls between classes. She frequently shopped at Myers Market after school when Jim was working. The feelings he had for her were buried beneath his grief, but they were there. Despite his attempt to suppress those feelings, the day she grasped his hand and gently squeezed it before departing school was the first day he allowed himself to think openly about her.

His body, more easily curable, was responding to the physical activity at the beach. When he did not have to report to work from school, he went directly to Collins Park to run. That included the weekends. The running became a salvation and the more conditioned his body became the harder he pushed himself.

Meanwhile the days got warmer and younger boys were showing up at the playing field for baseball games. Many knew who Jim was and spoke admiringly to him when he left the beach and went past the field on his way home. Those boys were pleased to call him by name. Jim always managed to force a smile and return their greeting.

The curiosity of some of the youngsters increased. Arriving at the park they made a point to go to the top of the long knoll overlooking the beach and observe a local hero. Soon the few became a large audience and they gazed in wonder at the running maniac below, churning up the sand as he dashed from one end of the beach to the other, again and again.

The first Monday in June was sunny and hot and Jim finished his workout bathed in sweat. He felt purged and he felt good. He had made up his mind he was going to ask Connie out. Spotting the young spectators on the knoll he waved to them for the first time and got an enthusiastic response. He also noticed someone sitting on the rocks at the east end of the beach. Immediately he recognized Connie. She got to her feet and walked toward him. She was barefooted, still in the dress she wore to school. She moved nicely, even in the sand. Not knowing what to do, he stood and waited for her.

"Hi, Jimmy!"

"Hi," his reply was subdued, but inwardly he was jumping.

She walked to him and placed a hand on his forearm. He nearly flinched. His instinct was to withdraw the sweaty arm. Somehow it did not seem appropriate for her to be touching all that perspiration. He forced himself to be still and found he enjoyed the intimacy.

"That was some workout!" she smiled.

"Yeh, .. I guess so," he responded shyly. He thought he should put on his shirt, but did not want to withdraw the arm, did not want to break from her touch.

"Would you walk me home, Jimmy?"

"Yeh, .. I guess so," he muttered looking downward. He raised his head and looked directly into her eyes. Suddenly filled with courage, he smiled, though again shyly, "Sure I will!"

Jim pulled on his trousers over his running shorts and struggled with the T shirt over his sweaty torso. He picked up his books and shoes and they walked to where she had been sitting when he first saw her. They picked up her books and shoes and continued to the park entrance. Approaching the boys playing ball, a few waved and one of them cupped his hands around his mouth and yelled, "Hiii, Constance!"

"My little brother Danny." Connie waved unenthusiastically and Jim suddenly realized how she found him and was thankful for 'little' brothers. They stopped at a park bench, slipped into socks and shoes and continued the short journey in relative silence. They turned into Warren Avenue, the Snyder residence three doors away.

Connie stopped and stepped in front of Jim. Looking directly into his eyes, very softly, yet deliberately, she asked, "Don't you like me, Jimmy?"

Completely off guard at her directness, he looked away stammering, "S .. sure ... sure I do." He was uncomfortable and angry at his ineptness. He forced himself to look into her eyes and took a deep breath. Thoughtfully he replied, "I like you a lot, Connie."

Her face turned soft and her eyes sparkled through a growing smile. Something passed between them in that instant and she took his free hand in hers and squeezed.

Jim Williams was not aware of the passing time as hand in hand they completed their journey to the front steps of the Snyder residence and onto the porch, only then realizing the blissful interlude was over.

Before they could speak the front door opened and Mrs. Snyder greeted them and was introduced to Jim. She invited them in for a snack. In his unease Jim made an excuse. He got through the goodbyes just less than tongue-tied and headed home happier than he had been in a very long time.

When he walked in the side door his mother was setting the table, "Hello, Jimmy!"

"Hi, Mom!"

She gazed at him seeking a clue to the tone in his voice, "You're later than usual tonight. Did you run longer?"

"No. I walked Connie Snyder home, Mom."

"Oh, Jimmy! That's fine. I'm glad to see you taking an interest in her again."

That night in bed, Jim Williams lay awake a long time. He was unable to keep Constance Snyder from his thoughts. But he did not care. He wanted her there. When he did sleep, he dreamed pleasantly and the last dream he remembered was Don placing both hands on his shoulders and smiling down at him. When he awoke there was an aura of peace in the room.

Jim's struggle with school work began to ease at once. His relationship with schoolmates, especially Buck, improved considerably.

*

Jim Williams was filled with anticipation from the time he awakened Friday morning. He and Connie had a date to attend the Centre Theatre that night. By five he was in the shower, not just washing his body, but standing under the pelting spray stretching and rotating his head and neck to soothe the tenseness. Twenty minutes later he was dressed and heading down to the kitchen to eat an early supper.

His mother smiled happily as she served him. His father stuck his head through the kitchen entry, "Are you sure you don't want a ride, Jim?"

"No thanks, Dad. I really feel like walking and we won't have any trouble getting to the Centre by seven."

He finished his supper, bid his family farewell and walked briskly, reaching the Snyder residence well before six-thirty.

Mrs. Snyder greeted him at the door, "Hello, Jim! Come in. Connie will be ready in a moment."

He followed her into the living room. She introduced him to Mr. Snyder, a distinguished looking gray haired man who shook Jim's hand pleasantly, but seemed somewhat aloof.

Turning to the other side of the room Mrs. Snyder continued, "And this is our son Danny."

"Aw, Mom! I know Jim! Hi, Jim!"

"Hi, Dan."

Taking the seat that was offered, he was about to speak to Mr. Snyder when behind him came a cheerful and excited, "Hi, Jimmy!"

His heart thumped wildly! He jumped to his feet and turned at the same time. Connie walked into the room wearing a yellow summer dress which fit her lovely form to perfection and accented her dark brown eyes and hair. On her feet were brown saddle oxfords over white socks, folded at the ankle forming a three inch cuff.

"Hi!" he replied enthusiastically.

Following Connie into the room was her older sister Barbara. Jim knew her by sight from her senior year at Shoreford High. Mrs. Snyder introduced them and concluded, "Barbara has finished her second year at Vassar and is home for the summer."

Jim smiled in acknowledgment and turned back to Connie. Overcoming his usual reserve in a group of strangers he eagerly exclaimed, "You look great!"

He was relieved when the last, "Good night," had been spoken and the door closed behind them. They walked briskly to the corner, turned north toward the center of town and slowed their pace, their shoulders and elbows touching frequently as they moved. He did not know how to react to this light contact and in his confusion clumsily grabbed her hand. She responded by arranging their grips comfortably. They continued the journey in wonderfully blissful silence.

Friday night at the theater was traditionally high school night and when they entered the center of town, friends and acquaintances were there. Jim let go of Connie's hand and did not attempt to hold it again in public. There was sufficient time to chat with some friends and have Cokes at Burndys.

They entered the theater before seven. The back row on Friday was quickly filled by young couples wishing to sit in semiprivacy. They found seats mid way down the center aisle on the left. They were not thinking of privacy, but wanted to be reasonably close to the two giant fans at the front of the theater. Air conditioning was not yet installed in this movie house.

The news was shown first. During a scene from the fighting on Okinawa Jim recognized the camouflage helmet covers and whispered softly, "Those are Marines!"

Connie leaned against him, "What, Jimmy?"

He leaned closer and whispered, "Those are Marines."

"Oh." she answered, smiling at him in the darkness. Their shoulders and arms were now in firm contact and suddenly they both wanted it that way. Their bodies warmed considerably yet they remained so during the entire first film.

"Jimmy, would you please excuse me so I can freshen up?" Connie asked as the film ended and the previews began.

"Sure. I think I'll go to the men's room myself."

They excused themselves as they squeezed in front of four people. When they were in the aisle their hands eagerly slipped together. At the back of the theater they faced each other. With great reluctance they loosed their grips and finally their eyes and slowly went to different sides of the theater.

In the separate rest rooms, two very warm and damp sixteen year olds splashed cold water on shiny and rosy faces.

Connie dabbed her face dry and wiped the moisture from her arm. Gazing into the eyes of her smiling reflection she saw the pure and simple joy that was there ... and the giddiness. But, there was something else. When she recognized it, the smile turned a bit smug. She was feeling a distinct and growing self confidence.

Across the theater Jim splashed cold water on his face and arms and vigorously wiped them dry. He too looked at his reflection in the mirror. He too saw joy ... and a growing confidence. He was surprised at the closeness he and Connie had so quickly shared, .. but it was great. He gave it no further thought. As he turned to leave he softly said out loud, "Wow!"

Jim was out first. He waited eagerly, then happily watched her come to him. She reached out a hand which he eagerly accepted and they walked hand in hand to the row of their seats. The previews was nearly over. They slid in with as little disturbance as possible. As quickly as they were seated they anxiously moved close. Shoulders touched and Connie slid her arm under Jim's and took his hand in hers. Their fingers entwined. He squeezed her hand hard and she turned her head and beamed her smile to him. By the time the feature started their legs touched from knee to foot.

It was a new experience for both and they lost themselves in the darkness of the theater. When the film ended it took the theater lights to return them to an embarrassed reality, but they left the theater holding hands, oblivious to the humanity on all sides. They lingered over each step and said not a word.

The front porch light was on and they walked around to the back door. Holding hands they faced each other for a long time, then slowly, timidly, haltingly, came together and kissed the kiss of inexperience, but somehow it was magical. When they disengaged Connie went up the steps. Hesitating at the top, she turned and whispered softly, "Oh, Jimmy!" Then she was gone.

Jim looked up at the stars, gave a deep sigh and walked slowly to the street. When he turned the corner at Warren Avenue exuberance overwhelmed him and he sprinted three blocks. When he slowed to a walk he jumped high in the air and just managed to stifle the yell that almost escaped his throat. The journey home was completed with a smile that never diminished.

*

Connie went to New York City with her family for the weekend. Jim worked all day Saturday till six o'clock. He was agitated when anything occurred that distracted the overpowering, romantic thoughts of the girl who had barricaded his heart in a fantasy world. There were times he had to ask a customer to repeat something. Occasionally Mr. Myers or Norm Kaus curiously glanced his way and sometimes with a peculiar grin. Jim was unaware.

The mile and a half trek home took about twenty-five minutes. He greeted his family and was glad that Bobbie was reading in the living room. He went up to their bedroom and flopped on his bed.

Both Jim and Bobbie insisted that their parents take back the master bedroom and this was accomplished over a month ago. Both boys were sure it was the right thing, especially for their mother. They were right. Being in the room her sons shared, seemed, for what ever reason, to add to her solace. Jim was pleased with Bobbie's desire to reach out to their parents. He came to the conclusion that his younger brother was OK. But at the moment it was not his younger brother who was in his thoughts while he lay on his bed in a hypnotic state, suddenly and clumsily leaping to his feet when his father called him to supper.

*

Sunday morning seemed to go on forever sitting with his family in church. When they finally bade the minister and fellow parishioners farewell, Jim could not remember what the sermon was about.

Dinner on Sunday was late in the afternoon and since his father was studying and things were quiet he decided he had to break out, .. to be free to run with his emotions. He told his mother of his plans, changed into running shorts and sneakers and headed for Collins Park. He ran with a vengeance until he could run no more. When he flopped on the sand in complete exhaustion, millions of the tiny, gritty particles adhered to his sweat bathed body, but he lay there, secure and content in the knowledge he would see her tomorrow.

*

In school earlier than usual Monday morning, Jim was thankful his tired body had given in to a restful and lengthy sleep despite being filled with wild dreams in which Connie was often present. Fidgeting at his locker, he did not know why he arrived so early. Connie was always late.

But there she was, ... coming down the corridor ... early. His heart beat faster and he exerted all his self control to keep from bounding to her. When they met, they could only utter a soft, "Hi!" Their expressions said it all. Their faces aglow they walked as far as possible together not allowing themselves to hold hands. That was forbidden inside the building. They did, however, caress finger tips moving along the crowded corridors.

The day was interminably long and those closest to them where sure they knew the reason for their unusual behavior ... and they did. The bewitched sixteen year olds, by going out of their way between classes, caught sight of each other only rarely and talked briefly but once, during the entire school day. It was good that the school year would be over next week. Jim could think of little else but Connie.

They met in the hall after the final bell. He walked her home. They held hands the entire journey to the Snyder back door. They were reluctant to let go.

Final exams were about to start and both knew a lot of hard studying lay ahead yet they dragged out their farewells for nearly an hour. Jim desperately wanted to kiss her, but the sunlight and the prospect of being seen by Mrs. Snyder intimidated him. His innards groveled in frustration. She moved closer to him, but his cowardice prevented any reaction. As they said, "Good-bye," for the tenth time, Connie in desperation leaned against him and softly brushed his lips with hers. Then she was bounding up the steps.

When Jim reached his own home his shirt was soaked with the perspiration of his run. His heart was still at the Snyder back door. Study that night did not come easily, ... nor did sleep.

*

The daily routine for Jim and Connie varied only when a prior commitment interfered with their inability to be together. Since Jim worked three nights after school he walked Connie home only once more during the remainder of the week. But that day at the back steps she pressed her lips to his and he answered her. His feet seemed to barely skim the earth on the homeward journey.

*

Saturday night Jim and Connie walked to the center of town at a brisk pace, full of the joy of being together. Connie had no trouble matching him stride for stride and they held hands and swung their arms with each step. They did not stop at Burndys. They wanted a seat in the rear, unmindful of the breeze from the fans. Their eagerness paid off. They got first choice in the middle of the back row on the left side. They were holding hands before the lights dimmed, arms entwined and legs touching.

Throughout the entire show Jim Williams experienced emotions that vacillated between wild joy and serenity. The young lovers waited for the theater to empty before leaving their seats. Their clothing was damp and in places stuck to their bodies. The walk to Connie's was slow at first, then slower still, hands held firmly, bodies brushing at hip and thigh, shoulders and arms.

The front porch light was lit and they went directly to the back. They faced each other holding hands, standing so close Jim could hear her breathing. She must surely hear his heart pounding, he thought. She released his hands and placed hers on his waist and drew herself to him, tilting her face upward. He instinctively encircled her with his arms. Holding her tightly he met her lips.

It was a hard kiss at first, but they adjusted and drank from each other greedily till their breathlessness had them gasping for air. Connie looked into his eyes, searching. In the dark she could not see the adoration, but felt it. Neither could she see the distress that was seeping into his features, but she felt that too.

A change was occurring in Jim's body and the reaction in his loins to their youthful passion was discomforting and embarrassing to him. He pushed himself away just far enough to break the intimate contact. There was a sense of relief, but a greater feeling of loss and disappointment.

In his confusion he leaned over and kissed her on the lips.

"I've got to get going, Connie," he said huskily. He did not want to leave. What was worse, he did not understand his emotions and the strange desire, .. the need to be crushed against her.

Aware of Jim's state of excitement Connie did not answer, but pulled him to her, startling him with the abruptness and strength of her move. She found his lips and kissed him hard, thrilled in her inexperience at her impact on him. But she was also confused about proceeding further. She was also scared. She pushed away and ascended the stairs, more to escape the uncertainty than the excited boy who excited her so.

On the top step, a hand on the doorknob, she turned and whispered, "Goodnight, Jimmy!" and before she vanished, puckered and smacked her lips, sending him a tender and sweet kiss that bridged the distance between them, accompanied by an affirmation in the softest tone, "Jimmy, ... I love you!"

Alone, he stood transfixed to the spot, her words piercing his heart, the result, decisive. It was nearly two minutes before he moved and then only languidly, his feet hobbling to some unknown command.

In her unlit bedroom Connie stayed at the screened window till she began to worry about him. Then he was passing below. She watched him walk slowly by, stifling the urge to whisper her love through the screen. Before he vanished from her sight he threw his hands up with wild abandon, leaped high and bolted into the blanketing shadows of the night.

Connie Snyder turned from the window smiling. It was a joyful smile. It was a smile filled with some very strong emotions for Jim Williams. But there was something else. She was pleased with her newly discovered power.

*

Sunday morning dragged until the time came to leave. In a departure with tradition Jim would not share Sunday dinner with his family. He was going to a picnic lunch with Connie, her sister and sister's boyfriend, Jason Parks. They were going to dine at Silver Beach, the exclusive beach for the residents of that part of Shoreford.

Jim felt like running, but had plenty of time and forced himself to a moderate pace. He would soon be with Connie and the anticipation gave birth to a tumult in his stomach that pummeled unmercifully the composure he desired. He breathed deeply and swung his arms. He talked to himself. By the time he rang the bell at the Snyder front door he had conquered some of his nervousness, but only some.

Exchanging greetings with the Snyder family politely, Jim was introduced to Jason, a tall, blonde, Ivy Leaguer. He was exceedingly happy he did not have to be long alone in this group.

Connie entered at once.

"Hi, Jimmy!" she pleasantly and excitedly greeted him.

"Hi!" He broke into a huge grin.

Connie was in her swimsuit and sandals, a towel around her neck and a much larger towel over her arm.

"Let's go!" she commanded grinning brightly at her companions.

"That's my little sister," Barbara smiled at Jim and Jason, "always the last one ready and the first out the door."

"Don't you want to change, Jim?" Mrs. Snyder asked.

"Thanks, Mrs. Snyder, but I've got my suit on under my pants."

They completed their farewells and left in a hurry.

Outside Connie placed her hand in Jim's. The two sixteen year olds rubbed shoulders and elbows and arms and occasionally thighs strolling unseen behind Barbara and Jason. Often they snickered silently as the body caressing turned to body bumping and was soon a game.

At the beach the sisters placed the large towels on the sand. Jason and Barbara headed for the water. Jim was warming to Barbara. As a senior in high school she came across as a snob. Her relationship with Connie, whom she was genuinely pleased to be with, was the reason.

Sitting on the edge of Connie's towel Jim removed his shoes and socks and watched them walk away. Barefooted, he jumped to his feet beside Connie who was feigning impatience and teasing him.

"Hurry up, slowpoke. What's the matter? Do you need some help?"

Loosening his trousers he removed one leg and lifted the other to free it. A smirk lighted Connie's face, but Jim recognized it too late. She lunged, pushing him onto his back, laughing all the while, then dashed madly to the water. Free of the trousers he jumped to his feet and raced after her echoing her laughter.

She was stroking strongly when he plunged in, arms in motion, feet kicking furiously. They sprinted fifty yards and he was unable to reduce the distance between them. She stopped. Treading water she turned to face him. He drew up to her. Giggling, she plunged her palm across the surface splashing him full in the face.

"Think you're smart, huh?" he shouted lunging at her, but she was gone.

Trying with everything he possessed he could not overtake her. Again he came upon her treading water. Again she attempted the previous maneuver, but he was ready this time. With a powerful lunge he caught her ankles the split second before she escaped.

Superb in the water, Connie knifed straight down pulling Jim, but his weight was too much for her aquatic brashness. She arched her back and headed for the surface pulling him along. Moving one hand from ankle to knee, then the other, he turned her body and pulled himself up slowing the ascent and skimming her lithe body with his face. Their heads broke the surface in unison. Breathing heavily from their exertions, he placed his hands on her shoulders. She grasped his elbows and they moved their limbs only enough to keep their heads above water. They stayed that way perhaps a minute, their eyes glued together, smiling the smile of adoration and exhilaration.

Connie's expression was first to change, her smile turning coquettish. Releasing her grip, she moved her arms vigorously in a circular motion that carried her beneath the surface feet first. Jim instantly imitated her, following her downward. Well below the surface she grasped him. He grabbed back and two bodies became one. They clamped lips together and kissed with a passion they no longer wanted to delay. Their stability gone, they twisted and turned out of control.

They shot to the surface, their lungs on fire as they gasped for air. They tread water to regain their composure. When their breathing returned to normal they were smiling and full of a confidence that was bred of their mutual and burning infatuation.

Without a word and as if by command they started swimming to shore. They swam with a slow, rhythmic crawl stroke. At the part of the stroke when heads turned to a side for air, they faced each other. Close to the shoreline they stopped swimming and walked through the shallow water onto the warm sand. Barbara and Jason were sitting at a picnic basket dropped off by Mr. and Mrs. Snyder.

Connie picked up a towel to dry her hair.

"You two were a long way out, .. just for a swim," Jason said, a mirthful grin on his face as he winked at Jim.

Uncomfortable with Jason's meaning, Jim looked away.

"Mom wasn't too happy about it either," Barbara added.

"Gee, I'm really sorry," Jim quickly replied. "I guess I just wasn't paying attention."

Jason wink went unnoticed as Connie gazed into Jim's eyes, tilting her head just a bit and smiled.

They ate the lunch savoring the delicacies Mrs. Snyder prepared. With the clean up complete, Barbara and Jason decided to explore the shoreline.

Jim had a lot of studying to do and knew their time together must be cut short. Likewise, Connie was allowed on this outing only after promising to be home early to hit the books. They were not sorry when Jason and Barbara departed. They contented themselves in their final hour together, lying on their stomachs, eyes partially shut for protection from the sun, but their gaze locked. In the midst of an ever increasing beach population, the sun warmed flesh of their arms was reluctantly, their only contact.

After lying still for some time Connie smiled, squeezing Jim's hand, "You didn't have to take the blame for us being out so far, .. but I love you for it."

Jim smiled shyly, blushing slightly. She quickly and neatly brushed his lips with hers. He hoped no one witnessed the incident, but immediately realized he did not care. He was in love, ... he was in heaven.

When it was time to go Jim dressed and carried the picnic basket in one hand and with the other, held tightly to Connie, fingers interlocked. Putting the basket down at the back steps he looked deeply into her dark brown, by now, subdued eyes. Courage came easily with her parents away. He reached with both hands into her soft, brown hair and pulled her lips to his kissing her hard. He did not dare linger, knowing that every passing second would make it more difficult to break away, ... more difficult to control his passions.

Connie watched him leave from the bottom step, her face alight with her feelings. He did not look back, for seeing her, he knew he would rush to her.

*

The final days of the school year Jim and Connie desperately sought each other between classes, between exams, whenever there was an opportunity. On two nights they walked to her home, glued together. It seemed only to intensify the desire to be together, a situation made worse by the coming events. Saturday morning Connie was leaving for the Snyder family's usual summer vacation at their beach cottage in Maine. She would not return till just prior to Shoreford Beach Days. That seemed ages away, almost an eternity to the young, energized and impatient lovers.

*

The first day of summer vacation, early Friday morning, Jim was cutting the grass. Mr. Kobak the Williams' neighbor on the other side of the street came out his side door. He crossed and walked over to Jim.

"Good morning, Mr. Kobak." Jim noticed the stern look on the neighbor's face.

"Morning, Jim. Have you heard the news?"

"What news, Mr. Kobak?"

"Jim, ... we .. we just heard. .. I'm sorry, .. but .. uh," he stopped and sighed, "we just heard that Tim Ryan and Tony Capoletti went down with their ship off Okinawa!"

"Oohhh, God! Nooo!" Jim groaned.

"The kamikazes hit them hard. I understand their ship took a direct hit. I'm sorry to have to tell you this, Jim. I know you were really close to them."

Jim stood transfixed, his hands on the handle of the mower, his head sagging and shaking slowly in disbelief. He stared at the ground. He fought with his emotions. He wanted to cry, but forced himself to hold back the tears. He was not aware of Mr. Kobak's departure.

Cringing at the thought of opening his mother's wounds he went inside and gave her the news. She remained composed despite the faraway look that clouded her eyes and the tears she wiped away. There had been too much suffering.

He called Connie. She sobbed, "Oh, Jimmy!" and cried softly into the phone. Again he wanted to cry, but again he smothered his tears and gritted his teeth.

The movies that night did nothing to elevate the spirits of Jim and Connie. The walk to the Snyder home was slow and sad. They walked with arms about waists, leaning on each other. They needed to lean, needed the mutual support each gave.

At the back door the many words Jim rehearsed would not come forth. Their parting kiss was long ... and their beings merged while their bodies clung. They were vulnerable to conflicting emotions and to each other. They did not want to loose their lips or let go. When Jim was unable to control the excitement in his loins he was angry with himself. Despite his intense desire to remain glued to Connie he pushed slowly, hesitatingly away. Today did not seem appropriate for such feelings.

Connie in her turn was wavering between common sense, the grief heaped upon them and passion for the boy she would not see again for weeks. The common sense prevailed and she allowed him to become separate from her. What little light there was reflected from the tears on her cheeks.

Standing apart now, Connie turned slowly. Holding the rail she walked unsteadily up the stairs. She did not want to leave him. When she reached the top she turned and made a move to descend, but instead, gave a feeble wave and entered the house.

The trip home for Jim was slow and tedious and a sojourn into loneliness. He arrived so much later than usual his mother was beginning to show signs of worry. Seeing her son's demeanor she was sympathetic and gave him a tender hug.

* * *

Jim was thankful for his job that summer. During July Norm Kaus took a two week vacation which meant that Jim had to work additional hours. It was at that time he decided he must visit the Ryan and Capoletti families. He did not want to witness grief like that again, but could not escape it. He was sure he owed that much to Tony and Tim.

There was a warm welcome for Jim at both households. After condolences and all were more at ease, the good memories were recalled and though there were tears of sadness, there were also tears of happiness, for the joy of having known those two. Jim was able to relate events that the families knew little or nothing about and there were smiles and even some laughter. The initial dread passed quickly and Jim was glad he came. The invitations to return were genuine. For a short time that day his thoughts were diverted from Connie.

* * *

Gasoline was more readily available. The first Saturday in August Jim was entrusted with the family car. He drove Shirley and Bobbie to a suburb outside of Boston to spend two weeks with their maternal grandparents. He enjoyed the rare visits with Gram and Gramps MacPherson. It would be a pleasant interlude to a monotonous summer. Especially enjoyable was their grandfather's droll humor and dry wit, which by now, Jim was used to. His sister and brother were occasionally caught off guard and Bobbie could frequently be seen casting an unhappy glance at his grandfather which turned to embarrassment when he saw the smiles on other faces.

Meals were always a delight. Their grandmother was superb at putting various vegetables and meats together in pies, stews and hashes. Overeating was the norm for the youngsters, but there was always room for the great fruit pies Gram baked.

Before Shirley and Bobbie retired that night, Gram served tea with her wonderful Scottish shortbread which could not be resisted. The conversation was light and cheerful and lasted till well after 11:00PM. It was a fun time for Jim and he was surprised that he was sorry to see his sister and brother go to bed. He sat much later into the night talking with his grandparents.

It was a healing conversation. They spoke at length of Don and later of Tony and Tim and later still, of Connie. Gram and Gramps listened and Jim was thankful for their wisdom. He secretly wished they had been closer when Don was killed. It would have made it easier. Then he scolded himself for the thought. He knew that his own mother and father had to deal with that tragedy from a very different perspective. He could not walk in their shoes anymore than his grandparents could. He felt better going to bed that night than at any time since Connie went to Maine.

*

When his grandmother shook Jim awake, everyone was up and dressed. His mind was groggy, but displeased at the mandatory church attendance his grandparents required. Besides, it was always such a long drive. Presbyterian Churches were not abundant in New England.

Gram started the Sunday dinner right after church. Jim had promised his mother he would be home before dark. Shirley, always helpful at home, was chased from the kitchen. That would change in the days to come, but today Gram wanted her to join her grandfather and brothers.

The foursome took the short walk to a pond a quarter of a mile behind the grandparent's home. Gramps loved bird watching and visited the pond at least weekly on a year round basis. In this environment he could talk non-stop about the winged creatures, displaying a passion unknown to any who had never shared these moments with him. Shirley hung to every word he spoke. Bobbie, with the loyalty to those he loved, listened attentively at first, then enthusiastically. Jim heard much of what was being said in earlier times when it was he and Don who were the students. Nevertheless, he still enjoyed listening to the strong, but gentle man who could hold his interest like few others. He had seen his grandfather coax chickadees to perch on a finger and eat from his hand.

Returning to the house the siblings devoured the dinner with gusto. Their grandmother enjoyed their enthusiasm. She packed a lunch for Jim's return trip that included an extra large piece of blueberry pie. Sadly, he made ready to leave and when he hugged his sister, he realized he meant it. It was not a bad feeling.

*

The following day, Monday, August 6, 1945, Jim was at work when the newspapers were dropped at the market. The headlines were huge. Something called an atom bomb had been dropped on a city in Japan called Hiroshima. Three days later a second bomb hit another city with the name of Nagasaki. The radio broadcasts and the newspapers were filled with reports of the terrifying destructive power of the new weapon. Consensus was, the end of the world's greatest conflict was near.

Six days later on a sunny Wednesday, the announcement came. Japan surrendered unconditionally!

Through the large front window of Myers Market Jim watched spellbound as Main Street, Shoreford, U.S.A. erupted and filled with frolicking, dancing, hand shaking, hugging, kissing humanity. Norm Kaus and two other employees rushed into the street. Mr. Myers thumped Jim on the back with an exuberance heretofore unknown. The expressions of overpowering joy and relief were unreal in their intensity. The inhibited became animated, the gloomy smiled and laughed, the staid became giddy and for a brief moment in history, there was peace.

After a short spell of observing the gleeful anarchy, Mr. Myers sent Jim to recall the employees, no easy task at the moment.

When the last reentered the store, Mr. Myers said, "Let's close up, folks. You'll be paid for the rest of the day." He paused briefly and softly added, "God bless us!"

The joy in Jim was blunted as thoughts passed through his mind walking home. Remembering that terrible night in February and the more recent news of Tim and Tony, he said to himself, "God, what a cost!"

When he entered the house his mother ran to him. She threw her arms about him sobbing uncontrollably, "Oh, Jimmy! Isn't it wonderful?"

* * *

Two more weeks before Connie was due home, two weeks that were exasperatingly long. As the time of that homecoming drew nearer, Jim grew more restless. In his thoughts she was so much a part of him. Thinking of her, which was what he mostly did when alone, he remembered happily the way they played and fooled around, her athleticism and ability to be physical and not need the pampering many girls desired. And boy! Was she great to be next to. That was the thought that aroused something primeval in him, something he did not understand, nor seek to understand.

They wrote detailed letters daily, but that only intensified his hunger for her. Her letters expressed a mutual burning desire to be with him. Sometimes though, like her letter today, she seemed silly. She and Barbara saw a movie about a gangster who called his girlfriend, 'Baby'. She said that every time the guy spoke that name she got goosebumps. He wondered if he called her, 'Baby', would goosebumps appear.

*

When Mr. Myers called Jim to the phone and he recognized Connie's voice he was transformed immediately. He beamed, he laughed and once again he could not remember the words he wanted to say. He was walking in the clouds. Connie would leave her home about the same time he left the market. They would meet somewhere on Carson Street.

Mr. Myers smiled knowingly when Jim was getting ready to leave.

"Jim, I've never seen you do the cleanup so fast. I thought for awhile the hurricane season was starting early." The older man grinned when they said, "Goodnight," and watched Jim hurry away.

East past the town green, then a block beyond and Jim turned south on Carson Street. No longer able to suppress his yearnings he broke into a run. About a minute later he spotted her, three blocks away. He increased his effort and when she saw him she started running, slowly at first, but picking up speed as they came closer.

It was fortunate they met at the wooded area of Carson Street where they came together in a gush of movement, unaware of the world about them, which miraculously they had to themselves.

In each others arms Jim had Connie off the ground swinging her wildly around. When her feet regained the earth, mouth sought mouth, missing badly, but swiftly the miscalculation was corrected. They remained glued together till the need to breath forced a return to sanity.

The day was unusually hot for the time of year and they were perspiring freely and breathing heavily. They collapsed to a sitting position on the grass between the edge of the sidewalk and the treeline. With their bodies riveted side by side, shoulder to foot, Jim took her hands in his. They reacquainted themselves visually and their eyes reflected the joy that inhabited their beings.

Connie was dressed in a sleeveless jersey, shorts, tennis sneakers and ankle socks. Jim was immediately aware of her tan. She was darker than he who had spent ample time in the sun. Her legs and arms were firm and he knew she had done a great deal of swimming. She looked terrific! When he gazed into her eyes he could see the sparkle. He was filled with confidence.

Their smiles turned to silly grins.

"That was the worst summer vacation I ever had!" Connie said, at last breaking the silence.

"Oh gosh, I know, .. I know!"

"I got mad at Barbara. Jason came up on three different weekends and all I had were your letters. I was really jealous of her," she hesitated, fixing her gaze deeply into his, "I think they might have been doing it."

"Doing what?!"

"Oh, you know," she grinned mischievously.

Jim's face turned red and he averted her eyes.

Her expression softened. She brought his hand to her lips and kissed it.

"I'm sorry, Jimmy, I didn't think you'd mind."

He smiled and breathed deeply, his embarrassment dissolving. He squeezed her hands quite hard.

"Aw heck, it's OK. I really don't mind. I guess I was just ... you know .. sorta surprised."

She kissed him on the cheek and once again he wished he could verbalize the emotions he was feeling. He could never put into words that which he desired when with Connie, but when she leaned her head against his shoulder and his head touched hers, it did not matter, they were together.

But being together was not enough to save them from hungry insects. The mosquitoes were vicious and the young lovers were forced to flee. It was impossible to make plans being bombarded by cannibalistic creatures.

They made their plans on the move and by the time they reached the Snyder back door, all was in order. They hugged energetically, kissed quickly and parted.

Rushing to be ready Connie dashed up the back steps while Jim broke into a run when he reached the sidewalk.

"Jimmy! What in the world have you been doing?" Sarah squealed as her son charged through the kitchen door, his shirt saturated with perspiration, droplets covering his face and arms.

"Just running, Mom, just running!" His face was a huge grin. He picked his mother from the floor and squeezed her tightly.

She gasped and breathlessly commanded, "Put me down, Jimmy, put me down!" Back on the floor she wiped her son's perspiration from her face with the corner of her apron all the while shaking her head, but smiling at his exuberance.

Helping her mother with supper preparations, Shirley shrieked when Jim turned his gaze on her.

"Don't you touch me, Jimmy Williams! Don't you dare touch me! Yuuk! You're disgusting." Jim reached out to pat the top of her head and she screamed, "Nooo!" and ran behind her mother.

Blowing them a kiss he laughed and bounded for the shower. Bobbie, drawn to the kitchen by the commotion, was greeted with a hard punch to the upper arm as Jim sped past. The retaliatory blow missed wildly. Jim raced up the stairs touching every third step. Quickly undressed and in the shower the hot water beat full force on his appreciative, needful body.

Bill Williams promised his son the use of the family car the week before Connie's return. This was their first date in an automobile and when Jim came to a stop in front of the Snyder home he was feeling good about his new status. He rationalized that he had become an adult with the turn of a key.

Mrs. Snyder welcomed him enthusiastically and Mr. Snyder exhibited less than his usual reserve. From Barbara he received a light hug.

Dan admired Jim. It showed in his face when he said spiritedly, "Hi, Jim!"

He was feeling good about himself.

Before they could be seated Connie's footsteps were heard running down the stairs. Entering the room she went straight to Jim. The yellow chiffon dress on her trim, athletic figure looked great to him.

Taking his hands in hers she searched his eyes, tilted her head slightly and with that coquettish manner she sometimes displayed, said softly and short of breath, "Hi!"

"Hi!" he answered, exhilarated with her presence, but uneasy with her expression. He hoped the family did not notice the dare in those eyes, or his own discomfort. He was sure he saw Barbara smile. He squeezed Connie's hands and tried to force the tenseness from his body and psyche. He did not succeed.

Mrs. Snyder's words broke the spell, "Are you sure you children wouldn't like to share supper with us on the patio? We're having many of the foods you enjoyed in the past, Jim."

"Thanks a lot, Mrs. Snyder, but we really want to try that new place in Crampton, the one the two wounded vets opened up. All the kids say they have the best stuff around and everything is charcoal broiled."

Connie enthusiastically echoed him.

Mrs. Snyder was disappointed, but did not pursue it further. She walked with them to the door. She took Connie's hands in hers and looked at Jim, "I know I don't have to tell you to be careful."

"No, Ma'am. I sure will be."

Mrs. Snyder kissed her daughter on the cheek. Jim and Connie went out the door, walked across the porch and down the steps and crossed the sidewalk. He opened the car door and she climbed aboard.

For as long as he could remember he liked looking at girl's legs, but only as a youngster had he observed legs, those of his cousin Kit, with the hidden intensity he now focused on Connie's and the perfectly straight stocking seams.

When beside her, Jim wanted to touch her, but refrained. Mrs. Snyder was standing in the door. Connie sat oblique, her left leg bent under her on the seat, her knee touching his leg as they pulled away. Before they reached Main Street, she placed a hand on his shoulder and before Main Street became the Old Post Road heading out of town and the half hour drive to Crampton, she was straddling the gear shift, their bodies touching all the way to the floor, her hand resting lightly on his knee.

The only sound was that of the engine and the warm air rushing past the open windows. Locked in their own little world, nothing else mattered. They rode happily in silence.

When they arrived at their destination they were momentarily disappointed the journey had ended. Jim got out of the car and placed their order. When he returned they enjoyed foot long, charcoal broiled hot dogs plastered with everything but chopped onions. As they ate, their eyes remained locked. Their contented, happy smiles never wavered. After washing the last of the hot dogs down with large containers of ice cold white birch beer, Jim got them ice cream cones. It all tasted delicious and for the moment was enough to distract them.

The sun was low in the sky by the time they finished. Dumping the trash in a large refuse can Jim reentered the car and they drove to the seawall at Crampton Beach, a favorite spot on summer evenings. They shared the area with dozens of others, including many young children, most of whom strolled the beach below the seawall with their parents.

Jim and Connie decided to walk. He removed his shoes and socks and got out of the car to allow her the privacy to unhook stockings from a garter belt.

Barefooted, they made their way down the seawall steps to the still warm sand. Hand in hand they strolled past the end of the seawall and slowly traversed the longest beach of any of the shoreline towns. When they reached the point where the salt marshes began, they found themselves alone and some distance from the nearest people. They sat in the sand and watched the last of the multipinks disappear from the sky and the horizon turn deep orange around the setting sun. They talked and talked some more to the accompanying sound of water lapping the shore. Their time together was enhanced by the beauty of the sunset colors before the darkness which in its turn gave birth to millions of bright, twinkling stars.

When they tired of sitting they stretched out on their sides. They rested heads on hands propped up by elbows and talked some more, oblivious to the passage of time. When that position required adjustment, they squirmed. Their toes touched. Electricity surged. Toe sought toe. In the fleeting silence that followed their abrupt intake of breath, the only sound in their world was the tiny wavelets softly crumpling over the sand below their feet.

Bolting to a sitting position Jim exclaimed, "Where the heck is everybody?"

"Oh! My goodness! They're all gone!" Connie echoed Jim's concern.

Jumping to their feet Jim grabbed Connie's hand and they walked rapidly to the only car left at the seawall. They scrambled aboard out of breath. Coming down the road to the seawall was a pair of headlights. They knew it was the police.

"Oh, boy!" Jim cried out, "We gotta get outa here!"

Hurriedly, clumsily, he searched for the ignition with the key. He found it and started the engine. He spun the wheels, backed up four feet and turned sharply. Connie slid down in the seat until they passed the police car.

It took a few moments to realize they had done nothing wrong. The police always checked such places after dark. They felt foolish for their reaction and giggled self consciously and finally laughed briefly. When the first street lights of Crampton center appeared ahead, Jim pulled off the road.

"This seems like as good a place as any to put our shoes and socks on," said Jim.

After Jim tied his second shoe he started to get out of the car to allow Connie her privacy.

"Don't get out, Jimmy, .. please!"

He was happy she wanted him there. It seemed natural.

Inserting her feet into the stockings she rolled them up her legs, twisting and turning and feeling for the seams, while in the dim glow from the street lights he observed. When she hiked up her dress to hook the stockings to the garter belt he was fascinated and feeling special, allowed to witness such a private ritual. She did not have to touch him to excite him.

Checking the seams for straightness one last time, Connie said with a giggle, "The next time I wear stockings with you, they'll be seamless."

She slid next to him placing a hand on his thigh. He started the engine and pulled onto the road. A few times along the way she squeezed his leg and lay her head on his shoulder. He could smell the sweet odor of her hair and feel the warmth of her body. Secure in their private precinct, their bodies sensing the intimacy, their thoughts wandering less cautious paths, neither wanted the ride to end.

By the time they came to a stop in front of the Snyder residence their desire was only to share their intimacy more deeply, but the silhouette of Mrs. Snyder standing in the front door splashed and soaked them with the cold water of reality.

Waving to them, Mrs. Snyder opened the screen door and motioned them inside. Jim took as much time as possible exiting the car before going to Connie's side to help her out. It was time he needed to annul his embarrassment.

"I was somewhat worried. I expected you sooner," Mrs. Snyder said, relieved. She kissed Connie on the cheek.

"Golly! I'm sorry, Mrs. Snyder. After we ate, I drove to Crampton Beach and I got to talkin and kinda forgot about the time. I'm really sorry."

"It's only because I'm a mother," she smiled pleasantly, "and this was Connie's first date in an automobile. Mr. Snyder went to bed for he has to catch an early train tomorrow morning. Danny is in bed and Barbara is not home. I had the time on my hands and that is not good for a parent waiting for a child to return. All right, enough of that. I've just baked an angel food cake. Come along to the kitchen and have a piece."

"Gosh, thanks, Mrs. Snyder, but it's kinda late. I ..," Immediately aware of Connie's unhappy frown, Jim changed course, smiling self consciously, "Uh .. gee, that really does sound good, Mrs. Snyder."

Leading the way to the booth in the kitchen Mrs. Snyder served them angel food cake and milk. She sat with them joining the conversation.

"The cake was really great, Mrs. Snyder ... and it was a great idea. Thank you."

"I'm glad you enjoyed it, Jim," the older woman smiled warmly, "and happy you joined us. You must come again."

"Thank you, I will. Well," he sighed, "I guess I better be going. Thanks again Mrs. Snyder."

When Jim rose to leave, Mrs. Snyder stayed in the kitchen. Connie walked him to the door and switched off the inside hall lamp. With only the light from the porch coming through the screen door the interior was in semidarkness.

Instantly they were crushed together. The blood gushed to Jim's loins. He tried to maneuver his lower body away, but Connie slid her arms down to his waist, holding him tenaciously. How long they stayed that way he did not know, but when they came apart his head was swimming and they were breathing as if they had completed a marathon.

"I love you, Connie!" he hoarsely whispered, stumbled out the door and staggered to the car.

Connie stayed where she was, not only to watch him out of sight, but to bring her own breathing under control.

He drove slowly going home. There were unusual thoughts in his mind he did not know how to handle.

Bobbie was sleeping peacefully when Jim climbed onto his bed and lay staring into the darkness. His mind refused to stop rethinking the events of the evening. He found he was concentrating more and more on the moments he and Connie were physically close.

"Boy oh boy!" he said over and over to himself. He heard a few of the guys at school talk about their prowess with girls, but Don had laughingly explained that this was usually exaggerated boasting. His sexual education did not extend much further. He did remember the gist of something his father said to him about a year ago, something like, he should think of a female as somebody's mother or sister and treat them accordingly. But crimany! Connie was not his mother, or his sister and the feelings he had for her were exciting beyond his wildest dreams.

Sleep came slowly and when it did it was filled with the most unusual dreams.

*

"Jimmy," his mother yelled up the stairs, "you're wanted on the phone, ... it's Connie."

He rolled to his back, struggled to a sitting position and tried to focus his eyes on the circular alarm clock.

"Crimany! It's almost eight o'clock," he said out loud. Overcoming his lethargy he vaulted from the bed, grabbed his robe and ran downstairs to the phone. "Hello?"

"Hi, sleepy head!"

The sound of her voice hurried his pulse and livened his face with a smile.

"Mornin," he replied sheepishly.

"Do you think you're up to a swim, or do you need more rest?" A soft giggle punctuated her jocular taunt.

"I'll fix you ... you ... you bet I'm ready and I'm gonna beat your pants off!"

"Jimmy!" his mother blurted.

Connie's laughter was as instantaneous as his embarrassment while Shirley giggled quietly and Bobbie grinned. But the momentary discomfort did not matter, Connie's invitation did. Filled with happiness, he hung up, knowing they would soon be together.

"Mom, I'm gonna meet Connie for a swim at Silver Beach, .. OK?"

"Doesn't the football team have a meeting today?"

"Yeh, but it's not till ten thirty and Mrs. Snyder has invited me to lunch after the meeting, ... before I go to work. And I'll cut the grass tomorrow. OK?"

"All right, Jimmy, but don't try to do too many things at one time or something will suffer."

"Thanks, Mom!"

He went up to the bathroom and removed the shorts with the large rigidified spot and remembered the wild dream. A smile lit his face. He was filled with wonder and a tiny guilt, which he did not question, but shoved aside. He showered, dressed quickly and packed a small gym bag. He gobbled some toast, cleaned his teeth, bid his mother and siblings farewell and left at a rapid pace, soon to turn into a run.

Turning into Warren Avenue he spotted Connie sitting on the front steps and sprinted to her. Their faces beamed. They enthusiastically uttered a soft, "Hi!" He reached out and took one of her hands and squeezed. She squeezed back.

"Good morning, Jim. How are you?" Mrs. Snyder greeted him from behind the screen door.

"Good Morning, Mrs. Snyder, I'm fine thanks. How are you?"

"I'm fine, Jim," she smiled, "would you like something cold to drink? You look like you could use it."

The morning was warm and Jim was thirsty from his exertions. He asked for a glass of water. She brought it in a large tumbler with many ice cubes. He gulped it down.

"Would you like another?"

"No thanks, Mrs. Snyder, that was great!"

"Would either of you like something to eat before you go to the beach?"

"No, Mom! We're going swimming, not lying in the sand. I'm going to teach Jimmy how to swim," she giggled.

"All right, but be careful," Mrs. Snyder smiled benignly. "Watch out for her, Jim, she's a showoff in the water."

The two youngsters waved to the older woman and cheerfully headed for Silver Beach. During the short walk Jim concentrated on the vivacious creature moving with effortless stride at his side. She was wearing the yellow woolen Jantzen which was not new, but her favorite. It allowed for the activity she so enjoyed. She had grown into the swimsuit that fit her lithe young body to perfection.

Connie placed the towel well back from the water's edge. The tide was out, but beginning to come in. Jim bent to unlace his shoes and she joyfully pushed him backwards to land on his rump, giggling softly, bouncing just far enough away to be out of reach.

"Jumpin Jehoshophat! Not again!"

He looked up into her broad, impish grin and sparkling eyes that flashed a challenge.

"You're askin for it!" he slyly grinned.

He wanted to jump up and grab her, wrestle her to the sand, but two elderly ladies, the only other beach occupants, deterred him.

He undressed to his swim trunks. Still grinning Connie held out a hand and helped him to his feet. Too conscious of the audience to retaliate he walked with her. She knew he would. They entered the water and started walking until it reached midthigh, then plunged gently in and began to swim to a raft and diving board anchored another twenty-five yards out. The diving board faced seaward and the depth at low tide was about five feet, permitting shallow dives.

Connie was as talented off the board as she was in the water. Jim sat on the raft and contented himself as a spectator to her performance. It was easy for him. Her marvelous figure and flawless form pleased his visual sense as she executed a half dozen beautiful dives.

Climbing onto the raft she gazed down at him, "Aren't you going to join me?"

"I really enjoy watching you, ... I really do. And besides, I would feel like a fool by comparison." He looked away from her.

Her face softened. She sat beside him and leaned her head against his, "Would you mind if I helped you, Jimmy?"

Taken momentarily aback, he hesitated. He had never been instructed by a girl. But Connie was a special girl, .. his girl. He smiled and replied shyly, but with enthusiasm, "That would be great!"

She went to work and he responded with alacrity. In no time he was entering the water cleanly and attaining heights off the board that impressed her. He was exhilarated with his new found talent. He was not sure whether Connie was an excellent teacher or that she brought out the best in him, or maybe both. Soon he was climbing onto the raft and diving in quick succession.

"Jimmy, I think you'd do this all day," she pouted good naturedly.

He was at once contrite. He was neglecting the one person that meant more to him than anyone or anything. He put his arms about her in full view of the beach occupants. He kissed her. Remembering her letter, he looked into her eyes, hesitated a moment, then smiled self consciously, "Oh, Baby! I'm sorry!"

She pressed against him and shivered. When she gazed up at him there was a sensuousness in her eyes. "Let's go for a swim," she said huskily. Taking his hand she led him to the edge of the raft. Diving in, they swam seaward with a slow rhythmic stroke, side by side.

Camel Rock was a large boulder formation over 250 yards from shore. It jutted five feet above high water and was about ten feet in diameter. At low tide it was ten yards wide and twenty-five or so long. The long side ran parallel to the shore. A gentle slope to seaward permitted habitation until about an hour before high tide.

Most of the formation was still exposed when Jim and Connie rounded the end and slid up on the smooth stone slope concealed from the shore. Lying face down they rested after the lengthy swim, feet and ankles in the water, the sun drying their bodies. With few boats about they were alone and secure in their private sanctuary. The wonderful tranquillity put them at ease and Connie soon closed her eyes.

Gazing at her inert and peaceful form Jim smiled to himself. He could not escape the mischievous thoughts that passed through his mind as he remembered her exploits on the beach. He could not resist a scheme to take his revenge when she was so vulnerable. Very carefully raising on an elbow, he moved his fingertips to the small of her back, lightly running them up her spine and back down.

"Ooohh!" she sucked in her breath shivering, her body responding to the exquisite tickle. "Ooohh, you rat!" she rolled partially to her side.

Grinning wickedly, she instantly slung a leg over his back and was astride him, digging her fingers into his ribs. He laughed, begging for mercy. With great effort he rolled to his back. She did not give up easily and was still astride him, but now, he caught her wrists and imprisoned them.

"Now I've got you and are you gonna pay."

He laughed a make believe, evil laugh and looked into her eyes, eyes that sparkled, eyes that were full of mirth, but slowly, willfully, turned sensuous. The playful mood dissolved. Ever more strongly their eyes locked in an erotic embrace. Neither had experienced the kind of excitement now surging through their beings, that locked them in its grasp, triggering a desire for more.

Their eyes still locked, he let go of her wrists and carefully slid his hands up her arms, grasping the shoulder straps of the swimsuit. Pulling the straps slowly and gently he set free her breasts, fixing his gaze there. White in contrast to the deep tan of her body, the small, pink nipples poked out from near perfect demispheres. He stared and she let him. She wanted him to. She was pleased with, filled with the wonder in his eyes. He wanted to kiss them, fondle them, do something, for they seemed to be sending an invitation.

At last she took his hands and placed them there, one on each and he wanted to squeeze them, but he was not sure that was the thing to do, .. but he wanted to.

Mouth open wide, sucking the fresh sea scented air deep into his lungs, Connie plunged downward, mashing her lips to his. They drank greedily, their tongues lashing wildly. She gripped the water covered rock with her toes. Their loins crushed together while they moved and rubbed aggressively. Within seconds Jim wrenched his mouth from hers and groaned loudly to the heavens.

They remained together a long time, her breasts crushed between them, he completely tranquil under her warm flesh until at last, the unyielding rock became uncomfortable. When it did, the water was lapping their thighs.

They would remain virginal. The swimsuits saved that much.

The swim to shore was effortless with the incoming tide. It was almost noon when they reached Connie's. Mrs. Snyder hurried her daughter to an upstairs bathroom and showed Jim to one on the first floor.

In the shower Jim realized he had missed the football meeting, but it did not weigh heavily on his conscience. It was with Connie he wanted to be. She ignited a fire within him, a fire that spread and grew, a fire of curiosity and desire.

Connie too, was undergoing something new and distinct. It was not love, though she was sure that it was. It was something that excited her, gave her a sense of power, something she wanted to experience more fully.

The lunch was good, but Jim was uncomfortable, wondering if Mrs. Snyder could look into his mind. When he went to work he was not sorry to leave the imagined scrutiny behind. Connie walked with him down Warren Avenue and up Carson Street, hands clasped tightly. They hurried to the wooded area and looked in both directions. There was no one in sight. They embraced, their lips coming together in a kiss that turned quickly to passion.

Connie was breathless and a little frightened when she pushed away. She suddenly realized she had been on the verge of losing control and they were in plain view on a public street. Her voice was husky when she spoke, "You're going to be late for work, Jimmy."

Parting was never easy and it was more difficult today. They would not see each other until tomorrow evening.

Backing away grudgingly, Jim turned and started up Carson Street. He looked back over his shoulder, shouting in a whisper, "I love you, Baby!"

A tiny chill preceded the goose bumps. She waved sorrowfully and watched him as he started to run. She did not turn for home until he was out of sight.

*

Jim worked till 9:00PM that day and Friday till 5:00PM, time seeming to stand still. He had a feeling he had not performed as usual, but at least he got through it. Right now all he could think about was Connie and the Olympian Bandstand in Peltshire. Vaughn Monroe and his band were there tonight. He bought the tickets while Connie was in Maine. They were going to be together for an entire evening.

It was 7:15PM when Jim turned the car onto the state highway and headed north, twenty-five miles to Peltshire. They arrived before the start of the performance, the parking lot filling rapidly. Hand in hand they walked slowly to the entrance, not participating in the hustle of many of the other couples. Younger than most, Jim would normally have been uneasy in such a crowd, but being with Connie transformed him. He was her protector and though he was not actually outgoing, he had little difficulty conversing with strangers that night.

The Olympian was a large, gym sized hall. In the summer three sides opened to the outdoors, nevertheless, it was hotter inside. At the enclosed end was a large stage. The band arrived amidst enthusiastic cheering. After a short introduction the lights dimmed and the rotating glass balls overhead, sparkled and blinked and threw various colored droplets of light over the dancers on the crowded floor.

On the dance floor Jim's ability was due to Connie. Under her tutelage he was a willing and speedy learner. They danced the few fast numbers with enthusiasm and the slow ones, arms tight about the other, oblivious to the heat and the increasing moisture on their bodies.

Intermission came and the interior was lighted. Seeing the shine on Connie's face, Jim laughed, "I think we better get some air."

Holding her arms parallel to the floor she shook her hands, "Boy! That's for sure."

Jim removed his damp jacket, slung it over a shoulder and grabbed her hand. They walked cheerfully to the outdoor refreshment stand, swinging arms as they moved. Each guzzled a large, ice cold mug of root beer and ordered a third which they shared and consumed somewhat more decorously. Numerous small flasks appeared and reappeared around them. There were many others drinking beer transported in ice chests. Uneasy, they decided to leave that environment. They searched out the car.

Jim let Connie in and when he climbed aboard, she was sitting with her back against the steering wheel, her knees slightly bent, her feet against the passenger door, her shoes on the floor. He slid to her wrapping her in his arms. She lay her head on his chest. He closed his eyes tightly, took a very deep breath and squeezed her to him. When he opened his eyes, he looked down at her in the darkness. He placed a hand under her chin and gently lifted her face. He stared only moments before placing his lips on hers, softly at first, then hungrily.

She responded and their tongues plunged furiously. She pushed her feet against the door forcing her upper body into his. His embrace tightened. Her hands gripped his head and moved through soggy hair, her fingers digging into his scalp. The soft brown hair that framed her lovely face was in damp ringlets. They struggled together. He loosed his right arm from around her, slid the hand down to her buttocks, enjoying the journey and firm roundness. He moved the hand again, down the back of her thigh to the back of her knee. The hand moved not with knowledge, but primal instinct. It went under her dress and traveled to the top of her stocking, resting momentarily on the flesh of her outer thigh.

The music had started and the parking lot was empty of people.

Their pulse was quickening with each passing second. He slid his fingers downward to the softer flesh of her inner thighs, so warm and smooth and tempting, so exciting beneath his touch. His being thrilled at the experience and his desire to explore was whetted to the extreme. The fingers slid between those inviting thighs and touched the warm, moist panty fabric. She gave a quick intake of breath before she shuddered. She squeezed her thighs together and groaned in subdued pleasure. Forcing her feet more strongly against the door she struggled and rolled to her back. She sought his mouth. He lifted her with his left arm, kissing with renewed vigor and passion.

Perspiration soaked their clothing and ran down their faces collecting on their chins till the drops became weighty enough to proceed to the necks and continue the journey further.

His right hand was still affixed to the juncture at her thigh tops when she forced her left leg outward. He rubbed his hand excitedly back and forth over the very moist fabric. She wriggled just enough to move the point of contact to where the pleasure was most intense. Soon she was writhing and moaning softly and he was fighting with the confinement to give himself more freedom.

"Baby, I love you! ... Oh, Baby, .. you're so beautiful!"

His voice was hoarse and husky, the words somewhat slurred, but she heard the words she wanted to hear and she tried to make it easier for him while they wrestled for position. He fought with her panties and got them free of her feet while his excitement built to a roaring inferno out of control. She struggled to a sitting position as he slid off the seat and onto his knees between her legs. He tried frantically to remove his trousers. She hooked her toes inside the waist band and with the will of her desires forced trousers and shorts down. He tried to find his way, but was clumsy and inept. She desperately grabbed him, guiding him to her sanctum. They forced themselves together in a violent collision. The pain she felt was blotted out by her own passion to which all her power to reason had long since surrendered. He was wholly unprepared for the intense sensation that generated from her hot loins to his and to his entire being as she pushed hard to meet him. Bodies and souls engulfed in passion, they mashed together in three frenzied lunges and with a wild roar he spent his fury and gave himself up.

It was awhile before he moved and only when he realized she must be uncomfortable. As he came away from her he could feel his soaking shirt plastered to his skin. She was no less drenched with the mingling of their youthful perspiration and his fructifying fluids.

On his knees he gazed shyly at her, his emotions uneasy. He could only say softly, "I love you, Connie! Oh, wow! How I love you!"

She tenaciously pulled him to her, holding him tightly, whispering into his ear, "Oh, Jimmy! Oh, Jimmy, .. how ... I love you!"

They were the words he needed. His unease turned to joy. The deed became a triumph.

At last they knew they must do something about the condition of their persons. They got out of the car and walked about tidying up and drying themselves as best they could. They pulled out of the parking lot just before the dance ended.

*

The sound of his mother's voice roused Jim and when he arrived at the breakfast table he was unaware of the smile on his face.

"You must have really enjoyed Vaughn Monroe," Shirley giggled, "or was it Connie Snyder?"

Jim Williams blushed. He could only answer his sister with a silly grin.

*

It was not a busy day at the market. It was the first day of Shoreford Beach Days and many of the townsfolk had done their shopping earlier and were now at Collins Park for the opening festivities. The holiday mood was enhanced by the joy of the first Labor Day weekend of peace. The terrible war had lasted nearly four years and Shoreford shared greatly in the sacrifice.

The Williams family was at the park, but Jim was thankful his father was picking him up after work and taking him home for a quick shower and change of clothes.

In less than an hour of leaving the market, Jim and his father were at the park. In the fireplace was a fire. Two neighborhood families shared the spot with the Williams. Greetings were exchanged and Jim dashed off to gather up Connie.

Two families also shared the Snyder's location. After more greetings and some introductions, many in the town knew who Jim was, the two youngsters at last got away and joined the group at the site the Williams shared. Connie was received enthusiastically, especially by Shirley and Sarah.

Jim had a hot dog and Connie sipped a lemonade. Their anxiety to again be away was increasing, but Sarah did manage to take Connie's hands in hers. She smiled and said sweetly, "I'm so glad you've come into Jimmy's life. You've made such a difference."

"Aw, Mom," Jim said softly, but inwardly he was pleased with his mother and surprised at Connie. She blushed, .. not much, but there was color in her cheeks.

"Thank you, Mrs. Williams."

After their goodbyes the youngsters walked away holding hands. Connie leaned her head on Jim's shoulder, "I really like your family."

The town band was playing as they moved among the cheerful crowd pausing occasionally for salutations with friends and acquaintances, but never for long. The sun was approaching the western horizon when they exited the park, the band working its way through the music of the armed forces. The strains of the Marines' Hymn reached their ears when they were a block away. Though with Connie and her hand in his, Jim could not escape the spurt of sadness as the vision of his brother flashed through his mind. But Connie's presence prevailed and when they reached a deserted Silver Beach, the sun was not far from starting its drop behind the horizon.

She squeezed his hand and excitedly asked, "Do you feel like a swim?"

"Yeh!" He was enthusiastic again.

They hurried up the private walk to the Snyder home and entered through the back door. Jim's suit had been left from their Thursday swim and she took it from a downstairs closet and threw it to him and dashed up the stairs to change.

Undressed and suited in record time Jim went quietly to the stairs. He bounded up without a sound. The bedroom door was ajar and he pushed it open and walked in as Connie was pulling her swimsuit over her hips. She straightened and gazed at him, surprise in her expression. It changed quickly to a smile. He thought her beautiful and his stare remained awhile on her young breasts. When he went to her, his breathing was more intense with each step.

They embraced with a youthful vigor, his arms wrapping hungrily about her, she, passionately responding. The feel of her warm skin and crushed breasts gratified him. Their hearts pounding, they groped and pulled at their partners swimsuits, clumsily hindering the others attempt. Despite the comic effort they were swiftly naked, tangled together on the bed, groping, searching and groping more fervently. Fiercely, but quickly, it was over.

They cleaned up, got back into their swimsuits and headed for the beach. When they reached the water's edge the tide was receding. Walking till the water was at mid thigh they slipped in and swam leisurely to the back of the raft. Holding to a metal support for the diving board they lost themselves momentarily in the day's closing glory. The sky in the west was loosing the last of the bright orange glow and the clouds were softly touched with the pinks that would linger only awhile, giving a final sweet beauty to the day.

"Ya know," he said, "that's some sight," paused a few seconds and looked into her eyes, "but it doesn't compare with you."

Her eyes shone in the reflection of the evenings faded brilliance and she released her hold on the support and wrapped him in her arms, "I love you, Jimmy Williams! I love you!" After a momentary pause, she giggled and added, "In case you didn't already know."

"Oh, Baby! You make me the happiest guy in the world!"

Lips touched and locked. Bodies pressed together. Passion returned, a passion that was becoming the most vital force in their young lives.

Breathing hard when their lips came apart, Jim held a support with one hand and with the other, removed her shoulder straps. Connie gripped the support with both hands as he went under the surface of the blackening water, pulling her suit down, kissing her body as he moved, feeling her shiver. When the suit was clear of her feet he deftly removed his own trunks and slithered up her body. Breaking the surface he swung the swimsuits onto the raft.

Awkwardly, unceremoniously, he searched for her without success, his ardor and expectation increasing with his frustration.

"Grab the bars, Jimmy!"

He obeyed and she reached for him, guided him, encircling him with her legs. It was a clumsy attempt, but with youthful energy it was accomplished. When Jim was finished, Connie clung to him. She wished it had not ended.

Leaving their swimsuits on the raft, they swam in the dark till exhausted.

* * *

In Jim and Connie an evolution had occurred with such rapidity they had no time to contemplate the consequence, or judge the morality. They could do little, but act out their dangerously desired rolls. Their lives were strung together on one course, with one purpose, one desire. That part of the day when they were together was the time they lived for and it falsely sustained them and the cost began to mount, .. rapidly.

***

School started. Football and cheerleading practice went into high gear, but the enthusiasm and energies of Jim and Connie were directed elsewhere. Before September came to a close, Jim was finding excuses to miss work at the market.

The first Saturday in October was Shoreford's first football game. They won, mostly from the outstanding performance of Milton Buchanan and the strong, accurate passing arm of quarterback Dom Ventura.

Coach Mullen switched the entire offense to the 'T' formation and Jim was no longer required to look between his legs to snap the ball, except on punts. He could now make his own blocks at the line of scrimmage and it should have inspired him. It did not.

During the following week at practice Coach got on Jim a few times, but he paid little attention. The meaning and the living of life was in Connie's ready embrace. In addition to work, he was making excuses at home to get out. At school he was doing the same for unfinished assignments. The excuses turned to small lies which increased in substance, proportionate to his hedonistic pursuit of Connie. His all consuming desire, albeit his only desire, was to spend every available moment with the thief of his heart and rationale. The young man who never in his life had been a liar, gave no thought to what he was doing. His judgment was so clouded it was nonexistent.

*

Disaster for the Bulldogs was not long in coming. Their second opponents were bigger and had more talent. They waited patiently between seasons to avenge the beating they absorbed last year. They were well coached and had done their homework. They keyed on Buck and only his raw ability kept him from total shutdown. Dom Ventura, however, could not dodge and dart like 'The Buck' and when he dropped back to pass, he was dumped more than a few times. Jim, unable to perform his blocking assignment on those plays, invariably ended on his back.

In the evening after the game Jim had the car and he and Connie were parked at a very private spot they discovered a few weeks earlier. She wanted to talk and he was disturbed at her reluctance to get into the back seat. He coaxed and cajoled finally with success.

Afterwards Connie was subdued. They redressed and returned to the front seat, sitting silently for a few minutes, each on their own side.

"What's the matter, Baby?"

"I can't see you tomorrow, Jimmy."

"Why? What the heck's the matter?"

He was stunned, in disbelief, but now she had his attention.

"I had a big argument with my folks today, ... after the game. They said we were seeing too much of each other and I lied and said that every time I was out, it wasn't with you. They said I had to start putting some real effort into my school work. I think somehow they musta got word on all the tests I've failed."

His thoughts stumbled over each other in the dark silence unable to contrive a course around the dilemma.

"Jimmy!" he looked in her direction, "We really hafta go. It's almost eleven. I promised I'd be home by then. I know they'll be waiting for me. ... Please!"

They arrived at the Snyder residence on time. All the downstairs lights were lit. Walking quickly to the front door, Jim brushed her lips. That was all she allowed before going inside. He felt they were being observed.

* * *

"Williams! Do you think you can join the rest of the team?"

The coach again! Heck, he only turned his head for a brief moment. His mind was elsewhere. So was his heart and both were confused. Connie was just not the same anymore.

The team was well underway on the lap around the field at the close of practice when the coach walked up beside him. "Do your lap, Jim, take your shower and stop at my office on the way out."

Jim shook his head in answer and took off at a jog around the field. He hated being singled out by the coach and he started making excuses and rehearsing speeches while he ran. When he got to the locker room many of his teammates were dressed and getting ready to leave. Some glanced curiously at him when he walked by. Buck came over and tried to be friendly, but Jim's response was mostly mechanical. He felt uncomfortable.

When the last member of the team left, he undressed. The shower, usually a warming comfort, did not help at all. He wiped dry and dressed slowly, then very deliberately packed his gear away and went down the stairs to the coach's office.

His knock brought a response from within and he walked through the door.

"Have a seat, Jim."

The brief silence before his coach spoke was agonizing and his mind was not capable of remembering the words he had rehearsed.

"Jim, when you came out for the team you were neither big nor fast, but you showed strength and agility, but even more important, you showed me heart, .. guts. I never saw a starter, let alone a new kid, get involved in as many tackles, except perhaps your own brother." Coach looked away a few seconds.

"You were the kind of player that gladdens a coaches heart. Your contribution last year played no small part in the league title coming to Shoreford. We don't have the same kind of team this year, but if you were playing like I've seen you play, it would be a big plus. But you're not! You're preoccupied, Jim. And worse, you don't seem to care. Your play lacks spirit. You're barely going through the motions. I told you after the first game that if something was bothering you to come and see me, but you seem to be doing your best to avoid me."

Coach had him on the ropes. He was being pummeled and did not know how to fight back, ... did not want to. Football had lost its meaning. All Jim wanted now, was to be gone. He had someplace he wanted to be, someone he wanted to be with.

"I know you've got all kinds of stuff you haven't shown, Jim, but we can't play a person in the hope that he will perform tomorrow when he isn't performing today. There is someone who is trying, trying with everything they've got, .. trying their heart out. I have to play those who show they are trying to work for the team. Saturday, I'm going to start Donner in your place. He's been coming on ... and he shows me desire."

Jim was staring at his folded hands. Lifting his gaze he looked into Coach's eyes. He could still do that, he thought, but then he dropped his eyes again and returned the gaze to his hands. He was on the outside now, no longer a part of the inner circle. For the shortest moment he was stunned, but it was only a short moment. He had already decided it meant nothing.

The coach said a few more things, but Jim did not remember for he did not hear. Then he was closing the door and walking down the hall to the exit. Out in the air the muddle in his head began to clear and his thoughts once again became definitive. He knew what he would do. The pay phone was three blocks away, one block from Myers Market. He ran all the way. He inserted the nickel, sighed audibly and dialed the number. His schoolmate Frank Palumbo answered.

"Frank, I'm feelin lousy. I'm not comin in tonight."

"Geeze, Jim, the boss'll be screamin if you miss another night. I'm gonna get him and you can tell him yourself. I don't wanna hafta listen to his tirade."

"Look, Frank, I just don't have time. I gotta go."

He put the handpiece back, sighed deeply, lifted it out again, inserted another nickel and dialed another number.

"Hello."

Jim sighed again, but more easily this time. Connie had thankfully answered.

"Hi, Baby! How about meetin me in a couple a minutes?"

"I thought you had to work tonight?"

"No! I got the night off."

"Jimmy, are you nuts? Supper's not that far off! I'd have to sneak out!"

"I know, I know, but I just want to see you and talk a little."

"How come now? You didn't want to be bothered talking Saturday night."

"Come on, Baby, .. just a short visit on my way home."

"Cripes, Jimmy!" a long pause, "OK, where are you?"

"I'm just leaving school," he lied, "why don't we meet on Carson Street?"

She was reluctant, but agreed. When he hung up, he ran. He wanted to get to the wooded area ahead of her. It was a beautiful October day, the sky beginning to show signs of what would be a gorgeous sunset. By running, he reached the site as she came into view. Stepping off the sidewalk and amongst the bushes and trees he was hidden from her sight.

She was wearing a cream colored sweater and dark brown skirt which swung side to side with her graceful stride. The skirt matched her eyes and hair, the natural curl which never needed the foul smelling home permanent the girls often performed on each other. Her feet were shod in loafers and white bobby socks and she carried a light weight jacket over an arm.

When she was a few feet away Jim jumped from behind a bush, arms above his head and uttered a soft, but deep, "Boo!"

Connie jumped backward. The look of fright on her face disappeared instantly as recognition occurred.

"Jimmy! Sometimes you're nuts!" There was a hint of anger in her voice.

He laughed, put his arms about her, lifting her from the ground in a firm hug, then a strong kiss. When she was returned to the earth, he became serious, "I love you!"

She smiled weakly, "How'd you get here so fast?"

He did not answer, but took her hand and led her to the interior of the wooded lot. When out of sight from the street, he turned and faced her, put his arms around her and drew her to him.

She was reluctant at first, but when he kissed her and explored her mouth with his tongue, she came hard against him. She was responding, but suddenly pushed away, noticeably flushed. Jim was breathing rapidly, his heart pounding.

"Jimmy! This is not the place! Are you mad!?"

"Baby! I really need you! I gotta have you, Baby, I gotta!"

He coaxed and pleaded. She did not respond with the alacrity that was missing of late, but rather acquiesced as she had done the last few times they were together. He threw his jacket on the ground and holding her arms helped her be seated, then pushed her gently backward. Quickly beside her he fumbled with her clothing and his own to bare their most private parts. She did not help him, but he energetically and hurriedly found the way.

Her feelings had changed. She did not understand her conflicting emotions as she became heated. She did desire him, the way she always had. But now, she did not understand why.

It was a frenzy for him and he was unleashed from his passion in no time.

With his first spasm she softly sobbed, "Oohh nooo." Tears flowed and she was shaking ever so softly.

He was confused by her reaction, .. even hurt.

They did their best in the gloomy stillness putting themselves together. When they finished, Connie stood, hands at sides, looking at the ground. Jim could neither feel nor understand her agony. He could do nothing to comfort her. He was baffled. Misery engulfed him. He did nothing, .. but remain silent.

At long last Connie spoke "Jimmy, every time we do this it's always the same. You make me want you so bad then you leave me hanging. Cripes! It's like you only do it for yourself. I feel more and more like I give you everything and you just take it and run."

"Oh, Baby! You know I love you!"

"Sometimes I'm not so sure, Jimmy. Sometimes I feel you just want me for what you get from me and I get mad at myself for giving it to you, for making it so easy for you. Jimmy, at every football game last year all I saw was you. You made my heart ache, because every time there was a pile of bodies I knew you were somewhere in it. When you asked me out, .. I thought I'd wet my pants. A lot of girls thought you were so nifty, but you were so bashful. But you asked me out.

"Then came the tragedy of Donald. I cried for you every night. Finally I decided I had to do something and when I heard you were running at Collins Park I went there and at last we were together. When you asked me to go to the movies, ... oh, Jimmy, did I love you! It was the greatest thing in my life. The movies, the picnics, the beach and swimming together, ... Jimmy, I was in heaven. You were a dream come true to me.

"Then we did it. I knew it was the first time for both of us. I felt a little guilty, but that went away, because it was you and me, .. doing it together." Connie paused, her hands clasped. She was looking into the distance and Jim saw the tears on her face.

"Then, Jimmy, it was every day, everywhere, whenever we could be alone. We've been skipping school and both of us are getting lousy grades. And I overheard Frank Palumbo asking Buck if anything was the matter with you, because Mr. Myers was not happy with you .. and neither am I! For weeks, all you've wanted ... was ...." She wiped her cheeks and straightened up. In the approaching twilight she searched for his eyes.

"Jimmy, I can't go on like this! I feel like my stomach is wrapping around itself. I love you, but it doesn't seem real anymore. I want to be with you, but it's making me miserable ... and you ... you've got a great family and you're not part of them any more. You used to help people, now you ignore them. And cripes, Jimmy, what if I was pregnant!"

"Connie!! Are you telling me you might be pregnant?"

"Oh, Jimmy, I'm a little late, but sometimes that happens."

"I'll marry you, Baby, I'll marry you!"

"Jimmy, that's dumb! What would we do? You've got till June till you graduate and I've got a year after that. Our folks would be furious. Look at June and Sam. They left school last year. Remember all the talk. Now they don't associate with their old friends and their life is no fun ... and that's from June's own mouth. I don't want something like that."

"We wouldn't be like that, Baby, .. I swear. We love each other. We've got a good thing going."

"We had a good thing going, Jimmy, but now ... I'm not so sure. How could you take care of me and a baby? You're having trouble taking care of yourself right now."

He felt the flush come to his face. How could someone he loved, who completely claimed his life, talk that way. He was confused and he was hurt. From that first moment that he knew he loved her and knew that she loved him it had seemed just natural that their lives would be forever. He could only plead, "Connie, .. Baby, .. I need you so much! .. You don't know how much. ... I'll change, Baby, .. you'll see. I gotta have you!"

His arms went about her and pulled her to him, "Oh, Baby! I love you! I need you!" His hands started moving upward, under the sweater to the bra strap.

"No, Jimmy! No more tonight! I've got to get home, ... please, ... let me go. I'm really tired and I have lots of homework. I'll meet you tomorrow night after work and we can talk."

"OK. Tomorrow night, .. yeh."

He watched as she turned and without kissing him, walked out of the darkened woodland to the sidewalk and dejectedly headed homeward in the October twilight.

It seemed as though it took Jim forever to reach home. His folks were out and Bobbie was sitting at the kitchen table doing homework. Shirley was preparing supper.

"Hi, Jim!" Bobbie greeted him cheerily.

"Hi, Jimmy, you look terrible," Shirley said gazing quizzically at him.

"Yeh, I don't feel so hot. I'm goin to bed," and went immediately up the stairs, undressed and crawled into bed. He did not clean his teeth, but that was not the reason he slept poorly.

*

After school the next day Connie had an excuse not to see him. Her parents she said, would not allow her out for she had too much homework to catch up on. She had excuses for every day thereafter, including Friday night when she was going out with some girl friends, because football players were supposed to be in early the night before a game. It had never mattered before. In school they spoke only briefly. A feeling of doom began to engulf Jim Williams.

The love for football had diminished in Jim as his passion for Connie increased. So had all his interests. His relationship with her superseded everything. As he sat on the bench for most of Saturday's game, his attempt to be stoic was betrayed by his mournful expression.

In the coming week he plunged into a deep depression and choking self pity. Connie was more distant almost daily. On Saturday she was absent from the cheerleading squad. Again Jim did not start. He forced himself to think he did not care, but belittled Coach in his mind for the stupidity of playing Donner who missed tackles on defense and blocked poorly on offense. Shoreford, Jim thought, was lucky to win the game.

Connie was absent from school on Monday and Jim worked up the courage and called her that evening. Her parents were out and she agreed to see him briefly. He borrowed the car, picked her up and they drove to Collins Park. It was dark and cool as November should be. They had the whole park to themselves.

He tried to move close, but she would have none of it.

"Jimmy, please ... don't!"

"Baby, I love you, don't you know that?"

"Jimmy, I don't believe that! And please don't call me Baby. I don't think you know what love is. I don't think I know any more. But it certainly isn't just for your gratification. Somehow it doesn't seem good to me any more. What started out as a dream for me has turned into something .. well .. dirty.

"I wasn't going to tell you this, but I really think you should know. I went to New York with Barbara on Saturday. Someone at college had an abortion there and Barbara was able to get the name and address of the doctor."

"Connie!! .. I .."

"Wait, Jimmy, .. let me finish! I didn't know if I could do it, but I knew I had to. Now it's over. I don't feel the same anymore. .. I don't know, .. I can't explain it, .. but I don't feel the same.

My parents would be mortified and so would yours. Thank God for Barbara. I don't know what I'd have done without her."

She looked at him, but he was looking elsewhere. She pulled hard at the fabric of his sleeve. He turned slowly, timidly. The expression on her face was stern, unforgiving.

"Three of us know about this now, Jimmy. I hope you'll have the good sense and decency to keep it to yourself!"

He felt like he had been kicked in the stomach. Numbness immobilized him. His mind became blank. He sat, staring somewhere beyond.

"Jimmy! .. Take me home! ..... Now!"

Like a zombie he started the engine and drove her home.

As she opened the door she said, "Good-bye, Jimmy!" got out and went inside.

He sat awhile, staring ahead and finally started for home. When he drove into the driveway, he sat for a long time before going inside.

His parents and siblings greeted him. He replied, trying to hide his dejection, but they were not fooled. They knew something was amiss, had known for some time. He told them he had homework to do and went up to his room. Instead, he lay on the bed in the dark, staring upward, unable to distinguish between his guilt, his self pity, or the anger that was coming to life within him. When Bobbie came in, Jim got ready for bed. Later he heard his folks going to bed and much later he stumbled into a troubled sleep.

* THREE *

A vicious wind gust rattled the windows. Abruptly he jerked to a sitting position. He smiled sheepishly to himself for his reaction. He readjusted the towel about his midsection and lay back, his head sinking into the pillow.

Having started this journey he found it difficult not to continue. It was as though some perversion was driving him. His time with Connie, his failure in school, was not a time of happy memories. His brother's death left him easy prey, less able to cope. Added to that, his youth and irrepressible and untamed infatuation destroyed his judgment. He had been very willing to give into the hedonism he consciously and shamelessly pursued.

He learned, but it took time. He hoped he had acquired some wisdom during a lifetime of shifting circumstances and unpredictable changes. His time with Connie held little relevance with his life today, but it did play a part in shaping the character of his transitory youth.

~ ~ ~ ~ ~

His mother was shaking him, "Jimmy, it's time to get up. You're going to be late if you don't hurry."

"OK, Mom, I'm awake."

She left the room and he groggily forced his feet to the floor. He sat with elbows on knees, head in hands. All the memories of last night were seeping back into his troubled, slowly awakening consciousness. The anger that he felt last night returned. He fumbled through dressing himself and his time in the bathroom. He stumbled down the stairs to pick at breakfast, most of which he left.

Shirley had informed their mother of his deteriorating relationship with Connie and now cast questioning glances in his direction. When Shirley left the table his mother sat opposite him, trying to console him, "Jimmy, you'll feel better with something in your stomach ... and things will be better before you know it, I'm sure." She hugged him as he was leaving. His response was mechanical.

Shirley went on ahead with some girlfriends and Jim walked alone, troubled and sullen, his eyes focused on his plodding feet. He walked to the center of town and got on a crowded trolley car going into the city. None of his homework had been done for weeks. He knew it was too late to face up to it in front of his teachers. He was out of excuses. He spent the day roaming city streets.

The balance of the week Jim skipped school. On Friday Mr. Myers called and asked him to pick up what pay he was owed. The meeting was not pleasant and his former boss berated him constantly. Jim said not a word. He took the verbal beating with little emotion at first, but his anger welled up as Mr. Myers proceeded. He almost confronted the older man, instead, he turned and left.

"Jim Williams, you're just one big pantywaist!" Mr. Myers called after him, "You're not worthy of your brother."

His soul was pierced. He sagged. The fight left him. He knew he was not worthy of Don. No one had to tell him. He walked into the cool morning, hands in pockets, head forced between shoulders, teeth clamped together, eyes somewhere ahead. Walking unfocused, unaware of time, he found himself at Collins Park.

On the beach he shuffled aimlessly. He felt the sand entering his shoes. He went to the rocks at the east end where Connie sat that day early in June, ... where their life together had begun. Now, just five months later, it was over.

It was a long time before Connie departed his thoughts and his anger cooled. Don's image and later still, those of Tony and Tim mercifully blotted her out. He grieved again and was sad again, yet when Connie returned so did the anger. He began to wonder about the anger. Loving Connie had been the ultimate experience for him. When he thought about that love which now turned so easily to hate, he was not sure it was love. Then he was sure it had been love. He wondered if he let her down, though he did not want to face up to that.

It was different, the way he loved his brother, but he soon realized he was letting his brother's memory down ... as he was that of Tony and Tim. He knew that now. The chance to right the wrong with Connie was gone, but maybe he could still do something about his brother and his two friends ... and maybe he could make some amends to others.

*

Jim spent much of Saturday at Collins Park, the day after the whipping by Mr. Myers. There was much to think about. He came in the door late, the table was set and supper ready to be served.

"In heaven's name, Jimmy, where were you?" Sarah asked, an edge to her voice.

"Uhh, .. just walkin around, Mom."

"Are you all right, Dear?" a deep, curious frown clouded her face.

"Yeh, I'm OK, Mom."

His father entered the kitchen and stood before his wife.

"Sarah, let's have supper and afterwards," he said softly, but firmly, then turned to Jim, "the three of us will sit together and talk."

The only conversation at the table was Bob's attempt to question Jim about football. Their father mercifully intervened. Despite his decision to stand and take his due, supper was over too quickly. Soon he was sitting in the living room with his parents while Shirley and Bob took care of the clean up.

There was a short, uncomfortable silence while thoughts were gathered and put in place, until his father spoke.

"Jim, we know you haven't been to school all week."

"Who told you that, big mouth Shirley?" Jim shot back angrily.

"It doesn't matter how we know. The point is, .. what you have done and how you have done it is wrong!"

"And Jimmy," his mother interjected, "you have lied about your whereabouts and your activities which is something you've never done before. ... Why?"

"I'm not sure Jim can tell us why right now, Sarah, but this behavior can not go on." A long pause made Jim more uncomfortable. "Did you plan to return to school, Jim?"

"Yeh," he replied, not really knowing how he intended to accomplish that.

"Were you going to come to us to get the note to get you back in?" his mother asked.

"I was going to write it myself."

He surprised himself at his quick and easy response.

"OK, Jim," his father replied, "I'll tell you what. I'll go to school with you on Monday and I'll talk to Mr. Melillo to get you reinstated. Do you have any intentions regarding football?"

"I thought about it a lot today, Dad. I think I'd like to get back on the team .. if they'll let me."

Football was the reason he must return. He knew he would only be eligible to play until report cards came out. Fortunately that was not until December. By then he would be finished with football and the second part of his plan would be operative.

"You've got to talk to Coach Mullen about that, Jim."

Jim knew that this was the way it must be done, nevertheless, his father's words caused his stomach to do flip-flops at the thought of going to his coach and begging.

"You owe him that, Jim. You have let him and your team down."

*

Lying in bed Jim listened to the scholastic scores on the radio. Shoreford lost. For the first time in weeks he felt bad for Coach and the team. When he went downstairs to say good night, his mother came to him. She looked deeply into his eyes. There was a softness in hers and a touch of pity. She hugged him tenderly. As he was leaving she patted his rump softly, the way she did when she sent him on his way as a young boy.

*

Sunday afternoon Jim was at Collins Park. He skipped church. His father gently turned his mother away from her attempt to coax him into going. He was glad. Who needed that stuff anyhow. God did not do him any favors.

Before he started running he experienced some changes of heart. The decisions he made yesterday were not easy ones. They would not be easy to stick to without tremendous resolve.

The physical exertions not only had a revitalizing affect on his body, but helped to cleanse his mind. Now there was order. His goals and plans were clear. Yesterday's scheme would remain unchanged. There was still some formulating to do, but he was making headway. The pity he lavished on himself was nearly gone and so was much of the anger. It was nearly dark when he got home, but some of the darkness had vanished from his soul.

*

Early Monday morning Bill Williams and Jim entered Shoreford High School through the back door near the gym. The coach was standing outside his office and Bill watched as his son approached the man. The two talked briefly and went into the office. Bill turned and headed for the principal's office.

It was torture at first.

"Coach, .. I'm here to ask you .. to .. to please let me come back to practice. I .. ah .. I don't .. I know .. I don't deserve it, ... but I promise, .. if you let me in practice .. you can use me for a tackling dummy. Coach, .. I'm really sorry I .. ah .. let you .. and the team down so bad. I'm really sorry!"

"I'm sure you mean what you say, Jim. You have let your team down. I think you know that better than anyone. .. Am I right?"

"Yes, sir!"

"You're the guy that's going to have to carry that burden. OK. Normally I would like some time to think about such a decision, but this time I'm going to say yes, right now. It's not going to be easy, Jim. When you suit up tonight, you will line up with the subs and all players on the starting team will have explicit orders to see what you're made of. Can you come to terms with that?"

"Yes, sir!!!" Jim's face was suddenly a huge grin.

The coach took in the expression. He was pleased with himself for the quick decision.

"All right, Jim, we'll see you tonight. Now get to your classes."

"Thank you, Sir, .. thank you, Coach!"

The grin did not leave Jim's face as he rose and reached for the door knob. He opened the door and started through.

"Jim," his coach called.

He turned, "Yes, Sir?"

"Good luck, Jim!" There was a warm smile on the coach's face.

Jim Williams almost skipped down the hall. He could play, he would play, he had to play.

Bill and Mr. Melillo were waiting in the corridor when Jim arrived. With greetings exchanged there was a short conversation before the first bell rang and Jim was told to report to his homeroom. As he was departing his father put a hand on his shoulder and gave it a gentle squeeze, then a wink, a nod and a smile. He knew his father loved him, but he had never seen a display like that from him. He walked happily to his homeroom, his apprehension noticeably diminished.

Sitting at her desk Mrs. Siptroth nearly smiled when she greeted him.

"Hey!" Buck yelled from across the room, leaped to his feet and met Jim halfway to his seat and pumped his hand.

Jim was embarrassed, yet was pleased to receive the joyful welcome from his best friend.

"All right, boys, take your seats."

And so the school day began. It was not long before Jim realized how far behind he was, but he had to make a strong effort, enough to get him through the next few weeks. Then he could take the next step.

Football practice was difficult, not so much for the lack of it in the recent past, but for the mental hurdles yet to be vaulted. Many of his teammates eyed him suspiciously at first. During the light scrimmage contact was fierce. He liked it. It hardened his resolve.

Sarah consented to hold up supper a half hour each night. Jim went from practice to Collins Park. He did some hard running, then jogged home. The first few nights sleep was fitful for his overtired body.

He struggled in despair with his studies, but he would do what he had to do.

Through much of Saturday's game he sat on the bench. He was used mostly in punting situations where his control of the long snap was a visible, viable asset. He got in the last few minutes with Shoreford leading. He played with such tenacity his teammates cast smiles his way. Shoreford evened its record to 3 and 3.

Bill was unable to attend the game and Shirley and Bob went home with friends. It suited Jim's mood to walk alone after the shower and change of clothes. There were still things he had to work out by himself.

The streets were quiet. He walked at a leisurely pace lost in his thoughts until he heard a car approaching and break to a stop. Turning, he saw Barbara Snyder hastily exit the auto and quickly approach. Not knowing what to do he greeted her, his head slightly bowed, his eyes focused through his lashes, the sound of his voice almost timid, "Hi."

"Jim! I used to think you were something special," her words came in a flurry, "but I find you are just another jerk like so many guys in this hick town."

She was gone before the icy glare reached his eyes and his words shot between clenched teeth.

"Go to hell!"

He had never used that epithet before and it was lost on Barbara as she roared away to the accompaniment of squealing tires.

*

Except for practice and the time at Collins Park the days dragged, but Jim was becoming more communicative with his family and his sullenness was gone. His only real friend at school was Buck. When they were together he found life bearable. By midweek Coach changed some of the rules for contact drills. He smiled frequently at Jim's fervor while playing with the second team and put a stop to some of the hitting, not to save Jim, but his first string.

On the bench at the start of Saturday's game, Jim was sent in the second time Shoreford had possession.

Dom Ventura handed off to Buck who dashed to his left. When he reached the spot he would normally turn upfield, he spun and lateraled back to Dom who was running behind him. The defense was converging on that spot and Dom planted his feet and threw to the right end Steve Goss, out in the right flat.

The guard opposite Jim was the first to feel his wrath. Never slowing, he turned immediately to his right spotting the only defenders who could run Steve down. The angle judged instinctively, he sprinted with all out effort toward the meeting point. Dashing side by side the two defenders were just yards from Steve when Jim launched his body in a perfectly executed cross body block, cutting them down as one.

The touchdown was easy and when cheering erupted from the Shoreford faithful, Buck was at Jim's side slapping his back and shouting, "Beautiful, Buddy! Beautiful! That was the nicest block I've ever seen."

Russell Donner did not need to be told his starting job was gone.

The tone was set and Shoreford never looked back, the final score, 26 to 0. Buck scored the last three touchdowns, one on a pass, two by lengthy runs. Jim played without peer and the local weekly in addition to lauding the efforts of one Milton Buchanan, Dom Ventura, Steven Goss et al, expressed the opinion that the return of Jim Williams was a thing to behold.

At home that evening, at supper and thereafter, Bob pestered his brother with questions and comments until Sarah and Bill finally and kindly intervened and sent their youngest to bed. Jim was home again.

*

The pep rally was held as usual on Wednesday. Immediately thereafter, Jim met Shirley and they hurried home together. Grandmother and Grandfather MacPherson were expected. They were going to stay over, go to the game and share Thanksgiving with the Williams. Jim's Uncle, Ed Macpherson and his daughter Kit were expected to arrive early Thursday morning to also share the day. Kit was home for the holiday during her first year of college.

The grandparents arrived soon after Jim and Shirley. After supper they had tea in the living room along with the shortbread that Gram baked for the visit. Always at his loquacious best in family gatherings, Bob took up all and then some, of the slack left by his brother. Unfortunately for Jim, his inability to get involved in the family discussion was responsible for some of the discomfort he was feeling. He frequently noticed his grandfather observing him.

The coming football game was the center of Bob's life, even more so since his brother had returned to hero status. He was constantly praising Jim and glorifying his deeds on the gridiron. During one unbridled discourse Shirley good-naturedly interjected, "Bobbie, for heavens sake, will you please slow down."

The room filled with laughter and Bob, his eyes open wide, stared curiously at his sister, "But how will Gram and Gramps know about Jim if I don't tell them?"

There were some more chuckles and Shirley smiled pleasantly at her younger brother, "They will see him play tomorrow, you know."

Bob scratched his head and muttered, "Yeh, but ... yeah, .. OK, Shirley, but they shouldn't be surprised." He held his chin up and smiled, proud he had the last word, but the conversation did go in other directions.

The first to excuse himself for bed was Jim. He was thankful to escape his grandfather's scrutiny. When he got to his room he knew he had not socialized the way he should, but there were big things on his mind, big plans. It was getting close to the time he must bare those plans to those he loved. It was not something he relished. Nevertheless, tomorrow there was a game to play and that game was a part of those plans. He must play like never before.

*

The Shoreford team was full of quiet confidence on the short bus ride to Newville. On paper they were not as good as Newville, but today, .. well, they had a feeling. They were filled with a renewed and vigorous spirit, born the past few weeks. Coach Mullen knew its origin as did a few of the more perceptive players. None of them said anything, but occasionally they smiled to themselves as they observed Jim or felt his punishing hits in practice.

The teams lined up on their respective forty yard lines. Newville won the toss and would receive. Moving into position for the starting kickoff Jim felt the familiar little knot in his stomach that would disappear the instant his body went into motion.

The kicker's foot met the ball. Jim burst downfield picking out the player maneuvering to receive. The ball hit the midsection of the runner, was instantly secured in the crook of an arm and his legs were churning upfield. Before his lead foot hit the ground for the third time, he was hit with such force that the grunt he emitted caused the Newville player nearest him to wince. He was noticeably slower getting to his feet than was Jim who bounced up and took his position behind the line.

The game was close for most of the first half. Newville was more talented, but today the intensity of the Shoreford team was the dominant factor. Newville could not grasp what was happening to them. Shoreford was inspired. They were infused with a spirit that had been building for two weeks and now they were playing beyond themselves. Buck had a great day as did Dom Ventura and Steve Goss, but it was Jim who was the catalyst. His superior blocking went mostly unnoticed to most but his teammates and coaches. His play on defense was an inspiration. Every time Newville got something going he was there to stop it. He had two interceptions. He recovered three fumbles, all of which he caused. And he was in on more tackles that day than anyone on the field.

As the game progressed, many began to look for Jim's number where ever a play concluded. He did not disappoint them. With less than two minutes to play and Shoreford leading 20 to 0, Coach took him out. He was exhausted and barely heard the ovation of a thousand plus Shoreford faithful. From the other side of the field a deep admiration filled the dignified silence.

Approaching the sideline he glanced at the animated cheerleaders. Connie was standing still amidst the jubilation, her expression, one of sorrowful adoration. When their eyes met, Jim turned away. He sat on the bench wearily and during the final moments of the game, the fatigue commenced the journey up his limbs and throughout his body. Sore muscles from too much punishing contact were spreading over his entire, worn out physical being. Strangely, it kindled exaltation. In his mind's eye he saw Don smiling at him while hearing the voices of Tony and Tim raised in the song of victory.

The game ended and the Shoreford fans poured onto the field. The team had difficulty getting organized and headed in the direction of their bus. Jim sighted two soldiers in the crowd pushing through to him. When George Olson and Eddie Jaskowski reached him, he was pummeled with undisguised affection.

"That was a helluva game, man!" shouted Ole over the din, "I'm glad I didn't have to play opposite you today. You might not be very big, but you looked like a giant on that field today, Jim."

"Yeh, man! It was a pleasure to watch you, Jim." Eddie chimed enthusiastically.

They exchanged happy talk and by the time they reached the bus promised to get together over the weekend. Then Jim climbed aboard.

Buck had a seat saved and when Jim sat down they shook hands and smiled, each congratulating the other for a splendid game. No words were necessary.

The ride through Newville and Shoreford, a convoy of autos in tow, horns honking and beeping, was a noisy and happy affair.

When the busses arrived at Shoreford High the players were up the steps to the locker room in no time. It was a joyful team that rushed for the showers and Jim for one brief instant thought how great it would be to have Tony and Tim leading the victory song with Don by his side. In that brief instant, he felt the emptiness and was glad for his laughing and boisterous teammates.

Showered and dressed, Jim blinked his eyes when he exited the dimly lighted high school and walked into the bright noontime sun. The sky was blue and the temperature pleasantly cool.

His father, Uncle Ed and Bob were waiting for him. Bob, face beaming, was quickly to him.

"Boy! That was a terrific game, Jim! Boy! Was it terrific! You were just great!"

Jim put his arm about the shoulder of his enthusiastic eighth grade brother, now only an inch shorter and they walked to the car.

His father stood in front of him looking deeply into his eyes, nodding his head and smiling proudly. At last he spoke, "That was a fine game you played today, Jim!"

"Jim, you did us all proud today," Uncle Ed smiled brightly.

The praise continued when they arrived home. Jim's grandfather, who brought the womenfolk home, was first, then his cousin Kit and before he could take a breath, Shirley called him to the phone.

"Jimmy," Gramma Williams greeted him from the other end, "your uncles tell me that you and your friend Milton Buchanan didn't make any friends in Newville today," she chuckled softly, "but don't you worry, there's one old lady in town who loves you and is very proud of you. Please come over and see me during the weekend. I've griddled a batch of fresh Welsh cookies. Bring Shirley and Bobbie with you. I've got to finish dinner now, but your uncles," she chuckled softly again, "want to say some unkind things to you."

Art and Owen Williams kidded him just a little, but their praise was lavish. After weeks of discontent with his life and disenchantment with himself, he was now distracted, even cheerful and for once, he was not too ill at ease with all the praise. For the moment, his thoughts of the future were buried.

*

When the cleanup was complete the families gathered in the crowded living room, a few uncomfortable from over eating. Additional chairs from the kitchen seated the extra bodies, but Bob squeezed into a spot on the floor. He lay on his back, belt undone, trouser top unbuttoned and at intervals emitted a subdued groan. Of course this did not please Shirley.

The abundance of bodies in the confined area created more warmth than was needed. Jim was not only too full of food, but his muscles and joints were stiffening. He wanted desperately to go outdoors and walk off his discomfort. He was also back to contemplating the future and he wanted to clear his head, .. away from the family. And he needed to work on his courage. He fidgeted a bit and finally asked to be excused to take a short walk.

"That sounds like a great idea, Jim. Do you mind if I join you?" Kit asked.

"No, come on."

He had thought he wanted to be alone and was surprised at the pleasure Kit's request elicited in him.

Jim had been fond of Katherine MacPherson from early childhood. She was always his favorite cousin. A month younger than Don, as youngsters, the three always played well together when the families visited. She accepted her younger cousin in the same way Don accepted Jim. In fact, she was a great deal like Don, except she had no athletic bent. This was because she had never given herself time to develop an interest in sports, but she ran beautifully.

Recollections of her as a young and growing lass, so pretty with her deep blue eyes and chestnut hair, her sensitivity and kindness, surged through Jim's mind. He remembered her limbs swiftly flashing as they ran around the back yard and rolled in the sweet smelling, fresh cut grass. Instantly he was reminded of his youthful curiosity, .. when he secretly stole looks at her as they recklessly frolicked in innocent immodesty, her dress swirling and bouncing, often revealing her underpants. And he remembered the strong desire to touch her, to run his hands along her enticing bare legs. Those were things he did not even divulge to Don, things that now, he hurriedly, ashamedly chased from his transient and momentarily disturbed thoughts.

The two cousins left the house with the temperature dipping and walked west. They observed the descending sun, the twilight glow permitting the day's radiance to endure a bit longer gladdening their beings with a warmth of color. They turned south and headed in the direction of Collins Park. About twenty minutes passed before Kit broke the silence.

"Jim, how are you doing? Sometimes when I looked at you today your eyes seemed to be focusing somewhere out there," she waved an arm toward the horizon. "Gramps told me that he was sure something was weighing heavily on you. It troubles him ... and now that I see the same thing, it troubles me."

The lovely young woman had inherited her grandfather's ability to see into people's souls. But there was much more. Kindness and concern in abundance were a large part of her personality. They walked almost a block while Jim mulled over a response. Kit did not pressure him when he did not immediately reply.

Stopping, Jim turned to face her, "Kit, I'm going to quit school."

"Why, Jim!? ... Why?" She was stunned and filled with disbelief.

He looked away, then slowly turned. His gaze sought the beautiful blue eyes now just barely visible in the distant glow of a street light. The outline of her hair, the deep chestnut color no longer discernible, framed her pretty face. Once again, but imperceptibly, he was drawn to this lovely creature and his normal reticence and shyness evaporated swiftly. Suddenly he wanted to talk, to bare his soul, to confess, as he had heretofore done only to his brother.

They started to walk again and the words spilled out in quick succession, "You know, Kit, when Don was killed, there was a time .. I thought I'd never make it through. He was such a great guy. He did more for me than anyone'll ever know. The first few weeks I didn't know what I'd do and I knew Mom and Dad, especially Mom, were goin through somethin like that too." He swallowed the lump in his throat, "I don't know if there's anyone like him in the world. I guess I loved him about as much as anything."

"You're right about that, Jim. Don was really one heck of a great guy. It seems that people like him come along so rarely. Too bad, isn't it?"

"Yeah," he nodded sadly and looked away.

They walked a bit in silence before Jim said, "Then Connie came along and I guess I forgot about Don for awhile." He paused briefly, "I did some pretty stupid things and got myself all fouled up. I guess with girls I don't use good sense, Kit." He was self conscious a moment, "Then I lost my job at the market, ... I got benched, ... I let my school work go down the drain. When I get my report card, .. all my marks will be failing. When it was too late, I knew I'd let my family down and more than anything else, I knew I'd let Don down and that's why I worked to get back on the team and finish the season. For the rest, .. it's too late."

"But, Jim, it's not too late! I know your ability, I know you can catch up."

"No I can't, Kit, no I can't, there's just no way, I'm just too far behind!"

She knew that he could, .. if he wanted to, but she sensed that he did not want to try. She hesitated a moment before tenderly asking, "What will you do, Jim, get a job?"

"Join the Marine Corps."

"Join the Marine Corps? That's crazy, Jim!"

"No it's not, Kit. They have a two year enlistment now and the GI Bill is in effect. That's the only way I could afford college."

They stopped again. She took hold of his elbow and turned to face him.

"How about a football scholarship, Jim?" Kit asked enthusiastically.

"Heck, I'm not big enough or fast enough for college ball."

"You looked like a giant on that field today. Nobody could stop you."

"Heck, Kit, it's one thing to play against a few big guys. It's somethin else if everyone is a whole lot bigger'n you." He looked down at the ground and added softly, "Besides, I was lucky today." Returning his gaze to her eyes he went on eagerly, "And with the GI Bill I'd get a little money too!"

"What do your folks think about it?"

"They don't know yet."

"Oh, Jim!" her voice filled with compassion, "So that's why you've been so preoccupied."

"Yeh, I guess that's about it."

"Is there any way I can help?"

"No," he replied softly, shaking his head. "Thanks, but I gotta do this thing myself."

A long pause followed, their breathing the only sound punctuating the still night.

"What happened, Jim? What caused this terrible change in your life? I heard from Gram before I went off to school that you were doing great and had a terrific girl friend. Then I heard that you broke up with her and in bits and pieces learned that things were not well with you."

"Connie broke up with me, Kit."

He turned away from her. They started walking again. His words stumbled at first, but as Kit put her arm through his and gripped him firmly the words began to flow.

"I never knew a girl .. like Connie before, .. Kit. She was really special ... and ya know what, .. she liked me as much as I liked her. It was great!"

Kit squeezed his arm and smiled unseen in the growing darkness.

"We just sorta wanted to do all the same things together ... and after awhile, .. well, .. you know, ... she got pregnant." He stopped short and turned. He took hold of her hand, "Kit, .. nobody knows about this!"

"Nobody will, Jim."

He let go of her hand and they returned to walking at their slow, but steady pace, Kit, her arm through his, her cheek against his shoulder.

"I really wanted to marry her, but she went to New York and got an abortion and I guess that's when she decided she didn't feel the same about me anymore. I guess it was as bad as when Don died, cause I went through some pretty bad stuff again. Well, it took awhile, but I knew the way I was feelin was wrong ... and so .. you know the rest. I guess you must really think I'm a real jerk."

"Ohh noo, Jim, noo!"

They reached the knoll overlooking the beach at Collins Park. He had spoken with honesty, something absent of late in his life. Kit had listened with great sympathy. His plight was her plight and she wanted to reach out, comfort him, take away his pain.

Stopping, they faced each other. He saw the tears on her cheeks which reflected the starlight. She pressed herself against him and wrapped her arms about him and lay her head on his shoulder. Her words were filled with a touching tenderness, "Oh, Jim, I'm so sorry. I would take your pain if I could."

He could feel himself wanting to reach out for her and embrace the solace she offered. She lifted her head and touched his lips lightly in an act of compassion that confused him. Something stirred within him. Old memories flashed through his troubled mind. Without conscious thought he wrapped her tightly in his arms. Their lips came hard together and she eagerly melted into him as his tongue plunged into her mouth. She responded. For one insane instant they shared a violent and unsought passion.

Suddenly she forced herself from him, her voice husky, her breathing labored, her chest heaving, her thoughts in complete disarray. "Jim! We really have to get going. Dad will be wanting to get on the road."

Smothered instantly in another guilt, another fierce anger, the black chamber that was his mind echoed, "Oh, God! What did I do now?" with the screams of his blasphemous act.

He wanted desperately to say he was sorry, to get on his knees and ask forgiveness, but was numbed into inaction.

They started homeward. It was an agonizing journey and he locked his mind so deeply in a dungeon that he never understood her efforts to soothe him, or to ease his guilt.

*

Jim's grandparents were leaving right after lunch on Friday. The drive was only an hour from Shoreford, but Gram, as always, was eager to be underway. They were going to stay the night with Uncle Ed and Kit before going on to their own home. Kit was preparing their favorite supper.

"That Kit certainly is a lovely young lady," Gram said before entering the auto.

Jim averted her gaze.

Soon after the departure of his grandparents Jim was on his way to Collins Park. His mind was in turmoil, not only because of last night, but the time was here for him to speak to his parents and running was the best way he knew to put things in perspective.

Arriving at the beach, the day was cool, but the sun was shining. He removed his shoes and ran bare footed. In no time he cast off his jacket, then his outer and undershirt. He traversed the beach end to end, again and again. The shadows had lengthened considerably when he collapsed on the sand. His sweat bathed, naked, upper torso, invited millions of grains of sand and adorned his bare skin. Sucking in huge quantities of air, exhausted, but reconciled to his decision, he scooped sand into his hands and watched as it flowed out. His mind was clear. He would do, what he had to do.

*

"No! No! No, Jimmy, you're not!" Sarah Williams was shouting, "No! It's ridiculous, you can't do it! I won't let you! I will not give another son to those Marines! I just can't do it!"

His father sat quietly, taken aback, but calm, "Why, Jim? What brought this on?"

Jim talked, hesitant at first, but gradually the words were what he wanted to say. His mother kept interrupting and shaking her head, but he was not deterred. His failing grades, the fact that no war was in progress and the GI Bill helped his cause. Finally he mentioned the Marine Corps Institute and the correspondence courses available. He solemnly promised he would finish his high school requirements and obtain his diploma. His father knew that his promise was good .. and so did his mother.

Ninety minutes passed before his mother, her will shaken, was coerced to let her son do his bidding. She did not cry, but acquiesced slowly and mechanically and toward the end, silently.

Bill Williams questioned his son occasionally, his voice somber and when the conclusion was finally reached, he said, "Jim, I hope you're not running away from something?"

"No, Dad," he lied, but he had not lied about any of the other stuff.

*

Monday morning Jim was waiting outside Mr. Melillo's office well before the first bell rang. The principal was genuinely disappointed. They talked for a bit and Mr. Melillo attempted to reverse the decision, but finally wished him well and sorrowfully and without rancor, bid him a kind farewell.

Books and supplies were turned in and the final chore was to see Coach. It turned out not so bad. Though he did not know what it was, Coach knew something was preying heavily on Jim, something that he needed to work out for himself. He hoped it could be accomplished in Shoreford, but felt Jim must march to his own drummer. He had seen enough of Jim to think he could do just that. He was upbeat and positive without preaching.

"It's been my privilege," Coach said when they were shaking hands, "to coach and observe a lot of good boys on the gridiron, but it was just four days ago that I saw the finest individual performance ever. Jim, if you tackle life the way you played that game, you will be a success at anything you attempt. I expect you to be a top notch Marine."

*

Because of his mother's insistence, Jim asked for and was granted an enlistment date after Christmas. He did not mind giving in to her on that. Luckily his father knew the owner of a construction company who gave him a job for four weeks. New housing was escalating rapidly and even in bad weather there was work to be done inside. Jim worked hard and earned more than he ever had. He felt good about having a large sum for Christmas gifts.

Jim did not visit Shoreford's center except when necessary. He did not want to make explanations to schoolmates and he certainly did not want to bump into Connie. He did get together with Buck whenever basketball or schoolwork permitted. Their friendship was solidified.

On Christmas Eve Jim did not wish to attend church, but disguised his feelings for his mother's sake. He did enjoy the Williams family get together. His grandmother, always his staunch supporter and his aunts, uncles and cousins did not pry into his decision. The food and singing were great and he was sad when leaving. All present took a special turn to wish him the best.

Two nights later he borrowed the family car and drove to the Buchanan's to bid his best friend farewell.

As he was leaving, 'The Buck' surprised him with a quick, hard embrace and said, "I'll miss you, Buddy!" There were tears in the corners of Buck's eyes.

The next morning his family dropped him at the recruiting station in the city. His mother did not cry and was at her most serious best. She was constantly giving one set of instructions after another, frequently repeating herself. Jim was amused, though he would never let on. His father too was enjoying it. Bob was completely disgruntled. He could not get a word in and he was bursting to talk to his brother. Shirley, now as tall as her mother, stayed at her side, quiet, but smiling. When it came time for the farewells, Jim and Shirley hugged and when he kissed her cheek there were tears. After the hand shaking it was his mother's turn and before she loosed her grip on her son, he felt her shudder. His father's first letter would tell of the stoic behavior she maintained until she crawled into bed that night and cried herself to sleep.

*

Within two hours of leaving his family, Jim was on a train for New York City with a lad named Salvatore Gennaro, a fellow recruit, or 'boot' as they would be known from now till graduation, .. at least in polite circles.

Sal was a dark, brooding kid who did not laugh easily or talk much. He smoked a lot. Jim maintained his usual reticence with strangers and the first half hour or so remained silent. The train wheels clacking over the track joints was the only sound.

Reaching for a cigarette, Sal fumbled through pockets trying to locate a match. Uncomfortable at Sal's frustration, Jim turned, hoping he could help and spotted the match book on the seat between them.

"Here they are. Must have fallen."

"Thanks." Sal took the matches and lit up.

Frustrated, Jim forced himself into a decision. He convinced himself that he must break the silence if any conversation was to take place. He asked the first and easiest question that came to mind.

"Why ya joinin the Corps?"

Inhaling deeply Sal exhaled the thin smoke in a quick burst and looked down at his cigarette. He was silent a moment before he muttered, "I don't know," and was silent again. He thought a bit, quite a bit, then looked deeply into Jim's eyes and continued, "I guess I just wanted somethin different, somethin different'an what I had, which wasn't much."

The tone in Sal's voice and his demeanor stirred Jim's emotions and he could not help but feel for the somber lad. He wanted to reach out to Sal, but did not know how. At the same time he did not want to press Sal, but he did not want to let go, so he took over the conversation. It was labored at first, but soon came more easily.

Telling Sal about Don and the great brother he had been and their life together, Jim's enthusiasm spilled over onto Sal and he turned in the seat and listened intently. It was a great feeling for Jim, not only to be able to reach Sal and see his interest aroused, but to once again bring his brother to life. There was some of the old pain that accompanied the telling of Don's death, but it was diminished and the pride now was stronger.

"You're a lucky guy."

Sal's comment puzzled Jim coming on the heels of the story of his brother's death, but he realized he was a lucky guy and he knew what Sal meant.

There was a short silence and Sal turned away and gazed out the window. He started talking, as if to himself, "My old lady is a drunk ... and a whore."

The words startled Jim. He stared wide eyed at his seatmate.

Sal turned back after a short pause, but his eyes focused on his hands, "Well, not always," he glanced up at Jim, "but when I needed a mom, she disappeared from my life." He looked down again, then directly into Jim's eyes, "Ya know, she was really good ta me when I was a kid. My old man slapped me around sometimes. I think I made it worse cause I didn't cry, but my mom was always there for me after. When I was nine, my old man and my two younger sisters got killed in a car crash. It was tough. Pretty soon she started drinkin and after awhile guys started comin home with her. It wasn't much fun. I even got in fights with somma them and got my ass kicked. I quit school at sixteen and had a couple a shitty jobs that didn't pay nothin, so I turn seventeen an I join up. Why not? I mights well be here."

The words riveted Jim to his seat. He had not known that life was sometimes lived like that. For Sal, it was the first time he had spoken of his family to anyone, let alone speaking intimately, something he did with great difficulty. Neither boy knew it, but it was precisely at that moment that the boy from the tenements and the boy from suburbia were pouring the mortar that would bind them together for the rest of their lives.

By the time they reached New York their number had swelled to six. A platoon sergeant met them and handed out food chits, gave instructions almost kindly and herded them to a nearby Y.M.C.A. where they were to spend the night. Two more bodies were added to the group and after supper they marched as one into the cold city night for their last fling at frivolity for three months.

They were seventeen year old boys seeking the spurious attainment of manhood in New York's bars and strip joints. No one in the group was eighteen, the legal drinking age in New York, but they had little trouble obtaining drinks. Jim did not enjoy the two beers he nursed. One lad from upstate New York named Steven Sellers was compelled to inform every waiter and bartender they encountered, that, "We're all Marines you know!" It was embarrassing to Jim at first, but as the evening wore on, he found himself liking Steve. Sal too smiled occasionally at the loquacious farm boy.

Heading back to the 'Y', a few were feeling no pain.

*

When the train wended its way through Washington D.C. the following day it was dark. The Capitol building was bathed by brilliant floodlights.

"Wow! Will you look at that," Jim uttered softly.

Sal, Steve and Tom Blatchford, another recruit who joined them in the seats adjusted to face each other, ended their conversation and quickly turned their gaze in the direction Jim pointed. They stared in silent awe until the gleaming building was out of sight. It would be a few years, but these young men would come to hold the occupants of that hallowed edifice in less than esteem.

At each stop a few more bodies were added to the group. By nightfall they were twenty-one strong. They were all headed for a great adventure and many could already see themselves as heroes and imagine themselves returning to the open arms of anxious and desirable females. Despite the noisy conversations and bravado most were asleep in their seats by eleven o'clock.

*

The train was slowing when the last of the new Marines returned from a hurried breakfast in the dining car. The coach was now filled with young men bound for Parris Island reaching clumsily for their gear in the overhead racks.

Before the train was completely stopped, a lean, unhappy looking Marine platoon sergeant was aboard.

"All right you shitbirds, listen up!" he bellowed in a voice that overflowed with frightening authority.

One of the boys in close proximity to the sergeant grinned. Immediately the man in green was in front of him.

"You see something funny, girl?" the sergeant sneered, his voice challenging.

The boy quickly came to attention, bending slightly to the rear, the sergeant so close their noses almost touched. The sergeant was the shorter of the two, but at the moment he appeared a giant.

"Did you hear me, girl?" the sergeant growled, his nearly black eyes impaling the luckless individual where he stood.

The youngster was instantly subdued. "Y .. y .. yes sergeant," he stammered.

"Don't call me sergeant you dumb ass shitbird! And don't you eyeball me! You stare above my head, asshole!" the D.I. shouted, "You see these emblems?" He pointed with a swagger stick to the black eagle, globe and anchor on his lapels and cap and growled, "They tell you I'm a Marine and all Marines will be addressed as, 'Sir!' by you and all your low life girl friends. Someday you might earn the right to wear these emblems," the sergeant sneered again, "though I doubt it. But if you do, then you may address a Marine by rank and name. Until that day you are the lowest form of life, .. a shitbird, .. a useless boot! You understand me, girl?"

"Y .. y .. yes," meekly, gazing as required, over the sergeant's head.

"Yes, what?" boomed the sergeant.

"Yes, Sir!" yelped the frightened lad.

"I can't hear you!"

"Yes, Sir!" shouted the red faced boot who had been reduced to a feeble nonentity.

Thus were James Arthur Williams and seventy-five other young Americans 'welcomed' aboard.

Platoon Sergeant Delbert Lightfoot, Satan incarnate, guardian of their transcendental journey into the Corps, their drill instructor, rushed them from the train onto the platform where they met a similar other, their second D.I., the junior member of the imperial pair.

Sergeant Francis Keefe reached for and caught a tall, gangly lad who was missing a shoe on his left foot. Spun around, the youngster stared open mouthed at the D.I.

"Stand at attention you useless shitbird!" the D.I. bellowed.

The boot came immediately to attention.

"What's your name, shitbird?"

The recruit, subdued, but not completely discomposed, answered in a thick southern drawl, "Jonnie."

"Jonnie what?" the D.I. shouted.

"Jonnie Phillips."

"Jonnie Phillips, what?" The voice was fierce.

Confusion for an instant, then, "Jonnie Phillips, Sir!" A smile started on the boy's face, but he quickly wiped it away as the D.I. leaned closer.

"Where's your shoe, shitbird?"

"I lost it."

"You lost it what?" Sergeant Keefe yelled, inches from Jonnie's face.

"I lost it, Sir!" was the instant reply.

"Marines don't lose their shoes!"

"Yes, Sir!" very loud.

"But then you're a far cry from a Marine," the D.I. sneered, "You won't make it into our Corps, will you, shitbird?"

Committing a cardinal sin, Jim moved his eyes just enough to observe with his peripheral vision. He saw Jonnie stiffen.

"Yes I will, Sir! Yes .. I .. will, Sir!" Jonnie shouted, his reply tinged with anger.

For the briefest moment Jim thought he saw approval in Sergeant Keefe's eyes, but he growled at Jonnie and sent him into the ranks.

And Jim got away with it.

Sergeant Keefe was the taller of the two D.I.s. His spit shined shoes reflected like a mirror. Spending two years in the Pacific Theater, his Asiatic-Pacific campaign ribbon contained three bronze battle stars. On Bougainville Sergeant Keefe served with the Marine Raiders and went to Saipan with the Fourth

Division where he was wounded. He ended the war with the Fifth Division on another bloody island called Iwo Jima.

Platoon Sergeant Lightfoot wore the larger silver battle star designating five campaigns. Refusing to leave his unit to return to the States at the end of two years, his time in the Pacific lasted over three years. A member of the 8th Marines of the Second Marine Division throughout the entire Pacific war, he went ashore in the latter stages of Guadalcanal, the first American land offensive of the war. This was followed by the bloodbath at Tarawa, then Saipan and Tinian. Finally, his regiment was called out of reserve and entered the last land battle of the war at Okinawa. A scout-sniper, he was wounded twice, but made it back. Jim was intrigued by the man's always quick, but cat like movements. He was a Cherokee-Creek Indian and like eighty per cent of those original Americans who served, he served in the Corps.

It would take time, but these boots would, by sweat and tears, bruises and exhaustion, pride ... and some fear, come to respect these two men who came thundering into their midst like a giant tornado. Jim knew they were in good hands and would learn and learn well from two who had survived the bitter experience of bloodletting. He was filled with far less trepidation than his fellow commiserables. After all, he had been prepared for this by his uncle and his brother. In his mind, there were none better.

But for now they were loaded onto a flatbed semitrailer with side boards. Ordered to stand at attention, they were forbidden to hold to the sides or overhead braces. When the air brakes were applied, those closest to the sides, fearful of hurtling into the unknown, did surreptitiously grab the side boards. That, along with the closeness of the bodies kept them upright.

Once through the main gate they came upon a group of Marines walking on the sidewalk. Halting their walk, the Marines turned and faced the boots as they drove by, shouting in unison, "You'll be sorreee!" This was repeated all the way to the administration building by every group and individual Marine they chanced to pass.

Paperwork complete, they were marched to the barber shop as Platoon 489. The haircut, to be deducted from their first pay, was about four swipes of the clippers. It took something like thirty seconds and left nothing but skin. Platoon 489 was then welcomed at the Naval dispensary where it ended as a naked mass of prodded, pricked, humbled, unenthusiastic humanity. It quickly learned the rudiments of the short arm inspection which would be repeated relentlessly during the early weeks of boot camp.

Still in civilian clothes, they marched to a mess hall and had their first taste of Parris Island sustenance. The mumbled, whispered critique that followed was not kind to the cooks and bakers. Marching away after the meal, Jim could see Jonnie Phillips limping up ahead, the holes in the bottom of his sock enlarging. They halted where they would live, in front of a large wooden 'H' shaped barracks of two stories. Platoons were housed top and bottom on each side of the H. The connector was the D.I.s quarters and contained the showers and toilets, now the 'head'. When the boots were rushed inside, they found the wooden floor, now the 'deck', to be squeaky clean and bleached from all the previous scrubbings.

Next stop was the quartermaster where they received the initial clothing issue. Back in the squad bay they dressed in their new, shiny, herringbone dungarees and learned how to stow their clothing and toilet articles in locker boxes, the same article in the same place in every locker box.

Bunks, or 'racks,' were made up under the tutelage of both D.I.s and were precise in every detail, at least they were supposed to be. Those who failed saw their workmanship violently torn apart and repeated the process as many times as necessary to get it right.

It was a very busy first day. The boots learned to call 'attention' the instant a D.I. or any other Marine entered the squad bay. Instructions and orders, orders and instructions were laid on the dumbfounded kids of 489 until 9:30PM, now '2130'.

The final order of the day from Sergeant Lightfoot was, "You will write letters home, .. now!" In the next half hour, seventy-six short letters and probably a few more were completed. Promptly at 2200 the D.I.s shouted their last epithets and the lights went out.

In seconds, the future Marines of 489, clad in skivvies as prescribed by Naval law, were between clean sheets. Many found the weariness did not help them sleep. They looked to tomorrow with varying degrees of anxiety, uncertainty and more than a little fear.

*

The shrill blast of the police whistle exploded the silence. The flagrant glare of the lights terminated the darkness. The unholy sound of Sergeants Lightfoot and Keefe shouting, "Hit the deck, you lousy shitbirds!" while walking along the bunks hitting each with a rod, sent the apprehensive boots scurrying for their lives.

"My God!" thought Jim, "This is for real!" Pulling on his dungaree trousers, socks and ankle high shoes, now 'boondockers', he ran for the head with the masses. He emptied his bladder and squeezed in at an open sink and washed his hands and doused his face with cold water.

"Those bastards really know how to make ya hate em." Sal said, standing next to Jim. He appeared not fully awake, but there was a fierce look on his face.

"Yeh," Jim replied, a sarcastic grin punctuating his response. "Let's go. We gotta get moving. We don't need the wrath of God this early in the morning."

Bunks were made up, some more than twice, before the overhead platoon was thundering down the outdoor stairs, now 'ladder', at the same time that platoon 489 below, was spilling outside into the blackness before sunrise. They joined the other platoons barracked on the inner edge of the paved parade ground to 'muster on the grinder' for P.T. Sweatshirts were worn, but the cold in early morning South Carolina chilled the unenthusiastic young Americans, but not for long. The large formation was called to attention facing a raised, wooden platform occupied by a well built Marine bellowing instructions. The workout began.

In great shape, Jim took to the P.T. without much trouble. There were others that experienced more than a few difficulties. They received a fair share of unkind advise. No one complained, ... out loud that is. The P.T. was concluded with a run in platoon formation.

Dismissed, they dashed back into the barracks. The deck was swabbed and they were shaved, whether they needed it or not. With field jackets over dungaree jackets, they dashed out the front door, now 'hatch' and marched to breakfast. On their heads they wore the forest green garrison cap, referred to by some as the fore and aft cap, but vulgarly by most as a 'pisscutter'. The left side of the cap revealed a small hole which would one day accept the proud black emblem of their Corps.

*

New Years Eve came and went. The mess halls added a few special foods, but the boots did not celebrate. It was just another day in the life of Platoon 489 and all the other recruit platoons at Parris Island. Some said the D.I.s on duty were worse than usual, because they had to spend time with a bunch of sorry looking boots and not the fine looking females they much preferred.

Towards the end of the first week, in the new year of 1946, the platoon was taking on a form and personality. Mistakes were made on the drill field and elsewhere, but there was improvement. The D.I.s' bellows and cursing were still a very prominent part of each day, but there was a lessening, if only a modicum, though many would say that was not so. A few members of 489, a very few, were beginning to experience just a twinge of respect for their tormentors and allude to the fact they might even be part of the human race.

Outdoors they did P.T. and drilled and drilled and drilled. Indoors their young minds were filled with the general orders which were committed to memory. There was Marine Corps history, Naval law and procedures, 'junk on the bunk' inspections and 'field days', that is, making the squad bay and heads spotless. All this was done to the accompaniment of boisterous and unending 'encouragement'. The spare time they received was well organized. They washed clothing with the issued scrub brush on the cement slabs between the barracks and they studied hard and wrote letters.

The reality of discipline, both individual and group, was achieved at once. For those that smoked, they could do so only in designated areas. Mostly they waited for, "The smoking lamp is lit." The extinguished butt was 'field stripped', the tobacco scattered, the paper rolled into a tiny ball and lost. When a non stripped butt was found, the entire platoon paid.

One lad did not shave on the third day and did so in front of the platoon, double timing in place on his locker box, the razor applied to his dry face and neck. Another called his field scarf (the terrible neck tie made of the same material as the khaki shirt) a tie and wrote five-hundred times, "I will not call my field scarf a tie."

And the platoon itself became an instrument in administering discipline. One individual did not shower daily. He was carried bodily into the shower and cleansed with multiple scrub brushes by his enthusiastic shipmates. Lessons were being learned and Platoon 489 was at the beginning of the journey to become a cohesive unit.

During that first week, during the brief lull after noon chow, Jim was about to exit the head and return to the squad bay. He knew by now that the platoon would be falling out in a matter of seconds. Sergeant Lightfoot rushed past heading for the squad bay before Jim got into the corridor. A split second later there was a loud thud, simultaneous with a high pitched, "Attention!"

Sprinting to the hatch that entered the squad bay Jim came immediately to attention. Lightfoot had rounded the first bunk and was confronting Steve Sellers who was glued to the wall, now 'bulkhead'.

Steve had been bending over his locker box when he spotted the D.I. Calling out and snapping to attention at the same time, he crashed backward into the bulkhead. His head hit hard, bringing tears to eyes, open wide in fear. The D.I. was standing less than six inches away. It appeared Steve was trying to force the back of his head through the bulkhead.

Zeus spoke loudly and frighteningly, "You're a clown, Sellers!"

"Yes, Sir!" in panic, Steve screamed high and squeaky, his eyes glued above the D.I.s head.

"Tell me what you are!"

"I'm a clown!" looking over the D.I.s' head.

"You're a clown, what?"

"I'm a clown, Sir!" squeakier.

"I can't hear you!"

"I'm a clown, Sir!" getting more squeaky.

"I can't hear you!"

"I'm a clown, Sir!" voice rising, quavering.

"Again!"

"I'm a clown, Sir!" voice higher, approaching soprano.

Sergeant Lightfoot's face twitched, his mouth tightened, his eyes for a fleeting moment lost their intensity. In that instant before his composure was whisked away, he turned on his heel, rounded the bunk and fled the squad bay.

The door to the D.I.s' quarters slammed shut.

Jim almost doubled over trying to contain the silent laughter and shaking body. The rest of the platoon remained stiffly at attention, doing everything humanly possible to contain their merriment. To lose control would bring disaster. Steve never moved. He was traumatized to the bulkhead, the only one in the squad bay who did not know he had bested his D.I.

But the concealed, cautious mirth did not last. Three minutes later the platoon was marching to the armory to take possession of M-1 rifles. Sergeant Lightfoot had regained his form and was calling cadence in that sonorous, "Awunhupparee-foryurluprightalup." Sergeant Keefe brought up the rear, his infallible eyes spotting and severely correcting the most minute flaw or malfeasance.

Jim was excited. He learned to shoot at an early age. His father taught Don and later him to respect firearms and handle and operate them properly.

Bill Williams worked hard for his family and there was never enough time to do all the things he wanted. The infrequent times he spent in the woods with his sons were happy memories for Jim. Bill would brook no nonsense where firearms were concerned. In the beginning Jim was harshly rebuked for a less than serious attitude. It never happened again. Jim would eventually out shoot his father and his brother too, who excelled at so many things. And it was Don who praised Jim's shooting excellence with such unenvious zeal.

Bill bought for them to share, a single shot .22, Marlin 'Tom Mix Special'. When the three hunted and it was Jim's turn to carry the rifle he always hit what he shot at unless it was moving very fast. With time he managed to excel at that too. Now as the M-1 was placed in his hands, that little Marlin seemed insignificant.

With rifle and bayonet they fell in to return to barracks. They marched back with rifles at the trail. Grasped at the forearm the weapon was held at an angle, butt to the rear a few inches off the deck. Time passed and the entire platoon was arm weary. A butt plate was heard striking the deck. Sergeant Keefe was instantly at the transgressor, roaring, "You will not allow your rifle to come in contact with the deck, shitbird! When you get in your rack tonight you will take your rifle with you and sleep with it. And it had better be very warm at reveille!"

The rifle, .. the weapon, .. the piece, the boots now possessed, must never be called a gun. A few days earlier the boots of 489 witnessed a lone boot from another platoon circling the grinder, rifle held aloft in the right hand, left hand clutching his crotch. As he ran he shouted over and over at the top of his lungs, "This is my rifle," and he shook the weapon, "this is my gun." He accented the grip of his left hand, "This is for shooting," again he shook the rifle, "this is for fun." And he accented again the grip of his left hand. The poor lad made a good show of it. To have done less he would have to repeat it till perfect. Four platoons witnessed the spectacle and no one in any of those units was a participant in a similar performance.

Much of the daily routine now revolved around their M-1's. The manual of arms was incorporated into close order drill. The rifle was disassembled and reassembled under the close scrutiny of the D.I.s. When there were odd moments between chow and falling out, the boots did it on their own. Soon they could do it blindfolded which sometimes ended in frustration. Some jokester would steal a part and replace it before the blindfold was removed. Steve Sellers became the platoon champ at completing the operation blindfolded and at stealing the parts from his buddies, who now good naturedly called him 'clown.' Steve was not a quick learner on the drill field. There was the time he knocked over a stack of rifles and had to sleep with all three. But at last, he found something he was good at and he was feeling better about himself. That tended to increase his pranks.

Things were moving more quickly. The future Marines absorbed more at a faster rate. As their minds sharpened, their bodies hardened. Their language was also changing. It was peppered with slang, vitriolic cussing, cursing and downright foul mouthedness. Jim was using words he almost never heard in Shoreford and never at home. He was at Parris Island about four weeks before he first vocalized the famous 'F' word. The sound of it spilling from his open mouth surprised him, not because the word was new to him, but that he had uttered it. After that experience he worked to clean up his language, but to his discomfort, a sudden bout of anger or some unhappy surprise, sometimes brought such language forth.

The weeks passed. They ran the obstacle course, got 'gassed' and spent many grueling hours at bayonet drill. They went from on guard to thrust, parry, butt stroke, smash, slash and withdraw. It felt as if their fatigued arms would fall off, would respond no more, but the arms did respond and so did their confidence.

489 got its second hair cut. It was kept close on the sides, but on the top there was some real stuff. They were starting to feel salty.

The day before they were to leave for the rifle range it was excessively hot for the first week in February, even for South Carolina.

After noon chow a large group was standing outside the barracks having a smoke before muster. Frank Hickey, not only the biggest physique in the platoon, but the biggest mouth, was leading the conversation. Hickey was not well liked, but no one disputed his statements. There were some who thought he was an outright liar.

Jim was standing with Sal and Steve Sellers close by, amused at the boisterous bravado. After one of Hickey's comments, Sal, field stripping a cigarette said to no one in particular, "What an asshole."

Steve winced as Hickey's head swung toward them, eyes glowering, mouth tight. At that precise moment the squad bay hatch opened and Sergeant Lightfoot emerged followed by Sergeant Keefe. Somebody yelled, "Tenshun!"

As the group stood at attention the sergeants observed from the top step. The boots did not know it, but the D.I.s had overheard much of the conversation. Lightfoot scanned the stiff standing assemblage. Keefe, somewhat behind, smirked.

"So you shitbirds think you're salty, huh?" Lightfoot said, followed by silence. "I asked you a question, shitbirds!"

"No, Sir!" sheepishly.

"I can't hear you!"

"No, Sir!" good and loud.

"That's not the impression I got. How about you, Sergeant Keefe?"

"Sergeant Lightfoot, these shitbirds are trying to snow us and show no respect for our judgment."

While the two talked, Jim was convinced, rightly so, they were looking for an excuse to order some foul deed. Things had been going too well.

"When you're dismissed," Lightfoot sneered, "you will fall out with rifles," and louder, "on the double!" He paused a moment, looked over the group before shouting, "Dismissed!"

There was a mad dash for the squad bay and the thunder of feet on the wooden deck. The young men dashed inside and grabbed ammo belts and weapons. The entire platoon was on the grinder, standing at attention in very short order. Not a muscle moved while Sergeant Lightfoot walked back and forth in front of them. Sergeant Keefe turned and entered the squad bay.

"Little girls could do better than that." Lightfoot shook his head sadly, "And you shitbirds think you are salty, .. my, my."

The members of 489 had experienced what followed on numerous earlier occasions, but never for so long. At attention, but with arms fully extended to the front, rifles were gripped by the finger tips and held horizontal to the deck. The 'old salts' were in much better condition than the first, second or third time they participated in this drill, but when the minutes dragged on, they passed that state of fitness and the agony set in.

Arms began to quiver inside the dungarees. Shoulders locked and turned numb. Surely someone had to lower his arms, or perhaps commit the cardinal sin and drop a weapon. But they hung on, teeth clamped tightly, eye muscles straining to keep their eyes from closing, gaze fixed straight ahead, unseeing. Every known foul word and phrase surged through their brains, all directed at the motherless Lightfoot.

Then it was over and they stormed back into the squad bay. They replaced the rifles in the racks and ammo belts over the ends of bunks and came to attention. The senior D.I. walked to the far end and joined Keefe who ended the short silence. He gave precise instructions. The overwhelming relief of moments ago was shattered.

Starting at one end of the squad bay, the first man ran to the side of the first set of bunks and plunged over the bottom one, squirmed under the next and over the next, going over and under every lower bunk in the squad bay. Each man in the platoon followed right on the heels of the man ahead. They accomplished the task with speed. They did not wish to repeat the wretched exercise. When it was over and the final entrant completed the course, they stood at attention in front of their racks.

The bay was a shambles That required a giant field day. It was indeed a thorough event, yet it was completed in record time by an angry and determined group of future Marines. Not an audible sound was uttered during the entire procedure and when they finally marched to evening chow, they were a tired, sore and bruised group, not quite as salty, but they marched straight and tall and they knew, they had not been defeated.

Perhaps Steve Sellers put it best when he said, "If those motherless bastards want to hand it out, we'll show em who can take it!"

*

When the platoon arrived at the rifle range, they did not go near the firing line for days. They learned positions and how to adjust and apply the sling. They learned sight pictures and breathing and trigger squeeze and they participated in many hours of dry firing, 'snapping in', an activity that was at first arduous, then boring. When the time arrived for the real thing, 489 was ready.

In the second week, the first day on the firing line, Jim, Sal and a few others witnessed Hickey receive a very swift kick to the buttocks followed by a severe tongue lashing from his shooting coach. He had turned just slightly around with a loaded weapon, an unforgivable cardinal sin. Safety was the first thing they learned and the first thing they performed. Any deviation brought instant retaliation.

The animosity Hickey had for Sal was building and that incident intensified the bad blood between the two. Sal had the misfortune to witness Hickey's humiliation.

The next time the platoon was in the butts pulling targets, Hickey 'accidentally' collided with Sal, knocking him to the deck on his butt.

"Geeze, I'm real sorry, Gennaro," Hickey said with a smirk.

Sal calmly got to his feet, brushed himself off and went back to the chores at hand.

Jim never cared for fighting as a means of settling personality conflicts, but he was certain this conflict was headed there. He liked it even less in this instance. Hickey was a few inches taller than his friend and probably fifteen pounds heavier.

By the end of the first week on the firing line, Jim and Steve were celebrities amongst their close buddies. Their prowess with the rifle was without peer. They shot possible after possible (all bulls eyes). At the end of each day they were requested to show their scorebooks. The tight groups were the envy of many.

Not so fortunate in the early days was Sal. He was having problems with the M-1 and received a few 'Maggie's drawers', the red flag waved across the target on a miss. Both Jim and Steve tutored him when there was a spare moment, there being more of those on the range, also occasional diversions, mostly athletic events. It was part of the substantial effort that was made to qualify every Marine with the rifle, for no matter what a Marine's specialty, he was always supposed to be capable of filling a rifleman's boondockers, something unique to the Corps.

On a Sunday after noon chow, Jim and Steve were coaching Sal. They occupied a small grassy area at the end of a row of quonset huts. While the three buddies were working together, Jim was increasingly aware of Hickey and one of his dubious associates passing a football. With each reception Hickey was getting closer. Sal, in the kneeling position, his back to the action, was suddenly bowled over by a charging Hickey.

Getting quickly to his feet Hickey forced a knee into Sal's thigh on the way up. "Shit, man, I'm real fuckin sorry," he sneered.

Sal rolled to his knees and stood erect, his eyes strangely calm, but intensely piercing.

"Su .. Su .. Su .. Sal!" stammered Steve, his voice fearful.

Jim stepped between Sal and Hickey.

"It's OK," Sal said, his voice calm and steady.

"Williams!" Sergeant Keefe's voice boomed.

Jim jerked around, surprised to hear his name, "Yes, Sir!"

He ran to his D.I. and came to attention while Keefe stood silently watching the group disperse.

"Damn!" thought Jim, "he knows something's wrong and he'll try to get it out of me, but heck, I can't tell him. ... I won't!"

"Stand at ease, Williams." Jim relaxed, but only slightly. "I understand you had a brother in the 28th Marines who won the Navy Cross at Iwo."

"Yes, Sir!" Jim answered with undisguised enthusiasm, so relieved at the D.I.s' comment that a smile lit his face before he had time to think. It was OK.

"I met your brother when he joined the division. I didn't know him on a daily basis. He was in another platoon in our company, but I saw him from time to time while we trained and I saw him after we landed at Iwo. We got the hell shot out of us on that stinking little island. Later in the campaign, for a short time, I was company commander with the rank of corporal. I went through that one without a scratch, but sure lost a lot of good buddies. It was a real carnage. What I wanted to tell you was, your brother, from everything I knew about him was a helluva Marine. If you're anything like him, you'll be a credit to the Corps."

"Yes, Sir! Thank you, Sir!" There was no need to hide the smile now and Jim did not. He was walking on air when Keefe departed.

Sal and Steve joined him from a distance.

"What the hell was that all about," Steve asked.

"He knew my brother, ... well sort of. He wanted me to know."

The three walked to their quonset hut and along the way Steve kidded him about brown nosing and Sal good naturedly punched him in the arm.

Fifteen minutes later the platoon was standing at attention in front of the row of quonset huts. A 'left face' and 'forward march' took them to the grassy area the three buddies had just vacated. Platoon Sergeant Lightfoot instructed the platoon to gather on the slight rise in front of him and Sergeant Keefe. Each D.I. held a pair of boxing gloves. They picked out a few pairs of opponents. Each pair boxed a few rounds. It was surprising to Jim how evenly matched they were. Next came the volunteers who were not always matched well, some taking their lumps. The D.I.s did some more choosing and again the matching was better.

Jim hated boxing. He hoped he would not be picked. Steve, standing behind Jim was trying to make himself invisible, but they were pointed to by Lightfoot and had to fight each other.

It was not scientific, .. or pretty, but after a slow start they got into it and did a fair job of pummeling one another. Just before the second round ended, Jim caught Steve with a roundhouse right landing him on his back. Steve thought it was good fun and so did Jim. Back amongst the spectators they were laughing and jabbing, but were returned to sensibility with a start.

"Sir, Private Hickey requests permission to box."

Almost the entire platoon knew what was coming.

"Do you have an opponent?" Lightfoot asked.

"Well, Sir, I figured maybe Gennaro wanted to fight me."

Jim and Steve grimaced. Sal, standing beside Jim, never moved or changed his expression.

"You're in a different weight class than Gennaro," Lightfoot continued.

"Sir, I get the idea he wants at me. He talks big."

Lightfoot turned to Sal who tilted his head to one side, then walked to the D.I., hands and arms extended to accept the gloves.

There was an electricity that surged through the platoon. All knew of Hickey's feelings. It was difficult not to the way he boasted.

Sal, mostly closemouthed, was an unknown factor. He was a close friend of the two best shooters in the platoon, but otherwise, little was known of him, though he always carried his load and was not disliked by anyone, unlike Hickey.

There were few present who did not hope for some kind of miracle.

It started slowly, Hickey moving around Sal who moved only enough to keep Hickey to his front. Hickey smelled blood and the lust was in his eyes. Sal moved on his feet like he knew what he was doing, hands where they should be, in a slight crouch. Cat like, his movements were precise.

Hickey's left shot out for Sal's head and before it was withdrawn, a powerful right came up for Sal's chin. Both maneuvers struck nothing but air. Within a second the moves were repeated missing by a greater margin. With Hickey off balance Sal quickly jabbed a left to his nose. As blood appeared, second and third more powerful punches scored in rapid and stunning succession.

"My God!" Jim said to himself, "he's so fast. He reminds me of Buck."

When the round ended, Hickey's nose was bleeding and there was swelling above the left eye and on the lips. He was so angry he would not sit and rest.

The new round began, Hickey rushing at Sal swinging wildly. Sal sidestepped and smashed a punishing right to the side of Hickey's head as he went by. Groggy and missing badly, Hickey was exhausting himself fast. He was losing his ability to defend himself. Sal stepped in under the wild swings and pummeled the midsection. Before the round ended Hickey was on his hands and knees, gasping for breath. He did not get up.

The platoon was cheering and Jim saw the D.I.s exchange a quick smile before helping Hickey to his feet. These two men knew more about the people in their charge than anyone in the platoon cared to acknowledge, .. at least for now.

*

The four weeks on the rifle range were over and Platoon 489 went back to mainside for a week of mess duty and after that, the final week before graduation. Sal qualified and made Marksman with a point to spare. His confidence bolstered he also qualified with the carbine.

Both Jim and Steve broke the range record for recruits and scored expert with the M-1 and the carbine. Being a rifle expert added an extra five dollars to the monthly pay which was a whopping ten percent for privates.

Additionally, all fired the B.A.R., rifle grenades and threw hand grenades. More would follow when they joined a rifle company, but for now, they were nearing the end of an episode in the life of every Marine.

*

Dressing for the final parade at Parris Island, the young Americans were excited, nervous and proud all at the same time. During the last week they had not heard the word shitbird once. Their D.I.s were starting to sound like members of the human race, at least as far as Marines were concerned. They were physically fit and they learned well the lessons of the drill field, the rifle range and teamwork. They were filled with history and tradition and were imbued with a spirit that was characteristic of the men of their Corps.

A few had not made it, but seventy of the starters were still aboard. As they were handed the black eagle, globe and anchor to be attached to the naked garrison cap, there were few present who did not hold it in a hand and fix their gaze thereon, for at least a few seconds.

The massed parade of all the graduating platoons of the Recruit Depot was performed to expectation and when they marched off, ramrod straight and all stepping as one to the Marines' Hymn, they were feeling something that would last a lifetime.

* * *

Three buddies debarked from the train in New York City, the new forest green uniforms showing signs of travel. The spit shined shoes sported a few bruises, for these new Marines had not yet learned how to evade the clumsy feet of civilians.

Seabags on shoulders and glad to be free of the confines of the crowded coach they entered the terminal to check the schedule board for departure time and track number of connecting trains. Steve had an hour and fifteen minutes until departing up the Hudson Valley. Jim and Sal boarded immediately. The shoreline train was leaving in ten minutes.

They quickly made plans to meet here six days hence for the return to Parris Island and orders to wherever. Steve shook hands with his two buddies and watched them rush off.

Jim and Sal found an empty seat. They were soon underway. Emerging from the underground maze of tracks into the afternoon sunlight Jim turned to his buddy, "Look, Sal, if things don't work out, give me a call. My folks would be happy to have you stay at our house," and smiling, he added, "and so would I."

Staring out the window, a cigarette between thumb and index finger, Sal turned. Their eyes met.

"I gotta give it a shot. She needs my help ya know," he paused giving Jim one of his rare smiles with his lips, but not his eyes, "but thanks."

He was again silent.

The friendship that had grown between the two never required conversation to sustain it. They not only had a strong respect for each other, but a respect for the silence one or the other might desire.

They parted at the station, Sal promising to call Jim in four days to make plans for the return trip. Jim watched Sal walk to the bus stop. He had been thinking so much about his friend sitting beside him that he had given no thought to getting from the station to his home. Trying to make up his mind about what to do, he wanted to be home as soon as possible. His mother he knew, would right now, with Shirley's help, be preparing supper. His father would be reading the evening newspaper sharing the living room with Bob who was reading either the sports page or comics.

About his time of arrival Jim was purposefully vague. He wanted to surprise his family. He had over one hundred dollars in his pocket so he decided to spend the two dollars for a taxi. The cab driver was instructed to drop him a few doors up the street.

He went up the front walk, up the steps, onto the stoop and placed his seabag down. Turning the knob of the front door as noiselessly as he was able, the opening measured about a foot. He saw his younger brother slowly lower the newspaper and peer nervously over the top, his eyes enlarging by the second. Dropping the newspaper, Bob jumped to his feet.

"Jim! Jimmy's here!" Bob yelled rushing to his brother, hand extended. They shook energetically and Jim punched his younger brother in the upper arm with his free hand.

Bill, his back to the door, jerked around and softly muttered, "Jim!" He was on his feet in an instant and Bob, still grinning, took a step to the rear to allow his father access to his other son.

There was a thud in the kitchen as a chair was accidentally knocked into the wall and Shirley was at the entrance to the living room. Jim released his father's hand and took his sister in his arms in a giant hug. Before he released her, his mother was standing at his side. She was bunching her apron in nervous hands, tears on her cheeks. He turned Shirley loose and she stepped aside to allow their mother her turn with her son. Jim hugged her so hard she gasped, but in that gasp was a mother's profound joy.

They stayed overlong at the supper table. Not knowing exactly what time her son was arriving Sarah had nonetheless prepared the meal for him. The table was covered with as many of his favorites as space would permit. Jim's appetite was ravenous and the family took delight watching him devour copious quantities.

In the living room later, they shared a relaxed, happy time. Bob was reminded periodically to allow others to speak and that too was a source of amusement. The gathering broke up well past midnight.

An hour later Jim was still awake listening to his brother's soft breathing and chuckling to himself at Bob's fight to stay awake and keep their conversation alive. Lying on his back, hands clasped behind his head, he was happy. He gazed through the window at the star filled sky. The wayward son had come home to a lavish welcome.

As he often did when alone or there was an incident or familiar setting to jog his memory, he thought of Don. The wonderful welcome he received was because he was deeply loved, but he wondered if it was greater now than it might have been had Don lived. He did not know the answer to that, but if his welcome was exaggerated, it was because he was filling a void larger than himself and he did not feel worthy. And because he did not feel worthy, his mind wandered through his failures and the romance with Connie. He had behaved badly in that ill fated affair.

Thank God only Kit had knowledge of it. Kit, the cousin he loved deeply and respected so much and he shamed himself with her too. Could he ever face her again and be at peace with her?

He was going to make amends for his failure in school. He promised his mother and father he would obtain a diploma. In that he would succeed. He owed it to them ... and to himself ... and to Don's memory. But that would not change what happened with Connie, .. or for that matter, Kit. He was glad he was getting out of Shoreford. Despite his family and their strong love, he was going off on his own and that was the way he wanted it.

*

Soon after five o'clock Jim was awake, shaved and dressed. The promise to himself to sleep late and lounge around was not kept. The recently instilled routines in his life were not amenable to deviation.

He was taking the metal percolator from the cabinet when his mother entered the kitchen. She was tying the belt of her robe.

"Good mornin!" he smiled, "What're ya doin up so early?"

"I heard you up and about so I'm here to make your breakfast. I see you drink coffee now."

"Yeh, Mom, I'm picking up lots of bad habits."

He grinned at her and she clucked twice and shook her head, but smiled back, her face softening and showing the pleasure of being with her son.

"Here, let me have that pot ... and sit down at the table so I can get your breakfast."

Knowing she would do what she had come to do, Jim reluctantly handed her the pot. She always seemed so at ease in the kitchen, never wasted a move.

Conversation came easily and she questioned him about his plans for the day. She never asked him anything about the Marine Corps. She did not want to know. Last night Bob's nonstop inquisitiveness about training made her edgy.

The smell of the frying bacon soon had Jim's father at the table. After their greetings Jim commented, "You're up early for a Saturday, Dad."

"How can a body sleep with all the confusion out here," Bill joked, then smiled at his wife and son, pleased to be with them.

His parent's good mood was not necessary to lift Jim's spirits for they were already high, but had they not been, Sarah's breakfast could have achieved much on its own.

Before eight o'clock Jim called Buck. He was elated to hear his friends voice to which he replied, "How the heck are you, Milton?"

"Jim!" Buck shouted, "Son of a gun! How ya doin? When'd you get in?"

"Last night."

"Why didn't ya call an let me know you were here."

"I got to blabbin with the family and next thing ya know, it was kinda late."

"Of course! I guess I forgot for a second that you have a family. Pretty dumb of me, cause they're some of the greatest folks in the world. But good as they are, it really is good to hear your voice you salty ole leatherneck. Look, I have to be to work by nine, but would it be OK for me to stop by for a quick 'hello' on the way?"

"You bet it would! That'd be great!"

"See ya in a few seconds."

Jim hung up the phone and Shirley walked into the kitchen in her robe showing signs of sleepiness.

"Good mornin, Sister," he smiled as he pinched her cheek. She did not respond verbally, but gave him a raised eyebrow and bleary eyed look. "Mom, Buck's gonna stop by for a few minutes on his way to work."

"Jimmy!" Shirley screamed, "How could you do this to me?" and speedily exited.

"What's up with her?" Jim asked, surprise on his face.

"Oh, you know girls," Sarah smiled, "they don't like to be seen before they've fixed themselves up."

Minutes later the car was heard stopping out front. Jim bounded out the kitchen door and before he reached the end of the short driveway, Buck was there. Their hands gripped and pumped and pumped, left hands fastened to forearms then thumped shoulders and backs. Their words tumbled out with enthusiasm and the love of reunited brothers. They made plans to meet that night, then Buck was gone.

At the breakfast, table Jim was sitting with his parents when Shirley returned, washed, combed and dressed.

"Where's Buck?" she asked.

"He only stopped for a second, .. had to go to work," Jim replied.

"Ohh!" Shirley exclaimed.

She sat down and Jim was sure he saw disappointment in his sister's expression.

*

The short leave passed quickly. Meetings with former teammates and schoolmates were few. Ole and Ski were on occupation duty in Germany and Japan respectively. Others from the football team were now in the service. He stayed away from school, mostly because he did not want to bump into Connie. He did visit the Capoletti and Ryan families.

He drove to the Boston suburb to see his grandparents MacPherson and came away with a large container of shortbread. Likewise, he departed his grandmother Williams with an equally large supply of Welsh cookies. He visited the

Williams aunts and uncles but briefly, missing some of his cousins. He did not drive up to his Uncle Ed's, using time as an excuse. He could not face Kit.

Time with his family consumed most of the leave and he and Buck were together whenever possible. He liked it that way. Now he sat between Shirley and Bob in the back seat of the car on the way to the railway station. His father drove and his mother sat silent, staring ahead, her mood infecting the family so that even his normally loquacious brother had little to say.

The automobile was parked and the family walked together, Jim shouldering his seabag and Bob carrying a duffle stuffed with an abundance of goodies. They entered the large terminal and Jim and Sal spotted one another simultaneously. Sal crushed out a cigarette, rose from his seat and walked to his oncoming friend. The two young men shook hands, Jim grinning. Shipmates again, they were happy to be reunited.

Dumping his seabag on the deck, Jim introduced Sal to the family.

Sarah and Bill knew all about the tragedy in Sal's life. Sal was somewhat ill at ease among people he heard so much about, but had not met in the flesh. Sarah hugged the uneasy lad, who surprisingly, responded with a slight, timid smile that was in his eyes too.

The family was swift to put him at ease and Sal was answering questions from Bob about the Marine Corps before he had a chance to think. He wanted to break away early to give the family a chance to be alone with Jim before he departed, but they were adamant and insisted he stay. They all walked to the train together, going down the stairs and through the tunnel.

Sarah was overcome by a strong desire to make Sal welcome. She was taken with him. Her maternal instincts replaced her earlier mood and set in motion the sympathy she felt for him. But there was no time.

Up the stairs and on the passenger platform it was now they must part. Sal said his goodbyes and boarded the train allowing Jim and his family the privacy of the final few moments.

Sarah quickly slid into the dark hole of sadness again and had difficulty being cheerful. Jim shook hands with his father and brother and hugged and kissed his sister. Placing hands on his mother's shoulders, their eyes met.

"You're going to be gone for a long, long time, ... aren't you?" she said sadly.

"Mom, I told you I don't have my orders yet. I really don't know."

She did not hear his words, "I know it's going to be a long time." She looked away and mumbled angrily, "I hate the Marines, .. I hate them."

Jim squeezed her hand hard, "Mom, it's gonna be all right ... and remember, before I get my discharge, I'll have my diploma. Come on, it's really not so bad."

She smiled weakly. He squeezed her to him kissing her cheek. When he released her he shouldered his seabag and took the package of goodies from Bob. Smiling one last time he boarded the train. His parents and siblings continued to wave until the coach disappeared.

It was almost ten minutes before Jim turned to Sal and asked, "How'd it go?"

A lengthy pause followed. Sal mashed out a cigarette. His eyes were half closed and staring ahead, "Not so good." Another long pause followed, "I dunno, maybe I did the wrong thing, .. joinin up, .. but I couldn't stay around and watch her die a slow death. God! I can't seem to do nothin ta help her."

Jim remembered Sal's words of last December when they approached New York City. They had perplexed him at first, but he had realized their truth. He was a lucky guy. He lost a brother, but that brother left him terrific memories and a great legacy. He had a great family, all caring and always available. He wished he could share that with his friend. Unable to offer verbal comfort he was deep in thought when Sal's words broke the silence.

"How was your leave?" then grinning he went on, "Didja get laid?"

Jim laughed out loud at the crass question, happy to be shed of the gloomy quiet.

"Who're you kidding? The only females who talked to me were my mom and sister and my grandmothers, .. oh yeh .. and a couple of aunts and cousins." Turning serious, he went on, "Ya know, the only person outside the family I spent any time with was my old buddy, Buck."

"He's that nigger ya told me about?"

Jim did not immediately answer, but looked at Sal a moment.

"Ya know, Sal, Buck's my good friend, .. same as you. I'd appreciate it if you didn't call him that."

"OK, Buddy!" Sal replied without hesitation, "You got it."

And true to his brief reply, Jim never again heard Sal use the word.

* * *

The former boots of 489 returned to Parris Island, but returned as Marines. They were assigned to a casual company and lived in tents awaiting orders. They had little to do, but clean up details, shop at the PX and attend movies at the open air theater in the evening.

Orders arrived and groups large and small left daily. There were less than twenty remaining on the fourth day when Steve Sellers departed for advanced infantry and then sniper training. Jim and Sal lost a good buddy and would miss his practical jokes and plain scooching around.

With the dawning of the fifth day Jim received orders for Treasure Island in San Francisco. Happily for him, so did Sal, along with the last two remaining members of the tent, Jonnie Phillips and Tom Blatchford.

Word came down that Sergeant Lightfoot was being processed for discharge, but his whereabouts were unknown. Sergeant Keefe was assigned a new platoon. Jim talked Sal into going with him to bid farewell to Keefe.

The company office contacted Keefe and Jim and Sal obtained permission to visit him at his newly assigned barracks at 1245. Promptly at 1245 and inadvertently, Sal leading the way, they entered through the hatch of the squad bay.

"Attention!" shouted some scared boot.

Bent over locker boxes, smoothing bedding, studying guidebooks or involved in other nervous activity, seventy odd skinheads jerked upright, one poor soul banging his head on a top rack.

"Jesus H Christ!" Sal muttered softly.

At the middle of the bay, before turning up the hall to the D.I.s quarters, they stopped. Looking up and down the bay, in his deepest and loudest voice, Sal shouted, "At ease!"

When they reached the hatch to Keefe's quarters Sal turned to Jim before knocking, "Wasn't that somethin?"

Finally allowing himself a smile, Jim answered, "You can say that again!"

"Wasn't that somethin?" They chuckled softly and knocked.

Sergeant Keefe had been promoted to platoon sergeant and the two friends congratulated him. They were introduced to Corporal Munson, the junior D.I. Keefe told Munson about Jim's record breaking score on the range and Sal's bout with Hickey.

"Excellent job, Marines," Munson said. "Well, I gotta fall this group out. Good luck to both of you."

The sergeant and the two privates were standing in the corridor when the corporal entered the bay to a high pitched chorus of, "Attention!"

"You sorry ass shitbirds, I'm gonna give you a command and all I want to see is assholes and elbows. You understand?"

"Yes, Sir!"

"I can't hear your weak, girlie voices!"

"Yes, Sir!" resoundingly.

"Did you shitbirds see those two Marines who just came through this squad bay?"

"Yes, Sir!" again, loud and clear.

"Well, shitbirds, you remember what you saw. One is a champion fighter, the other a champion shooter. That's what the

Marine Corps wants. Now I don't think you girls got that kinda stuff. Maybe we oughta get you dolls to play with. Goddam! What a sorry ass bunch! ... Fall out!"

Smiles touched the faces of Jim and Sal. They bid their former D.I. farewell and he wished them good luck.

Afterwards, back at the casual company, Sal commented, "Boy! All that stuff sure seems a long time ago ... and that's OK with me."

"You can say that again."

"Boy!" Sal grinned, "All that stuff sure seems a long time ago and that's OK with me."

Jim punched Sal on the arm and they chuckled, but Jonnie and Tom missed the humor. When the inside of the tent suddenly darkened, the four turned to see Sergeant Lightfoot standing in the tent opening. Tom jumped to his feet, standing at attention.

"At ease, Blatchford, at ease. Those days are over for you. Old habits die hard, huh?"

"Hiya, Sarge!" Jonnie yelled sitting up on his rack.

"Hello, Phillips," Lightfoot replied, then nodded to the others as he addressed them, "Williams, Gennaro."

Delighted that their former D.I. stopped by, the four kept him in a lively conversation until fifteen minutes passed and Sergeant Lightfoot glanced at his watch.

"Well, Marines, I've got to catch my transportation, so I'll be going. You were part of a good platoon. You'll do OK."

Handshakes were warm and they exited the tent with Sergeant Lightfoot. Before he turned to leave, he said, "Semper Fidelis!"

"Semper Fidelis!" they answered in unison, keeping an eye on him as he walked away, his quick, but cat like grace always present. Then he was gone from sight ... and from their lives.

* FOUR *

There was movement in the room. He opened an eye and squinted at the face above him.

"I didn't know if you were asleep, but thought you might enjoy this sometime before you dress."

"You're something."

He smiled a tender, contented smile as she placed the glass on the night stand, then he took her hand and squeezed it gently, but firmly. She returned the squeeze, smiled and raised his hand to her lips, then pressed it to her cheek.

He found her remarkably attractive for one in mid life. She was an active person and appeared younger than she was. As she backed away from the bedside, he turned his head to watch her go, finally focusing on her slim, shapely legs.

The tumbler was warm to his grasp as he lifted it to his lips sipping once, then a second time before replacing it on the stand. The warmth that journeyed down his throat, ending in his stomach, the pleasant taste lingering on his tongue and the light, peaty, almost fruity odor in his nostrils relaxed him. Soon again he was back in time.

~ ~ ~ ~ ~

The three thousand mile cross country train ride from South Carolina to Atlanta and Chicago and ending in San Francisco was five additional days of inactivity for the small group of Marines which included the last four remaining members of 489. They acclimated readily to the absence of authority and regimentation and enjoyed the contact with the civilians aboard, who were mostly the age of their parents, the reason for the good behavior of the Marines. The treatment they received was similar to what Don had talked about a year and a half ago when he crossed the nation. The war was still fresh in many minds.

Treasure Island was bustling. The barracks they were assigned was filled with veterans of the campaigns in the Pacific awaiting processing and discharge. Some of the new arrivals were disappointed by the lack of war stories. Most of the veterans were content to play cards, talk about home and family or just lie back and relax.

Once again there was little to do. There were periodic roll calls and some work details. The mitigating factor was liberty call. It was heavily attended by the newcomers from the east who were awed by the massive Oakland Bay Bridge overhead preceding them across the bay. They were a noticeable group walking to the ferry. Their forest green uniforms exhibited the nap of newness and there was not a single chevron on anyone's sleeve. This, in contrast to the veterans of war with their ribbons and at least a P.F.C. rating. Other than that, they looked like Marines with their shining shoes, sharp creases and erect posture.

Going ashore and proceeding on foot with his three buddies, Jim took an immediate liking to the friendly western city of hills. The four Marine buddies did a lot of walking that first night. They reached Fisherman's Wharf via Nob Hill, a cable car ride, a stroll through the major mercantile area and Telegraph Hill. By then they were famished and treated themselves to a delicious sea food dinner. They worked off the full bellies in Chinatown traversing the streets till weariness turned them back to the base.

*

All those fresh from boot camp were informed of their destination the next day. They were to board ship in four days and sail for the Orient. Jim was overjoyed. He wanted China duty, indeed had asked for it at Parris Island. That was where things were happening.

*

The four left the base the second night to continue their exploration of San Francisco. Jim's fascination with the city was not shared by all and they did not walk as far or stay as late.

They were returning to the ferry when approached by a taxi driver who greeted them.

"Hi, Marines, can I speak to you?"

The four returned the greeting and came to a halt.

"You see that young lady standing near my cab?"

They looked in the direction he indicated. On the sidewalk across the street a young woman stood close to a yellow taxi. She was nicely dressed and had a good figure and pretty face.

"Well, she's really down on her luck and in need of some cash and a place to sleep. I don't usually do things like this, but when I heard her story, I said I'd help. She'll sleep with one of you guys tonight for ten bucks if you'll pay the room rent."

Jim felt pity for the girl. She appeared downcast. He wanted to help, but mostly, the thought of lying next to a warm, lovely, naked female was provocative to him.

It was Tom who spoke first, however, .. quickly and excitedly, "No shit! How much does a room cost?"

"I can take you some place nice for less than ten bucks."

"OK! It's a done deal!" Tom replied eagerly, his face displaying his mood.

"Way to go, Tom!" Jonnie enthusiastically approved in his strong southern accent, "If I had the bucks, I'da beat ya'll to her."

His face a huge grin, Tom bid his buddies farewell and crossed the street with the driver. The three conversed briefly, got into the taxi and were gone. The three who were left behind headed again for the ferry. Jonnie conjectured all the way, in the most vivid detail, his perception of his buddy's anticipated activities. Jim was amused at Jonnie's descriptions and chuckled periodically. Sal remained silent.

*

Tom Blatchford returned in the morning with minutes to spare. His face was one huge grin. From roll call to the mess hall, breakfast and back to the barracks, he extolled the beauty and virtue of his overnight bed mate.

"Damn! I can't help it, guys, I'm in love," he happily concluded.

"For chrissakes, Blatchford," Sal interjected, "will you shut up and get with it. She's nothin but a fuckin whore with a taxi driver for a pimp!"

Tom remained silent and injured for much of the day when in Sal's company. He could not, however, keep the grin from his face when he sat alone on his rack.

* * *

The sea voyage via Pearl Harbor and Manila would take four weeks. The ship carried about five hundred Marines, a small Army contingent and a group of civilian dependents. The civilians were quartered amidships on the upper decks in officers country. The Marines were forbidden entry into that hallowed area. Only those who pulled guard duty had a fleeting glimpse of a female form.

Jim and his buddies were in a troop compartment in the bow, about the worst place to be in rough seas. The bunks of canvas laced to metal tubing were up to five high in most places. When sea sickness occurred in an upper, it could be a sad experience for those below. Unfortunately most of the Marines were new to life on the seas and more than a few were receptive to that malady.

All activities were preceded by long lines. For the Marines fresh from the recruit depots service life appeared a grim prospect.

The enlisted heads contained a long trough, slightly elevated at one end. It was spanned every few feet by a pair of boards, slightly carved out on the inner sides to impersonate a toilet seat. Sea water entered at the high end and ran down the trough to the low end transporting any prior deposit and emptied into the Pacific Ocean. The high end was in greatest demand.

Three nights out of Frisco, Jim and Sal entered the head and were greeted by howls and yells. From the high end of the trough to the low end, bare bottoms were excitedly exiting their place of residence in unorderly succession. Thus did those newcomers receive the initiation of what was called in polite circles, 'the flaming toilet paper'. The victim's chagrin was not shared by the spectators and even Sal's normally impassive expression turned to a wide grin.

*

All Marines not on duty were on deck when Oahu was sighted. The large ship seemed to stand still in the inky blue Pacific while the green island emerged from the clear, azure blue water of the coral reefs and came out to meet them. But it was the moving ship that slowly passed from the dark, deep ocean and crossed the demarcation line where the water color became the beautiful azure blue seen in so many pictures of tropical islands. The lush green vegetation and picturesque sandy beaches became increasingly visible. Those on deck were caressed by the aura of paradise. It did not last. The pristine beauty was soon swallowed up and vulgarly replaced by the sights and sounds of the giant Naval base at Pearl Harbor. The silent, meditative group at the ship's rail was unhappily returned to reality.

The reality, however, was painless. They were soon preparing to go ashore and live it up and make the most of a days pardon from their ocean going prison. This despite the inefficient ability of many young Marines to manage their meager pay. Quite a few were running low on funds. But if they could do nothing other than walk Honolulu's streets, it was better than the confinement and smells of the troop ship.

Honolulu was not much of a city, though it had its full share of bars. There were not nearly enough women to pacify the excessive abundance of servicemen. Alcohol consumption was the accepted activity. Most of the new arrivals were under age, but it was not impossible to obtain an illegal drink. Actually it was not even difficult if one went to the right places. Tom and Jonnic decided to give the drinking a try and left Jim and Sal to the sightseeing. The two buddies walked about six hours before returning to the ship. Weary, sleep came easily that night.

There were a few hangovers present at morning roll call, two, unhappily shared by Jonnie and Tom.

*

The Philippine leg of the voyage took twice as long. Various islands of the group were passed well before the ship came into Manila Bay. Soft exclamations were muttered by the spectators on deck. They became solemn as more and more partially sunken naval vessels revealed themselves. A bow, a stern, a superstructure protruded through the silent waters surface. A strange eerie mood pervaded the spectators as they glided amongst the derelicts of a life and death struggle that took place less than two years ago.

Liberty was short, but not sweet. With little money available activities were severely limited and the Marines were happy to be underway the next morning, the only passengers aboard the half filled transport.

* * *

The U.S. Marines came to China after the last land battle of the war on the island of Okinawa. They came to help repatriate the Japanese troops after the surrender. They were also assigned to guard bridges and outposts necessary to keep the coal trains running. Coal was vital to the survival of the Chinese. They rode shotgun on the trains.

The First Marine Division had landed at Tangku to be dispersed over a very large area of Hopeh Province. That province was not yet under attack from the Chinese Communist Army. Their brothers in the Sixth Marine Division went ashore at Tsingtao on the southern shore of the large peninsula of Shantung Province. Some 200 miles wide, it separated the Gulf of Po Hai from the Yellow Sea. Tsingtao was now surrounded on three sides by the Chinese Communist Army, but life in the city was peaceful.

The veterans of war were being replaced as quickly as possible for return to the States and discharge. They were replaced mostly by Marines like Jim and his buddies, right out of boot camp and lacking advanced training. To add to the problem, demobilization was already well at work. Regiments, through manpower cuts, were losing their third battalion and the supporting arms of that battalion, one third of their strength.

*

When debarking, the first recollection many had of North China was the smell. It was distinct, but not easily described. One thing was certain, there was an element of human waste in the composition of that smell.

Jim and his three buddies joined a battalion of the 5th Marines at Peiping, one of the two battalions remaining in the regiment.

In some of the older books Jim read about China, Peiping had been Peking, meaning, 'Northern Capital'. It became Peiping, the pei pronounced bay, in 1928 when Nanking became the capital. The name now meant, 'Northern Peace'.

The first recollection Jim had of Peiping was the Ch'ien Men Tower, a huge tower gate that separated the southern Chinese city from the northern Tartar city, names that were meaningful hundreds of years ago. Constructed in the early Fifteenth Century, the gate was formerly used exclusively by the emperor and his retinue who passed through only rarely. The wall extending on either side of the tower was nearly gone, but the tower was rebuilt after the Boxer campaign of 1911. The base of the tower rose to the height of the once formidable wall. An overhanging balcony atop the base served as a walkway above the teeming street. A four storied structure rose skyward from the base. The tiled roof sloped gently downward and outward forming graceful eaves. A second set of eaves jutted from between the third and fourth levels. An immense portrait hung between the second and third levels. Jim was certain it was a portrait of Sun Yat-sen.

The battalion and supporting troops and an artillery battalion of the 11th Marines were at various billets in and around the city. Peiping had two airfields which were utilized by two air groups from the First Marine Air Wing. Corsairs from these units were on patrol along the rail lines in support of their brothers on the ground. There were scattered incidents with the Chinese Communist forces.

The new replacements from the States quickly took over from the veterans of war. They were dispersed over the immensity of the area and were involved in much needed training exercises, ... whenever possible.

*

Two days after arriving in Peiping Sal was given emergency leave to attend his mother's funeral. He was flown home, the last surviving member of his immediate family. He left without any display of emotion. Jim was friendly with Jonnie and Tom, but soon realized that the dark, serious, quiet lad, with the lightning quick hands was a friend not easily replaced.

*

A few days after Sal's departure a Communist force of fifty to seventy-five attacked a recon patrol south of Tientsin. When the firefight ended one Marine lay dead and another was wounded. Two Communists did not survive and perhaps there were others for they always attempted to carry off their dead.

*

The Chinese Nationalist Army was still in control over much of the land, but they had overextended themselves with the ill conceived invasion of Manchuria. The Communists, or Ba Loo as they were known, were becoming more aggressive. The hands of the Marines were tied. They could not take sides and could not initiate any offensive or preventative action. They could defend themselves, but that was usually after the fact. The American presence was not the deterrent it should have been.

*

The service records of the new arrivals did not keep up with them. They missed midmonth pay call and would have to wait another two weeks in a destitute state. That did not stop Jonnie and Tom from going on liberty. They tried to coax Jim along, but the almost religious attitude he had about staying out of debt tied him for the most part to the barracks. His parents planted that seed well. Likewise, the sense of obligation from his promise to them to earn his diploma motivated immediate entry into correspondence courses with the Marine Corps Institute. Additionally he was able to catch up on his letter writing. Keeping so busy, Jim did not miss liberty during the first two weeks in Peiping.

*

"The girls in this city aint that bad. Not like the toothless peasants we saw comin north. And they aint bowlegged and I know ya like nice legs. I'm tellin ya, but what does it take ta make ya believe?" Tom Blatchford was doing his best to coax Jim into sharing liberty with him and Jonnie.

"I know, I know! You keep sayin it and I believe you, but I'm not goin on liberty till we get paid."

"Sheeit, man, we just got off that lousy train guard and ya'll don't wanna shake the dust off. Ya'll gotta be kidden me," Jonnie chided.

"No ahm not kidden," Jim laughed, trying his best to imitate Jonnie, "but I do have things to do. Tell ya what. Sal's due back on payday and we'll have about two months pay coming. We'll go out and have a big blowout, OK?"

"How can you wait that long?" Tom eagerly asked.

"For cryin out loud, it's only two days away."

"This guy's impossible. Times awastin. Let's go, Tom," Jonnie said grinning at Jim.

The two performed quick little Oriental bows, Hollywood style. They waved and laughing, exited the squad bay.

Jim watched them leave and stared ahead in thought, interrupting his letter writing. There were some attractive women in Peiping, not like most seen in the countryside. He wondered if they ate better here or if it was just different blood. He did not know the answer, but the idea of appealing women so readily available was exciting. But dammit, they where all whores. That thought did not please him and he wondered how Sal would react to such an encounter.

*

Alone in the small squad bay after supper the following day, Jim was lying on his wooden cot studying. None of the course materials from the institute had arrived, but he obtained some textbooks and was making a strong effort to be ahead of the game when the materials did come.

Though he loved history, other subjects were not always a pleasant pastime, yet he attacked the textbooks with the same tenacity he attacked opponents on the gridiron. He knew the diploma would be his anchor until he held it in his hand. That was the way it had to be. He and nobody else had created the situation. He and nobody else had made the promise.

About 2100 he heard the footsteps of someone returning from liberty. He glanced toward the open doorway. His face came alive with a huge grin. He tossed his book aside and jumped to his feet.

"Sal! You're back!" extending his hand. As they shook, Jim was instantly aware of a change in his friend. His somberness was barely noticeable.

"Glad to be back. How ya doin?"

"Great!" Jim searched the face, "How's it with you?"

"OK."

Sal tossed his pack on his cot, opened it and started restoring gear to its proper place. Jim did not press him. Ten minutes later they were sitting on their cots facing each other, sharing a box of Ritz crackers.

"You got back a day sooner than we expected."

"Yeh, I got all the details squared away. I only stayed this long ta please my aunts and uncles. I don't know why. Hell, we never saw em when she was alive."

The two buddies talked, or rather Sal talked and Jim listened, encouraging Sal on till lights out. Then they went outside into the warm spring evening and continued. Sal spoke of things very personal. He had not talked like that since the journey to Parris Island. Now he was laying his soul bare and it was evident he had acquired some peace in that soul. There was some guilt for his inability to aid his mother, but her suffering was past. He felt a sense of relief, a quiet passionless joy, as much for her, as for himself.

Winding down Jim sensed the relief and the change in his friend. Sal happily told of Jim's mother who had seen the obituary and made every effort and finally succeeded in getting in touch with him. She begged Sal to allow her and Bill to help, but there was little that needed to be done.

The funeral was private and without knowing why, Sal called and asked if Sarah and Bill would mind coming. They showed up well before the services and spent some time with him. His last night in the States, he went to the Williams home and slept in Jim's bed. Bill and Sarah drove him to New York's Idlewild airport the next day.

"Your folks are somethin. Pretty special I'd say." He smiled at Jim in the darkness and put a hand on his shoulder, "I guess that's why you're OK, Buddy."

*

Friday was the last day of May and it was payday. The newcomers received two months pay. They also received additional compensation with their overseas pay. Further, a new pay scale was approved by congress and the monthly stipend for privates was increased from $50.00 a month to $75.00. They were riding high. They decided to really see the town.

Before going on liberty Jim sent half of what he received, home to be banked.

Four shipmates walked the city's streets that night, Tom and Jonnie proud to lead the way and show off their meager knowledge. Jim was happy to be loose in Peiping. He acquired books about the city and the nation since his arrival in China. Now he was curious to experience the city first hand. He wanted to digest the sights and the sounds and experience the smells. He wanted to mingle with a populace that was largely peasant and merchant. His desire for historical knowledge had always been strong and his residence in Peiping was stirring that desire anew.

There was an abundance of Marines in the city and a few other Americans. There were other Caucasian civilians as well, many, White Russian refugees from the Marxist revolution. But it was the Chinese who dominated the swollen populace and the Chinese ladies of the night that made it impossible to go through an evening without a proposition to share a bed, though rarely for long.

The four soon built up a thirst and the two guides led them into a busy bar. Four Chinese beers were ordered. Waiting to be served, Jim felt a hand placed on his arm. He turned and looked down into a young, round face, with too much make-up and framed with shiny black hair.

"You buy me drink, Joe?" she asked with a thick accent. Her lips smiled, but the dark eyes were vacant.

"I'm sorry, not tonight, maybe some other time."

Tom and Jonnie were amused at Jim's polite behavior.

"Hell, Jim," Tom said, "you don't hafta be so gentle with these whores. Just tell em to get lost."

"Tom's right. Ya know, Jim, they're all around us and all they want is our cash. Sheeit, they'd yank the gold from outa your teeth before yu'd know it," Jonnie added.

"They are females guys ... and maybe they are whores, but I just don't see treatin them like ... sheeit." Jim smiled at his southern friend.

"Ya'll are too much, Jim."

"Ya know, maybe Jim is too much fer the likes of us," Sal interjected, "but we all got things to learn and maybe we wouldn't be so bad off ta listen to him."

Never much of a conversationalist, Sal's comments did carry weight and for whatever reason, those who knew him rarely argued with him. And it was not because of his ability with his fists, for he was slow to anger and not one to take offense at words. When he did speak, he made sense.

"Ya'll just may have a point there, Sal, ol buddy," Jonnie replied shaking his head.

None would have admitted that anything changed, but for the balance of the evening the females who chanced to chat with any of the four, were treated, if not respectfully, at least courteously.

*

Saturday morning they practiced perimeter defense. Liberty followed at noon and they again headed into the city, but this time for a specific destination. Jim talked the group into an excursion to the Forbidden City. Except for Sal, they were hesitant, but went along.

"Hey! Look at the totem poles," Tom yelled.

They did look something like totem poles, the white marble columns at the entrance to the imperial city. The poles were carved round with dragons. Artistic wing-like arms curved upward near the top. White marble lions with heavy manes and broad chests stood guard nearby. Five gently arched marble bridges with wonderfully sculpted marble banisters and balusters showed the way to the Gate of Heavenly Peace, a large gate house capped with a graceful roof and overhanging eaves. A second set of caves just below jutted from the building and extended beyond those of the roof proper, the double roof style so common on many of the older Chinese structures.

The four buddies crossed the center bridge in silence. Jim fondled the intricate and detailed carving of the marble banister. He had a sense of the thousands of peasants and artisans who must have worked and sweat and put it all together. They passed through the huge central portals of two more gate houses and emerged into the light of day on the other side. Beyond was a long walk to the imposing wall that protected the southern entrance to the Forbidden City itself.

Only the inhabitants were allowed to enter the City without special permission prior to 1911. The young men came closer and a thirty foot high, reddish colored wall loomed above them. Time was attacking the exterior. The color was flaking off in spots, creating a patchy appearance, yet it was still quite formidable. Two other like walls extended out perpendicularly, forming a gigantic three sided courtyard, where once the emperor reviewed his armies.

With this kind of protection Jim wondered how the dynasties had been so subjugated to foreign powers. Then he remembered from history that no static fortress was impregnable, especially from the onslaught of a determined enemy. But this place had not been attacked like Iwo Jima. It had fallen to greed and self interest and treachery, not only from without, but also, insidiously from within.

They entered the inner city via another massive portal and crossed one of another group of five bridges similar to the first group they encountered. The buildings before them had tiled roofs of yellowish glaze, many with the common double eave. The lions were now of bronze, the male with a ball under the right paw, the female with a suckling kitten under the left paw. It was the way gender was determined, for both lions had full manes. There were other bronze statues of storks and turtles set on marble bases full of wonderfully sculpted detail.

With his recently acquired knowledge of the events that gave birth to the opulence they witnessed, Jim's commentary kept his buddies interest. They remained enthused during the entire tour.

"That was great, Jim," Jonnie remarked on the way out, "really great. It's too bad tha ol dynasties aint aroun no more."

"Yeah, Jim, it was really OK," Tom added.

Sal grinned at their comments casting an approving glance at Jim.

"Well, life wasn't too good for the peasants back then," Jim mused, "but I guess it's not much better today."

The smells of the food of vendors outside the gates heightened their appetites. Much Chinese food was taboo for sanitary reasons, one being the use of human waste as fertilizer. They searched out a European restaurant and gorged themselves. They each had two French deserts. They did not leave the premises till after dark.

Attempting to work off the discomfort of over eating, they walked the busy, crowded sidewalks. The streets teemed with rickshaws and pedicabs, scores transporting Marines. Prostitutes were part of the masses, some very attractive. They were near the bar they visited last night when a young boy grabbed Sal by the arm. With reasonably good elocution he asked, "You wanna fuck my sister, Marine?"

Sal's relaxed demeanor turned icy. He yanked his arm away as his eyes bored into the young boy.

"Get outa here kid!" he growled. "Can you believe that goddam little pimp?"

Jim herded them into the bar and ordered a round of drinks. A few sips and the mood was relaxed. They dissolved into the crowd of Marines and bar girls. It was more than three hours before they departed and the night air was filled with raucous humor and laughter. Jim did not finish his third beer, but he was caught up in and enjoyed the rowdiness of his friends.

*

When Jim awakened, the entire squad bay was asleep. There was no reveille on Sunday morning for those not on duty. He thought about rousing his buddies for chow, but decided against it. They would probably wake with hangovers and be unable to look at food. When he returned to the bay after breakfast, he sat on the edge of his cot wondering what, if anything to do about his slumbering buddies. Finally he leaned over and gently shook Sal by the shoulder

Struggling to open his bloodshot eyes, Sal squinted to avoid the light, "What's up?" he grumbled.

"Feel like liberty? I was thinkin about goin to the Temple of Heaven today."

Sal did not respond, but rubbed his forehead. With effort he managed a reply, "No, .. not today. You go. I'll see ya when ya get back." He turned to his other side and pulled the pillow over his head.

Jim knew Tom and Jonnie would be worse off. He chuckled to himself and turned to get ready for the trek. He was glad to take a break from the books and in a way, he was glad to be alone. Tom and Jonnie often required effort to keep their attention on other than the mundane. And there were times he wondered if Sal enjoyed this type of excursion or if he went along because of loyalty to a friend.

When ready, Jim headed south and went through the portal of the Ch'ien Men Tower and into the Chinese city. He liked the tower as he liked so much of the ancient Chinese architecture. It pleased his visual sense and spurred his interest to learn of the culture that created such a structure.

Walking the busy streets among the peasants and vendors was no less a part of his interest, but he was unable to keep up his brisk pace. Some object or some occurrence would excite his curiosity and demand his attention. He was trying diligently to pick up enough of the language to converse with the street people and that slowed him further. The numerous delays were enjoyable, but prodded him to greater effort when on the move.

Arriving at the north entrance of the Temple of Heaven, he was damp with perspiration. The starch in his khakis was starting to give up and not wanting to wipe his brow with a sleeve, he pulled a handkerchief from a side pocket. Marine trousers, except for officers, had no rear pockets.

No one was about when he entered the temple, which was not a building, but the vast grounds that housed various structures and contained squares of miniature woodland of small to medium sized trees in close proximity. It was a place of religious eminence and Jim was immersed in the serenity and elegant beauty.

Passage through the gate house portal revealed the beautiful Temple of Happy New Year, a round structure of three tiers, the second and third progressively smaller than the one below. The roof on the top tier and the eaves that arched from the two lower tiers were of cobalt blue tile, distinctively speckled with a profusion of colors. The structure sat on a circular white marble pedestal, also of three tiers. Each tier was balustraded with the same marble, intricately sculpted.

As in the Forbidden City, he was compelled to run his hands over the carving. Three times he strolled around the top tier of the pedestal never removing his hands from the marble banister. When he went inside he marveled that no nail was used in the construction. Being alone, he was swallowed up in the silence and spirituality, some real, some imagined. He did not want to leave, but there was more to see and more to touch.

There were two more gatehouses at the beginning and end of a long walkway flanked by huge candle holders. In days gone by, giant candles lit the way of the emperor. Inside the circular Whispering Wall was the Temple of Imperial Tablets. In design it was similar to the first structure, but of one level and one roof. The base was a solitary balustraded pedestal of white marble. There were two main parallel stairways which flanked a slab spectacularly carved with a Heavenly Dragon deeply chiseled into the slab. Despite his desire to linger, he pushed on.

Another gate house, a pair of columned gates and he was at the Alter of Heaven, a replica of the three tiered pedestal which supported the Temple of Happy New Year. The exposed upper level had a darker colored stone at its center, said to be the mythological Chinese center of the universe.

He climbed the stairs and leaned against the marble railing. Lost in the dimension of time, the intense sun pummeled his over heated body. Heat waves bounced off the white marble in shimmering ripples that distorted his vision. With his eyes nearly closed his mind wandered dreamily.

At first he thought the movement was an illusion, but it developed form and the form materialized bewitchingly into a female. She had approached the alter and was moving gracefully up the stairs. She was attired in the typical Chinese dress that ended above the ankle and was slit up each side to slightly above the knee. It was not the normal dark color worn by peasants, but a rich gray. It was silk. She did not walk with the humility of a peasant. Her posture was erect. When she reached the top step, Jim saw that she wore no noticeable make-up and her face had classic, exotic features. She had the shiniest black hair, pulled tightly to the rear and tied in a bun. Slim, her figure as it formed the contours of the dress was most pleasing. Taller than most Chinese females, as she walked, Jim could see enough of her legs to know they were nicely shaped. Her hips under the dress moved noticeably and pleasingly.

He stared at her, not impolitely, but curiously, captured by her beauty. She moved across his front without acknowledging his presence. He could not take his eyes from her and his natural shyness with females did not deter him. In the present environment it was as if he was witnessing a dream come to life.

How long his eyes feasted he did not know. He had to bite his tongue for he almost said out loud, "My God! She's beautiful!" He did say it to himself. At last he realized what he was doing and turned away, uneasy with his brashness yet wanting desperately to continue drinking in her loveliness. While he was trying to decide what to do she moved down another set of stairs and walked to the nearest gateway, where for the first time, Jim was aware of an elderly woman with tiny feet and a young girl, perhaps twelve or thirteen. The three were companions and disappeared through the gateway leaving him disturbingly alone.

It was minutes, longer than he thought, before he made the decision and gathered the courage. Despite her two companions, he determined he would try to locate her. Walking the temple grounds he hoped fervently to see her again. He went over in his mind what he would do, what he would say.

The aura of the temple melted away as he moved aimlessly about the grounds in a hopeless quest, searching for the fantasy that displaced the reverence he felt so devoutly when he entered the sacred site. After nearly twenty minutes he admitted to the futility and gave up. Disappointed, he headed back to the barracks.

He did not have the same curiosity and interest in his surroundings on the return journey. He had been captivated in an instant by someone so alluring that she burned a vision into his mind and branded his psyche with her ethereal beauty. He thought of little else on the homeward trek.

Arriving in time for noon chow, Jim changed into dungarees and joined his buddies in the mess hall. Sal seemed to have recovered and was eating, but Jonnie toyed with the food on his tray. Tom sat with his head bent forward uttering intermittent soft moans.

"Fer chrissakes, Blatchford, you better stick to soda pop," Sal smirked and dropped his fork on the metal tray.

Tom scrunched his eyes and pulled his head down into hunched up shoulders, "Saaal! Pleeeas!"

Sal glanced at Jim and they both smiled at their buddy's discomfort. Jonnie continued to toy with his food.

"Hell! I'm glad I don't hafta depend on you two zombies fer anything today," Sal chided.

The two distressed Marines decided they had enough. With great difficulty, they rose and emptied their trays into a garbage bucket ... with as little banging as possible, scrubbed them down and returned to the squad bay and their cots.

The mess hall was nearly empty. Sal was sipping coffee and Jim was eating the desert of the day, powdered ice cream. It did not taste like that at Burndys, but it was not bad.

"Didja hear what happened to the 7th Marines up at Peitaiho yesterday?" Sal asked.

"No. I haven't heard any news since I left this morning."

"Well, some fuckin gooks attacked some bridge guards and five a the bastards were killed."

"How about the Marines?" Jim was excited, but concerned.

"All OK from what I hear. Guess the lousy gooks bit off more than they could chew this time. Those guys in the 7th are really out on a limb up there an I don't trust those gooks no how."

"It's strange isn't it? From everything I hear, when our guys first got here, all the Chinks were so happy to see them, yelling and cheering and all that stuff. Now all they want is our money. And all the Ba Loo want is our asses. And our government keeps cuttin back more and more on troops and all the rest. And they tell us we can't do this and we can't do that, but those guys up north showed em. Not just the gooks, but the guys in Washington too."

"You can say that again."

"Naw, it's too much to repeat."

Both laughed and took care of the mess gear and vacated the mess hall. On the way to the squad bay Jim related his experience at the Temple of Heaven.

"Ya know," he concluded, "I can't ever remember bein so taken with a girl, specially from just one look."

"Maybe she'll show up again someday, somewhere and ya can make her acquaintance."

"Yeah, big deal. What would a beautiful well to do lady like that want with a lowly gyrene?"

"Ya know, a lowly gyrene aint the world's worst."

"I wonder if she would know that?" They both chuckled. "Ya know, Sal, I'm sure she wasn't as beautiful as I think I remember her, but the doggone image she left in my mind is unreal. It musta been the heat waves and just the atmosphere of the place that made it all so ... so .. well, you know, .. kinda like a dream."

"Well it's no dream you're tellin me about, Buddy," he smiled and put a hand on Jim's shoulder. "Maybe ya will see her again. Hell, who knows. Ya know what they say, .. it's a small world."

* * *

It was a time of parsimony for the armed forces of the United States. A nation tired of war and thankful for victory was quick to dismantle that which made the victory possible. History was forgotten and new animosities disregarded in the rush to shed the heavy economic burden of support for the men and weapons of war. The Sixth Marine Division was disbanded and its personnel returned to the States except for the 4th Marines who remained in Tsingtao, the only infantry regiment to retain its three battalions. The regiment was renamed the Third Marine Brigade. The depleted First Marine Division, about two-thirds its original strength, still guarded the coal trains so vital to China's life. The Marines of that division remained at outposts and bridges.

The peacetime strength division was now filled with a preponderance of men straight from boot camp. There was a desperate need for training, which was given priority whenever possible, whenever the division's manpower was not stretched beyond the limit. On top of all this, the division was going to lose two of the air groups from the First Marine Air Wing. It was not a situation reeking of optimism. Fortunately, most Marines were not aware of the battles taking place in Washington to disband their Corps, or at least, merge its functions with those of the Army. For those who where, morale began to sag.

Jim Williams was one of the informed.

"My God, Sal! Can you believe some of the goings on in Washington?"

He put down a batch of news clippings Buck had sent and looked over at his buddy lying on his cot reading a letter from Sarah.

"Whadaya mean?"

"Remember what I told you before, about the other services, especially the Army, tryin to knock down the Corps? Well, they really mean business!"

"Aw, they're nothin but a bunch of assholes. Everybody knows the Corps the best. They aint gonna fuck with it."

Like so many of his brothers in green, Sal felt secure in the history of his Corps, its ability and its place in the scheme of things. Little did he and so many others know how desperate the struggle for life had become.

* * *

The summer was exceedingly hot. Guard duty, road patrols, recon patrols and convoy duty were not the most entertaining pastimes. Training picked up and bodies were shuttled hither and yon. The buddies of 489 were not always together in the field and did not always pull liberty together. When his friends were not around, Jim plunged into his schoolwork. There were times he regretted his promise to his parents, but he was seeing progress. It seemed reasonably certain he would finish before the year was out.

During this period Jim received a letter from Kit. It was upbeat and cheerful. He responded as he had in boot camp, very formally and without enthusiasm. She would write one more time and after a second similar response from him, her letters were less frequent.

*

In July all privates with six months service and no blemishes were promoted to P.F.C. Many did not bother to have the chevrons sewn on khaki shirts, but did rush out to Chinese tailors to have it sewn on the green blouse. The tiny bit of red that outlined the stripe brightened the dark uniform.

The middle of the month brought unsettling news. Some bridge guards were captured by the Ba Loo. A week and a half later they were released. Four days after that a convoy was ambushed with loss of life and wounded.

The Nationalists still seemed to be the prevailing force, but their poorly planned excursion into Manchuria was taking its toll. The American effort to bring the two sides together was heading towards hopelessness.

The luster of the Marine presence in China was wearing thin. Some of this was the fault of the Ba Loo who were winning the support of some of the people. Some of it was the fault of the troops and those who should have known better. There was a surprising lack of indoctrination on behavior in a foreign country where the culture and customs were so dissimilar to America.

The regiment's other battalion was garrisoned in Tangku protecting an ammo dump. A few brief firefights occurred in August and the anticipated full scale war between the Communists and Nationalists was beginning. Changes continued to occur for the Marines. Guarding the coal trains and bridges was being eliminated and outposts were being pulled in.

Both the Nationalists and the Ba Loo took prisoners in the growing conflict and some switched allegiance, for to join the fight meant food and it was better to face death than privation and torture. The civilian population became suspect in many places. When being observed, that population remained civilian, but away from prying eyes, some became guerrillas. Many individual Chinese were distrusted.

As the war became more brutal to the peasants and more personal to the Marines, they were more aware of atrocities. Knowing that both sides committed them, they were nevertheless unsettled when the Ba Loo took vengeance on a village that did not comply with their expectations quickly enough. The village ceased to exist and the bodies of the inhabitants were stripped and stacked like cordwood. A Roman Catholic priest was murdered and his penis amputated and stuffed in his mouth. Most of the dire conditions, however, were far removed from Peiping and when the Marines returned to their homebase from wherever, or whatever, the liberty was good within that ancient city.

* * *

On a Saturday after mid September, Jim and Sal shared the day off. They had no plans other than taking in the culture. Sal was a great companion on these outings, unlike Jonnie and Tom who were easily bored. Sal wanted to learn. He took pleasure from the substantial knowledge he was acquiring. He enjoyed the frequent stops when Jim practiced his improving linguistic skills on any peasant willing to converse and they were many. The conversations were usually quite animated. Unfortunately for Sal, language was not one of his gifts, but it did not stop him from trying.

As they walked, they came upon an elderly Chinese gentleman, standing, talking to another who was squatting in the familiar posture. Jim greeted them politely and they returned the greeting with easy smiles. The Chinese were drinking tea, yellow in color, from small, white bowls.

The squatter was wearing the black Chinese skull cap pushed back and revealing a lack of hair and a forehead generously furrowed with deep wrinkles. Smaller wrinkles around the eyes and the corners of his mouth were in abundance. There was a small patch of very short hair adorning his chin. A scraggly mustache in shades of gray drooped down over the extremities of a mouth that was barren of all but a few teeth. He presented an air of comedy along with his aged dignity. He wore a faded double breasted shirt with a Mandarin collar. The shirt was spotted from the work he did and not from food. Under the outer shirt, a darker collar of western style was visible.

His standing companion wore the same flat bottomed shoes and a sleeveless sweater over the high collared shirt. The summer sun had darkened his skin. He was hatless. Variously gray hair, in some places quite dark, that had abandoned the top of his head, circled the sides and back and straggled down over the tops of his ears. In the front, just shy of the temples, sideburns journeyed down, then across, to became a mustache. From the chin sprouted a luxurious goatee. The outer strands of the magnificent growth, like the frame of a lyre, flowed in opposition to each other, outward, inward, outward and in again, ending at mid chest. Despite the splendid beard, it was the face that set him apart. Furrowed wrinkles were present and the deep set eyes were surrounded by the bulges of age. But the mouth displayed a constant, sweet grin and the eyes, slitted from the sun, never ceased to twinkle and welcome. What child, Jim thought, would not want this grandfather?

There was a brief discussion and Jim introduced himself and Sal. The kindly 'grandfather' was Han and the gentleman sitting on his haunches was introduced as Lou. Sal removed cigarettes from his socks and offered one to each. They were very gracious as they accepted, then lit up and smoked them down to a nub while getting happily acquainted. Han gave the appearance of wisdom and the young Americans found it to be so.

The four hit it off right from the start. Neither Jim or Sal expected their visit to be a long one, but at the end of an hour they were going strong and no one seemed willing to break away. Han and Lou enjoyed a second of Sal's cigarettes. In the beginning Jim did a lot of the translating, but Sal was picking up on some words and phrases though he spoke infrequently. Occasionally he asked Jim to say something for him.

They were preparing to part when an elderly, small lady, walked from the building. Seeing Jim and Sal she slowed and approached tentatively. She was the wife of Han and he motioned her to join them. She came slowly on tiny feet, bound at an early age to retard growth. Except for the Manchus, the bound, small feet of women was considered feminine and was practiced till prior to the present generations. She was timid in the Marines presence and reluctantly joined the conversation. When she saw that Sal did not do much talking, she looked at him shyly, but quizzically.

Sensing her curiosity, Jim put a hand on Sal's shoulder and jokingly, as best he could, explained that Sal could not speak because he was a turtle, a name used in derision. Sal picked up on the word which he knew well, tilted his head to one side and played the perfect foil with a clownish shrug. The two older men giggled and shook, but the poor little lady did not catch Jim's jest until Han was able to reassure her. She did not share their humor.

The promise to come again accompanied the warm farewells.

As they walked away, Jim smiled to himself at the emergence of new moods in his buddy. Captivated by the people and culture, Sal was as caught up as Jim. Additionally, the last few months ripened a dormant sense of humor that blossomed from beneath Sal's brooding, serious exterior. Though it was not robust and visible to all, it was a definite part of the repartee between the two close friends. And Sal was becoming more tolerant of people who sometimes got under his skin, like Tom Blatchford.

*

The sun was approaching the horizon when they exited the restaurant and stood on the sidewalk discussing their next move. The street was coming to life with rickshaws and pedicabs. The rickshaws diverted Jim's attention and he watched a few go by. He marveled, as he had done so many times before, at the trotting coolie leaning forward over the yoke, pulling his vehicle and passenger with what had to be some effort, but which never showed in their expression of stoic acceptance, or maybe it was just Oriental inscrutability. He felt compassion for the men relegated to this chore. One day they would probably pass from the scene. Even now the pedicab which traveled much faster with less effort, was equaling, or surpassing their numbers and was more used by foreigners.

A bright splotch of color in a rickshaw some distance away unexpectedly caught Jim's eye. It was a vivid orange-red that bounced back the light from the low lying sun. As the rickshaw approached, Jim could see that the radiant color was from a dress which covered a female form. Shining black hair danced across the top of the bright dress. The face was set off with beautiful eyes and nose and a mouth painted to accent its sensuous shape. The hair hung differently and there was an abundance of make-up, but it was her.

Surprised and off guard Jim jerked alert and jabbed Sal in the ribs with an elbow, yelping in a loud whisper, "It's her!"

Startled, Sal's head darted right, then left before he replied, "Who? ... Where?"

Jim pointed instinctively as the rickshaw drew abreast.

A young pedicab driver about four feet away displayed a mouthful of teeth in a large grin and enthusiastically shouted, "You want?" Before Jim could respond the driver yelled, "I get!" and sprinted the short distance to catch and stop the rickshaw.

There was arm waving from the man while the woman sat calmly. After a brief conversation the intermediary motioned Jim, by now a bit ruffled, to join them.

"Go man! Go!" Sal said, giving Jim a nudge.

Reluctantly Jim walked to the trio. His discomfort was intense, but he desperately wanted to know the beautiful woman sitting elegantly in the rickshaw.

The pedicab driver said, "I talk ... you." Jim did not interrupt. He had no idea what to say. He had no idea what the intermediary was trying to accomplish. The driver spoke quickly, too quickly for Jim to understand many of the words. She shook her head a few times and turned just enough to inspect Jim. The expression on her face changed to a soft smile. Turning back to the pedicab driver, the smile disappeared. She said something and the pedicab driver grinned, baring his large teeth. He turned to Jim, "You have room, .. she go you. I know. Good, ... clean, .. only officer."

The remarks fell on him like a club. So much for visions. He felt betrayed by his imagination and the person he thought her to be. And now this lousy gook was pimping for her. Then she smiled at Jim, not much, but enough to mix him up. He took some change from his pocket and gave it to the spokesman and told him to leave. Pocketing the money the pedicab driver departed, a self satisfied grin on his face. The rickshaw driver stood patiently between the pull bars and the yoke, his face expressionless.

Jim was hesitant, but he spoke, choosing the Chinese words carefully. She never moved her arms from the rests at the sides of the carriage, but nodded and smiled slightly as he talked. She never spoke, but continued to nod, her expression becoming a constant, soft smile. When she did at last speak, it was to her driver. He leaned over the yoke and the rickshaw was in motion. She turned slightly for a final nod and a smile that completely confused Jim. They disappeared down the busy street.

Sal was field stripping a butt when Jim returned to his side. "She's beautiful, isn't she?"

"You can say that again!" Sal smiled and Jim returned a weak grin, but was in no mood to repeat himself. Sal finally asked, "Well?"

"She's a prostitute."

"A fuckin whore! You gotta be kiddin me?"

"No way, man! That's what she is."

"You didn't wanta go with her?"

Jim hesitated before answering sheepishly, "Tomorrow, ... I'm goin with her tomorrow. I don't know what got into me, Sal, but something did. I never thought I'd make a date with a whore, but dammit, I did! I never thought I'd pay money for it, but geeze, I'm gonna."

"Why didn't ya go now fer chrissakes?"

Jim hesitated, again searching Sal's eyes, "Because I left with you and I'm goin back with you."

Sal nodded and put a hand on his buddy's shoulder, "Let's have a drink."

They found a bar and had a few. They were silent for some time before Jim spoke.

"Remember when I told you she was probably not as beautiful as I remembered her?"

Sal shook his head, "Yeah."

"Well, she's not."

"Maybe her bein a whore has affected the way you feel about her."

Jim grinned, "Don't get me wrong, she's still one beautiful lady .. and pretty classy too ... and I guess I'd hafta say, .. about as desirable as they come, but I did see her in some kinda special circumstance when she wore no make-up. She was like a vision from heaven." He turned silent a spell before adding, "Yeah, ... you may be right. Maybe I do see her now for what she is. But damn! There's something about her ... ahh heck ... I guess I'm just a sucker for beautiful females, .. but dammit, there is something about her."

The drinks went down easier for Jim that night. When they left to return to barracks they were sober, but relaxed. They walked a long time in silence and Sal looked down at his spit shined shoes reflecting somewhat the artificial street light.

"Ya know," Sal said, pondering a moment, "ya know, I never had a close buddy."

Jim put a hand on his friend's shoulder and gave it a squeeze.

*

The drinks did not help Jim sleep. Thinking about the coming day, he saw again the horror movies on V.D. But hell, he knew guys that had tried and never got it. All you had to do was protect yourself and he would certainly do that.

The memories of being with Connie were still sharp and he knew he wanted to experience that again. Despite his inability to feel a fondness for her now, in his mind, he often relived the intimacies and thrills they shared. He wondered if he could experience something similar with someone else. Could it possibly be the same with a whore? Well, he would find out. He never thought he would give a girl money for it, but tomorrow he was going to do just that. Heck, maybe that was the best way. "At least," he thought, "I don't have to become involved. And nobody gets hurt, .. especially me." Well, he would give this girl money. She was not really a girl, but an immensely beautiful woman, .. an immensely beautiful whore whom he desired, ... perhaps for no other reason than her beauty, ... maybe.

When he at last thought of home so far away, his mother, his sister and finally his grandmothers who thought so highly of him, he said to himself, "Oh shit! Maybe I should stay in the barracks tomorrow. Hell, maybe she won't even show up. Hell, maybe the sun won't come up."

At long last he fell into an uneasy sleep.

*

The sun did come up and shined beautifully. The small squad bay came to life slowly. A few were sleeping off the excess of a Saturday night liberty.

Jim was lying awake when Sal returned from the head, "You goin ta chow?"

"Yeah."

Struggling to his feet he dressed in dungarees and boondockers and walked with Sal to the mess hall. He was thankful that Sal sensed when not to pry into his thoughts.

The food was tasteless and was followed by a lengthy shower and slow shave. In clean uniform, his appearance was what it was supposed to be, but his mind was not.

"See ya later," he said to Sal, waved to a few other mates and was on his way.

The streets were nearly empty. Since he had taken too much time in preparation, he hired a nearby pedicab. He gave the driver a destination a block from the hotel where they were to meet. When he arrived, he paid the fare without haggling and walked reluctantly to the hotel, conscious of his visibility on the street. It was nearly ten o'clock and she was nowhere in sight. He observed the sweep hand of his wrist watch make three revolutions. He had thought earlier that if she did not show, he would be off the hook, but now, disappointment was starting and growing with each passing second and though he tried to convince himself otherwise, he knew he did want to see her.

Then, there she was, still over a block away, but she was there and like it or not, way down inside himself, he was pleased. The rickshaw drew nearer and came to a stop in front of him. The hair was as yesterday, dancing across her shoulders. She wore a tan dress of silk with a soft luster. It covered the knees of her shapely legs as she sat easily in the seat. The coolie placed the pull bars on the pavement. Taking her hand, Jim helped her to the sidewalk. High heels adorned her feet. She was not only beautiful, she was elegant.

Jim asked the driver the price of the fare. At the answer, she touched his arm and shook her head. He haggled with the driver till she gave a positive nod, then paid and they went inside.

Jim was self conscious when they registered. He did not notice that no one seemed to care and the desk clerk did not even glance at her. "Her!" he thought, "Cripes, I don't even know her name."

After he signed the register and paid, they decided to walk to the second floor. He held her elbow as if to guide her when they ascended the stairs. Reaching the top, he released his grip and purposefully fell in behind her. The movement and curve of her buttocks was extremely appealing. Then they were at the door. He inserted and turned the key. They entered.

The room was of medium size on the south side of the building. The morning sun shined through a large window and bathed the double bed in a cheery glow. There was a large stuffed chair, also in the sunlight, near the window. Without time to structure his thoughts, Jim grabbed both her hands and enthusiastically blurted in English, "I'm glad you came."

She smiled, but it was a polite smile and he knew she did not understand his words. He stumbled over the translation, not because he was unable, but because he was self conscious. Her face turned softer when he spoke Chinese and she understood his meaning. Her smile was genuine. He asked her name and she pronounced it. He asked her to do it again, then a third time. Unable to mimic her Chinese pronunciation to his satisfaction, he asked if she would mind if he called her Soo-Ann, a phonetic similarity. She smiled approvingly, then nodded.

Soo-Ann pronounced Jim as, "Jeem". He liked the way she made it sound and squeezed her hands and said, "Jeem it is." Again she smiled, quite sweetly. He wondered how well she was playing her part, but decided it did not matter. He drew her to him, ... somewhat clumsily and hugged her. That affectionate behavior pleased his sense of propriety. She tilted her head back and looked into his eyes which in heels were only about two inches below his. She seemed pleased and kissed him on the lips. It was a tender kiss, devoid of meaning, ... he thought, .. but he liked it.

Riveted to the beauty of her face, he thought it close to perfection. The setting at the Alter of Heaven was missing, but she did possess something almost spiritual, which confused further his mixed assessment of her. Shaking those thoughts from his mind, Jim pointed to the bed. She smiled sweetly and nodded approval. She was not mechanically going about her business as ladies of her profession had done in so many of the stories he heard. She seemed very much at ease, even pleased to be with him.

Very carefully he slid the knot of his field scarf down, hoping to keep it neat for reuse. Slipping the noose over his head, he sat in the chair and happily observed Soo-Ann remove her dress. The smile in his eyes spread over his entire face as he filled with anticipation and was aware that his heart was beating faster.

Puzzled, she stared at him. She was unused to someone not undressing quickly and waiting for her in bed. Seeing the look on her face he struggled with his Chinese, conscious that his vocabulary was not adequate for this encounter, but did get her to understand that he enjoyed watching her disrobe.

Moving to the bed, she sat on the edge. Very slowly and methodically, even somewhat seductively, she removed her shoes and stockings, her smile broadening as she sensed his pleasure. Standing, she wriggled free of her undergarments. She was not bashful or uncomfortable undressing for him nor was she brash, but was amused at his enjoyment. When finished she stayed in front of him allowing his visual exploration.

Jim was mesmerized. His eyes traveled up her lovely body, back down, only to start over. At the Alter of Heaven he was sure she had well formed legs, but viewed in their entirety they fulfilled his concept of perfection. The downy hair at the loins was neither profuse nor curly, but delicately covered the tiny, beckoning hillock. Her belly, an almost imperceptible arc, was framed by lovely curved hips joined to a slim waist. Her breasts were not large, but perfectly round, the nipples poking proudly from their tinted base. Even her arms seemed shapely.

He rose and placed hands on smoothly molded shoulders which were remarkably firm, then moved them down to her elbows. Her skin was flawless. A slender neck supported the beautiful face that was indelible in his mind. She wore no make-up. He had requested that and there was nothing that covered or detracted from her genuine beauty. The jet black hair shined when touched by the rays of the sun.

He did not know how long he remained captive to her beauty, but while his hands were still on her elbows she started to unbutton his shirt, finished the task and slowly removed it and his undershirt. Pushing him gently into the chair, she removed his shoes and socks. She reached for his hands and he responded to the moderate force and urged himself upright while she worked at completing the task.

He remained standing in his skivvy drawers while she folded and hung his trousers. Watching her undress and now feeling her hands on him excited him greatly. Part of him popped through the opening at the bottom of the fly. He looked down and thought it comical.

She returned and completed her chore and he was naked. She took his hand and led him to the bed. Suddenly he remembered and broke free to get the rubbers. He had trouble in his nervousness opening the package. She came to him and touched his hand and gently took the package from him. Extracting one, she dropped to her knees, kissed him there, sending shivers up his spine and slid it on. Except for the kiss, she accomplished the task step by step from the manual, an efficient whore. Yet the young American was feeling something more than just lust. That was very present to be sure, but Jim Williams was experiencing something in his soul for this woman of unusual beauty.

Sliding between the clean, smooth sheets, she pulled the top sheet over them. When they embraced, his passion was intense. She helped him enter her and his ardor immediately transformed his body into a wild and vigorous action accompanied by noisy vocalizations.

The end came quickly. He lay atop her unable to move while the delirium subsided. She stroked his neck and the small of his back prolonging pleasant sensations and his inertness.

His mind slowly cleared and he was startled by his lack of concern for his partner. She was lying uncomplaining under his full weight. She not only continued to smile at him, she never stopped the gentle stroking.

He rolled off her and leaned over and kissed her nose and was surprised at the feeling of tenderness that came over him for this beautiful whore. He propped up on an elbow and looked into her eyes, so dark and appealing, then leaned over and touched her lips lightly with his. Her beauty was indescribable.

He wrapped her tenderly in his arms and they remained that way until perspiration collected between them and through miniscule routes, escaped downward to dampen the sheets. Lacking sufficient circulation, the arms beneath their bodies were numb. More sure of himself, he asked if she would bathe with him. She smiled and gave a positive response.

The notion that she was his for pay was not in his mind.

At the sink against the far wall Jim quickly cleaned himself where needed and got into trousers and shoes. Soo-Ann did likewise, then slipped her dress on and her feet into her shoes. Though it did not matter, he self-consciously stuck his head out the door to see if the hall was clear. They walked hand in hand to a large immaculate bathroom which served about a half dozen rooms.

They undressed, she pulling the dress over her head. Again he took pleasure observing her.

Along a wall was a huge tub and when it contained about eight inches of water at the right temperature, he climbed in and sat down. She started to get in facing him, but he gently turned her and she sat with her back to him. He wrapped her in his arms. He massaged her neck and shoulders and back. She looked over her shoulder, her expression puzzled. She was in the profession of being used and this was new to her, but she relaxed and enjoyed his efforts. Before long she was moving her shoulders and neck under his fingers in a subdued ecstasy and humming very softly.

Ultimately she forced herself free and turned half around. She pushed him gently against the back of the tub laying her head on his chest. It pleased him and he slid an arm about her and tenderly cupped a soft breast. The warm water and the soft pliant body fastened to him lulled him into a stupor of the mind while his body luxuriated in undisturbed tranquillity. She was similarly affected.

The cooler water was the first hint that nothing lasts forever. Jim stretched a leg toward the faucet, but his toes could not reach. Soo-Ann raised her head and looked into his eyes. He spoke to her in her native tongue, "It's cold!"

She smiled, but there was a veiled impishness in her smile. She moved a hand slowly across his chest, the fingernails the only contact. She moved them in circles a short time before proceeding enticingly downward to his stomach. She lingered and drew more circles. She worked one fingernail back and forth along the line where the leg joins the torso, tantalizing and caressing the skin.

Jim's body temperature rose rapidly. That was not all.

Soo-Ann, at first to her surprise, then to her pleasure, was undergoing emotions new to her. She rolled to her knees straddling his legs. Gliding downward she engulfed him. The desire was strong, but their movement more controlled, less severe, their stamina surprising.

Afterwards when they lay together in bed, limbs intertwined, their bodies contentedly immobile, Jim recalled something he thought he had seen. In the tub, in the moment of his own stormy excitement, his vision focused on her face but an instant. What he saw returned to his minds eye. Soo-Ann, her head thrown back, was moaning and crying out, but very softly. With his own delirium so intense, he could not be sure whether or not he imagined it. Could it have happened that way? Yes .. it did ... he was sure.

Reveling in his good fortune Jim turned suddenly sober and said out loud, "Damn! I didn't wear a rubber!" Soo-Ann opened her eyes. She gazed at him, then asked what he said. He rose on an elbow and smiled, "It's all right." He kissed her shoulder and said to himself, "Hell, if I get it, I get it. At least it can be cured. Besides, it's hard to imagine her with V.D."

He pushed the negative notion aside and ran a hand over her body pleasing himself with the exploration. She smiled and understanding his pleasure relaxed in consent and found it enjoyable. She was permitting herself to give in happily to this man she did not know, but found she wanted to know and she was allowing old inhibitions to fade, inhibitions she had forced on herself when she plied her trade.

When his hand gently wandered over her breasts, the nipples hardened. The covers moved downward with the hand and his eyes too caressed her. He was gentle around her loins, curious at the soft hair and pouting flesh. He was being stimulated. So was she.

Later they went out for a meal. When they returned they were together till after ten PM when he escorted her to the street and found her a rickshaw. He knew he would have liberty again next Saturday, but his funds had taken a beating. He asked her about Saturday evening when he could stay overnight. She was pleased and responded affirmatively. With some effort and a little embarrassment, he got her to understand that he could not again afford the luxury they shared today. She assured him that she would take him to a place he would like and could afford. She was enthusiastic in her desire to be a help and he wondered if she was for real. She did not fit the image of the Chinese prostitute he had heard of in so many unkind stories.

They confirmed the date and the meeting place while the rickshaw waited. He helped her aboard and watched till out of sight. He was glad he paid her when she arrived. Right now he did not wish to destroy the aura of their pretended love.

Jim Williams did not dwell long on the reality of his conduct that day, but returned to barracks at a snappy, happy pace.

*

Soo-Ann arrived promptly. That would be her way. Jim helped her from the rickshaw with one hand and with the other pressed the money for her fee into her free hand. She did not look at it. That too would be her way. She placed it quickly in a small purse. They went inside, transacted the routine business and were handed a key and walked up a flight of stairs. The room was small, but clean. There was a supply of various towels at the sink. The bed was diminutive, but that did not matter. There was a tiny window allowing some light into the room. He watched her slowly undress in the shadowy atmosphere and could feel his senses heightening. He wanted to grab her and pull her to him, but did not. It was worth the wait.

Soo-Ann seemed driven to please him, wanting nothing in return. It was infectious and Jim found himself wanting more and more to please her. He matched her vitality and she matched his ardor. It was getting dark before she lay still, clasped snugly in his arms.

Early in the morning, while still dark, they awakened sweaty and warm. They went to the sink and she bathed him with warm cloths. When finished, she started on herself, not yet used to his need to share in their ministrations. He took the cloth from her and gently bathed her. He lingered over her and her pleasure was equal to his. When he finished and they were standing in front of the sink, it was she who pulled his naked body to hers and held him tightly.

They stayed together until late Sunday afternoon.

* * *

Training exercises and static guard became the norm. There was time for close order drill and some of the more mundane aspects of barracks life. Jim tackled his routine duties with a renewed energy and some of his squad mates were amazed when on occasion he volunteered for some less than savory duty, or 'shit details' as they were commonly referred to. It was the beginning of an extended period of harboring funds which prevented him sending much money home. A good deal of his time in barracks was spent at study.

Sal contented himself with an occasional trip to the slop chute and a few beers. He missed the time with his best friend, but did not complain. Jim soon discovered he too missed a good buddy and it was not long until he decided it was time to make a conscious effort to spend time with his buddy. Thereafter, at least once a week the two pulled liberty or some such thing together. They also made certain to visit Lou and Han on a somewhat regular basis.

Jonnie and Tom joined another company. Only on limited occasions did the four former 489ers get together.

*

The platoon returned from convoy duty on Thursday, impatient to wash the grime from their bodies. Back in the squad bay, sitting on his cot drying his feet, Jim said to Sal, "Hey! Whadaya say we go to town and see if we can find Han and Lou and chat a little? And after, I'll buy ya a drink."

"Sounds good ta me."

"The days are getting shorter and cooler and they probably won't be hangin around too much longer," Jim commented taking a clean shirt from a hanger.

"I got some cigarettes for them."

"That's great! I got a couple a boxes of crackers from the PX. It'll be good to take them something."

"I sure am glad we don't hafta wear those damned starched khakis anymore."

"You can say that again."

"I sure am glad we don't hafta wear those damned starched khakis anymore."

Sal received a punch in the arm from his grinning buddy.

They checked out and set a brisk pace. The terrible heat of the oppressive summer was gone and the cooler air invigorated them. Their duties were behind them for the moment and they were clean and the smell in the air was not all that bad. It was good to be alive.

Han and Lou were at their place sipping tea. Greetings exchanged, the two Marines were offered tea, but declined. They handed over the boxes of cigarettes and crackers and were thanked profusely with words and rapid, diminutive bows. Conversation was light and good natured. Not only Jim, but the two elders, who were the epitome of patience, had tutored Sal with his speech. While he would never be a linguist, Sal's improvement was noticeable and the delight was evident in the smiles of Han and Lou.

Twilight was upon them when the group broke up. The two friends walked slowly away discussing destinations. They turned a corner and headed for a more affluent section of the city.

"Sonuva bitch!" Jim spat surprising Sal.

"What's the matter?"

"Soo-Ann was in that jeep with Captain Colbert."

"Who the hell's he?"

"You know, the C.O. of Headquarters Company."

Jim knew she had seen him, yet gave no sign of recognition. He was angry and hurt, not only because she had not acknowledged him, but he had seen her plying her trade. They continued their journey, Jim remaining silent, grappling with his vacillating thoughts and allowing self pity to seep into his feelings.

Sal did not say anything right away, but after a spell he stopped and faced Jim. He placed a hand on his friend's shoulder, "Ya know, Buddy, that's the way she makes a livin and it might be the only way she can get what she needs to live. Maybe she's got somebody in her family that needs takin care of. Anyhow ya can't change it. You accepted her on those terms and if ya still wanta see her some more, you'll hafta go on under those terms."

Looking down Jim nodded agreement. They were soon in a bar and Jim did some bona fide drinking. He did not allow Sal to buy a round. He did not get drunk and it was Sal who pulled him out of the place to return to the barracks.

They had not gone far when Jim turned to Sal, "Heck, I'm bein lousy company and you didn't have a thing to do with any of this. I'm sorry, Sal, but I sorta feel like I got kicked in the gut. I'm really sorry, Buddy."

"Hey! No apologies needed. I just wish I could do somethin ta help, but hell, I know you'll get through it fine. I know that, Jim!" Sal was smiling and Jim smiled back, feebly at first, but the smile grew and the two friends were soon conversing about other things.

The next morning Jim awoke to reveille with a modest headache. He had come to terms with himself, with Soo-Ann and with the circumstances of their relationship.

Saturday they shared the same small bed and did not part till very late on Sunday.

* * *

The Marines were relaxed when they entered the city. The convoy was almost home, the dangers of the open road behind them. The Ba Loo had been kicking up their heels on a more regular basis in the surrounding countryside. Railroad tracks were a constant target. Less than two weeks ago there had been a firefight at the large ammo dump to the south wounding a Marine. The Ba Loo paid a price. They left a dead body and a wounded comrade behind. Such an event was not conducive to a carefree patrol.

The brown countryside and faded mountains in the distance were so unlike the mid October brilliance flowing south in New England. Jim took a swig from his canteen to wash the road dust from his mouth and throat. Remembering those autumn colors, he realized he had not thought much about home of late, though he wrote with regularity and looked forward to receiving letters.

His mother's letters portrayed the sweet, caring, worrying person he loved, yet sometimes when Soo-Ann was in his arms and his mother fleetingly crossed his mind, he resented the intrusion.

Letters from his father were usually short and not too informative. Jim knew his father was struggling with time to absorb the knowledge and gather the wherewithal to get the new business in operation. He never doubted his father's success.

Shirley and Bob he considered just kids though Shirley was now a junior and Bob a freshman. Shirley was more like their mother every day, but more in control of herself. Bob was as tall as Don. He had the makings of a natural leader, though not in the way Don had those attributes. With Don there had been a special quality, a charisma that one naturally looked up to.

Jim's affection for his family was strong, but being far away, that affection was less constrictive. He did not need his family as he had growing up. More to the point, he did not need their disapproval of his off duty time ... and disapprove they would. It mattered little. He no longer lived in Shoreford nor in his mind was he a citizen of that town. He was a member of a dust covered group of Marines in vehicles, getting closer to home, ... his home ... and his girl.

* * *

Sunday, November 10th, the Corps was 171 years old. It was Jim and Sal's first birthday celebration as Marines. It was a celebration they would try to abolish, that is the powers in Washington unfriendly to the Marines. But for now, chow on that special day was abundant. It was a great day for contraband, the two becoming experts at removing surplus from the mess hall for delivery to Han and Lou.

So as not to miss noon chow, Jim regretfully left Soo-Ann before eleven o'clock and hurried to meet Sal. They would share in the plenty and hide some for transport out the gate. These gifts were greatly appreciated in a land where a native barber received twenty-five cents for a shave and a haircut and that included a four cent tip. In addition to the quantities of food, cigars were handed out and the two scrounge artists acquired more than a few extras from buddies who did not smoke.

The two elders did not hang about in the colder weather, but the four had an appointment to meet this special day and when they did, the Chinese acted like winners of a giant jackpot. Beaming and bowing, Han and Lou were finally convinced to get the foodstuffs into the building. With that accomplished the elders quickly returned to their friends. Next was the gift of the cigars. Han and Lou lit up and puffed happily showing off their newly acquired status to the few acquaintances who passed by. It bordered on the comic. The two Marines enjoyed their friends pleasure.

* * *

The temperature had not risen much since nine o'clock that morning. It was cold. Wearing his overcoat, Jim walked rapidly to his rendezvous with Soo-Ann. She alone was in his thoughts. Did she really care for him or was everything just one big act? He had mulled that thought over in his mind many times.

A month ago, to test her, he handed her half the usual fee. The following week he did the same. She never said a word. A week later he made up the difference. He lied and told her he had been short of money. She changed the subject before he completed the second sentence.

Last week they returned to the hotel of their first meeting partaking again of its more luxurious appointments. They bathed together and returned to their room. He spread his towel across the seat of the stuffed chair and sat, still naked. She stood in front of him not knowing what his intentions were. He asked her to sit on his lap. She came to him, this prostitute, a sweet smile lighting her face. She sat on his lap and wrapped her arms about his neck and lay her head against his.

She was as content as he and they stayed that way a lengthy time. Eventually he squirmed to get more comfortable. She stirred and their eyes locked. Jim's words came easily in Chinese, "I love you, Soo-Ann!"

Before he finished she was smiling happily. She repeated the words, but ended with the familiar, Jeem.

"My God!" he thought, "This whole thing is nuts."

As he neared his destination and his appointment with his whore. He wanted to be there as quickly as possible. He decided he wanted to run ... and he did.

*

November was the month James Williams turned eighteen. Christmas at home with all the family in Shoreford and Newville, had been in years past, the happiest event of the year for him. His first Christmas away from home, he knew, would be passed with few regrets. He was a young man on his own, doing what he wanted and doing it well. He was reaping huge mythical benefits.

Jim sent gifts home and received a substantial quantity. Sal was not forgotten, receiving a packet of baked goods and home made candy. The cookies did not do well in transport, but the crumbs were eaten with a spoon and enjoyed to the utmost. Sarah put together a large photo album. It piqued Jim's conscience when he realized it did not make him homesick, but Soo-Ann was salve for any temporary mental discomfort. It was an ironic love affair. He knew she could never be his completely. When they were together, however, everything else ceased to exist, along with his rationale.

When they were together, she wanted only to please him and make him happy. He struggled to keep from succumbing and permitting it, for he too desired to please her. His love, his obsession, was not as it was with Connie. At least he learned from that. He could now put things in perspective and would allow nothing to come between him and doing his duty properly and well. He worked at being a good Marine. He saw Soo-Ann mostly on the weekends when he was not duty bound. He worked at his studies. He made time for Sal and together they kept alive the friendship with Han and Lou.

There was one thing he shied from. He did not walk aimlessly about the city he had come to love. He did not want to chance seeing Soo-Ann with someone else.

The winter months off duty were pure pleasure. Jim and Soo-Ann shared far more than fleshly pursuits. They enjoyed sitting and talking. It was fun to eat together. She taught him how to use chopsticks and introduced him to Chinese food. He learned Chinese games from her and they played together. And she showed him parts of the city he would never have seen by himself.

Unaware that his buddies had anything but a meager knowledge of his activities, Jim contentedly continued on his merry way. Nothing was ever said to his face, but his buddies began speaking of 'Jim and his Whore' and how he had gone 'Asiatic'.

Sal threatened the entire squad bay. He informed them that if Jim ever heard a word of their description, either directly or by innuendo, he would personally 'beat the shit' out of the loudmouth who would end up toothless and very battered. Sal could not remember having ever threatened anyone with violence, but he was not sorry he made that threat. Jim was a buddy like none other. Actually, he was pleased with himself.

*

The Marines were issued winter clothing that was sorely tested. It was difficult to imagine how a place that got so hot in the summer was so cold in the winter. The long woolen underwear itched like blazes. The shoe pacs with rubber bottoms and leather tops were an impediment to walking and only kept the feet warm with layers of socks. Woolen shirts, sweaters and trousers were topped with heavy overalls and a lined jacket. Over this was a knee length, hooded parka.

Units of the 7th Marines further north were without heated bath water. Up there, the Gulf of Po Hai froze a hundred or more yards from the shore.

Much of the guard was static and training exercises were welcomed by many to warm cold bodies. After one such exercise, back in the barracks, a complaint was heard.

"Boy! These duds are one big pain!"

"They keep ya warm don't they?" Sal commented.

"Yeh, they do that, .. at least most of the time, but my bitch is tryin to take a leak through six inches of cloth with a three inch pecker."

*

In December the 7th Marines returned to the States with two battalions of the 11th Marines. Part of the First Marine Air Wing also moved out.

Jim was insensitive to the changes taking place around him. Things were going his way. He did not want it to change, could not even imagine it would. There had been too many hurtful changes in his young life and he did not want any more. He decided he had to do something to make his lifestyle permanent. This was where he belonged. He was a China Marine, like his forebears in the Old Corps.

Late on a Sunday, late in February, but early in 1947, Jim reluctantly kissed Soo-Ann just before she entered the pedicab. He had something on his mind. He got into the barracks in time to catch Sal on his way to supper.

"Hi, Sal."

"Hi, Buddy! How'd it go? Ya goin ta chow?"

"Yeah."

He turned around and joined his friend. They shared small talk during chow and returned to the squad bay. Sal sat on his cot. Jim unbuckled his fair leather belt and removed his blouse and hung it on a hanger. Sliding the knot loose on his field scarf he decided he could wait no longer.

"How do you feel about the Corps, Sal?"

Sal thought a bit before he answered, "I guess you might say I found a home. The thoughta goin home, .. hell, I got no home," he paused again, "and ya know, the thoughta workin in a shop is like a kick in the balls. Why'd ya ask?"

"Well, I kinda thought you felt that way. You've said things like that from time to time. I've been thinkin like that too. I've been thinkin of reuppin if they'd let me stay in China." Sal smiled, not only because he knew Jim's reason, but he too liked China duty. "Besides, I think somethin's gonna happen here sooner or later."

"Yeh, I think you're right about that," Sal paused and looked away, then cocked his head to one side and returned his eyes to Jim's, "Yeah, reuppin don't sound that bad."

Jim stuck out his hand. Sal grabbed it. They shook enthusiastically.

*

By the end of the week, James A. Williams and Salvatore A. Gennaro added two more years to their tour which would have concluded before the end of the current year. Saturday and most of Sunday, both in and out of Soo-Ann's arms, Jim was in heaven.

Monday night was different. Jim sat on his bunk, a pad resting on his thighs and knees trying to compose 'the letter.' He started four and threw them away. In agony, he said to himself, "My God! I've got to tell them and the only way is to tell them the truth. The truth, ... hell, I can't tell them about Soo-Ann. Well I guess not the whole truth. Geeze, I don't really want to go to college. Heck, I've got a job and I like it. I kept my promise about the diploma. I got it! Besides, it's my life. Who wants to go back to Shoreford anyway?"

Rationalizing to his own satisfaction helped, but the letter still took some time. It was a kind letter and did not mention that it was his life to live and he exaggerated some. In closing he wrote, "It doesn't mean I love you any less, but I really want to be a Marine." That was true. Sealing the envelope he thought, "Boy! Dad's going to have a time with Mom for a few days."

* * *

On April 4th, Good Friday, the ammo dump down south was hit again. The Ba Loo slithered in during the darkness of night. This time it was well planned and coordinated. Five Marines died and sixteen were wounded, but the kids in green recovered quickly and fought back with tenacity and skill. The Ba Loo left behind six known dead. The blood pools were further evidence of Communist casualties that were dragged away. They also left behind a huge crater when they exploded of a large cache of ammo at the dump.

Two prisoners were captured, one an officer, the other a Japanese now fighting with the Ba Loo. The officer carried plans for the attack and another to take place in a few days. It would not materialize.

The reinforcements who went into the nearby village in search of attackers were infused with an anger that energized their unsuccessful task.

* * *

Scuttlebutt was rife with all kinds of rumors about the future of the depleted division. It soon became known that the battalion was leaving Peiping. Jim took days to work out of his depression and accept the fact, never totally succeeding. His first visit with Soo-Ann during this time was a painful experience. He was certain she already knew of the order. The Chinese had a way of finding out those things. Nevertheless, when he told her, the anguish was unmistakable. She had hoped it was not true. When he spoke to her, he often had to repeat himself. She was far away. They spent a long time dawdling over the food he brought, eating little. They went to bed and just lay wrapped together, unmoving. When their body heat and perspiration drove them apart, they came back together in a passion like none before.

*

The last two weeks in Peiping was typical Marine Corps hurry up and wait. Jim and Soo-Ann conspired to be together whenever possible and Jim made more than one unauthorized visit. Those visits were, for the most part, heavyhearted. Neither was handling their emotions well. Often the intimacy they shared was just sitting together, mostly with Soo-Ann on Jim's lap and sometimes, she sobbed softly.

All at once D Day arrived. The convoy saddled up and was on its way. They proceeded down a main boulevard of the city passing under a graceful portal that spanned their route. The Marines were turned toward the roadside silently observing the masses lining the way. Sal jabbed an elbow into Jim's ribs. There was Lou and Han with his wife. The two elders waved cheerlessly and the little old lady stood motionless at Han's side.

The crowd was thinning as they moved out of the city. She was standing alone and Jim spotted her and yelled, "Soo-Ann!"

His buddies all glanced his way, but he was not aware of their attention, nor would he have cared had he known. All he could see was the lovely girl who raised a hand to the level of her shoulder and waved in a timid, almost imperceptible movement. She was crying and her body was shaking slightly, unnoticed to any, but Jim.

Slowly, but gradually Soo-Ann's form got smaller and when the road made a slight bend and the convoy followed that bend, Soo-Ann disappeared from sight.

* * *

The remains of the regiment was on its way to Guam, the last place Jim and Sal wanted to be. They were able to use the cause of their reenlistment to stay in China. They were reassigned to the Third Marine Brigade at Tsingtao. Jim actually entertained thoughts that somehow he might be returned to Peiping.

Tsingtao was a different city than Peiping. It lacked the grandeur of ancient China, so abundant in Peiping. It was a seaport, more Western, with a German background. It was filled with small bars sometimes overflowing with sailors of the Seventh Fleet who came ashore periodically in relief of their sea duties. By September Tsingtao was the final duty station in North China garrisoned by Marines. Two battalions with supporting arms was all that remained of the two proud divisions and air wing that landed in North China two years earlier.

Landing exercises and combat training commenced in earnest. For many of the Marines, it was their first experience landing on a beach from amphibious craft and landing boats. There were a few who gave up their Navy chow over the side of the hard riding boats. When it became evident that it was about to happen there was a scramble to position oneself upwind.

The city was surrounded on three sides by the Communists, but life within was peaceful, except for the occasional thief fired on by alert sentries. Liberty was remarkably good, at least when the fleet was out, but there were incidents outside Tsingtao. A landing party was sent to destroy a downed aircraft. They were attacked, fortunately with no casualties.

For awhile Jim had difficulty acclimating to his new station. He and Sal did some sightseeing, but little else. He missed Soo-Ann intensely. He knew he should not, but he did. He did not talk about it and Sal did not push it. Then one day during the warm summer Sal spoke up.

"Hey, Buddy, I think it's time we went out and blew away the cobwebs, whadaya say?"

Jim looked at his friend a long time, "Ya know something, Sal, I think you're right. I'm buyin. Where do ya want to go?"

"Hell, I'm sure we won't have any trouble findin a bar in this town."

They did find a small bar with the usual contingent of bar girls. They had a beer and all the while Sal was eyeing a cute little girl named Ruby. She made money from the drinks that were bought for her and was not a prostitute. Sal introduced himself. Almost instantly they hit it off. It was the start of a relationship for Sal. When he went into the city he always ended up in that bar. Jim on occasion accompanied him, but remained aloof to the female inhabitants, though Ruby's girlfriend Pearl took an interest in him. Eventually Sal made a date to spend a Sunday with Ruby in her cubby hole room in a huge apartment building filled with similar tiny rooms. Jim could not be convinced to join them and spend the day with Pearl who was more than happy to have him. Sal and Ruby were to make a habit of these Sundays whenever Sal was off duty.

Christmas, unlike the previous one, was lonely. Jim could not shake his thoughts of Soo-Ann. What bothered him most was her ability to survive under the Ba Loo. Prostitutes who cohabited with Western Capitalists, he was sure, would not escape the Red wrath. It scared him as nothing else did. Perhaps his relationship with her had been a death sentence. For that reason he often regretted their relationship, yet could not pry the memory of her from his mind, nor could he escape the loneliness. He could not repent despite his remorse, a remorse that was deepened from his neglect at any attempt to get her out of Peiping. He knew deep down that it would not have been permitted, but he had not even made an attempt to speak to anyone about the possibility. That omission was additional fuel that stoked his burning fire of guilt whenever he thought of Soo-Ann and her unlikely chance of survival.

* * *

The New Year of 1948 dawned. Jim joined Sal and they went off with Ruby and Pearl to their respective rooms and a tiny bed. Jim knew he should not have given in to Sal, but he did. Pearl made a valiant effort to please and it was not her fault it was an unhappy experience for Jim. He was still in love with Soo-Ann, though he tried not to admit it. The guilt too, of having to leave her behind to unknown and perhaps terrible consequences, refused to dislodge itself from his sometimes troubled thoughts.

During the coming week, Jim signed up for a history course with the M.C.I. He steered clear of any further trysts with the local ladies and tried to forget the last one ever happened. He also worked hard to forget Soo-Ann. He was not successful.

The second year in China was quite unlike the first for P.F.C. James A. Williams.

* FIVE *

He crossed his arms over his bare chest. He was slightly chilly, lying still for so long. There was plenty of time and he thought he might as well be comfortable. He got up and went to the closet and removed a light blanket. Lying back down, he pulled the blanket over himself.

He was enjoying the rare luxury of inactivity. Though the memories were sometimes sad and sometimes less than admirable, they were events that helped shape his life, much as his daily activities shaped his body. At fifty-two, he was firm and free of fat.

Picking up the tumbler he took a sip. The amber colored liquid flowed over his tongue and down his throat. A pleasant sensation, he waited almost a minute and did it again, then replaced the tumbler on the night stand.

The wind had lessened and a few nearly white clouds were visible. Maybe the weatherman was going to be right with that forecast of a sudden change.

His own life had experienced sudden change. Fate some called it. Well, fate was fickle like the southern New England weather, but maybe there were times he lent fate a hand.

~ ~ ~ ~ ~

A few hundred Marines boarded the ship for the long sea voyage to the United States. There was no Marine officer aboard. The highest ranking N.C.O. was a gunnery sergeant who was out ranked by any Naval Chief Petty Officer (C.P.O.). Four sergeants and a handful of corporals rounded out the meager body of N.C.O.s. As a group, they lacked clout.

"God bless the Navy!" Jim grumbled sarcastically, "With all the empty troop compartments aboard this scow they gotta shove us up in the bow again."

"You know the fuckin swabs. We're the poor relations and they don't wanna let us forget it," Sal responded, exhibiting the sardonic grin Jim had come to know.

The first morning at sea, breakfast was the third meal aboard. It was not the greatest chow, but more of it was fresh than the Marines were used to after two years in China. It was also the third time the Marines came in contact with the Master at Arms who disliked Marines more than he did the working sailor and those he hated. He was a surly guy who abused and used his power with sadistic pleasure. He constantly and with zest, chewed out any Marine who displeased him.

Jim and Sal arrived for breakfast at the last minute and the M.A. proceeded to read them the riot act. Jim, who would have been intimidated on the voyage over, two years ago, thought the guy a jerk. It showed.

"Wipe that smirk off your face, Marine!" the M.A. yelled.

The smirk magnified. The M.A.'s ire magnified.

"I told yo..," the M.A. was suddenly jerked away. The Gunny had grabbed him by the elbow, turning him to the side, motioning Jim and Sal to continue through the chow line.

The two could not resist the temptation to look back. At the same time, all over the mess hall, elbows jabbed into ribs, hands tugged at sleeves, heads turned and those at the tables whispered to those opposite. In seconds the mess hall was filled with grinning faces. Gunnery Sergeant Perkins was leaning into the M.A.'s face, laying down the law. When the gunny turned and walked away, the M.A., who outranked him, was deflated and defeated. He exited hastily, a very unhappy sailor.

"Hot shit! Looks like Gunny gave that asshole the word," laughed Sal.

One of the sailors in the serving line gave Jim and Sal a thumbs up and a big grin.

*

The Marines took advantage of warm temperatures and a lazy sea after chow. The cargo hatches were covered with stripped to the waist bodies and those who could not find space lolled at the ship's rail. Life aboard did have some rewards.

Looking around him at the total relaxation Jim chuckled and said to Sal, "Look at the old salts. Remember the trip comin over? It sure wasn't like this. Nobody knew what to expect right out of boot camp. A couple of years sure makes a difference."

"Yeah," his buddy replied not taking his eyes from the horizon.

Early that afternoon the ship's loudspeakers instructed all Marines to report to their troop compartment. With the usual grumbling they wandered unhurriedly through the hatchway and down into the compartment. They gathered around the raised platform in the rear. Gunny Perkins stood on the platform, arms folded across chest, an unhappy expression clouding his face.

"Tenhut!" the Gunny shouted.

An ensign came through the hatch and down the ladder. The Master at Arms was right on the junior officer's heels.

"At ease, men," the young officer said, his voice revealing his unease. "Now listen up. There is work aboard that needs to be completed and the Captain has ordered the help of the Marines. Deck paint must be chipped and the decks painted. The Marines will be responsible for the area from the bow on the main deck, aft to the forward bulkhead. You will be expected to work eight hours each day, but will be split into four shifts of two hours each. That will spread the work out amongst all, since there is not enough space to allow the entire detachment on deck at the same time. If you have any questions, Gunnery Sergeant Perkins will answer them. That is all."

The ensign left immediately, unable to clear the compartment quickly enough, the smirking M.A., again at his heels.

Called to attention when the officer left, the Marines stood in stunned silence. The Gunny looked over the group before speaking, "All right you guys, at ease, the smoking lamp is lit."

It was a surly group and a surly individual spit out, "What the fucks the scoop, Gunny, Marines don't chip paint!?"

"I know, .. I know," the gunny answered, "but I just came from a session with the Exec and he didn't take too kindly to my arguing the same thing. He told me that aboard an American Naval vessel, the captain decides who does what and he decided the Marines aboard will chip paint. He also told me that no Marine would threaten any of the ship's crew in the performance of their duties. Where the hell he got the idea that any of his precious crew was threatened, I don't know."

Raucous laughter echoed around the compartment.

"That lousy M.A. is hated by the crew as much as by us!" Jim chimed in.

A loud, "Yeah!" filled the compartment. Every voice echoed the sentiment.

"Be that as it may," continued Gunny Perkins, "but as long as we're aboard this ship, we have to obey the Captain. Now I can't tell you guys how to chip paint, cause I don't know. You're gonna have to set your own pace, .. if you get my drift. I'm going to turn this over to your sergeants who will assign the shifts and so forth. That's the way it has to be." He turned to leave. There was no doubt of his anger.

*

A grumbling, cussing, ill humored pack took their places on deck the following day. Without enthusiasm, without purpose, they went to work, if that is what it could be called. Almost from the beginning they were sitting with legs spread apart, the hammer blows falling haphazardly between. Soon after, organization was achieved. All the hammer blows landed simultaneously, roughly thirty seconds apart, to the accompaniment of loud groans.

Onlookers, mostly Marines, for none of the ship's company cared to venture into the area, found the display more than a little humorous. Their facial expressions and giddy chuckles said it all.

*

Reveille, breakfast and the shrill boatswain's pipe the following day, then the familiar announcement, "Clean sweep down fore and aft, ..." concluding with instructions to take all trash to the fantail and dump it overboard.

"That's it! That's it!" yelled Sal to Jim, "We gotta find Forbes and tell him."

"Tell him what?" Jim was surprised at Sal's excitement. He saw the gleam in his friends eyes and went with him. They searched out Sergeant Forbes, the N.C.O. in charge of the clean up that day.

When they were face to face, Sal blurted, "That's it, Sarge, that's it, .. the fantail, .. that's the answer!"

"Whadaya mean the fantail, Gennaro?"

Sal did not answer the sergeant, but turned to Jim, "You remember the trip over when those doggies dumped the trash over the side and the way they got their asses reamed?"

"Yeah!" Jim enthusiastically replied, his eyes lighting at his buddy's meaning.

"You mean for us to dump over the side?" Forbes caught on immediately, "Gennaro, you're a genius!"

"I don't mean just over the side, Sarge, but up in the bow where it'll really blow up inta officer's country amidships!"

"That's even better! We'll be behind the hatch cover, giving better concealment. Gennaro, you really are a genius!"

"Yeah!" Sal replied, his face a huge grin.

Jim slapped him across the shoulders.

Sergeant Forbes called the Marines in the detail together. They gathered around, serious at first, but quickly turned into a bunch that acted like silly grammar schoolers as the sergeant laid out the plan. When the plan was complete, the Marines that undertook the clean up that morning did so with greater enthusiasm than any prior Marine clean up in the history of shipboard life.

When the compartment was shipshape and spotless, two trash cans were full of all sorts of potential flying debris. A scout went topside to make sure it was all clear and the cans were carried up and into the bow. The deed was accomplished with great eagerness and abundant revelry. The open hatch was filled to capacity with curious and delighted Marines. They were not disappointed. All kinds of paper and other junk disappeared below the ship's rail only to be caught up in the ship's wind draft and carried aloft to the decks amidships where the officers were berthed.

The first shift of paint chippers was doing their thing by the time the announcement was made that concerned a terrible breach of proper procedure. Fortunately, the raucous display of sacrilegious merry-making by the Marines was not witnessed by anyone in authority.

No one was left in doubt by the announcement over the ship's public address the next morning. Proper procedure for a clean sweepdown would be strictly adhered to. However, Sergeant Bishop's crew was not about to be outdone by their shipmates. Later another announcement, most vehement, regarding perpetrators of improper procedure.

The fourth day of the paint chipping detail, the standard announcement was far from standard. Sergeant Greene and his crew seemed not to have heard the explicit instructions. Their ardor to at least match their predecessors was rewarded.

At 0800 an announcement on the PA ordered all Marines to report to their compartment. Ten minutes later the Executive Officer stormed through the starboard hatch and down the ladder. Observant Marines could only describe the man as humorless and angry.

Tall and lean, the officer had piercing, steel blue eyes that in days gone by had nailed many a hapless, malfeasant sailor to the bulkhead. But today, despite the anger and lack of humor, the more astute observed an uncertainty in those eyes.

In the officer's footsteps a young yeoman followed, a clipboard in his hand, his eyes affixed to his superior's back. The M.A. was nowhere in sight. Gunny Perkins was the third member of the party. He brought up the rear. He was apprehensive.

The compartment was filled with Marines. Displaying proper Naval etiquette they came to attention when the officer entered. Put at ease, the Exec started pointing fingers at various members of the detachment and asking questions about the clean up details. The answers were all the same, accompanied by a similar blank expression or shrug of the shoulder, "Sorry, Sir, I don't know." The replies never varied. No one knew who had issued orders to the workers. No one knew who was on the work details. No one knew anything.

The Exec stood silent. Only those close enough could see the slight shake of his head and the defeat that clouded the piercing eyes. He turned and walked to the ladder and disappeared into the sobering, sea sprayed air on deck and his real world, the yeoman glued to his tail.

"You know, .." Gunnery Sergeant Perkins said surveying the men to his front, "Marines have always prided themselves on their knowledge. They are aware of what goes on around them. You characters are the dumbest bunch I have ever served with." A sly, knowing smile lit his face as he was turning to leave. He gave a thumbs up and said respectfully, "Semper Fidelis!"

Maybe it was because so many were returning to the States for discharge, most at the end of two year enlistments. Maybe it was the parsimonious times and there was no brig space. Maybe it was decided there was not enough time or manpower to get to the bottom of the conundrum. Maybe it was that busy Marines were just as troublesome as idle Marines. Maybe it was just because they were Marines. What ever the reason, the paint chipping detail was over for the kids in green.

*

The transport had been at sea nearly three weeks. The ship went through a hurricane in the China sea and for most of one day maintained only enough speed to operate the helm. The mess hall could not even prepare coffee. The troops lived on sandwiches and then oranges for most of two days.

When the Hawaiian Islands appeared on the horizon, a calm morning in early June, the passengers were eager to get ashore and shake the inactivity and confinement and the smells of the ship.

Jim and Sal departed these islands more than two years ago. Like most of the Marines aboard, this would be their first contact with an American type civilization since that departure.

Liberty call was right after noon chow and every Marine, except the very few on guard, was in the line. Over two hundred snappy salutes were presented to the Officer of the Deck and at the top of the gangplank, the same number were executed aft, to the colors and quickly, the line of men in khakis and spit shined shoes was gone.

The city had changed in two years. Honolulu, Jim concluded early, had more glare, more commercialism, more hustle and less class.

Jim, Sal, and four buddies stopped first at a soda fountain, where to the clerks surprise, they ordered plain milk. Downing two glasses each, two of them polished off a third. They walked out into the brilliant sunshine licking large ice cream cones.

They walked a lot. They ate a lot. They swam in the surf at Waikiki. They ended the day in a burlesque theater, something new in town since their last visit.

At the conclusion of the erotic display, as they got to their feet to leave, the youngest member of the group pleaded, "Hey, guys, slow down a bit, will ya? I can't stand up yet."

"Whatsa matter, Buddy," one of the group asked amidst chuckles from the others, "those khakis so tight ya can't hide the little fella?"

"Aw come on, slow it down will ya?"

They were tired when they returned to the ship and slept well, that is until their digestive systems began to react to the over abundance of rich food so long absent from their diet. The heads were a busy place after that.

*

Six days later, in the fog of prenoon, the transport glided under the Golden Gate and into the U.S.A. Another seven days and Jim debarked at the railway station in that city in Southern New England. He took a bus uptown. The trolleys had disappeared during his absence. He transferred to another bus and headed for Shoreford and thirty days leave. Sometime after 2:00PM he exited the bus two blocks from home.

He did not want any fanfare on his homecoming and when he called his folks from Treasure Island, he was purposefully vague on the time of his arrival in Shoreford, only mentioning an approximate day. He wanted to spend the first few days at home with his family and soak up some of the new, 'foreign' culture.

Walking up the driveway he heard a sound from the past, still familiar to his ears. Sarah was running the vacuum cleaner in the living room. He entered quietly through the side door and into the kitchen. Gently, he placed his seabag on the floor and tiptoed into the living room.

"Hi, Mom!" he shouted over the noise.

Sarah Williams spun around, eyes wide, mouth agape. She nearly lept as she threw herself into her son's arms. She clung to him with a desperation born of anxiety and a mother's love. When he leaned back to look at her, there were tears on her cheeks. He had expected that.

"Mom, don't you think I should turn off the vacuum?"

"Oh, Jimmy!" was all she could say.

He freed himself and flipped the switch to off.

He returned to her and placed an arm about her shoulder and squeezed and said, "Come on, Mom, I'll make you a cup of tea."

"You'll do no such thing!" she exclaimed as they walked into the kitchen. "Sit down, Jimmy and tell me what you would like."

"Aw, come on, Mom, why don'tcha let me do it for you?"

"Jimmy, ... sit down! This is my kitchen," she smiled and brushed the stray strand of hair from her forehead with the back of her hand, "and I'm still your mother." Then she turned soft, "What can I get you, Dear? What would you really like?"

He knew any further discussion was useless. "How about a glass of milk, Mom?"

"My goodness! You must want something besides milk?"

"Milk's fine, Mom, .. honest." He spotted the fresh batch of Welsh cookies on the counter, his face becoming a wide grin, "I wouldn't mind some of those."

She was at her best doing what she was doing. She was more full of joy than she had been in some time. She had her son home again. The kettle boiled and she poured her tea and sat opposite him. He waited for her before he partook of the delights she placed in front of him. He studied her as he chewed. She pondered him and did not speak until he devoured two cookies, the sweet smile remaining on her face until she spoke.

"You were gone such a long time, Jimmy. I knew that would happen. It was really bad when we lost our Donald .. and now we never see you, ... except once in a great while." Her eyes filled with tears.

"Mom, I'm home now. I'll be here for four weeks." He stretched his hands across the table and lay them on top of hers.

"Yes, but if you're a Marine, we won't see you much anymore. Do you know something? Your father thought, of all his sons, you would be the one to join him in the business."

"Oh my gosh! The business, how's it going? The last letter I got before leaving China, you said Dad thought he had a location. When I called from the west coast I didn't even think to ask about it."

She was smiling again, "He opened the doors a week ago. He's already got enough work to keep him busy. You know, Jimmy, when you decided to stay in the Marines, I really think he felt bad. But you know your father. He never says much about things like that."

"Well, Mom, I'll sure give him a hand getting things shipshape while I'm home." He turned the conversation to more pleasing things and soon they were laughing as they reminisced about past happier events.

Stopping in mid sentence, Jim put a finger to his lips. Footsteps were heard coming up the driveway. He motioned his mother to silence. Placing his dishes on the chair, he slid it under the table. Grabbing his seabag, he slunk from the kitchen.

The screen door banged shut.

"Hi, Mom! What're you doing sitting here drinking tea by yourself?" Shirley picked up on the unusual expression on Sarah's face, "Is everything all right? Mom, .. are you OK?"

Facing her mother, she never saw Jim approach from the rear. He quickly wrapped strong arms about her waist, lifting her from the floor.

"Jimmy!" she screamed, her voice a high pitch.

Returned to the floor she spun and faced her brother and gave him a vigorous hug. He squeezed her to him, hugging her back.

She stepped back and gazed into his laughing eyes, "After all this time, you're still a big tease." Giggling, she chopped a right jab at his mid section which missed completely as he bounced lightly to the rear.

"Well, ..." he chuckled, "maybe just a little," and put his hands on his sister's shoulders, observing her at arms length. "Mom, will you look at her? She's become a young lady! My God! She's a young lady."

Shirley blushed, but recovered quickly, "Well, you know, Jimmy, you've been gone a long time and I do graduate next week." Turning serious she paused briefly and hugged him again. "Jimmy, I was so afraid you wouldn't make it on time," she smiled affectionately, laying her head on his shoulder, "but I'm glad you did."

House cleaning was over for the day in the Williams' home. The three sat together and resumed the quest to reacquaintance, including many questions about Sal. Sarah was disappointed that she would not see him, but did not pursue it. Instead, she made the most of her son's homecoming. She and Shirley soon turned to asking all kinds of questions about China. It surprised Jim, the curiosity they had for the place. Pictures he sent home were dug out and spread across the table top. They pointed to one, then another and bombarded him with questions. He enjoyed it and was glad he had taken an interest in that ancient land and was knowledgeable with his answers.

"Did you have a Chinese girl friend, Jimmy?" Shirley's question caught him off guard.

He recovered quickly, his response controlled, "Most of the people there were peasants and it wasn't easy for Marines to get acquainted with anyone. Besides, the language was a big problem."

"But you said in your letters that you were trying to learn the language."

"Yeh, but I was not really fluent. Mostly I could talk to merchants. That kind of stuff."

He was glad his sister did not pursue the matter. The guilt he carried for Soo-Ann was still heavy. Not for their relationship, which he thought he could have revealed to his sister or his brother somewhere in time. That was pleasing to his memory and for what ever reason, he felt no apology was necessary. Despite the circumstances of that affair, he knew he had truly loved Soo-Ann and was as sure that she had strong feelings for him. It was the way he left her and the constant wonder if she had survived that fueled his guilt and annulled his ability to speak of her.

"I think it's about time I gave Buck a call."

"He won't be home from work yet," Shirley replied. "After supper will be the best time."

"Too bad he had to drop out of school after only one year," Sarah lamented.

"But he's going nights, Mom," Jim replied, "I'm sure he'll get his degree. It may take awhile, but you know Buck. It's just a shame he doesn't come from a wealthy family like so many kids in Shoreford. He's all his mother's got and he is helping her. And ya know, I've never heard the guy complain."

Suddenly Sarah looked up, her eyes opening wide, "Will you look at the time. It's almost six o'clock. Your father and Bobbie will be home shortly and I haven't started supper yet."

Mother and daughter commenced a flurry of activity.

"What can I do to help?" asked Jim.

Sarah looked over her shoulder, "Stay right where you are."

Soon the cooking food was filling the kitchen with a pleasant aroma.

The car drove into the driveway a short time later. Bob was first through the door. Before Jim was on his feet, his younger brother reached across the table and grabbed his hand. The two pumped heartily. Bob was beaming, but did not speak. He was at a loss for words, so out of character for him. When Bob released his grip, Jim walked around the table. His father had stayed near the door enjoying the sight of his two sons. Jim stuck out his hand and they just grasped firmly without shaking. They searched each other's eyes. With a sudden move, Bill Williams put his arms about his son.

That night the family was up long past the normal bed time.

*

The next morning Jim successfully sneaked down the stairs without waking anyone. He opened the side door and the screen door only as much as needed to slip through. Sitting on the steps, he put on his boondockers. The air was fresh and sweet, so unlike the smells of China. The sky was exceedingly blue in the early morning as the sun began its climb.

He walked the residential streets near his home shaking out the kinks of the inactivity of the past month and a half. It was twenty seven months since he trod this area, but there was little change. The homes in this section of Shoreford had been here for forty years or more.

The change that had taken place was very evident. The empty lot behind the Williams home now contained a house. It had been built while Jim was in China. Jim's memories of 'the field' brought a smile to his face. It was to that lot that Don had taken him, he remembered, after that collision with Eric Olson at Collins Park. They tackled and blocked each other that day till they were both weary. After that, there were many more times that the two brothers used that field to practice, one against the other. He did not think about it back then, but now realized that Don had not pulled any punches when they played, even though Jim was smaller. And he also knew there was no competition between them, no desire to show one or the other up. It was Don's way of helping his brother become the best he could be. And while they played hard, Don constantly praised him for his accomplishments with such short tributes as, "That was great Jim!" usually accompanied by an arm about the shoulders and a firm squeeze.

It had seemed back then that he would always have his brother, that Don would always be with him, always be around to show him the way. The happiness inside him turned briefly sad, but it did not last. He remembered so many of the good things as he walked that he unconsciously picked up his pace. He smiled to himself. Memories of Don were like that.

Like the house on the former vacant lot, the town too was growing. There were whole new sections being added. New homes were popping up in clusters. He was glad his neighborhood had remained mostly as it was.

He enjoyed the solitude of the empty streets and silent homes not yet astir with morning activity. He also enjoyed becoming familiar once again with his old neighborhood and at least some of the town. He walked rapidly for twenty minutes before turning back.

Nearing home, the side door of the house across the street opened and the occupant emerged carrying a metal trash can to the curb.

"Good morning, Mr. Kobak."

Having deposited the load, the man looked up, "Jim! .. Jim Williams! Welcome home! We heard you were due soon." He extended his hand as Jim crossed the street.

Mr. Kobak was genuine in his enthusiasm and the two stood and conversed for a few minutes. When Jim recrossed the street he was thinking it really was good to be home.

"Hi, Mom!" he greeted her as he entered the kitchen and gave her a big hug.

"Where have you been? You're warm!" she smiled squeezing him to her.

"Just took a quick little walk. Needed to work up an appetite. It's not every day I get your home cookin and I want to be able to eat lots of it." He pinched her cheek, then added, "Boy! Mr. Kobak sure has gotten gray since the last time I saw him."

"Well, Jimmy, you know you were gone a long time and people do age."

"Not you, Mom," he grinned pinching her other cheek, "you look the same as the day I left, .. like it was only yesterday."

"James Williams, you know the Lord will punish you for lying."

She was pleased with her son and reached out to lightly slap his behind, but he nimbly jumped aside. She shook her head and happily went back to her chores. It was like old times.

Jim was seated at the table when his father entered and greeted his wife and son.

"Hi, Dad! It seems strange seeing you get up this late to go to work."

"Yeh .. and I'm not used to it yet. I like getting up early. One good thing though, I don't have to drive to the city. What's on your schedule today, Jim?"

"Heck, Dad, I thought I'd go with you today and give you a hand. I hear you still have a lot to do to get the place squared away and customers don't make it any easier. I can do some of the bull work for you."

"No, Jim! This is your first full day home and I don't want you to be tied down so quick. You can ride in with me and that way you'll have the car for the day. Besides, Bob comes in after school and gives me all the help I need."

"Sorry, Dad, I made up my mind. You can find something for me to do, can't you?"

Bill Williams looked down at his folded hands a moment, then into Jim's eyes, his pride in his son evident, "OK, Jim, ... if that's what you really want."

"That's what I really want, Dad."

And so Jim spent the day sweeping, scrubbing and painting at a fierce pace. When Bob arrived after school, he had difficulty keeping up with his older brother. When it came time to close up, William Walter Williams stood in the doorway and surveyed the interior. He nodded his head in approval at the results of the efforts of his sons. The domicile of the 'Triple W' was beginning to look for real.

*

That night after supper, a car was heard coming to a stop out front. Jim was out the door in an instant. Buck had arrived. The two friends met in the street, shook hands, slapped shoulders and just grinned.

"You salty old gyrene, you sure are a sight for sore eyes!"

They jabbered lightheartedly for about ten minutes before realizing the Williams family was standing at the front door waiting for them to come inside.

About an hour passed and Buck glanced at his watch, "Golly! I'm sorry, but I've gotta rush out. My mother has a late appointment with Dr. Chadwick."

"How is your mother coming along?" Sarah asked.

"She's coming along fine. This may be the last time she has to see the doctor." He looked around the room at the family, "Would you mind if I asked Jim to go along. She'd just love to see him."

"You boys go right ahead. It'll be good for you two to have some time together," Sarah answered.

"You sure you won't mind, folks?" Jim asked.

"Go on!" Bill replied motioning toward the door, "We'll be here when you get back."

"We won't be too long," Buck promised.

Mrs. Buchanan was indeed glad to see Jim. She hugged him like he was her own son. She asked him questions all the way to the doctor's office and all the way back. When Buck pulled into the driveway, she invited them in for pie.

Before Jim could respond affirmatively, Buck answered, "Thanks, Mom, but not tonight, please. OK?"

Sensing his friend's opposition to the invitation, Jim jumped in "Sounds great Mrs. Buchanan, but could we take a rain check for some other time?"

"Jim Williams, you don't need any rain check in this house. You just come when you feel like it."

"Thank you, Ma'am. I will, .. soon."

The two bid her good night and drove off. A block away Buck asked, "Feel like a coke?"

"Sounds good."

They drove to Collins Park and the snack stand now open for the season. They got a hot dog and a soda and returned to the car. A few bites and a few sips and Jim asked, "What's up, Buck? I kinda thought I noticed some edginess tonight and I've never seen you that way before."

"Aw ... it's Shirley, .. I just ..."

"My God! Don't you like her?"

"You know I do, else I'd never have written you about the whole thing. She's gotta be the sweetest, finest girl I've ever known."

"Well what's the problem then? Cripes, she thinks you're the greatest."

"I don't know. I seem to feel eyes on us when we're together."

"Damn, Buck, I never thought I'd hear talk like that from you. I know you're not afraid of stuff like that."

"It's not me I'm concerned about, it's her. I get scared for her. I know there will be times when I'm not there to protect her," a pause followed and Buck lowered his voice to nearly a whisper, "and then I get scared that maybe she'll change her mind."

Jim laughed out loud, "Ya know, you might think she's sweet and all, but she's a tough little cookie. She's got more of my folks in her than I have and she's a lot like Don, so I don't think you got much to worry about on either count. Besides, she's from a Marine family."

They chuckled, but Buck again turned serious, "Jim, I've really got to tell you something, cause I know you'll never hear it from your father. Last weekend he called me from his store and asked me if I'd stop in to see him some night. I said I'd come then if it was OK and it was.

"He didn't waste any time and started talking about Shirley and me right away. He said he didn't know how serious we were and that we were still quite young, but if we were serious, there could be problems. He mentioned the hate and the prejudices and the all round struggle. I sat silent. I never heard him talk much and I guess I was too surprised to respond.

"When he finished, I just kinda sat there, searching for words and after a bit he says, 'Buck, I think you're a great guy. It goes without saying what I think of my daughter. You two have seen a lot of each other lately and I know that both of you are serious kids. I want you to know that if you two have decided to seek a serious commitment, you have Sarah's and my blessing.'

"The only thing I could say was, 'Thank you, Sir!' and when I left, I was kinda like in a dream. Shirley and I had been talking for some time about how we were going to talk to our folks, but we never came to a conclusion. You're the only one who knew besides us. I don't know how the heck your folks knew."

In the darkened interior of the automobile Jim smiled the smile of satisfaction. He had never heard his father talk so to any of his children. Bill Williams acquired a new dimension for Jim. Despite never having heard such a conversation, Jim was not really surprised at his father's behavior. It was from their father that Don had acquired his straight from the shoulder honesty.

"I guess that makes it unanimous, Buddy. You know you'll get no less from me. I love my family, ... no matter how I've lived my life ... and I would lay that life down for them. I'd do the same for you, .. Brother!"

"Thanks, Jim. I guess I always knew what your reaction would be. I have never been able to think of you as anything but my greatest friend."

Jim smiled affectionately and softly punched Buck in the arm, "That's exactly the way I feel about you, Buddy."

Buck started the car and they returned to the Williams home, feeling good about the world.

*

Over the weekend the Williams family drove to the George and Mary MacPherson residence. Gramps had been failing badly for months. Kit MacPherson would be there when they arrived. She had completed her junior year at college and was spending some time with her grandparents, mostly to help care for her grandfather.

Jim's leave had been pretty good till now. That was changing. The closer they came to their destination, the greater became his misgivings. He was glad his father had asked if he wanted to drive. Giving his attention to the road helped some. He never stopped feeling the humiliation of that Thanksgiving day over two and a half years ago whenever Kit entered his mind. Fortunately he had not thought of her much during the prior two years. There had been other things going on in his life. Today, he could not help himself.

He steered the car to the front of his grandparents home and braked to a stop. Gram MacPherson and Kit were standing in the open doorway before the car emptied. His grandmother's exuberance at his entry into the house was what he expected, but he was taken aback by the warmth and affection of Kit. He was tense around her and was convinced he was not doing a good job of deception. Thankfully the group did not stand around talking, but were ushered into George MacPherson's room.

For a second time Jim was taken aback, but this time for a different reason. He struggled to maintain his composure. His grandfather not only looked much older than his seventy-two years, he was gaunt and worn, approaching macabre. The first to the bedside, Jim could not bring himself to ask his grandfather how he was feeling, "Gosh, Gramps, it's good to see you!"

From deep down George MacPherson gathered some inner strength. A grin seeped through. For a moment it overcame his ghostlike countenance. He extended a shaking hand. Jim placed it gently in his and felt the frailty. When he loosed it he bent and hugged his grandfather, all the time fighting for control.

Within a few minutes all but Jim were chased from the room to allow the two some time together. Jim loved his grandfather dearly and though his innards were being chewed to bits, his demeanor, accomplished with the greatest resolve, remained cheerful. In near desperation, his mind searched for a way to comfort. Soon, as if touched with some special power, he was speaking to his grandfather of China and its ancient culture. Jim's descriptions were vivid and his emotions came through and bouyed and captivated the older man who smiled proudly at his grandson. Jim told stories of Sal. He told of humorous events from their recent past, including the paint chipping incident aboard ship. He sensed the joy his grandfather was feeling. Their roles had reversed. Jim become the story teller and his grandfather, who was always capable of enthralling his grandson with his stories, was now a happy listener, all the while smiling and holding firmly to his grandson's hand. It was brief in the span of their lives, but it was something the grandfather would happily carry to his resting place and the grandson would never forget.

George MacPherson was petulant with his wife when she came to whisk Jim away.

"He's got to have his rest, Jim."

"OK, Gram." Turning to his grandfather he whispered into his ear, squeezing his hand gently, "Gramps, we'll talk again, later." He did not want to leave. When he got to the door, he turned and smiled, "I love you Gramps!" With a thumbs up, he softly added, "Semper, Fi, Gramps!"

His grandfather returned the smile and weakly raised his fist, thumb up.

*

Supper was a somber affair and afterwards the doctor called about writing a new prescription,

"Will," Mary said, "would you mind going to the doctor's for me and then to Lorenz Drug Store to have a prescription filled for George?"

Before his father could answer, Jim jumped in, "I'll go, Gram. I know where the drug store is and I'm sure I can find the doctor's office if you give me directions."

"I'll show you the way, Jim," Kit immediately responded.

Inwardly he cringed, but managed to speak without floundering, "OK, Kit. That'll be fine."

They waited, Jim uncomfortably, while their grandmother dug some money from her purse. They rode silently after Kit gave Jim the directions. When they arrived at the doctor's Jim went to the door and rang the bell. The doctor's wife answered and opened the door. After a few words she handed Jim a small piece of paper. He did not want to return to the car and Kit. The silence, his own doing, was eating at him.

Back inside the car Kit turned sideways pulling her left leg onto the seat as Jim steered the vehicle on its way.

"Jim, are you trying to avoid me?"

He caught his breath and struggled with the words, "No, ... not really, Kit. ... I .. uh.."

"Jim, I've had that feeling since you arrived. No! I've had it for sometime, ever since you answered my very first letter. Have I done something to hurt you, Jim? Please! Tell me if I have."

"Ohh, Kit! You hurt me? ... Never!"

"Then what's the matter, Jim?"

He drove in silence for a short spell.

"I guess ...." he took a breath and shyly continued, "I guess it's because .. I feel embarrassed and ashamed."

"Embarrassed! ... Ashamed! ... You feel embarrassed and ashamed! Why, Jim, why?"

"Dammit, Kit, don't you know?" The thought that he would have to explain himself left him more uncomfortable.

Her voice turned softer, "No, Jim, I don't." She was bewildered.

"Oh God, Kit, ... you must. I really made an ass of myself that night, .. forcing myself on you like I did. You musta hated me!"

She exhaled forcefully as part of a deep sigh, "Oh, Jim! So that's it! That's why you didn't write me or come to see us on your leave from boot camp."

"Yeah, .. I thought you were being kind to me when you wrote. You know, .. like it was the right thing to do for guys in the service."

"Ohh, Jim, I feel terrible to think that all this time you've carried that feeling around. As if you didn't have enough already. Do you know, ... that night, ... what was it, .. two and a half years ago, .. when I kissed you and you responded so fervently, I wanted you so badly. When you told me the story of your lost love, I was caught up in the tragedy. On top of that I was so impressed by your heroics on the football field, I was afraid we'd end up on the ground right then and there. I don't think, .. no, I know I've ever felt so strongly for anybody as I felt for you that night," then very softly, "no, Jim, I was not angry with you, I was really frightened of my own feelings, frightened of what I thought I might do, .. of what I wanted to do."

He did not speak right away, but savored the sense of relief and the warmth that engulfed him. He and Kit had been separated by self-inflicted, fraudulent misgivings for too long and now those misgivings were suddenly gone and he was again happy to be with her, or more appropriately, overjoyed.

When he pulled up in front of the drug store he turned off the engine and leaned back. It was a good feeling that permeated his entire being. He had loved Katherine MacPherson for as long as he could remember and it was good to know that he was OK with her.

At last he turned to her and spoke with humility and meaning, "Kit, you've made one dumb ass Marine, one happy guy."

She laughed the way she did when she was joyful. It was somewhat of a giggle. She swung her right leg around and rose to her knees and hugged him tenderly, as a mother might hug a child, his head on her breasts. When she pushed away he grasped her chin lightly and their eyes met in the diminished light of the car's interior.

"You are something really special, Kit."

"Then we're friends?"

"We are best friends!"

He got out his door and helped her exit hers and they went into the drug store and picked up their grandfathers prescription. When they were back in the car, she turned sideways in the seat, her left leg under her again and rested a hand very lightly on his shoulder. Before he reached for the key he turned and looked into her very blue eyes.

"Kit, you're the only person I've told about Connie and me. You're a special person to me, .. the way Don was."

"That's the most profound compliment you could pay me, Jim. Your secret, if that is your desire, will remain a secret. It will be safe with me."

"It's not that I want to keep some deep dark secret, I just think it would hurt my family, ... Connie's family too ... and crimany, it would sure hurt her ... and I've done enough to her already.

"I've done a lot of things I'm not proud of, that I wouldn't want my family to know about, .. for one reason or another. ... I guess I'm ashamed," he smiled self-consciously, "well, anyhow, there's one less thing chippin away at me, .. thanks to you. ... Boy! ... I sure have messed a few things up. Thank God my family doesn't know everything about me."

"Your family would never allow their love for you to be lessened by any deed you might think demeaning. I know them too well to believe otherwise. And Gramps has always been your champion ... and seeing the effect you had with him tonight, I don't wonder why. And knowing you, Jim, I suspect you are being overly hard on yourself. And since we're speaking of secrets, let me tell you mine.

"When Dad and I got home that Thanksgiving night, I couldn't get you out of my mind. I was experiencing all kinds of emotions, .. not the least of which was love ... and of course passion. I even went so far as to check the laws in our state and found that first cousins could legally marry. I began to romanticize briefly and during that time, I was in a real quandary.

"You know, Jim, there is something about you that is quite attractive to females. I'm not quite sure I know what it is. You're not ... overly handsome and you're not even a good conversationalist, .. at least not some of the time, .. but then, .. there are other times. There is just something about you that is appealing. I remember Mom saying something like that when I was a little girl and you were hardly old enough to have made that kind of impression. And Shirley has told me about the way the girls in school used to croon about you and ask her questions about you.

"Well, anyhow, I didn't know what to do and when you didn't answer my letters with anything but formality, time and common sense took care of it until Mal came along. So you see, you're not the only one with a deep, dark secret. Someday when we're old and gray, I may tell Mal. Maybe not. He is the only man I expect to know in my lifetime, but he almost became a close second."

She giggled heartily this time and squeezed Jim's arm.

"Kit, I love you! Thank you friend, thanks a million."

He started the engine and pulled away from the curb. They rode home side by side, Kit with her hand on Jim's shoulder, he, just happy to be there.

*

The following day, before the Williams returned to Shoreford, they bade their farewells to George MacPherson in shifts. Though Kit was staying on, she and Jim went in together. Gramps was very weak, but when he saw them together he made a special effort to smile. He knew that something had been amiss between them, but now, all was well. It was the last time Jim saw his grandfather alive.

* * *

He awakened well before her. That was normal for him. He could not escape the habits of the last two plus years. He had thought deeply about joining his friend on leave, but he was not ready for that yet. Someday maybe. It was as if he was afraid to commit himself to a relationship with a family. In fact, ... he knew he was.

Turning to his other side, he grinned. His bedmate was sleeping peacefully and as he observed her, he counted his good fortune at finding her, or perhaps she found him. While not beautiful, she was certainly attractive. Maybe she liked to drink too much, but then so did he at times. Most of all, they delighted in doing certain things together. It was that commonality of character that changed his grin to a smirk.

He abandoned the enjoyable thoughts of the warm body at his side, however, and decided something else demanded his immediate attention. The human bladder is not without limits. He slipped easily from the bed and headed for the bathroom. He did not close the door. She was sleeping soundly. Then he stood at the bowl.

At that precise moment, she was suddenly and rudely awakened. The frightful sound of his voice boomed from the tiny bathroom. Though her brain was fuzzy, there was no mistaking his resounding choice of words.

"Shhhiiit!!!" Sal Gennaro shouted at the top of his lungs.

* * *

Shirley graduated with honors and was one of the speakers at the ceremony. Jim was quite proud of her. He condescended to wear his uniform, for that is what she desired. He had not been in uniform since his arrival home and Sarah pushed him aside and starched and pressed a set of khakis. He spit shined his shoes to perfection.

Bill got to use the bathroom last. Everyone else was ready and Shirley wanted to have some pictures taken. They went into the backyard. Shirley asked Jim to be the first to pose with her in her gown. When he settled himself beside her she ordered, "Please put your cap on, Jimmy."

Standing behind his mother, Bob, two inches taller now than Jim, a silly grin on his face, was wearing the too small cap cocked at a rakish angle.

"Gimme my pisscutter, you little squirt!" Jim yelled jovially.

"Jimmy!" Sarah squealed.

"Oops! Sorry, Mom. I just wasn't thinking," he grinned foolishly at his mother. "Please hand me my garrison cap, Robert."

Shirley and Bob giggled and Jim tried faking penitence. Sarah looked into the heavens, sighed and shook her head. Jim had not seen her do that for some time. It was not only Jim and his sister and brother who enjoyed the moment. Sarah had difficulty pretending not to smile.

*

Over the years, Shoreford's wealthiest family, the Canterburys, had an open house the day after graduation at their Silver Beach estate. Buck and Shirley, after much persuasion, convinced Jim to go along with them. Buck drove up at six sharp, gathered his two best friends and drove away. Ten minutes later they were parked and crossing the huge manicured lawn. They passed under an arbor covered with roses, the only opening through the rose covered trellis fence and were in a gigantic rear yard, full of humanity.

Slightly behind Shirley and Buck, Jim passed by a small group of males, most of whom he did not know. He overheard the concluding words in a sentence uttered by a tall, lean young man, ".... little whore and her nigger pimp."

There were one or two stifled snickers.

With two swift and precise steps, Jim was in front of the speaker who was almost a head taller. His eyes were filled with fire, his demeanor intensely determined, yet deathly calm. His speech was precise and frigid and just loud enough to be heard by the thoughtless speaker and his immediate companions.

"You keep your fucking, ugly, dirty little thoughts to yourself, or you will not have another thought for some time!"

Jim could see fear in the eyes as they opened to their fullest. There was a slight quiver in the body. The mouth was silent and gaping when Jim turned with parade ground precision and walked coolly away.

"What's the matter?" quizzed Buck, waiting with Shirley for Jim to catch up.

"Not a thing, Buddy, not a thing. I'm glad I came. I think it's going to be a grand affair."

The three youngsters ambled around the spacious grounds and visited with friend and acquaintance. Jim began to feel like the spare tire. Having been away from Shoreford for more than two years, he was not acquainted with many of the younger crowd. Most of the people he went to school with were away from the town for various reasons. On the other hand, Shirley and Buck were well known and well liked by those who knew them. Those closest to them knew they were a twosome with promise.

"Look you guys, I don't want you to feel you have to ride herd on me and keep me entertained. Mix with your friends. I'll find my way around. OK? I've been gone awhile and I'm gonna have to reacquaint myself. Have some fun."

Buck and Shirley did feel obligated to Jim. They had talked him into coming when he was wavering, but they were also sympathetic to his feelings. They knew he meant what he said. Before they split up they made plans to rejoin at a specified time and location.

Jim was thirsty and walked to a huge punch bowl filled with lemonade. He poured himself a glass, took a swallow and scanned the large crowd for a familiar face.

"Is it as good as my mother's?"

Startled at the familiar voice, he spun around and came face to face with Connie. She had walked up behind him, unobserved. He could feel the excitement she generated, that sneaked surprisingly into his being as she moved closer, somewhat unsteady. Her words had a slight slur to them.

"No it isn't. How are you Connie?"

"I'm fine, Jimmy. You look wonderful. The Marines must treat you well."

"No complaints. How's your mom and Dan ... and the rest of your family."

"They're fine, Jimmy," she smiled and took the last step to his side, placing a hand on his arm, "they're away for the day."

He did not respond. She leaned against him, her eyes a bit fuzzy, but unwavering as they gazed into his, "Jimmy, we could stop by the house ... and have a few drinks, ... for old times sake."

Again he did not respond. Gazing at her he smiled shyly, swallowing hard to ease the tightness in his throat. His body tingled as memories of their tempestuous behavior surged through his mind. Suddenly he wanted to go with her, be with her and he castigated himself. He wondered why he was so foolish. He had wronged her and she threw him aside. He remembered the hurt and the anger and the crash of his dreams. Yet he still wanted to go with her. Then he saw the image of Soo-Ann. That helped.

Slowly and finally, he realized she was no longer who or what she was, ... nor was he. They could not restart their lives together and even if they could, he was not sure he wanted that. They could not begin again from some vague, passionate memory.

For reasons he did not fully understand, he felt sorrow for her. Maybe that was because she was getting drunk and it did not become her. Most of all, he did not want to hurt her, wanted to tell her he was sorry, but he also did not know how to do that, or how to make peace with her.

"Not tonight, Connie," he finally answered. "I really don't care much for drinking, but I can walk you home if you want to go."

"Why should I want to go?" she turned haughty, "I came here with someone. He'll take me home when I want to go." She removed her gaze from Jim and hesitated. Her demeanor changed once more. There was a hint of sadness in her voice when she returned her gaze to him, "Maybe I'll see you sometime."

"Right, Connie, maybe sometime."

He wanted desperately to put his hands on her shoulders, to look into her eyes and tell her he was sorry, really sorry, but she turned and walked slowly and uncertainly in the direction of a tall, fidgeting character, nervously casting sideways glances in their direction. It was none other than the bigmouth Jim confronted on the way in.

Connie spoke to the young man briefly and looking over her shoulder at Jim, put her arm through his. Extremely uncomfortable, her escort was more than pleased to hurry Connie from the grounds. They quickly disappeared.

* * *

The call from the clean little suburb outside Boston was a sad one. George MacPherson was dead.

Sarah took it hard in spite of the fact she knew her father's suffering was over. During her period of sorrow, Bill was able to offer her comfort, unlike when the news of their Donald was received. He held her in his arms for extended periods. Jim too was a comfort to his mother and she responded to the soothing influence in good time.

Bob spent three days in a state of bewilderment before he accepted the death of a man he thought would live forever.

It was Shirley and Kit who managed the chores at Grandmother MacPherson's and were towers of strength for their grandmother and Sarah. Through it all they maintained a quiet, dignified cheerfulness.

The funeral arrangements were handled by Uncle Ed, greatly aided by Jim. Buck drove up for the funeral as did Kit's fiancé, Malcolm MacDonald.

A large crowd gathered at the grandparent's home after the burial. When the chores were completed, Shirley and Kit joined

Jim, Buck and Mal in the back yard, slightly apart from the masses, which by now were thinning out. As the conversation progressed Jim became more of a listener, not because he was in any way bashful with these people, but he enjoyed listening to them. He liked being with them and he was sure the world was a better place for their presence.

Here he was at a funeral where he felt he should be mourning a man he deeply loved, yet he was feeling good about so much. His grandfather no longer had to suffer. That was a large part of it. Shirley and Buck, Kit and Mal were another part. And he liked what he was, .. well, most of it. That was the thing that puzzled him. Why was he unable to be like these companions he so admired. Oh well, every family had to have its black sheep. That thought created a tiny titter which he quickly suppressed, thankful no one had noticed.

*

Standing with his family and one of his two best friends, his mother, despite her attempt to lay some guilt on him, was quite jolly.

"Mom! I'm only going to be seven hundred miles away, not thousands, like before. If you get lonely for me I can be home for the weekend. How about that?" He pinched her cheek, "And you know, Mom, I'll be twenty years old in November. Don't you think that's old enough to be making my way in the world?" He grinned and pinched the other cheek.

"It's not too old to get a crack on your smart bottom. Which you should get anyhow for not bringing Salvatore along with you."

"Mom, you know Sal wanted to sow some wild oats and you would have cramped his style." What he said was true, but he said it like he was joking and his mother took it that way. He grinned broadly, "Moms are like that you know."

"Oh, the Marines has made you terrible, James Williams." She shook her head in mock disbelief, but was enjoying her son and his teasing.

"Anyway, Mom, I promise, we'll have Sal here before you know it."

When he climbed aboard the train, she was actually smiling.

It had been a good leave. No, it had been excellent, made the more so by the initial doubts and the guilty baggage he arrived with. True, his grandfather was gone and he would never see him again, but he had some wonderful memories. The way Gramps was with birds. The way he could relate to life and make an exciting story of it. The way he seemed to know when something was amiss, no matter how well concealed. And the dry humor that caught so many unawares, Bob so often the victim. And Jim would never forget that last night he saw Gramps alive, when their roles were reversed and his grandfather listened to him and was made happy, if but briefly. Lastly, the way he knew something was amiss between him and Kit, but departed this earth knowing it had been set right. He was truly someone special.

And there were the things he did by himself. He went to Burndys and had a milk shake, then visited the families of Tim and Tony. He walked the streets of Shoreford sure of himself. He visited the high school and some of his favorite teachers. The time with his former coach was great. Before he left the school he felt a secret pride in his own scholarly achievements, thanks in part to the positive comments of some of his former mentors.

At the Fourth of July celebration, he came upon Mr. Myers and walked right up to him and extended his hand and when they shook he said, "Good to see you, sir," and meant it, though his former boss got somewhat tongue tied.

He had considerably less irritation about Connie. He wished he could help her, but knew that was not to be. There were still twinges of guilt about the part he played in her life, as there was about the life of Soo-Ann, though for very different reasons. He knew he would continue to have those twinges, but maybe, he thought, he could better live with them. He was beginning to know himself. He could function and he could put things in some kind of orderly perspective.

And, there was that jerk he had threatened in a moment of extreme anger. Why did Connie choose someone like him? Secretly he was proud of that threat, only because it had been for such a just cause.

Looking up into the train's overhead rack, Jim smiled. The contents of the huge package of goodies would likely be in disarray by the time he reached Lejeune. Aside from all the stuff from Mom and Shirley, Kit, while at Grandmother MacPherson's made him a quantity of shortbread which his grandmother claimed was as good as hers. Grandmother Williams gave him a double batch of Welsh cookies and Mrs. Buchanan gave him a bundle of homemade chocolates. He would certainly be popular in his new outfit, .. at least in the beginning.

This leave, his father and he had conversed more than they ever had. They had always been close, but in a kind of formal way. The one thing Bill Williams did not tell Jim, was that he wanted him to join the business. For that, Jim was grateful.

Gramp's death hit Sarah Williams hard, but she recovered quickly and well. She looked great and was more like the person she was before Don's death. She could talk about Don now and relate openly to the happiness her oldest son had given her and the entire family in his much too short life, without that terrible sadness in her voice.

Bob of course would always be Bob. He was already a pretty good athlete and not a bad scholar. He would make his mark in his last two years at Shoreford High.

As for Shirley and Buck, Jim could not be happier. He had watched his sister come of age. She would not be eighteen for a few weeks, but she was so grown up. She knew what she wanted and she had guts. She met her match in Buck. He was as fine a person as walked the earth.

The final enhancement was Kit. They were once again best friends and he really liked Mal.

Yes, it had been an excellent leave.

* SIX *

He was warm under the blanket so he undid and removed the towel, almost dry from his body heat. The spread was slightly damp, but it too would be dry by the time he was ready to dress.

He sat up, swung his legs off the bed and took the towel into the bathroom, hanging it over a bar. Being neat was something that remained from his earliest days with Don. His brother was always aware of anything that would help others. Keeping their room neat meant their mother had less to do. When in boot camp, that trait became a way of life. It was a characteristic he passed on to his sons.

He crawled back under the blanket and squirmed into a comfortable position. He had never thought about the past in its entirety, only in segments when something jogged his memory. Those memories of his leave after returning from China were pleasing. Too bad all his memories were not as satisfying to recall, he thought. It was often his own youthful pursuits that were responsible for his displeasure with himself. He was better now at living within the bounds of his beliefs. He was not always that way as a younger man.

~ ~ ~ ~ ~

Jim Williams arrived at Camp Lejeune, North Carolina in mid July of 1948. The brick buildings, clean streets and manicured lawns were a far cry from the massive boondocks and beaches that occupied most of the gigantic, sprawling base which he would see much of in his stay here.

He joined the 6th Marines, the sister unit of the 5th Marines he served with in China. The two regiments fought side by side in France during World War I and earned great acclaim. He would continue to wear the small green and speckled red braid over his left shoulder, the forgierre, an award presented by a grateful French government, compliments of his forebears, one of whom was his Uncle Art.

Dress Blues were issued, something Jim had not worn in two and a half years of service. He received a green cloth belt to replace the fair leather belt and brass buckle worn with the forest green blouse.

Sal was in another platoon, but in the same company. He arrived two days ahead of Jim. The two walked to the slop chute on Jim's first night at the base. They had a lot to talk about since they parted a month ago. Enthusiastic about his leave, Jim did most of the initial talking, Sal listening attentively. He was visibly moved when Jim expressed his parents wishes that Sal return with him on their next leave.

"Ya know, Buddy, in all my life, I never had an offer like that."

"Well, whadaya say?"

"I sure gotta think about it. Thanks! That's some family you got there," he smiled putting an arm about Jim's shoulder, "but what about you? It sounds ta me like you had no love life."

"You can say that again."

"It sounds ta me like you had no love life."

They renewed their old game and chuckled. Sal gave Jim a slap on the shoulder.

"Hell, I've been doin all the blabbin. What about yourself, Sal? How'd it go with you?"

"Well, Frisco was OK. I met this babe in a bar one night and we got kinda chummy and a little zonkered. Next thing I know, she invites me to her apartment and shit, pretty soon we're in the sack."

"Just like Tsingtao, huh?"

"Well, .. not exactly. She works, but invites me to stay and that's OK with me, so I move in my gear and sight-see durin the day and woo her in the evenin. Since I give up my hotel and I'm loaded, we eat out and do a lotta boozin, .. which she loves. She's veeerry appreciative I tell ya."

"Well, about a week goes by and I'm thinkin, man this is really somethin. I go inta the head this mornin and there's a kinda white speck on the end a my pecker and when I start ta piss, it burns like hell."

"I'll be damned!"

"No, was me was damned," he chuckled. "Well, I really chew her ass out and she's bawlin like a baby and I grab my gear and go back to T.I. and turn myself in for the cure. Shit! Over two years in China and I gotta come back to the States to a round eyed, fair haired chick fer a dose a the clap."

Without waiting for a comment from Jim, Sal plowed right into a new topic, "Hell, didja ever see so many dress blues ... and no more fair leather belts either, .. it sure wasn't like this in the Old Corps."

They laughed, slapped backs and went into the slop chute.

* * *

It was a tough period for the Marine Corps. All the services were taking it on the chin, but the Corps was hit still harder. In addition to budget cuts, their role was being undermined, particularly by the Army. The new Air Force and even some in the Navy were also a party to this. Names like Eisenhower and Bradley and most especially President Truman were becoming anathema to knowledgeable Marines. Perhaps most surprising was the first Secretary of Defense, who had been Secretary of the Navy at the flag raising on Iwo Jima. He stated at that time, that that event meant there would be a Marine Corps for the next five hundred years. Even he was wavering, .. but he was a very sick man by now.

Jim followed the proceedings in Washington doggedly. Any feeling of kinship he had for the other armed services was diminishing rapidly. He kept all his mates well informed and Sal constantly prodded him for updates.

* * *

In late September Jim and Sal decided to go to D.C. for a weekend. The place was supposed to be loaded with females, which was not the case in the environs of Lejeune. They hitch hiked in their green uniforms, because rides were easier to come by in uniform. Arriving in the nation's capital in the late evening, they searched for about an hour until they acquired an inexpensive hotel room. The following morning, however, they did not descend upon the weaker sex. They took to the footpaths and sidewalks and visited all the places they heard about, but had never seen.

First was the Lincoln Memorial where they were taken under its spell and had difficulty tearing themselves away. By the time they did leave, they were filled with the emotion of the place. The Washington Monument followed and then the Capitol building and later the White House. They continued touring till their stomachs began to beg.

More and more Sal enjoyed the excursions with Jim. He was taken by, even somewhat in awe of Jim's grasp of history and the way he brought it to life. He fed on that knowledge and was himself learning and filling in on some of the schooling he had missed. Before dark they were sitting in an Italian restaurant enjoying some great spaghetti.

"Man, we sure covered some ground today," Jim said.

"Yeh! It's not the first time we did that. Frisco and Peiping, Honolulu, Manila and Tsingtao. And don't forget Jacksonville, North Carolina. Those places are filled with our footprints."

Jim chuckled, "Who could forget Jacksonville, North Carolina."

"You can say that again."

"Who could forget Jacksonville, North Carolina," he responded with a big grin.

Sal shook his head and sighed, then flicking his head quickly to one side asked, "Have ya noticed those two chicks across the way?"

Jim moved only his eyes in the direction Sal intimated. A pair of females was sitting a few tables away, "Yeah. So what?" Jim was careful not to look at the girls.

"Well, the short cute one, .. she keeps lookin at you and then says somethin to the other one and they both smile."

"So what?"

"Well I think we oughta have a go."

"Sal, you're nuts! You can't just walk up to a girl and put the make on her."

"Watch me."

Sal rose and walked to the table where the two girls were sitting. They watched him approach. Jim thought they looked pleased, but he wanted to get up and leave. Despite the intimacies he had shared with the opposite sex, his boyhood shyness, with girls he did not know, stuck stubbornly to him.

The girls received Sal cheerfully. They conversed at length and laughed easily. The taller of the two, the one Sal was most attentive to, took out a pad and pencil and wrote something. She ripped out the page and handed it to Sal. He stayed on a few moments longer while they paid their bill and prepared to leave. He graciously accompanied them to the door. When the shorter of the two passed by, she gave Jim a pleasant smile. He feebly attempted a response.

When Sal returned, Jim asked, "What in hell did you tell them?"

"I told em your mother never let you go out with girls and I had instructions from the skipper to watch over you, cause nobody knew what would happen the first time a female spoke to ya. Didja see when she walked by? She never said a word, did she?" Sal never cracked a smile.

"Boy! I sure don't need an enemy when I've got a buddy like you," Jim smiled, but was still uneasy. He was not sure what Sal had really said.

"Whadaya mean, look at this," Sal held up a small piece of paper. "Next time we're comin ta D.C., we're supposed ta let em know. They woulda gone with us tonight, but they had tickets to somethin. Ya know the cute little one's got the hots for you."

"Sal, you're nuts."

"Yeh, you'll see."

When the bill was paid they walked the streets in the early evening in search of a bar, though in D.C. bars were not in abundance. It was a partying city and parties were held in the home, ballrooms or wherever. Beverages purchased in stores were considerably cheaper than those sold in bars. The bars that did exist, were mostly frequented by the wandering servicemen.

The wine with dinner was enjoyed by Jim and was sufficient for him, but he would sip a beer for Sal's sake. They entered a place that had booths all around the walls and a double row in the middle. There was no drinking allowed while standing and the booths were all occupied. More than half the patrons were Marines.

"Have a seat, Marines, .. that is if you don't mind sitting with a couple of old farts." It was a gunnery sergeant, sitting with a platoon sergeant, who spoke. Both were in dress blues, as were all Marines present, being from nearby Quantico.

"Thanks, Gunny. Sure appreciate the hospitality," Jim answered and they sat.

The China Marines thought of themselves as salty. They were humbled by the hashmarks and battle ribbons of the senior Marines, who were most hospitable and drew the youngsters into their conversation.

About five minutes passed before Jim asked the gunnery sergeant, "Were you in the Fifth Division?"

"Yes I was. How'd you know?"

"The jump wings. My brother was in the 28th Marines and he told me a lot of Paramarines were in the Fifth."

"That's true. I was in the 26th. Was your brother at Iwo?"

"Yeah, ..." Jim answered, looking down for an instant, then back into the gunny's eyes, "he was there."

The gunny picked up on Jim's reaction and did not pursue it further. "We lost a hell of a lot of really good men on that stinkin little island."

The four got on quite well and during the second hour Jim endured a second beer.

Suddenly, a loud, rude voice boomed through the interior of the large room.

"I can lick any fuckin Marine in this place!!"

For the briefest moment, conversation ceased and ears perked up. In the open doorway was a huge soldier, his uniform in disarray, his words slurred. He was very drunk. Heads turned for an instant, then returned to prior activity. The soldier was accompanied by a buddy who was frantically attempting to pull him out the door. The big man had no intention of leaving.

Jim was uneasy. The man was well over six feet tall and no lightweight. He felt he should do something, though he knew not what and the big guy scared him.

The challenge was repeated. Sal clenched his fists and his knuckles whitened, the first time Jim had seen him react that way to a challenge. The platoon sergeant seeing Sal's discomfort said, "Don't mind that asshole. He's so crocked he doesn't know what he's doing. Probably won't remember this tomorrow."

For the third time the challenge boomed through the large interior.

"That's it! He's not that crocked!" Sal slid out of his seat and purposefully, calmly, walked to the entrance, confronting the soldier, "OK, doggie, let's go!"

He pushed by the soldier, almost a head taller and out onto the sidewalk. Jim was at his heels as was every Marine in the place. There was another bar diagonally across the street. As if the drums had sounded, it too emptied of Marines.

The antagonists faced one another. The onlookers gathered around. The soldier raised his fists as if he knew what it was about. Sizing up the big man, Sal stood for a few seconds. The spectators were silent, but there was a strong undercurrent of excitement. Sal finally put up his fists.

Jim expected to see a jab or a feint, but Sal came over the man's guard with a swift and stunning right that caught his opponent on the side of the jaw near the temple. The big man went down like a puppet cut from its strings. It was over. The soldier was on hands and knees, drooling and spitting blood.

A bus was approaching and the big man's friend said, "That's our bus."

With the help of a few Marines, the defeated warrior was pushed aboard. When underway, the soldier stood at a window shaking a fist at the crowd, which except for two sailors, was all Marines.

"I hate Marines," one of the sailors said to no one in particular.

"What's your problem, mate?" the platoon sergeant asked, standing next to him.

"Didja ever do brig time with Marine guards?".

"Can't say's I have."

"Well I did and I hate Marines!"

"I'll bet you do!" The platoon sergeant turned away and went back inside with the crowd.

One more time Jim was in awe of his friend's fast hands and cool behavior. He also wondered what would have happened had Sal lost. There were about thirty Marines at the site. Would each have taken a turn? He wondered?

Back in their seats, Sal remarked, "And the Army wants to get rid of us, .. fer that!" It was the only mention Sal ever made of the affair.

* * *

Combat training became the order of the day. It seemed to be one thing the Corps did not tire of teaching. Jim wondered if it would ever pay off. Too many in the nation were of the opinion the country would never again need a Marine Corps to storm some foreign shore. Many of the same individuals also believed that if there ever was another war, the Air Force and technology would be the answer. The Army would do any cleanup, .. if needed.

There were times during training when gasoline was in such short supply that tanks and planes were grounded and their crews could not join their rifle toting brothers as tankers and flyers. The finest combined arms team in the world had improvising to do.

* * *

It was nearly mid October when Jim and Sal exited the main gate with an overnight bag in hand. Their green uniforms and spit shined shoes were parade ground sharp. They would not be so when they reached their destination. They had the foresight to have the girls reserve a room in a city that did not always have one available. They arrived at the inexpensive hotel sometime after midnight. They slept late and showered and shaved and had breakfast. After that, Sal called Helen Darcy. They met an hour later and Jim was introduced to Jane Higgenbottom.

She was as cute as he remembered, short, with a full figure and nice brown hair in a page boy that bounced when she walked. Her eyes were light brown, her lips full, almost pouty. She wore a casual dress, as did Helen and their walking shoes were put to good use. After eating an early supper at the same restaurant they met in, they walked some more. Both girls were surprised at their escorts knowledge of the city, which was considerably more than their own. But the girls soon had enough and begged for mercy. Some gin and beer was purchased and they went to Helen's apartment, a modest flat where the living room became the bedroom when the couch was opened. There was a small kitchenette and tiny bathroom. It was neat and clean.

They talked, had a few drinks and laughed a lot. Jane was nervous at first, but lightened up considerably as the evening progressed. She did not drink much, but what she did drink had an effect. Slightly after midnight, Sal, who had been the perfect gentleman, said it was time to go. He grabbed Helen by the hand and they went into the hallway for some privacy before they parted.

Taking Jane's hands in his, Jim thanked her for the day together. He wanted to kiss her and thought she wanted the same, but shied away, "Good night, Jane, it was fun."

"Good night, Jim. I had a wonderful time. See you tomorrow, .. right?"

"Right you are." He knew she wanted to be kissed. He almost did, but instead, he smiled half heartedly and opened the door and went into the hall. Sal and Helen broke from a clinch, breathing hard.

The next day they went to the zoo and after a late lunch the two Marines had to start back. Jane gave Jim a soft kiss on the lips and he thought he would pull her to him, but did not. He walked close to a block before Sal caught up, breathing hard and sporting a large grin.

"Not bad, huh?" Sal gave Jim an elbow to the ribs, "It'll get better, I promise."

Jim glanced at his buddy and grinned as they headed for the highway and hopes of a quick ride.

* * *

The next two weeks were filled with hiking and sleeping out. The Marines in the battalion also readied themselves to fire the range. Jim and Sal had not done so since boot camp. In the evenings at the base, when time was available, Jim commenced some running. He liked the exertion, the sweating and the feeling of freedom and with time, forced himself to greater and greater effort. He even got Sal thinking about joining him.

* * *

D.C. was pretty much as before, but Sal and Helen were becoming more intimate. When parting time approached Saturday night, they went into the hallway well before Jim and Jane were ready to call it a night.

Jim thanked Jane anew. After some vacillating thoughts, he gently drew her to him. It was a nice, lengthy kiss, to which Jane responded eagerly. They tried it once more, warming to each other rapidly. Reluctant to part, their discretion bested their desire. When Jim was out the door and in the hall, Sal and Helen clumsily performed a massive disengagement.

Walking to the hotel in the cool night air, Sal said, "Pretty good, huh?"

*

Jim, Sal and the girls spent Sunday, or what there was of it, walking and talking. They ate lunch at Helen's. Readying to leave, Helen asked, "When will you come again?"

"We gotta build up some funds," Sal answered, "so I guess it'll be a month or so."

"Helen and I have talked it over," Jane spoke softly and shyly, yet was clearly excited, "and agreed that you can stay here and she and I will stay at my place ... if that's all right with you?"

"Gosh! That sounds great," Jim replied.

"We could go for that," followed Sal.

They made a date for two weeks hence and before Christmas leave, they had stayed at Helen's twice. She and Sal spent more and more time alone. They consummated their 'friendship' during those weekends. Sal would not talk about it, but it was more than sex that brought him back to Helen. It was a new and strange emotion he was experiencing. When he did take the time to think about it, he was not quite sure of himself. With Helen, there was no doubt, she was in love with the rough and coarse, but thoughtful and caring Marine.

Jim and Jane were more cautious, but were finding the growing intimacy was deepening their pleasure. Jane did not care for Jim's penchant for outdoor activity and she complained on occasion. Once she whined. That did not please Jim, but when they were alone, she was more and more excitable and exciting to be with. They were parting after an evening together in more agitated states, their clothing rumpled, their blood pressure reaching new heights. Yet Jim sensed that Jane was new to this and he did not want to force her into something she was not comfortable with. She, on the other hand, desired him greatly, but did not know how to go about fulfilling that desire. Fear had a lot to do with it. Jim was not aware of her desire, but he was sure she desperately wanted to be loved and that frightened him, though he knew it was love that should be the stimulus for what he hoped would happen.

Their last night together, before the holidays, they came very close to what Jim hoped would happen, but strangely, it was he who stopped it. He stopped because he was sure Jane was frightened. It was not a rational decision, but rather intuitive. For Jane's part, she was disappointed, yet at the same time, relieved. She was going home to Ohio for Christmas while Sal was going to spend the holiday with Helen, who like Sal, had no family.

The Williams wanted Sal to come to Shoreford and Jim lied and told them Sal could not obtain leave. Sal wanted to go with Jim, but was skittish about making his first visit to Shoreford over Christmas. Moreover, the allure of the holidays with Helen was the stronger desire.

*

Bill and finally Sarah Williams had come to terms with their son's vocation. Sarah vacillated now and again, but when Jim was home, she pampered him. It was her son's first Christmas at home since the one prior to his enlistment.

At first she did not allow him to lend a hand with anything. It became a game with him and he learned quickly not to ask her if she was in need of help. When she was doing dishes or preparing supper, he appeared at her side and dried the dishes or set the table. She argued, but he grinned at her and continued the task. When she was reading or sewing, he would sneak into the kitchen and make her a cup of tea. He persisted and she finally accepted his efforts. Soon she was smiling to herself at his actions and though she would be sad when he left, she made the most of his presence when they were together.

Two days before Christmas Jim drove Sarah to his Uncle Ed's. Kit was home from college and their Grandmother MacPherson was there for the holidays. She was slowly being convinced to give up her home and live with her son. Kit was graduating in June and she and Mal had a wedding date for soon thereafter. That was the deciding factor for Mary MacPherson. She was convinced that when Kit left, someone must look after her son. Jim and his uncle enjoyed a smile over that, but it was good for Jim's grandmother. She had something to look forward to on this first Christmas without her beloved George.

The gathering at Grandmother Williams was changing. The cousins were older and did not have the same youthful eagerness. There was also a new groom present. But the food was as good as ever and the sonority of the wonderful voices of the Welsh Williams was even better, for the glorious sound of Milton and Isabel Buchanan were a delightful complement.

During the singing, Jim often felt short changed with his own voice, but it mattered little. His ears were excellent and by singing softly, he could listen and be glad, even thankful for those ears and the wonderful sounds that passed through them.

*

The train was crowded the day after Christmas. Jim squeezed into a seat next to an attractive, slim, dark haired woman. He judged her to be in her late twenties or early thirties. She glanced at him as he tossed his pack into the overhead rack, then turned back to her book. He would have greeted her if she had not turned away, but now she was reading and paying him no heed.

The clacking wheels and the pleasant memories of the leave relaxed him, making it difficult to stay awake, but his seat mate moved and he was instantly alert. He turned slightly, mostly from curiosity.

She gave him a weak smile when their eyes met, "Do you mind if I smoke?"

"Heck no! I've got a buddy that smokes and he's not nearly as pretty as you." It was out before he thought and he was surprised, but also pleased with himself.

She smiled again, but openly and warmly this time. She pushed the pack towards him, "Would you like one?"

"No thanks, I have no vices," he chuckled and she smiled. "If you believe that, you'll believe anything," he chuckled some more.

She lifted her chin, just enough to look across her nose and studied him, "I don't know, .. I picture you as a fine upstanding gentleman."

"By golly, I think I like you!" Completely out of character, he was on a roll and had not even tried. He felt good. The conversation came surprisingly easy.

Before very long she said, "By the way, my name is Lucina Lucibello." She smiled, but there was authority in the statement that followed, "Please don't call me Lucy."

Jim cocked his head to the side and looked into her eyes, "That's a pretty name. It has a nice sound, ... sorta like poetry."

She had a wide mouth that displayed beautiful white teeth when she smiled and that was now. He continued to stare.

"Aren't you going to introduce yourself?"

"Sorry, beauty makes me tongue tied."

She stared at him as she had before and smiling, said, "You see? I told you I could envision a fine upstanding gentleman."

They both laughed.

Jim introduced himself. They talked for nearly an hour before he asked, "Where are you headed?"

"Washington, D.C."

"That's great!" he blurted enthusiastically.

"Why is that?" she looked at him again with the lifted chin.

"Because that's my favorite liberty city."

Turning sly, she egged him on, "Yeess?"

"Because I'd like to see you." He did not hesitate nor was he self conscious.

She had a way of taking her lower lip between her teeth when she was thinking, or perhaps, he fleetingly thought, it was an affectation, "I believe I would like that."

They never stopped talking all the way to D.C. She was from Providence and a wealthy family. She loved good food and she loved to cook, though her slender body showed no evidence of that passion. She had a PhD in psychology and was doing research on human behavior. Despite what he learned of her, he realized he was contributing most to the discussion. She was extremely clever in the way she drew him out. She was in control, but he did not mind. He was enjoying himself. He did not remember ever talking so much.

When they arrived in D.C. she went with him to the bus terminal. He bought two cokes. They sat on a bench, she with her appealing legs crossed, sipping slowly and exhaling smoke far into space. When the bus came, they stood together. He wanted to kiss her, but a sense of propriety stopped him. Then expertly, her lips were on his and the tip of her tongue brushed ever so lightly across the inner surface of his lips and it was over. It was exquisite.

He turned to board the bus and she touched his elbow, "You will call." It was not a question, but a command. It was unnecessary.

"You bet!"

He smiled one last time and climbed aboard, stowed his pack, sat down, waved as the bus pulled away, leaned back and said out loud, "Wow!"

*

Friday was New Years Eve. The barracks was empty. Half the battalion was on leave. Most of those remaining were on liberty or at the slop chute. Sal had pulled some strings and was back in D.C.

Jim lay on his bunk reading. He could not concentrate. He pushed the book away. "Nuts!" he exclaimed and went to the pay phone in the hall. He gave the number to the operator and inserted the coins.

"Hello?" the voice formal, unemotional.

"Hi, Lucina! Just wanted to give you a quick call and wish you a Happy New Year."

"Jim!" surprise in her tone, "How are you?" but it vanished immediately. "Are you in Washington?"

"Heck no, Lucina, I'm at Swampy Lagoon."

"You're where?"

"Camp Lejeune," he laughed.

"Ohh!" The tiniest hint of disappointment.

"I didn't know if you'd be home tonight, but thought I'd take a chance."

"I'm doing research, Jim. I choose my entertainment very carefully. One could attend a party every night in this city. I find diversions of my choice more pleasurable."

Without any difficulty on his part, they were conversing and when the operator cut in to tell him that his three minutes were up, Lucina interrupted and stated she would accept the charges. At other times he would have been uncomfortable with a female paying the way, but tonight, with Lucina, it did not bother him.

When they hung up, he knew it was an expensive conversation. For that reason he thought of trying to end it, but she kept him on the line. He was not sorry. They made plans for a meeting in two weeks. She was going to feed him and take him to a concert.

He took a second shower and got into his bunk. He was still awake when the sounds of the new year were heard, but he was not really trying to sleep. His hands were clasped behind his head and he was looking up into the dimness of the squad bay.

"Damn!" he said out loud, "She likes me!"

*

It was early Monday morning when Sal returned. He looked beat during the entire physically active day. He never complained and carried out all orders, albeit not always with enthusiasm. After supper when he came and sat on Jim's bunk, he was quite chipper. They had not been apart for long, but were happy to be together again. Both had things to say.

Sal was not jolly, but he was as close to it as Jim had ever seen him. His story, more detailed than ever, was at times humorously graphic and that was without the intimate details which he was wont to leave unspoken. The guy was in love and he was telling his best friend about it the only way he knew.

They traded stories and Jim mentioned Sarah's disappointment at Sal's absence. Sal was moved, but right now there was someone in his life. Jim told him about Lucina and their date two weeks hence. Jim and Sal would share that journey to D.C. The journey they would not share was the coming weekend when liberty was not available due to the port/starboard system.

Jim tried his best, but could not talk his friend out of going over the fence.

For the balance of the week, whenever they were together, Jim worked on Sal, but it was useless. Sal was going, liberty or no liberty.

"Look, I can get over the fence easy and when havya seen anyone check a liberty pass once yer out the gate? It's no big deal, believe me. Besides, if I don't go, Helen'll die." Sal laughed at his own humor. Jim did not share that humor. Sal was too good a buddy, too good a Marine to be heading down the road to trouble. It made Jim uncomfortable.

*

The hike lasted all day on Monday, a fair portion of it through sandy woodland. The temperature was in the high thirties, yet sweat was the order of the day. When it was over and they were back in the barracks the shower felt great and young bodies revived quickly and required other activity. Some went to Jacksonville and other North Carolina environs close by. Jim and Sal joined a large exodus to the slop chute. Over a beer and a ginger ale, Sal took the floor.

"See, I toldja it'd be easy. Nobody ever checks anything once you're out the gate. And boy! Was it cold in D.C. We didn't wanna go out so we hadda spend most a the time under the blankets ta keep warm." He chuckled like a young boy who had put something over on someone. "Jane called while I was there. She sure wants ta see ya, Buddy. Said she missed ya all the time she was in Ohio."

"I guess I'd like to see her too, but you know I have a big weekend planned with Lucina. Anyhow, we can ride up and back together."

"I'll call Jane and tell her ta come to Helen's on Sunday before we leave. Then you two can meet for a bit."

"No way, man! No way! Don't you even think of tellin her I'm in town!"

*

They split up early Saturday morning soon after arriving in D.C. It was cold and from the drop off point it was about four miles to Lucina's. Jim had more baggage than usual, but decided to walk. He did not want to arrive early and have to wake her. There was no traffic and he savored the fresh, cold air and the movement in his limbs after the inactive hours in various vehicles. He tried to keep his pace down, but found himself moving briskly in the frosty morning. Lucina's directions were precise and perfect. Jim turned into the street of her residence in just under an hour.

None of the buildings in the block were more than three stories. The fronts were of variously colored brick, some with simple ornamentation. There was an aura of affluence.

He thought it would be too early to awaken her, but from across the street he could see a lighted lamp in her windows. He crossed over and entered the building, searched for and found L. Lucibello on the mail box. He pressed the button. Immediately, the formal, "Yes?"

"Good morning, Lucina." He was not allowed to say more.

"Come right up, Jim. 2-A is the first door on the left, at the top of the stairs."

He went up the stairs two at a time. Lucina was waiting in the open doorway. He put his pack on the floor and she put her arms about him and kissed him on the lips. He responded, kissing her back. She pushed away. He felt like more, but instead, he stood while she unbuttoned his coat.

"You must be frozen!"

"It's not bad at all when you're moving." He told her what time he had arrived and where.

"Apparently you were moving. That is some distance to have walked in the time it took you. You did well, Jim. Are you hungry? Are you tired?" She moved her eyes over him and smiled, "You appear rather rumpled for a Marine."

"Yeh, I guess I do look untidy. I'm not very hungry, but I sure could use some sleep. I was surprised to see the lights on when I got here."

"I've been at work for some time. I have more to do, but first I'm going to make you a cup of hot cocoa and then I want you to take a hot shower and get into my bed. You can have your sleep while I finish my work."

She sat with him while he drank, not talking much, but observing. Once she put the lower lip between her teeth. She smiled occasionally and he smiled back. The taste was wonderful as the hot liquid rolled down into his stomach, warming and soothing him. The shower was even better and soon he was in clean skivvies luxuriating between the satiny sheets. The smell of her on the sheets was divine.

The bedroom door opened. She moved gracefully to the bed. Leaning over him, but holding his wrists at his sides, she kissed him very gently and did that thing with her tongue. Then she was gone.

*

Jim stirred and looked at his watch. It was eleven minutes past twelve and sunlight was pouring through the windows.

"Wow! It's noon," he said to himself while he lay on his back putting the pieces together. The bed was great and so was the smell. He stretched, spread eagling his arms and legs and forced his stomach up. Lucina was instantly in his thoughts. She must have come in and opened the drapes.

Thirty seconds later the door opened and there she was. She sat on the edge of the bed and handed him a cup of coffee. They conversed lightly and easily. When he finished the coffee she took the cup and saucer and said, "You may dress now," and left the room.

When he came out, she was putting lunch on the table. After eating and more light conversation, she quickly cleaned up and they left the apartment.

She took him on a tour of the city, including the Smithsonian. She was impressed with his knowledge and he did much of the talking. She held his arm as they walked, but it was more formal than romantic. They were back in time for showers.

Lucina showered first and dressed in the bedroom. Jim followed and dressed in the bathroom. He did not use the towel in his pack. There was no place to hang it. All the towel bars were occupied with large, plush, lilac towels and, he thought, much better than his.

She had pressed his trousers and sport jacket while he slept. He did not have civilian shoes and he touched up his spit shine.

In simple black dress, pearl necklace and earrings, she looked great. He enjoyed seeing her walk in high heels as she crossed the room in front of him, but the dress was long and he wished he could see more of her shapely legs.

When at last they were ready she stood back and observed him approvingly. A smile crept to her face, "You can take the Marine out of the uniform, but you cannot take the Marine out of the man."

They ate in the small dining area. She served him a delicious salad before the magnificent steak and baked potato along with the proper wine which he did not like as well as that served in the Italian restaurant. Conversation again passed easily between them, but something was gnawing at Jim's mind. He felt at times her purpose was not an interest in him, not romantic at least, but that she had him under scrutiny. He spoke of some things he might not have mentioned to another and he instantly had misgivings. He did not, however, dwell long on thoughts of that nature. Lucina was interesting when she spoke and she was very attractive. There was rarely a lull in their conversation until they were seated in the concert hall

The contemporary piece that opened the program was not something that stirred Jim and his initial reaction to classical music was not positive. Shortly after the opening of Brahms'

Third Symphony, he was deeply involved and during the second movement he felt emotions he had never known possible from music. He closed his eyes and allowed himself to be carried along. When the end came, he was profoundly moved. Without thought, he placed his hand atop her thigh behind the knee and squeezed. She turned just enough to look into his eyes and smile. It was a smile of approval.

When they returned to the apartment and put their coats away, she asked, "What would you like to drink?"

"I'm really not much of a drinker. How about some ginger ale?"

"I believe I can make you something you will like."

"OK, I'll give it a try." He was not enthusiastic.

Lucina went to work in the kitchen. Jim sat on a very expensive, very comfortable couch. It was his first real opportunity to visually explore the place. Behind the couch was an alcove with Lucina's desk. Two windows to the front of the desk overlooked the street. One window on each side, at an angle, with bookshelves from floor to window sills completed the cozy work place. Lucina had been working there when Jim arrived, the desk lamp being the light he saw from across the street. There was a speaker and mike close by, the reason she answered his ring so quickly.

The furnishings in the apartment were expensive. He had seen similar in wealthy homes in Shoreford. There were book cases throughout the large, open suite and all were filled to capacity. Everything had its place and was in it.

Lucina returned and placed coasters on the coffee table before handing him a tall glass with an orange colored liquid. She sat next to him, their knees touching.

"You do not have to worry," she smiled, "the drink is quite mild."

"That's not the part that bothers me," he lied a smidgen, "I just don't like the taste." He took a sip and there was a vague hint of something other than the orange juice. It was tolerable. He took another sip and placed the glass on the coaster.

Removing her earrings and necklace, Lucina placed them on the coffee table and positioned herself to look into Jim's eyes. As if it was planned, he slid his hands behind her back and she came to him. Their lips came together easily and tenderly in the beginning, but soon, their tongues were in a duel and excitement was building. She cleverly exposed her neck and ears to him and he explored those areas with lips and the tip of his tongue, then bit her tenderly about the ears. The swelling tempo of their passion increased their heartbeats as their breathing became labored.

Lucina seemed somehow to be controlling their actions, but once more, Jim gave it no thought. His enjoyment was immense. For most of an hour, everything took place above the shoulders. It was wild, passionate, unadulterated necking.

Her breathing was by now intense. Without warning, she released her hold on him, throwing her head to the rear, gasping greedily for air. When she had her fill, she groaned softly and exquisitely. Hands in her lap, she reached across her body with her outmost hand, placing it on his inner thigh. It rested there, only briefly, before she deftly slid her fingernails up the thigh and with one expert motion of her thumbnail, very adroitly, caressed the most shamelessly excited part of him.

Though covered by trouser fabric, the sensation sent shivers through his body. An unexpected, small groan escaped his throat. He was certain of the message she was sending. He wrapped her in his arms and pulled her to him, his hands on her back moving in ever larger circles, his fingers searching for the place he could unzip or unbutton the dress. He could find neither buttons nor zipper. When he tried to move his hands to her front, she incarcerated them with her arms. She did not say, 'No!' did not take his hands away, but calmly commanded, "Jim, I would like a cigarette."

He was befuddled as he watched her lean across to the canister and remove a cigarette. Aside from his confusion, he was too crushed to do it for her. She used the table lighter and when lit, she inhaled deeply and tilted her head back and exhaled powerfully at the ceiling, "Would you care for one? They taste wonderful at a time like this."

Still working at catching his breath, he took a deep one and exhaled, "No thanks. I'd probably stick the wrong end in my mouth and pop like a busted balloon."

Lucina giggled and when he heard her, he did too. It was the first time he saw her give in to humor in that manner. It passed quickly, however. She was serious when she looked into his eyes.

"There will be another time, Jim. You will come again. Go take a shower."

No explanation, just a command.

The shower soothed somewhat his battered psyche and he tried not to rationalize the experience. When he came out the couch was made up and Lucina was in the bedroom. When he was under the covers she came through and soon he heard the shower running. She was out quickly and when she made the return trip he said, "Good night, Lucina."

"Goodnight, Jim," she answered softly, but unemotionally. She shut the bedroom door and he was alone.

He lay awake thinking about his fortunes. This woman he found so attractive, had walked off and left him and he did not know the reason. To himself, he had thought of her as classy, but he had difficulty associating that word to her tonight. There was much unanswered by the time sleep finally came.

*

Reading and taking notes, Lucina was at her desk when Jim awoke. She got up and walked around to the front of the couch and a different character greeted him than the one he left last night.

"Good morning," she said cheerily, "are you hungry?"

He smiled back, albeit not through fully opened eyes and answered hoarsely, "Hi! For some reason, I'm starved."

"Good! When you finish in the bathroom, sit at the table and by the time you finish your juice, breakfast will be ready."

Not knowing why, he pulled on his trousers under the sheet as Lucina went into the kitchen. He grabbed his shoes and pack which she had placed at the side of the couch and walked bare footed to the bathroom.

When he came out, the couch was returned to normal. In uniform, he sat at the table and drank juice. True to her word, she arrived with a platter of pancakes as he emptied the glass and set it on the table. The pancakes were light and fluffy, the lean sausages beyond reproach. He was convinced she had made too much, but when he placed his utensils down, there were no scraps. She had not matched him morsel for morsel, but she ate heartily. With the second cup of coffee he lit a cigarette and handed it to her, trying unsuccessfully to subdue the cough seeking to escape his throat.

She thanked him and smiled sympathetically at his discomfort, "Would you care for more coffee?"

"Please. Then I'll get my gear together and hit the road."

He would have liked to hang around for awhile. He had a long wait for Sal. She did not ask him to stay. He was sure she wanted to get to her research, though it did not make him feel any better. She was on her feet after he finished the second cup of coffee. When he was up, she had already removed his overcoat from the closet and had it over her arm. She helped him on with it, then buttoned it for him as he stood near the door. Not knowing what to do, he did nothing. She slid arms about him and held him tightly, then kissed him passionately, her tongue stabbing, her loins pushing up into him, her finger tips digging into his neck and head. When they broke, they were breathing very hard.

"I will see you here in two weeks." Again, it was a command.

"Yeah," he answered, exhaling with force. He opened the door, "See ya in two weeks."

He thought of turning and blowing a kiss to her, but it did not seem appropriate. That was romantic and at the moment he did not feel romantic. He shut the door.

On the sidewalk he ambled along aimlessly, his mind confused. What was he trying to do? Hell, he knew what he was trying to do, but what was Lucina trying to do? Maybe she was having her period. That thought made him feel a little better. Damn! Why did she have to be so alluring?

He had not given Jane a thought all weekend. No reason why he should. He was busy elsewhere. Now he was concerned about bumping into her. Hell! She lived far from this area of the city. The worry disappeared and he did think of her. She was cute. Probably ten or twelve years younger than Lucina. Maybe Sal was right, maybe he should go and see her. No! That would have to wait for another time.

*

Much later, the two Marines met and started the long hitchhike back. They had good fortune and were picked up soon after their initial attempt, but there was enough time between rides for Sal to harangue Jim about Jane.

Since returning to D.C. from Ohio, Jane had made a decision. She knew that Helen and Sal were staying together and what they were up to. She decided there was no reason why she and Jim could not do the same. Since Helen was her good friend and she felt comfortable talking to her about such things, she did. Helen passed it on to Sal.

"For cryin out loud, Jim, she really wants ya to stay with her the next time you're in D.C. ... and ya know what that means," he chuckled.

"Dammit, Sal, I'm not going over the fence with you next weekend or any weekend. It's nuts."

"Come on, Buddy," Sal joked, "you're not afraid of climbin an jumpin, so it must be Jane you're scared of, but I don't know why, you're bigger an stronger."

Grinning broadly, Sal punched Jim on the arm.

*

For the first time in over three years, James Williams did not look forward to seeing the face of one Salvatore Gennaro. Every break from the drill field, the lecture hall, or in the field and worst of all, when the day ended, Sal was there. He had never been so persistent about anything.

"I'm tellin ya, Buddy, she really wants ta see ya."

"And I'd like to see her, Sal, but damn, don't keep askin me to go over the fence."

That was Wednesday after supper, a long three days since the weekend with Lucina and something occurred that brought a smile to Sal ... and Sal to Jim.

"I'm tellin ya, Jim, we don't hafta go over the fence!"

"OK, tell me again."

"I'm talkin to our buddy Stosh, about you not wantin ta go with me and he laughs and says, 'That's Jim, everything by the book. But maybe he's got a breakin point.' Then he tells me he's got the duty on Friday night and all I hafta do is come in and stand there when he goes to the head, our liberty cards will be on the desk."

"Dammit, Sal, it's one thing to do something and get caught and pay the penalty, but it's just not right to get caught and get a buddy in trouble when he's trying to help you."

"Stosh won't get in trouble an neither will we. And if we did get caught we'd never say that Stosh left the cards out. I'm right, .. you'll see ... So whadaya say? ... You'll go, right?"

"I don't know. ... We'll see. But dammit, you sure got me thinkin about Jane. You're incorrigible, Buddy," Jim said with a big grin.

"What's that mean?"

*

When liberty call came on Friday, Jim was sitting on his rack in his greens. While not privy to the intimate details, some of his mates knew he and Sal had dates in D.C. When they passed by they would tell him to, "Have fun!" or "Don't do anything I wouldn't do," or something similar.

Two of his squad mates came by together. "Don't be so down, Jim. Nobody ever comes in the barracks on the weekend and there's no such thing as a bed check, so you got nothin to worry about. Forget this crummy place and have a great time. In your position, I know I would. When you can get a date with a pretty chicky, grab it."

The other laughed and vulgarly added, "Yeah! Get laid, Buddy!"

At that point, Sal came into the squad bay and waved, "Let's go, Jim!"

He picked up his gear and joined Sal at the entrance. Sal handed him his liberty card.

*

It was 3:30AM when they got to D.C. A half hour later, they arrived at Jane's. Helen lived two blocks away. Sal showed Jim into the entryway to the basement apartment with the small windows at ground level.

"Hey! Good luck, Buddy. As if ya needed it. Have fun, yeh!" Sal whispered softly, giving Jim a smirk that was visible from the light of the street lamp. Then a wave and he was on his way.

Jim knocked three times very softly before he heard feet on the floor. Seconds later, a voice, "Jim???" She sounded frightened.

"Yes, Jane, it's me," he whispered, close to the door.

She opened the door, the chain still in place, the dim light of the hall lamp touching her soft, little girl's face. She squinted through the opening.

"Hi!" he whispered, then chuckled quietly when she opened the door wide to let him in.

"What's the matter?" she timidly asked.

Standing in a heavy robe pulled hastily about her, the hem on one side higher than the other, her hair was tussled about her head. Unsure of herself, her guilt diminished her more.

"You're rumpled," Jim chuckled, "but it's cute. I like it."

She put her hands to her hair as if to hide it and hunched her shoulders self consciously. Jim walked through the door and gently pulled her to him.

"Don't kiss me," she meekly pleaded, " .. my mouth tastes awful."

He laughed out loud, "It's OK," and held her more tightly, resting his chin in the rumpled hair. It smelled good. She was trembling slightly and he rubbed her back, seeking to soothe her.

Her face was against his overcoat. Her voice fragile and uneasy, "What do you want to do, Jim?"

"Right now, the one thing I'd like, is sleep."

She relaxed. After a hurried intake of breath and expiration, that was part sigh, she stepped back and looked up at him. A shy smile spread over her features. She said in an almost normal voice, "It's so good to see you, Jim," then hugged him sweetly.

"Let me wash up and clean my teeth and I'll be in the sack in a jiffy."

When Jim came out of the bathroom, Jane started in, but stopped and turned to face him.

"I'll turn out the light for you to get undressed."

She did, then entered the bathroom and closed the door. He heard the toilet flush and heard her cleaning her teeth.

The room was cold. Undressed to his skivvies, he moved quickly to feel the warmth of the bed. When Jane returned she took off her robe and timidly entered the bed. She turned her back to him, pulling up her feet. She was at least a foot away.

He lay quietly, sensing her discomfort.

"Jane," he softly called to her, putting a hand on her back. The flannel nightgown did not hide her chilled body.

She flinched, just a modicum and tried to control her voice, but there was quaver, "Yes??"

"Give me your hand."

She lay on her side, quite still, but slid her hand to the rear. He knew the feel. It was a small, soft hand, but right now, surprisingly cold. He held it gently for what seemed ages to his tired body. Her breathing eased and she rolled cautiously to her back. He squeezed the hand tenderly. She was relaxing and before he lost consciousness he felt movement and she rose to an elbow and looked down at him.

"Jim, ..." her voice was soft and apologetic, "I've never done .. anything like this before."

He forced himself awake and rolled to his side. Grasping her by the shoulders he gently eased her onto the pillow. He stretched and kissed her forehead, then lay beside her, both on their backs. When sleep came, he was still holding her hand. It was quite warm.

*

Jane was reading in the room's only stuffed chair when Jim squinted through a partially opened eye lid. She glanced at him sideways and when his eyes opened fully she quickly returned hers to the book. He stretched and moaned happily.

"Good morning!" he said.

She turned. "It's almost good afternoon," she answered, trying to be light hearted, but there was still a hint of self-consciousness.

"Did I sleep that long?"

"Yes, you did." She was easing up.

Jim sat up and swung his feet to the floor. Feigning embarrassment, he grabbed a blanket and covered himself and grinned, "Oops! Sorry."

Her cheeks became light pink and she started to turn away, but fought it and continued to gaze at him. A faint, timid smile crossed her face.

As he rose wrapped in the blanket, he put a hand in front of his mouth, turned his head away and with thespian aplomb screeched, "Aaaghh! Don't you dare kiss me! The birds have pooped in my mouth."

She giggled uncontrollably and when she was almost back to normal, laughingly said, "Oh, Jim, you're silly."

He stepped to her and carefully pulled her from the chair. She came happily. He hugged her to him, the blanket sliding to his waist. Her face was against his chest and when she looked up at him, her eyes reflected her good humor and her affection for him.

"Would you like something to eat? You must be famished."

"That sounds great! But would it be possible to take a shower first?" Then he grinned comically, "I brought my own towel."

She giggled again, "Of course, silly."

She backed away and the blanket fell to the floor. He was standing in his skivvies.

"Ooohh my goodness," he shrieked as he bent to retrieve the blanket, "you did that on purpose, you ... you voyeur!" She was shaking with mirth. Trying to appear cross, he went on, "Well, .. well, .. didn't you?"

It was awhile before she could speak. Even then her words were interrupted with chuckles, "Oh, Jim, ... you are ..silly." She tried, not entirely successful, to be serious, "Would you ... like .. eggs?"

"Sounds good to me." He picked up his pack and headed for the bathroom. He stopped, grinned and looked back over his shoulder, "Care to join me?"

She turned instantly red and blurted "No!" and looking away, added sheepishly, "I took one already."

Twenty minutes later Jim was at the table. Eating a quantity of eggs and toast and sipping down juice and coffee he was able to observe his surroundings. The apartment was a replica of Helen's, but smaller. The bed was again a couch. The appliances and furnishings were old as were the plumbing fixtures. Jane turned the heat off at night, but it was quite comfortable now. The place was clean, but unorganized and cluttered, quite unlike Lucina's.

Jane wore a plaid, flannel shirt, a few sizes too large. It probably belonged to her father, or a brother, he thought. The jeans were another story. They were the right size and fit her nicely, hugging her hips. Her hair was perfect and Jim enjoyed watching it bounce when she walked. She wore no make-up except for a light colored lipstick. She was at home in the kitchen and Jim thought her really cute as she moved about. When she served him she was pleased with his appetite and joined him for his third cup of coffee.

Jim wore civvies when they walked in the afternoon and they walked a considerable distance. The cool wind turned Jane's cheeks pink under the stocking cap pulled down over her ears. She did not complain once as she had in the past, but clung to him tenaciously, her arm wrapped tightly about his. Sometimes she lay her head against his shoulder. They did some shopping and when they returned to the apartment, the day was turning to night. When they removed their outer garments Jim mixed her a Tom Collins with ingredients they purchased. He sat in the stuffed chair and watched her sip her cocktail as she put away the inventory of the days outing.

With that accomplished, Jim commanded, "Comere!"

She obeyed with a smile. He reached out and took her hands and pulled her to his lap.

She came gladly. Her cheeks against his were cold still. He kissed her and she kissed him back. It was a light kiss, a friendly kiss, but it changed soon enough and the passion and easily lit fire of youth was consuming their practicality. He pushed her away.

"What's the matter, Jim?" she asked, both surprised and hurt.

"Whoa, lady! I can't take much more of that and do what I planned."

Realizing he was not rejecting her, she perked up and smiled. Her confidence returned. The smile turned to a silly grin, "What did you plan, master?" She bit his ear, surprising herself at the case with which she accomplished it.

"I want to take you out to supper."

"I thought we were going to eat here."

"Well, I've been thinking about that and I'd really like to take you out."

"Ooohh!" Her surprise turned to elation, "That would be wonderful, .. but where would we go?" Her eyes brightened even more, "How about the restaurant where I first saw you ... and we ate once before?" She looked into his eyes and pleaded, "Please? Their food is so good and it's very reasonable."

"How could I resist such a pretty damsel and her plea? Yes, Milady, that is where we shall go."

"Oh, Jim, I love you." She kissed him hard on the lips.

"You see, it's paying off already." He pinched her cheek. She stuck out her tongue.

"But I'll hafta wear my greens, .. cause I've got no jacket or tie with me."

"I'd prefer that. I like you in uniform. That's how I first saw you."

She showered, then he showered. She went into the bathroom in her robe while he dressed in the living room. He looked at magazines for no more than ten minutes when the bathroom door opened.

The dark green dress showed off her full figure much better than her earlier attire. In high heels, the top of her head was just below the tip of his nose.

Reservations were made. They called a taxi. She would not let go of his arm in the cab and out and into the restaurant.

With Jane's permission Jim ordered a bottle of Chianti. They had a salad and pasta on the side and Jane delighted in the veal parmesan while Jim enjoyed an eggplant dish.

The wine was loosening her tongue and she took heart in her new found confidence. Jim listened. When she was not complaining Jane had a pleasant sounding voice and tonight, she had not a complaint in the world. She was bubbly and straightforward and her happiness was contagious.

She told him how she had sat with Helen and after many quick glances at him had mentioned to Helen that he looked like the kind of boy she could bring home to her mother. Helen's reply, "What! A Marine!" They both laughed, but soon her eyes turned soft. She rested her chin on the back of her clasped hands and was content to just gaze at him, her face a silly grin. It made him uncomfortable and he got her talking again.

To complete the meal, a second bottle of Chianti was needed, at least, that was the decision. Neither wanted desert, but they did have Italian coffee and at the waiter's suggestion, a sambuca. Before they departed Jane's cheeks were ruddy, her eyes sparkling and she was finding humor in everything Jim said.

As they were leaving the restaurant, when the cold night air slapped her face, she whistled "Phheww!" Turning her gaze to his eyes, she smiled almost giddily till seriousness overtook her. Squeezing his arm, she softly, but with feeling said, "Oh, Jim, you're so nice to be with."

In the cab she lay her head on his shoulder. It stayed there the entire homeward journey.

After Jim paid the driver, he helped her exit the cab. She was a little unsteady and he asked for the key. She fumbled around in her purse before handing it to him. The hall was not well lit, but he found the lock and opened the door. He took her by the hand and led her inside.

The apartment was warm. He helped her off with her coat and removed his overcoat and blouse and hung them on hangers.

When he turned, she was standing in the middle of the room, her face a broad grin. Without ceremony she kicked off her shoes. One landed in a chair, the other skidded across the floor. He went to her and she forced her body into his.

"Aren't you going to take me to bed?" she giggled, the words coming out in a modest slur, spoiling her attempt to be nonchalant and worldly.

"Are you sure you feel up to it?"

"Are you sure, you, feel up to it?" she giggled loudly, "I sure do!"

They kissed so hard their teeth clinked. He released her and pulled out the bed and threw back the covers.

"Undo me!" she commanded impatiently and turned her back to him.

"Just a minute."

He turned on the small stove lamp and switched off the overhead light.

Unzipping her dress he reached for the hem to pull it over her head, but she slid her arms free and wriggled it to the floor giggling softly as it fell. He did pull the slip over her head and when it was gone, she crushed herself against him. They kissed passionately, their tongues dueling fiercely.

Finding the bra snap he undid it and slid it off, then held her at arms length. There was enough light to see her skin. It was without blemish except for a small mole on her right side. Her breasts were full and quite firm, the nipples small, hard and erect. She stood for his inspection which he enjoyed to the fullest. She stared back at him. He slid his hands through the waist band of her panties and pushed them down, lingering over the roundness of her buttocks. When the panties crumpled on the floor at her ankles, she energetically, but ungracefully kicked them away. He carried her to the bed, sat her on the edge and unsnapped the stockings from the garter belt and rolled them down her legs and off her small feet. She removed the garter belt and threw it across the room, then lay back, legs apart, arms straight out from the shoulder.

He was undressed in no time, then beside her. They kissed furiously. He held her to him with an arm underneath while the other hand traveled her body.

Arms tightly about his neck, she recited into his ear again and again, "Oh, Jim, I love you! I love you!"

He touched and twiddled her most sensitive spot. She shuddered, squeezed against him and asked in a plea, "How much do you love me, Jim?"

He could not give her the answer she desired, the answer she needed, but clamped his mouth to hers, his tongue working furiously. She shuddered again, but violently this time and wrenched her mouth away. Without warning, with all the strength in her body, she pushed him away.

"Ooohh, my God!" She gasped, starting to cough and gag. She rolled awkwardly off the bed and onto the floor, on all fours. She struggled, uncoordinated to her feet. Weaving clumsily from side to side, she ran, staggered, into the bathroom, her mouth covered by both hands.

On hands and knees, Jane was severely throwing up into the toilet when Jim hastily reached her side. He kneeled beside her, reached to his side and snatched a wash cloth. He soaked it with cold water and held it to the nape of her neck. The other hand he placed under her forehead for support as her body heaved and she emptied her stomach.

Sleep did not come easily for either of them. Jane was miserable. Her head ached and her stomach was in severe distress. Jim held her limp, naked body in his arms for a very long time. Occasionally she had body tremors. A few times he heard her whimper. He dozed, but only fitfully.

About two o'clock she got up and went into the bathroom. In the confusion of her mind, she wondered if her malady was an omen. She donned her nightgown and returned to the bed, quite unsure of herself. She curled into a ball and lay as close to the edge of the bed as she could get. She stayed there.

*

It was hot when Jim awakened. The heat remained on during the night. He did not feel rested. The early morning sun was beginning to light the interior. Jane sat in the stuffed chair. She wore the nightgown she had donned during the night and her legs were pulled up and encircled by her arms. Her chin rested on her knees.

She was not aware of his movement and he lay awhile studying her, wondering what he should do. He forced himself to rise, ignoring his nakedness. He went behind her and placed his hands gently on her head amongst the very tousled hair. She did not move and he bent and kissed the top of her head.

He removed his hands and picked up his pack and went into the bathroom. He splashed cold water on his face and gargled mouth wash. He pulled on his skivvies and trousers before returning to her.

Retrieving one of the cushions from the couch, he placed it on the floor at the foot of the chair. He took her hands in his. She neither resisted nor helped. He carefully pulled her from the chair, maneuvering her onto the cushion. She assumed her previous posture.

Working his way into the chair, Jim sat behind her and placed his bare feet along her buttocks. He rubbed her shoulders and back, tenderly at first, but with gradually increasing pressure. He used finger tips on her head further aggravating the hair. She sat without moving.

The sun was well up when she loosed and stretched her arms and unlimbered her legs. She pushed her feet off the cushion and forward across the floor, slowly and wearily rotated from the waist and looked up at him.

In a voice filled with pathos, her face covered in pain, her eyes somber and red rimmed, she asked, "Am I going to lose you, Jim?" Before he could reply she lay a cheek on his knee and sobbing softly continued, "I had such great plans for us this weekend. I always seem to mess things up. I thought when I came to Washington I was leaving all that behind, but..."

"Enough talk!" He stood up and forcibly lifted her to her feet. He wrapped her in strong arms. "Look! I want you in the shower in sixty seconds. What do you think you can eat?"

"I don't know, Jim. You can't fix breakfast."

"Yes I can! Now what do you want?"

She sighed deeply before answering, "Oh, just some juice I guess."

"You've got to eat something!"

"I can't."

"You must!"

She pondered and sighed again, "Oh, maybe some toast."

"OK!" He stepped aside, gave a gentle push to her slouching body and commanded, "In the shower!"

Her slow obedience elicited a sharp slap to the behind, "Go!"

She snapped upright and moved to the bathroom door, sheepishly glancing over her shoulder, not knowing what he might do next.

She was in the shower an exceptional length of time. He made the bed and folded it away. He did not feel like eating, but knew he too must.

When Jane reappeared she was in her robe and had a towel about her head. Her face was shiny and almost normal except for the bloodshot eyes. She appeared vulnerable to Jim. She smelled of soap and he hugged her. She was glad for his attention. Glad he was still there. He disengaged and pushed her into a chair at the table. She sat with her hands in her lap, her head slightly bowed.

She drank some juice, but would not touch any of the stack of buttered toast. Jim ate three pieces and pushed one in front of her and ordered her to eat. She dawdled with it, but finally nibbled till it was gone. He forced another on her and she repeated the performance and sipped a cup of coffee with cream and a lot of sugar, then half a second cup.

"Jane, I've really got to hit the road. I'm to meet Sal at ten. We really can't let anything screw us up from getting back on time," he grinned, "even if we have to take a taxi."

Sadness blanketed her expression, because he was leaving, but his comment surprised her, "Take a taxi, .. why?"

"Just joking. I'll tell you about it sometime."

"Then I will see you again?"

"Yes."

She was relieved, if only for the moment.

He rose from the chair, put on his blouse and stood near the door, overcoat and pack in hand.

She came to him with cheerless eyes and drained emotion. "Will you ever forgive me, Jim?"

He placed his gear on the floor. Holding her chin he smiled affectionately, "There's not a damn thing to forgive!" He paused briefly and studied her, "Do you hear me?"

Doubtful at first, she was pleased. It showed. She rose on her toes and kissed him hard, with ardor, her tongue plunging into his mouth. In an instant he desperately wanted to open the robe and fondle the soft, sweet smelling, clean, naked body underneath. He fought with his resolve and prudence prevailed, but even that could not stay his hands. He tenaciously grabbed the roundness of her buttocks, lifting her to him, her legs parting, hugging and squeezing his hips as their loins crushed magnetically together.

Frantically and clumsily he disengaged ignoring her desperate grip. He reached for his gear, picked it up and blurted, "Gotta go!" In one final impulsive act he slid the towel from her hair, bent and tenderly kissed the top of her head, then sped away.

It was five past ten when Jim stepped onto the side-walk. Sal was coming toward him and stopped to wait. When Jim drew abreast Sal was grinning and laughingly asked, "Well, didja get ..."

"Noooo!" echoed loudly down the almost empty street.

Laughing with rare raucousness Sal said, "You never tell me nothin."

The two Marines made good time on the return trip. Their liberty cards were back in the file and no one the wiser, at least no one who would give them trouble. They took no chances. A buddy would not be put on the spot, most of all, one lending a helping hand.

They were able to obtain some sack time before reveille, something rare when they made the trip to D.C.

*

Jim received his Good Conduct medal at midweek, almost a month late. He had completed three years of service with no disciplines and no infractions. The weekend's escapade he got away with. He felt lucky. He promised himself he would not do something similar again.

Sal, by his own admission, would probably never complete three consecutive flawless years. The skipper echoed that sentiment during one of Sal's extra duty levies. The sad part thought Jim, Sal was one of the best in the field and when trouble started, there was none better to be with.

On Thursday Jim went to the PX and bought a ribbon bar. It would hold the three he now possessed. A full row after three years. His brother had two full rows in less than ten months, but that was war. If wars accomplished anything, it was to add ribbons to the warrior's chest, especially Purple Hearts.

He attached the bar to his dress blues. It did not look bad along with the crossed rifles of his expert badge and his basic badge with three bars. He only wore the blues when necessary and he did not wear the decorations on his greens. He took an extra moment to stare at the blues before closing the door of the locker.

All the training and details that week were routine except for the extra consignment of drill. Long periods of field work depreciates snap on the parade ground. Jim and Sal joined a couple of buddies in the slop chute only one night. Conservation of funds was a prerequisite to the numerous forays to D.C.

*

Thoughts of Lucina were in Jim's mind as he readied himself for the trek north. Did she have class as he originally thought? Now he was not sure. He was sure that she wanted no entanglements in her life. She wanted to live that life her way and do what she wanted. But she was gracious at times and he was drawn to her, perhaps for some hidden, perverse reason, for she held out to him a promise of wild adventure.

With that in mind, Jim had the Corporal of the Guard wake him at 0500 Saturday morning. Sal went on ahead Friday. Lucina gave Jim specific instructions to arrive for supper at 6:00PM and he did not want to spend all that time in D.C. with no place to sleep and nothing to do. And he had no desire to bump into Jane, however remote that might be. He would return to Lejeune with Sal.

By 0625 Jim was on the road hitchhiking. He waited eighteen minutes for a ride. He climbed into a tractor-trailer going straight through. The cab was not especially warm, but the driver had removed his left shoe and sock, resting the left knee against the door. Jim watched fascinated as the driver rubbed between his toes and scratched his foot nearly the entire journey.

Lucina opened the door at precisely 6:00PM and Jim knew by the look on her face she was pleased with his surprised reaction. Her expression, while not smug, was certainly self-satisfied and more than a little confident.

"Do you approve what you see?" she teased.

"Approve? Wow! Your beautiful!" He could not take his eyes from her.

She bit her lower lip before smiling broadly. She took the few steps to him, kissed him on the lips and stepped back quickly, escaping his grasp, "My word, Jim, you are really cold! You must warm up in the shower. Supper will be another forty-five minutes."

He did not obey immediately. His eyes did not want to give her up.

She wore a gorgeous, black satin gown that matched her hair. The fit was perfect, not skin tight, but loose enough to move when she moved. Her arms were bare, the straps over the shoulders thin. The neckline plunged with abundant cleavage to a few inches above her nipples, which at the moment were prominent beneath the fabric. The gown caressed her hips and fell almost to the floor. When she turned, which she accomplished with a gracefully gentle spin, the fabric was released from her body, but came back to rest and cling to her buttocks, revealing two. There was nothing underneath.

He wanted to touch her, hold her, but he knew she would not permit it. He wondered about that characteristic.

She followed him into the bathroom and watched as he undressed, causing him some minor discomfort, but he did not hide from her. When he climbed into the shower, she returned to the kitchen.

Jim often had trouble understanding women. He certainly did not understand Lucina, but he did understand that her eyes on him excited him. He stood under the hot, pelting stream, not knowing what might be next. He never questioned Lucina about any of her actions. It was as if she had him in her spell. Maybe, he thought, he wanted it that way. At any rate, this was not the time for questions. He made the decision to be here and now it was time to reap the fruits of that decision.

Under the hot water in a semi-lethargic state he was unaware of any movement until he felt her naked breasts compress against his back. Instantly her entire nude body was crushed against him, her arms about his chest. He returned at once to reality and tried to turn and meet her head on, but she squeezed him and said, "No!"

She slid her hands slowly and erotically downward till she reached her destination, his response instantaneous. She fondled him only briefly, then moved her hand expertly and vigorously. He was soon loosing control, leaning forward, hands against the tile wall, groans escaping his mouth.

By the time he regained his strength he was more confused than ever and Lucina was gone.

A plush robe was hanging from a hook. He had been instructed to don it, which he did. Then he went to the kitchen.

Lucina was busy preparing their meal in the dress she had on when he arrived. Her hair was perfect and there was no evidence of her excursion into the shower. She smiled at his reappearance and showed no sign that anything unusual had taken place.

Sitting on a stool he gazed over the counter watching her at work, this alluring woman who was such an enigma.

Supper was superb. The spinach salad with Lucina's homemade dressing was a fitting beginning. Garlic embellished the leg of lamb to perfection. The yams, touched with brown sugar and blended with melted butter, an incomparable plate mate. Neither Jim or Lucina wanted desert. They were sated, but well into the second bottle of wine which Jim found he liked. Lucina's eyes were more alive than he had ever seen.

"I know you do not smoke," she smiled, "but I have something here quite different. You must try one. I promise you will find the experience unusual and enjoyable."

"No thanks. But you go ahead."

She eyed him disapprovingly, but went ahead and lit an irregular looking cigarette. It had a strange odor, not unpleasant, but unusual. Conversation was becoming less easy for Jim and mostly he listened as Lucina spoke of pleasure. It was weird coming from one who until today seemed so conservative in her pursuit of that adventure.

When there was almost nothing left to the cigarette, Lucina was very relaxed. She rose from her seat and without emotion ordered, "Come with me."

Jim obeyed, following her into the bedroom. She deftly removed her gown. He wanted to gaze at her, "Stay a minute. You look gorgeous that way."

Instead she got into the bed and commanded "Come to me Jim."

"Wait a second I have to get something."

"Never mind!" her words impatient "I have taken care of everything. I have no intention of becoming involved with my namesake."

He did not understand her remark, but removed the robe and joined her in the bed. He tried to embrace, kiss her, but she distracted him and handed him a small appliance. The expression on her face was new and different, excited ... and anticipatory.

"Many would pay for what you are about to learn Jim. Push the button, I'm going to educate you."

The little machine came to life in his hand. She put her hand over his, moving to places of extreme enjoyment, then with verbal instructions, allowed him to navigate.

She lay on her back, arms and legs stretched outwards, her body writhing and undulating in a deluge of excitement. She groaned and yelled three times in climactic ecstasy and whipped the machine from his grasp and grabbed his head and moved it over her. He obeyed without thinking. She screamed, but would not allow him to stop. He was so caught up in her ardor, he was startled when she yelled, "Fuck me you bastard, fuck me now!!!"

She accepted him, treating him to nearly violent action, catapulting her into a further frenzy of movement and vocalizations. He was carried along, lost in his own unremitting passion till at last, their efforts collapsed and they were used and exhausted.

Apart, they lay on their backs, chests heaving from laborious breathing.

Finally life seeped back into Jim's body and limbs. He rolled to his side. He would have embraced her, fondled her, but she would have none of it.

"Go shower, Jim."

When he exited the bathroom the couch was made up and the bedroom door was closed.

*

It was a restless night. Jim was awake before daybreak. He got up, dressed and got his gear together. He pulled the bedding off the couch turning it again into a daytime furnishing. He rolled up the bedding and placed it on the couch.

Lucina had not awakened. He wanted to write her a note, he felt he owed her that. Glancing at the desk he spotted a container of pencils, but no paper. He debated going through the drawers to find some, but then she was there, standing in the open bedroom doorway.

There were large, dark crescents under her eyes. The hair that was always just so reminded him of Medusa. Standing with shoulders slouched, she appeared drained, her naked body, previously enticing and desirable, sagged and seemed without tone or grace. Her appeal was gone.

Strangely, he felt a distant pity. He wanted to say something, he knew he should say something, but there was nothing there.

"I gotta go."

She did not reply, just stood, expressionless.

He took his eyes from her and walked out the door and into the rush of early morning chill. Roused by the cold, Jim Williams searched for lucidity. He remembered Connie's description about feeling dirty and right now he was feeling just that. He made this journey for one purpose and it had happened.

Why did he not feel elated, he wondered? He felt somewhat similar to the way he felt that day in Tsingtao, except much worse. But that was because of Soo-Ann. Today was not.

As he walked, he wondered where he should go to wait for Sal. He thought about calling Jane, if only to have a warm place to wait, but decided that was stupid. But the longer he walked, the more cold he became and the more cold he became, the more a stupid idea made sense.

"Hello?" was the somewhat tentative reply just after eight o'clock.

"Hi, Jane, it's Jim."

"Jim!" excitedly, "Where are you?"

"I'm passing through D.C. on a quick trip."

"Can you stop by?"

"I'd like that." He was not sure whether or not that was true, but he wanted to go someplace out of the cold and be with a friendly human being. "I'm about a half hour away."

"Wonderful! I'll see you soon." She sounded happy as they exchanged small talk before hanging up.

He dialed Helen's number.

It took five rings before a rough, grumpy, impolite voice barked into his ear, "Who in the hell wants ta know?" Jim started to whisper and Sal yelled, "What?"

"Sal, It's Jim!"

In the background he could hear Helen, "Give me the phone!"

"It's Jim!" Sal muttered and took a few moments to calm her. "What's up, Buddy?"

Jim explained that he was going to Jane's and they reconfirmed their meeting time, but changed the location.

Twenty-five minutes later Jim knocked on Jane's door. There was no fear this time when she threw the door open and rushed into his arms. Instantly she was on tiptoes and smearing his face with kisses. When she stood back to gaze at him he saw the shining skin, the smiling lips and eyes and the neat hair, damp, but all in place after the hurried shower. Suddenly he was glad he came. It felt good to be wanted.

She made eggs and toast and coffee and more coffee. She ate little, but observed him and was glad. When they were finished she did not clear the table.

"Why don't we sit in the chair, Jim?" It was her idea and he liked it .. and it helped him forget.

Immediately she was in his lap, arms about his neck, kissing him, kissing him with wild enthusiasm.

Time was passing, but he was unaware of the clock. He had not planned on this, but he liked it. It was not long before he was being aroused. She was aroused. It turned to passion. Their breathing became labored and their hearts were beating faster and racing unchecked.

A message went to his brain which hurried it to his muscles. He forced himself from the chair with her overheated body in his arms. A thought flashed through his mind, "This is the way it should be!"

He placed her gently on the couch and kneeled beside her squeezing her breasts through her clothing. She put her hands atop his and increased the pressure while she scrunched her eyes shut and moaned quietly. He worked a hand free and ran it down her body, under her dress, up the inside of a thigh. He touched and rubbed her mons pubis under her very wet panties. There was nothing to think about, least of all, that time was moving on. He pushed the dress up and clumsily pulled the panties down, impatient when they caught on her shoes. He stared at her most private parts completely vulnerable to his view.

Unbuckling his belt he fought with his own trousers and shorts. He got them to his ankles as she whispered almost inaudibly, "Jim! Please don't!"

It did not register, since her legs did not resist, but came easily apart. He fell upon her, searching for the breach in her nether realm which he swiftly found.

His ear was close to her mouth. Again she whispered, her voice weak, but frightened, "Jim, please, ..." and more weakly, meekly, "please!"

Again he heard without understanding. He was in a frantic struggle and he plunged forcefully into her. She whimpered and stiffened the instant she felt the stab of pain, but he was only aware of her burning internal flame which engulfed him and swallowed him up.

And yet again, weakly and almost unheard, she sobbed, "Please, Jim, .. please! Don't, ... I can't! I can't!"

Her body was vibrating and the tiny sobs were nearly imperceptible, yet somehow, suddenly, the words sunk into his frenzied mind and came crashing into his consciousness and he felt the agony and the shame for what he had almost accomplished and forced on her.

With all the will he could muster he came away from her, collapsing to the floor, his bare bottom on the cold linoleum.

She lay unmoving, legs spread wide, drained of emotion. He was as one defeated and could only stare at the glistening, pubescent mound, now just below the level of his eyes. Sadly, reluctantly, he forced her legs together, pulling her dress down as best he could, .. to hide her shame.

The clock continued to move.

She began to cry then, very softly, but steadily. She fixed her eyes on the ceiling and apologized extensively and his distress soared as she uttered those apologies. The apologies should be his. That is what he thought. He knew now ... he had heard her, but in his rush, in his haste for his own gratification, he had not listened.

Between sobs she blubbered, "Jim, ... I .. do .. love you ... and .. I do ... want .. you."

It took more time for she insisted on apologizing and professing her love for him. He held her hands and rubbed her cheeks and forehead and she was calmer and she listened while he sympathetically reasoned with her.

"Honey, you don't want me. I could never make you happy. I'd be gone for months at a time, maybe years. You need someone at home to care for you and love you. When I went to China I was gone for more than two years and P.F.C.s are not allowed to take dependents along on tours like that."

She cried some more.

"What am I going to do?"

"You'll do fine. Someday you'll find a decent guy, ... you'll see. There's more than one guy out there that can make you happy. You've got too much going for you for the good guys of the world to miss."

The crying and sobbing was subsiding. Jim patted her hands and tousled her hair and kept smiling and reassuring her and all the while, the hands on the clock continued to move.

When the banging on the door started, Jane bolted upright to a sitting position.

"Jim! Are you in there?!!"

Jumping to his feet where his bare bottom rested on the floor, Jim was tangled in his trousers which refused to set his ankles free. He plunged head first across the room landing near the door. His behind exposed shamelessly, he lurched and jerked and tried to cover his ignominy while struggling to the door on his knees, finally regaining his feet. Pulling his trousers and shorts up, he turned the knob to allow Sal to enter.

"Fer crissakes, yer an hour late aready!"

Jane was crying again. It seemed like forever, but Jim rubbed her back and head and held her securely and ultimately, she quieted down. At last she sat without his support. He wiped her eyes and when the tears were finally cleared away she looked down at the floor and saw her panties. Sal was looking there too. He quickly glanced at Jane, lost his composure and grinned.

Flinging herself across the couch, she scrunched up in the fetal position, facing the wall. She bawled like a baby. Sal very wisely went into the hall to wait while Jim went back to work.

He worked frantically, soothing and massaging and talking and it seemed longer than it was. When at last Jim felt he could depart, he pulled Jane to her feet and held her. She lay her head against his chest and he lifted her chin. Her eyes held a plea he could not satisfy. He kissed her with compassion and got out the door as quickly as he could. He heard the crying start again, but continued with Sal to the street.

At first Jim was fearful Sal would ask his usual crass question, but his buddy never said a word, though he glanced at

Jim on occasion. Jim thought, "Someday, maybe I'll tell him about it." For the moment, he was glad for the silence.

They got the first ride easily, but were stranded outside a diner on 301 until two Marines came along in a souped up jalopy. They had, to put it conservatively, an exciting ride, for there was much time to make up. They turned in liberty cards with less than an hour to spare.

*

Monday afternoon Jim was at battalion headquarters waiting for some paper work. Spotting the large dictionary he remembered Lucina's words. Searching for the letter L, he ruffled through the pages until he found 'Lucina'. There was something about Roman mythology and the goddess of childbirth.

He thought many times that day about his 'women' of the weekend. One was incapable of love and had used him and he had asked for it .. had wanted it. The other had so much love for him, yet he did not want it, but nearly used her for his desires. He was glad he failed.

Jim sat exhausted on his bunk after supper. He thought of his family and wondered why he was so different. From his parents, .. from Buck and Shirley, .. from Mal and Kit? He knew he was loved as much as any. Why did he do those things that betrayed and denigrated that love? During his leave when he came home from China, so many situations were set right not the least, a better attitude. Now he was chasing the flesh again.

He went to his locker and removed the new Good Conduct medal. He stared at it a long time, put it away and crawled into his bunk, the squad bay still brightly lighted.

PART II

* SEVEN *

She tried to be quiet, but he was not asleep, though he pretended to be. He eavesdropped as she prepared to shower. It was not as if she would have done anything different had she known he was observing her. He was getting away with something without her knowledge. Afterwards he would tell her and she would joke about his hopeless behavior. Then they would laugh together and she would kiss him. They enjoyed their little games which thrived in the love of their relationship.

If he had talked to her then, joked about sneaking a peek, it would have taken some of the sting out of the denigrating judgment he passed on himself. The bad memories of his misadventures in Washington D.C. were truly that, bad memories and though he almost never thought of those times, he gritted his teeth when he did.

She disappeared into the bathroom wearing a robe. It did not disguise the fact she still had a very nice figure. Like him she was an active person. She walked like an athlete, well coordinated, on nicely formed legs.

When at last her image left his minds eye he drifted back to yesteryear.

~ ~ ~ ~ ~

In the coming months Jim made every effort to forget the immediate past. He enrolled in two courses with the M.C.I. He stayed on base, especially on weekends and attended more movies than ever before. His savings grew.

The port/starboard liberty restriction was lifted and Jim was immensely relieved for Sal's sake. He was certain his buddy would be caught sooner or later on the constant excursions to D.C., excursions that were taking such a toll on Sal he was finding it difficult to live within the bounds of his pay allotment.

The two friends no longer frequented the slop chute. They did their socializing in the barracks and Sal joined Jim on his evening runs. Jim loaned him whatever he needed and it was always paid back promptly on payday. By mid April Sal owed almost his entire pay to Jim.

Then, one Monday morning, the two met as was their custom before falling out for PT.

"Hi, Buddy, how's it goin?" Jim greeted his friend cheerily.

"Ahh, .. you know, .. ya win some, ya lose some."

Jim stared quizzically, "What's up? You look beat."

"Beat up is more like it." Sal turned away briefly then looked down at his feet. "Helen and ... Helen and me ... we split."

"Damn, Sal, I hate to hear that. I'm sorry. I know how you felt about her."

"Ahh, .. it's OK. It just wasn't workin out. She really wanted ta get married."

They walked a way in silence. When Sal lifted his eyes he looked directly at Jim, "Ya know, I really liked that girl, but ... shit, Jim, marriage scares the hell outa me. Shit, with all the crap I've seen I just can't see me there."

Jim put a hand lightly on his buddy's shoulder and gave a gentle squeeze. PT was more challenging for Sal that morning and lack of sleep was not the reason.

And so, Sal Gennaro was plucked from financial ruin. His mood changed little, never evident to anyone but Jim, even the aura of thoughtful reflection, something quite new. Sal signed up for an English course with the M.C.I. Jim was so proud of his buddy he took him to the slop chute one night and Sal came away pleasantly tipsy, never having bought a drink.

There was one piece of good news Sal brought back from that final voyage to D.C. Jane had returned to Ohio. Jim was happy for her. He was certain she would find what she was looking for in her own back yard. He wished her well.

* * *

In October Jim took a leave, primarily to see Bob play football.

In his final year, Bob had been the starting quarterback since he was a junior. From the clippings the family and Buck sent Jim, his kid brother was pretty good, his customary ebullience a contagion to his teammates. According to Buck's observations, Shoreford displayed a remarkable enthusiasm on the field which helped to make up for their lack of talent. Buck was not alone in holding the view that the leadership of Robert Owen Williams had something to do with that enthusiasm.

Bob did not possess Don's quiet charisma or imperturbability, nevertheless, the younger Williams was a worthy leader and notable asset to his team. As Don had been, so Bob was elected captain for his senior year. Jim was looking forward to seeing his 'little' brother in action, but he was also looking forward to seeing his family, absent from his life for nearly ten months.

There was an added bonus. Sal was joining Jim. Sarah accomplished that. In a letter to Jim, she commanded him to call home on a certain night and to have Sal at his side. No match for Sarah's motherly expertise, Sal was easily convinced.

The entire Williams family, including those in Newville, were familiar with the tragedy in Sal's young life. Without exception, they wanted to reach out to him and share something absent for so long from his life. But most of all, it was Sarah and Bill.

Though outwardly reluctant to accept the invitation, deep down, Sal was pleased.

*

The two Marines arrived in the city during the late afternoon. Buck and Shirley picked them up at the railroad station. When the initial excitement of the homecoming was over, Sarah chided Jim for his long absence, but it was only a light case of planting her usual seeds of guilt. She then proceeded to make Sal very welcome.

"Salvatore, it's so good of you to come and bring Jimmy along. He has not been home much in the last three years. I do believe I can count on you to get him here more often. And then you will be here too," she said smiling cheerfully.

"Ma'am, it's not good of me to come. You asked me and that's what's good ... and I sure thank you. You and Mr. Williams have been swell ta me, Ma'am. I sure don't deserve it, but I'm glad you asked me. And ya know, Mrs. Williams, that's the first time I've been called Salvatore since my mom called me that."

Leaning back in a chair, Jim was grinning. It was not a grin of amusement. It was a grin of satisfaction and pleasure.

"Do you mind if I call you Salvatore then?"

"No, Ma'am, .. I guess I kinda like it?"

"That's fine, Salvatore, but you must remember to call me Sarah and my husband, Will, .. or Bill, which is what most of his men friends call him. Will you do that?"

"Gee, Ma'am, I .. a .. I don't ...," he looked at Jim and knew the answer immediately. He grinned and shook his head, "Yeah! I think I'd like that."

Thus did one Salvatore Gennaro begin his relationship with the Williams family. He accompanied Jim on visits to both Jim's grandmothers, his uncles and their families. They visited Isabel Buchanan, Kit and Mal. They spent a lot of time with Buck and Shirley. And as would have been expected, Sal got on greatly with Bob.

For Sal though, the best was his relationship with Bill and Sarah, especially Sarah. He was treated as a son and it had a profound effect on him. The reserve that was so much a part of him never had a chance to materialize. He was nurtured and thrived in an atmosphere like none he had ever known.

Aside from the pleasure of seeing one of his two best friends experience a positive change in his life, Jim got to know his brother better. Being four years older, Jim left home before he and his younger brother really had a chance to know each other as teenagers. Jim missed three of Bob's high school years. He had some catching up to do.

The night before the football game Bill discovered that Sal liked pinochle. Buck stayed for supper and when the kitchen was cleaned up it was decided to have a game. Bill took Sal for a partner and Buck teamed up with Jim. Bill enjoyed a cigar when playing cards and he gave one to Sal. They also had a beer while the nonsmokers sipped birch beer. Sitting behind Buck, Shirley was no help to him at all. Her advice often got him in trouble, but Buck smiled and played on, taking his lumps with humor. Bob sat between Sal and Jim and happily cheered on one side or the other. Unfortunately for Jim and Buck, Bob's more frequent comments were things like, "Oh, crimany, that's too bad." Sarah insisted on keeping the glasses full. It pleased her to stand behind any of the four and offer encouragement, though she had no knowledge of the game.

It was no contest. Father and Marine buddy shellacked son and civilian buddy. When it was over, they all sat around the table and talked till quite late. Bob, who was supposed to be in bed at an early hour would not be denied his place in the group.

After Buck departed and the family was in bed, when only Jim and Sal remained in the kitchen, Sal said, "You got a great family, Buddy and a great friend. Ya know, I've never had a Negro for a buddy, but I like that guy, I really like him."

"I guess I never thought of Buck as a Negro."

"Ya know, .. that's the way it oughta be."

*

The game was a win for Shoreford and Bob, despite his lack of sleep had a pretty good day. It was as if he saved his best performance for his brother ... and Sal. There would be a third Williams kid to be remembered on the gridiron.

*

On the day Jim and Sal were to depart, Buck arrived to take his two friends, one old, one new to the station. When Buck came in through the side door Sarah was fussing over 'her boys'.

"Now don't forget, Salvatore, put in for your leave the same time as Jimmy. I will certainly feel much better knowing the two of you are traveling together."

Three young men smiled at her attentiveness, but did so as unobtrusively as possible. Jim wanted to kid her about her mother hen attitude, but decided it was not the time. He could see where her emotions were heading. Sure enough, when they left the tears flowed abundantly.

At the station Buck parked the car and walked with them to the station, down the steps, through the tunnel and up to the platform. The Marines thanked him.

Shaking Buck's hand Sal said very seriously, "Don't give up on the reserves, Buck! The Corps can use a good man like you. I expect ta see ya at summer camp. Don't forget, keep after the bastards. Things're tight right now, but one a these days they'll be takin some people in. Don't forget!" then pointing a finger at Buck, "I mean it, Buddy."

"Thanks, Sal." Buck shook his head affirmatively grinning all the while at his new friend, "I will. I sure am glad you came home with Jim. I'm looking forward to the next time. You take care of yourself."

Sal punched Buck lightly on the arm.

"Take care, Buck. Thanks again for the ride. We'll be seein ya soon, Buddy," Jim said as he grabbed his friends hand and pumped vigorously, punched him lightly in the arm and started up the steps of the coach.

Aboard and beginning to move, Jim and Sal caught a quick glimpse of Buck waving from the platform and returned a snappy salute. Finding a vacant seat they stowed their gear before sitting.

After about a minute Sal turned to Jim, "Ya know, he'll make a helluva Marine if they ever take him. What's the matter with those assholes anyhow.?"

"It probably has something to do with quotas. I wonder when they'll wise up. But I think if anybody makes it, Buck will. He doesn't give up and I'm sure you know by now that he's pretty special."

Sal shook his head, "You better believe it." He paused a moment, "Ya think he'll ever drink or smoke or swear?"

They both chuckled. The train was picking up speed and they sat silent awhile before Jim spoke.

"You just heard me say that Buck was pretty special ... and that he is, but I want you to know, I think the same about you. I can't imagine having two greater buddies. Sal I've watched you go through hell and you never bitched or moaned and you've always been true to your beliefs and to me. I could never ask for anything more in a friend. But you've given more. And now when I see you with the family, I really feel great. Semper Fi, old friend!"

Sal self consciously punched Jim on the arm.

"You got one helluva family there, Buddy!"

Jim slowly and softly replied, "Yes, it is."

There was a long silence before Sal spoke again, "Ya know, Jim, ... I don't know what you think a me fer not comin to see your folks sooner, but ..."

"Sal, you don't owe me any explanations."

"Jim, I gotta tell you this. So listen ta me." Their eyes locked, Sal intent on his mission.

"When we got to the west coast from China, I really wanted to come east with ya and ... you know, .. spend some leave time with you and your folks, but I wasn't ready yet. Don't ask me why, cause I don't know, ... I figured I just wasn't ready. Well, you know what happened there and I guess that's what really made me think about it, ... after of course, ... but I still wasn't sure a myself. Then along comes Helen and I guess you know," he hesitated a moment and looked away, then back at his friend, "she really threw me fer a loop"

"Yeh, I knew, Buddy."

"Anyhow, I made it this time and I don't know if ya know it or not, but that's the best time I ever had with a bunch of people ... I mean with a family, ... since before my old man and sisters got killed."

He paused and looked out the window briefly, allowing himself the time to pass over a bad memory. Turning back, he locked into Jim's eyes again, "Anyhow, I've never been treated so ... so .. so great and I never felt so good about it. I've known a lotta shitty people in my life, but this leave was fulla somma the ... the best folks I ever knew lived. Geeze! I don't know how else ta say it."

"I don't think anyone could have said it better, Sal. You did just fine, Buddy."

"Well, anyhow, it's no fuckin wonder you're the way you are," Sal smiled self consciously. Jim laughed out loud. The train sped on to New York City. It was nearly there before Sal lit his first cigarette.

* * *

The year was nearing its end. Just before Jim and Sal went north to Shoreford, Jim was promoted to corporal. He did not have time to write his family. He was proud, even pleased, but was also concerned. The idea of being responsible for other men's lives was a staggering thing to him. At the same time he was thankful that the nation was not at war. He required experience in his first command. He would work hard at that and he would get it. Of that he would make certain.

* * *

Bob picked them up at the station. The younger Williams was quick to notice the new stripes on his brother's sleeve.

"Jim," he excitedly yelled, "you made corporal! Great!" He turned to Sal and without a thought asked disappointed, "Where's yours, Sal?"

Sal laughed heartily. "A guy has to be qualified to be promoted. Of all the guys I know in the Corps," he put an arm around Jim's shoulder, "this guy here's the one who is."

Bob beamed.

"That's a lotta bunk, Sal!"

"I know ya mean that, Jim, but so do I. You'll be a great N.C.O., so let's hear no more about it."

*

The gathering on Christmas Eve was mass humanity. Surrounded by her family, Grandmother Williams glowed. Not only was she 'Gram' to all the cousins and a new husband of one, so too was she to Buck and Sal. It was with a joyful enthusiasm that Sal responded to his acceptance into the family. There was a noticeable warmth about him when he was in their presence.

The Williams and Buchanans were in great voice. And so was Sal, a talent Jim had not known he possessed until he heard him singing hymns in the church. To add to the abundantly high spirits Buck and Shirley were engaged earlier in the day.

On Christmas day Sal was a full fledged family member and participated happily in the exchange of gifts. He spent a sizable sum, not the least of which was the expensive French perfume and the Havana cigars he presented to Sarah and Bill.

It was a great leave for both young men as it was for all who shared it with them. Aboard the train on the return trip to Lejeune Jim observed his friend sitting silently next to him. Sal was smiling, but to himself. It showed in his eyes. He had changed decidedly since their first meeting four years ago.

Jim smiled to himself. He liked the change. He also liked what his father had become. Jim had never conversed freely with Bill Williams, nor for that matter had his brother Don. But now, Jim and his father were more at ease with conversation. It started with the rapport between Bill and Buck and was enhanced with Bill's relationship to Sal. So the Williams family too grew in new ways.

* * *

On their return from Christmas leave Jim and Sal sewed on their first hash mark, the symbol of four years service. They would be able to vote and drink 'legally' all across the nation. That was the privilege of those who had lived an abundant twenty-one years.

In November when they had shipped over, they hopefully applied for duty on the west coast. They decided it was about time they saw some more of their nation. Early in February of the new year of 1950, they got their wish. Their orders came through and they reported to their former regiment and battalion from China. They were back in the 5th Marines, now at Camp Pendleton, California. Both were assigned to the same platoon.

Pendleton was faring no better than Lejeune in parsimonious times. The fight for a force in readiness in the Marine Corps was turning into a fight for its very existence. Truman's Secretary of Defense, Louis A. Johnson, was on the side against the Corps. He made a statement to a Navy admiral in part, ".... the Navy, is on its way out. There's no reason for having a Navy and Marine Corps. General Bradley tells me, amphibious operations are a thing of the past. We'll never have any more amphibious operations. That does away with the Marine Corps. And the Air Force can do anything the Navy can do, so that does away with the Navy."

Jim, the student of history, wondered how a man in such a high place could be so stupid.

For now, however, the Corps was alive and training was intense, though ammo and fuel were not always available. Ratings changed to match the Army's and the old gunnery sergeants and platoon sergeants became technical sergeants and staff sergeants. The straight bar staff N.C.O. chevrons disappeared. The black eagle, globe and anchor emblems of the Corps were added to khaki shirt collars for summer wear. There was one good thing, the ghastly field scarf gave way to a respectable tie.

* * *

On a mission to harbor as much of their funds as possible, Jim and Sal were preparing for a trip to Shoreford. Sal was excited about the trip, an emotion long absent from his makeup. He swore off going to the slop chute for more than a month before they embarked. Jim was convinced Sal would get a Good Conduct Medal yet.

In mid June the two buddies boarded a plane and flew cross country. They attended Bob's graduation. Three days later Jim was to be best man for his new brother-in-law. He got fitted for a tux.

The graduation ceremony was boring, especially for Jim and Sal. They had to sit through it in dress blues, a concession unhappily made to Bob. He wanted his 'two' brothers 'properly' attired.

The wedding was something else. Everyone had a great time. The reception was held in the Williams back yard. The two Marines, Bob and Mal got to Buck's car and left the newlyweds with a dose of outrageous graffiti and trailing noise makers. This time Jim did not escape the punch to the stomach thrown by a displeased sister. When Buck and Shirley drove away Jim and Sal gave them a snappy salute. Buck had finally succeeded in his quest. He was a new private in the Marine Corps Reserve.

When the bride and groom were out of sight and Sarah and Isabel Buchanan and others had finished wiping the tears away and returned to the reception, Jim found himself offering a silent prayer for his sister and Buck.

"What's the matter, Buddy?" Sal said moving to his side.

"Oh I was just thinkin about those two," Jim sighed. "They've got a tough struggle ahead. Not just the newly wed ordeal of two people trying to blend their lives together in some kind of harmony, but the struggle to survive socially in a society that won't accept them. And some who will even despise them, .. those two good and noble kids."

Sal put a hand on Jim's shoulder. "They got great families to give em support and they got the stuff themselves to weather the storm. Somehow, Buddy, I know they'll make it."

"Ya know what, Sal? I know it too."

*

It was the first church service Jim attended since Christmas. Half way through the opening hymn, Bob standing to the left of his father and Jim, leaned forward. As subtly as he was able, he gave a slight, quick nod to his left, rolling his eyes in the same direction. Sarah and Sal were sharing a hymnal and enthusiastically blending their strong voices to the chorus. Jim began mouthing the words, the better to listen. Bill and Bob had powerful voices, but there was no doubt about Sarah and Sal. It was as if all in their vicinity allowed them to take the lead. Another great leave was nearing its end.

*

A week later Jim and Sal were back at Pendleton in time for the news. Sunday, June 25th, 1950, the North Korean Peoples Army (NKPA) marched south and crossed the 38th parallel into South Korea. The small, peninsular nation was at war. The Army of the Republic of Korea (ROK) in the South, broke and ran. American Army troops on occupation duty in Japan were rushed in to stem the flow. They were too few and their World War II equipment was not the equal of the more modern arms of the NKPA, equipment graciously supplied by the Soviet Union. The American soldiers would become the sacrificial lambs for now.

Camp Pendleton closed its gates to liberty with the coming of July. The First Provisional Marine Brigade was born anew. The 5th Marines at approximately two-thirds war time strength was the nucleus, the 1st Battalion of the 11th Marines the artillery. Additional tankers, engineers, signalers, ordinance, recon and drivers lifted the Brigade total to 4500 combat ready Marines. A Naval medical compliment joined their brothers in arms. But that was not all. 1500 very important men of the First Marine Air Wing completed the initial Marine investment. Despite the small size, it was a potent force. All ground and air components were trained to operate as one cohesive unit, unique to the United States Marine Corps. These fine troops might not have existed had the President, the Secretary of Defense, the Army, the Air Force and some of the Navy brass had their way.

It was quite an accomplishment, but five days after formation, the Brigade shipped out.

*

Standing at the rail, looking out over the inky Pacific, Jim was excited, yet scared. He was going to war. He remembered Don's description of his feelings before the crucible of Iwo. At his side, Sal was relaxed.

"Remember that chicken shit master at arms on the ship home from China and the way we got treated?" Jim asked.

"How could I ever forget that asshole ... and his bosses."

"Well, what I see this trip is a whole different attitude towards us. We're being treated like human beings."

"That's war, Buddy, that's war."

"And I bet they don't take as long getting us there as that trip home took."

"You can say that again."

"And I bet they don't take as long getting us there as that trip home took."

Sal punched Jim in the arm.

*

The ship docked at Pusan on the 2nd of August. It was late when the Marines debarked with weapons locked and loaded. The morning of the 3rd they were back aboard for breakfast, then debarked again. They moved out traveling light, with weapons, ammo, packs and rations. The day warmed intensely and became unbearably humid. Somebody said it was 120 degrees. The strong odor was reminiscent of China, but Jim thought it worse. Refugees were coming from the opposite direction, pushing carts and carrying their meager possessions, accompanied by children. Fear and uncertainty was on their faces which belied their Oriental inscrutability. It magnified the doubt Jim was manufacturing. He focused on death and his brother and decided it could happen to him.

None were acclimatized and men began to drop. Canteens ran out of water. Many were too miserable to even bitch, but they trudged on and settled in on a hill south of a town. They were bushed, but they dug in and darkness settled over them like a blanket too heavy to move under. Phantom images materialized in the mind and played tricks on tired eyes.

A shot rang out! It was followed immediately by another! And another! A small war commenced.

Twelve years ago when Eric Olson bore down on him at Collins Park, Jim Williams had been wildly scared. By comparison, the fright of that day was mild. Now, his body numbed by fear, his mind refused to function. His knees came up into his chest, locked tight by hands and arms. The metal rim of his helmet cut into his knees and he tasted the blood in his mouth where he sliced through his lip with his teeth. Like a fetus in a womb, he lay in his hole unable to move, except for his innards which were grinding to bits.

Though he did not know, it was only seconds he cringed in that vile fear, until a hand touched his shoulder.

"Jim!" The voice was soft, yet powerful. For a fleeting instant he saw Don's face.

Something deep inside grabbed at him, prodded him. His head went up. He peered unseeing down the sights of his rifle and pulled the trigger. In the wild bedlam and confusion he could not feel the recoil.

Voices were screaming and cursing amid shouts of, "Cease Fire!"

The word spread quickly. Some spooked Marine and another and another opened fire at a shadow and the rest was history. There was not a North Korean within miles. The men heard later that the officers had been reamed out with a terrible anger and a harsh promise, should any such thing ever again occur. And Jim made his second vow about fear, thankful that he suffered his shame alone and unseen.

*

The Marines, to their chagrin, learned they had been put under the command of an Army division. They patrolled the next day and worked on field discipline. The terrible humid heat continued from one day to the next. So did the need for water which flowed from their bodies faster than it could be replaced. The supply of this life giving liquid seemed always on the verge of running out ... and at times, it did.

A relief force was needed on one of the ubiquitous Korean hills. The company got the job. It turned into a slugfest on the way up. Casualties were numerous, not only from enemy fire, but heat exhaustion. By late afternoon they had another third of the hill to climb and conquer before reaching the top.

Jim worked his fire team along with their squad. He had targets and saw some of them go down, but so did two of the Marines in his team, one the BARman. They were carried to the rear with wounds. Jack Taylor the assistant BARman picked up the weapon and together, the two pushed on amidst the heat and dust and the noise and confusion .. and the fear and carnage.

The company was being bloodied. Jim saw his first dead Marine. For a moment he thought he would throw up. By the time he saw the second, it was a lesser blow. The dead NKPA soldiers, the gooks, did not infringe upon his emotions, especially after the thirst and exhaustion and the need to survive and do his job dominated his being. He diligently covered BARman Taylor. The automatic weapon drew fire as soon as the staccato outbursts revealed its whereabouts. He felt naked with but half a fire team, but other members of the squad were nearby as was the rest of the platoon. All were heavily engaged. Then another problem pressed upon them. Ammo was running low, but the resupply finally got to the men in need on the hill. As darkness descended Jack removed the last empty magazine from the BAR. He and Jim wasted no time reloading the precious metal containers.

During the night the company moved and moved some more. Morning found them on the hilltop. Losses were heavy, especially among the officers. They were commanded by a senior N.C.O. The heat stayed with them. So did the lack of water which was worse than the lack of sleep. With all the adversity, they stuck to it and the next day the territory belonged to them. They gathered their dead and carried them down to a place where they were covered by ponchos and laid together. As they were in life, they were in death, ... side by side.

For the young Marines, the stifling heat rushed the foul stench of death deep into their nostrils to linger long after the bodies were carried away. But the dead made one last contribution to the living. Their canteens were left behind and the remaining water shared by the living. Two men from the platoon were added to the fire team which moved out with the battalion before sunset. There was little rest and no relief. There was always another hill.

Up ahead Jim could see Sal, now in command of his own fire team. After any confrontation the two found themselves searching the other out at the first opportunity. Jim smiled to himself as the words of an officer at Lejeune flashed quickly through his mind, when he said that Sal would never rise above P.F.C. Sal might be a P.F.C., but his ability to fight and lead had shown up early in the confusion of battle.

But there were other things too that were becoming evident to Jim and his comrades and when laid bare, created concern and even resentment. Performance and discipline in some other outfits was not what it was in Marine units. The Marines felt that others gave up ground too easily. Much had to do with training, or lack of it. Some had to do with equipment. But some was the system. A Marine company went to the relief of a unit that had their command post a thousand yards to the rear. A similar Marine CP would have been fifty yards back.

When Jim and Sal were discussing those events, Sal spit out his disgust, "What'd I tell ya about those fuckin assholes who want to get rid of the Corps. They'll be eatin crow before this thing's over."

*

The roads did not change. They were always rough and always dusty and the Marines kept moving, always thirsty and always tired. They passed NKPA vehicles that were destroyed or damaged by Air Force planes. There were roadblocks and some firefights. An old man was executed by the ROKs for carrying ammo for the enemy. Then the advance was halted and the attack called off. The Army unit coordinating to the north was mauled and lost artillery and supplies. One of the Marine battalions was sent to the rescue and routed the North Koreans in a substantial victory. When the shooting was over, the bodies of about one-hundred American soldiers were found. They had been executed with their hands tied behind them, shot in the head after they surrendered.

The Marines were sent to the rear and had their first hot chow in nearly two weeks ... and their first bath ... in a river. Finally, each man received two beers. They were not cold, but that did not deter anyone. Jim drank both of his.

*

Fresh white bandages protruded below the utility cap. The skipper was making his rounds with a lieutenant and the top. When he got to Jim and Jack Taylor he said, "You two did a great job on the hill." He smiled and nodded and continued on to see the rest of his company brood.

"The skipper's a good officer." Sal had just arrived and joined the pair. The three gabbed till Jack left to make a head call.

"Ya know, Sal, that night the shooting started when we were blasting the shadows, I was so scared, I didn't know if I'd ever function again. But somehow, things worked out and I'm beginning to feel like an old salt." He smiled, "Remember how we felt comin home from China? Remember? It's not quite like that. I still get scared, real scared, it never leaves me, but when things start to pop, the muscles kinda start to respond. I guess

I'm even more scared of lettin somebody ... especially my guys ... and the rest of the outfit ... of lettin them down."

Sal looked into Jim's eyes, a soft smile on his face. "You're in a boat with a lotta good people, Buddy. I told you a long time ago you were a good Marine. But you're more than that, you're a helluva friend." He put a hand on Jim's shoulder and gave it a strong squeeze, "But I guess you come by it honest. Your folks are somethin special. The letter I got from them today said they got me registered in Shoreford at last. I now got the same address as you so I guess that makes us real foster brothers, comin from the same home and all."

*

The sweet feel of coming through an action with the rewarding rest and good treatment was short lived. The battalion was saddled up and on the road again. The NKPA had broken through and created a large bulge in the lines. If they were not stopped, disaster faced the entire allied force within the last small perimeter around Pusan. The Marines were called in to stem the flow. Army trucks were to carry them to the front, but fewer arrived than were needed. Two battalions, one of them Jim's which would lead the attack tomorrow had to march. That was often the way Marines went into battle.

At 0800 they jumped off and started toward the ominous looking ridge line. The artillery barrage was late and inaccurate. The air strike was so late only one pass could be made. To worsen a bad situation, the Army unit on the right did not secure that flank. It was silent and eerie when the ascent of the hill began. Jim was overcome with the eeriness as he moved forward with his platoon in the deathly silence. His eyes were constantly darting and scanning the ground up the hill and to the sides. His plodding, cautious feet carried him to the mid point of the wearisome climb. He desperately desired the hot water in his canteen to dissolve the dry scales from his mouth and throat.

With a raucous crescendo of lethal violence, the stillness was brutally shattered! As one, the battalion went to ground, many in pain, some in death. Movement brought retaliation, but move they did. They took more casualties, but they inflicted casualties, ... many casualties. Jim's fire team was intact. With a handful of Marines they reached the top only to be pushed off by heavier forces. Back they went, this time with one less man in Jim's team. He caught a fleeting glance of Sal off to the left.

After all of that, they were recalled to lay on an air strike. While they waited to do it all over again, Jim marveled at the bravery of the Corpsmen moving amongst the wounded in complete disregard for their own safety. If a Marine called, "Corpsman!" and one was within hearing, that medicine man moved hell to get there.

When the air strike ended they charged again. By mid afternoon the battalion had too few effective combatants and a sister battalion moved through. Fresh blood routed the enemy. The regiment's third battalion took a second objective in a further rout. The victory was costly, but more so to the enemy. An entire NKPA division was soundly defeated and badly beat up.

Atrocities were again discovered. An aid station had been overrun and the wounded killed. American weapons and equipment, captured or left behind were turned against the Marines. It was an exhausted Marine Brigade that returned to their former resting place, a spot they named the 'Bean Patch'. They lived on the ground, but morale was high. They succeeded where others failed. It was a job well done and they knew it. Patrols and training kept them busy, but they stayed clean in the river, which alas did not fulfill its other function, .. that of keeping the beer cold.

*

The displeasure of the Marines with some other units was on the increase. Flanks were left unprotected and ground had to be retaken. Many in those other units were resentful of the Marines for the publicity they received. They were in the same war, feeling the same fear, subject to the same dangers and dying the same way. And of course they were, but the media was excited by success. Until now there had been little of that.

*

A lot of good buddies were put in the ground on a Korean hillside in a quiet, somber ceremony. Two from Jim's squad and three more from the platoon. Guys he had shared living with. Young guys, full of energy and a lust for life. Guys he liked, who had families at home as he had. He thought of his mother, of his family and what he imagined their reaction would be if it was him, .. or Sal who went down into that hole. He quickly rearranged his thoughts.

Letters from home caught up with them, for the most part upbeat. Sarah, however, was unable to hide her concern. Not only was Sal an added and strong concern, but Buck too was now gone. He was at Parris Island serving his rite of passage into his Corps. Shirley turned out to be a hardier soul than her mother. She was not going to allow herself to agonize as she had seen her mother do.

The stint in the Bean Patch ended abruptly on September 2nd when the Brigade was ordered to move out. Again the NKPA broke through at almost the same place as before and the Marines were needed again to halt the flow. Again protection on their flank collapsed, but again, within two days, the Brigade routed and decimated an enemy division and sent them packing. All of this was accomplished in pouring rain. It was accomplished in spite of being shot at by their own tanks, Air Force fighters and heavy enemy machine gun and mortar fire and visibility that was almost nonexistent.

On the night of the 5th, the exhausted, victorious Marines were withdrawn and returned to Pusan, eight miles on foot and the remaining fifty by motor transport. They received replacements for their losses. Each battalion added a third company, bringing them to full war time strength. They were needed once more. They would be the ones at the tip of the spear in MacArthur's bold plan.

* * *

For those who did not already know, it was during this period that every Marine in the Corps and out, learned of the 'love' Harry Truman had for them. A congressman believed that the Commandant of Marines should be added to the Joint Chiefs and that the Corps, especially in view of their deeds in Korea, should be expanded.

Truman answered him in a letter that stated in part, "For your information, the Marine Corps, is the Navy's police force and as long as I am President, that is what they will remain. They have a propaganda machine that is almost equal to Stalin's." He would live to regret those words and publicly apologize.

P.F.C. Salvatore A. Gennaro, U.S.M.C. put it well. "Can ya believe that fuckin little sawed off sonuva bitch? One of the few outfits that dumb bastard can depend on and he says that. He's our Commander in Chief!?"

* * *

Aboard ship the battalion was filled with new faces inhabiting new bodies. They were full of questions. Sal was enjoying himself. He could be counted on to have a comment about the 'gook bastards' whenever he or anyone nearby was asked. The English course he had enrolled in was not yet concluded, nevertheless, there was an improvement in his pronunciation and his speech. And he cleaned up some of his language in deference to his foster family, though he was still capable of barroomese when the occasion demanded. One thing did not change. There was no one better to be with in time of trouble, whether in a brawl or the heat of combat.

One day a group of newcomers was gathered on deck with Jim, Sal and Jack. After various subjects were discussed, including many and various characterizations of the female sex, marksmanship became the topic. Sal, heretofore less extravagant with his speech, decided something needed to be said.

"Why if everybody in this man's Marine Corps could shoot like the corporal here and our old boot camp buddy Steve Sellers, this here war'd be over in no time."

"You mean Steve Sellers the joker?" a new man asked.

"One and the same. Ya know him?"

"Hell yes! I served with that joker in '46 at Lejeune. It never ceased to amaze me that he could go through sniper school, as serious and tough as that was."

"You mean he still liked to fool around and practical joke?" Jim interjected.

"Hell yes! Almost got himself killed doin it."

"What'd he do this time?"

"Well, one Sunday there's a few of us hangin around the squad bay and there's a guy a few racks down an he's sound asleep and he's got his mouth wide open. Sellers has this banana he brought back from the mess hall and he gives it to a buddy and explains what to do.

"His buddy peels the banana and they walk down to where this guy's sleepin and stand on each side of him. The guy with the banana shoves it in the sleepin guys mouth and moves it up and down.

"Well shit! The guy wakes up and there's Sellers standin there with his dick out. You never saw anybody so hot. This guy jumps up and grabs his bayonet and goes for Sellers who runs for the door and his life, screamin his fool head off.

"We all had to jump on the guy and hold him down and talk to him. Sellers didn't show up for the rest of the day and when he did, this guy wouldn't talk to him for a few more."

"That's Sellers, that dumb ass," Sal shook his head in disbelief, "he'll get himself killed one a these days."

*

Everybody got acquainted and took their places for the next event. The Marines from Pusan, however, did not have to get acquainted with the ship's crew. The battalion came over on this ship and both officers and men had made friends. The crew was great. They felt the heavy losses the Marines suffered and extended their sympathy in many and various ways. Good chow was part of it.

There was good news also from Washington. Truman fired his Secretary of Defense. The news fell happily on the better informed Marines. The Marine Corps Birthday would once again be celebrated legally, not that it was not a joyous illegal event in recent years.

Jim's comment to Sal was simply, "That jerk Johnson is gone." Sal gave him a big thumbs up and Jim concluded, "Maybe the next Secretary will not be so hostile to the Naval services, ... especially the Corps."

"What you mean, Buddy, is you hope he won't be another dumb ass sonuvabitch."

But it was not all fun and games aboard ship. Much of the time awake was spent in briefings and studying maps and photos. Weapons were cleaned and checked and the process repeated many times. PT was sandwiched in when small groups could be accommodated. Crowding was the norm. Additionally they were hit with a typhoon and with it some seasickness. And the closer they came to their objective, the tighter stomachs became.

*

So the First Provisional Marine Brigade ceased to exist, its units integrated into the First Marine Division. The Brigade had done everything asked of it and more. Many in a nation on the other side of the world knew that it still had its dependable Marines and that is what the men in the regiments, in the division were, they were Marines. There were many in the Division's ranks, entire battalions who had been rushed there from the 6th Marines of the Second Marine Division at Camp Lejeune. It was not a regimental number or a division number that made these men what they were, it was the title they carried.

Ten days after withdrawing from their final engagement down in Pusan, the 5th Marines, First Marine Division, were chugging ashore in landing boats and amphibious tractors. They were joined by the reborn 1st Marines and the 11th Marines, the artillery regiment which was now at full war time strength. In a few days the 7th Marines, also reborn, would land. As these fine regiments had been from Guadalcanal to China, they once again constituted the First Marine Division.

More Marines, the newly formed First Marine Air Wing, the irreplaceable airdales, gave the kids on the ground a special punch. They knew how to work together. That was the way they lived and trained and fought. It was an extremely remarkable achievement putting all this together on such short notice and it was done entirely by the Naval service.

*

Landing boats and amphibious tractors were coming in at the precise moment the tide allowed them to get over the mud flats. A battalion of the 5th had gone in on the morning tide and secured the island protecting the entrance to the landing beaches. Now it was late afternoon, sometime after five. Heads were down as the landing craft closed with the beach. Combat veteran or no, it was the same tight knot that twisted the bowels of all aboard.

The boat stopped with a thud. A ladder went against the seawall. Without fanfare and lacking grace, the Marines scrambled up and over the wall. It was better to be moving than waiting in that bobbing craft. The driving legs started the heart pumping faster, not that it needed to beat faster. The senses were awakened. The moving body helped to ease the fear, ... but not enough. Confusion was intensely abundant in the beginning and units intermingled and were sorted out and sped on their way. Some Marines were hit by friendly fire from the landing boats bringing in the later waves. Rain was falling. The fighting was moving away from the landing sites and inland. Resistance was light in the battalion zone and would continue that way for a time. It was not so for Marines elsewhere.

*

The next day they saddled up and moved out early. The Corsairs, those wonderful birds of the Marine pilots had a good morning and knocked out some NKPA tanks. The column received sniper fire, but not enough to slow them.

Jim Williams matured during the month of heavy fighting in the Pusan Perimeter. Without conscious effort he had become a leader, after what he considered his humiliating failure. Of the two new men in his fire team, one was a former member of the team recovered from his wounds. Jack Taylor stayed with the BAR. For the newest member of the team, it was good to not be involved in anything heavy at the beginning. So far, compared to Pusan, it was easy. When the North Koreans did decide to fight, they were brushed aside.

After they dug in that night Jim had a chance to visit with Sal. He handed Sal the cigarettes from his rations.

"Thanks!" Sal smiled. He gazed at Jim a moment before continuing, "Ya know, from Mom's last letter, my name oughta be there by now, right up on the town Honor Roll with Don's and Buck's and yours. Aint it great? I feel really good about it. I feel like I belong someplace now. It'd never'uv happened if it wasn't for you and the folks ... and all the family."

There was a look on Sal's face that could not have existed in the not too distant past.

"You know how I feel, Buddy, we've talked about this enough. I know the whole family feels the same way. You know, I don't think Mom could ever feel right about you being out in the world with no family. And I don't know why," Jim chuckled, "because you're nothing but a scoundrel." He punched Sal lightly on the arm. Sal grinned. Then Jim got serious, "But I never saw her take to anybody the way she took to you."

*

A hint of morning light was beginning in the sky. It was Jack Taylor's turn on watch and he was shaking Jim and whispering excitedly into his ear, "I hear tanks! I hear tanks!"

Within seconds the team was awake as was the entire platoon on the hillside. They watched, frozen silent and still in their holes as a half dozen NKPA tanks and a few hundred infantrymen came down the road and disappeared around the bend. With only rifles and BARs, they did not dare open fire. But it was OK. The platoon knew what lay ahead for the hapless gooks.

The wait was short. Marine tanks and supporting heavy stuff opened up with murderous effect on the enemy tanks. The NKPA infantrymen did a wild about face and came running back in a frantic effort to escape with their lives. Then the Marines on the hillside took their turn in the brutal extermination. It was over so quickly that even the veterans of Pusan were caught up in the excitement and animated conversations.

"I wish to hell all our engagements were so one sided!" Jim said to no one in particular of the excited men around him.

"You got that right, man!" Jack replied.

It would not be so and there was no respite for the victors. They were soon saddled up and moving to the next objective.

*

The 5th Marines trod dusty roads, crossed rice paddies and secured an airfield. They climbed hills and crossed a river and daily, enemy resistance stiffened and casualties got heavier the closer they came to Seoul. But there were more of them now. The 7th Marines had landed. The entire Division was ashore.

The fight for Seoul was a lousy, stinking, dirty task. It was building to building, house to house, amidst the heat and the smoke of the burned out and burning structures. Jim eyed the men around him. He now commanded a squad. Faces were blackened with soot from the fires and eyes were bloodshot from the smoke. Sal Gennaro a lowly P.F.C. was also running a squad, albeit smaller than when it landed a week ago. Their squads had spearheaded much of the current street fighting.

The NKPA contested many of the buildings and erected road blocks behind tanks and machine guns at almost every corner. Every street was the same story. Yet in all the conflagration there were many animals that survived. Most ran berserk through the debris of war. And despite all the surrounding horror, civilians came forth to aid wounded Marines and carry them to aid stations, often on doors blown or kicked loose from their hinges. Rubble was everywhere. It was impossible to find an unbroken window. Electrical and telephone wires sagged from the poles or lay on the ground in utter confusion. Many of the buildings seemed to have no innards. NKPA prisoners were taken and suspected collaborators were rounded up by the ROKs. Civilian casualties, bewildered and frightened, wandered into the Marine lines. Their agony turned to wails as wounded children were presented for medical treatment.

The carnage continued.

"Four days a this shit and there's still more. Every time we knock out one roadblock or building, there's another right behind it. Reminds me of the song about the bear goin over the mountain." Jack spoke nonchalantly to his squad leader when Jim returned from a meeting with their platoon leader.

"Well you got no more to worry about. Seoul has been liberated."

Jack's tired, bloodshot eyes opened wide, his indifference turning to incredulity. "Where the hell didja hear that?"

Jim smiled wanly, "The lieutenant just told us. Seems ol Dugout Doug issued a communiqué or somethin to that affect. The gooks are supposed to be fleein the city. Sad part is, nobody told the gooks. I guess when you're a five star general you can say what pleases ya. Anyhow, we're movin out."

Sal's squad took the point and was soon under fire. Jim's squad bringing up the rear arrived in time to see Sal lead a few men into a building and minutes later return with a thumbs up. He was some guy, Jim thought, for someone who had trouble qualifying with the rifle and who did not impress some peacetime officers. He was quite inspiring moving from objective to objective. Jim felt his buddy's performance merited him a decoration, but he knew that the day to day drama was often swallowed up in the overall campaign and passed by as routine, which it did.

It took a few more days, but there was a celebration in a secured part of the capital. A portion of the city was returned to the South Koreans with whatever pomp MacArthur could muster while the rest remained under siege. Marines, except the very senior were noticeably absent from the affair. Most of their units were still engaged in the fighting. It was as well under the circumstances. The word Marine was not mentioned once during the entire performance.

But alas, the campaign was winding down. Scuttlebutt was the order of the day. The Marines were going home. There was to be a big victory parade. The filth of weeks of accumulated dirt and grime, the constant harassing movement and deadly competition was nearing an end. The city of Seoul was nearly secure and a smile appeared now and then on a tired and soiled face. One could smell the sweetness of victory amidst the stench of war. The Army had reached the 38th parallel. It was good to be alive. That good feeling belonged to all the men in Jim's vicinity who were settling in for a rest. They were returning from a platoon patrol. They went out and back without firing a shot in anger.

Jim spent some time checking out his men, talked to the lieutenant and was about to look for Sal when he spotted him. Sal was coming to him. They flopped down and Sal took a cigarette from a crumpled pack and lit it. He was as dirty as all the other men in the vicinity. His dungarees appeared to have had it. Even his camouflage helmet cover was ripped. He took a few drags from the cigarette and each had a swig from their canteens.

"You ready to head Stateside, Jim?" Sal was smiling.

"You bet! I've been ready since the first day we got to this stinkhole."

"You can say that again."

"Naw, I don't think I will, I'm too damn tired."

"You can say that again."

They both laughed out loud, not uproariously, but enough to bring some cheer to the moment.

"I've been doin a lotta thinkin," Sal continued, "about goin home, especially now, .. since I got one to go to." He paused and took another drag and blew the smoke skyward. "I think I'm gonna contact Helen when we get back. I know we got in the sack kinda quick, but she was a nifty person and we liked to do a lotta the same stuff together. I know somethin else, .. she was in love with me ... and I hafta admit, I had, ... deep down, .. still do have those kinda feelins for her.

"There was no way I could see me gettin married then, but she was willin to be a Marine's wife ... and somehow, .. I think, .. we could make it now, thanks to Mom and Dad. I see them and others in your family," he smiled brightly, "..our family and I know they've taught me some things, .. some a the things I put out of my mind ... and my life when my mom went to pieces.

"Maybe I'm not the greatest catch in the world, but I think I could be good to Helen ... and good for her."

The smile on his face was a pleasant smile, a smile he could not have until somewhat recently achieved.

Jim was smiling too, but his was one of restrained exuberance. "I knew you had something special with her, but I guess I wasn't really sure it was that strong. I betcha she wets her jeans when she hears from you. Damn! I think it's great. Damn, Buddy, I really think it's great!"

Sal hesitated a moment and looked away, then back at Jim. "And ya know what, Brothe? She was nuts about kids. I know she'll make a great mom." He hesitated briefly, glancing down, then quickly back into Jim's smiling eyes, "And ya know what? I think I'm ready to be a good ol man."

The Marines were smoking and eating from ration cans and talking and doing the things they did best when they were certain of their security. The unnerving crack of rifle fire came from outside the group. There was a mad scramble for cover.

Shouted orders sent men scurrying in the direction of the shot, but the tragic damage was done.

There was blood pouring from Sal's chest and the glaze was already over his eyes. Jim frantically lifted his shoulders from the filthy earth and held him tightly in his arms. There was a gurgling in Sal's throat.

"Don't die, Sal! Don't die, Buddy! Please!!! Please!!!"

The all but closed eyes opened just a bit. The very dark irises penetrated the glaze. In a tone that got softer with each word, Sal whispered, "I love .. you ... Brothe."

Then he was quiet.

* * *

The Marines were issued cold weather sleeping bags and went back aboard ship. They were not going home. They would not be there in time for Thanksgiving. They would stay in Korea, along with P.F.C. Salvatore Anthony Gennaro, U.S.M.C., but he would occupy a small plot in a military cemetery at Inchon.

* * *

The squad of Corporal James A. Williams was not entirely up to strength. There were not enough new replacements to fill all the gaps, but that was often the way things happened in war. They were together aboard ship for the sea voyage around the peninsula, from west coast to east coast. The voyage turned into one of absurdity.

They were to land at the port of Wonson, but the harbor was full of mines and the Navy had to spend days clearing them. Meanwhile, the ships, which could not land their human cargo, sailed north for half a day and then back to the south. The maneuver became known as 'Operation Yo Yo'. A week became an eternity. Ironically the port was occupied by ROK and U.S. Army troops who walked in after overcoming light resistance. A hostile amphibious landing was scratched and the fighting

Marines were the brunt of not a few jokes by those already in the city one of whom was Bob Hope.

Food aboard the ships was running low. Lines at sick call lengthened as dysentery felled hundreds. Few remained good natured. Finally on October 26th the Marines escaped the rolling, stinking steel prisons and trudged ashore.

From deep down and throughout his being, Corporal James A. Williams was surlily angry and the sea voyage did not help his mood. War had taken two of the people he loved most dearly. It was easy to hate. The hate helped free him of any self pity and permitted him to think of his mother. Therein was part of his salvation. The thought of his mother losing another, even though not of her womb, sobered him. Jim observed his mother and Sal become so very close. Sarah wanted to give Sal the life he had missed. They began to establish their bond from that moment she and Bill attended the funeral of Sal's mother, a bond that was nurtured and grew. Now it was severed forever.

So Jim wrote a letter to his parents, but it was mostly for his mother's sake. It took him all of one night while at sea and he had no idea how it would be received, but he struggled with it and said all the things he wanted to say about Sal and his place in the Williams family. He did not know it then, but it was a fine letter and he learned from his father later, that it was what Sarah needed, for the wound so insensitively inflicted on her. She cried a lot at the commencement of her grief, but a change started when Jim's letter arrived. The change took time, but it occurred and she cherished the memories more quickly this time.

Unfortunately for the many replacements in his squad, Jim was not in the same frame of mind toward them. He did not take kindly to a group of newcomers for whom he was now responsible. He was a Marine and he was a good leader, but right now he did not want to wet nurse and look after a bunch of amateurs, some of whom would probably become casualties. He was sharp tongued with his new charges and sometimes ill tempered. He would not permit himself to get close to them.

Through August and September the men of the 5th Marines suffered with the unrelenting Korean heat. Now, however, free of the confines of that roving sea scow and ashore for the second day, the temperature dropped to freezing. The rice paddies glistened in their new, icy attire and those who had been around from the beginning shivered in the cold and wondered what next.

Winter clothing was issued and the new people in the squad grumbled about the cold.

"If you'da been here sooner you coulda had all the heat your hearts desired. Yeh! And humidity that sapped your brain. You guys got a cakewalk. We'll probably be outa this beautiful country in weeks the way the gooks are runnin north as fast as they are." As soon as he spoke Jim was sorry for the sharp words.

He walked away, more angry with himself than his new charges.

Later he sat alone on the far side of a hillock and ate from a can. Conversation on the other side got loud enough for him to overhear. A couple of the new men were complaining to Jack about their squad leader.

"You dumb bastards, you don't know how lucky you are. You got one of the best squad leaders in the whole fuckin Corps."

Jim got up and left the area. He walked over to where his platoon leader was eating with the platoon sergeant. They talked about assignments for the night, had some small talk and before Jim left, the lieutenant asked, "You OK, Jim?"

"Yeh, I'm OK, Sir." Except that night, at that moment, he was not completely sure that he was. The lieutenant, he thought, must have seen or detected something different or unusual. He decided he would have to square himself away.

*

Jack woke Jim in the morning. He sat with him while he got out of his sleeping bag. Jack exhaled upwards observing the condensed moisture from his breath. About a minute passed before he spoke. "Ya know, Jim, the new kids'll be OK."

"What're ya tryin to say, Jack?"

"Hell, it won't hurt to ease up on them, talk to them."

"Yes it will!" It was a snappy reply. A short silence followed before Jim very deliberately continued, "I don't ever want to get to know them, Jack. We've been in this lousy place about three months and I've lost more buddies than I care to count. If I don't know them, it won't be so bad when they're gone. I don't want any more buddies."

Jack looked squarely at him. "Aint I your buddy, Corporal?" his words touched with a trace of sarcasm.

Jim took a deep breath of the cold air and exhaled a long spout of cloudy vapor.

"You know you are, Jack," he paused, looked down, then back into the eyes of his fire team leader. He was not hostile, but neither was he contrite, "But I think you know what I mean, Jack."

*

The word was out again. They would be home by Christmas. This time it came straight from the mouth of the great one, creating euphoria that sapped inertia in the regiment. They were division reserve and further removed from the day to day anxieties. There were many who thought the war was over for them.

But the war was not over and it was not long before things began to happen that were proof of that. In less than two days, a company from the 1st Marines traveled down the coast to the south and was hit hard by NKPA troops who were supposed to have disappeared to the north. It was a disciplined attack and positions were overrun before the Marines regrouped and the North Koreans disappeared.

November 1st the news was worse. Some fifty or so miles to the west and not tied in to the Marines and the divisions of their sector, the Eighth Army met a more formidable and frightening specter. They suffered some severely painful reverses as the Chinese Communist Army, the PLA, exploded onto the scene. It was a very bad experience for some units and they were extensively mauled and chewed up.

The following day, the 7th Marines, in the vanguard of the division leading it north, were headed into the already frozen, mountainous countryside on a narrow, winding and treacherous road when a full Chinese division attacked them. The battle lasted most of four days, an attack initiated by the PLA to test the mettle of the Marines. When they withdrew, the Chinese had been badly mauled. They were very unhappy with the results of that encounter and proceeded to make preparations for the annihilation of the U.S. Marines.

*

It was bitter cold now and getting colder daily. The Marines no longer wore boondockers and the canvas leggings which prompted the North Koreans to refer to them as 'yellow legs', respectfully distinguishing them from other troops. The rubber bottomed shoe pac that Jim wore in China became the footwear. On the march feet perspired. When they halted the sweat quickly turned icy and frost bite and frozen feet were the undesired offshoot of that sweat. Feet had to be kept dry the same as the weapons they carried, except with the weapons, it was grease or oil that froze them up.

Jim made certain his men replaced wet socks immediately when they came to a halt. He badgered them in the beginning and soon they were taking care of themselves, first to escape his wrath, but later they decided he had their well being at heart. Respect was growing for the man they learned more about daily, mostly from Jack's constant reminders, but also from other members of the platoon and their own observations. And despite his desire to remain distant, Jim did care. He wanted to bring them out alive.

*

When it seemed temperatures had reached the bottom, they went down still further. The winter of 1950 had Koreans searching their memories for one that had been as severe, but there was not one to be recalled by those living. In that devitalizing environment, Jim turned twenty-two and was not aware the day had either come or passed. When mail from home caught up with him, there were cards and that was when he was reminded and when he remembered. With that mail he received a letter from his mother that he read and reread. She sent him a clipping from the Shoreford weekly newspaper. It was about Sal and contained a photograph from a picture taken on the last leave in Shoreford. He was smiling happily. Jim recalled the way Sal had taken to the family and the way it was reciprocated. The smile, something rare for so much of Sal's life, was very real in the photo. The story in the newspaper told of Sal losing his family and how he had become a foster son of Bill and Sarah and a resident of the Williams home and Shoreford. It also told of his promotion to squad leader and something of the battle for Seoul. It left little doubt about Sal's place in the family.

All correspondence in that batch alluded to the end of the war. The family was overjoyed that Buck would soon be home on leave from boot camp. The possibility of an early end to the fighting buoyed Shirley immensely. Buck on the other hand, though he said nothing specific, seemed to Jim disappointed at the prospect of missing the conflict. Bob was another who was disappointed. His chance would never come. He had made a solemn promise to his mother that he would finish his first year of college before seeking enlistment.

For Sarah, it seemed a certainty to be over by then.

*

Thanksgiving all along the perimeter, the Marines ate in shifts so the defenses were maintained. The cooks did a superb job with the turkey and the trimmings, but there was a problem.

One could neither dally over the food nor take the time to savor it for if too much time passed from the serving lines to the mouth, the food froze on the plates.

Aside from the good food, there was good news that day. An Army unit on a road to the east reached the Yalu River, the border with Communist China. That probably was the reason the regiment received a change in their orders to continue north with the division. The change sent them up the east side of the Chosin Reservoir, but also with the Yalu as their objective.

That meant fragmenting the division. It created an uneasy feeling despite the sense of victory so close at hand. But that order too was changed in three days and the regiment was relieved by an Army unit. The 5th Marines rejoined their division, which now, was to push west over the mountains and link up with the larger U.N. forces in that sector, many days march away.

The leading elements of the division, including Jim's battalion, were seventy eight miles from the sea at the end of a tenuous and treacherous supply route. Purposely slowed in their advance, the division commanding general was wisely trying to bring the division together before committing it to the wishes of what the Marines considered, very bad judgment. Transportation was lacking for this type of operation and the Marines spent a great deal of time afoot and building supply bases along the way. The Army attached motor transport units, but it was just not enough most of the time. But while they may have lacked transportation, they did not lack élan and they had a talent for innovation and improvisation which did not fail them.

*

The artillery lifted on the morning of November 27th and the battalion jumped off. They headed west on the long mountainous journey to link up with the Eighth Army. They ran into some ineffective small arms fire, but the Chinese responsible, who MacArthur still believed would not intervene, backed off and just past noon, the last high points on either side of the road were cleared and in Marine hands. Fire fights erupted and there were scrambles to move into and onto dominant terrain. A few Chinese prisoners were taken. It was decided to dig in and form the perimeter by midafternoon. Most were dog tired and in need of all the rest a fifty percent alert and the terrible cold would permit.

*

"Cripes it's cold!" Jack was right.

The last time they had a temperature check, it was twenty below zero and that was some time ago. It was about five hours since the darkness crippled their vision. Jim crawled from hole to hole checking his squad. Jack was on the flank with his fire team and the last man on his rounds. Jim knew Jack and his men would be OK, but the rest of the squad was pretty green and up until today there had been little to test their mettle since coming ashore a month ago.

Moving north Jim stayed on top of his squad and they were shaping up. They grumbled amongst themselves, but they obeyed and they learned. They had, like so many of the replacements, a deep respect for the combat experience of their leaders.

Jim and Jack were just finishing their muffled conversation when shooting erupted.

"Holy shit! Here they come!" The voice was taut and excited and came from the left, along the path Jim had just traversed.

"That's Jorgenson!" Jim spit the words between clenched teeth and was instantly slithering back over the frozen ground rechecking his men and whispering sharp quick commands. The firing from the enemy was not heavy and he had to work at getting the men under control.

"Easy with the BARs! They're lookin for weak spots and automatic weapons, just probin. Easy! Easy!"

The Chinese did just that. They prodded and pricked the Marine lines and when it seemed things were about to intensify, they backed off. All the while infiltrators were moving through gaps between units readying for the knockout punch.

Without warning, bugles blared and the freezing darkness was shattered in a million intangible pieces tearing at the sanity of the defenders. Machine guns and mortars searched for fragile flesh. Soldiers who crept close enough bombarded the Marine lines with clusters of concussion grenades. Chaos and uproar were everywhere. Then the charging shapes of submachine gunners burst upon them, forced forward by the massed infantry on their heels. Hellfire and brimstone were real.

Jim emptied the first clip of eight rounds and reloaded without conscious thought. In the light of illumination rounds, faceless men, nameless forms hurtled into his sights and were falling and crumbling to earth in rapid succession, yet they kept coming and kept dying. It was as if a live soldier jumped from the pocket of a falling comrade and the living were too numerous, for there was always another. It was a bad dream and there was no awakening.

The Marine line was rolling back from the massive onslaught. Jim was among his men yelling and cursing, as much at himself as them, for there was something in him that wanted to cut and run like hell.

One of the new kids in the middle fire team was a lad named Knox who Jim had been concerned about. Behind an outcropping, he was in the initial stages of his fears. When he did not move out at once on command, he received a well placed kick to the buttocks from Jim. He was in motion instantly.

The line strengthened, but it was impossible, they had to move back and regroup. Corporal James Williams was shooting and shouting and cursing and holding his men together. They stayed together and they held and were resupplied with ammo and they held some more and Jim, here, there, wherever his presence was needed, yelled and cursed some more, at times dashing to a wounded man and pulling him back.

The attack let up, then became sporadic and in the early morning Jim led his men with the Marines all along the line. They went into the attack and ran the Chinese out shooting many in the back as they tried desperately to escape. Knox made up for any earlier shortcoming. Remarkably, every member of Jim's squad survived. The battalion similarly was lucky, sustaining only moderate casualties.

Other Marines in other places were not as fortunate.

The beautiful Corsairs came in with the daylight and the Marines on the ground had a momentary respite while their brothers in the sky performed to a grateful audience. Air cover and support was never better.

But daylight also displayed the grisly carnage. Jim was totally unprepared for the scene to his front. The montage of death stifled his senses. So many bodies, so many broken bodies. He remembered how his hate for the Communists had grown over the years reaching its apex when Sal was killed, but when he stared across that desecrated landscape now, his emotions were void.

The battalion contracted and consolidated its positions in the daylight almost immune from enemy harassment. Nobody seemed to know much of the overall situation, but scuttlebutt was rampant, made the more so by the complete lack of any legitimate intelligence from the commands at Tenth Corps or the supreme command in Tokyo. Some Marines were known to be cut off and surrounded which added meaning to the one persistent and depressing rumor.

The road behind the Marines, the road they had traveled so arduously to get here, that road had been cut.

*

When the Marines moved within their perimeter, they had to dig, but digging in the frozen ground was next to impossible, but they dug and while they dug they sweat and they hated it for they knew the aftermath. The terrible chill started in the toes and spread upward into the small of the back and finally, icy tentacles clutched the entire body in a deep freeze that numbed the soul.

The two Marine regiments in and around Yudam-ni continued to move and draw the perimeter tighter and tighter. When they changed positions they dug again.

The officers and N.C.O.s were always present, giving orders, offering encouragement or perhaps some inane comment. The lieutenant, who now walked with a limp he tried to disguise, could be counted on at least once a day to say, "Remember, you're Marines!"

And though they often answered silently, "Yeh, yeh," under their breath, deep down and away from conscious thought and the need to articulate it, they knew what they were and they knew what their buddies were and despite the constant fear and overwhelming discomfort, they would be what they were.

*

The small group of officers and N.C.O.s listened to the skipper, many incredulous when he lay the plans before them. Jim was groping for words, but a staff sergeant from another platoon was the first to speak. "Shit, Skipper, are you tellin us we're gonna retreat outa this fuckin hole?"

The captain's serious expression turned to a wry smile. He looked into the sergeants eyes, "I hardly think that what we are about to undertake constitutes a retreat, Sergeant Maschal. Our two regiments here in Yudam-ni are completely surrounded by as nearly as we can tell, three Chinese divisions. There are more divisions blocking the road south. We will have to attack to the south and secure our flanks and protect our rear. Does that sound like a retreat to you?"

"No, Skipper. Sounds like somethin we can handle."

*

The battalion was to be the rear guard for the two regiments. They occupied a hill south of the village. From those heights they would have box seats for much of the unfolding drama.

They could see for miles to the north and south. If they were attacked, they would have to hold and could expect no help.

It was the morning of December 1st, 1950 when the Marines on that hill watched their brothers moving out of the valley below. By evening, in the fading light, visibility was enhanced by the snow and those on the hill could still see the long column of men and vehicles who had started the trek during daylight. They were still trudging up the steep incline between the hills and out of that ghastly valley. The vehicles were loaded to capacity and what could not be taken was destroyed. Marines marched alongside the vehicles which carried not only supplies, but many buddies, both wounded and dead. Men with wounds who were ambulatory, marched. So did those with frostbite.

In the hills on either side of the narrow frozen road were other Marines. They were shooting it out with contenders for the right of way, contenders who likewise were suffering from the severities of that abominable Korean winter. The men of the battalion were unable to view the conflicts on the other hills, but they saw the Corsairs and they knew that anyone in the path of those death dealing birds would not long remain there.

"Look at that, will ya!" It was Knox.

Jim turned in the direction of Knox' pointed arm. Down in the valley the Marines had vacated, the Chinese were sifting through the burning debris, searching for anything that would relieve their own distress. Warm clothing or anything edible. The pickings lacked beneficence.

"Fuckin gooks, .. look like flies on a dung heap," Knox said.

Jim smiled wanly at the description. He was amongst seven hundred or so trusted buddies yet was engulfed at that moment with a terrible loneliness as he turned his gaze from the Chinese and back to the thousands of Marines leaving his battalion behind.

"Jim, do ya think we're bein left here as a sacrifice?" It was Knox again, his tone subdued and unsure.

"No chance!" Instantly Jim was the squad leader. "We'll be outa here tomorrow morning and if the gooks try to make a sacrifice of us tonight, we'll kick their lousy asses off this lousy hill just like we did back there!" Turning his full attention to his squad watching the spectacle in the distance, he loudly uttered, "OK guys, let's get squared away. It just might be a busy night." Sometimes command was good.

*

The Chinese hit around midnight. It was a frantic and savage time. Some fighting holes were lost, but the battalion stayed between the main body and the Chinese. With white-phosphorous markers they guided in Marine Tigercat night fighters and enemy reinforcements were prevented on the scene. With daylight the Corsairs returned and the air Marines and the ground Marines sent the Chinese packing. The victory had its price. A lad named Seeley from Jim's squad was carried away with a chest wound, but his chances appeared good.

Those who stayed were a tired lot, their stamina further depleted by the unrelenting frigidity of the air which hurt the lungs after exertion when open mouths sucked in that abrasive necessity. On the move they breathed through clenched teeth. They did not pay much attention to the sporadic, hostile fire that came their way. They were just too cold and too tired to care.

Eyes sunk and stared blankly. Clothing and faces got grimier. Digestive systems were disrupted and like the summer months, there was an intolerable lack of drinking water. Still, they kept going, but the gap between them and the forward units was increasing. When his own squad began to string out Jim moved to the rear and cajoled and encouraged and finally vilified them. They stared in disbelief as he rushed forward at the most rapid pace his benumbed feet and fatigued legs could achieve. Passing by his exhausted squad members faster than he should have been able, he heard grumbles and things like, "That sonuva bitch!" but they picked up the pace and closed some of the gap. He knew they would.

They marched and fought for more than three days to reach friendly lines and a moderately safe haven, fourteen miles from the village they vacated. They still had a long way to go to get to the sea, sixty-four miles, but they knew they would get there. They stuck together, froze together and fought together and though captive of their own intense afflictions, they reached out to each other, to share and to care and to help. They bested the Chinese, whether in attacking hordes or in ambushes and they did not succumb to the ice, or snow, or the bone freezing winds. And that night, inside the friendly perimeter, they ate hot food placed on pieces of cardboard or in helmets. They had reached Hagaru-ri and joined up with more of their division. The taste of the liquor from the medicinal stores lingered on the tongue and when they crawled into sleeping bags, they slept warm and long and almost safe for the first time in over a week. The next leg of their hazardous journey was eleven miles. When they reached that destination the entire division would be together.

*

Jim woke with a start. He remained motionless so as not to give away his position with movement. It was daylight. His foggy mind frantically sought the reason for the lapse. Had he let his men down? The ceiling came into focus and his face hurt somewhat as the smile spread. He was surrounded by sleeping bodies and he opened the sleeping bag enough to wriggle a hand and arm free. The air was not freezing. Heaters kept the interior of the building warmer than anything he had experienced in what seemed eons. He luxuriated in the sleeping bag and stretched and restretched. His muscles and joints were rejuvenating and his thoughts briefly escaped the war. It was one of those moments when being alive felt especially good. He carefully crawled from his comfortable berth and stepped among and around the sleeping Marines. Not one stirred. He exited into the cold morning air. He was not prepared for the scene that met his eyes.

All the troops had not been as fortunate in obtaining warm sleeping facilities. Many were in tents. Some slept on the frozen ground, parachutes or tarps wrapped around their sleeping bags as windproofing and barriers from the bitter cold. He walked awhile absorbed in the panorama. He knew the lines would be forming for breakfast and he argued with himself. He wanted to rouse the men and get them in the chow line before those lines became excessively long, but the sleep was restoring exhausted bodies ... and minds. He eventually decided he had seen enough and turned and headed back to the hut and his sleeping comrades. Once inside he was happy he did not have to worry about making the decision to rouse his men. Jones and Monzeglio were sitting up, feet still in their bags. MacLean and McManus were standing, searching for eating utensils. Most of the rest of the occupants were somewhere in between those activities.

In twos and threes and assorted sized groups they got to the chow lines. With whatever implements they found they gorged on pancakes, powdered eggs and coffee, some using grimy fingers as eating utensils. Mess hands serving the food were apologetic for the chow and for the circumstances, but for those who were eating, for those who had gone without for so long, it was an Epicurean delight.

After breakfast the lieutenant and Staff Sergeant Dombrowski made certain of the welfare of their platoon members. When they were satisfied, the lieutenant called them together and spoke to the group.

"I thought you might like to know what was broadcast from Peiping last night. The Chinese have announced that the annihilation of the First Marine Division is only a matter of time."

Of all the sounds, Monzeglio's Bronx cheer was the most audible. It was typical of the feelings in the platoon. Bodies were responding to much needed rest and nourishment and the empty stare in many eyes gave way to glints of renewed life and confidence and humor ... and hope shined through .. more brightly.

Other events occurred which reached the ears of the men who fought their way to this temporary haven. Doc Norton, the Corpsman who joined them at Wonson, arrived with another Corpsman while the platoon was still gathered together.

"Lieutenant!"

"Yeh, Doc?"

"I'd like you and the guys to hear something my buddy here witnessed."

The newcomer told of hearing the news that elements of the column were approaching and he went, along with some doctors and other Corpsmen to help with the wounded as they came in.

"When the Marines came down the road," the Corpsman said, "they marched through the checkpoint in formation, straight and tall and in step. I heard one of the doctors standing nearby say, 'Look at those bastards, those magnificent bastards.' It truly was a sight to behold. Here's these guys who looked like they'd been to hell and back, but you knew they could do it again."

The entire platoon was filled with the pride that Jim felt. He and his mates were part of what made that possible. They had accomplished something that would bring them much deserved praise in the days ahead, wherever and whenever there was talk of courage and sacrifice, duty and honor, but they would do more yet.

What Doc's friend related next was of a different tenor. He spoke of demoralized troops, those soldiers who had replaced the Marine regiment on the east side of the reservoir. They arrived without weapons and as stragglers. Their officers, those who were in warming tents at the haven, did not venture back into the cold to lead them in.

The platoon members were silent after hearing that. Some were shaking their heads slowly in disbelief.

Jim made the only comment. "Thank God I'm a Marine!"

*

That morning was a time to share with a friend or search one out from another unit. Many had not made it. But while the respite from war occupied the time of so many, others were frantically busy. The airstrip roared with activity. Casualties were flown out, about fourteen hundred of them. Supplies were flown in. So were five hundred Marine replacements grabbed from duty stations throughout the Corps. And so to were reporters, eager to see first hand the 'trapped and retreating' division. The reporters stayed just long enough to get their stories and were gone, unlike the handful of their more hardy compatriots who accompanied the column.

The story those reporters flashed to the nation, to the world, contained an inaccurate quote. The commanding general of the Marine division was a religious man with a vocabulary free of profanity. He quietly and patiently explained to the assemblage of news people that the division was not retreating, but rather fighting in the opposite direction. Within hours bold headlines spewed the words, "Retreat hell! We're just attacking in another direction." It was not an accurate quote from the general but the words were accurate and described the ordeal to perfection.

That same misquoted, but steadfast and farsighted Marine general refused a gracious offer from the Air Force to airlift the division out. To have accepted the Air Force offer, the Marines would have had to leave their equipment behind ... and their unburied dead. That was not the way of Marines.

*

The Chinese could only get stronger the longer the Marines remained at Hagaru-ri. Before noon the battalion was preparing itself. They were to secure the hills overlooking the road south. Every man and piece of equipment had to pass below those hills and they must not belong to the Chinese. Weapons were readied, sleeping bags tied on, ammo and rations stowed and large caches of candy were added to each man's load.

When they moved out the wind was miserable. It whipped the intense cold across their bodies as they slipped and slid on packed, icy snow, toiling to reach higher ground. The main column would not start south until early tomorrow morning and these men of the rear guard would protect that column as it passed below them.

Rear guard again. Jim mulled the thought, but only briefly for they were on the move and that required all his energy and concentration. But he did feel better about things this time. They were rested and their bellies were full and he knew they would reach their destination. He knew that for a fact. The colonel expressed it best. "We're coming out of this as Marines. We're going to bring out our wounded and our equipment. We're coming out as Marines, I tell you, or not at all!"

The main column was on the road well before the sunup that lighted the Chinese positions. Mortar fire plowed up those positions and was followed by the precision air strikes of the Corsairs. It was a terrible thing for the Chinese who were too busy trying to hide to bother the troops passing below.

It was now that the Marine riflemen on that hill rose as one and moved in, the attacking platoons taking fire immediately. Jim wondered how so many of the enemy could survive the viciousness of the mortar and air bombardment. McManus went down and Doc Norton went to his aid, but nothing could be done. Within minutes Jorgenson was hit, but he would make it.

The two sides were close. The lieutenant and Sergeant Dombrowski, with frantic effort, kept the platoon together and on the attack. Dombrowski went down with a leg wound, but struggled upright and stayed stubbornly in the fight. The Chinese came at them once, twice and again and Jones and Monzeglio were lost with wounds.

As darkness began to cover them they were exhausted and depleted, but still carrying the fight. Then it started to snow.

"Williams! We gotta get that machine gun out on that knob," the lieutenant shouted pointing to his right. "Take your squad around their flank and kick the bastards outa there."

The 'squad' was down to five beat up effectives, Jack Taylor, Knox, Willoughby, MacLean and Jim. They were gathered together quickly by Jim and briefed. They were moving out in seconds. They worked their way hurriedly and unseen in the snow to a steep slope, a slope which made it impossible to outflank the position. They had to do something and they had to do it quick and there was no way they could make the change of plans known to the Marine lines.

Jim spit out orders amidst the noise and confusion of the furious battle going on to their left. They were in motion at once. They slid and slithered down into a shallow ravine. It was nearly impossible to be quiet with the hazardous footing, but there was so much turbulence and mayhem taking place above that it made no difference. At the bottom they were able to move fast and reasonably silent. Reclimbing the slope behind the machine gun nest took time. Already it had taken too long, but they were soon in position to launch their attack, nearly ten minutes from the time they departed their own lines. It was unwise to try and take the position with firearms or grenades for they could expect the wrath of every Chinese in the vicinity if they were discovered and their small force could not withstand that retribution.

Instructions were issued in one great hurry and the order given. Taylor was left in charge of Willoughby and MacLean. Those three would cover Jim and Knox, especially if they had to beat a hasty retreat. Crawling, or rather sliding over the hard, icy snow, the Marines had to stay low to keep from being hit by friendly fire.

It seemed it had taken forever to reach the position, but now, Jim and Knox were there, behind a machine-gun nest that contained only two extremely busy Chinese. Their breathing and heart rates were on a rampage, but they could waste not a second to compose themselves. On a prearranged signal the two dove into the hole and fastened onto the enemy soldiers. Kabars slashed through quilted clothing and plunged deeply into flesh, driven by all the strength two young men could summon. Two hearts were racing out of control and two others ceased to function. The ill fated operators of the death spouting weapon were dead.

"Sonuva bitch!" Knox rasped, trying desperately to wipe the blood from the knife blade onto the Chinese uniform.

"Never mind that! Gimme a hand with this gun!" spewed Jim as he worked frantically, trying to heave the gun from the rear of the hole. With Knox on the other side, they got the gun out of the hole and slid out behind it. Seconds later, united with their three buddies, they were dragging it helter-skelter down the hill.

All five were sweating furiously when they reached the bottom despite the freezing temperatures. Having gone downhill much faster than intended, their momentum carried them further than intended. With the falling snow sure to cover their trophy they lodged it behind some rocks and moved rapidly along a path in an effort to locate a suitable place to climb back to the top. They must come up behind their own lines, for the Marines above were on the attack.

Visibility was getting worse and that was not the only bad luck.

Just short of colliding with a Chinese patrol in a gully that emptied into the one the Marines were in, Taylor breathlessly rasped, "Fuckin gooks!!!"

With the Thompson sub machine gun he had earlier acquired from a dead Chinese, Taylor opened up. The Marines, still keyed up from their escapade reacted before the enemy and six Chinese lay dead in seconds.

In the immediate stillness after the last echo died away, Jim hissed, "Quiet!" As all ears strained he spat between clenched teeth, "Shit! There's more and they're comin fast! Jack! Get the guys up the hill! Move! Move!"

Spinning, Jim fired eight rounds with the speed of life saving necessity. There were two squeals as bodies hit the frozen earth. He reloaded instantly and opened up again yelling in the same instant, "Dammit, Jack! Move out!"

There was firing behind him. He heard another go down. It got louder and was more rapid and he knew his people were still there, engaged in the firefight. Jack Taylor, that wonderful fool, had disobeyed him.

But suddenly and with awesome power, the sun burst brilliantly right before his eyes. It blazed in the night's terrible blackness and exploded in a cacophony of sound that crashed upon him and was quickly swallowed up in deathly silence.

* EIGHT *

When he closed his eyes tightly and clamped his teeth rigidly together, he vividly recalled the chaos in his mind and the pain in his body. Strange how it was so real so many years later. Thankfully it was only a memory. That was all that remained of Sal, just memories, but those memories, like those of his brother Don, were always fond memories. To this day, whenever either of those two were in his mind, a smile often appeared on his face before they disappeared again in the sands of time.

He remembered many other men from those days long ago. Some he had seen again over the years. They had been good men, .. the very best. A nation was blest to have such as them. He had been blest serving with them.

Suddenly that blessing was punctuated! The sun burst through an opening in the clouds! It was just for an instant, but the ray had been brilliant in its short life and the wind had relinquished its ferocity.

He reached for the glass. He toasted hope and those men ... and Don ... and Sal and took a sip. It was easy to slip away and live again in the yesterday of his youth.

~ ~ ~ ~ ~

Anesthetized senses were jarred and wakened, not to alertness, but rather a dim awareness of distant aches and incongruous thought. Jim Williams pain was tolerable, even acceptable, but his inability to sift out the details of a bad dream tormented his weakened intellect. The jarring continued. It was most noticeable near the feet, but traveled up and through his body to his head where the pain was most severe. A groan passed between his clenched teeth. The motion stopped and he could feel himself being lowered.

"Jim! You awake?"

His eyelids were heavy and seemed glued together, but one, then the other opened enough to catch the palled images against the icy backdrop. The voice he struggled to place at last registered in his foggy brain. It belonged to Jack Taylor. He tried to speak and his tongue got in the way, but he finally uttered a raspy, "Yeeaah."

From then on he was nearly unintelligible and Jack interrupted him, "Don't try to talk, Jim. You're gonna be OK. Don't try to talk."

Jack turned and spoke to other fuzzy forms. The conversation was in sharp whispers and clouds of vaporized breath rose from the group and vanished into the freezing darkness. It was bitter cold, but he was not cold, his main discomfort being the pain and the numbness that engulfed his head and upper torso. The ill defined scene he fought to understand accentuated the intolerance for his inability to grasp what was taking place. A figure knelt beside him, inspected him quickly, then rose and spoke. It was not a familiar voice and there was an accent, but it was an accent he felt he knew. The voice was a pleasant voice, but one with authority.

"Och, lads, we canna dally here. We'd best be underway."

The Marines gathered themselves together and Jim felt his head and shoulders rise and he was moving again over the irregular ground. He strained to move his head for a view of the proceedings and a moan escaped his lips. He recognized shapes, but could not give them names. He tried desperately to understand, to make sense of things. He became frustrated and that made him weary and he could no longer fight Morpheus. He slipped from consciousness.

*

The voices were exuberant. Corporal James Arthur Williams, U.S.M.C. awakened enough to sense the mood and feel himself being lifted and placed in the back of a vehicle. He wanted to urinate. He needed to urinate. He tried to hold it. He could not move. It was not only his lack of command of his muscles, but he was wedged between other bodies. He heard engines being gunned and they were moving. He was conscious enough to make the decision. The warm liquid quickly soaked his mid section. Before it cooled, he was out again.

*

There was a vague recollection of being loaded into an airplane and taking off and another of having clothing cut from his body in a warm, bright, white room, but nothing else till he woke, groggy and famished. He was fed, but did not remember the face of his benefactor. By the time the utensils were cleared away his mind had regained some of its clarity. When the doctor and nurse arrived he was very nearly capable of analytical thought.

The examination was thorough and he enjoyed the comments of the doctor which was a single word repeated often, "Good!" The physician explained what had happened to his body and the prognosis, which also was, "Good!"

The doctor was first to leave and the nurse, quite pretty and perky lingered but a moment.

"We've heard what you boys did. You're all so marvelous!" A tear escaped along her nose and she smiled sweetly and was gone.

The space she vacated was filled quickly by bodies pushing up to the bed. Familiar faces crowded around him. One was on crutches. Another had an arm in a sling. All were heavily bandaged, but they were five exuberant Marines.

"How're ya doin, leatherhead?" Jack was grinning broadly. "Boy! We thought you were a goner when you went down. How're ya feelin?"

Jim smiled gleefully. He extended his hand to Jack who pumped it vigorously, followed in turn by Knox and Jorgenson left handed, his right arm in a sling. Then came Willoughby and lastly, MacLean on crutches.

"I feel pretty good, especially after hearing what the doc had to say. And that pretty nurse did me no harm," he grinned. "I guess I look worse than it is. The arm is only a simple fracture and they got all the shrapnel outa the left side of my body and the piece that hit my head didn't do any permanent damage. I guess it was the explosion that gave me the concussion. Damn! Damn, it's great to see you guys! Damn! You sure look good to me! Geeze! It's really great! Damn!"

A joyous six Marines jabbered and joked, laughed and poked and made more noise than they should have. They were survivors and glad to be, Jorgenson from earlier fighting, the others from the patrol that eliminated the machine gun nest. Jim learned that Monzeglio and Jones also survived. When he was convinced that he knew all there was to know about each man's wounds and well being, he pressed them for details of the patrol after he went down.

Jack became the spokesman. He related how all of them were wounded in the ensuing fight that wiped out another Chinese patrol of eight men. MacLean with a leg wound needed support. Two tried to carry Jim in a makeshift sleeping bag stretcher, but required rest every few steps. It was a disaster going nowhere. With their wounds, they became so tired they thought of forming a perimeter and trying to hold out till help came, but were fearful they would not be found. They pushed on, though with scant progress and suddenly were confronted by two remarkably healthy Royal Marines who had been in a convoy ambushed and cut off a week earlier.

The British had carried a small war to the Chinese. They sniped when they could hit and run, killing five Chinese in a week long adventure, all the while searching for allied forces.

"Did you get the names of those two?" Jim asked.

"What names? ..... .Oh! You mean the Limey Marines?"

"Yeah, Jack," Jim grinned, "that's who I mean, .. the Limey Marines."

"Yeh, .. well, .. the guy who helped MacLean," he nodded toward the Marine on crutches, "was introduced as Tester. I don't think I ever heard his first name." The others agreed. "The other guy was a corporal and his name was Doug Cameron. He spoke kinda funny, even for a Limey."

Jim laughed, grimacing a bit at the pain in his side.

"That's because he isn't a Limey. He's a Scot. My grandmother's mother was a Cameron."

"Well, he sure was a helluva guy. He had some morphine and medical supplies that sure came in handy and he pulled you on that travois he made, .. most of the way to Koto-ri ... till we got picked up. None of us was worth a damn. The other guy held Mac up all the way, too."

*

In the days that followed Jim poured over casualty lists. He came across names he served with at Lejeune. He came across names from the past, former buddies who returned to active duty with the reserves. A practical joke, as Sal once predicted, was not responsible for the death of Steve Sellers. Snipers are too serious a group. And there was Jonnie Phillips who walked into Parris Island in one shoe and shared much of his first two years in the Corps with Jim and Sal. He would share no more.

*

During the passage of a week Jim graduated to a wheelchair. He and his squad mates visited at every opportunity. He was surprised at the number of people he came across from previous duty stations. He was also surprised at the Silver Star that caught up with him for that night at Yudam-ni ... so long ago. And he was promoted.

He had many mixed feelings about it all. He had been leading a squad in combat for sometime and squads were commanded by sergeants so maybe that was OK, but of the details noted in the decoration, he remembered little.

He did remember Sal and felt Sal deserved recognition for his valor. Sal died and he lived. He was recognized and Sal was not. As a survivor he felt the guilt that frequently accompanies survival. It led to the ambivalence he felt about his decoration. And before he climbed aboard the plane that was to take him home, he was touched by the respect and love of the men he led.

Though he had tried to maintain a distance from them, he did not succeed. They shared in something uncommon and were not found wanting.

* * *

It was December 22nd when Jim arrived at the Brooklyn Navy Yard. With leave papers in hand he was turned over to the people who would take him home.

His mother sobbed and sobbed some more as she hugged him and rehugged him. She refused to let go. Tears rolled silently down Shirley's cheeks. His father gulped and gulped again to hold his emotions in check, but could not. And Bob, the good looking college freshman, grinned and beamed and repeated again and again, "God, Jim, it's good to see you! God, Jim, it's good to see you!"

Bill Williams drove slowly on the return to Shoreford. They talked and laughed and cried. They lingered over supper, the conversation never lagging. It was after eight o'clock when Sarah shooed them into the living room. The telephone rang a lot. It was very late when they went to bed.

Sleep did not come easily. Jim was too wound up and Bob had difficulty ending their discussion. Jim did not mind his brother's conversation. Bob had assiduously followed the Marine Division's activities in Korea, especially the epoch fight to the sea. Jim was surprised at his younger brother's knowledge of the event and was reminded of himself five years ago. He knew his mother would be unable to deter the youngest of her sons from enlisting when his first year of college was complete.

Alas, Bob finally did go to sleep, but Jim was still awake with his thoughts, which were mostly of Sal. He was told at the supper table that his good friend, his foster brother had made Bill and Sarah the beneficiaries of his government insurance policy. That was like Sal. He did it without even telling Jim.

Don's ten-thousand dollar policy had helped his father get his business started. The surplus, went into the bank. Now another ten-thousand would give his folks a cushion for the coming years. It helped to relieve some of the grief he felt for Sal.

His feelings were further elevated by the knowledge that Buck was arriving home tomorrow, home from Lejeune where he completed his advanced infantry training. He and Shirley wrote daily and she had quite a stack of his letters. She also had a large quantity of his money. He sent home most of his pay. This was to be his first trip through the main gate. He had not gone on liberty once since arriving at Lejeune. Jim was glad, not for the sake of Buck's frugality, but because North Carolina still posted signs for Colored and White. He was glad his best friend and brother-in-law did not have to cope with that. Jim found it impossible to imagine Buck in a situation of that nature and thinking about it, he clenched his jaw in anger.

*

The agile young man in the forest green uniform bounded from the train and spotted her immediately. They raced to a point in between. P.F.C. Milton M. Buchanan, U.S.M.C.R., dropped his pack, plucked her from the cement platform and instantly they were wrapped tightly together, hugging, kissing and hugging.

Another young man in a forest green uniform, not so agile, smiled approvingly from the spot Shirley vacated. When together, Buck and Shirley always reminded Jim of the way he felt couples should be.

Two young men carrying suitcases with college logos stopped to stare, then smirk and make some inaudible comment. Jim took three quick steps, his limp quite noticeable, but they saw the fire and anger in his eyes.

"You guys better move outa here, .. now!"

They did, perhaps Jim thought, caught off guard, perhaps intimidated. It mattered little, for they were long gone and the platform nearly empty when the young lovers separated. Buck, an arm about Shirley saw his mother coming toward him on the arm of a gimpy Marine.

Mother and son embraced instantly and Isabel Buchanan like another mother, tears streaming down her cheeks, did not want to let go. But after a bit she did and the two Marines embraced with a vigor that sent a shot of pain through Jim's left side. They did not speak. No words were necessary. The four walked arm in arm from the platform. They did not mind the December chill nor where they aware of the world around them.

*

In the afternoon of the same day Bob took Jim back to the city to do his Christmas shopping. The huge amount of back pay in Jim's pocket permitted a grand buying spree.

Back home Jim struggled with the wrapping, but accepted no help. He was able to use his left arm and hand enough to do a neat, even artistic job. At any rate, he was satisfied with the results.

His mother returned to the kitchen and observed the large pile of neatly wrapped boxes tied with various colored and styled ribbons atop the table.

"Why, Jimmy, you certainly didn't need my help. That's a fine job of wrapping," she said smiling and hugged him.

He put his good arm about her and kissed her forehead.

"Thanks, Mom."

She squeezed him more firmly than usual and he felt her quick intake and expulsion of breath before she released him.

"Bobbie, come help your brother with his packages. I must start supper."

The two brothers loaded up.

"Bobbie, for heavens sake, don't try to take it all in one load!"

*

The church was warm and friendly coming in from the cold outdoors. The congregation rose for the opening hymn and Jim glanced sideways at his mother sharing a hymnal with Isabel

Buchanan. It was just over six months ago she had shared, maybe the very same hymnal, with Sal and the two, Mother and adopted son had sung with such gusto.

His thoughts stayed fixed on Sal, a friend who had been so much a part of his life for most of five years. They shared many adventures and Sal was never found wanting. Then his thoughts turned to Don. Did anyone ever have a better brother? He too had never been found wanting. Now they were both gone and so was a large chunk of his young life.

He stared at the pages of the hymnal. There were no words coming from his mouth. His lips remained closed. He was among family and friends at the beginning of the celebration of the greatest birth and all he could think of was death. It glared at him from images on the pages of the open book, the images of Don and Sal gradually replaced by other dead comrades, some in sweaty, soiled and ragged dungarees, while others wore layers of filthy and rumpled cold weather clothing. There was a blankness in their eyes.

Would Buck's image one day join this band of dead brothers and comrades in arms. Jim wondered, for now it was Buck's turn. That morning he confided to Jim that he was joining a draft, that scuttlebutt had it, was headed for Korea in less than two weeks. Buck, his sister's husband who exhibited so many of the fine qualities of Don and Sal. Buck, the last of his three best friends, all 'brothers.' Buck, a new body, a twenty-two year old Marine Reserve P.F.C., was to be fed into that ugly, far off and merciless battlefield.

But as Jim wondered anxiously about the future, he did not wonder about Buck's performance. He knew his friend, his brother-in-law, would not be found wanting.

*

The family gathering at Grandmother Williams repaired somewhat the terrible melancholy, but Jim could not erase his concern for Buck and his sister. He, Sergeant James A.

Williams, U.S.M.C., he was the professional. It should be he who was going.

*

Three days after Christmas Jim drove Buck and Shirley to the railroad station. Shirley was uncharacteristically quiet. She lay her head on Buck's shoulder and pressed against him. Jim dropped them at the station and parked the car a block away and walked slowly back. He rejoined them inside and told them he was not going with them to the platform. He believed that should be their time, a time not to be shared with anyone. He and Buck were less demonstrative than on Buck's arrival, but the emotion was strong. They shook hands and maintained their grips a long time. They smiled, but Jim's smile was an attempt at lightheartedness he had to fight to maintain.

"You take care of yourself, good Buddy."

"You betcha. And you get yourself well quick." Buck also worked at his cheerfulness.

"Take care, Buddy."

"You too, Friend."

They loosed their grips and each patted the other's shoulder. Jim watched them walk down the stairs to the tunnel. Taking the same path when they were out of sight, he waited at the bottom of the stairs to the passenger platform. When he heard the train pulling out, he walked slowly up to meet his sister and place an arm about her shoulder.

They were in the car and under way before she spoke.

"He's going to Korea, .. isn't he?"

"Gosh, Shirl, I don't know. You never know where you're going till you get your orders. That's just the way it works."

"You know! Both of you know and you're not telling me!" There was anger in her voice. "You two think you're big, tough Marines and I'm just a weak little girl so you tell me nothing. Don't you think I have a right to know where my husband is going. Don't you think that if I was told the truth and didn't feel so left out, I could be more supportive to my husband. You two guys ought to take a look at what you do to me."

The few tears of anger turned to a gush and she dropped her head to her hands and sobbed, her body shaking. Jim pulled the car to the side of the road and wrapped her tenderly in his arms. The shaking subsided after awhile.

"Oh, Jimmy, I'm sorry. I didn't want to do that. I don't know why I did, but he's such a fine person and so good."

"Shhh. It's OK, Shirl. I'm the one who should be apologizing. God! I had no idea you had any idea."

"What do you think I am? Some kind of dummy? When I see my husband and my brother trying to cover something up. Jimmy, I've known you too long and Buck, .. sweet Buck, he could never keep anything from me. Do you know we had our first bad argument. I wanted to get pregnant and he said, 'No!' He wouldn't tell me why, but I knew why. Do you know why?" Jim knew, but said nothing. "He was so afraid I'd have to bring up a child of mixed race all by myself and it would spoil my chances of any further marriage."

"He's quite a guy," Jim smiled, "but I guess I don't have to tell you that."

He started the car and put an arm about her, squeezed her and drove away holding her to him. He turned his gaze momentarily on her and their eyes met for a brief moment before he concentrated again on his driving.

"We think there's a strong possibility that Buck is headed for Korea."

"Thank you, Jimmy."

She cried awhile, very softly, but by the time they were home she was more like her old self.

*

During the final weeks of his leave and the first days of 1951 Jim returned to the Navy Yard for a check up. He was healing more quickly than the prognosis. At home he was doing a lot of walking, including a daily excursion to his father's shop.

Before the end of the leave he was traveling to Collins Park and walking in the sand. He could feel the response in his leg which would soon be performing normally. His side ached only slightly, when he pushed himself. His arm was almost to par.

While his body healed, so did his mind and the periods of melancholy became shorter and were spaced further apart. They would never disappear completely, but he could live with that ... and he could function as he was supposed to.

Buck shipped out and Jim retrogressed briefly, but bounced back and forced himself to be cheerful and responsive to his mother and sister and to Buck's mother.

Shirley was great. She would not allow her own fears to rule her life, though she had them in abundance. It was she, down the road, more than anyone, who was most influential to Sarah's well being and that of Isabel Buchanan.

Jim never spoke of one thing in front of his mother, but he knew that when the school year ended, Sarah would have to face up to another 'son' becoming a Marine and in all probability, heading down the path of danger.

Bob was really impatient. When he was home for the holidays, as they lay awake in their beds, he talked endlessly with Jim about his feelings. He wanted desperately to be part of the conflict. As with most youngsters who never experienced the horrors of war, there was a certain amount of glory involved. But that was minute. Most of his motivation bordered on a kind of altruism. He dearly loved his 'brothers' and his uncle who went before him. He wanted to share in their hardships, their suffering and pain and bear his share of the burden. And though it never entered his conscious thoughts, he wanted to avenge the dead.

Knowing those feelings and what was in Bob's heart, Jim liked what he saw in his kid brother. He remembered vividly what Don had said to him about pride and he knew he felt that for Bob.

* * *

When Jim left Camp Lejeune a year ago, the Second Marine Division was way under strength. Since then it had supplied thousands of men, including entire battalions to the First Marine Division for service in Korea. Despite that exodus the base was now bulging at the seams. Reserves flocked in. Also feisty young Americans aware of their valor in Korea, wanted to be U.S. Marines. The Corps was again a going concern. The death and destruction of a war and perhaps the indiscretion of a President had sown the seed of rebirth.

Jim went to N.C.O. School for a few weeks and received his orders to join a battalion, again in the 6th Marines. His platoon leader was a young second lieutenant right out of Quantico, the platoon sergeant, a reservist returned to active duty, a veteran of WWII, as was the company C.O., his new skipper.

As platoon guide he jumped into his new duties with vigor and enthusiasm. Not yet at his peak physically he made the decision to get there at the earliest possible. In addition to the normal P.T. he did some running before evening chow when not on duty. At first he struggled, but his body acclimated and finally accepted, then rewarded his efforts. He pushed himself and he liked it and remembered that in the past when immersed in such activity, he was better at what he did.

Jim often took charge of the platoon on the drill field. He was good and there was an immediate response from the members of the platoon. He fit in quickly, but he was restless at times and his dreams were not always good. He signed up for a course with the M.C.I.

Jacksonville, North Carolina was not much of a liberty town, especially for Jim who seldom drank. Besides, segregation still ruled here and his relationship with Buck tipped the scales against spending money for the economy of the area. He was extremely thankful that Buck was in a fully integrated division. The Corps initiated the integration of its combat units, the first small step out of a grievous past. Buck was in the heart of the Corps, not on the fringes and Jim knew his brother-in-law would be an asset to any unit in which he served.

Letters home were a daily occurrence. Jim gave special attention to Shirley and his mother. He also wrote to Mrs. Buchanan. Of course he wrote frequently to Buck and as Buck began to experience the war first hand, the two were drawn into an ever closer bond, which at times made Jim uneasy. He knew that the chord that connected them could be severed so quickly and finally.

Notices were posted that the Marine Corps was forming a new outfit. Volunteers were being sought. It seemed a worthwhile challenge to Jim and he chewed it over for a few days before he decided to see the skipper. He made up his mind and was about to make the trek to the company office when he was summoned by the captain's runner.

"Hey, Sarge, the skipper wants to see you."

"No kiddin, Monty. I was just gonna drop in on him."

"Well, he beatcha to it," the corporal grinned.

Jim walked the short distance to the office. He knocked on the captain's door as instructed by the first sergeant. The voice from within told him to enter, which he did and stopped in front of the captain's desk standing at attention.

"At ease, Sergeant, have a seat." Jim sat. "I have a request for you. The word is out. With all that's going on in the Corps there's a desperate need for drill instructors. Have you ever thought of becoming a drill instructor?"

"I guess the only thing I've ever thought of D.I.s, Sir, is I don't want to be one."

The captain hesitated and studied Jim, then smiled, "I think you'd make a helluva good one, Sergeant."

"I don't know, Skipper, I just don't think I have the mentality."

"My God, Sergeant, you have a terrific record, both combat and otherwise."

"I'm sorry, Sir. I really don't want to be a D.I. I appreciate the offer, really, but I was hoping to get in to see you just now to ask for a transfer to that new outfit they call amphibious reconnaissance."

The captain looked down, tapped his fingers lightly and returned his eyes to Jim's.

"Sergeant, I still believe my judgment of you is correct. I hated like hell to put this proposal to you for I didn't want to lose you, but they asked for good people and I feel you are one of those." He studied Jim again, "So you want to join recon?"

"Yes, Sir!"

"OK, I'll have the top draw up the orders."

"Thank you, Skipper!" Jim beamed.

The captain started to rise and Jim jumped to attention. The officer extended a hand across his desk. They shook firmly.

"Good luck, Jim. You'll have your orders in a few days."

"Thank you, Sir! I shall feel naked without the forgierre. I've worn it my entire life in the Corps, in either the 5th or 6th Marines. I guess it feels sorta special to me. One of my uncles was one of the guys that earned it during the First World War."

"You'll be missed, Sergeant," the captain said smiling warmly, "Enjoy recon."

"Thank you, Sir, I will."

Jim took a step to the rear, did an about face and marched from the room, his exhilaration increasing with every step.

* * *

Sergeant James A. Williams joined Recon in its infancy, still in the process of forming up. It was to be a battalion, but about a third the size of an infantry battalion, roughly three hundred officers and men. There was a headquarters company of sixty or so and two rifle companies, the first not yet up to strength, the second to be formed when the first was in place. The battalion was patterned after the WWII preinvasion and long range reconnaissance units with a strong dash of Marine Raider added. Jim liked the outfit and the men and once again was platoon guide. An officer and staff N.C.O. ran the platoon and with the present scarcity of ratings, corporals often commanded squads. To some extent, platoon guide was a position in which he found some shelter and comfort. Having a man in the middle job, he did not have to jump right into a command.

Training was constant and physical conditioning a religion. They double timed all over the place. Jim's body, already in great shape, was fine tuned and his mind was busied with myriad topics, some new, others familiar but in need of more intense scrutiny.

*

Time passed so quickly Jim was surprised to receive his mother's letter asking him to talk his younger brother out of enlisting. It was June and Bob had completed his first year of college. Having kept his promise to his mother Bob felt his obligation fulfilled.

Buck had completed five months in Korea. He was patrolling constantly, especially at night and had been involved in some intense fire fights. Jim was convinced that constant patrolling required a great deal of the hero, but those that constantly patrolled were just doing a 'routine' job that was rarely recognized as anything else. It could, however, take a toll. Nevertheless, Buck remained unscathed and positive.

But Buck and Jim did sometimes discuss in their letters to each other, the change in the conduct and purpose of the war. They both felt the war was becoming a political misadventure and the combatants little more than tools of the politicians on both sides. Buck passed a particle of those feelings to Shirley who unwittingly let it slip out in her mother's presence. Sarah was quick on the uptake.

Yes! Jim thought, he would try to talk his brother out of enlisting. He arrived home a few days later for a short leave, his first trip home since recovering from his wounds.

*

Robert Owen Williams would not, could not be dissuaded. He was not eloquent as Don had been. He did not plead or rationalize the way Jim had. He stated his case with authority and a touch of hostility. He would go. He would not return to college in the fall.

"Mom, I am going! I kept my promise to you and now I'm going!"

"Oh, Bobbie, why? Why? You heard what your brother said about the war."

"I don't care, Mom. I'm almost nineteen years old and that's old enough to know my mind. Besides, how can you expect me to do any less than my uncle and four brothers. I could never live with myself. I'm going to go, Mom!"

Bill Williams said little. Despite his concern, deep inside he was proud of his son and could understand many of his feelings.

Shirley said nothing, but her sympathies lay with her brother this time.

The fight did not stay in Sarah Williams. She seemed to age a little as she sighed and slumped rearward, allowing the stuffed back of the chair to support her dispirited torso, her arms and legs limp.

Jim kneeled in front of her and held her hands and talked soothingly, but unsuccessfully.

When they went to bed, her husband held her in his arms and took his turn at conciliation. He was not totally successful, but she did listen to his words and she did sleep, though it was a troubled sleep.

When the three siblings were alone in the living room, Shirley spoke first.

"Bobbie, I can understand your feelings, but you didn't have to be so rotten to Mom."

"Shirley's right, Bob. You could have presented your argument much better and been kinder to Mom."

Bob sighed deeply. "I'm sorry, guys. Maybe I was hard on her, but I have to do this thing and she doesn't try to understand."

"Understand, Bobbie?" Shirley at once retorted, "Don't you understand? She's already lost two of the sons whose path you wish to follow. Jimmy's been wounded and Buck is there now. Loosen up and try to see this from her point of view."

"Once again, Bob, your sister's right. Now you've got to do the right thing and set yourself right with Mom. She deserves that much and you owe it to her."

Again Bob sighed, "You're right of course. Thanks for putting me in my place. I guess I just feel so strongly about going that I didn't even give Mom a thought."

Very kindly, in the morning, Bob would make his peace with his mother, but there was no doubt of his intentions. He did make one concession to Jim. He would join the reserves and not enlist for four years. He would then be released at the end of hostilities.

Sarah Williams hostility, however, would continue towards the U.S. Marine Corps, but she did start to come around a bit with her son after she and her Bobbie had their time together.

*

It was a short leave for Jim, but he returned to Lejeune with a good feeling. He knew that his presence was a blessing to his mother with whom he stayed for long periods.

Now living with Isabel Buchanan, Shirley and Isabel also figured heavily in Jim's schedule. Brave as his sister was, he, most of all, was aware of the strain she was carrying and hiding.

And he made one visit to his father's shop for a few hours. He jogged there and back.

During that visit he went out to get some coffee for them, since ironically, the coffee maker was down and had not been repaired. In civvies, he ran into a couple of former schoolmates who greeted him enthusiastically.

"Hi, Jim! How've ya been? Haven't seen you around in awhile," one said.

"Don't live here anymore. Just home to see my brother off."

"No kiddin. Where's he goin?"

"Joined the Marine Corps."

"No kiddin. What for?"

Life was like that less than six years after the end of WWII.

*

Jim was back on base before Bob left for boot camp, but his brother pushed all the buttons to get there posthaste, which he accomplished. The most gung ho recruit Jim had ever seen, he often chuckled to himself when he visualized his kid brother coasting through that humbling ordeal. He would be nothing less than a benchmark for his mates and would always be ready for more. The tenacity with which Bob tackled his challenges was completely lacking in self-grandiosity. He was filled with the lore and love of the Corps, greatly enhanced by his powerful feelings for his four 'brothers' and uncle. He needed to share their heritage.

*

While Bob was in boot camp Buck received a head wound. Four days later he was back in the lines for ten days and to the rear again with a chest wound. He was out of action for two weeks. From the tone of Buck's letters, Jim knew he had gotten himself back to his unit before the doctors would have sent him. That was the way Milton Buchanan was. Before the end of August, Buck was on his way home. His third Purple Heart was a leg wound that would cause a minimal limp on the coldest, dampest days.

"Thank God!" thought Jim. "Now those two great kids can have their life together."

*

When Bob graduated from Parris Island Jim received a forty-eight hour pass and made the short journey to see the affair and spend a few hours with his brother. He talked to his brother's D.I.s and Bob was portrayed exactly as Jim knew he would be.

Robert O. Williams was the happiest and most easily trained boot either D.I. could remember.

* * *

The battalion was at full strength with the latest influx of men right out of boot camp. Jim had a new company commander, just home from Korea. He served under the officer before departing for Pendleton over a year and a half ago. One of the first men the skipper sent for was Jim who was offered a seat in the captain's office.

"Sergeant, what's this I hear about you not wanting to take the exam for staff sergeant?"

"Yes, Sir.. I'm still learning to be a sergeant which I haven't been for very long. And I like being in the same squad bay with my men."

"My God, man! You learned to be a sergeant long before you wore the stripes and the quickest way I know, .. in combat. And you have commanded a platoon on occasion. I would like to give you a platoon in this company, but you'd have to be at least a staff sergeant. As you know, our platoon sergeants are supposed to be master sergeants, but we're way below in our ratings."

"I appreciate the words, Sir, but somehow I feel .. sorta lacking."

"Why in hell do you feel that way? Your record shows you to be a superior Marine." There was curiosity and even some anger in the captain's tone and expression.

"Well ... I had a brother killed at Iwo who won the Navy Cross. He was a real superior Marine and a real superior person and he was only a P.F.C. One of my two best friends was killed at Seoul, another P.F.C. who was a great leader and I think he did more than me and I got the medal."

"You mean Gennaro?"

"Yes, Sir, that's who I mean. My other best friend just returned from Korea with three Purple Hearts. He came home a P.F.C. and I betcha he'd have been a lot more if he wasn't a

Negro. And something I've never told anyone, but I couldn't function the first time I heard shooting in Korea and we weren't even under enemy fire."

The captain leaned back in his chair and studied the serious young man sitting rigid, eyes boring into his own. The better part of a minute passed before the officer spoke.

"Are you telling me you were scared, Sergeant?"

"Sir, ... I'm telling you I couldn't function the first time I thought we were under fire."

The captains face became softer and his tone kindly. "And after that. Were you able to function?"

"I did, .. but I never got over being scared."

"Do you think you needed to make that confession?"

Jim did not answer. He looked away, then back, but did not answer. He did not know what to say, .. but he was glad he told the captain, .. glad he confessed. There was never time before, nor was the time ever right. He would have talked about it with Don. He had tried to talk to Sal, but had not been completely successful. Now someone really knew how he felt, .. that night so long ago when he thought he was under fire.

The captain continued to study him.

"You and I both know that being frightened is part of the price we pay in our profession. I spent three months on Okinawa and another eight in Korea and there was never a time when we were in the lines that I was not scared. There might be a few rare individuals who know no fear, but I've never met them and I know of no one who has. It's learning to live and operate in that atmosphere that's important and I know you did just that. The medal they pinned on you was richly deserved. That's for sure. I know two different officers who served with you."

He paused and looked away, then back at Jim.

"We all feel guilty about buddies we lost, .. when we survived. I could cry sometimes when I think about the great kids I left behind. So I know how you feel about that, but the Corps must go on and it must nurture and care for and impart knowledge on those who follow. It needs good people to carry out those tasks and to travel the paths of its destiny and those of us who survive are duty bound to lead the way ... and that includes you, Sergeant."

He paused again and flipped through some pages in a folder.

"Do you know what your GCT score is?"

"I guess I don't, Sir."

"It's in the one-forties which is very high. That, coupled with all the M.C.I. courses you have taken, added to a fine combat record makes you excellent material for Officers Candidate School, .. which is where I'd like to see you headed."

"Holy shit, Skipper!" the words jumped from Jim's mouth. "I have no desire to be an officer, .. uh, .. no offense, Sir."

The captain chuckled. "I won't take any if you'll take the exam for staff sergeant."

Jim did not have to think. He answered in the affirmative and was comfortable with the decision. The schedule was verified and the two talked a bit, .. about Korea, .. about Recon, .. about the Corps. At the conclusion Jim executed the proper military etiquette, but at the door he turned, "Thanks, Skipper!"

* * *

Corporal Milton M. Buchanan, U.S.M.C.R., was released from active duty in late September of 1951. He was promoted to corporal on his return to the States. He had served over a year and nearly seven months of that in Korea. The last of his three Purple Hearts gave him a ten percent disability and a tiny check each month.

Jim applied for a six day leave as did Bob who was also stationed at Lejeune for his advanced infantry training. It was granted to both and they rode home together and shared some happy days with the Williams and Buchanans. Much film was used and many pictures taken. During one session when the three Marines were in uniform and posing for Shirley, Sarah put an arm about Isabel. She was beaming.

"Aren't they beautiful!"

Buck was thinner, but otherwise looked great. There was very little outward presence of his wounds. He would regain the weight in no time. Not only did he have his wife to cook for him, but also his mother and mother-in-law. He had another important asset. He had enough time under the G.I. Bill to finish his schooling.

Many relatives from the Williams and Buchanan families came to call and it got to be a bit of a nuisance for Buck and Shirley, but the time ahead, after all the celebrating, would be theirs.

And Sarah, when she rode with Bill, her two sons, her daughter and son-in-law to the station was happier than she had been in some time, but did cry when the train pulled out.

Aboard the train Jim relaxed. It was a gratifying leave. The happiness at seeing his best friend alive and well after an excursion into deathly peril was inspiring and exhilarating. Shirley's joy, Isabel's and that of his mother, was a thing to behold. He was also more aware of the special relationship that had grown between his father and Buck.

On top of all that he was coming to know better and learning more about the young Marine in the seat beside him. He liked what he was finding out about his youngest brother. On their return trip to Lejeune, Bob took his place in Jim's heart alongside Don and Sal and Buck.

* * *

It did not seem that it was possible, but the training tempo within the battalion increased. The unit was moved to an immaculate tent town near the beach. The Marines were up well before the sun and oftentimes worked through the night.

Just behind the vicinity of the tent town, in a small open area of woodland, a square box was built with a number of holes, a community head. Every morning there was a long line of anxious Marines awaiting their turn over one of the holes. They might not have another chance for some time. Not everyone was successful.

One morning in the pitch blackness, amid the impatience of those in line and the straining of those on the box, a plop, plop was heard.

Someone, somewhere in the harsh darkness grumbled, "Lucky bastard!"

"Lucky bastard, hell!" a near tearful voice replied, "That was my knife and spoon."

* * *

Staring down at the clouds, Staff Sergeant James A. Williams, U.S.M.C. mused to himself at how quickly this trip came about. He was in the right place at the right time and with the proper credentials.

A major, three junior officers and three staff N.C.O.s were flying over the Atlantic for a three month tour with the Royal Marines. Jim was the junior Marine in the group. Thankfully he took the exam for staff sergeant and passed with flying colors. That was the lowest rating accepted for the assignment.

When Jim heard about the tour, he did something strange to his nature. He pulled all the strings he was capable of pulling to wrangle a place on the tour. The experience and training was an inducement to be sure, but there was a much stronger motive. He was hopeful of locating two men, one in particular, who had saved his life and by doing that, possibly the lives of his entire squad.

The Royal Marines was a much smaller outfit than the American Corps and Jim thought that if these men were alive, there was a good chance they had returned to Britain after their tour in Korea. The Commando Training Center seemed a good place to start the search.

*

The Americans spent most of their first day in Britain settling in and the second day being indoctrinated. On the third day, in the afternoon, they listened to a lecture with their British counterparts. The session was concluded before supper and the Americans were standing with a group of their British brothers and Jim mentioned a name to a Royal standing next to him.

"Sure I know him. He's with us right now." The lance corporal pointed to a group of British standing across the room, then said, "He's the sergeant."

Jim excused himself and walked over to an individual within the group. "Are you Duncan Cameron?"

A pleasant Royal Marine smiled and looked into Jim's eyes. "Aye, that's true." The burr was thick and broad. The last word was drawn out to trrrooo, the r's stumbling over each other and the o's multiplied. "That's what ma mum calls me and she never lies."

Jim smiled at the sound of the words coming from the friendly stranger. "Did you join up with some wounded Americans south of Hagaru last December?"

The Scot's eyes widened, a grin spreading across his face. The now familiar words were repeated, but with greater enthusiasm, "Aye, that's true!"

"I believe you might be the guy who hauled my ass south from there till you met up with the column."

Two pairs of eyes searched each other.

"Och! Are you the Yank?" His face lit with a huge smile.

The American thrust out his hand. "I'm the guy, .. Jim Williams."

The Scot grabbed and they pumped vigorously. They began to laugh and threw arms about the other in a great bear hug.

A small body of onlookers had gathered. Jim related the story of how Duncan built a travois and pulled him so many miles with no relief through hostile territory. Duncan, not to be outdone, started to tell of the devotion the Americans had for their leader, but before Duncan could elaborate greatly, Jim politely cut in, "I was just really fortunate to be with some good men and then to run across the paths of two Royal Marines. That's the reason I'm here today. What do you say? Can I buy you a drink?"

"Aye, that sounds great!"

Jim turned to the small group, "Drinks are on me!"

*

Duncan Robert David Cameron was from a family that had filled the ranks of the Highland regiments for generations, mostly the Queens Own Cameron Highlanders, but some in the Seaforths.

His father, a Cameron during WWI had been gassed and returned to Scotland and mustered out. In 1925 Robert David Cameron met a beautiful sixteen year old and they fell madly in love. Molly Shona MacGregor was ten years younger, but they were married. A year later Duncan was born. It was nearly four more years until a new sister arrived.

Duncan's mother, a widow now some eighteen years, never remarried. She gave her children the love of two parents and bestowed on them a strong sense of family and responsibility. Duncan still sent some of his pay home, albeit against his mother's wishes. Duncan was the first in the family to join other than a Highland regiment.

*

It was a long train ride from southern England to the heart of the Scottish Highlands. In a week and a half the American and the Scot had formed a strong friendship that had its beginnings back in the frozen wastes of Korea. Jim was going to the home of his new friend to share a long weekend with Duncan and his family.

They arrived very late, but Molly Cameron met them at the door. She hugged Duncan heartily and kissed his cheek. He squeezed her till she grunted and begged, "Let me go, you rascal." The burr was similar to Duncan's, but softer and more lilting.

"Och, Mum, you're a big sissy."

Smiling warmly she put a finger to her lips, "Shh, you'll wake your sisters."

Jim was introduced. Molly Cameron was a strikingly beautiful woman for one to whom life had not been kind. She had deep gray eyes from the ancient Picts in her ancestry. The fan like wrinkles at the outer corners of those eyes were the only deep lines her relatively smooth skin displayed. She was most gracious and the feelings of intrusion that Jim entered the house with disappeared instantly.

After the greetings there was some kidding and friendly conversation. Molly and Duncan had little trouble bringing Jim into the conversation. It was not only easy for Jim, it was enlightening for one who was often shy around strangers. He got over the first hurdle of intimacy quickly. He liked being here. He liked Molly and he wondered what else this friendly environment would bring forth.

Then in the soft tone they had been using Molly suddenly exclaimed, "My goodness! In all the excitement, I forgot the kettle."

"Och, Mum, no tea tonight. We only want ta get ta bed."

"But you will have the whiskey?"

"Aye! That sounds good. Just a wee drappie, Mum."

Molly went to the cupboard and took out two bottles, while at the same time Jim turned to Duncan and whispered, "I don't drink the hard stuff."

Duncan chuckled, "Hard stuff? This is the water of life and it comes from nowhere else in the world, but these God kissed Highlands."

Molly gazed at them curiously not knowing what to do. Jim felt a flush of embarrassment at her discomfort.

"It's all right, Mum, you can pour."

Jim did not argue.

Pour she did. Into two tumblers flowed two fingers from one bottle and a matching dose from the other, then just a splash of cold water. Into a third tumbler she poured equal quantities of smaller amounts. Jim hoped she would serve that one to him, but she took it for herself.

"You (which sounded like, yee) can smell and taste our country in your glass, Jim. ... Smell it, .. easy like, then take a sip, .. a wee one and let it slide ta the back of your tongue and down your throat."

Jim took a deep whiff and his nostrils burned.

"Easy, man! (which sounded like mon) Easy. You're not trying to suck it inta your nose."

Duncan was smiling, but Molly, watching Jim intently was concerned.

This time Jim followed instructions. He found the odor indescribable, but not unpleasant. He sipped carefully, then as carefully swallowed. His throat burned, but not badly and the warmth spread to his stomach. He was determined to finish the amber liquid and after a reasonable wait he took a second and a third sip and found that each one was less harsh and more pleasant. When a small burp passed in near silence he found the aftertaste most enjoyable. When the liquid in his glass was consumed, his taste buds were well on the way to being seduced by a foreign potation.

With the glasses empty Molly asked, "How did you find it, Jim? I hope you enjoyed it."

"It was a pleasant surprise for me, Mrs. Cameron."

"It was my husband, bless his soul, who kept the Macallan and Glennfiddich in the cupboard. Most folks have a favorite, but he preferred them together. It was only drunk on special occasions, for the malt is dear. He was gone ten years when Duncan enlisted and the day he left I took the bottles from the cupboard and shared a drink with my son. When Duncan was on his way over to Normandie we had another and when he came home from the war, we had another. Duncan has since replaced those bottles a number of times and we still enjoy it on these special occasions."

Maybe the whiskey helped, Jim thought, for he felt right at home amongst these two friendly people. When they rose to go to bed, he was sorry despite the late hour. As he crossed the kitchen, Jim's peripheral vision was alerted by movement. Still the Marine despite slowed reflexes, only his eyes moved. Sure enough, someone was peeking from behind a door that was open a tiny crack. Then it shut hurriedly without a sound.

Duncan and Jim went into the small bedroom prepared for them. It was not long before they were sleeping soundly.

*

The flump of a pillow smacking flesh roused Jim instantly. A form was standing over Duncan and from it came female giggles and a taunting command.

"Get up you lazy lout, Mum's prepared breakfast."

Duncan tore the pillow from her grasp and barely missed her fleeing body as he flung it after her. The door slammed shut and there was laughter in the kitchen on the other side of the door and from Duncan in the tiny room.

"Someday I'll spank that rowdy brat. Ceit just thrives on bein a tease," his voice lowered, "but she's only like that at home with me. She's really quite shy in public, .. except when she's angry."

They dressed hurriedly, for the unheated room was cold. In the kitchen Jim was introduced to Ceit, pronounced Kate. She had shed her rambunctiousness. It was replaced by the shyness Duncan spoke of. She awkwardly curtsied.

She was a fifteen year old stringbean with the most beautiful red hair (why they called it red he did not know) Jim had ever seen. It was braided in pigtails that ended below the mid point of her back. Above her slim neck was a strong chin and wide, sensitive mouth. She kept her lips together during the shy, forced smile. She had a cute nose, slightly turned up and lightly freckled. It was the eyes, however, that Jim studied. They were green and seemed ready to cast luminescent rays, like those of the aurora borealis he and Duncan saw coming from the bus stop on their arrival. But there was also a sadness hidden in those eyes, a deep down private sadness that only those closest to her were able to perceive. Yet now, during this first encounter, Jim detected it.

Ceit was a late bloomer, just beginning to show signs of her womanhood. Her legs, though slim, were quite shapely and showed muscle tone when she moved. It was on those legs

Duncan told Jim, that she was able to perform Highland dancing of a quality equal to many of the boys in the village.

Not actually Duncan's sister, Ceit Sheila Fraser was a cousin who had been orphaned at five and adopted into the Cameron family. Her mother, Molly's younger sister, was killed with her father, a Highland soldier in the Lovat Scouts about to leave for overseas, during a bombing raid on London in 1940. From that day forward, Ceit was Molly's daughter and a sister to Duncan and Moira. She did, however, continue to carry her father's name.

The same year that Molly lost her sister, she lost her younger brother at St. Valery with the Highland Division. She carried on by herself, raising her own son and daughter and a niece to whom she was 'Mum' in every sense of the word. She never formed an attachment to another man.

Jim and Duncan had become close and now Jim was drawn to Molly. He related to her much as he did his own mother. He had a strange desire to call her, Mum. Ceit was more distant, but Jim hoped she would learn to feel comfortable around him. He knew of her past and he knew the sadness in her beautiful eyes was a result of that past, despite the inviolable love she shared with Molly and Duncan and Moira. He hoped he could crack the shell of the skinny, and by Duncan's admission, sometimes exuberant, sometimes sad, tomboyish, soon to be young lady. On a full stomach however, delighted by an abundant Highland breakfast, Jim overlooked his concern for Ceit and allowed that he felt himself adopted into a new family.

Molly shooed all three from the spotless little house. She wanted Jim to be shown around and the cool morning was free of the rain that was a frequent visitor to the area. They walked into the rolling hills devoid of much of the timber. It was removed during the war. Ceit had no difficulty maintaining the pace of the two Marines. It was obvious she adored Duncan and often she was more like a younger brother than sister, punching him in the arm, or jumping on his back trying to wrestle him to the ground. Duncan in his turn did not handle Ceit daintily. It was another story with Jim. When she was close to him she was timid. She addressed him only when it was essential. She was polite when Jim spoke to her, but her conversation was mostly directed to Duncan. On occasion when Jim glanced in her direction, she quickly turned away, but she had been studying him.

Duncan was great company. He knew an exceptional amount of the history of the area and its clans. Jim, the constant student of history listened in earnest, often interrupting with a question. His grandfather told him stories of this land and under Duncan's tutelage the stories came to life walking through a countryside of unusual quality and beauty. Jim was captivated. The words of his new friend deepened his feelings and he was being drawn into a love affair with a country that time and progress did not seem to smother.

The three hikers were nearly home when on the road ahead four teenage boys appeared. The two groups met and exchanged greetings and Jim was introduced. The lads were polite and their admiration for Duncan was obvious. One of the group however, could not contain his urge to tease Ceit. She clammed up and mumbled to herself while Duncan enjoyed his sister's discomfort.

As the four boys were leaving, the kidder grabbed one of Ceit's braids and yanked. She never uttered a sound, but spun and grabbed his arm. Holding him, she plowed a small, clenched fist into his stomach. The youngster doubled over and gasped for breath.

"I told you never to do that to me again, Charlie MacPhee!"

Understanding some of the spoken words here about had at times caused Jim some difficulty, but there was no doubt about Ceit's words or their meaning. Charlie MacPhee's comrades laughingly hauled him away. He was a young man in pain and would probably think a second time before taking on Ceit Fraser again. Duncan put an arm about his sister in an attempt to calm her. He had difficulty suppressing the grin that sought to engulf his face.

When they arrived home, Ceit's eyes were still flashing fire.

*

She departed the house early in the morning, before Jim and Duncan were up. She had a long bus ride to the hospital. She was a nurse. She finished tending the sick for the day and now she was home. Her whole being seemed to be smiling when she walked through the door.

Jumping to his feet, Jim spilled tea from his cup into the saucer.

The movement of her body complimented her smile. She greeted her family quickly, "Hello, Mum. Hello, Ceit." She kissed them lightly on the cheeks, but stayed longer with her brother, hugging him to her. "Och, Duncan, tis so good to see you and feel you."

Jim was standing uncomfortably by his chair when she extended her hand to him, a hand that was female, but firm and strong. "Jim! I'm so happy to finally meet the one Duncan was so pleased to tell us about."

Jim had no doubt she meant what she said. Gazing steadily, but shyly into her eyes, he was certain she was incapable of a lie. Besides, Duncan had told him about her honesty, her inability to speak anything but the truth.

Caught off guard and slightly unnerved Jim dimwittedly replied, "Pleased to meet you too."

He wished instantly he could have said something different, but his mind refused to function. He stood there, looking into her eyes, so brown, so soft and so full of wondrous sparkle. He was befuddled ... and trapped by her charm.

Moira Lorinda Cameron was lovely. She was not beautiful in the classic sense, but the more you looked, the more you were convinced she was a classic beauty. It seemed to come from within her being. Jim continued to stare and realized he was squeezing her hand and abruptly released it. Her eyes continued to smile, a smile that was accompanied by a gentleness and kindness. The light brown hair, or maybe it was dirty blonde, he thought, fell below her shoulders when free of the bun she kept it in while at the hospital. It framed baby cheeks still touched with pink and a plain, straight nose and soft, full lips.

"Please sit down, Jim."

She moved away and removed her coat and hung it on a hanger and then a peg. The burr was like her mother's, but softer and not as noticeable due to her education away from home. She was trim and very feminine in her nurses uniform and Jim noticed the ankles when she crossed the room and knew immediately that the legs above were as shapely for they belonged to a ballerina. Since quite young Moira had been a promising ballet dancer, contrary to most youngsters in these parts who devoted themselves to Highland dancing.

They sat around the table and Molly made another pot of tea and they talked. Whenever Moira spoke Jim had no desire but to listen. The sound of her voice was enough to enchant him and he had difficulty taking his eyes from her when she was not speaking. He tried to release himself from her hold on him, but could not. Then he no longer wanted to and he said to himself, "My God! I must be nuts! She just walked in the door and I want to marry her."

*

A light supper was eaten and the members of the household readied themselves for the special occasion for which Duncan had invited Jim to Burrtown.

A ceilidh!

Jim finally gave up trying to make the letters of the word in Gaelic sound the way it was pronounced. Here it was again, the cei, which sounded like kay, as it did in Ceit, therefore, a ceilidh, was a kaylee.

All were ready ahead of time and Molly was sitting and inspecting her entourage with satisfaction. Ceit was fidgeting with the bow on her dress and Molly to distract her asked, "Ceit dear, would you honor us with a song. It would be a wondrous way to pass the time till we leave."

Ceit was standing near Molly and appeared uncomfortable, but Moira and Duncan clapped and Ceit blushed.

"Please, Ceit, let us hear your lovely voice," Moira smilingly pleaded.

"Come on, Ceit, twould give us all pleasure ta hear ya," Duncan added as he went to her and put an arm about her shoulder.

That was all Ceit needed. Taking a few deep breaths and focusing her eyes above her audience, she began. The first few nervous words gave way to a beautiful acappella rendition of Robert Burns, "My Love is Like a Red, Red Rose".

Jim sat mesmerized. Ceit had never received formal training, but it was difficult to tell and he had heard some great voices. She had a wonderful range and sang with passion, yet there was sweetness in her voice. There was something else. It took Jim awhile, but he recognized it, .. the same quality he had seen in her eyes, .. a touch of sadness. He really had to listen, but it was there. It added to the beauty. It was a sorrowful audience that sat briefly in silence when the song ended, before clapping enthusiastically.

Then it was time to partake of the ceilidh.

When they arrived the hall was packed. Jim wondered if it was the entire population of Burrtown and decided it was. He was in civilian clothes, but everyone in the tiny hamlet knew who he was, though few had met him. A handsome Highlander led Moira to the dance floor the moment she shed her coat. Jim spotted the teenage boys from the daytime encounter and one of them came over to Ceit and asked her to dance. It was not the MacPhee lad. He stayed well hidden. Ceit was reluctant, but went with the lad when Duncan led Jim to the beer keg.

The band, composed of accordions and violins, fiddles to the Scots, was lively and to Jim's liking. There was also a drummer and a bagpiper who did not join the band on every tune. That is when the piper did some serious drinking. At the end of the third piece an older gentleman climbed to the stage. It got quiet. In the thickest of burrs, helped somewhat by the drink, he spoke. "We have next, a welcome to present."

The piper stepped to the middle of the stage. He blew a few warm up notes and slipped into a lively, well played rendition of the Marines' Hymn. Jim was moderately acquainted with the pipes, but had never heard anything like this. He stood at attention, self consciously at first, but then enthusiastically. He looked past all the smiling, strange faces. When it was over, amidst much cheering, he and the piper were handed tumblers of whiskey and he finally got the message. He lifted the glass and following the pipers example, quaffed it down. There was more cheering.

The whiskey did not taste as good as that of last night, but it was not bad and it mixed well with the beer he and Duncan already consumed. This procedure occurred twice more during the evening and each time was more rowdy than the time before.

During the intervals between the 'welcomes', Jim searched for Moira, but she was constantly on the dance floor, usually with that handsome clod. He spotted Ceit frequently glancing in his direction, never happily, but he was not aware of that sentiment. She danced with many in her age group and on two occasions with Duncan. Molly was busy seeing that the refreshments were always available, but often danced with men considerably younger. She was as sprightly as any in the hall.

Introduced to a pretty, plump young lady by Duncan, Jim was tutored in steps that were foreign to him, but which he learned quickly and proceeded to enjoy. He danced with Molly and once with a stiff Ceit and every other female in the place, but never with Moira. When the band was on break he was at the keg, not by choice, but the insistence of the many friendly villagers.

Jim Williams, the once shy kid from America, found his niche that night and reveled in it. He ate, he danced and somehow his friends managed to supply him with copious quantities of beer and of course the whiskey he politely consumed during the 'welcomes'. After awhile he no longer sought out Moira, nor was he ever aware of Ceit's unhappy demeanor.

When the ceilidh was over and the struggle to get into outer garments was won, Molly gathered her brood and they stepped out into the cold, sobering, early morning air. It had little effect on Jim or his inability to walk a straight line, or speak articulately. He shuffled and stumbled home between Molly and Duncan, she humming softly, he laughing softly, mostly to himself.

Periodically Molly asked, "You all Right, Jim?"

His reply was always the same. "Cursshh I'm awright, shhank you."

But they did make it home and for the most part, Jim got himself into bed.

*

From far away Jim heard the swish and wack of the pillow and the female voice, "Get up you lazy lout!" and the feet scurrying from the room. He tried to take refuge under his pillow, but neither the world nor the ache in his head would go away.

"Can you make it, Jim?" his Scottish friend burred in his ear.

"Yeah, ... sure."

The words pounded in his head. His first attempt to sit, failed. He tried again and made it. He had to. He and Duncan made a promise to Molly last night. They would attend church, or kirk as Molly said it. He got his legs over the edge of the small bed and his bare feet on the very cold floor. He did not flinch. He had no reflexes.

Eventually Jim was washed and dressed and sitting at the breakfast table, but he could not eat. Molly cajoled him, pleaded with him, but he could not eat. Moira moved next to him with a look of sympathy and a piece of toast. She sweet talked him and assured him that everything was all right and tried to get him to eat. Because it was Moira, he nibbled the toast and finally it was gone. She next got him to drink some hot tea. Molly patted his shoulder. Ceit was stoic. Duncan was amused.

It seemed to Jim, though it was not, a very long walk to the kirk which was filled to capacity. The minister soon entered the pulpit. Jim reached for a hymnal. It slipped from uncoordinated fingers and landed on the wooden floor with a loud thud. He bent over and leaned unsteadily forward to retrieve the slippery book. It required all the energy he could muster. The congregation and the minister waited silently and expectantly.

Extended to his fullest when his fingers gripped the book, his innards were in a state of severe compression. The unrecognized, hidden gas bubble was forced vigorously from his body with a thunderous, vulgar sound.

Instantly his cheeks were on fire. So was his entire body, his embarrassment all consuming. He stayed bent over, hidden in the pew. There was nowhere else to hide. There was no way out. He must remain hidden. How could he sit upright and reveal himself as the culprit. He touched a cheek and felt the fire, his mind reciting a timid plea, "Oh, God, please!"

Finally and painfully Jim came to the realization he must return to the real world. Slowly and with eyes half closed he came to a sitting position.

"My God!" he thought, "Why doesn't the minister say something?"

Molly sitting to his right was shaking gently. Duncan to her right was not only shaking, but snickering. Moira, sweet Moira to his left was having intermittent tremors. The entire kirk was shaking and still the minister did not speak. It was some eons later that the service commenced and it was the most gruesome church service ever attended by James Williams.

Others would have different memories.

*

An early noon time meal was served before Jim and Duncan boarded the bus to the train station. The headache had lessened, but Jim moved with much less grace than his well conditioned body was capable.

The embarrassment was fading somewhat. After all, the congregation treated him quite kindly after the service. Elderly Mrs. MacLaren had called him 'a braw lad' and old Mr. MacNeil kept shaking his hand and telling him to come again, though his toothless grin seemed something of a smirk.

Maybe he would be invited back. Molly treated him much as she did her own son and told him numerous times that he must come again.

Moira too had said he should return. Ah Moira! She with the wonderful, kind, smiling face that tried so to put him at ease, but instead left him frustrated, befuddled and tongue-tied. He had heretofore thought he was a man of the world, but Moira negated all that. She befriended him much like a brother. Damn! He did not want to be her brother. He could be a brother to Ceit, but not Moira.

It was Ceit, the skinny, red haired, sometime spitfire who did not treat him as family. He was not sure how Ceit felt about him. He could recognize her deep love for Molly and Moira and the way she idolized Duncan was so obvious, but when she was close to him, she retreated and became shy. Often he found her studying him with a sad aloofness. He wondered if she disliked him.

The headache was still present when Jim and Duncan exited the bus and eventually boarded the rail coach. Sleep, healing sleep finally overcame Jim as the train carried them south. Back on the southern coast of England, they could once again ply their trade as Marines.

*

Training commenced with a vengeance early Monday morning. Most of the sleep Jim obtained was aboard the train, but by noon the last vestiges of his debauchery had seeped from his body. His dungarees, when he stopped to eat, were soaked. He wolfed down the noon meal and could again stare back at the world. He was alive once more and he made a vow. Never again would he permit himself to go through that horror.

* * *

The two week period since Jim and Duncan had been in Scotland was nearing its end. Jim did not remember, but he had been formally invited back for the celebration of Ceit's sixteenth birthday.

What really excited Jim was the prospect of seeing Moira again. In his own defense, he tried to convince himself otherwise.

On a day before the journey Jim and Duncan went into the city to purchase gifts for the event. The shops adjacent to the base catered to Naval personnel and it was not difficult to obtain articles for the fair sex. Duncan had all of Ceit's sizes and purchased a lime green slip with a lot of lace.

"I dinna think she's ever worn such frills," Duncan chuckled, "she's been more like a boy."

With no ideas of his own, Jim's mind was working furiously, but kept coming up empty. They exited the lingerie shop and turned left and something caught Jim's eye in the other direction and across the street.

"Wait a minute! Come on."

Jim grabbed Duncan by the elbow and turned him around. They crossed the street and stood in front of the shop window. The dress was on a mannequin. It was velvet and hugged the hips, then flared slightly to below the knee. It was flat against the mid section and cradled the breasts below a jeweled neckline. Three quarter length sleeves completed the elegance. It was the color, however, that attracted Jim, a brilliant green similar to Ceit's eyes. Jim gazed for nearly a minute. The dress seemed more mature than Ceit, but he could visualize her in it very soon. He did not know her that well, still, he was certain the dress belonged to her.

"Let's go in and get it. That's my present to Ceit."

"Och, Jim, it's quite dear. You shouldna spend so much."

"Hell, Dunk, a girl turns sixteen only once."

Without another word, Jim marched into the store followed by Duncan, who gave the salesgirl Ceit's size. Jim asked her to make sure there was room for growth. The salesgirl was very obliging and assured Jim her choice would be perfect and she did not expect to see him again, for an exchange.

Walking from the store with the package under his arm gave Jim a good feeling. He asked Duncan to show him to a store where he could purchase whiskey. Duncan did just that and he bought a bottle of Macallan and one of Glennfiddich.

"Och, man, you spend money like a drunken sailor."

They both chuckled as they turned in the direction Duncan pointed.

* * *

Moira came in while they were eating breakfast. Jim's heart missed a beat and he wondered how she could look so good and be so fresh, having just completed the night shift and the long bus ride home. The smile never faded as she kissed everyone on the cheek, including Jim. Suddenly he was tongue-tied. She joined them at the table for toast and tea before going to bed.

Whereas earlier Jim had conversed very much at ease with the family, now he could think of nothing to say. Periodically, after she spoke, Moira glanced his way with a sweet smile. She paused as if to offer him an opening, but he continued helpless. He inwardly chastised himself for his oafishness, but that only made it worse.

Graciously, Molly, Moira and Duncan addressed questions to him. He found the questions easy to answer. Soon he was speaking enthusiastically about his family and Shoreford. He got caught up in the subject matter. Stopping at the end of a description of his brother Bob, he glanced hurriedly at the attentive faces around the table and realized he was monopolizing the conversation in a manner similar to his brother, a manner he had just finished laughingly describing.

"Holy cow! Here I am telling you about my brother and the way he often gets carried away and here I am doing the same thing."

"Come on, Jim. Don't stop now," Duncan pleaded.

"Please, Jim, do go on. It is a wonderful opportunity to get to know about you and your family and your America." Moira certainly had a way about her.

Molly patted his hand, squeezed it and smiled, "Tell us more, Jim, please."

His inhibitions did not completely dissolve, but he did go on. He was grateful for the acceptance and grateful for these people. For the moment he was not cowering in Moira's presence. He was speaking and often looking into her eyes and smiling ... and she was smiling back.

*

The day passed quickly for Jim. He and Duncan took a short run through the hills and later visited in the village. Ceit spent some time with them. She seemed almost at ease. When Moira awoke, the entire group went out for a short walk. Later they had supper and tea and leisure time sitting around the table visiting together.

Before the birthday cake was put on the table Molly asked Ceit if she would honor them with a dance. She shyly consented. A space was cleared and a record placed on the phonograph. The first sound was the scratchiness of a worn record, but soon the skirl of the bagpipes came through.

Standing in the middle of the cleared space, Ceit placed fists on hipbones. With heels together and toes spread wide, she bowed, then was moving her feet, legs and arms in effortless grace and energy, in a flawless rendition of the Highland Fling. The bow at the conclusion was followed by enthusiastic applause and whistles from the Marines. Jim was impressed. He would have happily sat through more, but Molly came to the table with the cake.

The candles were extinguished with a gigantic puff and Ceit appeared happier than Jim had ever seen her. The cake was eaten, tea was drunk and Molly and Moira cleared the table. Duncan placed the presents thereon, the box from Jim at the bottom of the stack.

The excitement was unmistakable on Ceit's face. Her green eyes sparkled. Standing with Duncan, Jim looked down on her dazzling hair. She was without braids and strands of her hair were in striking tones of burnished gold to deep copper as they reflected the light. He was captivated by the vision.

After Ceit opened the first package, she pulled the long, sheer fabric up and across her cheek. "Ohh, Mum, thank you! My first nylons!"

"And a garter belt to hold them up," Molly replied and received a joyful hug and kiss.

The excitement was again there when she removed the simple, but beautiful gold bracelet from Moira. Her deep affection for her sister was evident by the glow on her face and the way she went to Moira and squeezed her.

"Oh thank you, Moira, it's so beautiful!"

Moira held her by the arms and smiling affectionately, kissed her cheek. Jim was moved by the genuine feeling that passed between them.

The slip from Duncan continued her excitement. She happily squeezed him as he hugged her. "Thank you, Duncan!" She smiled self-consciously, "I've never had anything so ... so feminine. It's gorgeous!"

His hands on Ceit's shoulders, Duncan smiled, "And you, Ceit, are a gorgeous young lady." He hugged her again.

She opened the last box, slowly and timidly. For a moment it appeared she would stop, but her youthful curiosity prevailed and she completed the task. She stared at first, as the color bloomed beneath the overhead light. She touched the fabric and rubbed a hand across, grasped the shoulders and lifted it from the box holding it at arms length to her side.

In words just above a whisper she exclaimed, "Oocch! Tis beautiful." She was for the moment oblivious of others in the room.

"Let us see, Ceit," Moira interjected.

Ceit slowly rose from her chair and stood. She held the dress to her front, against her body.

"Please come here, Dear." Ceit moved in front of her mother clutching the dress to her. Molly fondled the fabric and motioned Ceit rearward a pace. She studied her daughter, tilting her head to one side, then the other while cupping her chin in a hand. "Ceit, lass, it will look lovely on you." Molly rose and hugged her tenderly, the two now equal in height.

"Ceit," Moira excitedly added, "you will make that dress a thing of beauty!"

"Ceit, darlin," Duncan smiled tenderly, "I saw that dress on a mannequin and it was a thing of beauty, but seein it in front of you makes me realize how much you do for it." He cast his glance at Jim, "My good friend here truly knew what he was doin."

Ceit reddened more with each morsel of praise. She was often unsettled by compliments, but with Jim present she was downright distressed. With great courage she advanced awkwardly to Jim's front and timidly gazed into his eyes. There was happiness on her face, especially visible in the glow of her eyes. But there was more than that. There was something intense he could not put his finger on. He did not put much credibility in his ability to properly judge females and he pushed any further thoughts away.

In words just above a whisper, the burr barely noticeable, Ceit said, "I thank you so much for the beautiful dress." She stammered a moment, "I .. ah ..." then continued, "I've never had anything quite .. quite like it." Her voice got softer and she lowered her eyes, gazing through her lashes, "Thank you, Jamie."

Jim had to strain to hear the last words. She addressed him the way Scots sometimes did when the first name was James. She started to turn away and he reached out and gently held her shoulders. When she lifted her eyes to meet his, he said with great tenderness, "Ceit, it's you who makes the dress. It would be nothing without you."

Her face turned vivid red and thankfully for her, Molly started the birthday song.

Later, that jerk, by Jim's standards, Geordie arrived and Moira stepped outside with him. She was gone briefly, but Jim, sitting with people he dearly loved and felt comfortable among, was lonely ... and troubled, those few minutes.

*

"You boys don't be late for breakfast," Molly commanded.
"No, Mum, we won't."
"And don't forget, there's kirk after that."

Duncan pinched his mother's cheek and pulled Jim through the door. They immediately broke into a trot. The sky was overcast and there was a nip in the air, great for running. The two friends moved with ease along a dirt roadway for ten minutes, then veered off and headed up a low hill, which added little to their effort. Jim was still new to most of the countryside around Burrtown, but he had seen enough to form a deep attachment to the area. Not at all like the shoreline of southern New England, or the mountains in the north, it lacked the hardwoods which gave his homeland, at this time of year, a beauty unsurpassed. Yet here also was a beauty unsurpassed. The colors were different from home, as was the landscape, but there was something about the place that imprisoned his soul, yet exhilarated him. Some of it was the pure air that he wanted to swallow in huge chunks.

They ran along the all but flat top of a hill a short distance and turned perpendicular to that track and soon again, perpendicular to that. By now they were quite warm, but moving gracefully with the strength of well conditioned athletes, athletes who ran for the sheer joy of the run.

The downhill grade was slight, but made the pace easier and Jim, filled with being alive had the urge to break into a sprint, but held himself in check for the terrain ahead was very rocky. They swung around a large rock outcropping which hid a small stream. It ran parallel to their route, tumbling downhill in a rush. Ahead Jim could see the stream narrow and plunge ten feet into a pool about twenty feet in diameter. It was sheltered on the near side by a low cliff it had carved away in the dimension of time.

"Is that water as cold as I think it is?" Jim yelled excitedly.

"You'd best believe that!" his friend cheerily replied.

"Whadaya think?"

"Let's do it!"

Sweatshirts and dungarees were thrown aside as they ran and stumbled, trying to rid themselves of their footwear and under shorts. From atop the overhang, two naked bodies enthusiastically plunged, knifelike, into the depths of the frigid pool. Instantly they shot to the surface gasping and coughing, not for need of air, but the shock of the icy water. They laughed and yelled and scrambled for the shore and up the bank at high speed searching for scattered clothing.

Jim pulled on his sweatshirt and grabbed for his skivvies. He jammed a foot through a leg hole, glanced down and yelped, "Dunk! My God! It's gone!"

They laughed, but it was more like the giggles of teens. They reveled in the bawdy humor of their diminished assets while they swiftly dressed and were again on the run. Nearing the house, they slowed to a walk to conclude the final fifty yards.

Moira was home from her shift at the hospital and breakfast was ready when Jim and Duncan entered the house, so full of the wonderful odors of Molly's magical culinary triumphs.

When conversation was at a minimum during food consumption, Jim really had to discipline himself to keep his eyes from Moira. Even when she chewed her food, he found her enchanting. He was certain he must have given away his feelings for her, but if he had, no one acknowledged it.

Thankful when breakfast was over, Jim was not thankful, that next on the agenda was the mandatory church service. It was, however, vastly different for Jim than it had been two weeks earlier.

* * *

November was coming to a close. Jim's twenty-third birthday passed with no fanfare other than the cards and gifts he received from home. Thanksgiving was shared with the Marines at the American Embassy in London and Jim brought his Royal Marine buddy to the feast. The food was excellent and the dining hall warm and spotless, quite unlike a year ago in Korea.

Of late Jim was thinking more about Korea, that is, in those rare moments when he was not thinking of Moira. His brother Bob would probably be on his way there soon and Sarah Williams' letters reflected again the insecurity she experienced so much in recent years. In his letters to his mother, Jim did what he could, but it did not change her maternal fear for her youngest son and did not ease her suffering.

When Jim did think of the war, it angered him. It had bogged down into a political quagmire. It had lost its sense of direction and purpose. Soldiers gave up their lives daily in squabbles over terms and definitions. He did not want his brother sent into such a fray, but he kept those thoughts from his folks. He did write to Buck about his opinion and found his brother-in-law felt similarly.

Not knowing how his brother and brother-in-law felt, Bob was another story. If anyone personified the happy warrior, it was P.F.C. Robert O. Williams, U.S.M.C.R. He accepted his entry into the life threatening event with something approaching alacrity, never dwelling on the morality or the dangers. He certainly experienced the fears and frustrations, the terrible fatigue and the agony and remained filthy for prolonged periods, but he did what he felt he must and he did it with a sense of honor and dedication. He followed in the path of his four brothers and uncle. His naiveté was his armor, his love and respect, his strength.

And it frightened Jim and Buck. They knew too well, how suddenly, all that Bob exemplified, could be snuffed out.

* * *

It was two months shy of two years since Jim so much as dated a woman. His last date, ... or dates, was that ill fated happening in D.C. Occasionally in days gone by, when he thought of women, he recalled with certain pleasure the carnality of his youth. Now he refused to even indulge in that whim, .. thinking of other women. For him, .. life now, .. could only be a life of celibacy, not only in body, but also the mind. The reason of course, Moira Cameron. Yet he was incapable of doing anything about his feelings. What was most responsible, was the guilt he carried. What rationally followed, was the goodness of Moira and his belief that he was unworthy of her.

Twice more Jim traveled with Duncan to Burrtown and the Cameron homestead. On another weekend they were in Edinburgh. The two Marines treated Molly and Ceit to a night on the town and a night in a hotel. They did so to see Moira perform with her ballet troupe. She was in the chorus, but Jim saw only her when she was on stage. The tutus looked silly, he thought, but they did permit full view of those long and elegant ballerina legs that all ballerinas seemed to possess, but especially Moira.

The following day all five dined in a splendid restaurant. Jim still got mostly tongue-tied when Moira spoke to him and a reply was necessary. Her spell over him would not go away. He had never been forward with a woman, at least not at first, but it always passed. Not so with Moira. What was it about her that tied him in knots, he wondered? She was never anything but kind, warm and friendly, yet she never gave him any encouragement either. Perhaps it was because of that Geordie guy, but he had not been around on the last two visits to Burrtown.

And so, unable to carry on a conversation with Moira while they dined, Jim observed her whenever he could do so without attracting attention. He was fairly accomplished at that by now. As he discreetly observed her, he realized again that her face did not compel his gaze with sculpted perfection, but rather with eyes that sparkled and danced and reflected the depth of a beautiful soul and a mouth that persistently turned upwards at the corners, revealing her joy of life. She nurtured that joy in giving and compassion. She reached out to help, to comfort and aid healing and Jim knew she was an excellent nurse. She could be no less.

* * *

Since that first day she walked through the door of her home in Burrtown, Jim's love for Moira continued to grow. He had yet to hold her hand, yet to reach out and touch her. She always kissed his cheek when they met, or in parting, but it seemed to Jim a formal act, yet the kiss was accompanied by a sturdy hug, a hug that turned his legs to mush. He could do nothing to compliment her actions, or express what he felt for her. He was too inhibited to speak to anyone about his feelings, especially Duncan or Molly and that added to his preoccupation.

Extremely busy, both physically and mentally while on duty, even there, Moira Cameron was beginning to interfere. Finally he decided he must be realistic. Taking into account Moira's wonderful character ... and his own questionable past with women, he deemed his feelings for her a hopeless dilemma. Still, he could not escape what he felt, nor could he escape her hold on him. He decided he had to find a diversion.

*

With all the requirements earned for the green beret of the Royal Marine Commandos, Jim Williams searched further for the diversion he felt he needed. At last he was sure he had succeeded, but soon afterward, his success bred a new emotion. He was scared. He was sure he needed to be scared, for Moira at that instant was out of his thoughts. In some strange, perverted, masochistic sense, he was pleased with himself. He had found his diversion.

The basket hanging from the balloon broke contact with the earth and ascended into the heavens.

The people on the ground got smaller ... and smaller. The words inside his head were screaming loud and clear. "I must be out of my mind to try this madness!" His stomach was being strangled by a million tightening knots. Icy bolts were shooting up his spine and the chill was spreading over him, yet sweat was pouring from his armpits and trickling down his sides in crazy patterns. His legs seemed so weak, he wondered if they would hold him up, but somehow they did. He looked down at the once friendly earth. It was not the height, he could deal with that. It was jumping out of the rickety basket and plummeting down at fantastic speed, hoping the flimsy parachute would open and snatch him from the wrath of gravity's quickening pull, slowing him enough to be safely deposited on his mother, the earth.

There had been rumors in the States that his outfit was to be jump trained and he welcomed the prospect, thus he did not expect the fear that was now his partner. Maybe it was because over here, the damn fool British did not issue a reserve chute. Maybe it was because suddenly and with terrible anguish he could only wonder what it would be like never to see her again.

So again, there she was. There was Moira. She was as always in the depth of his subconscious as she was in his conscious. Even with the distraction, even with the diversion he so desperately sought, he still could not shake her. Moira Cameron remained the strongest force in his life. But he must at least give her up for a moment if he was ever to see her again. His possible survival depended on it.

He succeeded only when he imagined she was watching from below. By rote, he repeated over and over, as fast as he could force the words through his mind, all the instruction he had received about this jump, until he was satisfied he knew those instructions by heart .. and none to soon. The signal came and he was only moderately aware of others leaving the basket ahead of him. Then he was out and falling and the gigantic mushroom forcibly plucked his feeble body from the fearful action of the gravity and he swung once and again and was soon in a gentle descent.

From below the voice on the bullhorn was enthusiastic, quite unlike it had been for some of the previous jumpers. He was doing everything the way he was instructed and it was good.

During the brief fall he felt an exhilaration mingled with a detached peace. When it was over and he was safely on the ground, he gathered the chute and headed in, not knowing why he was so full of the desire to do it again.

Duncan, first to his side said, "That was a very pretty first jump, Jim."

He had survived his first jump and he would see Moira again. He smiled to himself. There really was no better feeling than thinking of Moira Cameron. Why try to fight it.

* * *

The nearness of Christmas caught Jim off guard. He just managed to get the gifts to his family shipped on time. He completed his parachute training and was awarded his British wings. In spite of all this activity, Moira was the inspiration and the frustration of most of his waking moments. It was a minor miracle that he performed his duties with the success he did. He could not be distracted, so he learned to use Moira as incentive for all he did. He convinced himself he was doing it for her. It did help.

Christmas was to be celebrated in Burrtown. It was long since past the time Jim felt he was imposing. He was one of the family. If that had not been the case, he did not know what he would have done. Just to be in Moira's presence had an effect on him, but he knew he had to make a move and yet it was as if something was holding him back. His thoughts ran rampant. Maybe it was the possibility of failure, he thought. Maybe it was better, just to be in her presence, rather than be denied. He castigated himself for his inability to talk to her and it made him wonder all the more if she would ever accept him. She must know he felt something for her, ... but maybe she did not. He had no idea how, or what she felt. Maybe she, like he, was good at hiding her feelings, like that first parachute jump when inside he was frightened silly and his bowels were in knots and Duncan had told the family how cool he was. Maybe he should approach her with his feelings. If she told him she was not interested, maybe then he could get her out of his system. Maybe, but would he then stay away from Burrtown and the family he came to love only less than his own and wished to be near. It was a real impasse. If he said nothing, at least the Cameron home remained open to him. Maybe it was better that way, for his experience with women never turned out well. Nor did those experiences leave him with any pride in his behavior.

"Cripes!" he said to himself, "How can I even think of Moira in the same way. I'm not worthy of her. How can I expect her to share a life with me when I did some of the things I did."

But his love for her would not go away, .. nor could it be resolved in his present state.

* NINE *

The brightness of the suns' rays from the western horizon squeezed between closed eyelids. He turned his head to escape the brilliance. The wind was nearly gone. It was a good feeling to return to the present in such an atmosphere. The good feeling grew as his mind focused on his family. They would be here some time soon.

And speaking of time, he would have to start getting ready before long. But he had to finish the journey he started, the journey that would deliver him to that place in time twenty five years ago, to the event that was the reason for tonight's gathering and celebration. There was yet enough time to do that and be ready. There had to be. He allowed himself to relax and drift away, to continue his excursion through time gone by.

~ ~ ~ ~ ~

Christmas in Burrtown was more religious and less materialistic than in Shoreford, but the dinner was as sumptuous as any Jim had enjoyed anywhere. Before the cleanup began, Molly put together a meal and many nonessential goodies for Angus MacNeil, who was one of two Burrtown residents in ill health and without family nearby.

"Moira, dear, would you take this packet to Mr. MacNeil?"

"Sure, Mum."

"If you don't mind, I'll walk along and carry the stuff." Without thought, without hesitation, the words were out.

"Why should I mind, Jim? Of course, please come along."

"I'll go too," Ceit chimed in.

"If you don't mind, Dear," Molly declared, "I'd like you to go along with your brother and this bundle for Mrs. MacNab."

Moira and Jim dressed warmly and walked out into temperatures in the thirties and a light wind that blew into their faces. The sun was nearing the horizon and the clouds were tinged pink, the air fresh and pure. There was no snow.

Jim carried the bundle and they walked in silence for about half the distance.

"Moira!" It was abrupt.

"Yes, Jim?" She looked at him, but his eyes were focused ahead, in the direction of their travel.

"Have you ever done something you were ashamed of?"

"Och, yes! When I was a wee bairn and Ceit came to live with us, I was jealous of all the attention she received from Mum. After awhile Mum took me aside and explained things to me. I was so ashamed, because I should have known better."

"God, Moira, .. I mean something really bad. Something you live with. Something that keeps getting in the way. Something that makes you .. unworthy. Something that was .. a lifestyle."

"Lifestyles change, Jim. We don't live in the past. We live right now. One of the things I find in my profession, is people's inability to forgive themselves. God through Christ forgives us, yet we often can't accept that forgiveness. How sad. ... Don't you think so?"

She glanced quickly at him, but he was staring ahead. He did not answer.

A short silence followed.

"You mention God. Well I guess I've broken every commandment ever made. Some a lot more than others."

"Do you love?"

"Yeah!" For the first time he looked directly at her. "You bet I love."

"I know that, Jim. I can see it when you talk about your family. I can see it in the way you treat Mum and Ceit and me and all the other people you've befriended in Burrtown. And I see you and my brother and my heart dances when I see that, for you two have become like brothers." She paused a moment before going on, "You've killed, .. haven't you?"

"Yeh."

She paused again while he focused on the path. Tenderly, she took hold of his hand, her eyes remaining on him.

"My father killed. My brother has killed. My grandfathers and uncles went to war. I don't have the whole answer for that dilemma, but you all tried to defend something, or stop something you felt was evil. It wasn't as if you took pleasure from the act, Jim. I believe the values in our hearts and the reasons behind our actions, have much to do with the way we are judged."

He was uncomfortable with, 'the reasons.' Then they were at Mr. MacNeil's door. He faced her, but looked away.

"What about adultery?"

"You mean infidelity with someone who is married?"

"No, ... not married, ... just .. just with .. with girls."

In the fading light she put a finger to his lips. "Yesterday was. Today is, Jim."

Turning, she knocked and a voice answered. They entered the house.

Angus MacNeil sat in a large, worn chair. He was ailing, but chipper. He opened the bundle and smacked his lips, sunken inward over toothless gums. His arms swung up and he clapped his hands together.

"Och! Tis quite a feast your mum sent."

Mr. MacNeil loved to talk. He was so talkative in fact, that Jim wondered if they would ever get away. Despite his anxiety to leave and continue the uneasy, yet compulsory conversation with Moira, Jim nervously became part of a three-way gabfest. At last they bid the old man, "Good night," and stepped into the waning twilight.

In turmoil from his anxiety, knowing his days in Scotland were numbered, he gave no thought to the subject matter, thought nothing of the consequences, thought nothing of where he was heading. At that moment, his only thought was of the young woman at his side, the woman he desperately wanted at his side, now ... and always. Being so certain of that, of his love for her, he crushed the objection of his inhibitions and plunged into the unknown.

"You know Moira," he blurted what came immediately to his mind, "military life can be really tough on a wife and kids."

She looked at him as she had done before. A tender, sweet smile touched her features.

"I've heard that, Jim. But many of us are products, more or less of that environment without ill effect. The military has been in my family for generations."

"A whole lot of love and understanding is needed."

She hooked her arm through his and turned her gaze in the direction they walked. "Aye, that's true, .. that's true."

"You live in places that are not always the greatest."

"Yes, Jim."

"I'm leaving in less than two weeks to return to the States. That could be a real problem."

"A problem, Jim, but not insurmountable."

"I couldn't put anyone through that." He stopped walking and stepped in front of her. He looked directly into her smiling eyes, still visible and full of sparkle. "Could you go through an ordeal like that?"

"Yes, Jim."

His heart was pounding. "You mean you'd leave a family and home you love?"

"If I loved a man the way I do, .. yes."

He thought his heart hammered additional beats. "Life could be really rotten."

"Life is very much what one makes of it ... and of course with whom it is shared."

His heart was beating out of control. She was smiling sweetly as she gazed into his eyes. His legs were wobbly. He thought they would snap at the knees.

"Dammit, Moira, .. I love you! .. Oh God, how I love you! .... Will you marry me?"

In the approaching darkness she placed her hands on his shoulders and looked more deeply into his eyes than he ever remembered anyone doing. He could see the beautiful glow on her face as she slid her arms down and around him and pressed into him with all her strength.

"Oh yes, Jim!"

Then she raised on her toes and placed her lips on his. It lasted a long time. He held her to him with all his might, compressing the layers of clothing, but their lips were tender against one another, until his lips moved, to her eyes and eyebrows, to her nose and cheeks and ears in a joyous Odyssey and at last were used to kiss away the tears.

They joined hands and she lay her head on his shoulder and they headed homeward without another word, until he squeezed her hand and said, "Oh, Moira, how I love you, how I love you, oh my God, how I love you!"

She turned her face to him and raised on her toes as they walked, kissing his cheek.

"Jim, darling, .. I've loved you from the very first time you came into our home. I wondered if you'd ever care for me."

"Oh my God, Moira! It's unbelievable. I think I've died and gone to heaven."

*

Staff Sergeant James A. Williams spent his last days in Britain in a flurry of activity, some of it in England. He took care of the paper work at the base and the embassy. The necessary permission was obtained from Jim's C.O. The British Naval Chaplain gave him some good time and advice. Two trips were made to the American Embassy in London, to clear the last of the paper work. He found an engagement ring that he knew Moira would find extravagant, but it was a beauty. More important, he purchased two wedding bands in plain gold, the style they agreed on.

Duncan stayed behind in Scotland. There was much to be done in Burrtown. His energetic presence was a definite help.

As Jim boarded the train on December 30th to return to Scotland, passengers close by turned when they heard quite loud, "Damn, I hope I didn't forget anything."

*

The following day was Hogmanay, the last day of the year and probably the most celebrated in Scotland. Preparations for the wedding were complete and the participants relaxed and enjoyed the festivities. With all the visitors coming and going and the whiskey flowing freely, Jim was very careful. Thankfully, he did not have to drink when frequent toasts were made to his bride to be and himself.

There was no time to spend alone with Moira, but they managed to hold hands most of the day. He enjoyed watching her join exuberantly in the toasts not aimed at their nuptials and sip just the tiniest amount from her glass. He followed her example. It was not a way he thought of her, or would have described her, but she certainly lent class to any affair ... and dignity.

"God! How I love her!" he said over and over to himself that day. When there was a break, or whenever a chance presented itself, he whispered similar words into her ear and each time her face would glow and she would look into his eyes and lean into him and kiss his cheek.

Duncan was having a ball. Jim wondered if he could have been happier had it been his own wedding about to take place. There were some brief tears from Molly at odd moments during the festivities. The drink increased her vulnerability. The emigration of Moira to America would take a large chunk out of her life, but this kind of thing had been happening to Scots for generations. But there was something that somewhat eased her pain. She knew her daughter well and from early on, she knew of Moira's unspoken feelings for Jim. She decided that Jim and Moira were made for each other, though she never uttered a word of it and especially tried to keep it from her own thoughts. Now she could love Jim as a son. She cried for joy that Christmas night, when he and Moira walked in the door and he asked her for Moira's hand and she cried again the first time he called her, Mum.

Ceit was trying valiantly, .. with little success, to hold back her tears, but when she and Moira were close, she hugged and kissed her sister and the droplets flowed unashamed down her cheeks. There were a few moments when Jim thought of himself as a heel for taking Moira away. But then he would gaze on her and that thought would vanish more quickly than it arrived.

Jim was convinced that every ambulatory resident of Burrtown had shaken his hand, or kissed him on the cheek. It was his Moira, however, who was the leading character in the proceedings. He would never forget the outpouring of joy for her happiness and the sorrow at her upcoming departure. As the day progressed, the crowds and activity in the small home intensified. The merriment and noise surpassed anything in memory, but as midnight approached, the emotions turned to the sentimental and when the hour struck, the cherished Robbie Burns classic was sung with great feeling. It was a very moving rendition and filled with melancholy. Many cried. There was a depth of meaning to the words that were born in this very nation. When 'Auld Lang Syne' ended and before all eyes were dry, the words of the birthday song were happily sung. Molly marched to the table with a huge cake and burning candles. Moira was twenty-two. The story of her birth on the first day of the new year had been told and retold to Jim by all the adults of this tiny hamlet, old enough to remember and some who were not. The townsfolk loved their gentle and wondrous Moira, .. about to pass from their midst.

*

All occupants of the Cameron household stayed inside the cozy confines of the dwelling on New Years day. It was cold and damp and the clouds somber and gray, but it was not the weather, it was Molly who kept her brood inside. A lot of time was spent around the table in conversation. Moira was frequently herded into a corner by her mother who proceeded, often animated, to instruct her daughter on the finer points of marriage or some aspect of her future life. Once, when Ceit tried to stand close by Molly shooed her away. Moira, was as usual, good natured about it all, often laughing. One time she exclaimed giggling, "Oh, Mum, I am twenty-two you know. And I've been a nurse all these years."

Duncan was amused at his mother's performance and occasionally jabbed Jim in the ribs, attracting a scornful glare from Molly, followed by a shaking finger and, "Never you mind, you!"

At last Molly sighed and got up and went about brewing some tea for the umpteenth time. Out of advice, she finally concluded that Moira and Jim would probably manage quite well without her counsel. They continued to sit around the table, but Moira had long since moved to Jim's lap. It was mostly happy talk, but as the evening was coming to a close, it turned sad and the attempts to hide emotions were poorly concealed.

*

The day dawned cold, windy and gray, but Jim's world was filled with light, his world was filled with Moira Cameron. He held Moira's hand while they ate breakfast. The wedding was to be held early, for they had a train to catch at 2:00PM and they had to get to the station by bus.

Moira was ordered from the room to prepare herself. Jim and Duncan were dispatched to their small bedroom to change into wedding clothes.

Two sets of blues, one British, the other American, hung on the outside of the wardrobe, the spit shined shoes on the floor underneath. The blues were a concession to Molly.

The room was cold and Jim was standing barefooted in his skivvies. He was wholly unaware of the temperature.

"You know, Dunk, you'll never know the debt I owe you. You hauled my ass back to life once and now, because of you, that life has been filled with such meaning that I can't even express it."

"Och, mon, you're daft. You've filled my life with a staunch friendship. My mother truly has another son and Jim, I know my sister would be bonkers without you ... so ya owe me naught."

The room needed no heat.

*

Jim walked alone to the church, his back straight, his arms swinging easily, his mind calling cadence. He wore no overcoat and carried his white barracks hat in his hand to keep it from blowing away. His eyes focused on the distant horizon where Moira's likeness smiled sweetly down on him.

The people arriving early were hunched into the wind, their coats pulled tightly about them, their heads scrunched down into upturned collars. Those few souls who saw Jim, smiled, shook their heads and rushed inside the building.

He walked around to the back entrance to meet the minister. The two talked, more to pass the time than for a reason. It was not long before the congregation started to buzz. They were informed the bride had arrived, though still hidden in the small hall at the back of the church.

Before they walked into the sanctuary, the minister turned serious and spoke to the cheerful and confident young man standing at ease in front of him.

"Jim, tis not fair to judge, but in this case I cannot help myself. Of all the people I've met in my lifetime, I consider none finer than Moira Cameron. I believe from what I've heard of you, that you share that judgment. We love her and will miss her dearly. I know you will protect her with your life."

The final sentence stated fact, but it was also a command.

Jim smiled. It was an earnest smile that made a response unnecessary. The two men turned and walked into the sanctuary, which by now was severely over crowded.

The small organ was played well, but Jim was not familiar with the hymn which had been played at Molly's wedding. As soon as the minister and Jim were positioned, Duncan escorted his mother to the one vacant, or almost vacant space in the front pew. When Molly was seated, Duncan turned and walked to the back and disappeared into the small hall.

Next came Ceit. She was quite pretty. Her hair was just the right contrast to the plain lavender dress. It was evident she was blossoming quickly into a young woman. She marched down the aisle, eyes straight ahead and came to a stop on the right side of the minister, to Jim's left. She was trying very hard to smile, but the sadness of loosing her sister was not something she could easily conceal.

Despite her beauty, Jim did not gaze long at Ceit.

The wedding march thundered into existence and his bride was coming to him on Duncan's arm. Jim beamed. The congregation beamed.

The cold had driven her blood inward, but the warmth of the church was coaxing it quickly back and her cheeks glowed a deep pink. Her beautiful brown eyes were shining and her soft, full lips, were slightly parted in a radiant smile. There was much more of her, but Jim's gaze was transfixed to hers. There was no other being in the world for either of them at that precise moment.

After placing Moira at Jim's side, Duncan moved to his final place on Jim's right.

The ceremony began and soon thereafter did the sobs. Molly was in tears. The tears of Ceit rolled down her cheeks and onto her dress. Then the entire front pew was in tears. By the pronouncement of their union by the minister, the complete building was filled with sobbing Scots.

The two young people who had just become husband and wife were completely unaware of the emotion around them as they smiled in adoration, one at the other, then came together in a kiss, not a hungry kiss, but a long kiss. When they parted, they again locked eyes for a further moment, before turning and walking up the aisle, hand in hand, smiling, but only to each other.

They stayed long enough at the church receiving the multitude of well wishes for Molly to intervene. "You've got a train to catch you know."

Jim and Moira set a fast pace going home and went directly to the small bedroom Moira and Ceit shared. Their bags were packed and everything was ready, but they did have to change clothing. Moira removed her winter coat and lay it on the bed.

"Wait a minute," Jim asked, "let me look at you."

She stood in the long, unadorned, white dress that hung to her ankles. Her hair was wind blown and she smoothed it out. The silver tiara was then visible.

"Turn around, please." She cheerfully responded, never losing the smile that was so much a part of her. "Slower, please." Again she turned, continuing to smile. He shook his head and said softly, "Wonderful!" He took a deep breath and exhaled, "Thank you."

"You don't have to thank me for that, Silly," she giggled. "Now unhook me, please."

She turned her back to him.

"And you don't have to say please for that. It's something I do gladly."

He gave her a risqué look when she glanced back at him over her shoulder. Inheriting his playful mood, her smile turned mischievous, but as quickly, became one of shock. She jumped instantly away and out of his reach when his fingers touched her neck and shoulders.

"Och! Jim! Your fingers are like icicles!"

"All the better to make you squirm, my lovely."

His grin was fiendish and he held out his hands as if to lunge at her. She again tossed him the mischievous grin and moved further from his grasp.

"We'll see about that."

She deftly removed the dress without his help. He proceeded to get out of his blouse and trousers.

When she was standing in bra and panties and stockings, held up with hospital tape, he scowled and asked, "Why that?"

"A garter belt would show the knobs through the dress."

"Ohh ... clever."

She sat and with practiced hands, ripped off the tape and uttered a soft, "Phew!" and started to roll the stockings down her lovely legs.

"Here, .. let me make it better."

"How will you do that?" she smiled quizzically.

He was immediately beside her.

"The way my mom used to soothe my hurts."

She was sitting on the edge of the chair, legs slightly apart. He bent and kissed the inside of each firm thigh, running his lips along the irritated, pink tinged skin. She had a quick intake of breath. He straightened and gazed at her face. Her cheeks were pink in a mild fluster, but that gave way to a smile of pleasure. She took one of his hands in hers and brought it to her lips and kissed it.

When she released his hand, he slid his hands about hers and gently pulled her to her feet. They embraced and kissed and stood locked together. For one frightening, passionate instant, he wanted to lead her to the bed, but what he truly felt for her drove that thought away and they remained wrapped in each other, her head on his shoulder. In the tenderness of the moment, they were oblivious to the world and very much in love.

The knuckles pounding on the door startled them and they were abruptly returned to reality.

"You have a train to catch, you know!" Molly shouted.

*

Jim looked down at the peaceful, smiling face. She was asleep with her head on his shoulder. He gently squeezed her hand and the smile broadened for an instant. They were on their way at last. Leaving Burrtown had been traumatic. Both Jim and Moira were thankful Duncan was staying behind for a few days to help Molly and Ceit close their wounds. Jim remembered his own mother's farewells, no less emotional, but the crying had been less boisterous. When the train pulled into London, he too was sleeping.

*

The hotel room was not pretentious, but it was sparkling clean and neat. His C.O. had pulled all kinds of strings, not only to get them on a commercial flight tomorrow, but had obtained the room through work done by his British counterpart. There was a wonderful view of the city, but the newlyweds took little notice.

"I really do need a bath, Darling. Do you mind?"

"Of course not," he answered, "I feel the same way. I'll follow you."

She undressed to her slip and went into the bathroom, but did not close the door. Jim stripped to his shorts and sat on the edge of the bed listening to the splashing and soft gleeful chirping sounds. He went in and sat on the toilet cover. She accepted his presence as if they were old marrieds.

"Would you mind terribly washing my back, Darling?"

He got up and walked behind her, rubbed soap into a large wash cloth and began to scrub.

"Oocch! That feels wuunnderrful." She hunched forward, took a deep breath and turned her gaze to him, "Wouldn't it be easier, if you were to sit behind me?"

He stared in surprise but a moment at her sweet smiling face, quickly kicked off his skivvies and slid into the tub behind her, all too conscious of his fomented condition. For the second time that day, he had to fight against the powerful passion that wanted to take hold of him. His heart won the battle.

"Ummm," she cooed, stretching her neck and moving her head in a slow circle, one way, then the other, while he moved the soapy cloth sturdily up and down her back and neck. When he finished and put the soap in the holder, she straightened and twisted till their eyes met. She spoke softly. It was not a plea, though it sounded like one. It was simply a request in the straightforward manner that was so much a part of her.

"Will you help me, Jim? This is all so new to me."

He did not answer verbally, but smiled and hugged her to him, his arms under her breasts. She was satisfied with his response.

"I do so want to be your happiness. I do so want to do all the right things ... and have them please you."

He could not help himself. He felt the moisture coat his eyes. He squeezed her so hard, she gasped for breath. He released her immediately.

"I'm sorry, Sweetheart, I'm sorry!"

"Och, Jim," she laughed joyfully, "don't be daft. I love to feel your strong arms about me and to know they are mine. I feel safe in your strength."

He wanted to say things to her, things never said before, express in a new way the love she filled him with. But there were no new words, no different words. And he wanted to speak to her poetically, but alas, he was no poet.

"I love you Moira Williams!"

At the sound of her new name, she gleefully lifted her shoulders till they almost touched her ears and moaned softly.

A wide smile spread over Jim's face. He said, as much to himself as to her, "God knows. I love you!"

He lay back and pulled her with him, clasping his hands over her stomach, a finger resting in her naval. She placed her hands atop his, their fingers entwined. Closing their eyes, they were content for awhile, until the water temperature turned cool. Reaching out a foot, with nimble toes, she turned on the hot water. When they were satisfied, she turned it off and squirmed and stretched and he could feel the muscles in her back and shoulders moving against his torso.

With hands now free, he tenderly cupped her breasts and she turned her head till her forehead was against his jaw. He loosed his hands when he felt the breasts become firm and lightly ran the palms circularly over the small nipples, which became even harder. A tiny involuntary shudder rippled the water. He stroked her ribs and she shivered again. He moved his hands inward till they met and slid them, fingers first, over her smooth flat belly until the fingertips touched and searched through her wet down. She forced her feet into the front of the tub and her knees out to the sides, unveiling herself to him. His fingers entered the exposed fissure and one found the diminutive dot and drew circles and crosses and all sorts of things. She was soon squirming and moaning in whispers and finally, in an unrestrained show of emotion, she arched her loins and shouted, "Oooohhhh, Jiiiiimm!"

When at last she was still, he closed his eyes and squeezed her firmly, then kissed the top of her head. They lay awhile, steeping in the afterglow.

As her strength returned, she sat up and tried to turn around. He saw her eyes all shiny and filled with sensuality. Desiring her as he did, he knew he could not long put her off.

"Let's dry off and go to bed."

She was disappointed. She loved him deeply, wanted him, wanted to please him, but the disappointment disappeared quickly when she realized she was going to have her chance. She climbed happily from the tub.

By the time he was standing on the drying rug with her, she was vigorously wiping his backside, all the way to his ankles. Moving to his front, she giggled, "Oh my!"

He snatched the towel from her and spun her around and started on her back. To have allowed her to proceed, he knew he would lose control and the fury of his own passion would prevail, so he fought his desire. As he dried her, he kissed her neck and shoulders, her back and the surprisingly firm outer cheeks of her buttocks. The backs of her knees received the last of the kisses to her appealing backside.

She was humming a merry rendition of, "Here Comes the Bride" and moving her head from side to side, in unison with the tune. He turned her by the knees where he knelt.

She looked down at him, "Jim, darling, that was the most wonderful bath I have ever had. We must take the tub with us when we leave so that no person will ever use it again and defile it."

She chortled and he was amused at this newly discovered, silly good humor, but his attention was not all on her words as he continued wiping her, moving up her body. When he put his lips to her inner thighs for the second time that day, his ear brushed the still wet fleece of her loins, which he lightly skimmed with his lips. She shivered once more before he rose to his feet and they came together, their lips meeting in a long, hot, moist, passionate kiss, their tongues darting and whirling. When at last they breathlessly separated, he lifted her clean, firm body and carried her to the bed, balancing her in one arm while he pulled the bedcovers away with the other. He placed her tenderly on the immaculate sheet and for an instant, devoured her with eyes full of wonder, then was beside her. They were inhabited by a fury that was subdued only by a wild expenditure of energy and a stormy and fiery conclusion.

Later, ... much later, they slept the sleep of the victorious.

*

Moira woke first. She was very careful in her attempt not to wake Jim, but when she was getting into her robe, he startled her.

"Don't put that on, ... please."

She had an arm in a sleeve when she turned toward the bed and stood looking down at him. Putting on an act of nonchalance, she lifted her chin and replied, "OK." and threw the robe back into the chair. Then she walked to the bed, sporting an impish grin and kissed his forehead. While she was bent over him, the strong urge to grab her popped into his head, but wisely, she quickly straightened and backed off a step, her grin becoming a playful frown.

"How long would you keep me naked, Sir?"

"Forever!" he grinned.

Again she lifted her head and replied as before, "OK," did a superb pirouette and danced into the bathroom.

After the toilet flushed, he heard her cleaning her teeth. She completed the task by gargling Listerene. He thought that was a good idea and jumped up and entered the bathroom as she was wiping her lips.

"Would you do a whole one of those for me someday?"

"A whole one, what?" she asked quizzically, her eyes wide as she gazed into his.

"A whole dance, .. the way you just did that one."

A light touch of blush touched her cheeks and she pointed to herself. "You mean dressed like this?"

He shook his head, grinning self-consciously.

The blush disappeared and was replaced with her sweet, wonderful smile. She leaned into him and kissed him and answered, "Yes!" and was gone.

Immensely pleased, he mimicked her deeds and returned to the bed. Moira was sitting up, the sheet across her lap. Jim leaned across the bed and kissed a nipple.

"I like it!" he grinned.

"You like what, .. this?" and she put a finger to the nipple, her eyes mirthful.

"No! ... I mean .. yes I like that, but what I really meant was, I like the way you always look, no matter where you are, or what you have on, .. or especially, .. don't have on." His self-conscious grin turned to a broad smile.

"You silly," she giggled, but turned serious. Taking one of his hands, she pulled him and he fell across the bed, twisting his body so his head landed in her lap and his eyes were staring up into hers.

"Oh, Jim, I truly love you! At this moment, as much as I love my family, as much as I love my home and Scotland, it is difficult for me to see my life before you came into it."

He was deeply moved. Had he been a person who shed tears of joy, he would have done so. Instead, he was silent, letting the words and their meaning sink in. He could not surpass what she said, yet he knew he loved her with the same intensity.

"Sweetheart, I feel so fortunate to be with you, .. to share my life with you, .. to be part of your family. Having known you, I cannot imagine life without you."

"Ohh, Jim!"

She reached for him and he dug his heels into the edge of the bed and slid his behind across and against her legs and came to a sitting position. They embraced and neither wanted to let go, but when at last they did, her cheeks were covered with tears and he kissed them away. They lay down in each others arms, content, to just be together.

When discomfort caused them to make adjustments to arms in need of blood flow, they turned on their backs, holding hands.

"Boy! Yesterday was tough, .. wasn't it?" Jim finally said.

Moira sat up and gazed out the window.

"Yes it was. I never saw Mum like that. I only have fleeting memories of my father." She looked down into his eyes, "Did you know Mum never dated another man?" Jim nodded. She flushed slightly and giggled, "After last night, I can't imagine her not wanting to try again."

"You mean you'd like to try someone else?" he teased, grinning up at her.

"No, silly! ... Oh! You know what I mean."

"Yeah," he chuckled, "I know." He paused and got serious, "Do you think all the people in the kirk were as sad as they seemed?"

"Don't be daft. That was happy sad."

He rubbed his chin, "That's it!"

"What's it?"

"Happiness is a melancholy Scot."

She looked out the window, then back at him. She was smiling. "You may have a point." Then her stomach growled and she scowled and asked, "What shall we eat, my husband?"

"I could eat you all up, just like Papa Bear."

"Never you mind that brazen attitude. I can see what you're getting ready to do, but I'm famished and if I don't get some nourishment quickly, my body will have no energy and fall into disuse. What do you think of that?"

"Ah for cryin out loud, I suppose we'll have to eat. You sure are one tough sergeant major."

Her eyes filled with glee and she tore the bed clothes from their bodies and swung a leg over him, straddling him as she sat on his belly and dug her fingers into his ribs. "I'll show you how tough I am!" She ran her fingers from his waist to his armpits with the verve of a pianist playing a wild concerto.

He squirmed and yelled and tried to cover up and grab her hands, but she had the initiative and he allowed her to best him. She was filled with the excitement of the moment and they were laughing so hard, they were soon gasping for air. She held his wrists to the sides and he stared as her gleeful eyes turned soft for a moment ... and then erotic .. and he kept pace with her and mirrored her and was immersed in the same fountainhead of emotions. Suddenly she was crushed against him and their mouths were locked and their movements were wild and the sensations delirious.

When it was over, they collapsed to their backs, completely exhausted. They lay unmoving until their bodies began to shake with tiny titters that turned to convulsive laughter and reached near hysteria.

"I thought you had no energy," Jim said between the less raucous chuckles when at last he could speak. "If that was without energy, .. wow!"

Moira jerked to a sitting position, pretending anger, "Never you mind, you .. you scoundrel, I want you to feed me! ... Now!"

He sat up, laughing all the more. When the hilarity again settled somewhat, he looked into her twinkling eyes and asked, still chuckling softly, "What would you like?"

"Lots! ... And lots!"

"OK! I'll order room service."

"Jim Williams, you just don't want me to get dressed," she giggled.

"Not a bad idea." He picked up the phone and ordered bacon, eggs, sausage, chips, toast, juice, milk, tea and coffee. He started to hang up, but snapped the phone back to his mouth. "And a bottle of champagne!"

"Champagne for breakfast?" she squealed, "Do you like champagne?"

"Not much."

"Why did you order it?"

"For our wedding!"

"You're daft," she chuckled.

When the knock sounded and the voice stated, "Room service," Jim jumped from the bed and ran for the door.

"Jim!" Moira squealed, but he stood behind the partially opened door and stuck the tip into the hand without a face and waited for the footsteps to die away, then briskly flung the door open.

"Jim!" Moira squealed again.

He yanked the cart into the room and slammed the door shut.

"You rogue, you," Moira giggled.

They ate all but one piece of toast and two chips. They did not like the champagne and had but one drink in a toast to their marriage.

When Moira swung her feet over the side of the bed, Jim asked, "Where ya goin?"

"A quick trip to the loo. That was a fair amount of liquid we consumed."

She came around the bed to his side and stopped at the champagne bucket, bent and kissed him. He started to put his arms about her, but she stood up.

"Darling do you remember when you said to me, 'All the better to make you squirm.'?"

"You mean with my icy fingers?" Jim chuckled.

"Yes, Darling, that's what I mean."

Unseen by him, she had gathered as much crushed ice in her hand as her closed fist would allow.

"Now it's your turn!"

In a satisfied, lethargic state and unprepared for any kind of retaliatory act, Jim's mind failed to keep pace with her intimations and before he could react, she threw back the bed covers and gleefully rubbed ice into his genitals.

"Squirm!" she squealed.

"Yyaaaaa!!!" he screamed as his legs slammed together, his arms flailing wildly, then grabbed for her.

But too late.

Instantly in motion, she sprinted away, beat him to the bathroom and locked the door.

He leaped recklessly from the bed and rushed to the bathroom door. "Come out here you wench!" he commanded, laughing all the while.

"No way!" she giggled.

"I'm gonna hang you by the toes and dunk that beautiful body in the ice bucket if you don't come out here."

She giggled some more. "No way!"

"The longer you stay in there, the more fiendish your punishment will be."

"I'll come out if you grant me one wish."

"How do you get off asking for anything?"

"Those are my terms for surrender."

"OK. I guess that's easier than busting down the door. I grant your wish."

She unlocked the door and pulled it open just enough to be able to see him while she sized him up. "Now go stand by the window."

He obeyed.

She dashed out, grabbed the ice bucket, ran back into the bathroom and dumped the ice into the toilet. By the time he reached her side, she had pulled the flush lever and the ice was disappearing from the bowl.

"Now I surrender."

Her face was a huge grin and her eyes sparkled as she gazed into his.

"I've been outwitted by a canny ... and devious Scot." His face was no less a grin.

She raised on her toes, leaned into him and kissed his lips, then comically assumed a knees together, pigeon-toed stance, her hands clasped prayerfully to her front in a playful plea. "May I now release my bladder from its terrible ordeal?"

Smiling and shaking his head, he kissed her cheek, gently patted a buttock and returned to the bed, but when she finished, she called to him and they shared a quick shower.

Bathed and filled with good food, incredibly happy in their burgeoning relationship and secure in their love, they returned to the bed, full of good humor and lay on their sides. Before long, their smiling eyes embraced. They caressed and traded kisses to the lips, the face and upper body. It was tender and slow and easy for a long time before it built to the dynamic conclusion.

They had to run for their plane.

*

Somewhere, .. high over the Atlantic the storm hit with terrible force. The plane was buffeted for twenty minutes, when suddenly, it dropped through a hole in the air, to pancake with a frightful thud and dreadful shudder, onto solid air again. For those first time flyers and some of the others too, it seemed the plane would break apart.

Moira bolted awake. She frantically reached for Jim, her eyes wide with terror. He held her, rubbed and patted her back like a baby's.

"It's all right, Sweetheart, it was an air pocket. It's OK, it happens sometimes when the weather's rough." He smiled down at her, "But I have to say, that's the worst one I've ever experienced."

They talked awhile, she to ease her nervousness, he to be the help mate. She got serious when things quieted a bit.

"Oh, Jim, when something like that happens, all I can think of, is what would life be like without you. I'm so sorry I was such a baby."

He squeezed her and she turned her head and stared out the window at the black sky. When she returned her gaze to his she was even more apologetic.

"I don't know what's the matter with me, but I'm awfully sore. I'm sorry, Darling, but I really believe we'll have to wait a bit for more."

He looked at her, not immediately aware of her meaning. When it dawned on him, he had the indelicate urge to smile, but he suppressed that and was immediately sympathetic. He did smile, but it was a smile of compassion.

"Sweetheart, I'm the one who should be sorry. I'm the one who caused it."

She sat up and looked into his eyes with great seriousness. When she spoke, it was not in anger, but there was authority in her voice. "Jim Williams, don't you be daft. You didn't do it all by yourself. You weren't the only one wanting it. If you think you're responsible for all the damage, you're very wrong. Now there!"

He pulled her head to his shoulder and lay back in the seat, smiling to himself and thinking only of his bride. He heard the words as if he had spoken them out loud. "My God, how I love this woman!"

*

The plane landed late in Boston and they got a small room for the night. Tomorrow they would be in Shoreford for three days before Jim had to return to Lejeune. They were very tired, but they spent an overly long time in the shower, allowing the hot water to soothe and warm their bodies, for Boston was cold and dank. Though the window was only opened an inch, the cold breeze blowing through, drove them in their nakedness, into the bed and beneath the covers where they huddled happily together, sharing the intimacy and warmth of each other.

"Oh, Jim, I love you so much ... and I want you so much."

"I know, sweetheart, but tomorrow's another day." He squeezed her to him and whispered into her ear, "I love you, bonnie lassie."

She squeezed him back and kissed his lips and he was glad she did not linger, ... he too wanted her. It was made easier when she turned to her other side and forced her back into him. He put an arm about her and they went to sleep, tired, but full of the joy of being together, a joy that sent them happy dreams and produced a restful sleep.

* * *

Bill Williams wanted desperately to pick his son and his new bride up at the railroad station, but Jim insisted otherwise. For one thing, when Jim called from the hotel in the morning, the time of arrival was unknown. For another, Jim wanted Moira to meet the family at home, away from the confusion and bustle of the train platform. Further, the prospect of arriving unannounced, as he had done on his return from boot camp and China, was more to his liking. This time, it would be the most special of all. In the end, it was as well that they had not made arrangements to be picked up. In their anxiety to be underway they were in motion sooner. They got an earlier train and would arrive sooner than originally planned.

When the train jerked to a stop, Jim glanced at Moira before he rose from his seat. Except for that moment in the plane, he had never seen nervousness in her. She had such inner strength. But today she was nervous. He grabbed the bags from the overhead rack and helped her up. She held his hand until in the aisle.

"Jim?" She paused until he looked into her eyes. "They are your family and I know I will love them, for you have told me so much about them, ... but do you think they might not like me? After all, I'm not an American."

His face broke into a broad grin, then he laughed out loud. She looked at him perplexed. He dropped the bags in the aisle holding up traffic. He placed his hands on her shoulders and turned very serious. "If they love you half as much, .. no, one tenth as much as I do, they'll know you're the finest person in the whole damn world!"

The lady standing directly behind Moira was a grandmother type. She heard Jim's final two words quite plainly and saw his serious expression after he placed his hands on Moira's shoulders. When he picked up the bags, she gave him a dirty look and forced her way to Moira's side. "Is he hurting you, dear?"

Moira giggled uncontrollably. The passengers behind, not knowing what was taking place, were becoming curious and impatient. Then with the giggles under control, Moira smiled sweetly, .. as only she could and said, "Och, Ma'am, I have nothing to ever fear from my gentle lover, but thank you for your concern."

They hurried from the train, the spell broken.

*

The taxi stopped and Jim helped Moira out, hauled out the bags and paid the driver. When he looked up, Sarah was on the front stoop and coming at them. Jim met her somewhere in between and grasped her to him and swung her wildly around and around. When he placed her on the ground, Moira was in front of her. Jim took one of Moira's hands and one of his mother's and joined them together.

"Mother, this is my bride, .. my sweetheart, .." he paused, turned his head and smiled into Moira's eyes, "my lover," then returned his gaze to his mother, "my very best friend, .. Moira Cameron Williams."

The two women came enthusiastically together in an embrace. There were tears on both their cheeks.

Sarah stepped back a pace, holding Moira's hands, "Oh, Moira! .. Oh, Moira!" She let go with one hand and wiped her eyes with the bottom of her apron. "Forgive me, Dear, forgive a mother's foolishness."

"Mother!" Moira exclaimed, while Sarah beamed, "If as a mother, I am as foolish as you, I will feel grateful."

"Oh, Moira, you are what Jimmy said you were. You certainly are."

The two women, arms about waists, walked up the steps and into the house. Jim shrugged, picked up the bags and followed.

Inside, Sarah was again excited. "I must call your father, .. I must!" She went into the kitchen and dialed the phone. "Will, is that you?" Jim knew what his father's response was to that question. "Will, they're here, .. would you believe it? They're here! Will! Will? He hung up on me. Sometimes I don't understand that man."

Sarah came back into the living room where Moira was sitting on Jim's lap and whispering into his ear, "I love her!"

"Oh my goodness, I forgot Shirley and Buck!" Sarah went back to the phone and dialed. "Where are they? Where are ... Shirley, they're here!" pause, "Yes, Dear, Moira and Jimmy." Another short pause, "Yes, Dear, we'll see you soon."

Returning to the living room, Sarah asked, "Would you children like some tea?"

"How about a shot and a beer, Mom?"

Sarah's eyes opened wide and her mouth dropped. Before she recovered, Jim was laughing. Moira, when she realized her husband was joking, gave him an elbow in the stomach to the delight of Sarah.

"Thank you, Dear. He always was too fresh for his own good."

The next sound was a car pulling into the driveway. Jim set Moira's feet on the floor and took her hand. They went instantly to the side door. Bill was placing a foot on the ground when Jim came through the door. They stood four feet apart, eyes renewing acquaintance. Then they were embracing and Bill was patting Jim's back. When they backed away, still holding upper arms, Moira was at their side.

"Hello, Dad! I'm Moira."

It was her, his beloved, vintage Moira. Jim swelled with his love for her. Bill turned from his son and the smile on his face turned him younger as he stepped to his daughter-in-law, took her in his arms and beaming, said into her ear, "Hello, Moira! We're so glad you're finally here." Then he held her at arms length and said to his wife, his eyes locked to Moira's, "Sarah, this is Jim's Moira, .. our Moira!"

Sarah was shaking her head and softly murmuring, "I know! ... I know! ... I know!" But she returned briskly to reality. "My goodness, let's go inside. It's freezing out here."

The teakettle had just come to a boil when a second car screeched to a halt out front. Jim charged out the front door and never touched the steps in a gigantic leap to the ground. The driver of the car was sprinting toward him. They met in mid flight and hugged and punched and danced around and when they stopped, Moira was there.

"You must be Buck."

The newcomer, eyes twinkling, looked into hers. With a huge grin he asked, "How'd you figure that out?"

The three laughed and Buck and Moira embraced. When they separated, Moira was the first to spot her, standing, smiling at the abundant good humor. The two young women each took a step and were together.

"Hello, Shirley!"

"Hello, Moira!"

There was more embracing and more smiles. A friendship, a relationship was born that day. Those two, Moira and Shirley, would become not just sisters from marriage, but devout friends for life.

Lastly, Shirley was picked up by Jim in a giant bear hug and before they could get a conversation started, Sarah was calling from the stoop, "Come inside, children! You'll catch your death of cold out there."

*

They sat a long time around the supper table, the dirty dishes, for once, not bothering Sarah. Moira was normally a slow eater, but she was slowed even more, for they kept her talking. There was no doubt about her impact. The family fell for her with celerity. It was of course, no surprise to Jim.

At 8:30, Sarah glanced at the clock. "For heavens sake! Will you look at the time? Get up everyone, .. into the living room, .. come now, get a move on, I must clean up." Looking at Jim and Buck, she asked, "How do you Marines say it? ... Move out, .. on the double!" She took pleasure in her attempt at humor and laughed at herself.

Bill led the way into the living room while the three women got into a heated discussion about helping. Sarah lost. She was overjoyed to have her two girls at her side.

Meanwhile, a letter had arrived that day from Bob and the three men went over the details, or at least what details escaped the censors scissors. After that, Jim talked of Scotland and eventually told them of the unblended malts and how he had acquired a taste. He asked if they would share a drink with him.

His story telling aroused even the curiosity of Buck, who rarely drank a glass of wine in a restaurant.

Out in the kitchen, Jim went in search of the bottles, some glasses and pitchers and water. The three females were in a group at the sink and he walked up to them, kissed his wife and engulfed the three with his arms in an expansive hug. It was an unspectacular moment, but none would quickly forget.

Back in the living room, the three men enjoyed the MacFiddich, albeit Buck with a large amount of water. They sat and sipped and shared stories and it was another of those unspectacular moments not easily forgotten.

Shirley came in from the kitchen. "Hon, could I take the car keys?"

"Sure. Where ya goin?"

"Just gonna take a quick run over to the house with Moira and Mom. OK with you, Jim?"

"Sure."

Buck tossed her the keys.

*

It was very late when Buck and Shirley left. Sarah went immediately to the boy's room, vacant about four months since shared by Jim and Bob when they came to Shoreford for Buck's homecoming. She returned and said, "Your room is ready."

Jim chuckled. "Mom, it was ready before we got here."

"Well, .. I just had to be sure."

Sarah led the way. Jim and Moira stood in the open doorway while Sarah pointed out all the things Jim already knew.

"And Moira, I hope the bed is to your liking. I know Jimmy will have no trouble sleeping in his."

"Mom, thank you for all your concern and taking so much time to make everything perfect, but if you don't mind, Jim and I will sleep in one bed?"

Jim had an arm about her waist and squeezed her tenderly, reminded again of how much he loved her.

"Oh, dear! Why should I mind?" Sarah was mildly embarrassed at first, but it turned to pleasure. Her smile showed it. "I'm sorry. I forgot that you two are newly weds. You see, Dear, it seems we've known you a very long time."

"Mom, don't even begin to be sorry. It's just that, .." she looked into her husbands eyes, "I love him so much and I don't want to be away from him."

Sarah beamed. "Of course, Dear." She patted Moira's hand and kissed her cheek and that of her son. Bidding them, "Goodnight!" she walked away, still beaming.

A quick shower and they were in bed, side by side, holding hands, their fingers entwined. They were tired, but had not yet unwound from the days events.

They lay in silence awhile before Moira whispered, "I love my new family!" She struggled to an elbow and looked down at him in the dark, "And you know what? I feel like one of them already."

He was smiling, but she could not see it. "What did I tell you, Daffy?"

She hugged his nakedness to her and whispered again. "Shirley gave me some ointment she had to use a year and a half ago and I believe it's still very effective." She nibbled his ear and his neck and kissed a hardened nipple. Her words and that little action had a remarkable effect on him. When her hand, moving downward, reached its nethermost destination, she giggled softly and whispered, "Oh, my!"

*

Moira was in the bathroom when Jim joined his parents at the breakfast table. Sarah waited excitedly for Jim to be seated and the words gushed out.

"Jimmy, we love her! She's wonderful!" Sitting opposite her, Bill kept nodding his head and grinning in approval. "Why she's even more than you said. Your descriptions did not do her justice. And her accent! My! How we love to hear her speak."

Sarah got up from her chair and moved to the stove as Moira entered the kitchen and greetings were exchanged.

"Breakfast will be a few minutes. Show Moira around, Jimmy, she hasn't seen it all yet. After all, this will be her home till you get something in North Carolina."

Taking his wife's hand, Jim showed her Shirley's old room on the first floor. Upstairs, he led her to his parent's room. Standing in the doorway, he kissed her lips lightly and squeezed her hand. She released the hand and slid her arms about him. She lay her head on his shoulder and hugged him, then looked into his eyes and when she spoke, he could see the way she felt.

"Jim, I truly love your family ... and you know what? I believe they like me. Don't you think?"

"Och!" he laughed, mimicking the Scots, "Och! Like you? That's the understatement of the century."

When they disengaged, they went into the room.

"This is the room my brothers and I grew up in."

They walked to the large bureau.

"Are those Donald's?"

"Yes." The Navy Cross and Purple Heart hung from the middle of the mirror at the top. Below, sitting on the bureau, another Purple Heart hung from a fancy shaped bottle, resting on a brightly colored box. "And that's Sal's, along with the perfume and cigars he gave Mom and Dad two years ago at Christmas."

"Oh, Jim!" she exclaimed softly. Her eyes glossed over and she wrapped him again in her arms, as much for her own comfort, as his.

As he held her, old memories flashed by and they shared a moment of sadness. He was surprised that the hurt was still real. But the warmth and substance of her body returned him to the present and he was grateful, grateful for the time he had shared with those stalwart brothers and grateful for the wonderful creature who now shared his life.

The three days in Shoreford passed remarkably fast. The newlyweds only time alone was in the confines of the small bed in Shirley's old room. Sarah felt that room would afford them more privacy since they were using but one bed. Jim and Moira happily made the move

All their waking moments during those three days were spent acquainting Moira with her new family and opening scores of gifts. Grandmother Williams and her progeny took up one day. Grandmother MacPherson, Uncle Ed, Kit and Mal another. Isabel Buchanan made two visits with Buck and Shirley. A few close friends dropped by, including Mr. and Mrs. Ryan and Mr. and Mrs. Capoletti. News traveled quickly in Shoreford, of Jim and his wonderful bride. It did not matter who it was that visited the Williams' home, by the time they left, they had a lasting affection for the sweet, caring, unassuming girl from Scotland.

Though an exhausting time for the young lovers, it was a fun time and very good for Sarah. Since Bob recently landed in Korea, she was back to worrying on a full time basis. For the time being at least, the happiness that now permeated her being, helped take the place of some of that worry.

On the last night, when supper's litter was cleared and put away, all hands participating, Sarah condescended to join the others in a glass of 'The MacFiddich'. The clean table was reoccupied with glasses and pitchers, one with water, the other with equal quantities of the two whiskies. Unlike Molly, Jim used a measuring cup.

Sarah sat wide eyed as glasses were placed in front of Shirley and Buck and grimaced when one was placed in front of her. She followed her husband's instructions and attempted the 'sniff'. She shivered, then took a sip, a fair sized sip and shuddered to the amusement of the other imbibers.

"Ugghh! That's awful!"

"Sarah, you're supposed to sip it, not toss it down like medicine," Bill chided.

"Well it tastes like medicine!"

"Mom, do you know, that in Scotland, they call it the water of life?" Jim smiled impishly.

"It tastes like the water of death."

At that point Shirley joined in the fun at her mother's expense. She sipped from her glass, albeit much diluted with water like her husbands. She licked her lips and smiling said, "Mmm, not bad."

"Oohhh, Shirley, how could you?"

"It's really not bad, Mom."

"Mom, you've heard of the great Scottish poet, Robert Burns?" Jim interjected. Sarah nodded. "You know what he said about it?"

"I don't care what he said."

"He said whiskey and freedom, gang together."

"Freedom my foot! It's just freedom to make a fool of yourself."

Moira was smiling with the rest, but reprimanded her husband good naturedly. "You leave Mom alone. Not everyone feels about the whiskey as you do." She turned to Sarah. "Don't you pay him any mind, Mom, he's a rascal." She jabbed an elbow into Jim's ribs and he reacted with the drama his family expected.

Sarah reached for Moira's hand and patted it. "Thank you, Dear." With a great display of haughtiness to her son she added, "Young man, this lovely child is more than you deserve."

It was fun and the occupants of the kitchen were filled with the good humor of the moment, but Sarah soon became serious.

"Will, don't you think it's time we told them?"

Bill squeezed and rubbed his chin. "Yes, I guess it is."

Jim and Moira looked curiously at each other, then at Bill.

"Moira, I don't know what Jim has told you, but thanks to some of the insurance our son Donald left us, we got off to a good start in our business which has done very well. Then Sal, God bless him, left us his insurance. We are really quite comfortable now. Ohh, not like the people down at Silver Beach, but our needs are much less. Yes, we're quite comfortable. We would like to start you off on your new life together with something, .. well, sort of special."

Her expression full of affection, Moira said, "Dad, having you and Mom and Shirley and Buck," she looked at each in their turn, "and all of the family is such a wonderful gift ... and we've received so many other gifts already. Why we will have to build something to take them away. It is you and Mom should take a vacation for yourselves."

Bill put up a hand. "We have everything we want right here. We've discussed building a new home, but all our memories are here. It was small when the kids were growing up, but now, it's as much as we need. And we've got room for you and Jim to come home to and bring some grandchildren with you. I think we might get a double bed for the small room though." He smiled sheepishly at Moira and Jim.

"But back to the matters at hand. Jim, do you remember the '49 Ford old Mr. Yates bought just before he died?" Jim shook his head. "Well, they had to settle the estate recently and it was put up for sale. Buck and I took a look at it and it's in beautiful shape. It's been up on blocks all this time, stored away in the garage. Only got a few thousand miles on it and the price was a steal. Anyhow, your mother and I want you two to have it."

Jim's mouth dropped and Moira's eyes widened. They looked at each other, speechless.

"Besides, our motives are selfish," Sarah happily pronounced. "We figure this way, you'll have to come and see us now and then."

"Mom, it's an awful lot. It just doesn't feel right to have you and Dad make such a sacrifice."

"Jim!" Buck jumped right in. "Shirl and I mentioned to you before that the folks were helping us with our home. How the heck do you think we were able to acquire a house so fast. You know how Mom and Dad are."

"That's right Jim," Shirley added, "we know how you feel, but Mom and Dad are what they are and we can only be thankful that they are and be thankful for their generosity. I hope our kids can feel the same about us, .. I mean the way we all feel about Mom and Dad."

Moira got up from her chair. There were tears running down her face. She went to Sarah, to Bill and kissed and hugged each and stood before them. "I don't know what we can say, ... except, .. thank you very much. Jim told me how wonderful you were, but ... thank you, .. thank you."

Bill and Sarah Williams sat, unable to speak, humbled by the words of those who were the future of their family. It was a spectacular moment, not to be forgotten.

*

It was the loneliest, the longest train ride of his life and Jim was happy to debark. The persisting loneliness in the coming weeks was helped somewhat by the nonstop schedule. The days and many of the nights were filled with training exercises and with what spare time there was, he was getting their future housing arranged. Back to his former platoon he went, as platoon sergeant. It was a lucky break all around. The technical sergeant he replaced was on his way to Korea and was vacating his housing off base, housing that was difficult to come by. Jim and Moira would move right in when the wife of the sergeant moved back with her folks. Jim was in the right place at the right time and he and his bride would accomplish the move during the first week of February. The papers were signed and the sparsely furnished apartment was ready. Additional furniture was to be towed in the trailer Bill had obtained for them, a trailer that would permit transport of their belongings on any future move.

Readying himself for the trip home, it became clear in Jim's mind that Shoreford was no longer his home, their home. His folks home had always been his home too and though he had been away from it much of the last six years, when he returned to Shoreford, he always felt he was going home. It was different now. When he went home, he would be going home to Moira.

He really missed her during the short separation and was extremely anxious to see her and be with her again.

She wrote him daily. She wrote long letters, intimate letters, cheerful letters. She frequently wrote of her good fortune, living with her new family and how wonderful they were, but she never failed to express the sadness at the distance that separated them.

When Jim finalized the deal on the apartment, she started her letters with the countdown of the days remaining, till they would be in each others arms.

Jim also wrote daily. Sometimes it was only a paragraph that time allowed. For the first time in his life, he used the pen to express his feelings, feelings so deep and tender that the words took on a poetic quality. Moira said she wished others could see his writings.

And he knew, she was the catalyst who exhumed so much of what was good in him.

*

He stepped from the train and she was running to him before he spotted her. In an instant she was in his arms. They squeezed one another so tightly, it was as if they expected life would slip away with anything less than a supreme effort. When finally they kissed, it began with a burst of passion that gave way to tenderness and her tears wet his face and the skin was soon chilled in the cold air.

"Hey, you guys! It's only been three weeks." Buck's cheerful comment was effective and they slowly, grudgingly turned toward the sound to see Buck and Shirley grinning broadly.

"Hello, Marine!" Buck stepped forward and the two young men embraced.

Next, Shirley clutched her brother to her. They hugged heartily.

The two couples walked along the platform, down the steps and through the tunnel, their steps sprightly, yet unhurried. They stopped frequently and talked excitedly and laughed.

At one of the stops, Jim said to Moira, "Can you believe this guy," he put a hand on Buck's shoulder, "trying to break up two people in a clinch. Why I remember him and this young lady here," he smiled at Shirley, "so glued together in this very station, I thought they'd never come apart. Talk about the pot calling the kettle black, why I'll never be as black as him."

Buck chuckled and Moira replied with a tiny giggle, "Oh, Jim!"

Shirley looked at her smiling husband and Moira. With a chuckle, she added, "A comedian, my brother's not."

*

Moira had all the help she could use as she prepared for the move to North Carolina. Sarah, Shirley and Isabel Buchanan never stopped until everything was wrapped and boxed. Bill and Buck packed the trailer to near capacity and the car was checked and rechecked and ready to roll.

With less than twenty four hours to spend in Shoreford, Bill and Sarah managed to get their son alone. They were exuberant in their praise and the expression of their love for Moira, much of which they had communicated in their letters to him. They were taken with her and would truly miss her. They also informed him that they were in correspondence with Molly.

Buck and Shirley stayed for supper and well into the evening, Buck having to nudge his wife a few times to get her to leave. Shirley loved her brother dearly, but she was even more reluctant to part with Moira.

Moira and Jim accompanied them to the car, spoke briefly and Moira ran back inside to escape the freezing February night air.

"Jimmy," Shirley said, "we're so happy for you. She is just such a fine person. I will miss her so much."

Buck clamped a hand on Jim's shoulder. "She's all of that, Brothe, but we think she got someone special too."

*

Wrapped together, the numerous blankets protecting their naked bodies from the icy drafts that blustered occasionally through the half opened window, he felt tears on her cheeks.

"You OK, Sweetheart?"

"Oh, Jim, I'm fine. A little sad perhaps, but also very happy," she paused. "A month ago, I left Mum and Ceit and Duncan and now I must leave my new family I dearly love."

A short silence followed.

"But you also said you were happy."

She pushed away from him and hoisted to an elbow.

"Of course, my braw lad. I've got you again." She leaned over and brushed his lips lightly with hers and leaned back and stared at the form of his head on the pillow in the frigid darkness. When she leaned into him again, she kissed him passionately and he responded happily, with renewed energy. She slid beneath the covers and pressed her body tightly to him. A tiny giggle escaped her lips. "Oh my! We must certainly do something about that."

*

They drove straight through, stopping only for fuel and bodily relief. They did not have to worry about food. They were given more than they could eat had the journey taken thrice as long. When Moira rested, it was with her head on Jim's leg. It was a good thing the steering wheel was in the way, otherwise, he would probably have wrecked the car, for the urge to bend down and kiss her was overwhelming. But for most of the journey, she was snuggled at his side, kissing his cheek recurrently as the road thrummed beneath the speeding wheels.

* * *

February turned to March and Jim and Moira turned to the realities of a new life. She obtained a drivers license and was soon doing volunteer work at the nearest hospital while waiting to take the boards for her American nursing certificate. It pleased her and it pleased Jim. She was meant to be a nurse. It was remarkable the way she was sensitive to peoples needs and the positive ways she applied herself to meet those needs.

They were invited into the homes of Jim's fellow staff N.C.O.s. Moira was not only accepted, but accepted with alacrity and looked to when opinions were sought. Jim was keenly aware of most of her qualities from the beginning, but seeing them at work on a daily basis always filled him with a sense of wonder. Except for boyhood prayers, he had almost never been involved in any prayer but the formal ones of church. Now a day never passed that he did not give thanks for her.

On a weekend in early March, Jim borrowed a second shelter half and they drove to Hatteras and camped. It was cold and windy and they had the beaches to themselves for as far as they could see in both directions. They climbed the dunes and ran barefooted through the sand and ate from cans. The sleeping bags were snug and warm. They returned home, filled with a zeal and yearning that would send them back again.

The following week, Jim was in the field for three days. It was a company sized exercise and they were kept hopping through woodland, swamp and sandy dunes with little sleep. It was exhausting. He called Moira from the barracks before he shed his filthy dungarees. He stayed over long in the shower. He hitched a ride home with a tech sergeant who lived nearby. He came close to falling asleep in the car. When he exited the vehicle, he trudged up the walk to the door. He thought how wonderful it would be to lie next to her lovely body and fall asleep in her arms. He opened the door and went inside.

"Be right with you, Darling!" her cheerful voice called.

He slumped into a chair, surprised she had not met him at the door which she always did.

She entered the room wrapped in one of the large towels she used after a shower. Her hair was pinned up, emphasizing the elegance of her neck. She came to him, bent and kissed his forehead. Before he could respond, she turned and walked to the phonograph and gently placed the needle on a record, on the turntable. He did not recognize the music, but knew it to be classical. She removed the towel rather matter of factly and stood for a moment in her nudity until the music reached the starting point. Then she became the ballerina. She danced and moved with wonderful grace. He did not know what the moves were called, but he had seen them that night she performed in Edinburgh. Now however, it was more beautiful, ... more exotic ... and yes, .. erotic.

He sat spellbound at the twisting and turning, the spinning, the bending and stretching and her joyous leaps, those wonderful legs and arms flung wide. The weariness rushed from his body. His heart beat more strongly and faster and his muscles responded to the increased flow of blood.

When the dance was finished, she came to him, her body glowing from her exertions, the sweet smell of the shower soap radiating from her skin. She slid into his lap, her small nipples erect. She looked into his eyes and more sweetly than coquettishly said, "Oh, my!"

Sleep would wait.

*

Moira met Jim at the door five days later. After they hugged and kissed, she led him to a chair, removed his shoes and slid his slippers onto his feet. It did not surprise him. She was like that. He pulled her onto his lap and they kissed happily. He loved coming home to her and did not always know what to expect.

She did not stay long on his lap. Struggling free, she was on her feet.

"I must prepare my Marine's supper."

She leaned over him, kissed his forehead and disappeared into the kitchen. He busied himself with the newspaper, but was soon distracted by the wonderful aroma of broiling steaks. Joining her in the kitchen, he came up behind her, hugging her to him, kissing the back of her neck and ear.

"Listen to me, Marine! If you want a burned steak, just keep it up. If you haven't learned yet, I am very easily distracted by your amorous endeavors."

He squeezed her hard and fast, eliciting a soft grunt from her and released his hold. He marveled at the rare good fortune that brought her into his life. He sat at the table and watched her at work. He picked up the bottle of burgundy she had opened and poured a small amount into his glass.

"Don't you dare touch a drop of that wine till you drink it with me!"

She was jocular, but he did feel sheepish, for they rarely drank with meals at home and somehow he knew this was special.

The steak was done just the way he liked it and she had prepared a small salad and a bowl of colcannon, something her mother made in Scotland. He had loved it then, but they had not had it since coming to America.

Before they married, Jim was not into saying a grace, but she made sure he always did when they sat down to supper together. Besides, his father did it, so there was no reason he could not at least imitate his father. They both said, "Amen." and he looked across the table and into her soft, sparkling eyes. She was serious for a brief moment, then smiled sweetly, her cheeks pink, her white teeth just visible through parted lips. There were dancing specks in her eyes.

She lifted her glass and he took the cue and did the same. The specks became more lively as her smile spread and she happily said, "To our growing family."

Jim's eyes popped open in unison with his gaping mouth, "You mean you're ... you're .. we're going to ... when did it happen, .. how did .. ?"

She giggled uncontrollably. "Och! Jim! You silly, braw lad."

The magnitude of the moment finally crashed upon him and he jumped to his feet, the chair toppling backwards. He rushed to her and lifted her from her chair and kissed her cheeks, her eyes, her ears and her mouth, all of her face and started again.

"We're going to have a baby!" He had never thought about this happening. This woman whom he loved with such intensity kept all other thoughts from his head, but now, she presented him with something else to think about. He was thrilled beyond belief, for now there would be more of her, flesh of her flesh ... and his flesh too.

Little was eaten and only a few sips were taken from the wine glasses. They did the dishes together and he asked her one question after another. He wanted to stay up late talking about it, but felt that now, she needed her proper rest. So they went to bed early and he did not snuggle next to her as he usually did. He feared hurting her or the baby and she instinctively knew and squeezed him to her.

"Darling, you won't hurt me with your strongest hug."

"Are you sure?"

"Of course I'm sure," she giggled.

But he still did not press against her and mimic her. He was still uncertain. He put a hand on her stomach and moved it carefully up and down and around. "I don't feel anything."

"Of course not, Silly," she giggled again, "you're not feeling in the proper place and even if you were, you'd feel nothing yet for it's only a tiny, tiny being. Soon enough you will be able to feel our son or daughter and the growth will become visible and one day it will decide it is time to join us."

She squeezed him to her again and this time he hugged her back and was filled with the wonder of it all and his love for his wife and he knew she would be a fine mother and for an instant, he wondered if he would measure up as a father.

"I hope it's a girl, just like you."

"Oh Jim, it will be its own person, whatever it is."

He was quiet awhile and when he spoke, there was a troubled sound to his voice.

"Moira, I hope you will help me?"

She quickly raised herself on her elbow.

"Of course I'll help you, but whatever for?"

Her face was puzzled but he did not see it in the darkness.

"Well, I'm so used to us making love that I'm afraid I'd do something without thinking, .. or maybe lose control of myself and hurt you or the baby and then I could never forgive myself."

"You sweet, sweet darling, you. One of the last things I would ever worry about is you losing control, .. my gentle lover, .. or not thinking. Further more, it's a long time till we must stop our bodies loving one another."

"It is?"

"Of course it is. Did you think we must cease our," she giggled softly, "lustful activities?"

"I guess I didn't know for sure."

She slipped from her elbow, sliding the arm under him. She clutched him to her and kissed him, gliding her tongue into his mouth. She explored leisurely at first, but it became sensuous and he answered her call and soon they were in the throes of passion, a passion made more so by the simple knowledge that it was OK.

Later, their bodies still entwined, bonded by their perspiration, she kissed his ear and whispered, "Jim, I love you so much!"

He squeezed her so hard, they both sighed when he loosed his hold. He shuddered a little, because he had not thought and immediately she knew why.

"It's all right, Darling. I love your strong arms about me, ... about us."

* * *

Now more than ever, Jim missed Moira when he went into the field or on maneuvers. He not only missed her, he worried about her. She constantly reassured him and when he arrived home, she was always the same, cheerful and positive. He often felt a twinge of shame for his worry, for she was so capable and so full of faith. He forced discipline into his thoughts with some success. He was a Marine and had become a leader. He loved his men and his Corps, but a pretty, sweet, caring Scottish lass was his ultimate concern. It was no wonder marriage was considered by many to be the chain around the neck of the warrior.

If homecomings were a joy before, they were now the highlight of his life. As time passed, Jim and Moira spent more and more of their time at home snuggled together on the couch. She would sit with her knees drawn up, as graceful as possible under her enlarging belly. Because the summer had been so hot, Jim purchased a fan for her and it blew on them during these times. They took turns reading to each other, he doing more in the later days of her pregnancy. They read a variety of stuff, from the newspapers, to novels and Shakespeare, history and some, from the Bible.

In the hotness of the late summer, Moira began to glow. It was not from the heat and perspiration, but emanated from within her being. She always reflected her joy of life and her love for her husband, but now there was something additional. The new life within her was not only enlarging her body, it was enlarging the joy in her soul and it could not be hidden. She was a delight to behold. It was at times like this that Jim knew why he worried, ... he could not imagine life without her.

Moira's condition was a tonic for Sarah. The two had become extremely close. Moira was such a gem when present, but when she left Shoreford, there was a terrible void and Sarah returned to old ways. She worried more each day about her youngest in Korea. It was easy to turn too much time and loneliness into worry. But Moira's pregnancy buoyed Sarah immediately. It placed a positive force in her life and it eased, though it did not displace her fears. She began to make plans at once. There was clothing and all sorts of other things both baby and mother would need, especially care. Her shopping excursions were happy adventures.

* * *

James Arthur Williams, Staff Sergeant, United States Marine Corps, had seen many beautiful and inspiring sights in his nearly twenty four years on planet Earth. Sunsets at sea and in many lands. Autumns in New England. The rugged hills and watered valleys of Scotland. And of course, those frigid, often sunless life saving daybreaks in Korea. Amidst all these, the vision of his wife on their wedding day remained paramount. Now another scene was added to that portfolio. When he walked into the hospital room and saw Moira, holding their new son, cradled in her arms, it was for him, the perfect picture.

The smile on Moira's face hid the weariness in her body and the pillow supporting her head seemed to form a halo. Her eyes were shining as she gazed at their son.

Jim said to himself, "Oh, God! How I love her."

When she spotted her husband, her face brightened even more, then turned to a lively grin. "Do you think we should keep him?"

He laughed out loud and leaned over the bed and very gently placed a hand under his son's head and the other hand under her head. He wanted to hug them so very badly, but he was still in the throes of ignorance about his son's sturdiness, so he kissed her eyes and cheek and very carefully, his son's forehead.

When he straightened, he said the name that Moira felt their son should carry. He required no convincing.

"Welcome aboard, Donald Salvatore Williams!"

*

The news was announced in Shoreford and Burrtown via the telephone. Molly was ecstatic and despite her frugality and the knowledge that the call was quite expensive, she was reluctant to let Jim go and they talked for over twenty minutes. Sarah was no less emotional, but they talked just long enough for her to be certain that all was well and to obtain the vital statistics. She had to spread the news post haste. Further, her plans had been finalized months ago and she felt the need to start getting them ready for execution. Jim chuckled to himself. He knew what his father would have to contend with in the next few days.

*

Just over forty eight hours passed before the new grandparents walked into the hospital room.

Bill Williams, often the spectator, was a happy participant, a dominant, happy participant. When Sarah nagged him for holding the baby too long (depriving her of that privilege) he very calmly, but firmly, explained that she would be staying on while he must return to Shoreford. She would have more than enough opportunity to hold their grandson at that time.

Bill returned to Shoreford when Moira came home. Sarah stayed for two weeks and took over the entire household operation. At the end of that period, Jim took her to the bus station. She was reluctant to leave the baby and Moira and before the departure, she clung to her son tightly. When she finally let go of him to board the bus, she looked into his eyes, hers now filling with tears. "Jimmy, you have a wonderful family! I can't think of anything I could wish you more."

She was wiping her eyes when she waved through the window of the departing bus.

Though Sarah was leaving behind three she dearly loved, the long journey home was not sad. There was great joy in her heart and enormous relief, emotions born when it was learned that another son was returning home from the war. For the better part of ten months, Corporal Robert Williams fought and won and survived. Now he was coming home, whole and well.

With her family safe, Sarah could ask for no more.

*

In bed that night, Moira talked at length of her good fortune at being part of such a wonderful family. She was truly sorry to see her mother-in-law leave, not for the chores Sarah relieved her of, but the genuine bond that had grown between the two.

"It's no wonder I married you," Moira light heartedly added, "look at all the benefits I've acquired." A tiny giggle followed. "But I think there might be other reasons too." She slid against her husband and whispered, "I will be grateful when I can throw away this ugly nightgown and lie next to my braw lad the way God intended."

He turned to his side and kissed her lips softly, but, longingly. "You know, I think I might like that."

* * *

Donald Salvatore Williams was in his car bed six weeks later, wedged between the front and back seats. With his father and mother, he was heading north on Route 301 and a six day leave. Moira, minus shoes, knees drawn up, feet on the seat, her body against Jim, was massaging his neck. She turned to look down at their son and when she returned her gaze to her husband, her face was all smile.

"Och! Jim, twill be such fun, together again with the entire family and my first American Thanksgiving. And we'll really have something to be thankful for with Bob's safe return."

Jim nodded and turned for just a second to smile at her. It would be fun. Buck and Shirley would be there with Mrs. Buchanan. Uncle Ed was bringing Grandmother MacPherson and Kit and Mal. And there would be plenty of time to visit with the Williams clan. But best of all, Bob would be there. Jim was smiling to himself, not just for his own joy, but for what he knew Sarah Williams was feeling.

They drove through the night and Moira was able to sleep as before, her head on Jim's leg, that of course when she was not nursing, changing diapers, or otherwise caring for Donald, who by and large, was well behaved and slept for much of the journey. Jim was tired by the time they pulled up in front of the Triple W. They visited with Bill only briefly for Donald was asleep. When they turned into the driveway of his folks home, Sarah and Bob were out the door before they came to a stop.

Bob had his brother's hand before the car door closed, but the first words came from Jim. "Damn, little brother, it sure is great to see you!"

He quickly pulled Bob into an embrace. When they parted, Bob had the same dazzling smile on his face that Jim remembered so well.

"Jim, I've waited so long for this. It's great to see you looking so good, but from what I hear," he glanced quickly at Moira standing at Sarah's side, each with an arm about the other's waist, "someone pretty special is responsible and I can't wait to meet her."

Stepping away from Sarah, Moira was almost to him. Bob reached out and folded his arms about her. She squeezed him and after they kissed cheeks, he held her at arms length.

"It's really, really special to finally meet you, Moira."

There were tears on Moira's cheeks and she was smiling that soft, sweet smile.

"Oh, Bob, I'm so happy you are finally safe at home. We have waited so impatiently for this moment and now that you are here, we are profoundly blessed."

Her face beaming and tears on her own cheeks, it was Sarah's turn to speak. "Well now that we are all acquainted, don't you think it's time we examined Donald Salvatore?"

Though he did not awaken, Donald was carefully and quietly examined in his car bed before being taken into the bedroom and allowed to continue with his baby dreams.

Jim revived with the conversation and had to be forced by his wife, mother and brother to go to bed. He at last relented and when he kissed Moira before turning in, he marveled at how fresh and wonderful she appeared.

*

The house was bustling with activity when Jim awoke. Buck and Shirley had arrived with Isabel who just had to meet the newest Williams. Besides, she was very fond of Jim and of course, she adored Moira. Jim greeted everyone dressed in a robe, then hurried to shower and shave. While standing under the pelting spray, it dawned on him that this was his first Thanksgiving in Shoreford since becoming a Marine.

A joyful mood filled all present when Jim rejoined them. He could not recall ever seeing his mother more ebullient. She chortled and cooed with Donald Salvatore. She was the only one to call him that, but it was beginning to catch on with Isabel. Sarah hummed and even sang a little when she was in the kitchen. She tried to be hostess and waitress and fairly well succeeded, notwithstanding the profuse attempts by everyone to help.

They stayed at the supper table as they always did at times like this, long after the last morsel was consumed. The conversation was happy and lighthearted and Jim saw in his mother, unbridled joy without a single constraint for the first time in over eight years.

Later, all, including Isabel, but not Sarah, shared the MacFiddich. Later still, when Shirley and Isabel had gone and Moira and Sarah had long since retired, Bill entered his bedroom.

Sarah awakened groggily and asked, "Will, are the boys still up?"

"Jim and Bob took Buck home and they'll be in bed as soon as they return." He paused for a few seconds. "You know, Sarah, we have some pretty special kids and they have some pretty special mates, ... but you already know that. We do have our regrets. We lost our Don and then Sal, .. but they left us with some fine memories. It's just right that today is Thanksgiving, .. don't you think? Yep, the day is already three hours old."

He looked down at his wife in the darkness. She did not answer. She had returned to her own happy dreams.

*

Jim and Moira and Donald Salvatore Williams returned to North Carolina. The youngest of them had been pampered and spoiled by many in a few short days, but he would again become acclimated to a more Spartan lifestyle. His parents too would change their habits on arrival home. Both had gained a few pounds, but it would be gone in a few days. Their eating habits would return to normal, as would their active lives. Aside from an overabundance of excellent food, they were overflowing with good memories.

* * *

Duty in China first revealed to Jim the fear and death tactics that made the Communists no better than any oppressor they sought to replace. During his Korean service, he witnessed the aftermath of their inhumane treatment of prisoners and their indiscriminate value of life. The name of their cause, Communism, was a misnomer. They were not seeking a common equity, nor a common justice, but attempting to impose their own brand of totalitarianism.

A new president was elected and would take office in January. His platform contained a promise to end the war in Korea. But for now, that war ground on taking more lives in a relentless pursuit of the status quo. Politicians were in command.

The Recon battalion was reduced to company size to fill manpower needs in that war. Jim watched the men leave. In a small unit such as it was, he knew them all, many quite well.

Despite Moira and Donald, he felt twinges of guilt at not returning to the fight with his buddies. He had been there and done his tour, but that was part of the reason for his guilt. His combat experience would be an asset and a help in saving men's lives. It was a guilt he could live with, however, for though he did not like the insidious spread of Communism, he hated the current no win, attitude born of incompetent leadership and the massive Chinese intervention.

MacArthur, a man who apparently thought of himself as invincible, had fallen from grace with the gods of war and plunged his command into chaos. The imposition of limits that followed the great one's demise, left no chance of victory, only stalemate. That could only perpetuate the useless squandering of precious lives.

But if the cause was just and the strategy sound, Jim was sure he would be willing to give himself to it without hesitation. Yet he was glad he was not faced with that choice.

* * *

Sarah Williams was filled with more than the Christmas spirit. She was imperturbable, yet exhilarated. She was to be surrounded by her family for the second time in the span of a month. Before Bob landed on the West coast, she procured the services of a special person. A project was undertaken known only to her, her husband and her good friend, Isabel Buchanan.

Because the Williams cousins now had their own families, Christmas Eve was celebrated in the homes of their respective parents. Grandmother Williams took turns with each. Tonight was to be a special night at the home of Bill and Sarah and it was arranged for Grandmother Williams to be there. Grandmother MacPherson was also to be present, as was Isabel.

While the others attended church services, Sarah and Isabel stayed at home with Donald Salvatore. Bill sat with his mother and mother-in-law and his youngest son. The two married couples sat in the pew behind. After the service, there was an abundance of parishioners who decided they wanted to talk to various family members and the group returned home later than anticipated.

A bit impatient, Sarah was waiting for them at the kitchen door. Her first concern was to put Moira at ease.

"Donald Salvatore is sleeping and doing fine, Dear. Now everyone hang up your coats and go into the living room and face the tree." She glanced at her husband. "Please stay with Isabel and me, Dear."

Her hands folded to her front, Isabel watched the seven adults enter the living room. She had a look of excitement that betrayed the nonchalance she had hoped to convey.

The tree lights were the only illumination in the room. When all seven were facing the tree, Sarah, standing at the side with

Bill and Isabel, instructed them to turn around, then she flipped a switch.

A light atop a very large painting illuminated the scene.

The grandmothers sighed in unison.

"My God! It's so real!" Shirley excitedly cried.

"It's beautiful!" Moira said softly, "Oh my! It's so beautiful!"

The three young men stared unbelieving at the nearly life size and life like images. Five Marines in green uniforms smiled back at them. They were without hats and every detail, ribbon, badge, emblem and button was correct and in its proper place. It was as if it was a photo, but it was a painting and it captured something photos sometimes missed.

Buck sat on the right, on the left side of the portrait. Jim was in the middle with Bob to his left. The faces all wore smiles, but there was more. You could see the kindness and understanding in Buck's expression and the enthusiasm and cheerful confidence in Bob's. And there was an endearing quality about Jim that he thought he had never seen in a mirror.

Best of all, standing behind was Don, his hands on the right shoulders of Buck and Jim and Sal, his hands on the left shoulders of Jim and Bob. There was no escaping the integrity, the wholesomeness and intellect that showed through Don's smile, nor the devil may care, yet full of the charm and goodness that came with the smile few had known in Sal. The background around the heads of Don and Sal was painted lighter in a cleverly imperceptible manner, creating an aura of barely visible halos.

On the bottom of the frame was a brass plate which very simply stated, 'Our Boys' and below, in the words of Shakespeare, from King Henry V, 'We few, we happy few, we band of brothers'

* TEN *

Right from the shower, she trod noiselessly through the bathroom door, her feet shod in fluffy pink slippers, her freshly scrubbed body covered by a large pink bath towel. A smaller towel of the same color was wrapped turban like about her hair.

This time, his eyes were open. Moving to the bedside, she smiled sweetly down at him, lightly running her hand along his arm as she passed by. He smiled back.

Exposed from midthigh to the slippers, he observed her legs. The muscles formed, stretched and reformed as she moved along his line of vision and crossed the room. Nice, he thought, but he always thought that. She sat at the dressing table.

She had danced as a young woman and she was good. She still performed for him, for his eyes only and though she did not have the verve of her youth, he had yet, not to be pleased with the unique recitals she presented.

She turned on the hair dryer. It droned monotonously and soon his eyes were closed and he was traveling again in the past.

~ ~ ~ ~ ~

Back home in North Carolina, Moira and Jim shared the KP after supper. It was Hogmanay in Scotland. New Years day, tomorrow, they would celebrate Moira's twenty-third birthday and the day after, their first wedding anniversary. But tonight, during those long intervals when their son slept, they would celebrate their togetherness, something they had not done in abundance of late.

Christmas in Shoreford had been great. They were still feeling the euphoria it had generated. But, they missed those times of quiet conversation, side by side, or Moira in Jim's lap. They missed also those uninhibited, exhilarating moments alone together, when they gave to and received from the other, so much of themselves.

They did not have a drink after supper and when Donald was put to bed, they sat on the couch. They talked for awhile, but a kiss led to some petting and they made wild love right there, alone together.

When they finally freed themselves from their entanglement, they were in the midst of strewn clothing and rumpled confusion. Looking about her, Moira started to giggle. Jim, caught up in her lightheartedness and the absurd appearance of their immediate surroundings, was soon laughing with her.

"Holy Moses, we just behaved like a couple of raw teenagers," he said between chuckles.

"Of course," she replied, biting his ear, "we can't allow the teenagers to have all the fun. But, Darling, I do believe we're in desperate need of a shower."

"You just may be right."

Somewhere near nine o'clock, they were snuggled in bed and they fondled and kissed and explored for a very long time and made love, alone together.

They napped for a short time and afterwards, before Midnight, they showered again and went to the couch wrapped in towels which they removed and used to sit on. There, in the nude, they ate a bowl of ice cream, sitting cross legged and facing each other.

Moira returned the empty bowls to the kitchen. The minute hand was thirty seconds from twelve. She sneaked ice cubes from the freezer and rushed back to her lounging, vulnerable husband. From behind, she energetically rubbed the cubes over his torso

"Happy New Year, Darling!" she giggled joyfully into his ear.

"Oooh you ...."

Reaching behind him, he clasped his arms about her and pulled her wriggling body over the back of the couch. She fell victim to her own devilish prank. He never took advantage of his superior strength, but he did wrestle with her and they rolled onto the floor and amongst the melting ice. As they laughed and frolicked, their bodies became immune to the cold puddles of moisture dampening their skin and their exertions turned to passion and afterwards, tenderness, alone together.

They slept long and well, an exceedingly happy pair. In the weeks that followed, they received news that they traced back to that night, alone together.

* * *

As the early months of 1953 raced into spring, it was evident that Moira was nurturing life within her body. Jim began to take good natured ribbing from his fellow staff N.C.O.s. The First Sergeant called him, quick draw and the Skipper, not to be outdone by his senior sergeants, asked him what he did in his spare time. It was fun and in good taste for Marines, ... in deference to Moira, known personally to many and to others by reputation.

This time around, Jim was a pro, or so he thought. He did not worry like the first time, but he did wonder if it would have any effect on the leave he had applied for, the one he and Moira were so looking forward to.

It did not.

* * *

Jim, Moira and Donald were off to Scotland for most of the month of June. Moira was larger than she had been with Donald and Jim was glad there were no travel restrictions to hold them back. The growing Williams family arrived in that misty land and breathed the sweet air and shared the happy tears of an emotional homecoming.

If the Scots were supposed to be dour, it did not show up when Jim was there. They had not exhibited that characteristic on his previous visits to Burrtown and if anything, this time they were further from it than ever. Some did look askance when learning Donald's middle name. The town's people crowded into the Cameron household as if the new queen was in residence and holding court. There were so many trinkets presented to Donald, many home made, that they would have to be shipped home separately.

Molly was exceedingly protective. She spread her matriarchal wings over her clan, especially her grandson. She would not permit anyone or anything to separate them from her. She knew too well that this visit had its ending and it would be a long time before it could be repeated.

Ceit was in the middle of every activity. When Moira was not caring for Donald, or Molly monopolizing her grandson, he was in Ceit's arms. She sang softly to him in her beautiful and effortless voice. Donny, she called him, responded to her and they shared a love that nurtured Ceit's self esteem and infused her being with a wonderful joy.

*

They had been in Burrtown nearly two weeks. Duncan was due in three days and Jim knew they had to make their move quickly or they would have to cancel their plans.

"Moira, I think if we're going to make that trip to Wales we talked about, we better plan on doing it tomorrow or the next day."

"I think you're right, Sweetheart."

"Wouldn't it be easier to leave Donald here with us?" Molly asked.

"Oh, Mum," Jim answered, "it's terrific of you to want to make it easier for us, but we planned on taking him right from the beginning."

"I know that, Jim, but it would not only be easier for you and Moira," Molly hesitated and smiled, "but it would please us no end. Right, Ceit?"

"Oh yes, Mum, it truly would!"

Jim glanced at his wife. "What do you think, Hon?"

"Oh goodness, I don't know. I've never been away from our son for that long. I really don't know, Jim."

"It's only for the day, Dear," Molly said, "and he would be well cared for. You know that."

"Yes, Moira. It's only for the day. Please, .. please?" pleaded Ceit.

Jim and Moira of course knew their son would be in excellent hands. As their eyes met, they smiled and nodded.

"OK, Mum," Moira replied, "Donald can stay with you and Ceit. It is really sweet of the two of you to do this."

"It sure is," Jim echoed his wife's sentiments.

"Oh wonderful!" Ceit clapped.

"It's nothing of the kind. You must know it will please us no end to have Donald to ourselves," Molly grinned.

Ceit was still shy with Jim and rarely addressed him by name, but she turned to him and asked, "What is the place you are going to in Wales?"

"I'm not sure I can pronounce it, but it's the place my grandfather was born. His family lived there for generations, much as your family has lived in Burrtown for many generations."

"Hmmm. I don't know much about Wales."

"Not many do, Ceit. Actually, the Welsh and the Scots come from Celtic (Jim pronounced it with the K sound as the British did) backgrounds. The Welsh may very well be mixed in the ancestry of the Picts. And one of Scotland's greatest heroes, William Wallace, why his very name means, the Welshman."

Ceit turned to her mother, her eyes filled with wonder, "Oh, Mum, he's so smart, isn't he?"

"Yes, Dear, Jim is quite smart," Molly answered.

At the same time, Moira smiled, but tried to hide it from her sister while a quick trace of pink touched Jim's cheeks.

"No, Ceit! Just because I said that doesn't make me smart. It's some of the stuff I've read about and I hope I remembered it correctly. Anybody can read books and gain knowledge, but often, people with a lot of knowledge aren't necessarily smart. Anyhow, Ceit, historians don't always agree on things and I'm not sure they all agree on this."

Molly gazed approvingly at her son-in-law while Ceit smiled timidly, her eyes on Jim through lowered lashes.

Moira just smiled at her husband and squeezed his hand under the table.

*

Jim was especially pleased that Moira was accompanying him. She was so much a part of him. Whenever they did things together, it always seemed more meaningful. Her soft smiling eyes, cheerful mouth and demeanor were such a contagion, he often found himself gazing at her, just to be infected by her spirit. He had seen animals take to her without introduction. To be loved by her was something indescribable. He wondered if even the great and romantic Robert Burns could have come up with a description of that love.

In the strength of his bond with her, he was nurtured and the best of him was displayed to the world and to those he loved and the one he loved most of all. And while they walked through the Welsh village hand in hand and she sometimes lay her head against his shoulder, he wondered why someone so independent, someone with so much faith, someone who could make their way in the world alone, if need be and happily at that, could merge her being with his and want him and find such fulfillment with him.

They had come to the village to get a sense of the past, a past inhabited by human beings, human beings motivated by love and joy, pain and hunger and all the emotions shared by their progeny of today. Jim did not put much stock in ancestry as a source of pride, or self importance. His father and older brother taught him that. More recently, it was Moira. He was never far from the words she profoundly spoke the night he proposed to her, "Yesterday was. Today is." Nevertheless, today, he was looking back to yesterday, but it was to get a sense of a man he could barely remember and who gave such strong direction to his son's lives. Part of the answer was in the villagers with whom they talked. They seemed a sensible lot, not pretentious, but steadfast and loyal. Historically, they had displayed those traits at work, many in the mines, no less so, in the pay of the Crown. They were excellent soldiers.

They located the house Jim's grandfather was born in and the church in which he was baptized and worshipped. They stood outside the mine Jim's great-grandfather had worked in those many years before taking his family to America.

The world knew so little of these people, Jim thought. While sharing a Celtic background with the Scots and Irish, they did not have the notoriety of those cousins. They were frequently overlooked in the make-up and character of the island of Great Britain, often erroneously referred to as England. The name itself, Britain, he mused, has its roots in ancient Wales and the Welsh people.

When it was time to head back to the train station, they were filled with regret, but were anxious to return to Burrtown and to their son. It was a tired, but satisfied couple who wended their way north, asleep in the seats of a train speeding through the darkness.

* * *

The reunion was great for all and Jim would have been the last to say that it was more meaningful to him than to a mother and sisters, but Duncan Cameron held a unique place in his heart. Dunk stood shoulder to shoulder with Don and Sal and Buck and of late, his brother Bob. Jim had not seen this good friend and brother-in-law in a year and a half, not since the day he and Moira married.

The Royal Marine looked terrific, .. to everyone but Molly. She insisted the Marines were not feeding him enough. Donald observed the emotional, happy proceedings with curious eyes. It was not long before his uncle held him at arms length for inspection.

"Och! He's a braw lad, .. sturdy, .. well made. I'm thinkin he'll make a fine Marine."

"He'll make no fine Marine! He'll most likely be a fine doctor." Molly rebuked her son and as quickly screamed, "Duncan!!!"

She was wide eyed as her grandson was tossed high and caught smartly, Donald, full of animated, giggling, gurgling delight.

Moira turned aside and smiled, as much to herself as she was able. She had seen her husband do it many times and her son always reacted as he did with his uncle. It took awhile before Duncan was willing to give his nephew up, but eventually Donald was seated in a borrowed high chair and the five adults were sitting around the table.

"Now's the time!" Molly cheerfully pronounced.

She rose and went to the cupboard. As she was returning with two bottles and a pitcher, Ceit briskly got up and collected the glasses and another pitcher with water. Molly poured from each of the bottles into the empty pitcher with the confidence that comes from never using measuring devices.

"Just the tiniest drop for me, Mum," declared Moira

"I know, Dear."

The amber liquid barely covered the bottom of Moira's glass. Ceit received about the same.

"Och! Don't I get more than that? I'm not pregnant!"

Three onlookers found it difficult to disguise their humor at Ceit's chagrin.

"It's not funny!" Molly declared, turning to her youngest with a touch of displeasure, "Ceit, you're but a wee lass of seventeen. You shouldna be into the whiskey at all. It's only because this is such a special occasion that you're allowed a tiny dram."

"Mum! I'm a grown woman, .. look at me!"

Ceit jumped to her feet and spun around. She had grown and filled out decidedly in the last year and a half.

"Yes, Dear. You're body seems to say that, but you still have some growin to do."

The short lived pout disappeared when the glasses were raised. No toast was made. None was needed. Ceit allowed the whiskey to slowly pass over her tongue and trickle down her throat as she closed her eyes in a dramatic display of ecstasy. It went completely unnoticed. Donald decided it was time to be fussy and started to cry. The events of the last hour hastened the passage of time and one so used to eating on schedule took offense at the neglect, though his food was only ten minutes late. Those at fault were in action immediately and the misdeed rectified quickly.

Meanwhile, Ceit sat and mulled her overlooked performance. Being the mistress of impulse, she snatched Duncan's glass and took a large swallow. She repeated her earlier display to the accompaniment of watery, wide eyes and astonished, but amused stares from all, all that is but Molly.

"Ceit!!" Molly screamed from across the kitchen.

Donald, with much of his food outside his mouth, started up again, but with more volume.

"See! I am grown up!" Ceit declared, her chin jutting upwards in pride of achievement.

*

It was a fun day and Jim and Moira sat up late with Duncan. They talked considerably about Malaya. Duncan volunteered to go because he believed in what his government was attempting to do, especially, after the way Korea turned out. There was an additional reason. An uncle owned a rubber plantation very near to where the Marine Commandos were stationed.

Dougald MacLeod had been financially helpful to Molly after her husband died. He also helped with the children when they were young. He was not then a wealthy man, but was on the way when the war came along. He was interned during the war and his property worked by the Japanese. It had taken considerable time and money to rectify the abusive practices the Japanese used in working the place.

Now again there was turmoil. Another totalitarian group under the Communist banner was seeking the overthrow of the peninsular nation. The weapon was terrorism. Workers of the rubber trees lived in fear for their lives. An innocent was as liable to be slaughtered as a soldier. Fear worked wonders when intimidation was the goal.

Jim garnered as much information of the situation in Malaya as the news presented. That was little in the United States. There was small interest by the media to sell a colonial war so far away. Besides, it was not a sensational war with mass killings and vast movement of troops. There were days at a time when nothing seemed to be happening. That was not worth much as news. Jim listened intently as Duncan narrated events until now unknown to him.

Duncan explained that one of Winston Churchill's first priorities on being returned as Prime Minister, was Malaya. The High Commissioner of that nation had been assassinated, during daylight hours, while traveling under armed escort. His successor was given broadened powers and when he arrived at his residency, he shook the hand of every servant, something heretofore without precedent. He also saw to it that repairs were made to the servants living quarters. Jim liked the guy already.

It was a slow process. The hearts and minds of the people had to be won and they had to be protected from terrorist abuse.

The people were being protected and the prospect of independence for the nation was an added and remarkable incentive. The tide was turning and the hamlets were being made secure and the protective forces, civilian and military, were inflicting telling losses on a diminishing enemy and their infrastructure. Hearts and minds were being won.

Jim was quiet when Duncan finished and he realized he was envious of his friend. He too was a professional soldier and if men had to go to war, it should be just and based on a common good. That was present in this conflict.

*

The war was put behind them and they concentrated on enjoying their limited time together.

Every morning for the balance of Duncan's leave, he and Jim ran together before breakfast. It was a fun thing for them and whereas most of the conditioning runs while on duty, were done in cadence, these runs, cross country, uphill and down, were at varying speeds. Often they pushed themselves to limits beyond the reach of many. No matter what route they traveled, they always arrived at the Falls Pool on the way home. And they always had a hurried, naked plunge into those frigid waters and redressed, would sprint about a hundred yards before slowing to a jog. They walked the last fifty or so yards that ended at the breakfast table and their appetites did justice to Molly's culinary delights.

Ceit begged to be included and got into a friendly argument with Duncan about her ability to keep up.

"Now, Ceit," Molly, more serious said, "you know the boys don't want to have to watch over you lagging behind."

"No, Mum, it's the boys don't want me watching over them when they swim naked in the Falls Pool."

"Ceit!!" Molly squealed, "have you been spying on your brother and Jim?"

"No, Mum!! Twas Timmy Gordon who saw them!"

"Ceit, I think you know why you can't go along."

"But I could too keep up with them, Mum!"

"Ceit, dear, let's hear no more about it, .. please."

Moira had to busy herself with Donald. She did not know how else to hide her sniggers. Jim and Duncan kept their eyes focused on their plates, not daring to glance in Ceit's direction.

As for Ceit, she played with the food on her plate. In a voice her mother could not hear from across the room, she had the last word.

"I could too keep up."

*

Duncan readied himself for departure and the household displayed its sadness in various ways. Some scattered tears rolled silently down Moira's cheeks and she hugged her brother hard enough to make her believe the life inside her was kicking in dissent. Ceit sobbed openly. Molly sent her son off the way she always sent him off, with a drink and a stiff upper lip. This was for her a time to be brave and not add to his burden. She would cry later. Jim tried to be jolly in an unsuccessful attempt to cheer the group.

Molly's last words to her son were, "Remember, Dear, the whiskey's here, awaitin your return."

Donald slept through the entire proceedings and his uncle had to content himself with silently kissing his nephew's forehead, the last thing he did before he walked out the door.

*

It was a great visit for both families and for Burrtown. Jim continued to run in the morning, because he enjoyed doing it, but without Duncan, it was not the same. He did not plunge into the Falls Pool again.

He and Moira took frequent walks, even when it rained. Sometimes Ceit accompanied them. Less frequently Molly joined them, but that was when they took Donald along. They visited the village and its inhabitants and as much as Jim liked the people of Burrtown, it was the countryside that lured him and captured his heart. It was a magic land for him, but that was because his Moira was always at his side and this was the land of her birth.

Together one day on a hill path, they heard a lone piper off in the distance playing a lament. It was a rain free, beautiful day, the sky exceedingly blue and filled with puffy cumulus clouds. The sun warmed and brightened the varied colored landscape and Jim and Moira stood motionless, holding hands until the tune was ended.

When the sounds faded, he looked into her shining eyes. She was wearing her usual sweet smile. The music and the day and her love for him filled her eyes with wonder and a joy which engulfed him. He let go of her hand and drew her to him. She melted into him.

"I love you Moira Williams! You are everything to me. You are my life. Without you, there is no life."

She squeezed him with a wonderful vigor.

"Oh, Jim! How could God have blessed me so?"

He felt the lump rise and fall in his throat and when he moved his head and her hair brushed his cheek, a tear was wiped away.

* * *

The fan was on high, but the bedroom was abominably hot. As the fan oscillated and forced the air over their damp skin with its rivulets of sweat, their naked bodies rejoiced in the momentary chill.

Moira was large. They had known for some time that she was carrying two in her womb, but they kept it to themselves. They believed it would be a pleasant surprise for their anxious families when the births occurred.

Jim put a stop to their after hours activities before the mandated time. Moira was often uncomfortable and it seemed the right thing to do. She tried to reassure him, but he was not swayed and in the end, she was grateful for her husband's thoughtfulness.

"I love you, Jim."

She squeezed his hand, the only parts of their bodies in contact, except for the small toes of their inmost feet.

He turned on his side and propped up by an elbow, bent and kissed her lips and moist neck. She shivered a little, the way she sometimes did when he kissed her there. He looked down at her and saw the smile in the moonlight. He moved a hand carefully over the surface of her enlarged breasts, feeling the fullness and sensing the nurture being manufactured within. He moved and touched his cheek to the roundness that had been a lovely, firm and flat belly. He stroked her solid dancers thighs and kissed them and returned to the elbow propped position.

"Mum thinks you're someone very special," she said, gazing up at him, "and Duncan says the best thing he ever did was drag you down that path in Korea."

He knew Moira loved him deeply, but he never spent much time thinking about what others thought of him. He thought of himself as lucky as opposed to being a good person and he was happy with that judgment of himself.

"And Ceit loves you."

"Of course she does, I'm part of her family. She has to," he chuckled, "she probably thinks I might keep her Donny from her."

"No! ... I mean she truly loves you .. and not like a brother."

Jim sat upright, stunned by her words. "How can you say that?"

"Because it's true."

He shook his head, more like a shudder, in disbelief. "Did she say something?"

"She would never say anything."

"Then how can you be sure?"

He was impatient with his wife. She had made him uncomfortable.

"As sure as I am of my love for you, Darling. I've known it for some time and when we were in Burrtown, I became certain of it."

"But when we left and I hugged her, I felt her body stiffen and she pulled away in a hurry."

"That's exactly what I'd expect her to do. She would never do anything to hurt me, or for that matter, Mum and Duncan. She's fighting with herself, perhaps frightened with her feelings. She will never allow herself to be in a position of vulnerability. Mum has been keenly aware of Ceit's feelings. We have spoken of it."

"But why tell me, Sweetheart? Now I won't know how to behave around her."

"That's precisely why I'm telling you, because I hope you will be tender with her. She will never allow you to be aware of her feelings for you and because she does have them, she will always be a bit distant, or maybe shy around you. Time may be kind to her and maybe next when we see her, she will have met someone who has turned her head. She is such a dear child and her life has not been easy."

Jim fell backwards onto the pillow. "Phheww!"

Now Moira elevated herself to an elbow, albeit not with much grace. She gazed down at him and smiled, the way only she could.

"I cannot imagine Ceit not falling for you, my braw lad. But I am the one who has you, ... right?"

With her free hand, she deftly reached out and tickled him from his armpit, down his ribs to his groin. She knew he would not fight back in her present condition and she really did a job on him.

"Do you understand?"

He had difficulty answering. He was writhing and laughing and trying desperately to keep from accidentally jarring her, but he finally got the words out.

"Yes, ... yes .. I understand!"

When again they were still, bathed in the sweat of that minor exertion, he rolled over and kissed her lips.

"God! How I love you!"

* * *

The Korean war ended less noisily than it began. About 54,000 Americans died in the three years the war blundered bloodily on, yet life had been going on in the United States, sometimes as if there was no war. There were probably large numbers of Americans who knew little about the war, or perhaps found it easier to pretend it was not taking place.

But the Marine Corps lived. A staunch band of officers fought ferociously for the life of their Corps. The readiness and performance in Korea did not hurt the cause. Neither did the president's ill chosen words. From the remnants of the plundered battalions of post WWII years, emerged three divisions and three air wings, voted into permanent existence by an enlightened congress. Many of the nation's top military leaders and the American President himself, were the ones who would have done away with the Corps, or severely limited its function. Thankfully for America, that was not to be.

* * *

Cooling breezes lessened the heat wave somewhat. Moira sat in the new chair Jim so diligently shopped for. There was support for her back and she was comfortably relaxed, wearing a very loose sleeveless blouse. Her lovely legs were exposed from the bottom of the maternity shorts and her feet rested on the elevated foot pad. She felt she could sleep in the chair and would have tried, but when Jim was home and it was more frequent of late, she would only sleep at his side.

She watched her husband and her son with great delight. They were playing on the floor, Donald in a diaper and Jim in his running shorts. This was a ritual every night Jim was home and he was always reluctant to part with his son at bed time, but eventually Donald was put to bed.

Jim and Moira sat together with a tall glass of lemonade and talked. In the past, this was done on the couch, but now, with the new chair, Jim sat at Moira's side, on the floor. He rested an arm lightly on her thigh. He frequently chuckled to himself when in this position. More than once, they had used ice or some cold object on the other during periods of levity. He could easily slide the cold glass between her thighs. The way she occasionally looked at him, he knew that she knew what he was thinking. Fortunately for Moira, Jim was extra careful around her these days and would not attempt such a trick. She would not always be in this condition, however. So tonight they sipped their drinks and talked of the leave and the many moving and sometimes humorous things that had occurred while in Scotland. As for Shoreford, they decided they would probably not be able to get there again before Christmas.

There was a long silence before Moira asked, "You have something on your mind, don't you?"

Silent seconds passed.

"Yeah," a sigh, "I guess I do."

"I've noticed your thoughts at work for some time." She smiled sweetly at him, but there was also a questioning look on her face.

"I guess it was the last letter we got from Dunk. You know, Hon, the British sometimes seem to do things better than Americans do. They're doing a great job in Malaya and we mostly made a mess out of Korea. I know I'm comparing oranges and apples, but there is room for comparison." He paused, "I've never liked what I consider the British class system, but there they are in Malaya, working with the peasants and the farmers, the real people, in an attempt to win the lousy war and by gosh, they're doing it."

"Yes it does seem that way. Mum is so proud to send those news clippings whenever they tell of the Royal Marines."

Jim stroked his chin and looked at the ceiling before returning his gaze to his wife.

"I saw them send so many good people from here to Korea that it bothered me, because I thought I should go back. Heck, I was only there four months."

"Oh my braw lad," Moira smiled down at him, squeezing his arm, "you always think you have not done enough. That's one of the many reasons I love you so much. But, Darling, you gave so much when you were there ... and the battles you were in, ... especially the last one. Why that will probably go down as one of the most heroic of all time. You see, I know my history too."

She continued to smile as he looked at her sweet face and shining eyes. He smiled back, then looked away and took a deep breath that bordered on a sigh before returning his eyes to hers.

"Maybe so, .. but I feel I should be doing something more than sitting back and being a spectator. Then I start to think about you and Donny and the future Williams," he rubbed a hand over her growing roundness and smiled at her, but again turned serious, "and I get all mixed up and wonder what I should do."

She grasped his hand and carried it to her lips, kissed it and pressed it to her cheek.

"You've been thinking about what your colonel said to some of the officers and senior N.C.O.s, haven't you?"

"Yeh, I guess I have."

"Why didn't you tell me sooner."

"There's really nothing to tell. I can't ask to go as an observer to that war."

"Did you know the British have put out a plea for nurses?"

He slowly sat up straight, never taking his eyes from hers. He was startled at her prescience, but instantly knew he should not be. She saw into him so much.

"Honey! You're pregnant! You can't go there! You don't belong in a place like that!"

"You would go, wouldn't you?"

"Yes, I guess I would, ... but deep down I don't want to leave you and Donny, ... and the twins."

"Well, that settles it. If they decide you are right for the job," she smiled sweetly, "and how could they not, my braw laddie, we can all go. I know Uncle Dougald will gladly put up with us. He has always had a soft spot in his cantankerous heart for Mum and us."

"Moira! I refuse to let you and Donny and the twins be exposed to that danger!"

"Darling, there are all kinds of British dependents there, in addition to all the families who have lived there from the beginning of the conflict."

"Yeh, and some have been killed!"

"That was in the early days. It's become safe in the hamlets and on the plantation were Uncle Dougald is. Why it's more dangerous on the weekends on the highways of North Carolina. And I'd be able to do some good in my profession after the twins are born. Don't you see, it's an ideal situation."

"But how about medical care for you and the twins?"

"Darling! They are not in the dark ages you know. They have hospitals and all the rest. And you know what the doctor said about me, .. that I was made to have babies."

"Damn! I must be nuts to even listen to you about such a dumb idea."

"It's not a dumb idea. It would be wonderful for all of us, Jim. The children and I would get good care. Uncle Dougald has servants that he treats like family and we would be there with you, that's all that matters. It would be a wonderful adventure, don't you see?"

"As I said, I must be nuts to even listen to you! ... But it would be great being near you and Donny," he chuckled, "and whatever."

She put a finger to his lips. "You are not nuts, Darling. Remember, your family is part of everything you do, no matter where you might be. We, especially me, would find it difficult to be so far from you when we could, .. should, ... be at your side."

He thought about it for nearly a minute before he looked up into her shining eyes, a tender smile on his face.

"In case you don't know it, .. you're something pretty special. You and Donny are just the people I would keep away from such a place as Malaya, but here I am being talked into taking you there, just like I'd take you shopping or somethin. God! I love you, Moira!" He kissed the top of her thigh, then was silent a few moments before he soberly added, "Heck, they might not even take me."

"They will, Darling, they will. You'll see."

She brought his hand to her lips and kissed it, then pressed it firmly into her cheek.

* * *

When Jim was accepted for the mission, along with five others, he and Moira let it be known in Shoreford and Burrtown at once. No one in either place was pleased. A good deal of unhappy correspondence passed back and forth before acquiescence occurred. During those unsettled times, Jim wondered about the wisdom of the decision. He was frequently unnerved when alone. But in the end, it was Moira who convinced everyone they were doing the right thing, she, with her faith and positive outlook. She created in each of the dissenters, a similar, if not wholly satisfactory conviction.

* * *

Moira and Donald arrived in Singapore before Jim. Her uncle, Dougald MacLeod, after a long absence, came back into her life like a windstorm. The American government made no provisions for dependents in a situation of this kind and in fact would have tried to discourage it had they been involved. The British government wanted nurses in Malaya and though they would have to wait a few months for Moira, it made it that much easier for Dougald MacLeod to pull strings and get his niece to that destination. And it was necessary to pull strings, but Dougald said he would get them there and get them there he did. When Moira and Donald arrived in Singapore, they were met not only by Dougald, but a grinning Duncan. Without hesitation, or without seeing the sights, mother and son were whisked away to the northwest and ensconced on the plantation for four days before Jim landed in Singapore.

*

Having earned the green Commando beret while in Britain, Jim placed it smartly on his head. It exhibited the black eagle, globe and anchor of his American Corps. Along with three officers, he was one of three enlisted men. Of his companions, a major, two captains, a master sergeant, and technical sergeant, Jim was once again the junior man. From here on, however, he would see little of the Americans.

Eventually, after a very long wait, they boarded a rickety railroad coach with a darkened interior. At last they were under way amidst great confusion. The few British soldiers aboard had weapons and Jim felt naked without his.

The wood burning engine huffed and puffed great clouds of smoke filled with blackened cinders, most of which found their way through the opened windows and onto the passengers. It was a tediously long journey, but thankfully, uneventful.

The Royal Marine Commando camp was in a jungle clearing. It supported a troop of seventy odd souls split into two half troops. It was a self sustained unit with its own cooks, drivers, etc. The Marines lived in tents, canvas roofs with side curtains. The shape of the structures reminded Jim of small circus tents. A large wooden hut was the men's mess and social club, or canteen. It also housed supplies. Another wood hut was headquarters and the residence of a half dozen officers and senior N.C.O.s. This would be Jim's home. It had numerous partitions and reminded him of a shack they built as kids from a refrigerator crate.

The good news was, that Jim was less than ten miles from the MacLeod estate. The bad news was, that he could not get there on a daily basis and sometimes not on a weekly basis. It was nothing new for Moira and Jim, but he felt better about it than he had at Lejeune. She was with people who would look after her and care for her.

The three months in Britain with his Royal Marine brothers acclimatized him to their manners and customs and he fit into his new troop readily. His life with Moira tempered him and he found the transition to new places and people much smoother than before she came into his life. Of course, his nearly eight years in the Corps added much to his confidence. He would do the job he was sent to do. He started that job almost immediately. He would see Moira and Donald soon, but not yet.

*

Canvas jungle boots, a jungle hat, a machete and other accessories the British carried, were issued to Jim. He was here to observe, but had to fit into a combat situation and was briefed accordingly and accordingly armed. American weapons were shipped with the Americans, along with a supply of ammunition, all .45 caliber. The ammo would be used if need be in the Colt pistols and Thompson submachine guns. The Thompson was an issued weapon in Recon and Jim was proficient with it. He was able to fire in short bursts of two or three, within the range of the weapon, with deadly accuracy. It was an admirable weapon in the jungle where the enemy was not often in a fire zone until very close. He was also proficient with the pistol, but chose not to carry one.

The initial patrol that Jim joined, lasted the better part of four days. Most of it was in sultry, stinking swamp. One high point for him was his first contact with Dyaks, a small, dark skinned people from Borneo. They performed tracking duties for the Marines. Handsome, aboriginal people, they were well proportioned, with mouths full of gold teeth. They were very trusting, yet extremely superstitious. They had been head hunters in the old days and rumor had it, old habits die hard.

The patrol was a fruitless, uneventful, boring excursion through wretched flora and immersed terrain. The mosquitoes and leeches were voracious. The rotting vegetation and mud that was disturbed by tromping feet, stank disgustingly. The early nighttime jungle noises, when rest was strongly desired, were a cacophony of sound from hell. On the march again, the repetitious, strength sapping drudgery made staying alert a Herculean task. The training and the will of the Marines prevailed, however, despite the complete absence of bandit activity. They returned to camp, supplies and bodies exhausted, ragged, filthy and bleary eyed, but in high spirits. They were ready for a cleanup and a night in the canteen with quantities of beer and more lack of sleep.

Staff Sergeant James Williams was not present in the canteen that night. Thoroughly showered and in clean clothing, he hitched a ride and was on his way to the MacLeod rubber plantation. On arrival he was greeted by a joyful, enthusiastic woman with an expansive girth. She did not release him in a hurry and that suited him fine as they hugged and kissed, many of the kisses covering the entire face in a joyous display of their reunion. When they did separate, the man standing nearby seemed slightly embarrassed.

Dougald MacLeod would not stand out in a crowd, except perhaps for his ramrod straightness and perfectly trimmed gray beard and hair, which was completely absent from the top of his head. From a distance, a youngster might take the face as belonging to Santa Claus, but up close, his eyes did not have a twinkle, but a piercing, almost fierce look. Perhaps here was the dour Scot, thought Jim. He was of medium height, with a strong handshake, more noticeable by the rough, callused hands. He asked quick, piercing questions, never beating about the bush. He treated his help well, but it took on the tone of a benevolent monarch. He was not cowed by the terrorist activity. He was a man in charge and had been for most of his seventy-two years. Never married, he had bedded with a variety of native women. He was good to them and when they left, they were far better off than when they arrived. He did not like Americans, but Duncan had told him much of Jim, as had Molly's letters. If Dougald was not yet convinced, Moira had been in residence for more than a week. He was kindly to Jim, but there was no effusiveness, which he allowed himself to dabble in with Moira and Donald.

Jim's standing with Dougald was enhanced when Donald arrived in the arms of a servant lady. The son greeted his father highly excited. The father responded with equal enthusiasm. There were hugs and kisses and some tosses high in the air. The relationship that existed between them was undisguisable.

A hint of smile crossed Dougald's face.

Jim and Donny were not easily separated at that early hour, but the little guy was put to bed sooner than at home. The household went to bed early, for the day started early. Jim and Moira were locked in an embrace as soon as they hit the bed. After the initial squeeze, it turned to a tender embrace, a blissful embrace. They were together again. They conversed happily. He kissed her cheeks and eyes. She nestled her face where his neck joined his shoulder and her body gave a little shiver of ecstasy, because they were together again.

Jim was in excellent physical condition, but the patrol and all the days in transit had taken their toll. Nevertheless, he would not allow the exhaustion of all those days to deny him the pleasure of his wife's company, until he was sure of her well-being and sure of her satisfaction with the present. He stroked her arms and back and neck and ran his hands over her still enlarging tummy. The last act he performed before he was finally subdued by his weariness, was to slide under the covers and kiss that tummy. He was sure he could sense the two unborn at play.

*

Dougald left the house immediately after breakfast, giving concise instructions where needed, in a burr, after all the years, still strongly Scottish. Jim did not have to report back to the camp that day. He was playing with his son when Dougald left the house. Soon Donald was in need of a change. One of the female servants present, expecting to be called upon to do that task, was astonished seeing Jim undertake and complete the chore. Moira looked on happily, pleased with her husband and full of the joy of being a whole family again.

By lunch time, three contented people sat and ate together. The servants cleaned up and Donald took his nap. Moira excitedly grabbed Jim by the hand and pulled him to the door.

"Come on, it's time, I want you to meet her!"

Moira told Jim about 'her' last night. They met in Ipoh, which sounded like eepo, she and Moira, though she lived but a short distance from the MacLeod plantation. Moira, while in that city, found a theater where an amateur ballet troop was rehearsing. She went inside to observe. Moira picked her out immediately for she was exceptional. They talked afterwards and learned they were neighbors and coincidentally and happily for both, she was studying to be a nurse. They were friends from the first.

She visited the next day and was taken with Donald, as he was with her. Moira told Jim of her shyness, yet strength of spirit and irrepressible desire to reach out and help. Of her mannerism of covering her face with her hands and giggling at some unexpected humor, especially if it was comically embarrassing to someone, especially herself. In such a short time, the bond between Moira and her was secure.

And Moira told Jim of her beauty.

*

After knocking on the screen door, footsteps could be heard approaching. With a happy smile, she opened the door and said, "Please come in."

She was slender, but shapely, her hair long, shiny and jet black, falling half way to her waist. Her eyes were dark and bright, but shy, yet she always made eye contact when she spoke, though sometimes under lowered lids. She was taller and longer legged than most of her female Chinese counterparts and the ballet was playing a role in nicely shaping her legs.

The surprise was so complete, Jim almost gasped and wondered if it showed on his face. It was not the beauty, though that was evident in abundance. It was the resemblance. It was uncanny. He saw again in his minds eye, that image at the Temple of Heaven seven years ago, the image that became flesh and so much a part of his young life. Holding Moira's hand, he gave it a quick, involuntary squeeze.

Then he heard Moira say, "Sweetheart, I'd like you to meet Liang Sung Wellesley. Liang, this is my husband Jim."

She came to him with outstretched hand and when she placed it in his, she bowed her head just slightly, looked into his eyes and said softly, "I am very proud to meet you. I truly feel I know you."

Her English was close to perfect with only a slight accent. Her final words rattled his brain.

"I'm very pleased to meet you, Liang." He almost caught his breath before the next words, but remained composed, "I too feel I know you."

He smiled at her and relaxed. He knew that his mind was playing tricks. She was only nineteen years old. Moira had told him that. She could not possibly be eight to ten years older.

Besides, there were differences and the longer he stared, though he tried not to, the more evident they became.

She came here in 1948, nobody knew from where. She was then fourteen years old. Missionaries picked her up and adopted her, taught her English and encouraged her desire to dance ... and she became a Christian, because that too was her desire. Those same missionaries, the Wellesleys, her adoptive mother and father, were killed by the Communist terrorists a year and a half ago. She went through her mourning and decided this was the place she wanted to plant her roots. She was a quick learner and had no trouble obtaining employment as a bookkeeper, which she learned almost entirely on her own.

Despite the differences, Jim could not get over her features and form being so like those of his beautiful Chinese whore. But as the days passed and Jim began to know Liang better, he was surprised at the traits she possessed that were so similar to those of his wife.

*

Liang came into their life at once. When she was not at work or studying, she was a constant and sisterly companion to Moira and an ever present baby sitter for Donald. The relationship between Liang and Donald was magical, meanwhile Liang and Moira became inseparable.

Being the only other female close to Jim, Liang chose to call him James, for Moira called her husband Jim and Liang felt that appellation belonged to Moira alone. Besides, her English father's name was James and he was an honorable man, so the name fit well.

But apart from honor, there seemed to be something about Jim that defied description. That is what Moira had told Liang and as Liang came to know him better, she sensed Moira's meaning. To Liang, Jim was someone to look to, someone to admire, but from a distance. He was her dearest friend's husband. Then, at one of those too frequent times a bad dream kept her awake, she struggled to escape the demons of that dream, seeking a haven. In one insane instant, the image of the husband of her dearest friend appeared and she had a thought that was not honorable. She was ashamed and rebuked herself, forcing the wickedness from her mind. She vowed to never again give in to such horrid weakness.

* * *

In the weeks to come, Jim followed and observed and learned in the Commando. He had not yet come across Duncan, who was in another troop and whose path was always ahead or behind. He was able to spend three days with Moira and Donald and a single day, but not the night. And he slowly, but steadily, became a friend of Dougald MacLeod. He anguished, however, when he left Moira and Donald and once briefly, he had an adverse thought about his vocation and the many times he would have to leave them in the future. But the jungle continued to beckon and other thoughts eventually took precedence.

Officers and N.C.O.s were called to a briefing. The C.O. of the Commando Brigade received some intelligence that based on previous incidents, appeared credible. An entire Commando was set in motion to infiltrate a large area with half troops and sub sections. Two N.C.O.s in the troop were in the hospital with some kind of bug. The captain asked Jim if he would be willing to command a sub section on the mission. He accepted with alacrity, though the reason for his presence here was to observe. He had, however, done more than observe on earlier operations.

Known to be expert with map and compass, Jim had shown an uncanny ability to lead the way to a pinpoint objective. He had an excellent grasp of tactics and was known to be quick with sound decisions. Better yet, he had earned the respect of the officers, his peers and the Marines who would follow him. The troop was short of manpower and the sub section totaled fourteen men, including the radioman. They had the furthest distance to travel on this mission, a testimony to Jim's ability.

It was a cheerful lot that jumped from the truck and headed into the outcroppings of the jungle. Jim was reminded of the birth of the Royal Marines and a nickname they acquired in their early days, 'Jollies'. Those old time Marines had nothing on this bunch. But the high spirits would settle into resolve and forbearance as they marched, or rather slogged for three days, through swamp and jungle that was close to impenetrable. They had to stay clear of the trails.

The maps they used were not always accurate and the radios not dependable in the terrain they tromped. They were resupplied by air drop at the end of the third day. They arrived at their ambush site with time to spare, but the price was torn clothing, ripped boots and a thousand and one cuts and slashes to the flesh.

They radioed the code that told they were in position, a site that was thought to be the back door of an alleged escape route. Jim went over the positions till he was satisfied every man was in the right place and knew precisely what was expected of him. The forceps were already starting to close below them and any of the bandits taking this route of escape, should be on their way.

When all was in readiness and all were silently in place, the clamminess of sweaty clothing gave way to the cool, soaking discomfort of rain, which lasted most of two days. Bodies were sore and cramped and chilled when the rain stopped, an hour before they were to move out to a prearranged rendezvous with the troop and be trucked back to camp. The one consolation on the return trip was that they would follow the trails to the truck site.

Glancing at his watch, Jim knew he would soon have to haul the sub section out. He had one of those irrational impulses to stay longer and argued with himself, for there was no logic to such a decision. Anyone who had escaped the closing net below, should have been through here, maybe yesterday, at the least, hours ago. Nevertheless, he made the decision to stay. He knew the men could make it to the rendezvous on time if he kept them here up to another hour. Quickly and noiselessly, he got the word around. Soon after, he was telling himself again, that it was a dumb idea to stay on.

Fifteen minutes went by, then twenty. All of a sudden movement was heard down the trail. A small figure came into view. He was coming up the trail right into the ambush site. The man moved hurriedly, but seemed to lack confidence. He stopped frequently and nervously searched the area ahead and behind, listening with keen attention. He carried a Soviet rifle clutched close to his body. His hair was mashed around his head from the incessant rain and sweaty exertions, his clothing soaked. His eyes disclosed the fear that must have overtaken him after some traumatic encounter.

The ambush was set up with an alternative purpose should the opportunity present itself. Corporal Mooney, the second in command and Marine Elliot were strategically placed to snatch a straggler. The hidden Marines knew a straggler was at hand.

The enemy guerrilla's nervousness, as he came closer, was evident. Finally, he forced himself to stop when it appeared that was the last thing in the world he wanted to do. Within seconds his facial expression changed to instant relief as he urinated into the bushes at the side of the trail.

Mooney, set to grab the man from behind in a strangle hold, while Elliot disabled him from the front, stared dumbfounded as Elliot exploded from the brush, smashing a vicious punch that propelled the enemy backward. He was out cold before he hit the ground. Elliot was instantly on the path staring angrily down at his victim.

"The bastard pissed on me, .. he pissed on me!" he hissed through clenched teeth.

His mouth open, about to chew Elliot out for not following the plan, Mooney broke into a grin. He busied himself searching and tying the captive, doing his best to keep from laughing.

Jim arrived and before he could say anything, Elliot blurted, "He pissed on me, Sarge, the bastard pissed on me!"

"It's OK, Elliot, no one will ever know. You're soaked all over," Jim said turning away. It was not easy keeping a straight face.

"Did you have to do that, Elliot. We'll probably have to carry the bastard now," Mooney taunted, unable to hide his grin.

"He pissed on me, didn't you see that!" Elliot replied sullenly. Then he looked around at his buddies and pleading for mercy, dejectedly added, "The bastard pissed on me!"

His buddies had a different reaction to his dilemma.

It took some doing, but the bandit, a youngster of perhaps fourteen or fifteen, was revived and able to walk, albeit unsteadily for a time.

Aside from the fact that the captive did not have to be carried, the men of the sub section were pleased with their accomplishment. Captives could become informants and informants were more useful than dead bodies. But it was more than their success that kept all of the sub section smiling as they headed for their rendezvous, all that is, but Elliot.

When the sub section walked into the rendezvous site, there were six bodies laid in line. The fright of the bandit on the trail became apparent. He was the only survivor of a very successful ambush, something far too rare for the many days and weeks and months these men laboriously spent in the jungle.

Trucks transported the troop back to camp. When they arrived there was a large crowd awaiting them. It was mostly the police, there to identify the bodies.

The Sergeant Major looked into the trucks as they went by. He spotted the right one and ran to it. His hands on the tailgate, he smiled broadly and said, "Jim, your wife is in hospital and doing fine and so are two healthy boys."

"Yahoooh!" yelled Jim and threw his crumpled, sweaty hat into the air. He cleared the tailgate of the truck with more energy than should have remained in his tired, aching and stiff body.

A stranger soon appeared amongst the rowdy and raggedy sub section, busy congratulating their leader. He wore the pip and crown of a lieutenant colonel. It was the commanding officer of the Commando. They had not met, but he walked up to Jim who snapped to attention with the entire sub section. They were put immediately at ease.

The C.O. stuck out his hand. "May I offer my congratulations, Staff Sergeant? My driver will take you to the hospital."

"Thank you, Sir, thank you!"

"I understand," the C.O. added, "you had a good patrol, Staff Sergeant. Well done!"

"Thank you, Sir!" Someone handed Jim his hat. He mashed it on his head and saluted smartly.

The C.O. returned the salute and said, "All right now, be off with you and give them my best wishes."

"I will, Sir! I will! Thanks a million!" Jim raced to the vehicle, jumped in and hollered, "Give er the gas!"

The driver gunned it and chinks of mud flew from the tires as they sped away to the cheering of many Marines.

When they arrived at the small hospital, Jim was out in one leap. He looked back just long enough to shout, "Thanks!" and disappeared inside.

A nurse tried to stop him, but he rushed by her, not knowing where he was going. Confused, he finally halted and looked about, the nurse overtaking him. Before she could scold him, he spotted Duncan coming toward him sporting a huge grin.

Duncan put a hand out. "Hello, Papa!" They shook vigorously while the nurse smiled and turned away. Jim beamed and Duncan put an arm about his shoulder and steered him along. "My God, mon, but you're ripe!" Duncan laughed.

It was not until that moment that Jim realized he had not bathed in nearly a week, had not shaved in three days. His uniform was ripped and covered with all the grime it could retain.

"Oh brother! What a mess I am. My poor Moira. What a beauty she got for a husband."

Duncan, smiling all the while, filled him in on many of the details as they walked. They stopped in front of a door and still grinning, Duncan said, "Go in, mon! Go in!" and gave Jim a gentle shove.

Jim saw her instantly and moved quickly to the bed.

"Hello, Sweetheart," he happily greeted her.

She appeared a little tired, but otherwise was vintage Moira. The sweet smile and the sparkling eyes were there in abundance.

"Hello, my Darling!" she giggled and added, "Or should I say, my dirty Darling?"

Jim blushed slightly. "I'm sorry, Honey, I just got in from the boonies."

"Oh, Jim, I'm teasing you. I don't care how you arrive here, just so long as you arrive."

She held out her arms to him. They hugged and he kissed her, but cautiously, for his beard was prickly and he felt his mouth was unclean. It mattered nought to her and she clung to him, her joy evident.

He did not want to give her up. He had done that while in the jungle. He had given her up. He had little time to think of her, for there were other things that required his complete attention. All of a sudden, that did not sit well with him.

They chatted happily. He asked her all kinds of questions. Was she sure she was feeling good? Was the labor and birth as easy as he had been told by Duncan? She smiled and answered in the affirmative to all his inquiries and kept patting his hand, seeking to put any doubts to rest. He was finally convinced, then started asking all kinds of questions about the boys.

"Wouldn't you like to see them, Darling?"

"You bet I would!"

"Duncan, will you please show Jim to the nursery?"

"Twill be my pleasure."

Duncan took him by the elbow and led him down the hall to a large window. They peered through and a nurse inside recognized Duncan who pointed excitedly at Jim. The nurse smiled and shook her head knowingly. She motioned to a comrade and each picked up a bundle and walked to the window.

The new father was filled with the kind of pride that has filled new fathers for eons. He stood silently, not moving. A tear was visible, because his face was so dirty and the tear cleared a path down the inside of his cheek.

When they returned to the room, Moira's eyes were closed and she looked like an angel. That was as it should be for Jim could think of her in no other way. He walked to the bed, bent and tenderly kissed her lips. Her eyes opened just enough for her to be aware of his very cheerful and satisfied expression. Smiling, she very softly said, "I love you, my Darling!"

He swallowed the lump in his throat and kissed her forehead.

"I love you, my Darling!" and added, "You are my life!" He gently squeezed her hands and softly brushed her lips with his. "I'll see you very soon, Sweetheart."

It was time to go, time for his love to rest. When he got to the door, he looked back and her eyes were closed, but her face was covered by the same angelic smile. He had missed the event by three hours. Moira would never complain about that, but he wondered for a moment if he ever wanted to miss such an event again.

Outside, Duncan had a jeep from the plantation. He drove Jim back to the camp, still brimming with the excitement of a successful mission without friendly casualties. The filthy Marines were showered and in clean uniforms. Jim was debriefed and back in the jeep with Duncan and off to the plantation.

The servants and he happily exchanged greetings on his arrival. They had heard the news and were excited. He went directly to the bathroom and handed his squalid clothing through a partially opened door to the laundry lady. The bath water had been drawn and he climbed into the tub and scrubbed his body unmercifully with a thickly bristled brush.

Bathed and shaved and dressed in wonderfully clean and sweet smelling clothing, Jim joined Duncan and Dougald for relaxation and libation. It was not the first time that Jim felt fully at ease with Dougald, but it was the first time he enjoyed his company to the fullest. He slept almost ten hours that night.

*

The day Moira came home from the hospital, Jim started a seven day leave. It was not standard operating procedure, but then, nothing here was. He walked among the Marines of the troop as one of them, not as an outsider come to observe. His role had changed from the first few weeks and he was skeptical that many in Washington would approve publicly, had they known. But he was little fish and his deeds would not come to light in the eyes of the politicians. He wondered if privately, they would care. Probably not, but their words did not always reflect honest, or sound judgment. That was the way it was. But he would do his job and do it to the best of his ability. That was the way he was.

The leave was a tonic for Jim. Happy ovations were received from Shoreford and Burrtown. Some members of the troop showed up with gifts for the newcomers. Duncan came and went a number of times. Dougald was seen to smile frequently. Liang spent all her spare time with Moira and the boys. Moira began to complain of her uselessness, good natured of course. Jim had time with Donald and had a chance to become acquainted with his new sons.

The newest Williams, Duncan James and Robert Milton, were changed and bathed by their father, at least as much as by Liang and then Moira would permit. It was not easy doing things for his youngest, for even two of the female servants competed for turns. Best of all, there was time alone with Moira and conversation was plentiful, though he did not discuss his ambivalent thoughts with her.

When the leave was over, Jim had some very real mixed emotions. On the one hand was the strong sense of duty to his Corps, a labor of love, on the other, his devotion to his family and his duty to them. It was mostly the time away from them that bothered him most. He knew that his present situation would never come close to being repeated. It was a dilemma that gnawed at his innards.

* * *

Nineteen fifty-three was a good year for the good guys. Terrorist incidents were in steep decline. Some were saying that half the enemy strength was eliminated. Jim wondered if that might not be a conservative estimate. Contacts were fewer and fewer and more and more jungle bashing and back breaking work was required to dig out even a single bandit. With fewer bandits, their boldness was disappearing. They were retreating further into the jungle and their sources of supply were drying up. The prognosis was good. What was not good for the good guys, was their time in the jungle. That did not change. It remained arduous and monotonous, occasionally frightening and always dirty. Sweat was a constant companion. Insects and leeches were ravenous. There were hours and sometimes days in ambush sites and there were cold nights and the relentless swamp. Sometimes, .. there were casualties.

* * *

During every available moment of time off, Jim was at the plantation. In the months following the births of Dunkie and Robbie he was finding himself in greater conflict with himself.

Moira nursed the boys briefly until her milk dried up. She was selfish about giving up time with her sons, but eventually, thanks to Liang, she forced herself away and did some volunteer work at the hospital.

Liang was a wonder. She was not only an excellent surrogate parent, she became a sister to Moira and eventually came to live at the plantation. It was a pleasure for Jim to observe the friendship and emotional bond that developed between the two.

The two possessed many of the same traits. Though shyness was very much a part of Liang, she had Moira's courage. Her faith was a growing thing and was rooted in her character and the influence of her adoptive parents.

When Liang first came to the plantation, close as she was to Moira, when Jim and Moira sat together in the evening, she often went to her room. Both worked on her to stay and soon she was more comfortable with them.

Liang would never speak of herself, but Moira knew intuitively, the way she often knew about a person with wounds, that tragedy and trauma were locked away in Liang's cerebral crypt. Moira was certain that bringing it out would help her friend and ease the torment she sometimes saw, sometimes sensed in Liang, something Liang was able to hide from so many. Moira spoke frequently to Jim of her hope and desire to be blessed with the wisdom to help her dear friend.

*

Dougald was away on business and the boys put to bed. A pitcher of lemonade was made. Moira, Liang and Jim sat in the living room, Jim and Moira on a wicker couch, Liang opposite, on a similar couch. They sipped lemonade and the conversation was cheerful.

Liang was more at ease than Jim had ever seen her. They traded stories about the boys. When Liang spoke of them, she became animated, her joy in being part of their lives, abundant.

Soon Moira was telling of her childhood in Scotland and got Jim talking about his in America. In that environment, Moira was able to draw some stories from Liang. Hesitant at first, she warmed up as she told of her earliest years.

Born in a town in North China, Liang remembered the bound feet her mother walked on and her mother's beauty. She had a sister ten years her senior who was considered even more beautiful than her mother. Her father, as Liang remembered him, was a gentle man who loved her in spite of the fact she was not a boy. When she was about five years old, her father was killed by a war lord and her mother was taken to be a concubine.

She stopped, sadness masking her features. Moira went to her and held her hands.

"I'm so sorry," Liang said looking downwards, but returned her gaze to Moira and continued, "but it's been so long since I've spoken of this .. and then .. only to my sister Jiwon ... and my second mother and father, who loved me very much. Until now, they were the only ones I would speak to about such things."

"Oh, Liang! How awful it must have been for you."

At that Moira loosed her hands and hugged Liang before looking into her eyes. "You must know that you are with people now who also love you very much," Liang nodded her head, "and I hope you will consider me your sister, .. though I'm sure I cannot take her place."

Liang's expression turned deadly serious. Her eyes locked to Moira's. "But you have taken her place! You have! My sister Jiwon is gone and you have taken her place and I know that I love you as I loved her. ... You are the finest person I have known and that is why I speak to you as I do."

Moira's cheeks tinted pink at the sincerity and power of Liang's words. She pulled Liang to her again and tenderly embraced her. When Moira released Liang, she held her at arms length, a hand on each shoulder, her eyes smiling into Liang's. "It is a wondrous thing to find such a sister as you at this stage of our lives." She studied Liang's face. "Maybe we should talk about pleasant things for the rest of the evening."

"But I want to tell you more. I want to tell you everything! I have told this story only to my parents, ... who are no longer with me. You are now my family." Liang took a large sip of lemonade and a deep breath. "My sister Jiwon fled with me and we lived among peasants for sometime. When the Japanese arrived we had to move many times to escape their brutality. My sister never allowed me to be anyplace I could be injured. She protected me always." Liang smiled. "I remember nothing of the dangers we must have faced for she was always protecting me.

"I do not remember how we got there, but we finally settled in Peiping, just after the war ended. My sister obtained employment with the Americans and earned a great deal of money. She worked mostly during the evening hours and fell deeply in love with an American. She said very little to me, but I knew she loved him very much. I saw her cry just before the Americans were to leave ... and even more, the day they left. How sad.

"Then the Ba Loo came. Jiwon said we were not safe and we again had to flee. We walked many days and received a few rides on ox carts. .. I was so tired. .. We finally crossed into

Thailand. I did not know that at the time, but have learned since, that is where we were. I remember it so well, for it was there we were captured by bandits, .." she turned to Jim, "not the kind you have been fighting, James."

She tried to smile when she looked at him, but was only moderately successful and looked away, starting to cry softly until her body was shaking.

Moira held her tightly. Jim moved to the couch and sat on her other side. Holding one hand, he rubbed her back with his free hand. She fought through the demons of her past and slowly, determinedly continued.

"The bandits forced us into a small, dirty building. I was very frightened. I hid under a table. It was my sister they wanted and ..." She slipped her hands from the grasp of her friends and dropped her head into those hands. A great shiver went through her body. "They wanted my sister, ... they wanted Jiwon!" She again stopped, took a deep breath and grasped tightly again the hands of Moira and Jim.

"I think there were five of the bandits, .. maybe six. ... They took my sister ... and ..... and they raped my sister, ... they raped Jiwon, .. each of them! They were dirty ... and they were ugly! .. I remember!"

She paused, seeking control of her emotions, but her terrible anger could not be quashed, an anger that flowed with her words.

"When they finished with Jiwon, they left her on the floor. ... She was bleeding and naked ... and they were laughing ... and I was so numb with fright, .. I could not move, ... I could not help her ... and I remember Jiwon trying, with great difficulty, to turn her head in search of me. ... When she saw me, .. she smiled ... and they shot her .. and I could not stop screaming."

Moira's arms went again about her, but Liang did not cry. When Moira released her, she looked directly into Moira's eyes, her expression without emotion.

"They pulled me from under the table." Her breathing got deeper, "They ripped my clothing and tore it from me and threw it on the floor ..." her voice got softer, but more intense, "and ...

and .. and they formed a circle about me and prodded me with their fingers ... and they laughed .. and laughed .. and I screamed and screamed!"

She uttered a huge sigh. "I did not understand their language, but they were suddenly very excited when there was some shooting outside. They ran quickly from the building and there was more shooting and a great deal of confusion. I did not think, ... I could not think. I ran frightened from the building and into the jungle. I wandered without food and clothing for three days I think, except for some berries I picked near a clearing. There was ample water about, ... but I remember very little of the wandering, except my feet hurt so very much.

"At the end of that time, I came to another clearing and heard voices. Suddenly my spirits revived. I knew the language was the same as I heard the Americans speak in Peiping. I was exhausted and nearly delirious, but stumbled onto a road and into the arms of English missionaries. They clothed and sheltered me and they loved me and I loved them. They adopted me and educated me and helped me became a Christian, .. but I must admit, my faith was truly shaken when their lives were taken."

Jim was mesmerized as Liang floundered and struggled through her story. He had seen much of human perversity and brutality in his twenty-five years, but never the equal of this. He was thankful for Moira and her gentleness and responsiveness. He too wanted to comfort Liang. She acquired an added dimension and the special place she already occupied in his heart, would be inviolable.

"Oh, Liang, you are so brave and so wonderful. I am proud and so pleased you are my friend ... and my sister."

"I am not brave! I am a coward! My story must tell you that."

"Liang, your story tells me you are very brave. You have picked up your life, with all its tragedy and carry on with great courage. You never shy away from what you sense as duty and you have the most wonderful capacity to love. That requires courage under normal circumstances, but you do it after living through things that would turn many away from the goodness of life. You are truly brave and as I said before, I am proud to be your friend and be accepted as your sister."

"Oh, Moira! You are so wonderful. I feel so blessed to know you."

A long affectionate embrace followed. When they separated, Liang was more like her old self. A cleansing had taken place. The transition was good. They talked until quite late.

When Liang went to bed, Jim and Moira sat side by side, Moira's head on Jim's shoulder. They were full of Liang's life and their feelings for her where more of love than sympathy. They knew Liang did not need sympathy, nor would she accept it. They did not speak, but sat and took comfort from the other's nearness, till Moira sat up and looked into her husband's eyes and smiled.

He wrapped her in his arms and kissed her as his thoughts flashed back to when they first met. She had no idea then that he loved her. Maybe, he thought, that was because her own ungratified love for him clouded her insight into his mind. Now it was different. She seemed to have access to most of whatever he was thinking. He wondered if she knew any of the thoughts that passed through his mind as Liang told her story. It mattered not, for even if she did, it would make no difference.

Seven years ago, when he spoke Chinese and asked a beautiful woman her name, she answered in the sing song manner of the Chinese, the proper form, family name first, Sung, ... then Jiwon, her given name. He thought quite wrongly that Sung Jiwon was her first name and they agreed on an Anglicized version, .. Soo-Ann.

He now knew Soo-Ann's younger sister, the sister he had seen near the Alter of Heaven as a youngster of twelve, the sister he unknowingly helped support.

Over the years he pushed the anxiety of Soo-Ann's safety from his mind. His total love of Moira and her love for him, more than anything, helped him overcome the feeling of foolhardiness and guilt of his past, but now, it came dimly to life again. Soo-Ann had not been murdered by the Ba Loo, as he thought she might, but had been murdered nevertheless.

Later, in bed, Jim pondered the guilt. It slowly dawned on him that Liang, so full of goodness, was here now, because of Soo-Ann. For that he was thankful and though it did not immediately relieve his feelings, it did help.

"I hope we can give her the sanctuary to bury her suffering for good," he said to his wife.

Moira pulled his head to her breasts and gently rubbed his neck and scalp and replied softly, "We will, Darling, we will."

He fell asleep in the arms of his love, but his dreams were troubled. The specter of that grisly murder could not easily be erased. During the night he woke in a panic. Moira was not beside him. An instant later he looked through the darkness in the direction of a faint sound. His breathing eased when he saw her nude form fussing over Dunkie and Robbie.

He got up and went to her side and whispered, "Can I help?"

"Everything is fine." she whispered, "Go back to bed."

She gently pinched a buttock when he turned to walk away.

He went into the bathroom and drank a large glass of water and with another, rinsed his mouth. Returning to bed he slid up to her and kissed her on the forehead. "Sweetheart, I love you so much, sometimes it scares me."

She put her mouth to his and spontaneously their tongues were in a fierce duel and they hurtled into their passion with a savage energy.

*

It was great for Moira to have Liang about. The boys thrived with all the love and attention. It was also great for the local population when Moira spent some time at the hospital. If only for a short period each week, she was the nurse of her calling. An excellent and compassionate nurse, she was soon well known to many. Liang also did some duty at the hospital.

And as his sons and his wife did, so did Jim loose his heart to the graceful and exotically beautiful Asian girl of nineteen.

He was glad he loved his wife with such totality, otherwise, Liang could have been a sore temptation. As it was, Liang's presence was a good presence. She gave her share to the energy of the recently born happiness on the plantation that began with Moira's arrival.

As it was Moira who helped Liang be rid of her demons, it was Moira who convinced her to share in something daring and uninhibited.

The two young women secretly choreographed and practiced a ballet with a mix of Oriental and Western flavors. Purchasing some fabric of flamingo pink, one of Liang's favorite colors, they made themselves loose, but form fitting gowns that ended above the knee and were slit up the sides to nearly the waist. White ballet tights and slippers completed their attire.

One night when Jim and Duncan were present, they were invited with Dougald and all the servants into the large living room. The chairs and couches were arranged in a semi-circle. When all were seated, a melody unknown to Jim was played from the phonograph and the dancers went to work.

It started slowly, most of the moves strongly Oriental with an abundance of hand and arm movement. As the tempo increased, the East gave way to the West and Jim recognized moves he had seen Moira perform. Well into the piece, the dancers neared a frenzy, with wonderful leaps and twists, spins and rapid foot movement, only to slow to a beautifully graceful conclusion.

When complete and the dancers were still, they curtsied in the manner of the ballet, their exposed skin showing the glow of their exertions. The audience clapped and cheered with the fervor of an audience that had witnessed a world class performance. When the loud acclaim was over, the servants jabbered excitedly while Dougald stood transfixed, full of delight, something he rarely gave in to.

And Liang was filled with emotions, very strong emotions. She was full of wonder at the pleasure she derived from the performance, but she was more full of the devoted love she had for Moira. She knew that if Moira had not entered her life, it would not be as rich, not be as good. It showed in her features as they curtsied and their eyes met and they shared their smiles.

* * *

More and more, Jim Williams was having thoughts about his lifestyle, thoughts that were in conflict, for he had deep feelings and respect for the men he served with. He would rather be in his own Corps, but that was not the reason, for the British left nothing to be desired. It was as Moira said, "A Marine is a Marine, wherever he may be."

Oh, God! Moira! Sweet, wonderful Moira, he thought. She was a tonic and a salve all at the same time. An inspiration and a shelter, she was his lover and friend, the perfect mother to their sons. And it was those sons, even more than his wife, who were the catalyst for the all to frequent, recurring thoughts and doubts.

* * *

In the United States, Thanksgiving was approaching and remembering with fondness that celebration in the U.S., Moira thought it a good idea to celebrate at the plantation. Dougald concurred without hesitancy, something he was inclined to do at anything Moira suggested.

Jim was going on a short patrol, but would return in time. The planning began and the entire household was caught up in the excitement.

As they often did when everyone retired and especially when Jim was leaving for the jungle the next day, Moira and he sat together on a couch. They were silent awhile, content like so often, just to be together. Moira sat next to him, her legs drawn up, her bare feet protruding from under her dress.

"Sweetheart," Jim said softly, gazing into Moira's eyes, "I've been giving something a great deal of thought."

She had a sweet smile on her face and knowing her like he did, he wondered if she knew what he was going to say. She waited for him to continue.

"I'm thinking about leaving the Corps after this enlistment ends and I wanted to run it by you."

She sat up straight. "Whatever for? You love the Corps!"

Her eyes were open wide in wonder as she gazed into his.

"That's true, I do, but I've been looking at the boys growing up and thinking of how much of that growth I'm going to miss. Already I could have spent more time with Donny."

"But the time you spend with him is such good time. I believe most parents would envy the way you are a father to him," she paused and smiled sweetly again, "and a husband to me."

"Well, maybe so, but we may never have another tour like this one where we are out of the States and can be together like we've been here and Marines do spend a lot of time away from home ... and usually alone. We have been more than fortunate in our time together so far. This tour has been really special."

She got to her knees on the couch and threw her arms about him. She kissed him all over the face and once, hard on the lips. When she pushed back, she held his shoulders and smiled into his eyes.

"Oh, Jim! You know I would follow you if you walked the plank, but this is a supremely happy moment for me. I would never ask you, but if it is your decision, I accept it gladly. I too love your Marine Corps, but a life in Shoreford is very appealing and you must know how your father would like to have you with him."

"Yeah and I think I'd like it too."

Her expression turned serious and she reached for and took his hands in hers before saying, "Jim darling, I knew something was bothering you and for awhile I was hurt that you didn't confide in me, but now I know that was only self-pity. In this case I'm glad you thought it through and made the decision on your own, for I believe I might have influenced you and I would never have wanted to do that, certainly not in this case. Oh, Jim, you've made me supremely happy!" She paused and looked deeply into his eyes, "But you remember, .. I'm here to help you, .. if ever you're troubled again."

He kissed her forehead. "I love you, Moira Williams!"

She gazed at him a few seconds. "Have you given any thought to Liang?"

"Yes I have. Do you think she would come with us?"

"Oh, Darling, I know she would!"

"Well, I really have thought about it. She could train for her nursing right in the city. And ya know what? She'd make someone a heckuva wife. And guess what? I keep thinkin of Bob. I think he'd flip over her. Wouldn't it be great to have her in the family?"

"You're an incorrigible romantic," she giggled as she squeezed him with amazing strength, "But that's why I'm so in love with you. Let's go to bed," and she gave him that impish grin, "we'll have a lot to talk about when you get back."

They loved tenderly that night, at least for the most part.

*

In the morning Jim was up early, to shave and have plenty of time to share breakfast with Moira and play with the boys. The twins were in their own room by now and as was his custom in their private bathroom, he remained unclad. Moira came in to use the toilet. She washed her hands and then reached for her toothbrush. She lightheartedly pushed him aside and he gave her a mock dirty look. They stayed side by side until she finished. She put the toothbrush away and moved behind him, running her hands, then fingers, up and down his back and buttocks. She encircled his midriff with her arms, bringing her nakedness to his and moved her fingers in circles on his chest and down to the top of his loins.

"Stop it, you wench!"

She laughed and continued downward with her fingers. When she reached her destination she peeked around him and giggled, "Oh my!"

"Oh, are you gonna pay for that."

Her giggling infecting his mood, he chased her to the bed, some of the shaving cream still on his face.

When he ran from the house, he had managed to give the boys some time, but his breakfast had been a quickly gulped glass of juice.

* * *

The patrol was out three days. It was a lucky three days. The intelligence reports were right on the money. They got close to the enemy camp without being discovered. Some members of the patrol were working their way around the camp to cut off any retreat. It was not necessary. The three bandits were in the front. They engaged the Marines before they attempted to run. That was their mistake. Jim took one of them out with an accurate and lethal burst from his Thompson. The fire fight lasted a portion of a minute. Marines poured through the camp to gather what equipment they could find, while Corporal Mooney and another checked out the bodies. When Jim was sure all was under control, he walked over to Mooney.

Staring down at the open shirt and bare chest of the bandit he had taken out, Jim winced. There were three, small, neat holes punched diagonally across the chest, the first through the heart, the other two progressively higher, toward the left shoulder.

"Hey, Sarge this bugger's a girl!" Mooney exclaimed.

The small breasts were nearly non existent, but there was no doubt as to what they were.

Jim knew there was an occasional female amongst the bandits, but the thought that he had killed one did not sit well with him. He ground his teeth together and said under his breath, "Shit!"

The radio brought trucks to the rendezvous site before the Marines arrived carrying the bodies. During the three mile hike out of the jungle and the ride back to camp, visions of the dead girl periodically popped into Jim's imagination. He argued with himself about her death. He knew she was trying to kill him or his men. She put her life on the line as a wager in that gamble and lost. She paid the price. He was certain she had shared in the execution and atrocities of innocent people. He knew his reasoning was sound, even just, but the image of her lying there, dead from his hand, continued to erupt recurrently in his mind.

"Damn!!!" he said to himself, "It's a good thing I'm getting out of all this. I think I'm losing my stuff."

But for the others aboard, they rode into the camp triumphant. Also dirty and tired. The triumph they would savor, the dirt they would wash off and the fatigue would disappear with the first beer.

The trucks came to a halt and the men jumped off and unloaded the bodies. Jim was directing his men and did not see the man approach.

"Jim," the Sergeant Major said softly, his face somber and grim. "Jim!" his voice more tense. "There's some terrible news! .... There's been a bloody, nasty ambush, .. some deaths."

Jim Williams turned ashen, "Moira?"

"Yes, goddamit!"

Barely able to speak, his body lifeless and numb, he sagged like a used rag thrown into a pile of refuse. His words sounded far away. He did not recognize his own wavering voice, by now a heart-rending sob.

"And the boys?"

"No! They were safely at home. It was your wife and Dougald MacLeod."

* ELEVEN *

The pillow was damp with his tears. He got up and went into the bathroom and splashed cold water on his face. He looked at his reflection in the mirror and his eyes displayed redness. He wanted to wash the redness away and wondered why. Maybe, he thought, it was because today was a happy day in memory of a happy event and red eyes were inappropriate.

The tears came easily today as he wandered in the past. He had never been one to shed tears until Moira came into his life and left it so suddenly. Now tears were sometimes there when he was sad and sometimes when he was happy, or filled with pride. He lived life differently now.

Back on the bed, he closed his eyes when the bedroom door opened. He waited expectantly as she came to him. The blanket was pulled back and finger tips dug into his armpits and ribs. He rolled away and onto his stomach laughing loudly.

"No! Please! You fiend! Please!"

In his present mood, he did not want to fight back, yet he was glad for the chance to escape a sadness that could still engulf him so many years later.

"Will it be necessary to do something more drastic to get you up?" She was smiling down at him, but there was a gleam of mischief in her sparkling eyes.

"No! You sadistic ogress," he chuckled, "I promise, I'll be up soon."

"You'd better be!" she emphatically stated, the smile still present, the mischief still in her eyes. She quickly and firmly pinched a buttock before leaving, knowing full well a further call would be needed to get him moving. He seemed to have a goal and at such times, he was difficult, even impossible to discourage.

As soon as the door closed he rolled to his back and pulled the blanket up to his chin. He chuckled to himself at her antics, thankful she had turned a moment of sadness to one of frivolity.

He closed his eyes and slowly, painfully returned to the chaos of that horrifying ordeal.

~ ~ ~ ~ ~

He tried in despair to awaken from the terrible dream, but it was the dream that kept him awake. His ravaged mind conjured up all kinds of ghostly images, fed by his guilt and horrible grief. It consumed him and forbade his mobility. He did not want to see his sons. He could not understand it.

In the bedroom he had shared with her, he sat on the edge of the bed and cried, then sobbed, his body wrenching uncontrollably. He had to get out of there. Struggling to his feet, he walked unsteadily, without a destination, without purpose and escaped the room.

Duncan was helicoptered in from his troop in the jungle. He held Jim like a father, his own grief almost too much to bear.

Liang stayed out of sight and tended the boys with a tenderness and love bred from her own urgent need for compassion.

The servants padded about in sullen silence.

Unable to take himself to their bed, Jim at last lay on a couch, long after everyone was in bed. He was still in his filthy jungle uniform. He got to his feet sometime in the early hours of the morning without having slept. He paced and paced some more, his mind trying to face up to his plight.

Neither his folks nor Molly had wanted them to come here, yet it was from the clippings that Molly sent to Moira that they learned of the need for nurses. But, he thought despairingly, he was the one responsible for her lost life. He could not seek to pass the blame to anyone else. He knew that. He had wanted one more crack at the bad guys. Finally, but not wanting to, he remembered the words of the minister that wonderful day in the church, just before they were married, " ... I know you will protect her with your life."

He went outside and walked, or rather stumbled about. He did not recognize the familiar surroundings. The sun came up in the beauty of a Malayan sunrise that had always made him glad for his sight, but he did not take notice. The sun was well up when he went back in the house.

The occupants had risen and were moving about in numb disbelief. Duncan was there. His eyes showed his anguish. He gently placed an arm about Jim's shoulder, supporting him to the table where Jim's breakfast was waiting. They did not speak, nor did Jim eat, just sat with head in hands, eyes closed, his mind deprived of any normal function.

Liang was caring for the boys in their room. Her early Oriental heritage was in conflict with the Western culture she embraced, the culture in which she desperately desired to live. She could not bring herself to look at Jim when he appeared briefly in the doorway, for there were thoughts coming to life in her mind, thoughts she did not, could not understand, but when understanding, minute as it was, began to seep through, she knew she did not want to understand, for it filled her with a sense of perversity that fueled a desire to flee and she knew she could not do that.

Jim went into the bathroom and lethargically removed his stinking clothing and crawled into the tub. He filled it to capacity with water so hot his skin appeared sunburned. Two hours later he returned to the world, shaved and clean. Yesterday was, ... but today was not as it should be. He did not want today.

* * *

Her body was prepared swiftly for shipment home. She would lie at rest in a small cemetery in Shoreford next to the resting places of Don and Sal.

Sarah had worked relentlessly with Graves Registration to have their remains disinterred from Iwo and Inchon and brought home. Now Moira would share common ground with them.

Before the casket was sealed, Duncan and Liang paid a final visit. Jim waited until they turned to leave before he went to stand beside her. He stayed only a moment. He could bear it no more. He kissed her cold lips and squeezed her stiff hands and softly sobbed, "I love you, Darling. Yesterday was, .. today is ... I'll see you tomorrow."

He turned and walked quickly out, his legs unsteady, his body an indistinct quaver, tears streaming down his face.

* * *

Telegrams arrived from Shoreford and Burrtown where the grief was horrendous. People arrived at the estate, most of whom Jim did not know, to present their condolences for Dougald and the wonderful Scottish-American girl who had won so many hearts. The entire troops to which Jim and Duncan belonged, showed up at onetime or another.

The will had not been read, but Duncan was informed by his uncle's solicitor that Molly and her children would inherit the estate. Someone had to be found to run the place until the family could become involved.

Normalcy returned to Duncan more quickly than anyone and by the time he was back in his unit, he was mostly his old chipper self. During the bad times, he had taken charge, issued orders and generally pulled things together.

Liang was the greatest blessing to Jim, however, though he did not realize it, nor did he realize that because of her, he allowed himself to degenerate into incapacity. She cared for his sons while he was without inertia. She cared for them with a love and a compassion she could not have surpassed had they been her own. And she began to wish they were. Soon, she could think of little else.

The other outrageously powerful yearning that was maturing within her, she refused to acknowledge, refused to accept its existence, its hold on her, or believe its truth.

*

The wheels were set in motion for an immediate hardship discharge. It would take time, but Jim was not in any hurry to return to the real world. He was not ready to face his family, his friends, anyone, at this moment in his life.

* * *

Ten long days passed torturously since he walked out of the jungle and was greeted by the horrendous news, ten days of tormented emotions and memories he wanted, needed desperately to force from his benumbed mind .. and soul. But there was pity brewing too, for himself, for his loss, but he did not recognize it as pity, for another emotion, a much stronger emotion, was taking form and clouding the pity. A savage anger was boiling deep inside him, an anger that had grown, intensified in the passing days, an anger that was destroying his judgment, an anger that was intensely directed against himself, .. waiting to explode.

*

In all the months Liang had known Jim, he was never anything but an exceptional friend. She had long since forgotten that one, instantaneous, shameful thought and she did not understand that it was because of Moira, she had never felt anything more, that if Moira had lived, she never would have felt anything more. But now, after lying dormant and unperceived deep within her soul, this alien yearning was coming to life, but it was a yearning in conflict with her virtue, a conflict she was fearful of, fearful it would provoke her into something she felt to be unforgivingly shameful.

*

The evening of the tenth day, when the house was vacated by all who did not live there and the servants, Liang and the boys were in bed, Jim went to his sons' room and lifted the netting of their beds, one by one. He looked at each in his turn. Tears began to form and flowed down his face in profusion. He felt a dreadful pity for his sons. They had lost their mother, a mother who could never to be replaced.

Jim made no sound while in the room, but Liang, who slept there with the boys was conscious of his presence soon after he arrived. She observed his shadowy form in the darkness. Tears escaped her eyes and flowed delicately down her cheeks, .. as much for him as for herself. She could sense his remorse, feel his grief. In her compassion, she wanted to reach out, .. touch him, ... share his agony, .. their agony, but right then she did not know why. The truth she refused to acknowledge, muted her understanding

When Jim left the room, Liang, confused and uncertain, donned her robe and tiptoed silently to the open doorway of the room where now Jim slept alone. She could make out his form in the darkness, sitting on the edge of the bed, his head in his hands. The crying was not perceptible, but she knew he was crying.

She walked to him and knelt at his feet and pried his spiritless hands loose and held them in hers. She stayed with him, stayed that way a very long time, her emotions in complete disarray, her mind frantically searching. Why, she thought, why do I feel this way when I know it is so wrong. But there was no answer.

At last he mumbled, "My sons have no mother!" He paused, his jaw clamped tight, his vicious anger pouring forth in the words he spit out. "Just like that! ... She was taken from them! ... Now they have no mother! It's my fault!" and louder, " My fault! Do you understand? It's my fault!"

A second emotion, as powerful as the first, her love for the boys, stirred Liang.

"I will be their mother!"

Jim did not understand her meaning, yet her words soothed his troubled mind. For the moment, his anger took refuge in that solace. He could feel her nearness. There was comfort in her presence. Without looking at her, he muttered softly, "Thank you."

He allowed his head to rest against hers.

She was bewildered. Conflicting messages pounded back and forth through her distraught mind. Without warning, one dominated, something she could not understand, something she refused to accept, but something that assumed control.

Without knowing why, without caring why, she got to her feet and urged him up. While her heart pounded and raced, she removed his short robe and pushed him gently downward on the bed. She went to the opposite side and removed her own robe and climbed in beside him. Sliding her submissive body against him, she encircled him with her arms.

*

When Jim awoke, he was extremely groggy. He lay for awhile trying to remember where he was and where he had been. Then he remembered Moira and the terrible anger, the anger that was his companion of late, the anger that welled up in him, crushing his intellect, negating his rational. And he remembered Liang, her arms about him, his struggle to put an end to the anger, the anger that tore at his reason and dominated his soul and his body.

He was scared. He turned his head timidly, hoping she was not there, but she was beside him, her beautiful shining black hair in disarray on the pillow and around her face. She was staring at him, her features filled with tender compassion. She reached out a hand and touched his lips with her fingertips and moved them over his face, not smiling, but there was a softness there.

In a moment of horror, he saw the bruises on her upper arms where he had held her so tightly, .. used his powerful grip to shake her, vent his terrible anger, .. as Liang crossed over the boundaries of wisdom and moved into the realm of her own repressed and secret desire, responding with passion.

It had been a savage encounter as he gripped her tenaciously and she took him to her, helped him as she thought she must, as she unwittingly wanted to, helped him tenderly amidst his bout of bitterness. All her thoughts of the last ten days, her love of the boys, her desire to remain with them, to be a continuing part of their lives, .. but most of all, the out of sight, unaccepted love for the man in her arms, amassed, transcending reason.

"Ooohhh noo!" he groaned, "What have I done to you?"

There was a tender smile, paired with compassion in her expression.

"You have done nothing that was bad, James. It is good. You have done what you needed to do. You have freed yourself of the demons that gripped your soul."

He did not understand her words.

"Liang, ... Liang, .. my God, .. I'm so sorry!"

He thought of holding her, seeking to comfort her, but he could not bring himself to come in contact with her.

"I'm sorry, Liang. God! I must be losing my mind! Will you ever forgive me?"

"There is nothing to forgive, James. Please do not feel as you do." She smiled tenderly, her accent more pronounced than he remembered as she struggled to be precise, .. to ease his pain. "Please, James, ... please, .. do not feel as you do. Everything is quite all right." She was quiet a moment, her courage insufficient to say more. Then she smiled sweetly and reached out a hand and placed it gently on his cheek. "The boys will awaken soon. I must be ready for them."

She pushed the sheet back and slid from the bed and into her robe, walking to the bathroom.

He watched her go. In the prison of his guilt, he thought of himself as immoral.

* * *

For two days, Jim was intensely attentive to his sons. He reentered their lives as the father he had been. His guilt, however, would not go away, not only for what he had done to Liang, but for the lost love he believed he had betrayed, yet Liang was always there, though she made no overtures to him and he was not comfortable in her presence. And she did a good job of hiding her own deep mourning, but Jim soon sensed what she was experiencing, while trying to help him through his. It humbled him.

Thankfully, two days with his sons had a softening effect on his judgment of his errant deed. Despite his anger with himself, he was thinking of Liang differently. Anchored solidly in his heart from the very first, she filled that spot more fully now, caring for his sons with a devotion and selflessness ... and a love that no mother could surpass.

The two days also eased the burden of his grief somewhat. He could not escape it, but he knew he had to live and function.

He finally faced Liang, spoke to her and she smiled and answered him. At the end of the day, Liang made iced tea and she and Jim sat in chairs in the living room and talked endlessly of Moira. There were tears shed, but there were smiles. It was a cleansing time for both.

*

During the next day, Jim started speaking of going home. He asked Liang if she would mind caring for the boys while he spent the balance of the day setting the wheels in motion for the return to the U.S. and civilian life.

Her reaction was anything but stoic, though she tried desperately to control her feelings. She felt her life slipping from her.

The following day Liang was preoccupied every time Jim attempted to speak to her. He was curious at first, but eventually concerned. He tried to draw her out. She was polite, but remained distant and vague. Once he spotted her wiping tears away. The only thing she did not falter at, was her care of the boys.

Jim lay awake well into the morning hours that night. He knew of Liang's profound love for the boys. He thought he might know the reason for her reaction, but he was not really sure. Could his judgment be flawed, he wondered. He remembered he frequently failed to know the female mind. That was enough to give direction to further thoughts. Her words, after his shameful misconduct four nights ago, kept repeating themselves in his mind and he saw again and again the way she looked at him. He battled with and succumbed to, only to battle again his vacillating thoughts. It was something that unsettled him, something that created conflict in his mind, something he was not comfortable with, yet something that made a great deal of sense. When finally he did sleep, it was a troubled sleep and of short duration. When he awoke, his thoughts were still at war. The sheets were rumpled and soaked with sweat.

He lay in bed until one thought was victorious and the other finally surrendered, certain at last that his decision was just and correct.

In the bathroom he drew water for a hot and calming bath. Tentative, he wanted to linger in the tub, but cut it short and dressed and went to the breakfast table, late, but determined.

The twins were in their playpen and Liang had just finished feeding Donald. Her own plate was barely touched.

"Good morning, Liang."

She smiled timidly, but did not speak. He ate sparingly, then left the table and found the most trustworthy of the female servants.

"Mrs. Peng, would you be kind enough to stay with the boys while Liang and I take a walk? It will only be a short one."

Pleased to do something she enjoyed, something that would relieve her momentarily of her grief, she replied affirmatively with a smile, her English atrocious.

When he returned to the dining room, he stood beside Liang, looking down, "Liang, would you please take a walk with me? I'd like to speak to you about something. ... Please?"

She looked up and into his eyes, but turned immediately away, fear in her expression. The tears began to flow. He walked behind her, placed his hands on her shoulders and squeezed gently, then helped her from the chair.

"What of the boys?" She had trouble with the words.

At that point Mrs. Peng arrived with a toy for Donald who was reluctant to give up Liang, but he allowed himself to be taken from the highchair by Mrs. Peng and before Jim and Liang closed the door, he was laughing happily.

"It's OK. Come on."

Jim took Liang by the hand and guided her out the door. They walked down a short path to a bench that overlooked a small fish pond. All the time they walked, she was tense. He led her to the bench.

"Please sit down, Liang."

When she was seated, he stood in front of her, a little apart. He turned and walked to the pond, searching the water with his eyes while he searched his mind for words. About a minute passed and he turned again and walked the few steps back to her. His mind was not at ease, but he was convinced his judgment was not only right, but necessary, necessary for all concerned. He enunciated the words with great care.

"Liang, you know the boys and I will be leaving soon to return to our home."

She stared at the ground and gave a slight nod, but he was more aware of the shudder in her body.

"I treated you badly a few nights ago, when you were being kind to me. I'm extremely sorry for that."

Her body continued to quiver very slightly.

"I'm hopeful you can forgive me, .. can you?"

In tones so low he could barely hear, she answered, still looking at the ground.

"There is nothing to forgive, James."

"I guess," he took a deep breath, "I knew that would be your answer, .. but I want to tell you I'll never be like that again."

She looked up and into his eyes, her head cocked slightly, her expression puzzled. She did not understand why this conversation was necessary, why he did not take his sons and depart and not prolong her suffering. Immediately she was angry with herself for the loathsome thought.

"What I really want to ask .... is ... is .. will you come home to America with us, ... the boys and me?"

Her eyes were suddenly huge in astonishment. She could not bring herself to speak, only stare back unbelieving as the meaning of the words sunk in and even then she could not be convinced of what at she heard.

"Will you, Liang? Will you come to America with us?"

She jumped to her feet, instantly against him. She flung her arms about him, crushing her cheek to his shoulder, her sweet smelling hair touching his cheek. Between sobs, she got the words out.

"Yes! ... I will come to America, James ... and I will be a good nursemaid to the boys!" She paused, then softly, timidly continued, "And if you desire, ... I will be your concubine."

He squeezed her and holding her tightly laughed. Stepping back he gripped her shoulders tenderly, his merriment confusing her abundantly.

"Oh, Liang! I'm sorry. I didn't make myself clear. You silly, beautiful, wonderful girl, maybe it doesn't make much sense now, ... but what I mean is, ... will you come to America as my wife and be a mother to the boys I know you love?"

Her mouth was open wide. Her arms hung limply at her sides. At last, when she regained a modicum of her composure and a smile crept across and finally engulfed her face and the tears cascaded down her cheeks, she was back in his arms and the words gushed out, "Yes I will be your wife, your most happy wife, James! ... And I will be a good mother, .. a wonderful and joyful mother to the boys!"

"Oh, Liang," he sighed smiling down at her, "I know this is really sudden and I know you must think me nuts when I have just lost the woman I loved more than life, but I believe you are so very like her and the boys love you so much and you love them with such intensity. You are the mother they need. I promise to be good to you and I'm hopeful you can learn to love me over time."

Without removing her head from his chest she spoke very softly, "I do love you, James."

He took a step to the rear, smiling tenderly. Grasping her upper arms gently in his hands, he gazed into her eyes, "You are a very special person, Liang. Come on, let's go home."

Her cheeks were covered with teardrops, but she was glowing as he slid his hand into hers.

They turned and walked back to the house.

*

Within the hour Jim was on the phone. He had to locate Duncan and he called his troop. The Marines in that troop shared in the tragedy of Moira with Jim and Duncan and they went out of their way to run Duncan down and get him to the phone. He was to lead a patrol into the jungle in a few days, but the C.O. turned him loose for the balance of that day, which was what Jim requested.

At first shocked, next surprised, Duncan did not dwell on that. He knew his friend well enough to know he had not reached this decision without a tremendous amount of soul searching. When he arrived at the plantation, Jim greeted him.

"Dunk I know you must think I'm crazy .. I guess I do myself, but I've done a lot of soul searching and the boys ..."

"Stop, Jim!" Duncan held up a hand, "You are the finest friend I've ever had and ya were my sister's beloved husband. I would trust ye with my life. I know you that well. I trust your judgment every bit as much. You owe me no explanation. That's all there is to it."

What Duncan's comment meant to Jim, showed on his face, but left him speechless. Duncan smiled and put an arm about his shoulder. "What're we waitin for? Let's be on our way."

Jim went inside and gathered up Liang. They drove away in one of the plantation vehicles. When they arrived at the ministers home, they were invited inside. Duncan asked to remain outside with Jim and Liang for a moment.

"Och, man," Duncan said as they stood together, "I want ya to know, I love ya dearly and I know ya loved my sister more than life itself." He stopped and smiled, "And God knows, .. she loved you. But life goes on and so must you and the boys. As Moira herself always said, 'Yesterday was, today is."

Then he reached out his hands and placed them tenderly on Liang's shoulders, "And you, Lassie, are as fine a lady has lived. I know ye loved my sister deeply, as she did you. You are quite like Moira, you know. I believe you and my best friend deserve one another dearly. And ya go with my heartfelt blessin!"

The tears on Liang's cheeks were absorbed by Duncan's shirt as she stepped forward and threw her arms about him. He held her lovingly as Jim stepped in and put his arms about both. They stayed that way for a time and when they parted, there was more than one glossy eye.

Inside the house the minister took Jim and Liang into an office and talked to them briefly. He was almost at once convinced, that marrying them was not only proper, but the right thing to do. He was not blind to the things he already knew of Jim and Liang.

Duncan stood up for Jim for the second time in the span of less than two years. The ministers wife stood in for Liang. None else was present.

When Duncan returned to camp, he went with one disquieting thought. He wondered how Ceit would take the news, for both his mother and Moira had talked to him of their certainty of her feelings for Jim and he had seen enough of Ceit to believe those thoughts were correct.

* * *

Jim Williams had unusual thoughts for a wedding night. He had moments of misgiving. He knew he could never love anyone the way he loved Moira and yet he was bringing another into his life already. He wondered about his sanity. What happened to the grief, so real and intense? At that point, he remembered that every day, at various moments, he did feel grief and sporadically, unintentional shudders deep within his being. The grief was still present, it had not left him. There would never be another Moira, there never could be another Moira. His grief for her would not end because he made a commitment to another, yet he would learn to love another, that was happening already.

The ability to love another, he thought, was not a bad thing. Though it started as a love born of necessity, even that was not a bad thing. His sons had a need and he would see that need filled. There was none better than Liang. It should not have surprised him that he found himself loving her, though not yet with the intensity and in all the ways that would come and grow in time. It would become a good love, he knew, not in need of excuses. It would stand by itself, ... because of his wonderful Moira.

So Jim took Liang to bed. With the utmost patience and tenderness, the last vestiges of tentativeness were dispelled. In the silence of the darkened room there were subdued sounds and they knew each other as man and wife.

They washed afterwards and he held her hand on the way back to bed. When under the sheet, he again reached out and took her hand. He did not sleep deeply, but dozed an hour or so.

He was awakened by movement and a pleasing sensation. Liang was resting on an elbow. She was studying him by the light that came through the windows from the moon and the stars. Periodically she bent and kissed his forehead or caressed his lips with hers. He smiled in the darkness, rolled to his side and tenderly touched her lips with his. She came to him, slid her arms about him, while he locked her in his arms.

Lying pressed together, she put her mouth to his ear, "I love you, James." she whispered softly, "It is only you I can love."

He gave her a quick, firm squeeze and she gasped. He kissed her with deep feeling, his tongue entering her mouth. She responded with a passion that not only surprised him, but aroused him. Feeling her fingernails in his back, he continued to explore her mouth with his tongue and the vigor of her response increased as she pressed herself ardently into him.

"I am yours, James!" she whispered softly, but excitedly, "Please, .. please take me!"

But he would not give in to her until he teased and thrilled her sensual receptors and she cried out for him in a frantic plea.

"James! James! Please!"

It was then that they came together, uninhibited and noisy, exhilarated and wild.

When they were spent, they lay on their backs exhausted. Working to return her breathing to normal, Liang turned her head to Jim.

"Oh, my husband, that was very bad!" She had a quick intake of breath, "Oh, no! ... I mean ... it was wonderful, .. but I mean it was bad, because ... Oh James, I mean ... I know we must have awakened the boys."

Rolling to his side, he wrapped her in his arms and kissed her cheek and chuckled, "So much for inscrutability." He disentangled himself, rolled off the side of the bed and went directly to her side, taking her hand, "Come on. We'll take a peek and see."

They had nothing to worry about. The boys slept peacefully on.

"Come on," he said, "lets go wash up."

Taking her hand, they walked to the bathroom. The doorway was not wide enough for both and he released her hand, reaching in to turn on the light. She entered ahead of him and as she passed by, he gently pinched a buttock.

She turned with just the touch of a blush on her cheeks and a beautiful smile.

"Oh, my husband," she said taking his hand which she kissed and placed firmly against her cheek. Then she hugged him and tenderly kissed his lips.

* * *

The news, when it reached Shoreford and Burrtown was staggering and confusing, but in time would be accepted and love would come forth for a young woman so easy to love.

One, however, had difficulty concealing her anger. Life, she knew, was surely unjust. She went to bed infuriated, pummeling her pillow with smashing blows. Ceit Fraser would grow a profound hate for the young Chinese girl she knew nothing about and refused to accept. She would nurture that hate and it would grow and fester and negate her judgment.

***

For three days, Jim, Liang and the boys were inseparable. Liang nurtured and cared for the brothers with an escalating happiness, but when they were asleep, she clung to Jim as though she was dreaming and to let go, would be to awaken from that dream.

They spoke frequently of Moira. Neither had lost their grief and both recurrently had guilt pangs. Often when they spoke of her, a tearful eye would show itself, but more often, they expressed thanks for having known her and to have been touched by her life. Then one night, they both had dreams of Moira smiling.

They were at the start of putting things in perspective. Their emotional wandering was ending and their lives were starting a journey with a destination. Three young and very energetic boys helped immensely.

*

On the day before they were to depart the plantation and head home to America, Jim and Liang left the boys with Mrs. Peng and another female servant only to happy to oblige. They went to the small hospital to bid farewell to friends.

There was a bustle of activity when they arrived. In an aboriginal village to the north, some inhabitants had stumbled into an old terrorist minefield. The extent of the injuries was uncertain and a doctor and nurse were making preparations to go there and treat the wounded. There was no other medical help available.

Hearing the story, Liang asked Jim if she could assist. He did not want her to go, but when he saw how pleased the doctor was, he relented. He knew by now that people like Liang, as Moira before her, were true to their calling and could be no other way. He knew what a calling was. He had had his own. In the end, he realized he was proud of his new wife, for her decision and desire to help. The flight up and back and the time in the village would probably require no more than six hours.

Helping ready the gear and carry it to the copter, Jim's love for Liang became more tangible. He smiled at her enthusiasm and dedication. On the last trip, he held her hand all the way to the pad while she leaned her head on his shoulder. When they arrived at the open door, she raised his hand and pressed it firmly to her lips, then solidly into her cheek. He slid his arms about her, holding her tightly as he kissed her. She hung on fiercely.

Not knowing he had never spoken the words to her, he said, "I love you, Liang! Hurry back to me!"

Her tears started immediately. "Oh, James! I love you so much!"

She kissed him very hard and turned and fled. She knew that to hesitate another second would have made it impossible to leave him.

He watched her run under the whirling blades that rumpled her clothing and blew her beautiful, shiny hair around her in a million black wavelets. She sat in the seat and buckled the belt and turned one last time, kissed her hand for a long moment and threw him the kiss.

The copter lifted noisily away.

Jim stayed until the aircraft and its valuable cargo disappeared from sight.

*

The twins were in bed and Jim and Donald were having their last play on the floor, before Donald's bedtime. It was getting late. Jim was certain he should have received the call from the hospital by now, telling him Liang was on her way back. He should, he thought, be on his way to pick her up. He was uncomfortable and found himself losing his concentration with his son.

As his mind wandered, it was Liang who was very much in those wandering thoughts. For the moment, those thoughts helped ease his discomfort. He did love her, of that he was sure. Yet he was still in love with Moira. It was different, but it was also the same.

He wondered about that some, until the image of Liang at their first meeting caused him to smile to himself. He was knocked for a loop that day, but it had been easy to rationalize, convincing himself it was a coincidence, only to be shocked again when Liang revealed she was Soo-Ann's younger sister. And he wondered if it was possible that the guilt he carried for Soo-Ann had anything to do with the way he felt about Liang? No! That could not be. He was certain of that. He loved Liang for what she was, a gentle, sweet, kind and wonderful person who treated his sons ... and him with the utmost love and who had a miraculous sense of humor, especially when you knew what her experience with life had been.

And though it had nothing to do with his reasons for loving Liang, he happily remembered her dancing with Moira that special night and he saw them again in his minds eye. It had been a brilliant display, the entire audience captivated. As he thought of that evening he could not control the strange notion that accompanied the memory. Would Liang dance for him as Moira had? He was momentarily embarrassed for having the thought, but then smiled to himself. He knew she would.

The phone rang noisily!

Jim jumped aggressively to his feet surprising Donald who started to cry. He tenderly picked his son from the floor, calming him a few seconds before going to the phone.

He picked up the handpiece and answered, but never said another word, except for a mumbled, "Mmm." at the end. When the line went dead it took some time for him to replace the handpiece as he stared into space.

Gently picking Donald from the floor, he walked unsteadily to a chair and sat, holding his son tightly to him.

Radio contact was lost with the helicopter just after an emergency message was received. It had to be presumed down. No one knew for sure at the time, just what its fate had been, but it did go down and it would be months before the crash site was located and bodies recovered, in the most impenetrable jungle.

Jim sat in the chair with his oldest son. He did not shed a tear, he was completely numb. When the first rays of the morning sun sneaked through the windows, he was still awake, still tenderly holding Donald, who slept peacefully, unaware of the terrible void and crushing pain in his father's heart.

Jim Williams wondered that day if his grieving would ever end.

* TWELVE *

The wind was still blowing, but in a much diminished capacity. He opened his eyes. The sun was remarkably visible as it continued its descent below the horizon. It turned the clouds pink, now just wispy vapors that hurried through the twilight. With the approaching darkness the sky would soon be filled with flickering, visible stars.

The day's weather had changed completely during the time he lay on the bed wandering in the past. It was a good change, unlike some of the changes in his life-span. But there were good changes too and whatever the change, his life altered and he carried on. He was better at that now.

He remembered vividly the numbness, the lack of tears, the unreality, the feeling that his life would forever be filled with grief and mourning. After all the sorrow, he wondered why, today of all days, he found it necessary to travel the paths of yesteryear, but before he could decide on a reasonable explanation, he was on that road again.

~ ~ ~ ~ ~

Duncan Cameron sent his brother-in-law home to America with three young, motherless boys. He wondered why some must suffer so much. His own suffering had been terrible, but Jim Williams had borne more than most, at such an early stage in life.

And Liang, who's young life had been crushed so quickly, when she lived, experienced dreadful sorrows and never had a chance to share but a few happy moments with the man she loved, the same man who had been loved deeply by his sister.

Before he went back into the jungle, he thought of his other sister. He was certain of how she felt about Jim. Was it possible the two of them ...... ? He would not allow himself to linger on that. He was convinced ... or rather he knew, .. it was too preposterous.

*

Shoreford was depressing at first, mostly because people were trying too hard.

It was the first day of the new year of 1954. Yesterday was Hogmanay. Jim thought that day would never have meaning for him again.

When he visited the cemetery, he stood in the cold at Moira's grave for a long, silent time. His mind was blank, his emotions bankrupt, yet the tears would not stop. His face was chilled where the watery drops flowed over his skin, changing quickly from warm to icy cold.

A few steps and he was between the resting places of Don and Sal. He did not stay long. He was frozen stiff. His mood diminished his ability to stand against the cold. As he made the lonely return to the car, he wondered where Liang's body lay.

He was glad that he and his sons arrived home too late for Christmas. He could not have dealt with that. It had been difficult to contend with members of the family and also friends arriving at the house, in attempts at consolation. There was none to be had.

But at last, with slow appreciation, he came to realize that the efforts to show sympathy by so many of his family and friends, was simply, that he was deeply loved. That love would help his terrible wounds heal and though the scars would remain, he would function again as a father, a son, a brother and a friend.

Most new days it was easier than the day before, but not always. There were so many things to turn his memory backward. But those memories too were more easily borne with time's passage. And the days passed and he knew he had responsibilities he must shoulder.

*

Jim was fiercely independent about his sons and insistent that he care for them, but Sarah, captivated by her grandsons, overpowered him. Watching his mother at work, a labor of love, playing and laughing with his sons, her grandsons, was ultimately good for him. He was, in a short time, a participant and he too laughed and slowly his sense of humor returned.

Herself two months pregnant, Shirley and Isabel Buchanan were on hand assisting Sarah and Jim whenever there was a spare moment from their own chores. What with the grandmothers and Aunt Shirley and visits from uncles, aunts and cousins, the three little guys were cared for in resplendent style.

While at first Jim was resentful of all the attention lavished on the boys, feeling it cut into the time he should be with them, that attitude, along with others as faulty, disappeared. He was eventually pleased with the attention his sons received and at ease with others when he was able to see through his short sided opinions. But despite all the affection from others, his sons left no doubt in anyone's mind as to who their father was. A very special greeting was always there for him when he returned to their presence, no matter what duration the absence. That demonstration played a great part in the healing.

*

Bill wanted his grieving son to take all the time he needed, or wanted, before taking on a job, but Jim was at the Triple W the second Monday of the new year, January 11th. He was eager to start work. He was certain that doing something that occupied his time, would occupy his mind and ease his melancholy and the self pity that at times slashed at his soul, a self pity that angered him for its hold on him. He had his share of bad moments, but as the days passed easier, his burden lightened.

His father was great and along with his mother, they allowed him the space he desired in the beginning and reached out to him when they sensed his need.

There were others who reached out a hand to Jim.

At every opportunity Buck came to the aid of his friend. Jim never asked a thing of his brother-in-law, but Buck was always there, giving and helping, binding the wounds. And of course there was Shirley, caring, mothering to the boys. They became closer than ever. Likewise, Bob, now out of the Corps and returning to school in February, leaped to his brother's side, his enthusiasm and forthrightness, good for Jim. And despite their strong love and devotion to Moira, it was these three, along with his father and Kit, who let Jim know privately that they approved his marriage to Liang and shared his grief.

Isabel Buchanan became another grandmother to the boys and the spot in her heart she had for Jim grew. He accepted her like a mother, for he loved her as he did his own mother. He remembered what Sal said to him about being what he, Jim Williams was, because of his parents. Though he often thought he fell far short of that, there was no doubt as to where Buck came from. Returning to church with his family, Jim was pleased that Buck and his mother were now members. They transferred from their old ethnic church in the city, so much further away.

The Capoletti and Ryan families paid Jim a visit. Before long, he went into town, often with one, two or three of his sons in tow. Most of Shoreford knew of his ordeal. Some knew him only from his play in high school, yet they too, when they chanced to recognize him on the street, or more especially at the Triple W, were quick to make him aware of their thoughts for him.

Duncan called repeatedly from Malaya. Early in February he urged Jim to go to Scotland with the boys. He wisely knew such a visit would be a large part of the healing process, of not only his mother and Ceit, but also, for Jim. He would not admit it to himself, but deep down, he was hoping Jim and Ceit could come to peace, no matter what the conclusion.

Jim too knew he must go. He loved Molly and he was certain he owed that much to her. His sons were her grandsons, flesh of 'their' Moira. Duncan was certain that together, Jim and his mother would help each other.

"I think it's a great idea, Dunk, but I would need help taking the boys along."

"Now listen ta me, Jim. I know yu'll protest, but I'm goin ta stand the fare for you and your folks. That way yu'll have plenty of help."

"Dunk, that's a great offer, but I ..."

"Jim, please! Listen ta me. I have more money than I've ever had and I want ta do this thing."

"Dunk ..."

"Jim, didja no hear me! Please mon! It's not only fer you, but Mum needs it. And haven't yor mom and her gotten to know each other so well with all the writin they've been up to?"

"Dunk .."

"Please, Jim! Listen, will ya?"

There was a short pause when an idea suddenly popped into Jim's head, an idea he was surprised had not previously entered his mind.

"Dunk, for cryin out loud, all of us goin there is not the answer. My dad would have difficulty leaving his business for an extended period and he and Mom have talked a lot about having Mum and Ceit here. The twins are still quite young for such a trip, what with formula and all, it would really be tough on them. And there's plenty of room for Mum and Ceit right here. I think it would be great. They could stay as long as they want."

There was a short spell of silence at the other end of the line before an excited, "My God, mon, you're right. Jim, that's brilliant. I say we get things in motion."

Hurriedly and excitedly, the two, like happy young boys, began to make the plans, though there were many others needing consultation before finalization could take place.

*

Molly had called Shoreford periodically since Moira's death, the telephone calls being her one concession to monetary gain. It was during those conversations that she and Sarah became close and meeting face to face seemed past due.

Molly took some convincing, but she was convinced. Nothing short of death would keep her from her grandsons.

Ceit said nothing to try swaying her mother one way or the other. She knew what the decision would be. Outwardly she portrayed one who showed little interest in going to America, other than exclamations about her Donny and her desire to meet the twins. Her innards, however, were on fire. She did not fool Molly.

The Williams family was excited about the visit. They started planning at once. For Jim, it was a very positive happening.

* * *

Three, four inch Ws were painted on each front door of the new station wagon. William Walter Williams purchased the vehicle to double for family transportation and business use. Jim wanted to drive his Ford to Idlewild, but Bill insisted the wagon was more luxurious and more comfortable to ride in, especially for two ladies just off a flight across the Atlantic.

While the three boys stayed with Aunt Shirley and Gramma Isabel, Sarah accompanied her son. She breathed a sigh of relief when the car was parked and they were at last in the terminal. She became impatient when the landing was announced and it took the passengers so long to show up, .. but then, there they were.

Molly was the first Jim picked out in the crowd. As soon as she spotted him, the tears started. She struggled impatiently to move ahead, but was slowed by the crush of bodies. Jim moved as close as permitted. When Molly came through the gate, he grabbed her in a breath quenching hug. Her tears turned to crying. His arms stayed about her, holding her shaking body. He gritted his teeth, but some tears escaped his eyes.

Unable to remain in the background, Sarah was quickly at their side. Jim released Molly and she excitedly searched the strange face she knew so well by voice, through watery eyes.

Molly's face became a huge smile. Instantly her arms opened and she and Sarah came together. They were both crying.

As yet, not a word had been spoken.

Glancing about, Jim spotted her. She was standing a little to the side, hands to her front, holding the straps of a purse.

"Ceit! My God! I left you there all alone." He went to her and placed his hands on her shoulders, shaking his head in disbelief. "You've grown into a lady," he smiled brightly "A beautiful lady, I might add."

"Some would question the lady part." She was serious.

Wearing high heels, her forehead was at Jim's eye level. The brilliant and beautiful hair was there in abundance. It touched her shoulders at the sides and hung slightly lower in back, full of natural wave. The freckles that traversed the cute, gently upturned nose, were lighter and her mouth had a hint of sensuality. But as it was at their first meeting, so it was this time. Her eyes captured him with green luminescence .. and the touch of sadness. When he ran his eyes over the rest of her, he saw that her clothing, like her mother's, was new.

"Come'ere!" he commanded and pulled her to him.

She came willingly and pressed into him, then stiffened and eased off. The quick, tiny shudder was imperceptible to Jim as she backed away.

"It's good to see you, Jim." It was very formal.

He studied her face, thinking he saw an indication of tears about to form, but she gained control and Molly intervened and introduced Ceit to Sarah.

They stayed where they were, their animated discussion giving life to their small, intimate group. When the other passengers were gone, Jim got the bags and led them from the terminal. They continued their eager conversations all the way to the car.

At the beginning of the journey to Shoreford, sadness was the dominant mood as they spoke at length of Moira. Not a word was uttered of Liang. It did not surprise Jim, but he felt the ache for Liang. It seemed to him they did not wish to recognize her existence. But then the grandsons became the topic and Jim was relieved of the unhappy sentiments as they rolled cheerfully homeward.

They stopped briefly at the Triple W.

On arriving home, there was no doubt Donny remembered Ceit. The two had a grand reunion. Then she was torn. It was impossible to ignore his brothers and she found herself bouncing from one to the other, when they were not in Molly's loving arms.

It seemed to Jim more like a homecoming than the welcome of foreigners. Sarah and Molly carried on like they had been intimate for life. When Buck and Shirley arrived with Isabel, a new family group was in the making.

Sarah did not have an abundance of close friends. She and her brother's wife, Kit's mother, had been close, but Nellie MacPherson was gone nearly eighteen years. She liked her husband's sisters-in-law, but they had growing families and most of their meetings were during the holidays and on formal occasions. Sarah and Isabel became close, very close, when their children married. They visited almost daily. Their relationship was cemented by a strong mutual respect and a genuine affection.

Isabel had tragedy in her life. She lost a husband and infant daughter. She raised her only son to be one of the finest of human beings. This she did in the shadow of the hate sometimes heaped on her race, a hate she was incapable of reciprocating.

With the addition of Molly, the duo of Sarah and Isabel soon became a trio.

It was not instant with Ceit, the way it was with Moira and Shirley, but their friendship was nurtured and grew. It was a healthy environment for all and Jim admitted to himself, but no one else, that a match up between Bob and Ceit would be great.

*

Jim poured himself into his work. He was learning. That was one thing he did readily. There were sufficient baby sitters and the burden of caring for his sons during working hours was nonexistent.

Within days of their arrival, Ceit was driving the boys to the shop on a daily basis for a prenoon visit and to bring fresh lunches to Jim and his father. She drove Jim's Ford and required no practice switching from the left side of the road to the right. She was an excellent driver, or she would not have been entrusted with the boys, nor, would she have allowed herself that privilege. Her love and concern for them was paramount and was not only good for them, but greatly cheered her.

Bob returned to college without having shown any interest in Ceit, other than a cheerful friendship. Ceit reciprocated.

*

Three weeks and most of a fourth went by so quickly that when someone mentioned the date, it came as a shock.

Molly knew that she and Ceit would have to return to their home in Scotland sometime. She did not like the idea of leaving, but she also did not like the feeling that they might be overstaying their welcome. That did not lessen the pain of leaving her grandsons who were now a huge part of her life. Further, she was closer to the Williams and Buchanans than she had ever been to anyone. She had another reason to stay, but that was locked in her heart. Nothing she had seen to date gave her any reason to think that would become a reality.

* * *

Having finished the dishes together, they went into the living room and sat in chairs that faced. Buck picked up the evening paper and started to read. Shirley sat for some time, her expression clouded with thought and a dash of uncertainty.

"Buck, honey, what do you think of Ceit .. and ... and Jim?"

He lowered the paper and glanced at his wife, a soft smile on his face.

"I don't have to tell you what I think of Jim. You know that. And you know what I think of Ceit too. Like I've said before, I think she's sweet, very pretty and quite bashful. She's a bit of an enigma though and I'm not certain what's behind it, though I have my suspicions."

"That's what I mean, not what you consciously know of her ... and Jim too, .. but what you think, deep down."

"Whoa, Honey! I see some dark motive in your thoughts." He chuckled, but turned serious and pondered her words a bit, then grinned, "You're putting me on the spot, Babe. You know how I feel about judging what I think might be people's innermost feelings, .. or whatever, .. especially someone like Ceit, who we know so little about."

Shirley got up and crossed the distance to her husband and wriggled into his lap. She put her arms about his neck and looked into his eyes.

"Don't be silly. You know I feel the same as you do about things like that. What I really want to know is, if you've ever thought about what she might be about, ... the same as me."

He laughed loudly, "You vixen, you. You know I've been thinking about her and Jim, don't you?"

"Come on," she teased, wrinkling her nose, "tell me. I really have to know if we're on the same track."

"Well, ... I do think she's got something for Jim, but it's more intuitive than observed. With Jim, I'm not sure either, but he may very well have his guard up, in view of the recent tragedies. What's happened to him, could make him unwilling to even think about romance. But back to Ceit. She sure does love the boys and there's no doubt about the way they feel about her."

Shirley smiled down at him, hugged and squeezed him, then sat up and gazed into his eyes, her smile more pronounced.

"Oh, Sweetie, I've been pondering nearly identical thoughts. I think it's time somebody tried to help them. You know what my brother is like. He's so dumb when it comes to females, bless his heart. And you know what? I think you're just the guy to make it happen."

Buck's eyes opened as wide as his mouth.

"Shirley Buchanan, you're out of your mind! I can't do anything of the kind.!"

"You can to. If anyone can, you can. You're one of the few people who probably can. You're honest and people listen when you say something. And Jim thinks the world of you. I know you can plant a seed. You're just the guy that can. It's got to be done."

"You know what? I think something should be done too, but I have to admit, the idea fills me with trepidation. Suppose we're wrong. Suppose one has strong feelings and the other doesn't. Do you want to be responsible for something that might break a heart, something that might not work?"

She did not answer, but leaned down and kissed the end of his nose and smiled sweetly.

He sighed deeply and looked to the heavens.

* * *

It was during the fourth week of their stay that Molly spoke to Ceit about returning to Scotland. Ceit never offered a comment. She became sullen and withdrawn. Molly was not puzzled by her behavior.

The afternoon of the next day, when Ceit visited the Triple W with the boys and the lunches, she asked Jim if she could take the car for a drive after returning the boys safely home.

Jim smiled and said, "Sure. Enjoy yourself."

Ceit's heart was in no mood for enjoyment.

She drove to Collins Park. Jim had taken Molly and her there. He told them how he went there as a youth when his mind was troubled ... and Ceit's mind was sorely troubled.

It was a gloomy day and the wind was blowing from the northeast. It suited her mood. She sat on a bench on the grassy knoll, back from the beach. She drew her feet up and wrapped her arms about her legs. She stared across the water, her chin resting on her knees while she continued to brood. She knew she could not dwell on her bad luck forever, anymore than she could return to Scotland without some attempt at what she came here to do. She tried to think, but her mind seemed hopeless. She was certain that any kind of plan was better than no plan and some kind of action was better than no action, yet even the hint of a plan eluded her.

She slid her feet to the ground, got up and walked uneasily to the sandy beach. Slowly, but deliberately, she traversed the high water mark to the west end of the beach. When she reached the furthest point and turned to head back, the cold wind whipped across her face and rumpled even more, her tousled hair. She looked into the heavens at the fast moving gray clouds, then across the water, the force of the wind lashing her hair into fiery tails.

The buffeting of the angry wind stirred her anger.

Ceit had no control of her thoughts as they sped through her disordered mind. She spoke loud enough to hear the words above the sound of the wind and surf.

"What did that Oriental witch do to him, to my Jamie? She got him to marry her when poor Moira was not even cold and I, .. Ceit Fraser can not even get him to turn his head and look at me. Maybe he thinks I'm too young and that's the reason." Her voice grew louder, "No! She was almost the same age as me. Could she have been that beautiful? Can I be so ugly?" She hesitated and her voice softened, "Yet he said I was a beautiful lady and Mum keeps telling me how pretty I am and all the folks here about have said nice things. And that lout Geordie, .. he said I had a gorgeous body."

Her anger swelled and her jaw set. She continued to speak the words of her thoughts to the blustering winds which carried them away, but left behind the venom in her soul.

"I knew she was bad news the first time Moira wrote home about her, I just knew it. Sweet and kind Moira said, .. my foot! She must have been a witch to capture my Jamie so ... so quick. If only she were here, I would strangle her and do it gladly. It is good she is dead!"

The vitriol of her words astounded her, but she could not repent of her misguided anger and extreme frustration. She convinced herself it was because of Liang, that she, Ceit Fraser had taken up with that phony Geordie MacBean who tried so hard to win Moira. He was a mean person and their relationship had been a trying ordeal for her. She had lain with him like a slut, never feeling much but shame. He took everything she carelessly let him have and when she had the sense to shut him off, he sneered at her and walked out of her life. She was angry, giving up her virginity to a clod like that. She wondered what Moira ever saw in him. Maybe, she thought, Moira saw him for what he really was. Moira had that sense about people. She only dated him a few times and soon after Jim entered their lives, she kindly told Geordie they had no future together. Ceit was certain Moira would have done that even if Jim had not come upon the scene. At any rate, he had a big mouth and it was good to be in America and away from his pub talk. She was grateful she came away from that bitter experience without getting pregnant.

*

While Ceit was at Collins Park, Molly asked Sarah if they might have a cup of tea and talk. When the tea was poured, they sat together. After a few sips Molly broke the silence.

"Sarah, we have been here nearly a month and you and everyone have been so wonderful and kind, but it is time for Ceit and me to start readying for our return to Scotland."

"Whatever for, Molly?" Sarah was visibly upset, "Why you and Ceit are part of the family. And what of the boys? How would they be without their grandmother? You can't go just yet. Please! Do you know that Will and I were just talking about this the other day and he said he considered you and Ceit as part of the family and even with your lovely accents, he thought of you as Shorefordians. Honest, that's exactly what he said and I agreed with him. And we secretly hoped you might live here some day."

"Oh, Sarah, my dear Sarah, that is a beautiful thought, but we have a home in Scotland and we stay here imposing on your wonderful hospitality."

Sarah jumped up and went to the phone. She was emotional. "I'm going to call Will. He'll know what to do."

"Oh, Sarah, please! Don't bother Will with this."

Before Molly finished the sentence, Sarah was dialing the number. When her husband answered, she excitedly spoke. "Will, do you remember what we talked about concerning Molly and Ceit?" A pause. "Well Molly just spoke to me about them returning to Scotland." Another pause. "Yes, Will, .. yes, .. we'll be here."

She hung up the phone.

"Sarah! You can't bring Will home just because we have to return to Scotland."

"He'll be here in a few minutes and then we can talk. He'll know what to do."

"Oh, Sarah!" Molly scolded, but she realized she was pleased. She did not want to leave, but felt she must, her Scottish prudence prevailing.

In less than ten minutes the vehicle pulled into the driveway and Bill walked through the door.

"Molly, what's this Sarah tells me about you and Ceit wanting to leave us?"

"Oh, Will, ... I don't really want to leave, but we must. We've been here ..."

"Whoa! Hold on there. Did I hear you say you didn't want to leave?"

Molly could only shake her head meekly.

"Well that's it then. You have to stay, ... not only because we want you to, but the little guys would miss you badly and you wouldn't want that now, would you?"

Molly shook her head as before, but this time there were tears in her eyes.

Sarah walked to her and hugged her.

"You see, you know it too. Molly, dear, I don't know why, but I just feel you must stay, at least for a while longer. I have this feeling it will be good if you do."

Stepping back, Sarah, along with Bill, observed in suspenseful silence as Molly pondered, her eyes gazing down.

The tears continued to flow. As she returned her gaze to Sarah, then Bill, she spoke, "Yes, Dear, we will stay on a bit more. Thank you both for your very kind thoughts."

Moving quickly again to the phone, Sarah dialed. When she was answered, she blurted excitedly, "Isabel, Molly and Ceit are going to stay on. Isn't it wonderful.?"

"Sarah! I only said for awhile!"

"That's all right, Molly. We'll face awhile when it comes."

Bill held up a hand to his wife.

"Hold Isabel on the line for a second. I believe this calls for a celebration. Ladies, I'd like to take all of you out to dinner. Whattaya say?"

"Isabel, Will wants to take all of us out to dinner. Can you make it?" A short pause. "That's wonderful!" Then she turned to her husband. "What time?"

"We'll call her right back as soon as the reservations are confirmed."

"Did you hear that? ...... OK. I'll call you right back." Sarah hung up the phone.

"I think it's a wonderful idea, Will," Molly smiled, "and I will go if you make me a promise."

"OK, that I will."

"Then the dinner must be on me."

Bill opened his mouth to object.

"Now, Will, you promised! I have more money than I've ever had in my life and I've spent almost nothing since Ceit and I arrived here and I'd like you to share in some of my good fortune."

Bill and Sarah looked at each other. He grinned, slightly embarrassed, at his wife and turned to Molly. "That's fine, Molly. We accept. It's an honor and we thank you."

A table for four was reserved at one of the city's elegant restaurants. Bill had a connection and was able to purchase theater tickets as his treat for the pre-Broadway performance currently in town.

*

Ceit's thoughts continued to run rampant through her troubled mind. She did nothing to rein them in or give reason a chance. She made excuses. She fantasized about Liang, fantasies that were counterfeit, but appealed to her distraught mentality. Liang became licentious in Ceit's mind. That was surely how Liang conquered her Jamie, Ceit thought. From that faulty and unjust illusion, her plan took form. It was an utterly foolish plan, but frantic and dispossessed of sound judgment, she allowed her mind to be persuaded to recklessness, something that often motivated her actions. At any rate, she thought it not the time to be sensible and doing something reckless appealed to her impulsiveness. It was time to do something, for doing something, even if unsuccessful, .. even if wrong, was better than languishing in nothingness. If her plan failed and they returned to Scotland, there would be good reason for their return.

She walked to the car, determined and fatalistic ... and the fatalism helped a bit to allay her fears.

*

Bill called Jim and asked if he would mind closing up. He told his son that they were going out to dinner and to a show, but nothing more. Jim was pleased they were doing something frivolous for a change and was happy to take care of the store. The older adults would give over the baby sitting to Jim and Ceit when they returned home.

On his way home from school, Buck stopped by the Triple W to chat with his buddy, ten minutes before closing time. No sooner was he inside, when Ceit arrived. Buck and Ceit greeted cheerfully, but to Buck, she seemed stiff and preoccupied, especially when she greeted Jim. Buck observed them. He could not help pondering the recent conversation with Shirley. As he surveyed their actions, he wondered if he and his wife had not been involved in wishful thinking. But then, if not, Jim would never make a move on his own. Did Ceit, he speculated, have feelings for Jim as he suspected, despite her indifferent behavior.

Moments before closing, two young women, former classmates of the young men, came into the store. After greetings, Buck stayed near the end of the counter with Ceit. He continued to observe her as Jim conversed with the females. All at once, he was certain he and Shirley were right.

Jim went over the time he or his father would arrive to check out the errant electric stove. There was little doubt that the women enjoyed their time with Jim. They lingered longer than necessary to conclude their business. On the way out they bid Buck goodnight, addressing him as Milton. They acknowledged Ceit's presence with a nod and a wan smile.

When the door closed behind them, Buck was grinning. He remembered Shirley's words. Jim would never make a move. Like it or not, he would make the attempt. Ceit needed something to think about.

"You've still got it, Buddy."

"Got what?" Jim said puzzled.

"That certain something that attracts the females."

"You're crazy!"

"I am, am I," Buck laughed, "That's what makes you even more of a challenge to them. You don't know a thing about it. It's a kind of innocence, wrapped in a ... sorta .. sorta spiritual quality. Even now, after all you've been through, it's still there. I see the way they look at you."

"You're nuts!"

Buck laughed again. Ceit fidgeted.

"Heck, I remember when you first came out for football and the guys talking about the way the girls were attracted to Don's little brother. And Don used to tell us how even your aunts treated you diffcrent. And when you started dating Connie, the groans I used to hear in home room. And Sal telling me about the way girls looked at you when the two of you were on liberty and you never knew a thing about it."

"Come on, Buck, ask Shirley. She knows better."

"Your sister has told me. Remember, quite a few girls in school talked to her about you, you know."

"My God! What a lotta bunk!"

Laughing gently, Buck shook his head. "Jim, you're a wonder." He turned to Ceit. "He's something, isn't he?" Ceit forced a tiny and uncomfortable smile. Buck started for the door, glancing at Ceit out of the corner of an eye. "See you folks tomorrow. Take care, Buddy. Goodnight, Ceit." She forced another smile and a subdued wave. At the door Buck turned, exhibiting a huge grin. "Just you be careful in Elaine Crocker's house tomorrow."

Jim threw a cleaning cloth at his laughing friend as the door closed behind him.

Outside, in the cool evening air, Buck felt devious, something which made him uncomfortable. What he had said was the truth, but trying to bait Ceit was not his nature. He questioned himself and then his wife. He glanced upward and thought, "Well, my heart was in the right place." He sighed and remembered about the road to hell and good intentions and gritted his teeth and said out loud as he entered his car, "Oh, man! I sure hope I didn't foul anything up."

In the final minutes before closing, there was no conversation as Jim turned out the lights and checked the locks. It was dark in the car, but when Jim glanced at Ceit he could make out her face. She seemed far away. She was actually deep in thought. She knew what Buck said was true. She heard Mum and Moira talk about Jim. She had kept her own feelings about him bottled up for so long. She had fought terrible fights to keep those feelings from erupting. That was no longer necessary. He had married that witch, hadn't he? There was no reason to keep her feelings rooted in the past any longer.

Arriving home, Ceit's mood was sweetened by the boys and the departure of the grandparents. She enjoyed Jim playing with his sons. He did, she thought, have a sort of spiritual quality and his devotion to them was wonderful to behold. Before long, she was among them, part of the group. Everything for now, was all right.

Jim watched her. She had always been excellent with the boys. There was no doubt about the love that passed between them. He thought of his good fortune, the way his burden was eased by so many and Ceit was right at the top.

They did not linger over the supper prepared for them by their mothers. Ceit was a dervish with the dishes, while Jim played with the boys, until it was time for their baths in the kitchen sink. Father and surrogate mother dried them, diapered them and put them to bed in flannel sleepers. The adults kissed them goodnight, listened at the door briefly and returned to the downstairs.

Jim went into the small room where he slept, took his robe from the closet and went into the kitchen, where Ceit was putting the finishing touches on the clean up.

"I'm gonna take a shower."

She turned to glance at him and offered a weak smile. He started to leave, but hesitated and walked to her.

"Ceit, you really are terrific and I don't know how to thank you in the words you deserve. I'm really glad you and Mum are here. I wish you'd stay forever."

Her heart skipped a beat.

He hesitated before reaching out and touching her hair.

"Your hair is really beautiful you know. I remember the first time I saw you and thinking it was the most gorgeous color I'd ever seen."

Looking into her eyes he wanted to say something about those eyes, but did not. He saw a look he could not describe, a look he had seen before. Walking away he tried to shake his memory. Then he remembered. Jane Higgenbottom had the same look that day, just before he walked out the door. It was a plea, but hell, Ceit had nothing to plea for. He had to be mistaken, he thought, yet he felt as though he left something unfinished in the kitchen.

The hot, pelting spray felt great and Jim stayed under longer than usual. It relaxed his body which in turn consoled his mind. His mind needed consolation. The problem was Ceit. He had never been good at understanding the female, except for Moira.

They had become one. Their love was so deep, they had a feel for the others thoughts much of the time. Their trust was so great, there was never a moment either felt one might do something to hurt the other. Strangely, that same type of connection was being forged between him and Liang, at a time when he was suffering the most profound grief of his life.

"Damn!" he thought, he hated self-analysis, was not good at it either. He was less good at knowing what was in Ceit's mind. The look in her eyes confused him. He was certain that what was in her mind had nothing to do with him, ... it could not. What he should have remembered, he did not. What Moira once told him about Ceit, his confusion obscured.

"Hell!" he thought, "I need a nap."

Right after Jim left the bathroom, Ceit was under the shower. With the pending return to Scotland and Buck's words ringing in her brain, she was certain she must act now. She could not allow a moment of hesitation or she might lose her nerve and all that careful, .. well maybe not so careful, .. but the plan she concocted at the beach today, .. that audacious, shameless plan would be for nought.

*

The small light on the table beside the bed cast enough light to give the room a warm glow. Jim lay with his hands locked behind his head, his legs apart, wrapped in a terry cloth robe that extended to his ankles. He was starting to doze, but the sound of the doorknob turning, caused his eyes to open enough to satisfy his curiosity.

A head poked through the partially opened door. The eyes were curious, yet revealed a touch of fright. The hair reflected the modest light and tossed it back in resplendent color. The eyes searched the interior, becoming more confident, but when they locked on his eyes, there was a moment of indecision, an indecision that was briskly conquered by determination. The door opened wide with a hard push.

His mouth opened wide. He thought his eyes would leave their sockets. He was not surprised that she possessed other hair the color of that on her head, but what shocked him was, that it was plainly visible.

For a fleeting instant, she thought she would turn and run, accepting humiliation and defeat. With savage resolve, she straightened, planted her feet and jammed tightened fists into her hips. "Jamie! .. Jamie! I love you, you bastard."

She stood in her nudity for what seemed an eternity to her, but was no more than a second or so, then gritted her teeth and was instantly on the bed between his legs. She ripped open the robe and stared but an instant, before she crashed down on him. His mouth, still open wide, was mashed beneath hers. Like an expert with a foil, she thrust and thrust her tongue. Almost at once, caught up in her zeal, he accepted her, then eagerly responded. He parried and riposted and was carried by her energy. She forced his legs together and was astride him, taking him into her. She was immediately astir. It was as if she planned every move, so quickly and flawlessly was it achieved.

She dominated his body, his entire being. He was at once in the extraordinary chaos of sensory excitement. The sounds came from deep within his throat and were so loud, she thought the boys would awaken, but her own being, wildly beyond control would not quit and when the untamed, orgasmic adventure was done, they were helpless.

The boys did not awaken.

Ceit lay glued atop Jim's motionless body. Beads of moisture slithered down her sides, from her arms and legs and mingled with his. She was glad they lacked the stamina to move. She did not want to look into his eyes. She did not know what they would reveal, what his reaction would be.

At long last, when their breathing had quieted, when there was a modicum of strength in their bodies, he grasped her arms near the shoulders and pushed her gently upwards. He sought her eyes, but she turned away, unable to escape the shame that nagged at her.

"Look at me you little vamp!"

The sound of his voice made her uneasy and her eyes slowly and awkwardly focused on his, but his eyes were dancing merrily, his expression a huge grin. Her relief was instant and overwhelming.

"You raped me you vamp!"

He laughed until his body was shaking.

She fell joyfully back on him, kissing his face and neck, over and over. She forced herself up. Her joy made her giddy.

"Oh, .. Jamie, .. oh, .. Jamie, .. Jamie, .. Jamie, .. Jamie!"

She fell on him again, hugged him with all her might. He returned her hug as strongly. They lay still a very long time, soaked in perspiration like the sheets below them and lost in the emotional radiance of their coming together.

Much later, when he rolled her off, he propped himself on an elbow. He kissed her face and neck and breasts and the very pink nipples, which came quickly to attention. He eventually stopped and gazed at her. She opened her eyes. Her expression was angelic. He smiled and wondered how so much passion and purpose could lie beneath such a look. She reached up and ran a hand through his soggy and rumpled hair. She pulled strands of her own jumbled hair across her line of vision.

"Och! We're a mess."

"Aye, that's trooo," he grinned, mimicking her accent.

They laughed and she pinched his cheek and her body gave an involuntary shudder. He put his lips to hers and soon she was holding him tightly, afraid he might escape. Then her nails were digging into his back. He caressed her with hands and fingers and sometimes tongue and she became the victim of her desire and that desire was him. She asked for him, but he stayed awhile at what he was doing and when they did merge, the activity was furious and at the end, quite noisy.

The boys continued to sleep.

Worn out, they lay on their backs, one of his legs over hers, staring at the ceiling, lost in the reverie of complete contentment. They had no idea how long they stayed that way, but the sound of a car pulling into the driveway sent them into a frenzied flurry.

Jim leaped up and off the bed. His feet tangled in the twisted and damp sheets. He plunged head first to the floor. The loud thump brought Ceit swiftly to her knees at the edge of the bed.

"Jamie!? Jamie, are you OK?" her voice frantic, "Please, Jamie, are you hurt? .. Jamie!"

With an arm pinned beneath him, Jim struggled to raise the other in a gesture of silence.

"Shhhh!" he hissed.

Not knowing what else to do, Ceit obeyed. The silence lasted a few seconds.

"That lousy SOB," Jim grumbled, "was just turning around in the driveway."

"Jamie!" she pleaded, concern in her voice, "Are you all right?" as she leaned over the edge of the bed and peered down at him.

"Yeah," he groaned, struggling to his feet, a lump already sprouting from his forehead. "Damn! Damn! Damn that jerk!" He paused and grinned. "Heck, I don't know why I'm calling him a jerk. It was me who got all tangled up like an uncoordinated clown."

He turned his gaze to Ceit. Her hair lay in a tousled mess on her head and over her face. She reminded him of a comical witch. She saw the smile start on his face and knew why. It was contagious as she viewed his absurd appearance. The smiles turned to laughter. They pointed fingers at each other and the laughter grew. It was difficult to stop. Their comic images, their wild adventure and the imagined near discovery of their indiscretion was too much. Drained of his energy, Jim fell on the bed. Ceit fell across him. Their mirth continued till they were gasping for breath.

It was the knowledge of the ultimate arrival of their parents that at last sobered them. Ceit rose to her knees to allow Jim to get up. He struggled to his feet and stood, head sore and tired, but euphoric. Ceit shared the fatigue and euphoria.

Jim opened his arms. She crossed the bed on her knees and came to him. He held her gently for the first time that night. Encircled by his arms, she slid her arms about his waist and lay her head against his chest. They remained together, two contented human beings, until the realization of passing time forced them apart.

"Ceit, I guess we better get ready for the folks return. You can take a shower while I straighten up here and while you get dressed, I'll take my shower. That way, if the folks get here any time soon, they'll be none the wiser."

Unknown to either, neither was concerned that their parents should find out. They did not know precisely why, but that is the way each felt.

Eleven thirty-five and Jim was showered and dressed and walked into the living room. Ceit bounded from her chair and went to him. They embraced energetically and kissed longingly, but did not allow themselves more. They disengaged slowly and sorrowfully. Jim gazed into eyes that filled him with desire.

"Come on, we've got to find something else to do," he regretfully said.

This time when the car came into the driveway, it was the right car. Jim and Ceit were looking at picture albums when their parents entered the living room. Before the greetings were completed, Sarah interrupted.

"My word, Jimmy, what did you do to yourself?"

"Jim fell ..." Ceit was instantly interrupted.

"That blasted, stupid rug! I tripped over it and whacked my head."

"You sure the rug was stupid, Jim?" Bill smiled.

His son sheepishly smiled back.

"I should say you did fall, Dear," Sarah frowned. "Do you have a headache? I'll get some aspirin."

"No, Mom! It's OK. I don't have a headache. Thanks anyway."

Ceit was snickering, as much from what really happened, as from Jim's attempt to cover it up. She looked at Bill who always took her part.

"You're right. All the rug did was lie there."

"Ceit!" Molly scolded, but Bill joined Ceit with a grin.

"It's OK, Mum," Jim chuckled, "what can you expect from such a little girl."

"Jimmy!" Now it was Sarah.

"Mom, I'm only teasing her."

"It's not nice to tease Ceit like that and call her a little girl when she's such a fine young lady."

Ceit had arrived. Jim had never teased her before, never treated her any way but seriously. Now, even more than at the end of their escapade, she knew their relationship was on the track she desired. She smiled smugly at him and stuck out her tongue.

As the slight tint rose to his cheeks, Jim changed the subject quickly.

"How was the meal and the show?"

"Jimmy, we went out tonight to celebrate," Sarah replied enthusiastically. "Molly and Ceit are not going home. They are going to stay with us for awhile. Isn't that wonderful news?"

"That's great, Mom!" Jim replied as Ceit broke into a wide, happy smile. Jim wanted to run to her, squeeze her, but discretion prevailed. Instead he walked to Molly and gave her a hug. "I'm really glad, Mum!"

The three elders talked eagerly for a spell, but they were tired and soon on their way to bed.

Alone at last, Ceit came into Jim's arms. He squeezed her, bringing forth a faint grunt and soft response.

"Och, what you do to me, Jamie Williams."

She pushed up from the heels and bit his ear.

"Oooh," he grinned, roguishness in his eyes.

Her grin turned playfully smug.

"You didn't appreciate my effort to save your honor, did you? You had to interrupt me, didn't you?"

He tickled her ribs lightly with one hand and held a finger to his lips with the other, softly hissing, "Ssshhhh."

She deftly jumped to the rear. When she returned to his arms, there was a devilish gleam in her eyes as she whispered, "And you called me a little girl, didn't you?"

She pressed tightly against him and moved her pelvis across his loins in a tiny ellipse, never taking her eyes from his. She could feel what was happening to him as she pulled his head down and bit his ear again, then pushed away giggling, "I think I should be off to bed."

She quickly reached the stairs, but not before he smacked her bottom, .. softly.

Out of reach, she turned to face him and backed up the stairs grinning impishly.

"I think you better go to bed, you little vamp," he whispered after her.

When at last they could sleep, .. when their weariness overcame their excitement and their very active minds, Jim and Ceit slept very well.

*

Ceit arrived with the boys and the lunches much earlier than usual. Jim was overjoyed. It was almost time for him to leave for Elaine Crocker's and he knew that his father would now go in his stead. Bill played with his grandsons briefly before he left. Leaving an employee to mind the store, Jim and Ceit took the boys into the office where there was a playpen for the twins. They gave Donny a toy auto which he played with on his grandfather's desk.

"Mum told me this morning how happy she is that we're not returning to Scotland right away." Ceit's eyes lowered, "I wouldna go anyway."

Jim put his hands on her shoulders as she locked her eyes into his.

"You would stay in Shoreford?"

"Yes!" She was silent briefly. "Jamie, no matter how you feel, ... I can't leave you."

The tears were starting in her eyes and he gently pulled her to him.

"Ceit, will you marry me?"

She knew as surely as she breathed that this was going to happen, but the swiftness caught her off guard. Her eyes opened wide as she stared up into his eyes. She could not move, till suddenly her body responded to her emotions and she squeezed him tenaciously.

"Oh, Jamie, you know I will!!!" she replied breathlessly, clinging to him.

He was content to hold her close, drinking in the pleasure of the moment.

"It's a heck of a spot to put you in. You'll never have a chance to be a bride. You'll have so much of a burden right from the beginning."

She pushed away, holding his hands and gazing deeply into his eyes, very seriously.

"Jamie, I said yes. I mean just that. I love you. It seems I've loved you all my life. But that's not all. I love the boys as if they came from my own womb, just like Mum loved me. She never loved me any less than she loved Moira and Duncan. And to them, I was their sister through and through. I've had very good teachers you know. And if I ever give us children, they will take their place in our whole family."

"Ceit, I love you."

"Oohhh, that sounds so good. Jamie! .. Even if you didn't love me, I think I would will you to. I know I can never take Moira's place. She was such a wonder. She.."

He released one of her hands and placed a finger to her lips.

"You are not taking Moira's place. We come together for us. She taught us that. We'll never forget her and we'll always be thankful for her life. We'll both have memories. We wouldn't want it any other way, but when you and I step off together, we'll be making our plans and setting our goals, OK?"

He smiled at her, but she could only shake her head. The tears were fast flowing streams. He placed his hands on her shoulders and looked into her lovely eyes.

"Ceit, would you mind if we didn't tell our folks for a week. I'd like to court you for seven days, ... before we make a formal announcement. And during that time, I won't do anything but kiss you. Would that be OK? Would you mind?"

"Of course I wouldna mind," she smiled through her tears. "The idea pleases me."

But being wiser, she wondered if they could conceal their emotions in front of others for that long. And when she left with the boys, she wondered if the kissing only, would be successful.

*

Jim took Ceit to the movies. He took her out to eat. They went for drives together, with and without the boys. They ran together at Collins Park.

The family knew what was happening. They not only approved, they were jubilant and soon making plans. Molly called Duncan on the other side of the world. Sarah called Bob. Jim and Ceit did not catch on to all the knowing looks and whispered activity. Even the three youngest sensed that something unusual was taking place.

Saturday night they went dancing. Ceit was a beautiful dancer, but she was more than that. Whenever she knew the words to a song, she sang them softly and effortlessly into Jim's ear.

Afterwards, on the way home, on the coldest night of the week, he drove to a private spot overlooking the water. When he turned off the key, she was instantly in his arms and they came together in an energetic and wild passion. On the way home, Ceit's huge grin was hidden by the dark interior of the car.

"That was some kiss, my Jamie."

* * *

The event was planned around Duncan. He obtained enough leave to have seven days in Shoreford. During the included Saturday, the small chapel in the wing of the church was reserved.

Molly wanted to make Ceit a simple white dress, similar to the one Moira wore.

"Mum, I want to wear my green dress."

"You should wear a white dress, Dear."

"Mum, I can't wear a white dress."

"Why can't you wear a white dress?"

"Because I'm not a virgin!"

"I know that, Dear, but that fling with Geordie MacBean doesn't count."

Ceit giggled, "Why doesn't it count, Mum?"

"Because I say so."

"Oh, Mum, you're funny." She giggled some more. "Even so, Jim knows I'm not a virgin."

Molly's eyes opened wide, "Did you tell him of Geordie?"

"No!" she blushed, the color in her cheeks not quite matching her hair.

"Ceit!" Molly scolded, .. unconvincingly. "Oh," she exhaled, "I think I really knew that, Dear." She walked to Ceit and hugged her and patted her back. "It's all right, Dear, you may wear the green dress." She leaned back holding Ceit by the arms. "But you haven't had it on in ages. Put it on and I'll let it out if necessary."

*

The chapel could hold but a few dozen people and that day in mid March, it was filled to capacity and a few more. It contained only family and one dear friend. All the Williams clan was there including some fourth generation. Though fewer in number, the MacPhersons were present, including Kit and Mal and their young son. And Isabel Buchanan was present as were the young sons of Jim and Ceit.

Bob escorted his grandmothers in, then his mother. Duncan escorted Molly and returned to the rear to fetch Ceit and give her away. Shirley with her budding stomach was matron of honor and Buck stood beside Jim as best man.

It was a short ceremony. The minister spoke briefly and read from Genesis, 2:24 and I Corinthians, chapter 13. By the time he got to, "Do you, Ceit Fraser ..." there were some tears and by the time the couple turned to leave, lace hankies were in use by many of the ladies present and some of the gentlemen were swallowing throat lumps.

The guests were returning to the Williams', but Jim and Ceit left right from the church after the well wishes, hugs, kisses and hand shakes. Underway, they stopped as soon as they were clear of the merrymakers. They cleaned the confetti and graffiti as best they could and drove to the airport hotel. Jim put in an early call to give them plenty of time to catch their flight.

When their outer garments were on hangers, Jim flopped into a large stuffed chair.

"Come'ere! I'm gonna squeeze you till you beg for mercy."

"No!"

She grinned devilishly, kicked off her shoes and executed a beautiful Highland reel turn. The skirt of the green dress flowed artistically outward and upward in a perfect circle. Jim's eyes popped open as the white flesh and sunset hued hair passed before his probing, incredulous stare.

"Did you walk into that church and marry me without wearing panties?"

"Yes I did!" she answered haughtily and repeated the act.

"You are a vamp, woman! No! A tart! No! A trollop!"

He lunged from the chair. She yanked up the hem of the beautiful green dress and leaped to the bed and off the other side, he right behind her. Giggling, she made the frantic loop one more time before he caught her from behind and dragged her down on the bed, one side of the dress above her waist. A white orbed buttock was marvelously and voluptuously exposed. Out of breath and full of the spirit of the moment, he bit her there. He had to restrain himself. His impulse was to clamp down, but he was careful, if not totally gentle.

"Oooohhh! You lout!" she giggled, glancing over her shoulder, her eyes wide and filled with delight.

She struggled with great effort to turn to her back and swung at him. He caught her wrist and pulled himself to her. Their eyes locked and the laughter gave way to grappling, then kissing. Snared in their disheveled clothing, they groped and searched and stoked the fires within and began their lives together as husband and wife.

*

In Florida between the tourist seasons, Jim and Ceit had miles of uninhabited beaches to themselves. One blustery day when there was not even a soul walking the streets, Ceit kicked off her swimsuit and ran for the ocean waving her arms, hopping and jumping till she plunged into the roaring surf.

Jim was amazed, not at her, for he was well acquainted with her imprudent, uninhibited impulses, but at himself. He quickly imitated her and joined her exuberant play. When she sprinted from the water, he chased her and they wrestled in the sand. They went back into the water to wash the sand away, only to spot a couple and two small children about fifty yards away. They were coming down the dunes in search of seashells. It seemed they would never leave, but at last they did and the laughing nudists dashed from the water and dressed in a hurry.

For five days the honeymooning couple lived and frolicked and loved in that Florida town some miles north of Miami. They did not wish to be away from the boys any longer. Their parents tried to talk them into staying, but they were ready for home and their family.

Jim liked that about Ceit and he liked what she had become. The sadness had disappeared from her beautiful eyes. She was the person she never allowed herself to be. She was free from the impediments she so often permitted to regulate her conduct. Though not yet nineteen, she was loving and caring, thoughtful and generous, graceful and desirous and to Jim, she was all woman. It was a wonderfully wild and wacky and loving five days.

* * *

Duncan stayed in Shoreford for three days after the wedding. It was not much time, but it was enough. He went on a tour with Bill and Buck and saw a location that appealed to him. His companions concurred. He had carried an idea in his head for years, but it was an idea that had been nearly impossible. Now it could be a reality. He knew that it would never have been practicable if his uncle had not been killed and left the family with enough to be reasonably free from financial worry and that humbled him.

He was convinced that Molly would wish to remain in Shoreford and during his brief stay, he had become very fond of the Williams and Buchanan families. He saw enough of rubber farming to know it was not for him. He knew that if he suggested selling the plantation, his mother and sister would agree. He could rationalize that he had seen enough war. He would leave his Corps.

"Mum, I've looked at some land here in Shoreford that I'd like to put that pub on, the one I sometimes spoke to ya about in the past. I'm hopeful yu'll agree to sell Uncle Dougald's place and settle here in Shoreford with Ceit and me."

"Oh, Duncan, I do believe that is a wonderful idea. I have thought much about buying a home and staying here and you have just made it very easy for me to reach that decision. I have come to feel that I would like to live in Shoreford. I love Sarah and Will and Isabel. They have been the greatest friends I've ever had and I cannot imagine life without Ceit and Jim, or the boys. My Moira is at rest here. Och, Laddie, and to have you at home! Yes! Sell the plantation! We of course must confer with Ceit, but we both know what her response will be."

*

The day Duncan departed, Bill had Molly in touch with a real estate agent. Sarah and Isabel were overjoyed. Their trio would remain intact. When Jim and Ceit returned, the happy surprise was unveiled to them.

*

A small bungalow between Silver Beach and the more moderate homes along the western beaches of Shoreford was purchased by Molly. She had the place renovated and furnished. Though at ease financially, she was not lavish with the renovations or extravagant with the furnishings. She and Ceit and Duncan decided to keep their small house in Scotland, to serve as a vacation home.

Jim and Ceit wanted to build and started a search for land. They found a site that they fell in love with. It was on a knoll, high by Shoreford standards, about a hundred and seventy-five feet above sea level. It was heavily overgrown with scrub, but Jim could visualize the gentle slopes planted with Red and Sugar Maples not far from the imaginary house site. Some birches and beeches further out and maybe some oaks around the periphery on the nearly three acres.

Ceit, lover of colors and flowers, had visions of where the garden would be and the variety of flowers she could plant. There was one other desirable feature. From the top, where the front yard was imagined and the windows would look out, the sound was visible.

The drawback was the expense, not the building, that they could afford. Utilities would have to be run a long way and a very lengthy driveway was needed. Much clearing and blasting were required. It was a one time expense that would make for a valuable property. It was a beautiful dream and one Jim and Ceit passionately shared, but he, being the bread winner, was convinced his salary alone should be enough. It was not.

Ceit could have handled the finances by herself, but Jim was adamant. They had some very strong arguments. One day she doubled her fist and smacked him hard in the ribs. He was sore for a few days. Another time she plowed a fist into his midsection and doubled him over. He did not get angry, he felt responsible for her disappointment. Finally, one day, in severe frustration, Ceit broke down.

"Jamie! Yu ... you're a selfish man!" she cried and blubbered, "Don't you know, .. it's for our children .. and me too!"

He was beaten the way women sometimes beat their men, but most of all, he was ashamed of her accusations. He took her, sobbing and trembling, into his embrace. He soothed her a very long time. When she left the shelter of his arms, they never said a word about the decision silently reached. They both knew it and though it was not immediately evident, she was full of joy.

When they crawled into bed that night, very tired, there was a sense of release in Jim and contentment in Ceit. They fell asleep with their arms about the other. They woke hours later, sweaty and numb and sore. When the blood was circulating again and feeling returned to their limbs, she bit his ear and whispered, "Let's take a shower!"

Bill and Sarah awoke to the sound of running water. The tiny giggles were barely audible, but they decided everything was OK and went back to sleep.

*

On Wednesday, July the 7th, four days after the evening fireworks display, Ceit picked Jim up at the store prior to noon. She did not have the boys with her. Jim did not know where they were going until it became evident by the direction of travel. At their destination, they debarked from the car and holding hands, walked slowly up the hill. At the top, she put an arm about his waist and he squeezed her shoulder to him. A far away look came into his eyes.

"It sure is beautiful, isn't it?" he said in a hushed tone.

She released her hold on him and reached under her shirt and withdrew a paper and handed him the deed. He took her in his arms and was infected by her emotions. With a finger, she wiped a tear from the inside corner of his eye.

To punctuate the high spirits, that night, Shirley gave birth to a beautiful and healthy girl.

*

Jim and Ceit drew up the floor plan of their home to be. It was a ranch that would sit snugly atop the hill. It could be added to easily should the family continue to grow. There was nothing pretentious about the plan, but it would have two and a half bathrooms and a large dining room that would accommodate their extended families for holiday events. A number of large windows for the wonderful views, was additional appeal.

Clearing was started in two weeks and building soon after. Bill and Buck both had important connections that helped immensely. The construction was not always a happy affair, what with delays and coordinating the sub contractors, but it was almost always exciting for Jim and Ceit. They participated in the construction wherever and whenever their talents could be applied. They watched their house grow and during that same period, they took joy in the growth of Ceit's belly.

*

Ceit had a difficult time with her pregnancy. There were some bad moments. Nevertheless, on November 8th, nineteen days after her nineteenth birthday, she gave birth to a fine specimen of femininity. The only problem with this little bundle, was the difficulty she gave her mother in trying to bring her into the world. But the newest Williams was ready to go from day one. Ceit, however, required more time to return to good health.

Mother and father talked considerably about names, but Ceit returned time and again to the same one. Jim had doubts, but he was alone. And so a second Moira came into the Williams home. This tiny bundle caused an entire family group to fall madly in love with her. She joined her parents in their new home.

Molly had moved into her home by now and when Jim and Ceit moved out, it was not a happy time for Sarah. She gave them up grudgingly, but became a traveling grandmother. She went to Jim and Ceit's and Buck and Shirley's with joyful and unsurprising frequency, usually accompanied by Isabel or Molly or both.

The entire family group broke bread at the home of James and Ceit Williams on Thanksgiving. The large dining room passed the test admirably. The preparation, serving and baby-sitting was shared in abundance. There was a vast amount of food. When the meal was finished and the clutter cleared away, Bob, home from college, lay on the living room floor, his belt undone, his oldest nephew astride his uncomfortable stomach, bouncing with delight. The younger brothers played on the floor with their father and Uncle Buck. On the couch, Heather Buchanan lay nestled in Molly's arms, her two grandmothers on either side, smiling approval. Moira was asleep in her grandfather's arms.

Shirley and Ceit stood together at the entryway observing the idyllic scene. They could not resist putting an arm about the other's waist and squeezing.

*

Early in the spring of fifty-five, the chores complete, the children in bed, Jim was in the living room reading a book, his feet on a hassock. He heard her soft steps and looked up into her smiling face. He dropped the book to his lap.

"What's up?"

Ceit reached down and took the book and placed it on the end table. She slid into his lap and put her arms about his neck. Still smiling, she kissed him gently on the lips. When she leaned back, she told him the news.

He was surprised and they waited a few days before passing it on.

*

"My, God!" Bill was astounded.

"Jimmy!" Sarah was angry, "What's the matter with you. You know Ceit had difficulties the last time and it's so soon. My goodness, Ceit is only nineteen years old and her body is not yet fully mature." Then she turned to Ceit, "I'm sorry, Dear, I didn't mean to talk as if you weren't here, but he should know better."

"Oh, Mom," Ceit smiled sweetly, "he does know better. I am the one who wanted this. Five is a lucky number. Don't you think? And I have a feeling this will be our last. And we can raise our family while we are young and full of energy. That's not so bad, .. is it? Besides, Mom, it's been me who's been seducing him. Isn't that right, Jamie?"

Jim blushed slightly without acknowledging her question. She had been persistent of late. He would never admit that to his mother, but with Ceit's straightforwardness, it was not necessary.

"Well, .. isn't it so, Jamie?"

His sheepish grin was the best he could do.

Later that night, he lay on his back in their bed, waiting for her to finish in the bathroom and join him. He remembered her words to his mother. Ceit was that way. He never sought her defense, but he liked that about her. As she crawled in, he looked up into her eyes.

"I love you, Ceit Williams."

She smiled down at him, then leaned and nibbled his ear, the way she had been doing quite frequently in the recent past.

"Do you think my body is not yet fully mature," she whispered sensuously, " .. as Mom said?"

Before he could reply, she pressed her nakedness into him and grasped his hands, moving them slowly over her breasts, sighing softly. When she let go, he fondled her tenderly, moving his hands slowly downward.

"Ooohh, you have such nice hands, Jamie Williams, but you didna answer my question."

He wrapped her in his arms, holding her tightly. He kissed her with feeling and she responded happily. Their kissing continued and soon he was fondling her. They were breathing heavily by now, but she managed a giggle between quick breaths.

"Does that mean no to what Mom said?"

His excitement rising, he exhaled forcefully, shook his head and gasped, "Yes! Yes! That means no!"

*

With the passage of a few days, everyone came around and accepted the fact of Ceit's pregnancy. Over more time, enthusiasm surfaced, but Sarah and to a lesser extent Molly, did some worrying. Buck and Bob teased Jim. Shirley did the same to Ceit when the men were not present. That part was fun.

On an evening in May, when the kids were in bed, Ceit came into the den where Jim was writing checks. She sat in the stuffed chair and came right to the point.

"Jamie, you know I was studying to be a teacher in Scotland. I would like very much to teach. Not high school like Buck, but kindergarten or first grade, even if I could only substitute."

He pushed the chair back from the desk and studied her.

"I got some materials from the state teachers college in the city. I know I could get my degree going part time. It would take maybe six or seven years. Oh, Jamie, I do love children and ours, even this one," she patted her belly, "will be in school by then. I could do something more useful than staying home alone and it would give me plenty of time for the chores and I'd be home when the children were. Please?"

As she spoke, her excitement had grown and her face was lightly flushed.

Getting up, Jim walked to her. His initial reaction was to tease her and drag out his consent, but her seriousness dissuaded him. He took her hands in his and gently pulled her from the chair and into an embrace.

"Mrs. Williams, you know what? I think you should be a teacher."

She smiled happily, then kissed him hard. Backing away, she took his hand and led him from the den.

"I was all set for an argument, but you're so nice, I think you deserve something."

She had that devilish look in her eyes.

"Come with me."

As he went with her, he thought this was much better than the punch he would have received had he teased her.

* * *

Duncan obtained his discharge in September and came directly to Shoreford. He had earlier established residency with Molly. In a days time, he was reacquainted and acclimatized and went to work. He had left a deposit on the piece of property he desired. The old rickety building that presently occupied the site would come down. It was a great location. On the Post Road, it was on the west side of Shoreford near the Newville town line and about ten minutes or so from the city. Bill was an immense help, steering Duncan through the town hall, getting the paper work completed and sending him to the right people at the state capital.

On October 20th, Ceit had her twentieth birthday and Duncan stayed for the party. Next day, he was in the air and on his way to Malaya, to clear the final elements of the sale of the plantation.

*

Two weeks later preparations were in progress for Moira's first birthday. Apart from the party, there was further anxiety in the family. They had not yet heard from Duncan and were impatiently awaiting his call to let them know he was on his way home. They had expected the call days ago. When the phone rang that night at 9:00PM, Jim was really pleased to hear his brother-in-laws voice.

"Hi, Dunk! It's about time. We thought you would have wrapped things up before this," Jim said, but then remained silent a long time as the color drained from his face. He finally dropped into the chair at the phone table. His face now ashen, his voice barely audible, he could only repeat again and again, "Oh my God! Oh my God!"

Ceit was now directly in front of him, her bulbous belly making her appear uncomfortable, which she was, but her discomfort was far more than physical.

"What is it, Jamie? What's wrong!?" she pleaded with her husband, her voice high, "For heaven's sake, tell me what's wrong!"

The connection was not good and Jim was having difficulty hearing. He put a finger to his lips and muttered at intervals, "Yes," at length softly saying, "Yeah, we'll await your call." He had to repeat the words louder. He did not say 'good-bye', but placed the handset mechanically on the cradle. Sprawled in the chair, his face an image of anguish, he was a man defeated.

Kneeling in front of him, Ceit tried to look into his eyes. He would not meet her gaze. He continued to stare downward, his eyes out of focus, his demeanor, lost in some unfathomable dimension.

"What is it, Jamie?" her voice nervous and filled with anticipation and distress, was nearing a fever pitch. "For heaven's sake, what is it!? Please tell me!! Please, Jamie, for heaven's sake, .. tell me!!!"

* THIRTEEN *

Lying on his stomach, he shuddered as he remembered that telephone call and the feeling of doom that came over him and the sense of foreboding, before he repeated the news to his wife and family.

The door opened a crack and she peeked in, then pushed it fully open and entered. His meandering in the past ended abruptly and his mind was suddenly uneasy. He knew he was fighting the clock and she was here to remind him that it was getting late. He was determined to finish the journey he had begun. He heard her coming toward the bed and lifted his arm just enough to gaze through the space between elbow and pillow. He could see her shapely legs until she was against the side of the bed and her hips blocked his vision.

In the next instant the blanket was yanked briskly and impolitely away. She pinched a buttock, .. hard.

"Hey!" he yelped, more for the drama, than any pain, as he rolled quickly to his back. He grabbed the blanket and pulled it up to his chin, feigning modesty. He stared at her sheepishly, continuing his act.

Her face displayed her amusement.

"You are something when you choose to be obstinate, ... but I think you'd better make an effort to get yourself dressed, or you just may be sorry."

"You're determined," he chuckled, "to make me move before I'm ready, aren't you? Well, begone, I'm not finished yet. You're not going to throw cold water on my reverie."

"That just may be the answer," she said, giggling as she left the room.

He was pleased with himself. She did not often give up so easily. He tightened the blanket about him and closed his eyes. Her playful presence disrupted his mood and he had some difficulty returning to those fracturing events of yesteryear, but he did succeed and was one more time caught up in the emotion of those events, events that not only changed so many lives forever, but were to have such a profound effect on those lives.

~ ~ ~ ~ ~

As her mind came grudgingly awake, the pain in her body was so overpowering that she tried to slip back into unconsciousness. She did not want to open her eyes for she was filled with the fear of what she might see. She remembered terrible vibrations. She remembered voices that were shouting loudly, but were drowned out by all the other frightening noises. She remembered the sputtering and the violent spinning. That was vivid in her mind. But it had plunged her mind into incoherence. She did not hear the last awful sound of metal being torn apart and crumpled into unrecognizable shapes. Her consciousness had been mercifully, ripped away.

Despite the pain and her desire to escape again into that unconscious state, she could not ignore the gentle hands that were ministering to her needs. She made a valiant effort to force her eyes open and when they were at last able to focus, she could make out the satisfaction on the strange, shy brown face that hovered over her. There were two other similar faces nearby. They also seemed pleased. One of them bent over her and tenderly raised her head, just enough for her to feel the rim of the vial pressed gently between her lips and the warm liquid pass over her tongue and soothe her innards as it traveled downward. Soon she was relaxed and peaceful and despite the exploratory hands moving over her body, was able to enter a restful and healing sleep.

*

The passing days relieved her pains and returned her strength. She was soon up and able to walk about and converse with her benevolent guardians, albeit only minimally. The language of the aborigine was just a vague recollection in her mind, never having been mastered well, but the signs that passed between them, helped to bring her to near complete understanding.

She instinctively loved the gentle and timid folk who cared for her and lived in the cluster of little huts built on stilts, some five feet above the ground. Their clothing was simple. A few of the women wore one piece dresses, but many wore only skirts that left them bare above the waist. The men and children were adorned with pieces of cloth wrapped about the loins. The youngest required nothing.

She knew she had known them, or some just like them in her previous life, the life that was torn from her memory that dreadful, shadowy, frightening moment, just before she arrived in this beneficent village to be nurtured back to health. These same saviors informed her that she was the only survivor of a terrible helicopter crash, having been pulled free of the wreck just before the explosion and horrible fire that followed. The others aboard were killed. Their bodies were burned beyond recognition and buried by the aborigines.

Even her name was not known to her, but young and strong and a survivor of past adversity, she would get well, but for now, as her body healed, her mind was in constant struggle. She was fervently seeking to grasp the tiniest fragment of what came before.

Then one day, slowly, yet steadily, an image began to take shape in her mind. It was a sweet and kind lady who held her in her arms and comforted her, in another time and place when she was in terrible pain and anguish. That woman loved her and became her mother. Soon thereafter, she remembered her mother's name, .. Genevieve. Her spirits soared and for the first time, the shy villagers saw their beautiful visitor smile.

She at first remembered her name as Sung Liang, that is, until her father was returned to his place in her memory and Wellesley came to mind. Then she realized she was not Sung Liang, but Liang Sung Wellesley and was no longer bewildered when her mind was active, that her thoughts were in English, not her native tongue.

Liang smiled more frequently as time continued its journey, for not only were bits and pieces of her memory returned, but she was soon to feel the new life forming within her body and that became her greatest cause for hope.

The months that followed were kind to her. As the child within her grew, she was content to look forward to motherhood and was not as anxious about the past, though she was troubled when she searched for the reason behind her condition. But for now, she turned her thoughts to the future and opened the fullness of her heart to the defenseless bundle who would someday soon, enter her world.

*

Her disjointed intellect was nearly stitched together. All but those from her most recent past had retaken their places in her memory by the end of her pregnancy, a pregnancy that ended with a labor and birth that was difficult and exhausting.

Liang delivered with the help of an excellent midwife and some fine assistants. A healthy and beautiful baby girl was instantly a celebrity in the village. The child was given the name of Liang's English mother, the first name that had returned to her memory. It was a humorous thing for her to listen to the villagers trying to enunciate that name, for Genevieve was not among the sounds of their language.

*

Genevieve grew and Liang nursed her child with a joy and quiet passion and she sang to her in wonderful cooing sounds. It was during one of those moments that her memory gave birth to an image. That image was a young boy whose name she knew instantly. One to whom she had sung these same songs.

She said the name out loud.

"Donald!"

Filled with happiness at her discovery, she excitedly continued repeating the name. Soon other images and other names followed. She repeated those names out loud.

"Dunkie! Robbie!"

Her joy continued to grow, not only for the return of memory, but of knowing that she was connected to others by love, others who were alive and who would return her love. It set her heart pounding and forced the blood more quickly through her body and her face showed her joy in a radiant glow.

That euphoria was short lived, for her curiosity began to burn anew and with more intensity. When she went to her bed that evening, her mind was racing furiously. Sleep was nearly impossible. It finally did come, though it was not a restful sleep. Her body twisted and turned and she awoke sometime in the middle of the night. She was shivering, chilled from the perspiration that soaked her body and turned cold. The streams of tears that also came during her troubled sleep, were cooled as well by the night air.

The tears were caused by a new image in her dreams. It was fuzzy at first, but it came to life, only to die again. The sadness of experiencing Moira's death one more time was appalling.

Wide awake, she got up and searched for additional covering which she found and returned to her bed. She began to feel the warmth return to her body, but her mind was severely unsettled. She lay there, thinking about her dearest friend, tears flowing across her temples and into her ears.

As she reminisced, the last piece of the puzzle fell into place. She did not sleep anymore that night. The excitement was too great. By daylight her plans were complete. She knew what she must do. She could not stop her thoughts from returning repeatedly to Jim, ... to her James ... and the boys. She knew she must return to the place where she would find them. It had been too long. She could remember no time in her life when she was so obsessed about doing something.

Clutching her daughter to her breast, she gazed lovingly into the tiny face.

"You will love your daddy, Genevieve, for he is such a fine and wonderful man and he will surely love you. And you will love your brothers as they will love you. And oh! There will be so much love when we are all together." Then she turned her head and looked about her before returning her gaze to her child. "But it will be sad to leave this place. We have had our home here all this time and these wonderful people have been so kind to us and now I must convince them to lead us out of here."

It took some convincing, but Liang did convince her hosts to take them to the south in the hope she might find her way to the place from whence she came. It would take time for these villagers would take her to another village and more convincing would be needed. That might lead to yet another village and perhaps another, but Liang was certain it would be accomplished. Her faith was strong.

*

The parting was sad and sometimes stoical, but mostly sad. Despite Liang's desperation to be underway, she was as sad as any. She was relieved and thankful when they cleared the outskirts of the village and entered the deep jungle on a well worn trail.

It was not an easy journey, but there was plenty of water for drinking and bathing. Liang became more conditioned and attuned to the journey daily. Her own needs were easily met and Genevieve's nourishment was a simple matter. They did stop some when Genevieve nursed, slowing the procession, but it made little difference. The guides would not be hurried.

The closer they came to the plantation, the more excited and ebullient Liang became. When she finally left the last of her aboriginal guides, she was on the outskirts of a 'civilized' village that was less than a days ride to the MacLeod plantation. The new year of 1955 was a week old.

*

"Thank you," Liang said as she exited the vehicle with Genevieve in her arms and grasped the small bundle of belongings. The driver waved and drove away. She was very excited and wondered why she had not seen someone she knew, long before this. She walked up the path and onto the porch and knocked on the door. She was aware of the complete lack of activity, very unlike the days when Dougald MacLeod was alive. In those times, she would have seen servants when they drove on to the estate. Nevertheless, she was filled with excitement.

The girl that answered the door was very young, the daughter of a servant.

They exchanged greetings in Chinese and when the proper etiquette had been observed, Liang smiled and asked excitedly, "Will you be kind enough to inform Mrs. Peng that Liang Williams," she looked down at the baby in her arms, her smile broadening, "and daughter Genevieve are here."

With a confused look, the young girl answered, "Mrs. Peng does not live here."

Liang turned quizzical, "I hope she is well."

"I know of no Mrs. Peng."

"Perhaps you would inform Lai or Lee?"

"I do not know them."

Liang frowned and followed with a half dozen more names, one of which was Chin.

"There is one called Chin who is working down by the pond. He may be one of those you seek."

Continuing to frown, Liang asked, "May I walk there?"

The girl, pleased that someone older had asked her permission, perked up and tilting her head to one side replied simply, "Yes."

"Thank you."

Liang turned and walked off the large porch and toward the pond. Her excitement diminished, she was anxious to pursue her search elsewhere. As she approached the pond, she could not help but remember that it was there that her James had proposed to her and her emotions again quickened as she thought about that day. She had been willing to be his concubine. How silly that all seemed now. She blushed slightly. She should have known her husband better.

The man was bent over at the edge of the pond cleaning up the growth at the shoreline.

"Chin! Is that you? It is!" she said excitedly, speaking Chinese.

He turned at the sound of her voice, slowly at first, then jumped to his feet, his expression complete horror.

"Chin! What is it?"

"You are dead! You are dead!" he screamed.

Her face turned softer as she began to understand his reaction. She spoke soothingly, knowing the superstitious nature of some of the native people.

"I am not dead, Chin, I never was. I am not a ghost. Can't you see? I am flesh and blood, as you are. Come and touch my hand and look upon the face of our daughter, James' daughter and mine."

He stood transfixed and trembling. She walked slowly to him and put her free hand on his shoulder. He flinched slightly, but did not move away. She smiled at him, the smile he had known when he had been in her presence. He finally relaxed a bit and returned a weak smile. He gazed shyly at her when she started to speak.

"I lived through the crash, Chin. I have been all this time with the aborigines in the north. Genevieve was born in their village. I was without my memory for many months and did not know who I was. When I finally remembered who I was, I got those wonderful people, in that village, to start me home, to find my husband and the boys."

By the time Liang was finished, Chin was staring at the ground, bewildered. There was a long silence before he lifted his eyes to hers and spoke slowly and hesitatingly.

"Jim has returned .. to America. They told him ..." his face got very sad, "you were dead."

She was silent a moment before a soft, sad expression spread and covered her lovely face.

"I wondered. No one came searching for us. I thought he might have returned to his home, ... but I must contact him there and ..."

Chin was unnerved by now, his face, complete agony.

"What's the matter, Chin?"

"They thought you were dead. ... Jim has married."

"Married!!!?"

She almost shouted the word, but with the sleeping child in her arms, she managed to control herself. She stared in disbelief at Chin.

He gathered his thoughts before he continued.

"Jim was very sad, ... very sad. He has been gone these many months. On one of Duncan's visits, he told us that his sister, ... who is Moira's sister, ... she and Jim were married. They have given the boys a sister."

Liang Williams was stunned. She could not speak. There was no need to speak. She wanted to cry, but Genevieve kept her from that.

The minutes passed agonizingly before Chin clumsily, but tenderly took her free hand.

"Liang," he said softly, "come with me, ... please."

*

Liang and Genevieve stayed that night at the estate, thanks to Chin and the generosity of the head planter. None but Chin knew who she was. That was her desire.

As she lay in bed that night, freshly bathed and quietly crying, her hand was on the crib that had once held one of the boys. She thought briefly of taking her life, but pushed the thought away. She had a responsibility now, for someone other than herself.

Chin informed Liang that it was not the same on the plantation any more. He had been planning on leaving and seeking opportunities in the city. He was the last employee left from the days of Dougald MacLeod.

Two days later, Chin, Liang and Genevieve were in Ipoh. The day after that, Chin helped Liang locate Mrs. Peng, who now lived in Ipoh. Liang was able to obtain living quarters near the older woman, who would care for Genevieve when Liang found work.

Employment came as quickly as Liang's trip to the hospital. There were enough people in authority who had heard of her and remembered. They were not about to let such a prize escape. She contracted to work the night shift, so she would have the most time with her daughter.

It was now that her early Oriental heritage took over and ruled her life. She accepted the fact that her husband was no longer her husband, that he belonged to someone else. If that someone was Moira's sister, it was all right. Moira was the finest person Liang had ever known. She would no longer search for Jim, nor try to make her existence known to him or to anyone who could pass that knowledge to him. She kept those thoughts to herself, but asked those coworkers who knew of her marriage, to respect her desire for anonymity. Her daughter was the reason for her life. That was the way it must be.

* * *

Liang was on duty the day Duncan Cameron came to bid farewell to a miner friend recovering from an injury. When Duncan saw her, he did not believe it was her. He was about to turn away, but could not make his feet obey. He went up behind her.

"Liang?" he asked softly.

She turned and when her eyes made contact with his, her body stiffened and she was unable to move or speak.

"Liang?" again Duncan asked.

He took her hands in his. She was so overcome with emotion she fell into his arms and cried, then sobbed, her body shaking out of control.

Dumbfounded as Duncan was, as mixed up as his emotions and thought processes were, when he learned of her child, .. Jim's child, he knew he could not walk away from her and leave her to an unknown fate. With tremendous misgivings, he knew he must allow others to work out a solution, others who unfortunately had much, perhaps everything to lose.

His heart ached for Ceit. His heart ached for his mother and all the others in the close family in Shoreford. It ached greatly for Liang. And it ached so very much for his best friend and brother-in-law.

* * *

The birthday party was at best, a morose affair. No one was capable of changing that. No one was capable of anything like positive thinking. Usually a bulwark in any tribulation, Buck was as stunned as the rest. Three year old Donald kept asking his mother if she was sick. The two year old twins were thoroughly puzzled by the mood. Only Heather Buchanan and one year old guest of honor, Moira Williams, had fun, .. splashing ice cream all over themselves and everything within reach.

Jim received two more calls from Duncan that day. Duncan related most of the tragic story of Liang's terrible ordeal. Jim in his turn passed it on to the family, except for Ceit. She would not listen to any of it, nor speak about it with anyone, most especially Jim. Her world was crumbling and she could not face it. She was in complete denial.

The disruption in the lives of the entire family was nearly as bad. Jim's marriage to Liang had not been happily received two years ago, until the story of the tragedy in her life was divulged. Except for Ceit, it did touch everyone. The families, the Williams, the Buchanans, the MacPhersons and Molly, by the time Liang's story was known, were convinced they would love this young woman, not much older than Ceit, with all their hearts, but they never had the chance.

Liang's presumed death made it abundantly easy for Jim and Ceit to form a different and joyful union. It was also easy for the entire group to happily develop along changed lines. Now, the latest ordeal, of Liang's still young life, tended to confuse and elude the rationale of the family. It further disrupted any reasonable hope for Jim and Ceit and discredited their plans for the future. Nevertheless, as the story of Liang's latest ordeal unfolded, Ceit alone, turned to stone, shutting out the words and closing her heart. All others were moved once again, but this time, with different and very mixed emotions.

* * *

"You're not going without me!!!" Ceit was angry.

"But, Ceit, you're so close now. They'll never let you fly."

"We don't have to fly! We don't have to be there for at least five days! Didn't Duncan say they still had stuff to clear up in Singapore and it would be at least five days before she would arrive in the States."

Disgruntled, Jim shook his head affirmatively.

"Well, I am going with you, Jamie! Besides, I can drive too and I know Dad will let us take the station wagon." She thrust her chin out and glared into his eyes. "I am going!!!"

He did not want her to go, only because he was concerned about her condition and the fact that she had so much trouble when Moira was born. He did not wish to do anything that might create greater difficulties for her.

Mostly, it would be Sarah and Molly, but the entire family would not take kindly to Ceit accompanying him. He knew that. He could perhaps stand up to them, but he had no fight left for Ceit. He had an instantaneous thought of his own death and how much better it would be for him. Immediately he was angry with himself. There were too many people depending on him, people who needed him. That kind of thinking was cowardly. His actions created this situation and he must be the one to clear it up. But he had no idea what the first step should be, or even could be. His head was filled, not with ideas, but with anguish and despair.

That Jim loved Ceit, there was no doubt. There was no doubt either, that he did not want to lose her, did not want to see her hurt, but he could not allow Liang to be tossed aside. He remembered that he had loved her and strangely, when he thought of her now, he still did. He was legally married to Liang and she bore a daughter as a result of that union, but Ceit also bore a daughter as a result of their union. There was another child on the way and he was legally married to Ceit, ... or was he? Was he a bigamist? The more he tried to think it through, the worse it got. He decided to give up thinking about it, but could not. There was no solution, but it would not go away. He had to play the cards he was dealt, .. no matter what the outcome, .. no matter who lost the game.

*

The decision by Ceit to accompany him, did not, as Jim expected, sit well with the family. They were unable to hide their feelings and Sarah blamed him for not putting his foot down. Molly was a bit easier on him. She, best of all, knew how Ceit was. Bill was the one who would not allow himself to become emotional and cast stones at either his son or daughter-in-law. He said little, but his concern sometimes showed. Shirley especially, but Buck and Bob too, were against Ceit making the trip, but they kept those thoughts between themselves. No one of course, could relate to Ceit's feelings, whether irrational or not. In the end, they all unhappily accepted the decision.

*

The station wagon was packed. Air mattresses, sleeping bags and pillows were carried in case of emergency or they were caught on the long uninhabited sections of open road and needed rest. Thankfully, it was November and they could travel the southern route in relative comfort. There was emergency food, paper towels and toilet paper. Two, three gallon water containers for drinking, or filling the radiator, should the need arise, were in the back. All this was in addition to the normal clothing and toilet articles. The last things they put in the car were two quart thermoses, one of tea, the other of coffee.

They confirmed they would call home every day, sometime close to 7:00PM, not only to check on the children, but in case Duncan left any additional instructions.

Ceit gave Sarah and Molly two sheets of paper with written instructions, but was not satisfied until she repeated them verbally, word for word. Shirley and Isabel too, were going to be involved with the care of the children. Ceit was doubtful that all this help could accomplish what she did by herself. She was nervous and frightened and embarking on an emotional journey of unknown destination. She had difficulty when she kissed the children and tears flooded her eyes, but she stuck out her chin and forced her over large body into the car seat.

The 'good-byes' were no less easy for Jim, or the other family members present, though the family did their best, not entirely successful, to send them off on a positive note.

They got underway later than expected. Backing out of the driveway at 10:30AM, Wednesday the 9th, Jim did not feel well. He had very little sleep. With all the preparations and the packing, he had allowed his anger with Ceit to enlarge during those furious activities. He had difficulty keeping it under wraps. He was sure, that had he been able to fly, it would have been much easier on him. But towards the end, he felt guilty for blaming her. He knew, had he been in her shoes, he would have insisted on going.

The only stops they made prior to the telephone call home, were for fuel, refills on the coffee and bodily relief. Their supply of sandwiches would last beyond the coming day. The tea was untouched.

It was past midnight when Ceit spotted the vacancy sign at the motel in Kentucky, just south of Cincinnati. Jim wanted to catch a nap in the car, but Ceit would have none of that.

"Jamie, we are not poor. We can sleep in a motel. We need a bed and we need a shower. You've been pushing yourself and the car ... and me, all day! I want a bed and I want a shower, .. now!"

Since leaving Shoreford, that was more than all the words she spoke all day. He knew she was right and he was immediately full of guilt for not taking her into consideration. He decided he would have to be more aware of her and her needs. As for himself, it was as if he was punishing himself for their dilemma. His body was stiff and tired. His eyes felt like the proverbial 'two pee holes in the snow'. They were constantly in the rear and side view mirrors, on the lookout for police cars, as he severely exceeded speed limits, while draining the thermos of coffee three times.

He pulled the car up in front of the motel office and stopped. When he was out, he wanted fiercely to stretch, but would not allow himself the luxury. After he registered, he drove to number 3. They debarked from the car and he unlocked the door for her, turned on the lights and went back to the car to get the proper luggage.

In the shower when he returned, she remained for a long time. He laid out and arraigned her clothing for the next day, as he did his own. When she finished, he went in for his shower. When he returned, she was in bed, close to the edge on her side. He did not think she was asleep. He turned out the lights and wearily entered the bed without a word. He wanted to take her in his arms and tell her everything would be all right, but how could he do that when he did not know how anything would be. Nevertheless, he felt he should do it. He reached out and touched her, but she flinched and drew away.

*

The revitalizing rest Jim needed, he did not get. He tossed and turned and when he did sleep, his rest was disturbed by terrible dreams. He was also aware of Ceit's unrest. He wondered if maybe his locomotions disturbed her, but thought it more likely was the baby. She complained of late, about the discomforting activities within her.

Showering again, because they both required the prod of the pelting spray to awaken them, the only conversation they had was when they went to breakfast and he asked her what she wanted. Before the meal arrived, he reached across the table to touch her hand, but she instantly pulled away.

During another day of almost no conversation, he thought she was crying once and he desperately wanted to hold her. He asked her if he could make up a bed for her in the back, but she refused. She did finally fall asleep, her head on the pillow he insisted she place against the door. It was a fitful sleep. She twitched and jerked about and her eyes opened periodically, showing surprise and fear at her surroundings. When she looked across at Jim in one of those moments, she saw the man she loved and was calmed, but her anger with him quickly returned, as the haziness cleared away. When at last she was fully awake, she retreated once more into her sullenness, but her eyes were clearer and her color a bit improved.

* * *

"Oh, Duncan, are you sure?" Liang ruefully asked.

"You must go, Liang! Tis the only way. We dinna ken what will be the outcome, but you must go. I only wish I could diminish what you must be feelin, but I can not. Maybe fate will be kind to all of you."

"But, Duncan, it is a day sooner than was originally planned ... and I am truly frightened."

"Would you be less frightened if you waited till the scheduled day, .. or the next and the next?"

She looked at the floor and hesitated before shaking her head. When she returned her gaze to Duncan, she repeated her answer verbally, but softly, "No."

"Then it's settled. You and Genevieve will leave tomorrow. Jim is already on his way and should be there before you. But twill make no difference, for if he's a wee bit late, the rooms are reserved and you and Genevieve will be well cared for. Everything has been arranged and prepared for your arrival."

* * *

They called home before 8:00PM the second night. Liang and daughter were to arrive on the 12th at 9:10PM Pacific time. It was a day earlier than they anticipated, but it was OK. They were making good time and would be on time.

Stopping short of Oklahoma City that night, they were in bed right after their showers. Jim reached across the distance separating them. He touched Ceit's shoulder. She pulled away and he could feel her hurt. He could also feel his own sharp ache. He felt better when he heard her rhythmic breathing. Her well being was more important to him than his self pity, especially when he realized how much he loved her.

In the morning, they showered as they did yesterday, not because their bodies needed cleansing, but rather revivification. They ate breakfast and were underway with little wasted effort.

They called home that morning, west of Oklahoma City. Jim desperately wanted to hear the voices of their children. It was something he needed, something positive to help him through the day. Unknown to him, Ceit had similar desires. Both of them had some brief moments of pleasure, which temporarily eased their tension and anguish.

They took turns listening to Moira do her "Blablabla" on and on and the twins jabber disjointedly. Donny had lots of exciting news about the adventures he and his siblings were having with their grandparents, et al.

Bill, Sarah and Molly were staying at Jim and Ceit's and Isabel, the third 'Gramma' of the Williams children, was present much of the time, as were Shirley and Heather. Buck arrived after school and the group ate supper together. It was a good idea. Each was able to take some comfort from the group and the children were a blessing to all during this time of collective disorder.

The children had a positive affect on Jim and Ceit and he thought he had not heard his parents or Molly sound as good in days. For a brief time, Ceit was somewhat cheerful. She slept in the front seat again that day and it was more restful than the previous day. When they called home that night, they learned Duncan had called to confirm Liang's time of arrival.

Ceit lost whatever cheer she had, the news returning her to sullen silence.

A small town west of Flaggstaff, Arizona was their stopping point that night. The distance they needed to travel tomorrow was less than half of what they had been doing daily. They had plenty of time. Jim hoped Ceit would rest better if she knew. He sat with her and made sure she was aware of the easier day ahead. She listened without comment, or any change in her moody expression. He decided he would let her sleep as late as she could.

The motel was immaculate and the food excellent. They showered and went to bed. Before he fell asleep, Jim wanted to reach out and touch her, but decided against it. He slept well for the most part, except for the moments Ceit's nervous body wakened him. One time, during one of those moments awake, he put a hand on her, but before he fell back to sleep, she pulled away.

*

For the first time in four days, Jim came awake feeling moderately refreshed. He knew he should not feel that well. They were getting closer to whatever fate had in store for them, .. their family ... and their future. Ceit was still sleeping and her breathing seemed normal.

Dressing hurriedly and quietly, Jim exited to the outdoors with less noise than a mouse. The sky in the east was overpoweringly beautiful and he realized, they had come so far across the country and this was the first time he was conscious of the surroundings. Taking deep breaths, he forced the pure air into his lungs. When he started to walk, his body, his physical being, wanted to break into a run. He knew it was not for the usual exhilaration he obtained from running, but a subconscious craving to flee the events of his life. He would never, .. could never, do that, but, it was for an instant, an appealing alternative. Maybe, he thought, someday, when all of this was behind them, he could come to a place like this and run. Perhaps then he could run with the free spirit that normally was his companion at those times, when he ran just for the exhilaration.

But someday, a someday when all of this was behind them, was not a pleasant thought. The outcome of the dilemma could not have a happy ending. He returned to the motel in a gloomy mood.

Entering quietly, he found Ceit still asleep, but showing signs of restlessness. He went into the bathroom, undressed and stayed under the shower a lengthy period. When he returned to the bed room, Ceit was stirring and when she first opened her eyes, her face lit up when she saw him, but it was only for an instant. She quickly returned to her anger. During breakfast, she was silent and sullen.

By the time they were driving away, Ceit was glum and preoccupied, more so than at any time thus far. They were getting closer to their destination, a destination that reeked of uncertainty, bad omens and the end of life as she knew it.

They were on the road about an hour.

"Why did you do it, Jamie!?" she angrily asked out of the blue, without turning her head to look at him.

It startled him and he gave her a quick glance.

"Do what?"

"Marry that woman. What did you see in her? What was she like? What did she do to turn your head? Especially after Moira. How could you?"

He did not answer right away, but thought about what his answer would be.

"I had no intention of marrying Liang, Ceit, ... things just happened. She passionately loved the boys. I'm sure you can relate to that." He paused and glanced quickly at her, but she continued to look ahead, mouth clamped tightly shut, lips a thin line that remade their graceful shape. "She was a dear friend of Moira, ... the best she had outside the family. It's strange, but she was a lot like Moira. She di ..."

"How could you say she was like Moira?" Ceit turned instantly, cutting him off, her eyes full of rage, "How could you even think something like that?" There was vitriol in the sound of her voice and the meaning of her words as she spit them out. "No one ever has been or ever will be like Moira! You know that! How could you ever say a thing like that!!? It's unthinkable! It's terrible! You're terrible, Jamie!"

Jim was stunned by the intensity of her words. He did not answer, but stared ahead at the road, not sure what to do or say next. He realized that what Ceit said was true, there was no one like Moira and yet, what he said, was also true. He never believed his own dead brother could have an equal, but he often thought of Buck as similar in many ways. He glanced quickly in Ceit's direction. She had turned away and was again staring straight ahead, her jaw set, her cheeks crimson. He could only imagine what was in her eyes, .. and worse yet, .. her mind.

It was a very disturbing thought.

Wanting to explain himself, he started to mouth the words, but decided against it, decided it would do no good. Ceit had made up her mind and now was not the time to try to reason with her. The conversation was over for now and for what remained of their journey.

* * *

High over the Pacific, the sun was approaching the western horizon. Genevieve ate a good supper, but Liang hardly touched hers. She looked down at her daughter.

"Oh, Genevieve!"

There was fear and uncertainty in her eyes and in her voice. It was unnoticed by the lovely child beside her. Genevieve smiled up at her mother. Finally Liang smiled back.

"I am sorry, my Dear, but I have not been a good mother to you recently. I have been thinking too much of myself. I know it should be you that is in my mind, but I have let you down by my concern for the future. I am sure you will have a good life where we are going. Your father is a kind and wonderful man, you will see."

She stopped for a moment and looked away, tears clouding her eyes, but then returned her gaze to her daughter.

"Do you know that when Duncan first came back into our lives and I learned the truth about everything, I wished Moira was alive and married to your father. But you know, if she was, you would not be here and if I had to choose between you, it would drive me insane and I think I might die. .. So you see, we must accept our gifts and our lives for what they are, for there can be no other way."

Genevieve, still attentive, still gazing up at her mother, smiled so sweetly Liang was convinced in her heart that Genevieve understood every word. As Liang smiled back, then wiped her eyes, she was at peace. She had confessed and was repentant.

* * *

Still beautiful, she appeared somewhat older and her eyes had a hint of sadness, but there was no hate in Liang's eyes. There was confusion and fear. Liang turned her gaze away from him and nervously on Ceit and forced a weak smile. Ceit returned an abrupt, expressionless nod, but Jim was not aware of their undesired attempt at cordiality. He only had eyes for the fourteen month old child at Liang's side, a beautiful child, holding her mother's hand. He went directly to her and picked her up in his arms. She accepted him and allowed him to crush her to him. When Jim released her from the embrace, he held her in his arms and smiled.

"You shall be my Genny."

For the longest time possible, Jim would take refuge in his love for his child, a child he knew he loved even before he set eyes on her, a love spawned the instant he knew of her existence. And now, today, she not only accepted him, she responded to him. He kissed her cheeks and when he held her at arms length and looked into her eyes, she looked back and smiled, the way children do when they are happy. He wanted to strut and brag and tell the world about her. It had been the same with all his children when they came into the world and today this child of his came into his world.

But alas, he must return to reality and face impossible prospects, completely undesirable. Yet when he made his daughter comfortable in the crook of his arm and turned to Ceit and Liang, he did not feel foreboding, or remorse or anything similar, but an overwhelming desire to protect them and show his love for them.

Reality, however, was not that way.

*

The reservations at the hotel had been made by Duncan through an agent in Singapore. There were two bedrooms. Jim was certain that everyone would be hungry, but Ceit and Liang did not want a thing.

Jim went out and bought some ice cream for his daughter, with enough extra for everyone, should they have a change of heart. While the females took turns in the shower, he fed his Genny and himself and between them, they managed to spill a fair portion while they ate. He made faces and she laughed and he returned her laughter, as if everything was right with the world.

Liang returned to the room and sat in a stuffed chair. She observed Jim and their daughter, with sadness at first, but she was soon smiling. The interaction between them filled her with a quiet delight. It returned memories and she was once more, aware of the kind of father he was.

Jim wiped the excess from Genny's mouth and cheeks and chin and removed the bib. He studied her Eurasian beauty and liked what he saw. She had her mother's hair and mouth, but her nose was more like Shirley's and her eyes were not as dark as Liang's.

Some of Shirley's features were strongly evident in another child of mixed race. Taking the balance of the ice cream into the bathroom to dump down the toilet, he wondered why children of mixed race were sometimes not happily accepted.

"What a strange world," he said aloud, shaking his head.

Returning to his daughter and thinking of his own status, he smiled at her, "I guess a strange world is where your father belongs."

"I'm sorry, James, I did not hear what you said."

"Sorry, Liang, I was just talking to myself."

She eyed him curiously and he quickly turned the conversation away from himself.

"How does Ceit seem?"

Ceit had gone right to bed after her shower. Liang sat with her, questioned her, seeking some clue as to her well being. Ceit was negative and mostly unresponsive.

"I don't know, James. She has not said anything about feeling badly, but I wonder if she may be trying to hide it." She paused a moment. "Or it may be that she does not wish to speak to me about it."

Having taken Genny from the highchair, Jim handed her to Liang and went to see how Ceit was doing. She appeared to be asleep, but he knew she was pretending. He did not attempt conversation. Instead, he kissed her on the cheek and the forehead. He wanted to be next to her. He was certain she needed him, but he was also certain she would spurn him and would fight against that need and try to hurt him in the process. He did not wish to be hurt. Suddenly he was thankful the room was furnished with twin beds.

*

Liang was patient and gentle with Ceit, trying to help her prepare for the trip home. She was persistent with the questions she asked, but Ceit was completely uncooperative. Liang's eyes studied Ceit at every moment her attention was not required elsewhere. She was as concerned about Ceit's well being as Jim was.

On the way to breakfast, Jim carried Genny. Liang tried to stay close to Ceit, but Ceit would have none of it. She walked alone as she hurried along the sidewalk. Just before entering the restaurant, Ceit stumbled and Liang was instantly at her side, but Ceit regained her balance and shrugged Liang off. Ceit stared at Liang for an instant, a stare that was as curious as it was hateful.

*

They started east later than Jim planned. It was Liang's concern for Ceit that slowed them. Liang was adamant when she spoke to Jim about slowing the pace, but did so out of Ceit's range. Jim was not unhappy about slowing down. He also wanted to return at a more leisurely pace, for Ceit's sake. Moreover, he was in no hurry to arrive home and face the dilemma head on. Happily for Jim, with Liang along, she lifted much of the burden of Ceit's well being from his shoulders. He used that time to get better acquainted with Genny. She was bringing smiles to his face, smiles that had been missing for days.

*

The Arizona border was a short distance to the east when they stopped for lunch. Ceit wanted to return to the motel they stayed in two nights ago. She really liked the place and Jim wanted to please her. It did mean giving up the more leisurely pace, but only for a short time. With extra effort they would arrive in time for a late supper. Maybe, he thought, in the morning, he could talk them all into taking a walk into the countryside, as he had done on the way out. It would be good for everyone. Maybe getting there that night was not a bad idea.

As they rolled eastward, Genny was good as gold, sleeping when tired, playing with her mother when awake, or engrossed with the scenery flying by. Apart from the road and the constant surveillance of the auto's mirrors, Jim's eyes took in Ceit whenever she was unaware. There were occasions when he saw her smile at Genny. That pleased him. He was also mindful of Liang's increasing attention to Ceit and her intermittent questions. Ceit did not respond pleasantly to Liang, but at least she was beginning to respond. As time passed, a tiny bit of civility crept into her answers.

The station wagon was big and comfortable and the V-8 engine took the task at hand with ease. It was a good thing. There was a fair distance to cover and less time than there should have been. At sunset they were climbing. As twilight turned to darkness, they were the only travelers on the road.

Without warning, the engine sputtered and the vehicle lurched. The engine recovered for a moment, only to die with a wheezing cough. They coasted off the road onto the shoulder.

"What's the matter!!?" Ceit fearfully squealed.

Genny started to cry.

"I don't know. I'm gonna hafta look and see."

Jim got out and hurried to the back and opened the tailgate. His father kept an abundance of tools there and fortunately there were two six volt lanterns and a flashlight. He grabbed the flashlight and went to the front and opened the hood. He thought it was the fuel line and disconnected it. Sure enough, there was nothing coming through. He climbed back in and pumped the pedal repeatedly.

Outside again, he stared at a dry gas line. His mind worked frantically, but he realized their only chance was to stop a passer by and send them for help. Unfortunately, they had not seen another vehicle for some time.

Rolling the window down, Ceit leaned her head out.

"How much further do we have to go?" she asked meekly and frightened.

"I'd say twenty miles or so. Are you all right, Sweetheart?"

She took a deep breath before she answered.

"I'm not sure. I'm soaked. I think my water broke."

Liang was out of the car in an instant. Jim quickly joined Liang at Ceit's door. Liang handed Genny to him.

"Hold her and keep her warm! I want the rear seat out of the way and Ceit in the back where we will have some room. How do you move the seat?"

Holding Genny in one arm, Jim in haste opened the tailgate and climbed into the rear of the wagon. He struggled, but collapsed the seat and got it forward, opening the large rear area.

"I can blow up the air mattresses."

"Never mind that!" Liang ordered, "Can you get the suitcases and this other stuff out of here?"

He did what she asked as she worked with him. The area was clear of everything very quickly. The lanterns were lighted and the sleeping bags were spread over some car blankets. He took one of those for the child he so tenderly guarded in his arm.

"Get the whiskey from my bag, James, either the Macallan or the Glennfiddich that Duncan sent you."

Liang was full of authority, but it pleased Jim. He knew that she was the one person who had the capability to do something. She appeared calm, but he could detect the tiniest edge in her voice.

"Now take a walk and make sure you stop the first car! Tell them to get to the nearest phone and get an ambulance here!"

"Can't I help?"

"No! You'd only be in the way and you've got to care for Genevieve. I think there could be some noise."

Liang carefully helped Ceit into the back and made her as comfortable as she was able. Jim walked back and forth along the road with Genny. He had no idea how long he walked while his daughter drifted off to sleep wrapped in the blanket and held snugly in his arms. It seemed an eternity.

When he could stand it no longer, he went to the car. He opened the rear passenger door just enough to see inside. Along with the lanterns, the dome light was on. The lighting was poor, but it was enough to make his stomach do flips. He saw Ceit's ashen complexion and heard her mournful groans. Liang was squatting between Ceit's bent legs in the Oriental fashion, her dress about her waist. When she looked up from her labors, he saw the concern on a face soaked in perspiration.

"It's a breech, James! I have helped on one. I'll do everything I can. Oh James! I see headlights! Please tell them to hurry!"

It was a Sunday evening, quite late by now and traffic had been nonexistent. Jim stood in the middle of the oncoming lane and waved frantically with one arm. To get by him, the vehicle would have to run them over.

An old pick up with a lone occupant came to a screeching halt a half dozen feet from where Jim stood. Within seconds the driver had the truck turned around and was heading back to the nearest telephone.

Alone again, Jim was shaking. In his effort to get the truck to stop, he stood directly in the path of the oncoming rattletrap, with Genny in his arms. She did not awaken during the noisy, jerky stop of the truck. Gazing down at her he calmed down. He squeezed her tightly and kissed her forehead.

Next on his agenda was prayer. And he did pray. ... He prayed desperately and constantly for the lives of Ceit and their unborn child. He did that while his mind ruptured from the awful sound of Ceit's anguish, heard clearly through the closed windows of the station wagon. He prayed for Liang's ability. He did that when he looked through the rear side window and saw her working frantically, never taking her eyes from her task, never giving in to the possibility of defeat, never acknowledging anything, but Ceit and her unborn. And he prayed for the driver and for the old truck itself.

His prayers were at last graciously interrupted by a siren's wail, way off in the distance, but coming nearer with every second. Then the siren died in a fading whine as tires screeched and an ambulance came to a halt right in their midst.

The attendants were out in an instant and Jim showed them to the tailgate which he carefully, but quickly opened for them.

From the back of the station wagon, Ceit screamed as she was tenderly, but briskly moved and placed in the ambulance. Before they traveled the first mile, the medical technician was extremely grateful that Liang refused to leave Ceit. There was no doubt as to who was in charge.

Jim held Genny, clutched tightly to him in the front seat of the speeding vehicle of mercy. Behind them lay Ceit, moaning, sometimes screaming, in terrible pain. Liang and another, but mostly Liang, were busy beyond belief.

Unable to see anything that was taking place behind him, he regularly heard Liang calling out instructions. His eyes, when they were not closed in prayer, were glued to the road, as if his added vision, would aid the maniacal driver in keeping the racing vehicle on the road.

The ambulance did stay on the road and pulled safely into the emergency entrance of the hospital. Ceit was hurriedly and expertly removed and hustled off, Liang still there, still at work.

* * *

It was over! Jim Williams was drained, .. emotionally emaciated. He slumped in a chair, legs spread limply to his front. His mind was blank, at last released from the macabre scenes and terrible thoughts that raced through his tortured head in the last few hours. He wanted to sleep, but he could not do that until he did what he promised himself he would do.

There was movement. A form materialized and he looked up and into tired, but smiling eyes.

"Would you like to go in and visit now?" the doctor said. "Only for a few minutes, mind you."

"Yes!"

Jim came alive and jumped to his feet. He looked over at Liang in the other chair, a sleeping child in her arms. She smiled pleasantly and nodded. He stepped quickly to Liang's side, bent and kissed her forehead and that of the child. A smile seeped through his tired features, for Genny appeared to him, so angelic. He turned back to the doctor and walked with him down the hall.

He paused at the open door and caught his breath. She looked like a ghost, her pallor so unearthly, her hair accentuating the portrait, as it coiled untidily about her head. He walked in, suspicious of the prognosis, which was good, .. but she was alive, so maybe it was true. He stood beside the bed and she feebly reached out a hand. He gathered it in his and bent and kissed her very dry and rough lips.

"I love you, Sweetheart!" he said softly. "And she's a fine daughter!" showing his delight with a tired, but broad grin.

"I'm glad you're her father," she returned the smile weakly. "There's no one else ... Oh, Jamie!" Tears welled up and flooded her eyes. He bent down and kissed them away.

"Don't talk anymore, I can only stay a second, but I told the doctor I wouldn't leave till I saw you and could tell you that I loved you."

She squeezed his hand with all the strength that was left within her and in a voice that was a hoarse whisper said, "Oh, Jamie, I've treated you so badly and you don't deserve any of it." He put a finger to her lips to silence her, but she shook it off and struggled with the words. "And it wasn't ... it wasn't Liang's fault .. I went with Geordie MacBean."

He did not know her meaning, but when she said it, some kind of peace settled over her.

The doctor came to his side and put a hand on his shoulder. Jim turned and put his index finger up and turned back to Ceit.

"Go to sleep now. I'll be back after we've both had some rest."

He quickly bent and lightly kissed her dry lips and was gone.

Before he returned to the waiting area, he went again to the nursery, as if to reassure himself. As he gazed on Sally, he sighed deeply and when thoughts of the future started to run through his mind, he forced them aside and smiled at his tiny daughter. When they left the hospital, the sun was coming over the horizon. He knew he would be able to sleep.

*

The shower felt great. He stayed under and felt his body returning to life. Liang had allowed him to sleep. It was nearly noon.

When he came into the main room, Liang was feeding Genny. He went to them and bent and kissed his daughter and without a thought, kissed Liang lovingly, on the lips. It was natural. When he straightened up, he knew he loved her deeply.

Jim called the hospital to get an update and then called home with the good news of Ceit and Sally. Molly would pass it on to Duncan.

The car had been towed to a local garage and would be ready that day.

After lunch they made ready to visit Ceit. When they arrived at the hospital, Liang asked, "James, would you kindly care for Genevieve while I talk to the doctors. I promise I will keep you from Ceit only moments. I know you are desperate to see her."

He smiled and reached out for his daughter.

"Sure. Take your time, Honey. We'll wait right here for you."

"Thank you. I will return quickly."

She leaned to kiss him, but thought better of it and turned abruptly and left. He was disappointed. She went immediately to the nursing station on the floor of Ceit's residence. She was pleased to find a doctor. She asked him all kinds of questions about Ceit, her well being and also about Sally. When she was satisfied, she thanked him profusely and returned to the lobby.

"Thank you so much, James. I am so sorry to hold you up."

"Oh, Liang, ..." he smiled tenderly. He wanted to say more, but he handed Genny to her.

"We will await your return, James."

He was on his way and soon at Ceit's side. She did not look great, but had improved immensely.

"Hello, Sweetheart."

She returned his smile and reached for his hand. He leaned over and kissed her. They talked a bit. He asked her many things about the way she felt. He did not want to tax her, but she was eager to keep the conversation alive.

Jim was sitting on the edge of the bed when a doctor he did not know, came in to check on Ceit. He had many questions for the doctor, who answered with great patience. Jim was considerably relieved to hear the responses.

About to leave, the doctor hesitated and turned to Ceit.

"I think you should know, Ceit, your friend Liang is a very special person. She is one of the most compassionate and gifted people it has been my good fortune to come in contact with. I hear she's not yet a full fledged nurse, but what she did last night, without any help, should have been handled by an obstetrician. She's had some excellent training somewhere and performed magnificently. Turning your baby and helping her into the world, most of it in the back of a car or an ambulance was no mean feat. And then she refused to leave your side, Ceit, till she knew you were in the clear. I'd be proud to work with her any day. You must be proud to have her for a friend."

Ceit was crying softly when the doctor left.

*

The car was repaired and they were able to drive to the hospital for the evening visit.

"I wish only to see Sally, James. I am sure Ceit will be happier seeing only you."

He did not try to dissuade her, but when they arrived at the hospital, she asked Jim to hold Genny one more time and again Liang searched out the people who could fill her in on Ceit's condition. When she was completely satisfied, she returned. She was pleased with the information she had obtained and there was a soft smile on her face.

"It's wonderful, James, Ceit is doing extremely well! She is quite a fighter, you know."

The three then went to the nursery together. Standing in front of the large window, the newborn was displayed by a nurse on the other side.

Holding Genny in one arm, Jim gazed into her innocent, sparkling eyes.

"That's your new sister, Genny. When we get home, you're going to meet your other sister and three brothers. Isn't that great?"

The child stared into her father's eyes and smiled lovingly.

Liang slipped her arm about Jim's waist and lay her head against his shoulder. He put his free arm about her and could feel her softly crying. He turned his head and kissed the top of her head.

"I love you, Liang."

It only made it worse. When they left the window, only Genny was in a good mood.

* * *

Waiting the four days for Duncan's arrival was not a fun time for Jim. Fortunately he never had to contend with Ceit and Liang together. When with either of them, he found conversation difficult. In the beginning, he was affectionate with Ceit, as he was with Liang, but that tended to confuse more his already mixed up mind. He decided he must try to touch them less and kiss them only on the cheek, but that was definitely no help and he felt himself a coward. So he reneged and went back to being affectionate That was the way he really felt. That was the way he wanted to be. It was his nature. Once again his emotions went topsy-turvy.

Thankfully for Jim, Duncan arrived and the pressure was somewhat relieved, if only because when Duncan was about, Jim could be a spectator. It added a new dimension to the play.

On the second night after Duncan's arrival, when Liang and Genny were tucked in the double bed, Jim and Duncan were in the room with the twin beds, which they now shared.

Seeing the bottles on the dresser, Duncan asked, "Aren't you goin ta ask me ta share some whiskey?"

Jim blushed. He could not believe he had been so thoughtless with his good friend.

"Sorry, Dunk, I guess the last thing on my mind was the whiskey."

"Don't be sorry, Jim. I didna mean ta shame you, but tis not a bad time for good friends to sit and have a sip and forget soma the troubles about."

Jim retrieved the bottles. When Duncan looked at the bottles, he was surprised.

"Have ya decided ya like one whiskey by itself now?"

Jim laughed heartily for the first time in days.

"That's the bottle Liang used to disinfect her hands and whatever else needed it the night Sally was born."

Duncan chuckled.

They poured and sat on beds opposite each other. For awhile, their conversation was lighthearted. It did not last. Reality was close at hand and Jim could not escape it.

"I have a great favor to ask of you, Dunk."

"Just ask."

"Would you be willing to go with the girls on the train?"

"But why, Jim, whatever for?"

"I really don't think I can face the two of them all the way home, especially in a place we can't escape from. At least when we're all at home together, we'll be in friendly territory and maybe it will help us do the right thing, whatever that is. .. Please, Dunk, if you do this, I will owe you my life again."

"Och, Jim! Tis no problem. I will gladly do it for you, but I really thought I would drive the car back to Shoreford. .. And you'll no owe me your life. It's little enough I can do for you."

*

Ceit was picked up at the hospital about an hour and a half before the train departed. They kept her there till the last, as much for her to regain her strength as to heal.

The mothers and daughters would return to Shoreford in a Pullman compartment. Duncan would sleep in a lower berth, in the car behind them. He would be with them during the days to handle whatever needs they might have.

As soon as the train pulled out, Jim was on his way. He sped through a sunny day and then a cloudy day and through many hours of darkness. He slept in the car when he needed rest and arrived home in under two days.

His emotions improved vastly when he stepped from the car and into the arms of four happy and eager children. His first night home, when all the visitors were finally gone and they were alone, he played with his children long past their bed times. For two days, the only joy, the only respite Jim had, was with his children and to a lesser extent, his father and Shirley and a brief visit from Isabel Buchanan.

Bill wanted desperately to ease his son's burden and that of two lovely young women. For all concerned, he hoped for a just, painless and loving conclusion to their daunting situation, but felt that a bit much to expect.

Buck was at a teacher's convention. He was sorely tempted to return home to be with his friend, but when he talked to Shirley, she advised against it. She was convinced that Jim needed some space right now and though she was deeply sympathetic to her brother, she came to him only to give him a hug and tell him that she and Buck were available for whatever his needs might be. She offered no advice, only support.

Away at college, Bob talked to Shirley and felt as she did. He called Jim and repeated much of what Shirley said. He knew he could not do more right now.

The two who loved him as only mothers can, gave him the only difficult time. Before he was home less than an hour, Sarah and Molly questioned him about the future, less than objectively. Both had similar views, very biased toward Ceit, especially as to how all this would be handled by the courts.

Jim was close to venting his anger on them, something he normally would have been incapable of, with either of them.

Bill and Shirley got them out of the house.

Soon after they were gone, Jim was angry with himself, but he could not easily get over the hurt Sarah and Molly uncharacteristically and unknowingly heaped on him. But he made a promise to himself, right then and there. He must never again allow himself to reach such a point with his mother, or with Molly.

Isabel came the same evening after the others had gone. What Jim did not know, was that Shirley called her and told her about her brother's ordeal with his mothers. Isabel decided that Jim needed some loving support right then. She stayed just a short time and did not say much, mostly fussing with the children. When she was leaving, she hugged him sturdily.

"We all love you very much, Jim, each and every one of us, no matter how it might seem. Somehow, I know the Lord will see you through this."

There were tears in her eyes when she walked out the door.

*

Most of the second day home, Jim spent alone with the children. When the telephone rang and Sarah or Molly asked if they could do anything, for him, or the children, he kindly put them off. He told them they would all get together tomorrow, or sometime soon thereafter, when everyone was settled in.

He was not happy with himself for keeping them away, but his troubled mind was in enough of a spin and with his sons and daughter, he felt secure, or at least comfortable. He did not know how much confusion Sarah or Molly would add to his already befuddled mind, but he certainly needed nothing additional.

As it happened, Sarah and Molly talked with Bill and Shirley and were soon aware of what they had done. Immediately they were sorry. They truly wanted to go to Jim and express that sorrow and ease his mind, but that would have to wait.

*

That evening, Jim went into the city to pick up five weary travelers. When he reached his destination, Genny was fussing and Sally was crying. He quickly kissed Ceit and Genny, who was holding Ceit's hand. He did the same to Liang and Sally, who was in Liang's arms.

After shaking Duncan's hand, the two of them loaded the luggage into the rear and drove off. There was little conversation.

It was decided that Bill would stay alone at the house with the children when Jim went to the station. Sarah and Molly returned to their homes, hopefully to make it easier for Liang to settle in. It would certainly be easier for Jim, at least that is what he thought.

When the station wagon pulled up in front, the occupants made their way inside. Bill held the door open and did an excellent job welcoming them home. He was of course, joyful to see Ceit, but he managed to convey the same welcome to Liang. Jim was pleased with his father. Bill also managed to spend a fair amount of time with his two new granddaughters.

Amazingly, Donny went to Liang with unrestrained enthusiasm after he welcomed Jim and Ceit, who said softly, "My God! He remembered her, the same as he remembered me."

Liang was uncomfortable with Donny's affectionate display in Ceit's presence, but she did not want to let go. Neither did Donny.

Bill and Duncan were great. They stayed and helped get the clothing put away, continuously stopping to play with the children and to and make sure Ceit and Liang were comfortable. Jim wished they would stay forever, but sighed inwardly at the wishful thought. Sooner or later, they had to depart and allow the occupants of the house to get on with whatever life had in store for them.

When the two did drive away together, Jim felt like an old traditional ship's captain, standing on the bridge, while the crew climbed into the lifeboats of a rapidly sinking ship.

Jim was soon on the floor with all but Sally. He was having a ball, helping five peppy children become thoroughly acquainted. It was where he wanted to be, but it was also an escape from Ceit and Liang and thoughts of the future. As he stole glances at Ceit and Liang, sitting side by side in cushioned chairs, resting and sometimes smiling at the happy activity on the floor, he wildly hoped. But he did, finally, have to return to reality.

Sleeping arrangements were made. The boys slept in their room. Liang would be in with Genny and Moira. The crib had been resurrected in the master bedroom and Sally would sleep in there with her mother.

When the children were at last put to bed and no longer an excuse to dawdle over, Ceit and Liang were able to shower in the separate bathrooms. When they returned to the living room in their robes, at about the same time, they were shiny clean and even relaxed. They seemed more at ease to Jim than he felt. They bid him and somewhat shyly, each other, "Good-night."

But, .. there were no kisses and no hugs ... anywhere.

With the living room deserted, Jim went into the den and sat with his elbows on the desk, his head resting in his hands. He could not concentrate. His ability to reason had long since vanished. There was no way he could make a decision. There was no way he wanted to make a decision. There was no right answer. There was no good answer. There was not even a justifiable compromise.

At 4:14AM he glanced at his watch. He had done that too many times already. He had yet to sleep, yet to feel anything but total confusion, total disaster, total defeat. He got up and paced. The room was small and his pacing limited, but he kept at it. At 4:37AM, he looked at his watch again. What could he do? What could he do? He sat in the stuffed chair and again rested his head in his hands. He heard the words of his prayer as they come from his mouth, not loud, but quite soft, yet very audible.

"Please, Father, don't let my family be hurt. I don't care what you do with me, ... or to me, .. but please, .. don't let my family be hurt. Do with me what you will, .. but please, .. don't let my family be hurt."

He slumped back in the chair, his exhausted body and mind capable of no more. In an instant, he was in a deep sleep.

*

The den was lighted, not from the bulb that burned through the night, but from the rising sun. It was nearly 7:00AM.

The house was filled with an inert silence. Jim sprang to his feet and ran noiselessly to the first bedroom. The three boys slept peacefully. In the next bedroom, Genny and Moira did not have a care in the world. Liang's bed, however, was vacant and made up. He rushed into the master bedroom. Sally was asleep, her tiny body taking up little space in the crib. He went over to the crib and observed his daughter breathing and smiled down at her, forgetting for just a moment the turmoil that was tearing at his mind. The large master bed was vacant. It too was made up. As he glanced around the room, he saw them through the large, bow window, opposite the foot of the bed and at the side of the house that overlooked Ceit's summer flower garden.

Ceit was pacing as he had done during the night, but much more energetically. She was waving her arms and hands, the way she did when very excited, .. or very angry. Could she be that angry?

Liang was standing, her shoulders and head slumped forward, her face shielded in her hands. She was crying and her body shaking badly. Could it be that bad, .. could she be that sad, .. could her plight be that demolished?

For a second, Jim was transfixed, like one hypnotized, by a cobra about to strike, but his muscles came to life and he bolted for the front door and into the front yard. He sprinted with all his energy by the front of the house, to the side yard and the dormant garden. When he got there, it was over.

Ceit had won! She tried to be rational, but that failed. She pleaded and finally poured out all the emotion she could muster. It worked! She won! Overwhelmed, Liang, with extraordinary emotion, accepted the decision.

* EPILOG *

In the coming years, Shoreford grew considerably. Some of that growth was the newborn, but much of it was new residents who moved there because it was a good town to live in and raise families. Like all towns in America, some of its natives moved away when offered employment elsewhere, commensurate with their talents and education.

Of the latter, Robert Williams graduated from college and was employed in Boston and lived in its environs. He married a girl from that area. They came to Shoreford every other Thanksgiving and every other Christmas in alternate years and all the time in between when they were able, especially if it was November the 9th or 10th. Bob's wife was a delicate lass and had three miscarriages. They adopted a little boy who thrived when in Shoreford, in the presence of loving grandparents, aunts, uncles and friendly cousins.

The new residents included one Duncan R.D. Cameron, former Colour Sergeant, Royal Marines. He had a building constructed on the piece of land he purchased near the Newville town line, about ten minutes from the city. He opened a pub that succeeded, because it was a friendly place and served excellent fare and he was able to operate at a loss until the business grew. And grow it did, in substantial fashion. He did not permit drunkenness or troublemakers. The picture that hung in Bill and Sarah Williams living room, was photo copied and hung on a wall with other Marine memorabilia and every November 9th and 10th, the birth dates of the Royal Marines and the United States Marine Corps respectively, any one who served as Marines, or was attached to them, especially Naval Corpsmen and later Army helicopter pilots from the Vietnam War, got a free pint. Jim joined him in the pub when his father was able to take in another at the Triple W. When that event occurred, ... well, that is another story.

Of course, native Shorefordians remained and of course, one was William W. Williams. With his business in capable hands and additional help on hand, he was able to slow down a bit and become a professional grandfather. His grandchildren were not only an exceptional joy to him, but an escape. When Sarah was joined by Molly and Isabel, which was quite frequently, he did not stand much of a chance. If he stayed in their presence, the grandmothers took charge of him, for that was his nature, ... at least some of the time. So he found ways to gather up one, or two, or three, or more of his grandchildren and spend time with them and do things with them, which they all thoroughly enjoyed.

The three grandmothers were into everything, including helping Duncan and Jim on special days at the pub. Best of all for the pub, they cooked up some very unique dishes that brought patrons back again and again. But busy as they were, it never interfered with their grandmothering, which was not only rewarding to them, but to the children who called them, "Gramma." And there was nobody in the town that would go up against them when they decided to take a stand on something they believed in.

Two natives who added to the population, were Milton and Shirley Buchanan, who gave Heather, a brother and a sister. Shirley took over the books at the Triple W and the pub and was soon a strong presence with the handling of their funds and quite good at it. Buck became principal of Shoreford High School. He really wanted to teach and was extremely happy doing so and very good at it, but when the former principal retired, he was urged by so many, including his fellow teachers, to take the job, that it seemed like a duty and Buck could never turn his back on a duty. The town was never sorry.

~ ~ ~ ~ ~

He was aware of movement in the room, but paid it no heed. He was comfortable, .. content to just lie there and smile within himself and bask in the glow of his good feelings.

Without warning, the blanket was stripped away, roughly and impolitely. He blinked his eyes open in astonishment and squinted up into the glowing, grinning face.

"Jamie Williams! Do you know that great numbers of our family will be here in no time at all?"

He saw her arm move. He saw the large mug in her hand. He knew it was filled with ice cold water.

"No, Ceit! Don't you dare!"

He was immediately transformed from his lethargy and burst into action. Vigorously, he rolled away from her and onto his stomach, to protect his private parts, which he knew was her target. In shocking disbelief, he felt the water splash into the small of his back.

A high pitched, "Yiiii!" came from his wide open mouth. Forcing his shoulders up, the water flowed swiftly between his buttocks before he rolled rapidly to the other side of the large bed.

"I'll get you, Ceit Williams!" he yelled, but the red hair, that still beautiful hair, had disappeared through the bedroom door, her silly giggles tickling his ears.

He jumped to his feet at the other side of the bed.

A palm pushed hard into his chest and shoved him backwards. Off balance he flopped clumsily to the bed. It was then he saw her, was first aware of her. He knew in an instant his ordeal was not over. In her hand was a mug exactly like the first.

"No, Liang! No!" he screamed, but the frigid water, zestfully tossed, came splashing, crashing into that most delicate area.

"Yaaah! You, .. you wench!" he yelled.

He saw her eyes fill with mirth. She dropped the empty mug on the carpeted floor and laughingly shrieked, "Ooh, James!"

For an instant, she covered her face with her hands while her body shook with glee. When she took her hands away, her face was a huge, victorious smile. She ran around the bed and fled through the door in joyful hysteria. Her beautiful hair, still so shiny, still so black, was the last of her he saw.

In the living room, as they clasped hands and danced in a circle, their joyful giggling echoed through the partly opened door.

Well, they did it again. They seemed to take a sadistic pleasure in ganging up on him. Thankfully, it was most always in fun. Tonight they would celebrate twenty-five years together, born that eventful November morning, just before Thanksgiving, in a dormant flower garden, on the side of their warm and often lively home. Yesterday was, today is!

Reflections

The seed for THE LEAVENING took root while traveling with my wife. I came across the picture and story of a wonderful girl, wife and mother in her mid twenties who was tragically killed. She seemed very real to me and I felt almost like I knew her, or perhaps wished I had. She personified the old saying, 'The good die young!' Her vision stayed with me a long time. It seemed that such a character belonged in a story. As time passed, Moira was born and I found myself, without any purpose at first, concocting a plot.

With Jim, I pondered a bit. I wanted someone with vulnerability and remembered a novel I read in the '50s which took place prior to our Revolutionary War. One of the characters was a Dutch boy who was indentured and earned his freedom during the tale. I remembered liking him when I read the book. He was a humble lad and innocent in the ways of the world, but a loyal and gritty kid. I wanted that in Jim.

From the picture of a lass with the most exquisite red hair came Ceit. At almost the same time, an ad in the Wall Street Journal for Singapore Airlines showed the face of a beautiful Oriental lass. From that picture came Soo-Ann and Liang. After that, the characters fell easily in place and the plot developed at a pretty good clip.

I needed a vehicle to get Jim around the world and what better than the Corps. It was perfect and gave me the opportunity to mix fiction with some little known facts and do something for my Corps, especially to make known its struggle for existence during a difficult time and relate some of its fighting ability, esprit and fidelity. Not having been part of any of the actions in chapter Seven, it was researched diligently, as were parts of other chapters that contained historical events, to make them as realistic as possible.

The ending was not there in the beginning and did not come as easily as most of the plot, but suddenly, one day, while operating a lathe, I realized a Merciful Father might not find it difficult to smile on such an outcome. It seemed not only OK, but correct.

I hope the characters were real for you and you experienced some of the feeling and passion I tried to bring to the story.

About the Author

Forced into early retirement, but with no formal education, Ed Owen started this first novel at age sixty-two. The original manuscript was completed in longhand while working part time. Learning word processing and the minor intricacies of the computer followed. The manuscript was typed twice more, using hunt and peck, along with, over time, the legion of necessary revisions and corrections.

Ed lives with his wife Harriett in Connecticut.